KU-314-485

ANGÉLIQUE AND THE DEMON

Also available in Pan Books

ANGÉLIQUE I
ANGÉLIQUE II
ANGÉLIQUE IN REVOLT
ANGÉLIQUE AND THE KING
ANGÉLIQUE AND THE SULTAN
COUNTESS ANGÉLIQUE I
COUNTESS ANGÉLIQUE II
THE TEMPTATION OF ANGÉLIQUE I
THE TEMPTATION OF ANGÉLIQUE II
ANGÉLIQUE IN LOVE

CONDITIONS OF SALE

This book shall not, by way of trade or otherwise, be lent, re-sold, hired out or otherwise circulated without the publisher's prior consent in any form of binding or cover other than that in which it is published and without a similar condition including this condition being imposed on the subsequent purchaser. The book is published at a net price, and is supplied subject to the Publishers Association Standard Conditions of Sale registered under the Restrictive Trade Practices Act, 1956.

ANGÉLIQUE AND THE DEMON

SERGEANNE GOLON

Translated from the French by
Marguerite Barnett

PAN BOOKS LTD
LONDON AND SYDNEY

First published 1972 by Éditions de Trévise under
the title *Angélique et la Démone*
First published in Great Britain 1973 by
William Heinemann Ltd
This edition published 1975 by Pan Books Ltd,
Cavaye Place, London SW10 9PG
ISBN 0 330 24245 8
© Opera Mundi, Paris, 1972
Translation © William Heinemann Ltd 1973
*Printed in Great Britain by
Cox & Wyman Ltd, London, Reading and Fakenham*

PRINCIPAL CHARACTERS

Angélique, Countess Peyrac: an aristocratic French lady of the seventeenth century; after an early marriage to the Gascon nobleman, Joffrey de Peyrac, by whom she had two sons, Florimond and Cantor, she becomes separated from her husband who she believes has been executed for sorcery. She herself regains favour at court as a result of her second marriage to her cousin Philippe du Plessis-Bellière, who is killed shortly afterwards. In order to escape the King's attentions she flees the country and is captured on the Mediterranean by the Berbers and imprisoned by Sultan Mulai Ismail at Meknès in North Africa. There she is rescued by her fellow-captive, Colin Paturel, who accompanies her across the desert to Ceuta. She is taken back to France by the King's agents but escapes and leads the people of her native province, Poitou, in their uprising. She is condemned to death and once more obliged to flee France with her youngest child, Honorine, and a party of Huguenot refugees. On reaching America she is reunited with her long-lost husband, Joffrey de Peyrac, and with Florimond and Cantor. Together they survive their first winter in the inland fort of Wapassou, in the mountainous country of Upper Kennebec near the Canadian Border. When spring comes they set off down the river to visit their settlement of Gouldsboro at the mouth of the Bay of Fundy, then known as French Bay. Misunderstandings between Angélique and her husband and a string of false messages separate them. Angélique is captured by the pirate Gold Beard, who turns out to be Colin Paturel, sent from France to capture Peyrac's lands. Peyrac, however, defeats Gold Beard, pardons him, and makes him Governor of Gouldsboro.

Joffrey de Peyrac: a high-born Frenchman. His great learning and considerable fortune arouses the envy of King Louis XIV, who contrives his ruin and has him condemned as a sorcerer. After many adventures, he is reunited with his family and disembarks on the shores of Maine where he founds the colony of Gouldsboro. By setting up inland mining communities to exploit the vast mineral resources of the region, he establishes a claim to a large part of the territory of Maine and New Brunswick, then known as Acadia, the sovereignty over which was disputed between France and Britain.

Cantor: Angélique's and Joffrey's second son, aged about sixteen at the time of the action.

Honorine: Angélique's illegitimate daughter; about four years old.

Settlers in Gouldsboro:

  From La Rochelle:

  Gabriel Berne: leader of the Protestant community.

  Abigail Berne: his young wife.

  Sévérine and *Laurier:* Gabriel's children by his first wife.

  Monsieur and Madame Mercelot: paper-makers.

  Bertille: their daughter.

  Madame Carrère: the innkeeper.

  Monsieur and Madame Manigault.

  Jeremy: their son, and *Siriki* their African servant.

  From the defeated Pirate vessel Heart of Mary:

  Colin Paturel: her captain, now Governor of Gouldsboro.

  Barssempuy: his lieutenant, in love with Marie-la-Douce.

  Aristide Beaumarchand: a pirate whose life Angélique once saved after he had attacked her.

English Protestant settlers awaiting repatriation as soon as their homelands are free from marauding redskins.

The Reverend Thomas Patridge: Protestant Minister.

Miss Pidgeon: a schoolteacher.

Elias Kempton: a tinker from Connecticut.

Mr Willoughby: his tame bear.

Adhemar: a French soldier and a buffoon.

Piksarett: Chief of the Patsuikett tribes. He had claimed Angélique as his prisoner during a fight but had allowed her to go free, reserving his right to claim her ransom.

Michael and Jerome: Red Indian Catholic converts, devoted followers of Piksarett.

Clovis: a blacksmith from the Auvergne, who had worked for Joffrey de Peyrac in the mine at Katarunk.

Ambroisine de Maudribourg: a noble French lady, young, intelligent and beautiful, who is shipwrecked off the coast of

Gouldsboro with the 'King's Girls', her protégées, whom she is supposed to be escorting to Quebec.

Her followers:

Job Simon: Captain of the *Unicorn,* now wrecked.

Petronella Damourt: duenna and companion to the Duchess of Maudribourg.

Armand Daveau: her secretary.

Marie-la-Douce, Delphine du Rosoy, Jeanne Michaud, Julienne: 'King's Girls' on their way to Quebec.

Phipps, Sir William: first Royal Governor of Massachusetts.

Father de Vernon: a Jesuit priest, who had travelled as the sailor Jack Merwin, and come to know Angélique well.

Brother Mark.

Father Quentin: once chaplain to Ambroisine de Maudribourg and her girls on board the *Unicorn.*

Monsieur de Ville d'Avray: a dapper 'bon vivant' from Quebec, Governor of Acadia.

French Acadian Settlers:

Hubert d'Arpentigny: a young nobleman.

Baron Saint-Castine: betrothed to Mathilda, a Mic-Mac princess.

Nicolas Parys
Big-Woods ⎱land-owners in Acadia.
The Defour Brothers⎰

Marceline Raymondeau, also called *Marceline-la-Belle:* Acadian settler, mother of many children, including *Cherubino,* whom she had by Ville d'Avray.

Yolande: Marceline's eldest daughter.

Madame de la Roche-Posay: chatelaine of Port-Royal.

Radégonde de Ferjeac: governess to Madame de la Roche-Posay's children.

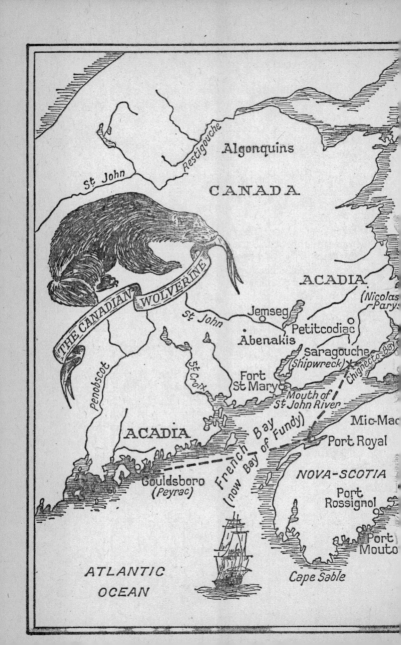

THE CANADIAN WOLVERINE

Algonquins

CANADA

St John

Restigouche

St John

ACADIA

(Nicolas
Parys

Jemseg

Petitcodiac

Ābenakis

Saragouche
(Shipwreck)

Chignecto Bay

Penobscot

St John

St Croix

Fort
St Mary

Mouth of
St John River

ACADIA

Mic-Mac

Port Royal

French Bay
(now Bay of Fundy)

NOVA-SCOTIA

Gouldsboro
(Peyrac)

Port
Rossignol

Port
Mouto

ATLANTIC
OCEAN

Cape Sable

Gulf of
St Lawrence

ISLES
DE LA
MADELEINE

CAPE
BRETON
ISLAND
OR
ISLE
ROYALE

ISLE SAINT-JEAN
(NOW PR. EDWARD IS.)

Shediac

Trantamare

Tormentine

Tidmagouche

Malecites

(Marceline
the Defour Brothers)

(Nicolas Parys)

Mic-Macs

Parsboro

Truro

Canso

Cobequid
Bay

ACADIA

PENINSULA

OR

La Hève 1604

(Hubert d'Arpentigny's
domain)

MAP OF
CANADA

PART ONE

Gouldsboro
or
Early Beginnings

CHAPTER 1

A TINY SHIP'S kitten, that somehow or other had succeeded in getting ashore, a little, forgotten kitten, stood before Angélique.

It was a skinny, scruffy little waif, but there was command as well as trust in the golden eyes that implored her help. Angélique did not see the little creature. As she sat at the Duchess of Maudribourg's bedside, her mind was taken up with melancholy thoughts.

The kitten stared intently at her. How had it ever managed to get so far? It was sickly and mangy, and it could only just have been weaned when it was cast up on the shore, perhaps thrown there by the hand of some impatient cabin-boy, a minute little thing with nowhere to go, too weak to find something to eat and to fight for it with the other cats and the dogs of Gouldsboro. And yet it had somehow made its way into the fort and then into this silent room, perhaps looking for nothing more than a quiet, shady corner to die in.

Now, it looked at this seated woman and seemed to be wondering what final appeal to make to her. It summoned up its last remaining strength and mewed. The sound it managed to produce was husky and almost inaudible, but succeeded in rousing Angélique from her reverie. She looked up and gazed at the kitten for a moment. It was so barely alive that she took it for a phantom of her weary mind, like the visions of diabolical animals that had beset her over the past few days. Then she bent down towards it.

'Where on earth did you spring from, you poor little wretch?' she exclaimed, picking him up as light as a feather. The kitten at once clung to the velvet of her dress with its delicate little claws and began to purr.

'Ah! you saw me,' he seemed to say. 'Please don't turn me away!'

'It must have been abandoned by one of the ships,' she thought. 'Perhaps Vanereick's or one of the English vessels . . . dying of starvation and weakness.'

She got up and went over to the table. There was still a little of the egg-flip that had been brought as a pick-me-up for the Duchess in the bottom of the bowl. The kitten drank a little.

'It's shivering. It's cold.'

She sat down again at the foot of the bed holding the kitten on her lap to warm it. She thought of her little girl, Honorine, who so loved animals and who would have made a tremendous fuss of the kitten.

These memories made her heart still heavier. She saw in her imagination the wooden fort of Wapassou, where she had left Honorine in the care of their devoted servants, and it seemed to her as if she was conjuring up memories of a paradise that was never to return. She had had such happy times there, with her beloved husband Joffrey de Peyrac. And now it seemed to her that all that happiness had been utterly shattered and broken.

What was it that had been brewing during those past few terrible weeks, and had finally set them against one another? She was torn by an agonizing doubt: Joffrey did not love her any more.

She paced up and down the room, unconsciously holding the kitten to her while he snuggled against her shoulder, with closed eyes, in an attitude of mingled love and abandon. It was as if life was flowing back into him through the touch of Angélique's hands.

'You're a happy one, you are,' she whispered to him, 'you're only a tiny, innocent, brave little thing asking nothing more than to live. Never fear, I'll look after you.'

The kitten began to purr louder than ever, and with one finger she stroked his soft, frail head. The affectionate little creature's company was a comfort to her.

Was it possible that she and Joffrey could have become such strangers?

'I too showed a lack of trust in him. I should have told him straightaway about Colin when I got back the other day. What had I to fear? It would have been so much easier to explain how things had happened, how Colin had come upon me asleep.[1] But perhaps my conscience was not altogether easy ... and I am always so frightened of losing him a second time, as if I refused to believe in this miracle ...'

She analysed the overwhelming sense of anxiety that held her in its grip, discovered that its source lay far further back than the tension of the past few days. It was something ancient,

1. See *The Temptation of Angélique*.

a lurking fear ready to spring out and cry in despair: 'My love! My love! I shall never see you again. "They" have taken him away . . . and I shall *never see him again.*'

And suddenly something within her revolted and gave up the struggle.

'Yes, that's it,' she admitted to herself. '*That* is what's wrong. I was very young when it happened. Really only a spoilt child to whom life had given everything . . . and then suddenly there was nothing.'

That great sun that had shone on her eighteen years,[2] that sun of love, discovered, shared in the dazzling atmosphere of carnival time in Toulouse, that dawn of life flooding her whole being, every day, every hour . . . 'I had begun to believe in the magic of life. And then suddenly all was cold, all was solitude. I have never really accepted that. I have gone on being frightened . . . and feeling a certain resentment towards him . . . fearing that he will leave me without giving a thought to my agony. We have found one another again, but my confidence has been shaken, my confidence in him, in life, and in joy.'

At Wapassou the almost superhuman effort to survive with their followers had helped them to re-forge the links that joined their lives.[3] But that warm sense of loving unity had masked different aspects of their personalities that had developed from their long separation, the haunting sense of the unknown that arose from those fifteen years of absence.

She thought back to his devastating anger . . . but also the gesture he had made that morning in offering her so magnificent a gift, the Spanish pistols, that lay in their open box on the table. And then he had clasped her passionately in his arms . . .

But then the benefactress of the King's Girls, Duchess Ambroisine of Maudribourg, had been rescued from the sea, and her arrival had been reported. So they had had to go to meet her and attend to her when she fainted on the shore.

Angélique had spent the whole afternoon in an attempt to revive her. Now she seemed better and had been resting quietly for the past hour in the big bed. Angélique had sent the girls away, for their despair at their benefactress's condition risked disturbing this health-giving rest. But Joffrey had not come to inquire about her and had sent no message. She longed to go and look for him.

2. See *Angélique.*
3. See *The Countess Angélique.*

She also regretted that in her first impulse of pity she had installed the benefactress in their room in the fort.

'I should have asked Madame Manigault to look after her. Or Madame Carrère. I believe they have built rooms above the inn to lodge visiting officers. But of course they must be rather uncomfortable and noisy, and the poor woman needs careful nursing.'

She went back to the bed, but, she knew not why, her eyes refused to rest on the face of the sleeping woman lying on the lace-trimmed pillow. It was so young a face, of such fragile beauty, and so ravaged that it left you with a sense of uneasiness.

'Why had I imagined the Duchess of Maudribourg as a stout old lady rather like her lady-companion Petronella Damourt?' Angélique wondered. 'It all seems like a bad joke to me.'

Madame Carrère who had helped her to undress the Duchess of Maudribourg must have been equally perplexed to see the marvellously comely figure of this benefactress; for Angélique had heard her muttering under her breath and shaking her La Rochelle head-dress disapprovingly.

But neither she nor Madame de Peyrac, as women of the New World, accustomed to coping with all kinds of unexpected situations, had said anything. One couldn't spend all one's time being astonished and throwing up one's hands to Heaven. Madame Carrère had merely muttered as she looked at the shipwrecked woman's clothing, her yellow satin skirt, her duck-blue mantle, scarlet modesty-vest, and her azure bodice, 'Jest look at them glad rags! She's not a woman, she's a parrot.'

'Maybe it's the latest Paris fashion?' Angélique suggested. 'Madame de Montespan, who was setting the tone when I left Court, loved showy things.'

'That's as maybe, but for a woman engaged in charitable work, like they say she is . . . *well*!'

Both her skirt and her mantle were torn and dirty, and Madame Carrère had taken them away to wash and mend them.

The red stockings with the golden clocks had been thrown on the ground and made a scarlet patch beside the bed. They caught the kitten's attention and he jumped down from Angélique's arms, curled up and settled down on them with a proprietary air.

'No, puss, you can't sleep there,' Angélique protested.

She knelt down beside him and had some difficulty in convincing him that this delicate silken bed was not for the tabby

fur of a sickly kitten, but eventually, after she herself had
settled him on a soft piece of blanket in a corner of the room, he
agreed to the exchange; as he looked at her through his half-
closed slanting eyes he seemed to be saying:

'As long as you look after me and understand how important
I am and go to a deal of trouble on my behalf, I am prepared to
give up those red stockings.'

She picked up the stockings and ran them through her hands
in a kind of dream . . .

'I bought them in Paris,' said a voice, 'at Bernin's. You know,
Bernin, the haberdasher in the Galerie du Palais.'

CHAPTER 2

THE DUCHESS OF MAUDRIBOURG had woken and for some
moments had been lying propped up on one elbow watching
Angélique.

As she turned towards her Angélique felt the impact of the
'benefactress's' magnificent eyes.

'What is the attraction of these eyes of hers?' she wondered
as she drew closer. The dark eyes seemed to swallow up the
whole of that lily-white, young-looking face, lending it a kind
of tragic maturity, like the eyes of certain over-serious children,
precociously matured by suffering.

But it was only a fleeting impression.

As Angélique bent over the Duchess of Maudribourg, her
expression had already altered. Her eyes now shone with a
calm, gentle light and she seemed to be examining the Countess
of Peyrac benevolently while her lips curved in a sophisticated
smile of welcome.

'How do you feel now, Madame?' Angélique asked her as she
sat down beside the bed.

She reached for the hand that lay on the sheet, and found it
cool, with no trace of fever. But the pulse in the delicate wrist
was still racing.

'Were you admiring my stockings?' Madame de
Maudribourg asked. 'Aren't they lovely?'

Her harmonious voice held a trace of affectation.

'They are made of a mixture of silk, Afghan goats' wool and gold thread,' she explained. 'That's why they are so soft and shiny.'

'They are very pretty and elegant,' Angélique agreed. 'Monsieur Bernin, whom I used to know, continues to live up to his reputation.'

'I also have some amber-scented gloves from Grenoble,' the Duchess went on eagerly. 'Where are they? I would love to show them to you . . .'

As she spoke, she kept glancing about the room and seemed not fully to grasp where she was and who this woman was, sitting beside her holding her red stockings.

'I dare say your gloves were lost with the rest of your luggage . . .' Angélique said carefully, in an attempt to help her take in the facts of her situation.

The patient looked up sharply at her and an expression of anguish flashed across her expressive face, fading away again immediately beneath her lowered eyelids. She fell back with closed eyes. She was very pale and breathing rapidly. She raised a hand to her brow and murmured:

'Oh yes, you're right. That terrible shipwreck! Now I remember. Please forgive me, Madame . . .'

She lay in silence for a moment then went on:

'Why did that captain tell us that we were about to arrive at Quebec? We are not in Quebec, are we?'

'Far from it! With a good wind it's three weeks' sailing from here.'

'Where are we then?'

'In Gouldsboro, on the coast of Maine, a settlement on the northern shores of French Bay.'[1]

'Maine! French Bay! Then somewhere the other side of Newfoundland we must have lost our way and gone right round the southern end of the Acadian Peninsula instead of entering the Gulf of Saint Lawrence in the north . . .'

She at least knew her geography or had taken the trouble to look at maps before setting off on her American adventure. She seemed quite shattered.

'So far away!' she murmured. 'What is to become of us now? And those poor girls I was escorting to New France to get married . . .'

1. *La Baye Françoise* (or *La Baie Française*) was the name given by the seventeenth-century French explorer de Monts to the famous stretch of water now known as the Bay of Fundy. (Translator's note.)

'They are alive, Madame, that is the main thing. Not a single one was lost, and, although some of them have been seriously injured, they will all recover from the ordeal, that I can promise you.'

'God be praised!' Madame de Maudribourg murmured fervently. Then, clasping her hands and closing her eyes, she appeared to lose herself in prayer.

The sun was already low on the horizon and one of its beams lit up her face, making her look astonishingly beautiful. Lying in prayer, this young woman somehow seemed not quite real.

'How can I thank you, Madame?' said the Duchess, coming to herself once more. 'I understand that you are the chatelaine of this place and that it is no doubt to you and your husband that we owe our lives.'

'It is a sacred duty in a wild place like this for people to help one another.'

'So here I am in America! May God give me strength!'

Then, recovering her self-possession, she went on:

'And yet that was where Our Lady told me to go when she appeared to me. So I must resign myself to her holy will! Don't you think that the fact that not one of the girls lost her life is in itself a sign that Heaven is protecting us?'

'Yes, I do indeed.'

The light from the setting sun was growing pinker and flooding the room with a rosy glow whose fiery reflections fell upon the Duchess's thick dark hair. A subtle perfume that seemed to come from this very beautiful head of hair, had from the moment Angélique first bent over the Duchess, stirred within her a strange, indefinable sense of misgiving.

'You are intrigued by the perfume in my hair,' the Duchess broke in, guessing exactly what Angélique was thinking. 'There's nothing quite like it, is there? I have it made up specially for me. I'll give you a few drops so that you can see whether it suits you too.'

Then remembering the disasters that had befallen her and the fact that her precious bottle of perfume must now be bobbing about somewhere in the sea, she broke off and gave a deep sigh.

'Would you like me to fetch your lady-companion, Petronella Damourt?' Angélique suggested, anxious herself to go and look for her husband.

'No, no,' Madame de Maudribourg retorted sharply. 'Not her, please, I couldn't bear it. That poor woman . . . she is most loyal but so exhausting! And I feel so tired. I think I shall sleep for a while.'

She lay down between the sheets in a stately pose, her arms stretched out beside her body, her head thrown back, and seemed to fall asleep immediately.

Angélique got up to close the wooden shutter so as to shield her patient from the light. She stood for a moment looking at the shore in the purple sunset glow and noticed the bustle of evening activity in both fort and village. It was the hour when, with the departure of the heat of day, smoke began to rise from the hearths as people prepared the evening meal, and when the sailors and redskins lighted their fires along the beaches and on the cliff tops.

She realized that it must have been the monthly bread-baking day in Gouldsboro, the process being carried out in ovens hacked out of the ground and heated with glowing embers and red-hot stones. The delicious smell of hot bread rose towards her like a subtle, familiar incense, and she saw some children climbing back up the hill towards the houses carrying handbarrows laden with huge golden cobs.

In spite of the recent battles that had shaken the little colony, life went on.

'Joffrey wanted it this way,' she told herself. 'What a will to survive he has, to carry on with life! Everyone who comes in contact with him seems to be possessed by it too. He is frightening . . . frightening in his energy . . .'

CHAPTER 3

THEN SUDDENLY Angélique put her face in her hands and was shaken by a sob that swept over her like a tidal wave. Why had her husband not come to inquire how she was?

Throughout the whole day that she had spent in that room in the fort at the Duchess of Maudribourg's bedside, she had gone on hoping he would come . . .

Nothing! So he *was* still angry with her. Yet, that very morning, for all too brief an instant, he had cried out his love for her . . . And suddenly he had clasped her to him with such violence that, whenever she thought about it, she was profoundly moved. She could feel his arms about her like steel bands, imprisoning her with such fierce passion that her whole being had been stirred with deep, sensual feelings . . .

But now her fear returned once more.

During the recent upheavals, she had been at a loss to understand many of Joffrey de Peyrac's reactions. She thought she could predict how he would behave, but now she was no longer certain! He had shouted things like an angry man, like a jealous lover, things she would never have thought him capable of before.

Yet she had preferred that violence, that brutality, to some of his wiles. To have lured her on to Old Ship Island with Colin,[1] so that he could catch them in one another's arms . . . was that not unworthy of him? . . . She kept on turning the question over and over in her mind, each time suffering a thousand deaths. The blow he had struck her on the face was nothing beside *that* blow. She *must* understand, for she was tormented with the fear that she had lost him for ever.

She kept on re-enacting the events in her mind, trying to find some lead, trying to see how it was that in so few days so many sinister coincidences could have occurred to force them, such loving partners, such devoted friends, so passionately in love with one another, to tremble in one another's presence. It smacked of witchcraft and nightmares! . . .

It seemed as if it had all begun at Houssnock when Joffrey had sent her off to escort the little English girl Rose-Ann home to her grandparents who were New England settlers on the frontiers of Maine. Called away himself on some matter of a treaty by an Indian chief he had sent her his instructions via Cantor, it being agreed that they should eventually join forces at the mouth of the Kennebec.

After that, events had followed one another with all the momentum of a dramatic avalanche.

There had been the attack on the English village by the Canadians and their allies, the Abenaki Indians, the object of which seemed to have been to capture her, Count Peyrac's wife.

Angélique had managed to escape thanks to Piksarett, the chief of the Patsuiketts; she had reached Casco Bay, and found that the pirate Gold Beard, prowling in the region, was none other than her erstwhile lover Colin Paturel, king of the slaves

1. See *The Temptation of Angélique.*

in Meknès, who had saved her from Mulai Ismail's harem, possibly the only man among the many who had once loved her, to have left in her memory and in her body a sense of regret, a vague nostalgia, a special feeling of tenderness.

Of course this bore no comparison to the great, devouring flame, the torment, the passion, the imperious desire, impossible to explain on rational grounds or to analyse, which she felt for Joffrey; nothing could be compared to that. But she had loved Colin, once, she had been happy in his arms, and finding him again in a moment of solitude, of demoralization and weariness, something had begun to tremble within her, something happy, gentle and sensual, sensual above all. She did not want to deceive herself nor to make excuses for what had happened. She had almost succumbed to a moment of giddiness, as the thunderbolt of desire had struck her as she lay half asleep, when Colin had taken her in his arms, covering her with kisses and caresses.

She had been at fault. She was too fond of love-making with its secret, heavenly ecstasies.

But it had been Joffrey – for ever Joffrey the magician – who had opened for her the gates of this enchanted domain, the first, in her youth, to teach her the meaning of pleasure; it was he too, finding her again after fifteen years of separation, during which she had thought him dead, who had brought her back to the life of the senses, awakening her once more to love with such delicacy, such care, such infinite patience . . . How could she ever forget that?

So easy was it to make her happy that this weakness had set her feverishly a-tremble for a moment in Colin's strong arms, when he had taken her by surprise that night on his ship the *Heart of Mary*. It had been an effort to tear herself from him, to make her escape . . .

Why had chance willed it that the soldier, Kurt Ritz, escaping from the ship, happened to have caught sight of them at that very moment, through the window of the poop-castle, as she lay 'naked in Gold Beard's arms'?

Why did it have to be that this mercenary of Joffrey de Peyrac's, not realizing the identity of the woman he had glimpsed, should repeat the story in front of the Count himself, and not only in front of him but in front of all the bigwigs of the Gouldsboro colony?

What a terrible moment for everyone! And for *him*! To be flouted in this way by her in front of everyone.

She could understand his violence towards her when she had found herself face to face with him. But now what could she do to calm his anger? How could she make him understand that she had never really loved anyone else. That if he no longer loved her she would die, yes, she would die . . .

Suddenly her mind was made up. She would not stay where she was, stupidly waiting for him to come. She would go and see him again this evening, would beseech him to listen. Never mind if he did say more hurtful things to her. Anything was better than being separated from him like this. Anything rather than his coldness. Let him take her in his arms again. Even if he were to stifle her, to crush her in his anger.

She dashed over to her dressing-table, and seeing in the mirror that she had tears on her cheeks, she put a little powder on her face.

She unpinned her chignon, and, taking her brush with its gold-encrusted tortoiseshell back – yet another present from him – swiftly brushed out her hair. She wanted to look beautiful, not hunted and strained as she had been over the past few days.

The kitten had not moved since she had settled it down on the piece of blanket; it lay curled in a ball, beatific with comfort it had not known long since, possibly never on this earth, motionless, gentle, patient, and almost ethereal in its delicacy and sickly fragility. But when she spoke to it, it began to purr loudly, expressing as best it could its gratitude and contentment.

'I'm going out,' she said to it, 'be good. I'll be back.'

She gave one last glance towards the bed. The Duchess lay still, stiff and straight in her bed. Angélique, brush in hand, tried to call to mind some vague memory.

'Why are you looking at me like that? Is there something about me that worries you?' the invalid asked without opening her eyes.

'Forgive me, Madame. It's nothing serious. I think it must be the way you are lying that caught my attention. Were you perhaps brought up in a convent from early childhood? When I was sent to one as a boarder, we were forbidden to sleep otherwise than lying very straight on our backs with our arms and hands outside the blankets . . . even in winter. Needless to say, I never slept like that. I was very disobedient.'

'Your guess is right,' Madame de Maudribourg replied with a smile. 'I spent all my childhood in a convent, and I must confess I still find it impossible to sleep in any other position than the one you reproach me for.'

'It wasn't a reproach. Where did you board?'

'At the Ursulines' in Poitiers.'

'At the convent in the Rue des Montées?'

'The Ursulines in the Rue des Montées are the only ones in Poitiers.'

'But that was where I was brought up too,' Angélique exclaimed. 'What a coincidence. Are you from Poitou yourself?'

'I was born in Rallenay.'

'Near the Forest of Mervan.'

'At the mouth of the Vale of Janot. You know the Roué runs through there,' the Duchess of Maudribourg went on, suddenly livening up. 'Our château was at the edge of the forest! Huge chestnut trees. The smell of fallen chestnuts and acorns there, it's like food and drink. In the autumn I walked for hours just to hear them scrunching beneath my feet.'

Her eyes were glistening and a pink flush had risen to her cheeks.

'On the other bank of the Roué lies the château of Machecoul,' said Angélique.

'Yes?' replied the young woman. Then, lowering her voice: 'Gilles de Rais?' she whispered.

'The Accursed.'

'The Devil's Man.'

'Who used to murder little boys to get the Philosopher's Stone from the Devil!'

'And who was hanged for his crimes on the gibbet of Nantes.'

'The very man! Gilles de Rais!'

Together they began to laugh, as if they had been talking about a mutual friend.

Angélique sat down beside the Duchess's bed.

'So we're from the same province. I was born in Sancé, near Monteloup above the marshes.'

'How delighted I am. But do go on doing your hair, please,' said Ambroisine picking up the brush Angélique had let fall on the bed. 'You have the most wonderful hair. Like a fairy.'

'In Poitou when I was a child the local people liked to say that I was a fairy.'

'And I bet they suspected you of dancing round the druidic stone in the forest when there was a full moon?'

'How did you guess?'

'There's always some fairy stone nearby in our part of the world,' Madame de Maudribourg replied dreamily.

There was something warm and gentle in the look she gave Angélique.

'How strange,' she murmured. 'People had warned me to be on my guard against you, and suddenly I find you are so close, almost like a sister. So you are from Poitou, Madame de Peyrac. What a happy chance!'

'Who told you to beware of me?' Angélique asked.

The Duchess averted her gaze, and with a slight shudder replied:

'Oh, you know, when people in Paris mention Canada, your husband's name often crops up. He's ... rather too close a neighbour ... to territories of the King of France. And I wager that they talk of him in London too.'

She clasped her arms round her knees, which she had raised under the blankets as she sat up. In this position she seemed very young, a woman devoid of affectation. Angélique noticed that her hands were clasped tight together, a gesture that may have revealed her control of some powerful emotion, but she continued to look Angélique straight in the face with a serene expression.

'She looks as if she had gold in the depths of her eyes,' thought Angélique. 'From a distance they seem very black, jet black. But, from close to, you can see that they are like amber.'

They looked at one another in silence. The Duchess tilted her chin a little and half smiled. Her bold confidence seemed to have been acquired by some act of will. As if she forced herself not to give way to an instinctive desire to turn away and avoid exchanging glances.

'Well, I find you very nice,' she concluded as if replying to some inner indictment.

'And why should I not be nice to you?' Angélique retorted sharply. 'Who could have painted such a black picture of me to you? Who knows me in Paris? I disembarked here last autumn and spent the whole winter in the heart of the forest ...'

'Don't be cross,' Ambroisine said, laying one hand gently on Angélique's wrist. 'Listen, my dear, I think it's wonderful to have met you as soon as I reached the New World, you and your husband. I don't pay much attention to gossip, to slander. I usually wait to form my own opinion about people I have

been warned against, and, maybe out of a spirit of independence or simply of contradiction – I am stubborn like all
women from Poitou – I tend to be prejudiced in their favour.

'I am going to confess something to you. From Paris
America seemed to me to be vast, endless, as indeed it is. And
yet I felt convinced that sooner or later I would meet you . . . I
felt certain . . . the day I first heard your name mentioned,
shortly before we embarked, a voice inside me said: "You will
get to know her!" And now . . . maybe God willed all this to
happen.'

Her hesitancy gave a certain charm to the way she spoke.
Her voice was soft, slightly muffled, and faltered occasionally
as if she had run out of breath. Angélique caught herself listening to it very carefully as if trying to discover the hidden personality that lay behind it.

Did not the Duchess's affection, slightly theatrical as it was,
stem from a certain effort on her part to make contact with
other people?

'She's a woman who stands alone,' Angélique caught herself
thinking.

Such a diagnosis did not tally with the dazzling youth and
beauty of Ambroisine de Maudribourg. In addition, there was
something girlish about her, a kind of childishness. Her upper
teeth, which were small, beautiful and evenly spaced, pro-
truded slightly, lifting her well-defined upper lip, and occasionally giving her the fleeting expression of a little girl who
has been crying. And when she smiled, it was also with a kind
of trusting innocence that was touching. But her expression was
shrewd, mature and dreamy. 'I wonder how old she really is?
Thirty? More than that, or less?'

'You're not listening to me,' the Duchess suddenly said.

And she gave that disarming, confiding smile, throwing back
her heavy black hair that had slipped forwards over her
cheek.

'Madame,' she asked mysteriously, 'since you are from
Poitou, did you ever hear the cry of the mandrake as it was dug
up on Christmas Eve?'

Angélique became aware of a sense of complicity stirring
within her on hearing this strange question. Her eyes sought
those of Ambroisine de Maudribourg and saw, as in the shaded
depths of some forest pool, the reflection of stars.

'Yes,' she replied, likewise in lowered tones, 'but it was in
September. People in our area used to go in September and

find a black dog to tear the magic root out of the ground.'

'Then you had to sacrifice the dog immediately to the gods of the earth . . .' Ambroisine went on.

'And you had to wrap the root in a scarlet cloth to keep off the demons that tried to take possession of it,' Angélique added.

They burst into peals of laughter.

'How beautiful you are,' Madame de Maudribourg said suddenly. 'All the men must be absolutely mad about you.'

'Oh, don't talk to me about men,' Angélique replied in irritation. 'I've just had a terrible quarrel with my husband . . .'

'That's a healthy sign,' said the Duchess approvingly. 'It's a good thing for husband and wife to quarrel from time to time.'

Her comment revealed a character of some maturity. Angélique was beginning to understand the influence she had over her dependants. She felt a sudden desire to confide in this woman, who so recently had been a stranger to her and whom she now felt to be very close. Perhaps she would be able to help her to understand herself. The Duchess of Maudribourg's gaze held something tender and sweet, a kind of ageless wisdom. Angélique pulled herself together and changed the subject.

'Is that a piece of mandrake root you have in that reliquary?' she asked, placing one finger on a gold chain the Duchess was wearing round her neck.

The latter gave a start.

'Oh no, I'd be much too frightened. That is accursed! No! Those are the medallions of my patron saints, Saint Michael the Archangel, Saint Lucy, and Saint Catherine,' she said.

The medallions were warm from contact with feminine flesh and gave Angélique a strange sensation.

'I have worn those ever since I made my First Communion,' the Duchess went on in confidential tones. 'When I can't sleep at night, I feel them there and they calm my fear.'

'What are you frightened of?'

The Duchess made no reply, but closed her eyes and an expression of suffering passed over her face.

'About the mandrake,' Angélique went on, 'were you trying to test me a moment ago? Were you perhaps trying to find out whether I am a witch as they so stupidly will have it in Quebec, and even in Paris? Well, my dear, let me explain to you that I do in fact use mandrake root to make medicine of Arab origin which is known as "soporific sponge". Mixed with a little hemlock and blackberry juice it deadens pain. But I have never bothered to look for it or to have it pulled out of the ground. The few pieces I possess were obtained for me by an English apothecary.'

Ambroisine de Maudribourg, as she listened, had been observing her through her long eyelashes. She suddenly asked:

'So it's true, then, that you have dealings with the English?'

Angélique gave a shrug.

'There are Englishmen everywhere in French Bay. This is not Canada, this is Acadia; in other words we are next-door neighbours to New England. Such a fine mess was made of drafting the treaties that the King of France's possessions and the English trading posts are hopelessly intermingled.'

'And the domain over which you are chatelaine is an independent one in the very heart of these two zones of influence?'

'You seem to be well informed,' said Angélique with a rueful smile.

When she had first set foot in Gouldsboro it had seemed to her to be the most remote shore there was in the world. But the hands of men and of kings had already set their stamp on these semi-virgin lands.

Suddenly she gave a start. What was she doing here? Had she not decided earlier to go and look for Joffrey? It was as if a sudden spell had paralysed her, had held her back ... She rushed over to the window.

Night was falling. In the gathering dusk a ship had passed through the narrows and was entering the port.

'Another visitor, some foreigner or other, a Frenchman, an Englishman, a Dutchman or a pirate, heaven knows what, someone who will persuade Joffrey to follow him heaven knows where on who knows what expedition in the name of order or justice. Never! This time he's not going to slip away under my very nose without warning, leaving me to rot here ...'

She grabbed her sealskin coat and threw it over her shoulders.

'Please excuse me, Madame,' she said to the Duchess, 'I have to leave you. Whatever you say, I am going to send you one of your girls. She can light the candles and if you feel better we'll have some supper sent up to you. Ask for anything you need.'

'Oh, please don't abandon me!'

'But you are perfectly safe here,' Angélique assured her, conscious of the note of anxiety in the Duchess's voice.

Beneath her plucky exterior she was a frail woman and was not finding it easy to recover from the horror of the shipwreck. Had she not said that she had had visions as if this was something quite natural?

'I shall send someone immediately to your bedside,' Angélique insisted, reassuring her like a child. 'Have no fear.'

Suddenly on the alert she caught the sound of male footsteps climbing the stairs. Enrico, the Maltese, appeared in the doorway as she opened the door.

'Countess, my lord Rescator wishes to see you.'

CHAPTER 4

WHENEVER HE was back by the sea again, Enrico resumed the habit of referring to his master by the title of Rescator.

Angélique followed him, her heart thumping, torn between apprehension and relief. So he *had*, after all, sent for her.

She hurried along behind Enrico. They left the fort and climbed up towards the trees. As they reached the edge of the village Angélique could hear the surf beating against the rocks and she remembered how a similar message had once before led her into a trap. That had been some evenings previously, when an unknown sailor with a pale face and strange eyes had come to her and said: 'Monsieur de Peyrac wants to see you' and had lured her away to Old Ship Island.

Instinctively she raised her hands to her belt. She had forgotten her pistols. How stupid! Turning towards Enrico she exclaimed in spite of herself:

'Was it really Monsieur de Peyrac who sent you? Or are you betraying me too?'

'What's going on?'

The Count was standing on the threshold of the last of the wooden houses, his tall silhouette sharply delineated against the light cast by a fire burning brightly in the rustic pebble fireplace.

Angélique gave a sigh of relief.

'Oh, I was afraid of falling into another ambush; the last time it was a white-faced demon come from the sea . . .'

'A white-faced demon?!'

Peyrac stared at her, intrigued.

He came down to meet her and help her over the stone threshold.

He dismissed Enrico with a wave of his hand and closed the heavy wooden door which was so thick that it immediately muffled the roar of the waves.

The tiny room was filled with the crackling of the fire. Angélique went up to the fireplace and held out her hands towards the flames. She was shivering with emotion.

The Count watched her.

'You *are* on edge,' he said gently.

She turned and looked at him with those beautiful eyes of hers that anxiety and unhappiness had darkened until the irises had taken on the colour of a storm-tossed sea.

'Do you wonder, after these terrible days? And I feared that you might have forgotten what we said to one another this morning.'

'How could I forget it, especially when you look at me with such lovely eyes.'

His familiar voice with its soft inflections struck right to her heart and she looked at him adoringly, unable to believe she had been totally forgiven.

He smiled.

'Come, my love,' he said kindly. 'Sit down.'

He pointed to one of the two stools which, with a roughly-made table, a trestle bed and some fishing equipment formed the entire furnishings of the hut.

He himself sat down on the other side of the table. He looked at her attentively and an inner passion sparkled in his sombre gaze, as he saw in her face, framed by her sumptuous pale golden hair, the traces of sorrow and the mark of the blow that had bruised her. He was distressed by the memory of his own violence.

'Oh, my beloved!' he murmured in a stifled voice. 'You are right: let us not allow our enemies to prevail against us. No offence warrants the destruction of what binds us together.'

'I have not offended against you,' she stammered . . . 'or hardly.'

'I like the qualifications,' said Peyrac, and he burst out

laughing. 'My love, you are wonderful. You have always delighted me with your spontaneity.'

She did not know if he was making fun of her, but the warmth in his voice eased the tension she was suffering. Already beneath his loving gaze her fear was evaporating.

'Perhaps we have been alone too long?' he said as if in answer to her innermost thoughts. 'You know, I have learned something during the past few days. Long ago, when the King's sentence of banishment tore us apart I was mad about you, and yet I managed to survive without you. But now *I could no longer do so*. This is what you have done to me, Madame, and I must confess, it is not an easy admission for me to make.'

He smiled, but behind those chiselled features, where life had set its cruel seal in the form of the great scars that stood out pale against his sunburn, his burning glance rested upon her with a kind of astonishment.

'What a strange thing love is,' he went on as if speaking to himself. 'How many times over these past few days have I seen you in my mind's eye arriving in Toulouse once again, beautiful, proud, both childlike and shrewd. It may be that in those days I would not admit to myself that I found the sweetness of your personality even more fascinating than your beauty. Does one ever know what it is one loves in that first glance that binds two people together, often without knowing it? ... Don't look at me like that, my love, you move me to the very marrow of my bones.

'But it was your eyes – that new, unfamiliar look that you revealed to me later in La Rochelle, as you appeared up out of the darkness and the storm to ask me to save your Huguenot friends;[1] that look in your eyes that turned me into a man I no longer recognize. I fear you weaken me. You make me different from the man I used to be ... Do you know what happened to me, my love, when you sought me out that night in La Rochelle? I fell in love with you. Crazily in love. All the more so because I did not want to understand what was happening, knowing who you were. The result was confusion and often torment.

'What a strange feeling it was! And then, when I watched you going about the *Gouldsboro*, with your little redheaded daughter in your arms among your Huguenot friends, I would forget that you were the wife I had once taken in marriage. You were only a near stranger whom I had met by chance, who

1. See *Angélique in Revolt*.

tormented me with her beauty, her sadness, the charm of her rare smiles, a mysterious woman who eluded me, whom I must win at all costs.

'So you see, in my ambiguous situation of a husband who had fallen madly in love with his own wife, I tried to cling to the things I had known in the past, to bring you back to me and although I was clumsy in brandishing the title of husband over your head in order to hold you captive, it was because I wanted you at my mercy, close to me, my mistress, my passion, you, my wife who for the second time had captivated me. Then it was that I began to fear that I might find your heart indifferent to me or that you had forgotten the husband who had been so long banished, and in my fear – oh, how elusive you were – perhaps I never won you over properly. I began to realize that I had treated life too lightly where women were concerned, and you in particular, my wife. And what a treasure I had neglected!'

Angélique was listening to him with bated breath and each word brought life back to her. The caress in his muffled voice, in his burning glance was, in her eyes, worth the sacrifice of all her freedom. What was solitary flight through dangerous open space, compared with the warm certainty of having found a haven beside him? This kind of confession he had had the courage to make to her out of love, revealed to her just how much sway she held over his heart. He had never ceased to think of her, to try to understand her in order to draw closer to her.

'Your unpredictable independence of mind used to cause me agonies. The fear of losing you again was my main concern, and I realized that you belonged only to yourself. It is not so easy to recover from the deep wounds such as you had suffered when you were far from me. I would have to be patient, but the fear was always there, bottled up inside me, and that was what burst out when suddenly ... Tell me, Angélique, my love, why ever did you set out from Houssnock for the English village without letting me know?'

'But ... it was you who told me to,' she exclaimed.

'What do you mean?' he asked with a puzzled frown.

Angélique ran her hand over her brow:

'I don't remember now exactly how it happened, but what I am sure about is that it was on your express orders that I set off to take Rose-Ann to her grandparents. I was in fact rather put out at not being able to make the journey with you.'

He reflected. She saw him clench his fists and murmur something through his teeth.

'So it was "they" once again who contrived the whole thing.'

'What do you mean?'

'Nothing . . . or rather yes, I am beginning to understand a great many things. You opened my eyes this morning when you said: "Our enemies are trying to separate us. Shall we let them triumph? . . ." That is another of your new powers that bind me to you in so exclusive a way. The way you help me through all the snares and difficulties that beset our path, with a skill which could only be yours – I have come to enjoy having a woman beside me who shares my entire life.

'Then came your disappearance, suspicions of your un-faithfulness! . . . How could I have borne that now! I would rather go back to the torture chamber.

'Forgive me, my love, for my anger. But consider, dear heart, to what lengths my love for you drove me, for it even made me lose the sense of justice I try to maintain throughout the many duties I have to perform. You made me lose my temper, made me act unjustly, even towards you my only love, my wife . . . for it is no light matter to discover a truth which in the past Count Peyrac would have been reluctant to accept – that love can cause suffering. So you see, what the Angélique of long ago, delectable and unselfconscious seductress that she was, had not awakened in me, the woman I found in La Rochelle, with her new soul – that irresistible mixture of gentleness and violence – Angélique, almost a stranger, who came and asked me to help a group of people in danger, succeeded in awakening.'

He paused, pulled a wry face then gave her a caustic smile, which did not however efface the passionate look in his dark eyes.

'Of course it is not a pleasant situation suddenly to find one-self a cuckold in the eyes of the world,' he went on, 'but that was not what hurt me most . . . although we had to make sure that the incident did not upset our people . . . but there you helped me . . . Yes, during that storm you never let me down over that . . . you were really . . . everything I could have wished and even through my anger I was forced to admire you and love you . . . But my sufferings were those of a jealous man. Jealous, is that the right word? Rather were they the feelings of a man who was in love but who had not yet won his conquest and who saw her escaping before he could reach that incom-municable meeting-point of love – certainty. Mutual certainty. As long as one still trembles with uncertainty, pain stands ready to rear its head, along with doubt and a fear that everything might be over . . . before you have touched one another in that nameless encounter that fills you with joy, strength and a sense of permanence.'

From the other side of the rough wooden table Angélique had never taken her ardent gaze from him. Nothing remained on earth but him, and their life together.

He misunderstood her silence.

'So you are still angry with me!' he said. 'Angry about what has happened over the past few days . . . I have hurt you! . . . Come now, tell me which of the unspeakable things I did, hurt you the most. Complain a little, my love, so that I may know you better . . .'

'Complain,' she murmured, 'about you, to whom I owe everything? . . . No, it's not that . . . let me just say that there were certain things I failed to understand because I too did not know you well enough . . .'

'For example?'

She could no longer think. Her grievances were melting away beneath the sun of so tender and deep a love.

'Well . . . you made Colin governor.'

'Would you have had me hang him?'

'No, but . . .'

He smiled indulgently.

'Yes, I understand! The complicity between two men who ought to be enemies on account of the beauty of Helen of Troy. Did that hurt you?'

'A little . . . a feminine trait, isn't it?'

'Yes indeed . . . and you are adorable,' he replied. 'What more?'

'And you flirted with that woman Inez!'

'What woman Inez?' he asked.

'Vanereick's Spanish mistress . . . during the banquet . . .'

'Ah, yes, I remember . . . a host's duty! Was I not obliged to console the charming young creature for all the attention our man from Dunkerque was paying you? When one is poisoned by jealousy, one feels a certain pity for others in the same boat . . .'

Angélique lowered her head. The memory of it all brought back her pain.

'There is something more serious,' she murmured. 'That trap you set on Old Ship Island. It was not like you to have lured Colin and me there as you did!'

33

Peyrac's face darkened.

'No indeed . . . it was not me.' He drew from his doublet a crumpled piece of paper which he handed to her.

She made out the following words written in a clumsy hand.

'Your wife is on Old Ship Island with Gold Beard. Land at the north end so that they do not see you coming. You will then be able to catch them in one another's arms.'

Angélique gave a shudder. The terror that had occasionally seized hold of her during the past few days swept over her once more, freezing her to the bones.

'But who . . . who could have written that?' she stammered. 'Who gave you that note?'

'One of the sailors from Vanereick's crew, who was only acting as a messenger, brought it to me. He and I tried to find the man who had handed him the message with instructions to give it to me, but in vain. That is how "they" do things. "They" take advantage of crews coming ashore and of the activity this creates in a port, to slip in amongst us and take action, then "they" vanish like ghosts.'

' "They"? Who are "they"?'

Peyrac's expression remained thoughtful.

'There are strangers in the bay,' he said at last, 'an unknown ship, manned by people who, I am now quite certain, are far too interested in us.'

'Are they French or English?'

'I don't know. Probably Frenchmen, but they sail under no particular flag, and seem to be bent on creating trouble amongst us.'

'Do you think the man with the pale face who came to tell me that you wanted me on the island is one of their men?'

'He must be, and so must the man who met me on the way to Houssnock and told me – falsely, that you had escaped and were on board the *Rochelais* sailing towards Gouldsboro . . .'

'But who can "they" be? Who are "they" sent by?'

'It's impossible to say yet. What we do know is that "they" were well informed about all our movements and that "they" will stop at nothing, for, among seafaring folk, it is a much more serious offence to send false messages than to commit a crime. These people are the scum of the earth, of that I feel convinced.'

'So I was right,' she murmured, 'right to fear some diabolical plot being hatched against us . . .'

'Then I saw you on the island with Gold Beard. And that was something our enemies did not know, something they could not know – that Gold Beard was Colin. And that altered everything. Colin Paturel, King of the Slaves in Meknès, almost a friend of mine too, at any rate a man of whom I thought highly, for he was famous throughout the Mediterranean. Yes, that made a big difference. Colin! . . . a man to whom it was no dishonour for you to grant, let us say . . . your friendship . . . but I had to make sure I captured Gold Beard. I sent Yann back for reinforcements with orders to return along the fairway only when the tide was going out.'

'And so you stayed.'

'Yes, I stayed.'

'You wanted to find out what sort of a person I was?' she asked, looking him straight in the face.

'And I found out.'

'You might have had a very unpleasant surprise.'

'I had some wonderful ones that fortified my heart.'

'You are forever taking crazy risks!'

'It wasn't only that. My reason for remaining on the island and hiding there until my men returned was not only because I wanted to know more about my beautiful, unknown wife. Curiosity alone would not have been enough to involve me in so awkward a situation had I not been obliged to do so. You must bear in mind, my love, that it was a delicate situation. If I had approached you alone, do you think that Colin would have been easily persuaded that, as your husband, my intentions were peaceful? And do you think that, as a pirate worthy of hanging, he would easily have allowed himself to be apprehended by the master of Gouldsboro? You accuse me of taking up impossible wagers all too easily, but the idea of facing him in single combat on that beach, without any other witness than you and the seals, which would certainly have resulted in his death or mine, struck me as being neither sane nor profitable. Your Colin never did have the reputation of being easy to handle.'

'And yet you have managed to persuade this unmanageable man to serve you, you managed to lure him into your charmed circle.'

'Only because he was brought to me in chains surrounded by four armed men. That was not how things were on Old Ship Island. Given these facts, what could I have done other than remain the invisible witness of your meeting? A fortuitous and involuntary meeting, as I was later to find out. There again our

35

enemies were playing a winning game by getting all three of us together on the island. The only way to counter such diabolical schemes is to do exactly the opposite from what everyone expects. Thank God that all three of us were given enough moral strength to resist.'

'Diabolical,' Angélique repeated.

'Don't worry, I shall know how to forestall their plans, whatever they are, and to get rid of them. While we did not suspect their presence, we fell into their traps. But even when I received that note on the evening of the naval battle against Gold Beard, I had begun to feel wary. I knew that sooner or later "they" would make contact with us. For a brief moment I thought that Gold Beard was in it, but as it happened I received proof to the contrary. I went to the island along the fairway with a boat and only one man, but I remained on my guard against anything unexpected and . . . against myself, since the note could have been a trick to draw me into a snare or it could have been true, in which case "they" counted on my wrath to make me do something irreparable, particularly towards you. I began to note this desire to harm you, especially you.

' "Be careful!" I told myself. "Remember that no matter what happens, nothing must harm *her*. Especially not her." My anger swung round against those wretches who were trying to use me against you through their Machiavellian plans. This time at least I had to defend you from their attacks, at no matter what cost. Did I not win you in Toulouse, by fighting a duel with the Archbishop's nephew?'

'That was not the same,' Angélique exclaimed passionately, 'it will never again be the same. Who do you take me for? Now I love you! . . .' Then – surprised by her admission as if by some revelation – 'Yes, I love you . . . too much! More than you deserve. Are you so remote that you cannot even begin to imagine how much I love you? Have we not fought together against the Iroquois, against the French and their savages? Against winter, sickness and death? Have I been unworthy of you? . . . I beg you, if you don't want to make me suffer, keep yourself safe for me, my dear love. Stop playing games with your life, for if I were to lose you again I should die, I should die!'

He had stood up and he came towards her with open arms. She clasped him to her, her forehead against his shoulder, losing herself in this wonderful refuge, where her whole life seemed to dissolve, and she felt, in this contact she had at last

36

regained in his warmth, in his familiar scent, a moment of acute happiness.

'I too have been guilty,' she murmured, 'I doubted your love for me and mistrusted your feelings. I should have said to you straight away: "Look. I have found Colin again . . ." but I was frightened. Some inexplicable fear held me back. Having grown accustomed to fight against mean and petty snares, I have become used to silence rather than truth. Forgive me.'

He took her face in his hands and tilted it back to look into her eyes and gently kiss her lips.

'We could scarcely have come together again without encountering difficulties after living through so much that transformed our hearts and marked our minds. The fear always remained, on the threshold of this wonderful new discovery of love, that we might again be frustrated . . . Now we must take cognizance of one another and say it. My dear, sweet little stranger, whom I have still not entirely managed to tame, forgive me, forgive me . . .'

And with infinite gentleness he kissed the bruise on her temple.

'My new love, my ever beloved, my too silent girl . . .'

She ran her fingers caressingly through his thick hair then across one silver temple.

'You always did know how to talk of love. The ocean adventurer and conqueror of the new world have not killed the troubadour from Languedoc.'

'He is far away. I am no longer the Count of Toulouse.'

'What do I care for the Count of Toulouse? The man I love is the pirate who took pity on me at La Rochelle, and who gave me a cup of Turkish coffee to drink when I was dying of cold, the man who had the guns fired on the King's dragoons to defend my hunted Huguenot friends, and the man who, in spite of their ingratitude, was able to pardon them at my request; the man with whom I slept in the depths of the forest with so deep a sense of security that it would be impossible to find its like on earth save in childhood, the man who said to my small daughter: "Young lady, I am your father . . ." You are so dear to me. I would not have had you indifferent to this . . . this incident. I need to feel constantly that I belong to you . . . truly.'

The physical bond which had always been so strong between them added a sense of giddiness to this moment of unclouded happiness, and their lips met in long, passionate kisses interrupting with their intoxicating silences the murmur of their avowals.

'Magician! Magician! How can I defend myself against you? But one day I shall find out how to win you over for ever ...'

Joffrey de Peyrac looked up.

'And now, what can we do, treasure of my heart? These people are swallowing us up. With all these pirates and ship-wrecked people in hospital, there is nowhere left for us. Did you not give up our room to the Duchess of Maudribourg?'

'Yes, I did. But I really didn't know where to put her so that she could have a bit of comfort, and you had gone away and left me there.'

'Let's go on board the *Gouldsboro*,' he decided. 'That's where I have been these past few nights to get some rest, away from the temptation of joining you in the fort and forgiving you too easily.'

'What false pride men have! If you had come you would have made me mad with joy. Instead of which I cried and cried ... I was no longer myself. You destroyed me!'

He clasped her tight in his arms. Then Angélique picked up her cloak.

They left the log hut and slowly walked down through the darkness towards the village taking care to keep their voices down in order not to attract attention.

They feared, as lovers do, being recognized and stopped and asked to face further obligations. Then suddenly, aware of their furtive reactions and their fears, they both began to laugh.

'There is no heavier burden than being responsible for people,' he remarked. 'Here we are obliged to keep to the deep shadows in order to have a few moments of privacy together.'

The Spanish soldiers, the Count's constant guards and companions, were following close on their heels but they were no more troublesome than ghosts.

'Let us pray to God that they are our only escorts and that we shall manage to reach the beach without hindrance,' whispered Angélique.

CHAPTER 5

IN SPITE of her prayer, as they passed close to the fort, a female silhouette that seemed to have been watching for them, slipped out from the doorway and ran towards them.

It was Marie-la-Douce, the young serving maid of the Duchess of Maudribourg.

'Ah, Madame, there you are at last,' she said in anguished tones, 'we've been looking for you everywhere. My mistress is dying.'

'But I left the Duchess of Maudribourg in excellent health only a short time ago?'

'It came over her suddenly. She lost consciousness, then began to run a high fever, and now she's delirious. Oh do come, Madame, I beg you!'

Angélique turned towards her husband. Panic was taking hold of her, the result of days of fatigue and superhuman tension. Every incident was suddenly taking on unreasonable proportions and she had the impression that the whole world was in league to separate them. Now that they had at last sorted things out after that dreadful quarrel, she no longer wanted to leave him, even for a few moments, before they had been able to rest and seek reassurance from their torments in one another's arms. Beneath the folds of her cloak she clung to his hand, warm and vibrant with life.

'But what is going on? I'm exhausted. And I want to be alone with you,' she added softly, turning towards the Count.

He replied calmly:

'Let us go and see how the Duchess is. I doubt whether things are so serious. If necessary you can give her a calming potion and then we shall be able to withdraw in peace.'

Inside the bedroom there was high excitement. Petronella Damourt was lamenting noisily, rushing round in circles, while Delphine du Rosoy and Antoinette, another of the King's Girls, were doing their best to bring the Duchess round. Jeanne Michaud was praying in one corner while her child sat beside her philosophically sucking its thumb. Madame Carrère whom they had summoned to help them was grumbling to herself as she brewed up some herbal tea.

Among all these women, the presence of the bespectacled secretary, Armand Daveau seemed incongruous. He came and went wearing an expression like a lost owl and kept on knocking into things.

On the other hand, the soldier Adhemar was standing motionless in a pool of water in the middle of the room, having been sent to fetch first hot, then cold water for compresses. Finally, the scraggy kitten had taken refuge on a console-table where it stood, hair abristle, spitting furiously.

It was the kitten whom Angélique noticed first.

'Poor little creature,' she thought, 'these silly women will make him really ill.'

She went over to the bed and leaned over the prostrate form of the Duchess. When she had left her, she had been calm and rested, but now she was burning hot. Her eyes were half-closed and she was muttering a string of disjointed, strange-sounding words.

Angélique lifted her eyelids and saw that the pupils had almost disappeared, felt for her pulse which she could not find, noticed the rigidity of her arms and hands, then, to make certain once more that no internal injury could be the cause of this alarming condition, she threw back the cover and once more carefully palpated her body, studying Ambroisine de Maudribourg's reactions to the touch of her fingers. But the Duchess remained in the depths of unconsciousness, with a vague, staring glimmer filtering through her half-closed eyelids. She neither shuddered nor seemed to feel any pain while being examined. Angélique tried to move her legs which were equally rigid. Her toes were contracted and icy cold; so Angélique rubbed them gently and noticed as she did so some relaxation of the muscles.

'Get some hot bricks ready,' she told the women.

While trying to get some warmth back into them, Angélique noticed that the Duchess of Maudribourg's feet were exceptionally pretty. She must take great care of them for the skin was supple and satiny.

Preoccupied as she was by this alarming condition, Angélique had not noticed that the young woman, abandoned to her care, was revealing to all present, through a thin lawn shift, the semi-nudity of an admirable body.

Adhemar's voice suddenly broke the silence.

'That's what you'd call a handsome woman,' he said nodding his head several times in a knowing manner. 'You really can say that that's a fine figure of a woman, can't you, Monsieur le Comte? . . .'

'Adhemar, what are you doing here?' Angélique asked. 'I thought you were on guard duty tonight.'

'They sent me to fetch water,' said Adhemar, 'they settled on me like a cloud of hens . . . It's not rightly a job for a military man who has his dignity . . . But you have to lend a hand to the ladies . . . Especially in a damned country like this . . . the poor things! . . . If I hadn't been there . . .'

Angélique had gently covered up the invalid again, who now seemed better although still unconscious.

'I think you're right,' she said turning to her husband. 'It's some kind of hysterical attack, no doubt brought on by the horror she suffered during the shipwreck. I'll give her something to calm her.'

'The infusion is ready,' Madame Carrère announced, coming towards them with the bowl in her hands.

Angélique fetched her bag and swiftly made up the mixture she needed.

Suddenly the Duchess's voice rang out through the room, clear and well modulated. She said:

'The volume of water q is equal to K, constant, multiplied by the square root of 2gH, where g is the acceleration of gravity and H the height of the waterfall . . . but he's wrong, I'm sure . . . K also depends on friction . . .'

The rest was lost in an indistinct murmur.

'Whatever is all that rubbish,' exclaimed Adhemar aghast, 'are those cabalistic formulae to bewitch us all?'

'Great heavens, she's delirious again,' Delphine lamented wringing her hands.

An enigmatic smile suddenly began to play about Count Peyrac's lips.

'She has just recited the theorem of an Italian hydraulics expert and I think that she is quite right to correct his formula,' he said, 'there's no need for you to be so worried, young lady. Don't you know that your benefactress is one of the most learned women in the world, always exchanging mathematical postulates in Paris with doctors of the Sorbonne?'

Angélique listened to him without really taking in this astonishing information.

She had leaned over Ambroisine and slipped one hand

beneath her head in an attempt to make her drink something. Once again the subtle yet spellbinding perfume exuded by the Duchess's thick black hair made her feel strangely disturbed. Like a kind of warning.

'What does that perfume mean?' she asked herself.

Then she saw that Ambroisine de Maudribourg's eyes were open and staring at her. She smiled at her.

'Drink up,' she urged her, 'come on, drink up, it will do you good.'

The Duchess raised herself with some difficulty. She seemed exhausted by the attack she had suffered. She drank in tiny sips, as if drained of all strength, and Angélique had to urge her on several times before she managed to finish it all. Then she fell back again and lay still with her eyes closed. But she was better.

'The fever is leaving her!' Angélique noted after laying one hand on the Duchess's brow, now cooler. 'There's no need to worry any more.'

She went and washed her hands and put away her remedies.

Madame de Maudribourg's followers gathered round her in anxiety.

'Oh, Madame, do not abandon us,' they begged her. 'Do stay with us tonight to look after her. We are so frightened for her.'

'No! you are wrong to be worried, I tell you.'

This kind of anxiety all these women were manifesting on behalf of their benefactress began to strike her as overdone.

'She will sleep, that I guarantee. And you too must sleep,' she advised them. 'Adhemar, pick up all your buckets and take your leave of these ladies! Come on now, you can light our way to the port with a lantern.'

Why did all these people cling to her and Joffrey like a lot of creeping plants, as if to paralyse them? It was like a nightmare.

She moved closer to him. He was still standing staring at the recumbent form of the Duchess of Maudribourg. Framed in that sumptuous black hair that spread over the lace-edged pillow, almost too heavy and opulent, her sleeping face appeared smaller, like that of a child.

Angélique said in a half-whisper:

'Are you coming?' But Joffrey de Peyrac did not seem to hear her.

Angélique's head began to swim and she felt a headache coming on. More than anything else on earth she wanted to get away, to make her escape with him. Not only was it a question of her need to be in his arms. It seemed a vital necessity, a matter of life and death. She must not lose him again tonight, or else . . .

She felt her nerves about to crack.

'Madame, please stay,' the young women moaned in chorus.

'She may die,' cried Delphine du Rosoy, in tragic tones.

They clustered still more closely round her.

'Do stay! Do stay!' they chanted. 'For pity's sake, dear lady!'

Their eyes shone with a strange fear. In a flash it occurred to Angélique that they were mad. With an instinctive gesture she grasped the Count's arm, begging for help.

He seemed to come to himself, looked at her, and saw her pale, tense face. Then, in front of everyone present, he put his arm round her waist.

'Ladies, be reasonable,' he said, 'Madame de Peyrac needs rest too, and I am going to take her away, if you don't mind! If you have any more worries about your mistress, send for Doctor Parry. He will give you good advice.'

Upon these words, whose irony was lost on them, he took his leave of them very gallantly and went out taking Angélique with him.

CHAPTER 6

'THAT DUCHESS OF MAUDRIBOURG and her retinue make me weary,' Angélique remarked as they walked down towards the shore. 'It's as if she drove them all crazy. Never have I felt more astonished than when I saw her. Why had I imagined her as a fat elderly lady? The title of Duchess, I suppose, and that of benefactress . . .'

'And also the fact that you knew she was the widow of the Duke of Maudribourg, who died only a few years ago at a ripe old age. If I am right in my calculations, he would be over

43

eighty now . . . and still the husband of that very pretty woman with more than forty years' difference in age between them.'

'Ah, now I understand,' Angélique exclaimed, 'so that's it. A marriage between fiefs such as all too many young girls, sometimes almost children, have to submit to to please their families.'

She gave a shudder and pressed her cheek against the Count's shoulder.

'I too can remember on my way to Toulouse I thought I was going to marry an old man . . . a monster, a Gilles de Rais . . .'

'The Duke of Maudribourg was all those things rolled into one: debauched, unscrupulous. It was said that he had pretty orphan girls brought up in convents so that as soon as they reached puberty he could either make them his mistresses or, if they were of noble stock, marry them. It seems that he tired of them quickly and after the death of his first three – no, four – wives, there was talk that he had had them poisoned. The young king even had him banished from Court for a time, although that did not stop him from attending the royal wedding in San Sebastian. But I refused to meet him . . . precisely on account of your youth and beauty. He had been to visit me before in Toulouse for he wanted to learn secret formulas to conjure up the Devil.'

'Heavens, how horrible! Was he already married to the present Duchess at the time of the King's wedding? No, he couldn't have been, she was too young still, the poor child!'

'She isn't as young as all that,' Peyrac replied somewhat caustically. 'And I don't think she's all that childish. She's a person of great intelligence and exceptional culture.'

'But . . . it seems as if you know her too!' Angélique exclaimed.

'By reputation only. She defended a thesis at the Sorbonne on the infinitesimal calculus invented by Monsieur Descartes. It was in that capacity that I, wishing to keep abreast of the progress of science in Europe, heard people speak of her. I even read a short treatise of hers in which she questioned not only Descartes but also the laws concerning the gravitational pull of the moon . . . When the duenna of the King's Girls mentioned the name of their benefactress I was not sure that it really was the same woman. For I too thought it somewhat unlikely, but it is indeed true that Gouldsboro has within its walls one of the foremost doctors *honoris causae* of our time.'

'I find it hard to believe,' murmured Angélique. 'What a lot has happened in a few days!'

They reached the edge of the water, and Jacques Vignot came towards them holding a lantern. The night was thick with mist yet not altogether dark. An invisible moon, filtering through the fog, left a murky trail of light glittering like mysterious fire-flies on the rippling waves, between the leaden-hued network of headlands and the reefs. There was something vaguely disquieting in the play of these dim, fleeting lights. Those swathes of ever-shifting mists seemed like monstrous lurking presences.

They were about to set foot on the jetty when, coming from they knew not where, far away, and yet distinct, they heard an agonized wail, the cry of a woman. It rang out, terrible, interminable, a cry that seemed to be caused by some unspeakable agony that would not end. It seemed to issue from the night itself, from the farthest point of the black storm clouds above them.

It rang out through the darkness, and the wind seemed to take it, amplifying its piercing echo, vibrant with a nameless pain, so that it resembled a shriek of hatred and demonic rage.

The hearers felt their blood run cold in their veins and stood still, petrified.

Adhemar dropped the lantern he was carrying. He was trembling so much he was unable to cross himself.

'The Demon . . . the Demon . . .' he stammered. 'That's it all right! You heard it, didn't you?'

Tough as they were, the other sailors were shaken too.

'Something not right going on over there, don't you think?' said one of them, staring into the depths of the night. 'What do you think, my lord? . . . a woman in distress?'

'No, it's the voice of a spirit,' said another. 'Don't make no mistake about that. I heard things just like that around the Demon Archipelago in the Gulf of Saint Lawrence . . . And yet that one didn't come from the sea . . .'

'No, it came from the village,' Peyrac remarked, 'almost as if it came from the fort.'

Angélique thought of the Duchess of Maudribourg.

Such a cry could only have come from someone in their death throes. Suddenly convinced that the sick woman had died, Angélique ran back towards the houses, reproaching herself for having abandoned the unfortunate woman at her last hour.

She arrived breathless and saw two silhouettes framed in the lighted open window from which they were leaning.

'What's happening?' she called.

'I don't know,' Delphine du Rosoy's voice replied. 'Somebody shrieked outside. It was dreadful! We are all still trembling.'

'It was as if it came from the forest,' Marie-la-Douce added as she stood beside her.

Angélique remained perplexed.

'No, it came from this direction. It's strange that you didn't have the same impression ... Was Madame de Maudribourg not disturbed by the cry?'

'No.' Marie-la-Douce glanced behind her into the room. 'She's sleeping peacefully, thanks be to God!'

'Well then, close the shutters now and get some rest yourselves. It may have been an animal caught in a trap in the woods. In any case, Marie, you oughtn't to be up and about like this, you've had enough for one day! Go and get into bed quickly, my child, to please me.'

'Yes, Madame. You are very kind, Madame,' the young girl replied, her voice suddenly cracking.

'Goodnight, Madame,' Delphine called sweetly.

They stepped back and closed the heavy wooden shutter.

For a moment, standing there in the darkness, Angélique listened once again for the echo of that dreadful cry.

'Who is suffering like that in the dark?' a secret inner voice asked her. ' "What distraught demon succubus?" Oh! I'm going mad. "They" will drive me crazy ... Joffrey! ...'

Then she realized that she was alone again, and she was seized with a sudden terror.

'Joffrey,' she shrieked in her turn, 'Joffrey, Joffrey! Where are you?'

'But I am here,' the Count replied as he walked up the hill to meet her. 'Come, what is it now, my dear? Why all this panic?'

She threw herself at him and clasped him convulsively.

'Oh, I suddenly felt so frightened. I beg you, let us not separate again this evening, let us not separate again or I shall die.'

CHAPTER 7

AND NOW it was morning, a white morning heavy with mist, yet bright and luminous enough for the horrors of the night to have seemed to vanish with the dawning day.

Angélique and Joffrey stood leaning on the rail of the *Gouldsboro* waiting quietly for the boat that was to take them back to the shore, still enveloped in the solitude and mystery that the fog had created around them.

From the invisible land they could hear the sounds of activity in the colony. This morning they felt happy and full of strength, keenly aware of the intense life the echo of which reached them through the mist, the calls of fishermen coming down to the shore, the sound of carpenters hammering nails into planks, beams and laths, women shouting to one another . . .

The cries of sea birds and the more distant cooing of doves in the woods rose above this noisy background and the smells of life pierced the fog, the smell of fires, of smoke-curing, of tobacco, of rum, of freshly sawn wood, the typical aroma of a fort along these shores, mingling with the iodine tang from the sea and the pungent exhalations of resin from the forest.

'I must go and make things up with the ladies of Gouldsboro,' said Angélique. 'They are not easy . . . but then neither am I. But all things considered, we are fond of one another and find our disagreements stimulating. They are intelligent and welcome the fact that I bring them a certain something from the outside that helps them widen their horizons. What I have always liked about the Huguenot women is that they have not got, as all too many Catholic women have, that overwhelming sense of their femininity, that unthinking docility before their husbands or the parish priest.'

'Hum!' Peyrac replied. 'It's obvious that you have managed to shake off the Papist yoke.'

'I have shaken off all yokes,' Angélique replied with a laugh, 'except that of your love.'

And she gave him her most passionate look. Those hours that

47

had just passed, that marvellous night, would forever remain something beyond price to her; everything they had said to one another the previous day in the turmoil of their first attempt at reconciliation, later in the blind raptures of their lovemaking, in the glow of those hours when, their bodies assuaged, but still stirring with delight at the joy they had felt, their minds freed from worldly anxieties, they had been able to communicate without shame, their hearts bare. All those words would remain in her like a treasure that she would never tire of contemplating, re-testing their sweetness and savour. Soon there would be a day when she would be able to draw from the memory of them the spiritual sustenance to enable her to live through a terrible ordeal.

She did not know it yet on that calm morning, permeated with light through the rising warmth. Alone and far off the demoniacal cry from the Lost Tower sent a tiny stab of anxiety through her. She wanted to ignore it. She felt renewed, even different, and looked the man she loved straight in the face with a smile. Everything about him stirred her and made her feel happy.

A rhythmical splashing sound told them that the boat was approaching.

They passed through the gang-port from which one of the sailors had removed the panel. The man went down on his hands and knees and let out a rope ladder.

'And I forgot about my kitten,' Angélique reminded herself. 'I hope someone gave him something to drink . . . and that the Duchess of Maudribourg hasn't died. I must also go and see Abigail now that things are a bit quieter. Her child is nearly due . . .'

They took their places in the longboat and the sailors strained at the heavy oars to cover the few fathoms that separated them from the shore.

'And I must go and ask Madame Carrère to find suitable lodgings for the Duchess so that we can move back into our room in the fort – you aren't going off again, are you? I cannot bear to feel you somewhere else. The hours seem so long and so bitter when I don't know where you are. I am prepared to devote myself wholeheartedly to Gouldsboro, but with you beside me . . . What was that ship that came into port last night?'

Peyrac nodded his head.

'I very much fear that it may be yet another lot of those

people coming to tear me away from you, on a police mission in French Bay.'

'Englishmen?'

'No! Frenchmen. The Governor of Acadia in person, Monsieur de Ville d'Avray. His arrival was announced to me yesterday evening, but I asked Colin and d'Urville to receive him as I wanted to devote myself to you, to nothing but you.'

The boat drew alongside the jetty and as Angélique began to walk across the beach she caught sight of something tiny, something alive and struggling desperately among the seaweed.

'What is that? A crab? Oh, my goodness, it's my kitten!' she exclaimed. 'What is it doing here? It was sick enough already.'

She picked him up; covered with scum and sand sticking to his fur and his frail limbs, the kitten seemed once more on the point of death. But, as on the previous day, his golden eyes besought her help and recognized her.

'It's as if he'd come down to the beach to wait for me, as if he knew I was coming back this way . . .'

'I was waiting for you along of that critter,' whined Adhemar out of the fog. 'That there Governor of Acadia who arrived yesterday evening says as we are deserters, me and the other soldiers who were at Fort Saint Mary. He says he's going to have us tried by court martial. He wanted to take a fat stick to the bigwig who brought us here.'

'Ah! So Defour is here too, is he?' said Peyrac. 'That spells trouble; the Defour brothers don't like officials from Quebec. And who's this coming now?'

Three or four shapes loomed up out of the mist. Colin, his quartermaster, Vanneau, d'Urville and Gabriel Berne. They wished, they said, to discuss several urgent matters with Monsieur and Madame de Peyrac before the French Governor, who had been their guest the previous evening, and who seemed to be about to cause a lot of trouble, took up all the Count's attention with his claims and his demands.

Colin was already well in the picture. The competence he had shown in taking over the running of Gouldsboro was gradually winning him support from the Huguenots.

He said that he had two projects about which both the Huguenot and Catholic population had already given their verdict. First there was the construction of a small fort with four corner turrets at a place known as Cayugas River, which was situated halfway between Camp Champlain and the port of Gouldsboro. It was down this river that hostile redskins came to attack the white settlers in the area.

To build a look-out fort to protect local people going about their business there had become a matter of urgency, especially at this time of the year when Iroquois war parties would soon be on the move again.

The other project concerned the building of a Catholic chapel on the far side of the promontory where the new arrivals on the *Heart of Mary* seemed inclined to settle.

'Right!' said the Count. 'Let us settle these thorny questions, but to start with, let's go and eat at Madame Carrère's – some of her shellfish soup or her hot cinnamon wine.'

He led Angélique off towards the inn, from which there rose the goodly smell of a wood fire; the others followed them, and finally Adhemar who always looked as if he were following a hearse.

Angélique had slipped the kitten beneath her cloak and noted anxiously that it was shivering.

Gabriel Berne came up to her and drew her aside.

'Just a word, if I may, Madame, but I have a feeling that Monsieur de Peyrac will have to leave us for a few days on an expedition up the Saint John River and I expect you might like to accompany him ... So I wanted to ask you ... my wife's time is almost come ... I am very worried. Your presence here is the only thing that will reassure us ...'

'Don't worry, my dear Berne,' she replied, 'I shall not leave Gouldsboro before Abigail has had her child and is completely recovered from her confinement.'

But she added, with a tightening of the heart:

'Do you really think that my husband will have to leave Gouldsboro? What business could he possibly have in the Saint John River?'

'The situation is extremely complex. That Englishman from Boston, Phipps, who came here with Admiral Sheringham, has managed to block the mouth of the river to certain important persons from Quebec. The Governor of Acadia with his chaplain and a handful of young hot-heads just managed to get through and have come here to ask for help; once again this is the sort of issue that might start a war between the two kingdoms, and your husband is the only one who can prevent it.'

He motioned with his chin towards Count Peyrac who was crossing the threshold of the inn.

The soldiers stood guard at the door. Don Juan Alvarez followed the Count inside. He never left his side while he was on land but kept a discreet yet unwavering watch on him.

CHAPTER 8

THERE WERE already a large number of women in the main room of the inn.

It was a custom, that had grown up among the ladies of Gouldsboro from the time the inn had been built, to foregather there in the morning after the children had got up and their husbands had left for work. They held counsel there and enjoyed something to eat, sitting quietly in front of their plates as a relief from the cares of serving the family table. Then they would all go back to their housework.

Angélique immediately caught sight of Madame Manigault who stood up and dropped them a little curtsey.

Some of the children and teenagers who were scaling fish over a wooden bowl also gave them a cheerful greeting. Madame Manigault was smiling as much as her habitually grumpy face would allow.

Peyrac smiled back at her.

'I see that the crates of china have been opened,' he said. 'All that porcelain was a pretty delicate cargo to bring from Europe, but Erikson did not spare the straw and it looks as if there were not too many breakages.'

'No, except the handle of one Limoges basin and a few things from a Dutch kiln.'

A few of the ladies carried over to the table various pieces of the china which was providing the subject of conversation that morning, a more cheerful and absorbing subject than piracy, fighting and hangings, treachery and shipwreck, which had wearied them over the past few days.

The presence of Count Peyrac and Angélique sitting side by side and apparently reconciled added to the general feeling of relaxation.

Every family in Gouldsboro had been given a present to hang up or stand on their dresser, some a soup tureen, some a few plates, or a jug, a bowl, a serving dish, something useful and of good quality that would lend new lustre to their rustic homes.

'And you, my love, have you had time to look at your presents?' Joffrey de Peyrac asked Angélique softly, leaning towards her.

'Oh no. I didn't have the heart.'

She remained preoccupied by what Berne had said and seemed distracted as she ate. Peyrac watched her.

'What are you worried about now?'

'I am thinking about the French Governor who has arrived so inopportunely. Are you going to have to go off up French Bay?'

'We shall see. Just for now, even if every man jack in Canada was in danger of being scalped or clapped in irons in the very next hour, I would not leave you for at least two days.'

This promise comforted Angélique. Two days. An infinity! ... She gave the kitten something to eat and drink beneath the fascinated gaze of a few small children, then spoke to Madame Carrère about finding the Duchess somewhere else to live. There was a house on the edge of the village whose owner had gone into the interior to barter furs. The Duchess and her suite might find it a trifle cramped but they would have to rough it; when you set off for Canada you must be prepared for anything ... Angélique also inquired whether it had been possible to mend Ambroisine de Maudribourg's clothes.

'Not yet. I have had to find thread of all the colours in the rainbow to mend things like those! ... You know, there was something odd about those clothes...'

'What do you mean?'

'Those stains, those tears...'

'After a shipwreck how do you expect them to be?'

'I don't mean that! Something, I can't explain...'

Angélique left the inn after making her husband promise to join her at the fort towards the end of the morning so that they could rest together, and also not to leave the colony suddenly on some warfaring expedition without warning her. He laughed, repeated his promises and kissed the tip of her fingers. But in spite of this she felt uneasy. The fears of losing him once more had opened before her like a deadly chasm.

Yet when she saw the sun finally break through the mist and saw Gouldsboro all a-glitter with its pale wooden houses, its cliffs with their emerald wash of thick trees, its beaches, its headlands of tumbled rocks, blue in one place, mauve or pink in another, happiness won the day and she told herself that she was the most fortunate of women. No matter what happened, they would overcome all obstacles.

As she approached the fort carrying the kitten, she breathed a prayer that the Duchess would be sufficiently recovered to be able to move, so that she could once again enjoy the privacy of her room, alone with her happiness, her new heart. She decided to examine the contents of the crates brought over on the *Gouldsboro*. So far she had only rummaged quickly through them in search of a dress to wear to what might well have been Colin's hanging. What a horrible memory that was; it made the serenity of this new day even more welcome.

As she was about to climb the staircase inside the fort, she heard voices that seemed raised in heated argument; then Captain Job Simon came out of her room bending his tall frame in order not to bang his already wounded forehead. With his head sunk down between his shoulders, as if weighed down by some crushing burden, he almost looked like a hunchback. He glowered at Angélique.

'There!' he said. 'Not only have I lost my ship, but I've come in for a tongue-lashing as well. Would *you* say that was fair?'

In spite of his hideously ugly face, so disfigured by the crude red birthmark on his temple, the humanity in those grey eyes buried under those enormous eyebrows made him look like a sad dog seeking a little affection.

'You did save your unicorn,' she said by way of comfort, 'isn't that a good sign, an omen for the future?'

'Yes, I s'pose it is! But I'll have to regild it. Where am I going to find any gold-leaf here? It'll be a long time before I can get that back on the prow of a ship! I'm finished. And on top of all that I get told off.'

'Just between us, Captain, are you not somewhat to blame? If you were supposed to be going to Quebec, how did you manage to stray into these parts?'

He considered her remark thoughtfully, then gave a great sigh.

'Agreed! But as for the shipwreck, that was not my fault!'

'Whose was it then?'

'Those filthy wreckers who waved lanterns about on the cliff-tops to lure us on to those blasted rocks . . .'

He suddenly seemed to think again.

'My unicorn ... My father was a gilder and I know a bit about it ... but I'll have to find some gold. Where do you think I can find gold in this damn country of demons and wreckers?'

'Who knows? Perhaps we'll find some! Don't you know that gold is the devil's affair!'

'You shouldn't joke about those things, Madame,' cried Adhemar, who had followed her.

The captain crossed himself vigorously, but added nevertheless:

'Never mind! Never mind about the devil. You find me some gold-leaf for my unicorn and I'm your man! Thanks in advance, Madame! You at least have a good heart.'

And he went off apparently feeling much better.

The kitten jumped down from Angélique's arms and began to sniff at the door.

'Be careful he doesn't get away again ... catch him, Adhemar! Why do you always follow me around like this, you poor boy?'

'Do you think I want to be hanged like that Governor of Acadia said? ... And anyway I had to tell you my dream. I saw an angel that was all red, entirely red from head to foot; now that's not normal for an angel ...'

Angélique entered the room. The kitten went in with a proprietary air. Tail erect, he made a beeline for the piece of blanket she had given him the previous day, settled down on it and began to give himself a thorough wash.

CHAPTER 9

AMBROISINE DE MAUDRIBOURG was sitting by the window wearing a black velvet dress with a lace collar. The dark dress accentuated the pallor of her complexion. She looked like an orphan infanta. With her hands clasped round her knees, she seemed to be plunged in deep meditation. Her followers respected her silence.

As Angélique entered, the Duchess looked up briskly. Her movements had distinction, but betrayed a natural impulsiveness which was not without charm and made her appear even younger.

'Ah, there you are, Madame,' she said. 'I have been waiting for you. There you are at last!'

Her eyes glistened with contained joy.

'I see you are up,' said Angélique, 'and, I trust, cured of your indisposition? Did you have a good night? You still seem very pale.'

'It's nothing. I was just thinking that I have troubled you enough, by occupying your private accommodation. Now I can move elsewhere, although I must admit I still feel very stiff. Captain Simon has just been to tell me that our ship is a total loss. But I think that by signing the necessary bills I might find a ship that will take me and my girls to Quebec.'

'Do not speak of leaving us to soon, Madame,' Angélique replied, thinking of the elaborate plans that had been made for the King's Girls. 'Neither you nor they are really recovered yet.'

'Well then, at least let me get out of your way here. Any old hut will suffice. When I left for New France, I placed the sacrifice of comfort on the list of things to be offered up to Our Lord. I am not afraid of hardship.'

'We shall put you somewhere with your girls,' said Angélique, 'and in spite of your desire for self-denial, I shall make sure that you have everything you need.'

She felt relieved that the Duchess of Maudribourg had been tactful enough herself to suggest leaving the room in the fort. This young woman with the strange personality had nevertheless absorbed the excellent training that all girls of the nobility received in convents, and seemed to have a natural inclination to consider the feelings and wellbeing of others.

She had smiled slightly at Angélique's words. She motioned towards the dress she was wearing.

'Another thing I must ask you in your kindness to forgive me. Look how forward I have been. Not knowing how to clothe myself, I borrowed this dress from you.'

'You could have chosen one that suited you better,' Angélique retorted spontaneously. 'That one doesn't suit your colouring. You look like someone from a convent, or an orphan.'

'But I *am* from a convent,' the Duchess retaliated, suddenly laughing as if she found it funny, 'didn't I tell you so already?

And I *am* also an orphan,' she added more quietly, but simply.

Angélique remembered what Joffrey de Peyrac had told her about this young woman's marriage to an old man and she felt a vague sense of remorse mingled with pity. Beneath that air of self-assurance worn by the Duchess of Maudribourg, who was reputed to be not only extremely learned but an acute business woman, she was possibly alone in discerning a chink in the armour, something childlike and broken. She felt a desire to protect and help her, to bring some distraction as well into a life which seemed to her to have been too austere.

'I shall find you a more cheerful dress.'

'No, please,' the Duchess replied shaking her head, 'allow me if you will to wear this in mourning for the poor wretches who died two nights ago without the sacraments. I can think of nothing else.'

And she let her face fall into her hands.

Angélique did not insist.

The girls and Petronella Damourt were standing as if ready to leave the room at their mistress's bidding. Everything had been impeccably tidied and cleaned and they seemed calm, quite recovered from the upsets of the previous day. The bespectacled secretary was just finishing off something he had been writing, sitting at the table which was normally Joffrey de Peyrac's work table. He had borrowed Joffrey's pen shaped like a perfect albatross's wing, a fact that instinctively annoyed Angélique although, when she thought about it, the Duchess's poor secretary, having lost everything, had little alternative but to do so. Armand Daveau, secretary to the Duchess of Maudribourg, was ageless. His slightly corpulent figure and his somewhat pedantic solemnity must have made simple folk look up to him. For some indefinable reason Angélique did not care for him. In spite of his good-natured manner, she had the impression that he was not at ease within himself nor with his position. But after all it was only an impression. And in any case the job of serving a person of high rank, necessitating as it did both servility and boldness, was not one that made for a cheerful type of character.

'Monsieur Armand is drawing up a list of our losses,' Madame de Maudribourg explained.

In spite of having said she would move, she remained seated where she was, hands clasped on her knees, and Angélique noticed some boxwood rosary beads between her fingers.

56

'Have none of the higher clergy asked to see me?' she suddenly inquired.

'Here?' Angélique exclaimed. 'But, Madame, we are a long way from any town, did I not explain to you already? There are indeed some Jesuits who move around Acadia, chaplains to some of the concessions or military posts . . .'

She broke off, struck by a sudden idea. Ambroisine de Maudribourg continued briskly:

'My confessor wrote to inform all the religious authorities in New France of my arrival. A member of the Society of Jesus should already have been informed that I have been shipwrecked on the coast of Maine and should have come here to bring us the succour of our Holy Faith.'

'There are not many of them and the distances are enormous,' Angélique remarked vaguely.

The Duchess seemed to be listening for something.

'One doesn't hear the chime of bells here . . .' she murmured. 'How can one tell the time? . . . I should have liked to attend Mass, but I'm told there is not even a church here.'

'We shall soon have a chapel.'

Angélique felt grateful to Colin who had enabled her to announce this fact.

'How can you live like this without ever assisting at the Holy Sacrifice of the Mass?' asked the young benefactress, looking at her in wide-eyed astonishment. 'You haven't even a chaplain, so they tell me. So all these people live and die like animals, without the sustenance of the sacraments.'

'There is a minister . . .'

'A Protestant!' the Duchess exclaimed, horrified. 'A heretic! That is even worse. Is it not written in the Bible: "Give a heretic one warning, then a second, and after that avoid his company; his is a perverse nature, and whoever lives with him is also perverse." '

'All right,' Angélique replied, mildly annoyed, 'but don't forget that our perverseness here in Gouldsboro does not prevent us being charitable to our neighbours, which after all is the first commandment of the New Testament. Whatever that precious pilot of yours, Job Simon, says, we are not wreckers and we have done everything we could to help you.'

During this exchange of words with Ambroisine de Maudribourg she moved here and there about the room, putting some of the furniture back where it belonged. What was that strange idea that had occurred to her a moment ago, when the

Duchess was talking about a member of the higher clergy? It had crossed her mind in a flash. Something important ... but she could no longer remember.

She opened the box that held the pistols Joffrey had given her and examined the various objects that completed the set within the casket. She became aware that the Duchess was watching her closely.

'So you carry arms,' the Duchess said. 'You are even said to be a first-class shot.'

Madame de Peyrac swung round towards her.

'You seem to know far too much about me,' she cried. 'There are times when I think it was not pure chance that brought you here ...'

Madame de Maudribourg gave a cry as if she had been struck to the heart and covered her face with her hands.

'What do you mean? That it was not chance? If it was not chance, what was it?' she said in a staccato voice. 'I cannot believe that it was Providence, as I still thought yesterday it might be. I have only just realized the full horror of our fate. All those poor people dead, drowned, torn to pieces so far from their own land. I feel as if their curse will weigh on me for ever ... If it was not chance that brought us to these lands, then who was it? Unless it was Satan himself ... Satan, oh! my God. How can I find the strength to fight him?'

She seemed to make an effort to regain control of herself.

'Forgive me,' she said gently. 'Please forgive me, Madame. I fear I must have hurt you with my comments on your life in common with these heretics. I am too impulsive and am often reproached for expressing my views too frankly. I reason things out logically and I do not give enough thought to the instincts of the heart. It is you who are right, I know. What does it matter whether there is a chapel here or not? What does ritual mean without goodness? "Though I speak with the tongues of men and of angels, and have not charity, I am become as sounding brass, or a tinkling cymbal ..." It was Saint Paul who said that, Saint Paul the master of us all ... My dear friend, will you please forgive me?'

A shadow of suffering darkened her magnificent eyes that glowed with a moving brilliance. As Angélique listened to her she wondered about the dual personality of this woman who was both too clever and too defenceless. A strict religious upbringing combined with scientific study had made her live beyond the bounds of reality, in an atmosphere of mystical exaltation. She would no doubt have been more at home in Quebec, received by the Bishop, the Jesuits and the nuns, than cast up on these independent shores of Gouldsboro. The tough land of America would show no indulgence to such frailty, and Angélique immediately felt pity for her.

'I don't hold it against you,' she said. 'And of course I forgive you. You have every right to seek information about the place you find yourself in and the way of life of those who welcome you. I too am impulsive and come straight out with what I think. Don't be upset. You will make yourself ill again.'

'Oh, how weary I feel,' the Duchess murmured, running one hand across her forehead. 'This heat, this interminable wind, the smell of the sea and the ear-splitting shrieks of the birds that never stop wheeling across the sky in great clouds, like souls in pain ... I would like to tell you something that happened to me this morning but you will laugh at me.'

'No, I shan't. Tell me!'

'Satan appeared to me,' the Duchess said very gravely, while the others crossed themselves in fear. 'Actually it was not the first time, but today he came in a most unusual guise: he was entirely red ...'

'Like my angel!' cried Adhemar, who delighted in these kinds of confidences and seemed almost to provoke them.

'Red and hideous,' the Duchess went on, 'sniggering and bristling all over like a hairy, stinking beast. I scarcely had time to begin to cross myself and say the first words of the sacramental prayer when he fled up the chimney.'

'Up the chimney?'

'That was what my angel did too,' Adhemar shouted in delight.

'I know that Satan can take any form he likes, and that he is fond of red and black,' the Duchess went on, 'but this time I was particularly frightened. I can't help wondering what this new form the Devil has decided to adopt to upset me can possibly herald. Misfortunes, torments, new temptations to inflict upon me ... So you can understand why I wished to receive help from a properly qualified priest, had there been one in the area,' she concluded in a voice that trembled in spite of herself.

'The chaplain of the *Fearless* has left, but maybe Father Baure is still in the neighbourhood. He is a Recollect Father who is chaplain to Monsieur de Saint-Castine in Fort Pentagouet.'

'A Recollect,' the Duchess protested, 'no, he's not important enough . . .'

Meanwhile Angélique was examining the fireplace up which Madame de Maudribourg claimed to have seen the Prince of Darkness fly away. There was some ash in the grate, for in spite of the heat of the July night a fire had been lighted for the invalid.

As she leaned forward she noticed the imprint of a bare foot. An odour hung around, still almost tangible, but one which was familiar to Angélique: 'A redskin,' she thought, 'one who got in here with his particular brand of effrontery! . . . Perhaps he was looking for me? Who could it have been?' She experienced a sense of relief, even of pleasure.

'I think that you were right,' she said to Adhemar with a laugh, 'I think it must have been an angel.'

'I can see that you don't take my vision seriously,' the Duchess of Maudribourg complained.

'But I do, Madame, I am convinced that you did see something . . . but I don't think it was a demon. Adhemar is a simple soul but on this score his instinct concerning the supernatural is pretty good.'

At that moment someone hammered on the door, and Madame Carrère's sons appeared, sent by their mother to help show Madame de Maudribourg to her new accommodation.

With their skin tanned by the sea air and the out-of-door life of hunting, fishing and heavy work these boys and youths looked fit and healthy. They had the confident manner of those who are masters of their own lives, far from a society stifled by centuries of civilities and finicky rules of polite behaviour.

'Where's the luggage?' they asked.

'There is hardly any,' the Duchess replied. 'Monsieur Armand, have you finished your scribbling?'

Her secretary sprinkled sand over his sheets of parchment then rolled them up with a deep sigh and stood up.

The company went down the wooden staircase of the fort. Angélique, in spite of the Duchess's protests, took her arm to give her some support.

It was a good thing that she did, for, as they reached the bottom of the stairs, Ambroisine de Maudribourg collapsed again.

She had every excuse.

Barring their way out of the main door, in all his splendour, stood Piksarett, chief of the Patsuiketts, Piksarett the Convert, the finest warrior of all Acadia.

It was undoubtedly he who had appeared that morning without warning, to the still wondering eyes of the new immigrants. It was not surprising they had taken him for a demon.

On that day he was looking particularly frightening. Dressed in nothing but a simple loin-cloth, he was painted from head to foot in dark red, scarlet and violet with stripes whirling in skilfully drawn circles round his pectoral muscles, his navel, his thighs, knees and calves, as well as on the arms. His nose, forehead, chin and cheekbones had not been spared the same ornamentation, which gave him the appearance of a man skinned alive, while through it all shone a bright smile like that of a carnivorous weasel and his little piercing eyes with their mocking expression.

Angélique hastened to acknowledge him.

'Piksarett!' she cried. 'How nice to see you again! Come in, make yourself at home. Sit down in this room here, and I shall send for something for you to eat. Are Jerome and Michael with you?'

'Here they are,' Piksarett announced, moving his spear to one side to allow the two inseparables to pass. This increase in plumes and war-paint completed the discomfiture of the King's Girls and their benefactress. But Madame de Maudribourg had considerable self-control. One felt that Satan himself could not make her lose her dignity in front of the simple women who were in her charge.

Even when Piksarett walked right up to them to touch them and laid a greasy hand on Angélique's shoulder, the Duchess managed not to flinch.

'You waited for me to come, you did not run away; it is well,' Piksarett said turning to his captive Angélique. 'You have not forgotten that I am your master, for I laid my hand upon you in battle.'[1]

'Of course I have not forgotten. And where do you think I would run away to? Sit down! Let us talk.'

She led them into the main hall of the fort where there were tables and stools, then returned to the Frenchwomen who stood there still wide-eyed but beginning to feel reassured.

'That is a very famous Indian chieftain,' she said gaily. 'You see he was not Satan. On the contrary, he is a Catholic and a very devout one at that. A great defender of the Holy Cross and of the Jesuits. His two companions are two of his braves, converts also.'

1. See *The Temptation of Angélique*.

'Savages!' Ambroisine whispered. 'The first we have seen, how exciting!'

They continued to examine the redskins with a mixture of fear and distaste as they sat down noisily in the main hall, gazing about them curiously.

'But ... they are hideous and terrifying,' the Duchess went on. 'And they smell dreadful.'

'That's nothing. It's only bear or seal grease which they smear on their bodies to protect themselves from the cold in the winter and from sandflies in the summer. You get used to it. I think he was what you saw this morning, when you were half asleep, and thought it was an apparition, don't you?'

'Yes ... I ... I think so. But would he dare to enter your room like that without any warning?'

'Anything is possible with them. Savages are shameless, and so proud that they understand nothing of the etiquette white men observe among themselves. But I must leave you now to entertain them or they will be horribly put out.'

'Go along then, my dear. I can appreciate that you must show tact towards these natives, for whose souls we say so many novenas in our convents. Nevertheless they are terrifying. How can you be so bright and gay with them and bear them touching you!'

The Duchess's reticence amused Angélique.

'They are great ones for laughter,' she replied. 'You must honour them by laughing with them. They enjoy nothing better.'

CHAPTER 10

PIKSARETT ACCEPTED the Virginia tobacco, refused the beer and, with still greater indignation, the brandy.

'The demon of drunkenness is the worst of all: he takes our life from us; he is the cause of murder and makes us lose our minds.'

'You speak like Mopountook, chief of the Metallaks, on the Upper Kennebec. He taught me about spring water.'

'Spring water transmits to us the strength of our ancestors who are buried in the earth through which it passes.'

62

Angélique sent someone to fetch the coldest water obtainable.

Then suddenly Piksarett became pensive.

Did he find the colony of Gouldsboro intimidating, this ally of the French and of their spiritual leaders the Jesuits? Did he perhaps feel uncomfortable at having wandered into an almost English colony to obtain the ransom for a captive whom he could not even baptize a Catholic since she was one already?

Angélique thought she would please him by assuring him that here he would be able to find steel of the best quality for his tomahawk and those of his warriors, and that if he wished for pearls, Monsieur de Peyrac had some blue and green ones which he had brought from Persia, put aside specially for him, the great chieftain. But Piksarett suddenly put an end to the conversation, saying that it was not seemly for a female captive to discuss her own ransom, and that he himself would bargain with Ticonderoga, the Man of Thunder.

'Would you like me to take you to him?' suggested Angélique, accepting his ill-humour.

'No, I can find him,' Piksarett stated in peremptory tones.

What had come over him so suddenly? Piksarett, the joyful, playful Piksarett, had suddenly grown anxious. The expression of deep thoughtfulness that made his dark eyes shine like blackberries, gave a sinister look to his face, suddenly impassive and hard beneath the twirling vermilion stripes of the painted mask. He began to glance around him as if he were sniffing out something. Then he laid the tips of his fingers on Angélique's forehead.

'You are in danger,' he murmured, 'I know it, I can feel it.'

This statement kindled a sense of alarm in Angélique.

She did not like to hear these savages, nor indeed that simple soul Adhemar, blurting out their secret premonitions. They were all too often right.

'What danger, Piksarett, tell me?' she asked.

'I don't know.'

He shook his tresses that were plaited around foxes' feet.

'Have you been baptized?' he asked, darting her a look like a Jesuit confessor, incongruous as it was coming from that grotesquely striped face.

'Of course I have. Didn't I tell you so already?'

'Well then, pray to the Virgin and all the Saints. That's all you can do. Pray! Pray! Pray!' he solemnly exhorted her.

He raised his hands to his oily knot of hair, felt around for something and removed one of its many ornaments, a mendicant friar's coarsely-made rosary beads with a wooden crucifix on the end, and slipped them round Angélique's neck. Then he blessed her three times with the hallowed phrase:

'. . . Patris et Filii et Spiritus Sancti . . .'

Then he leapt to his feet and seized his spear.

'Quick now,' he urged his two faithful companions, 'I must be on my way before the Iroquois over-run all our forest lands. The summer brings those coyotes out of their stinking lairs. Now that we have dealt with the English, let us finish the works of righteousness to please our brothers in God, the French, and satisfy our beloved fathers, the Black Robes. Otherwise the prowling demons will get the better of us. Sister, be of good cheer; I must leave you. But remember, pray, pray, pray!'

And with these solemn words he vanished in a few strides, while his two acolytes leapt after him. Their musky smell lingered on for some moments in the fort.

Angélique stood aghast, anxiously wondering about Piksarett's unpredictability.

Had something in Gouldsboro upset him?

The storm she and Joffrey had been riding out on a personal level, their fight against the pirates with its final outcome, the totally unexpected arrival of a contingent of King's Girls with an aristocratic French lady, none of these things could make her forget that a few miles to the west a gory tragedy was still being played out: wave upon wave of Indian tribesmen were pouring out of the forest to bear down upon colonies of white settlers, killing, burning, and scalping.

In contrast to the horrors that might well be occurring at that very moment, the relative calm enjoyed by Gouldsboro and the surrounding countryside seemed nothing short of miraculous.

This miracle was entirely due to the strength and authority of Count Peyrac, making the most of his alliances with Baron Saint-Castine and the local Indian tribes, and to the understanding he had with the French settlers in Acadia and the traders in the English posts.

People arriving in Gouldsboro passed from one world into another. In spite of clashes between local inhabitants or trouble with pirates, there was a kind of security, protection by invisible frontiers now set up for miles around them by the sheer reputation of this French Count, Peyrac, yesterday an unknown figure, today rich, independent of Kings, a man of liberal principle. In Gouldsboro, although war threatened so close, they could still elect a Governor, trade, welcome theologians from Boston one day and representatives of Quebec the next.

On the strength of the will and intelligence of a single man, here they were creating a small free state, free from the constraints of the distant, tyrannical kingdoms of France and England, their only preoccupation being to build, to make the land bring forth fruit, and lay down roots for succeeding generations.

But perhaps the coming, short, fiery summer would bring the moment of truth for all of them. Would it spell defeat or victory?

Angélique went up to her room.

She felt empty, rather like before a battle; when everything is in order, every detail settled, and one simply has to wait. What was about to happen?

CHAPTER 11

ANGÉLIQUE PICKED up her two pistols. They were light and precise. They would be easy to handle, twice as fast as any other known weapon.

She fastened the belt with its leather tie embroidered in silver filigree work. The weapons could almost be concealed in the folds of her skirt. The handles, made of precious woods encrusted with mother-of-pearl and enamelled flowers, might easily be mistaken for novel items of costume jewellery. She practised seizing rapidly one or the other of the pistols and cocking them deftly. She accustomed herself to the use of the 'miquelet lock' which, although far more efficient than any other system, was new to her.

Knowing herself to be armed, she felt easier in her mind.

The kitten had jumped up on the table and was following intently every movement of her fingers on the guns, furtively darting out one paw as if trying to catch her fingers. Then he bounded away. He managed to get hold of one of the bullets, sent it rolling across the room, and stood for a long time like a pointer, his tail bolt upright, before the piece of furniture beneath which the ball seemed to have taken refuge.

When Angélique went over to the chests that had been placed in a corner of the room and lifted a lid, he dived inside and buried himself among the trinkets and silks. His little head kept popping up triumphantly, draped in a ribbon or a ruffle. Angélique laughed at his tricks.

She must have removed him twenty times, but he always managed to get back again, sometimes without her knowing it. She could not resist playing with him, he was so full of life and character. His sprightly presence made her more cheerful.

That morning, when she had commented to Joffrey on the Duchess of Maudribourg's elegance and in particular on how novel her red stockings were, he had said:

'There are several pairs of stockings like that among the things from Europe that I have taken to your room. Haven't you looked through them yet?'

And it was true that there were marvels there, to delight the heart of the most Parisian woman. She had not noticed them on Sunday when she had tried feverishly to find a dress she could decently wear before the scaffold where Colin Paturel was to be hanged. At that time her choice had fallen upon the black dress with the Mechlin lace collar – the one the Duchess of Maudribourg had borrowed that very morning – which, although severe, was becoming and very sumptuous thanks to the beauty of the velvet. The other clothes were all of choice material, delightful in their novelty and their priceless accessories. She was touched to discover some little girl's frocks and two outfits for a small boy, made from strong woollen cloth in bright colours.

'It is as if Joffrey himself had done the choosing. But he must have kept so many contacts in Paris, in London and in all the other capital cities, people who know his tastes and will serve him with care. In spite of what he himself says and although he is apparently far from the civilized world, he is still the Count of Toulouse!'

As she thought of her husband, Angélique impulsively kissed the garment she was holding in her hands, which happened to be the boy's jerkin. Honorine, who so regretted not having been a boy, would inevitably appropriate this garment . . .

A sound of footsteps on the stairs.

Angélique rushed towards the door, her heart thudding.

It was he! . . .

Joffrey de Peyrac appeared accompanied by a Spaniard

66

carrying a light wooden box which he laid on the table in front of Angélique.

'Come and see what I have brought you,' said Peyrac. 'It's a medicine chest for all your phials, pots of ointment, bags of herbs and surgical instruments. The arrangement of the compartments can be varied as you like. I had it made in Lyons. The craftsman added to the illuminated paintings decorating it pictures of Saints Cosmas and Damian, the patron saints of the pharmacopoeia, so that they can aid you, and I think he was right; when it comes to saving life, we should not disdain any form of intercession, should we?'

'No indeed,' Angélique replied, 'I am very fond of Cosmas and Damian and shall be glad to have their help in my work.'

'And what about these things you are unpacking, are you pleased with them?'

'Delighted. I have a feeling that a certain ubiquitous Count of Toulouse must have been on the spot over there in Europe to choose them.'

'I have always loved to encourage feminine apparel with its inexhaustible fantasy.'

Angélique smiled gaily. 'But what shall I do with all these dresses in the depths of the forests of Wapassou?'

'Wapassou is a kingdom, and you are its queen. Who knows what festivities may be held there one day? You have already seen that even here we have no lack of high-ranking visitors. And I want you to dazzle them in Quebec.'

She shuddered. She was holding the kitten in her arms to protect the precious silks from his tiny claws and was stroking him mechanically.

'Quebec!' she murmured. 'That snare laid by the King of France? That nest of all our worst enemies, pious fanatics, churchmen, and Jesuits?'

'That's where everything is arranged. We shall have to face it sooner or later. Of course I don't wish to put you in any danger. I shall arrive with my ships and cannons. But I also know that the French will bow more readily before a pretty woman decked in all her finery than before a threat of war. And in any case, we have friends there: the Duke of Arreboust, Count Loménie-Chambord, and even Frontenac, the Governor. The assistance I gave to Cavelier de la Calle has created, whether one likes it or not, a kind of alliance between New France and me. Monsieur de Ville d'Avray told me as much just a short time ago.'

'The Governor of Acadia? What kind of a man is he?'

Peyrac smiled.

'You will see. A kind of Péguilin de Lauzun, crossed with a Fouquet for business sense and dilettantism, with a dash of Molière for a critical view of his contemporaries. And also better informed about all kinds of matters than he appears. But he tells me it is *you* they want to see in Quebec and he reckons that your presence far more than mine will be decisive.'

'No doubt on account of the legend concerning what the prophetess said about the Demon of Acadia?'

Joffrey de Peyrac gave a shrug.

'It takes very little to crystallize popular feeling. Let us take things as they are. The Church's opposition to us is founded on mystical elements which are far more important than any annexation of so-called French territory that I might ever make. We must destroy these fears that belong to a past age.'

Angélique sighed. It was not by force that one would ever conquer the intolerant soul of Quebec, worthy new-born daughter of the Roman, Catholic and Apostolic Church. Its inhabitants who had come to bring salvation to the savages and drive the spirit of darkness from the pagan forests of the New World still held in their hearts something of the spirit of the crusaders of yesteryear.

'Quebec! . . . Face that city?' she asked with some anxiety. 'Shall we be able to get back to Wapassou for the winter? You see, I am not used to society any more and I want to get back to Honorine.'

'The summer is short. First we must bring some order to French Bay . . . Talking of Honorine, can you imagine her going off hunting in this gentleman's jerkin?'

'Those things were in fact for her, then?'

'Yes, she is every bit as enterprising and tough as a lad. During the winter in the snow her girl's skirts get in her way and make her furious. These clothes are just what she wants.'

'You really do understand her.'

'She is very close and dear to me,' said Peyrac with one of those strangely charming smiles he gave her occasionally when he wanted to reassure her.

That he should be so concerned about Honorine did indeed bring her so much happiness that she found it impossible to express her feelings.

The kitten leapt down from Angélique's arms then on to one

corner of the table, where it began to wash its face with a look of detachment, as if it was noticing nothing.

Angélique had clasped her arms around Peyrac's neck. Talking about Honorine had further strengthened the bond of their love. For Honorine could have been the rock on which it foundered; instead she had become a further reason for them to feel themselves indissolubly linked. Whenever Angélique felt anxious about her, poor little bastard child, the thought that Joffrey de Peyrac had taken charge of her and loved her would calm her panic. 'Because I am your father, young lady!' What an unforgettable moment! Never had she seen so clearly as in that moment the profound goodness in the heart of her husband, whom life could have made intolerant, indifferent or even cruel.

Angélique wondered that she among all creatures had managed to captivate and hold this man, who was at the same time intractable and tender, superior and modest, a man who never bared his heart nor easily revealed himself, but one whose intentions were trustworthy and straight. Their recent dispute had proved this, and she had emerged from it with an extraordinary feeling of security where he was concerned.

Her anxiety came from another quarter.

She let her hands slide down her husband's shoulders. To touch him, to feel him, was a comfort to her, a joy, and she asked herself with some fear how she could ever survive without it.

She let her head fall. At last she asked him hesitantly:

'You are going to have to go away again, aren't you? To help the Quebec officials who are trapped in the Saint John River by Phipps's vessel?'

He lifted up her chin as one might do to an unhappy child.

'I must. It is an opportunity not to be missed to render assistance to those difficult customers in Quebec.'

'But can you tell me once and for all,' she asked impatiently, 'why the Canadians are hostile to me? Why do they see me as a Demon, and consider you a dangerous invader of French territory? This land belongs to you according to the treaties of Massachusetts, you acquired it perfectly legally ... the Canadians surely can't claim control over the whole American continent?'

'But they do, my dear! That is precisely their ambition, in the national as well as the religious sphere ... To serve God and the King is the first duty of a good Frenchman, and they are prepared to die for it, even if they are a handful of six thousand souls pitted against two hundred thousand Englishmen in the south. They consider *all* the territory around French Bay as French. But in the course of time the Acadians have begun to consider themselves independent, somewhat like Gouldsboro, and that is why Castine came to ask me if I would take under my protection all the different settlers who live in the Bay, French as well as Scots and English. Of course there has been talk of this in Quebec, I can hardly be in very good odour there and still less with the French Governor of Acadia, especially at a time when he is about to visit his recalcitrant subjects to collect their taxes. So you see it seems only politic for me to help him out of his present difficulty.'

'What has happened to him?'

'By way of reprisal for the massacres which the Abenakis, under French leadership, perpetrated over in the west in New England, Massachusetts has sent an admiral with a force of several ships on a punitive expedition to take action against any Frenchmen who might happen to fall into their hands. Although there is some justification for this they really ought to knock the nonsense out of Quebec rather than attack a handful of small Acadian landholders who are doing their best to cling to the lands they inherited from their forefathers. Having heard that a number of officials from Quebec, among them the Governor of Acadia, Ville d'Avray, and also Carlon, the Administrator of New France, were actually in Jemseg, Phipps from Boston has gone and blockaded the mouth of the Saint John River, thus preventing them from sailing out to sea again. Monsieur de Ville d'Avray, who is a restless man, chose to make good his escape on foot through the forest. Under cover of fog he boarded a cod-fishing vessel without attracting the attention of the English and came here to ask for my help. Although he considers me a hated rival and a potential enemy, his chief concern is to save his ship which I suspect to be full of precious furs collected during his tour as Governor. It would make a bad impression if I refused him this service.

'If Phipps succeeds in capturing these people, and taking them back to Boston or Salem as prisoners, and if this is reported to Versailles, the King might consider it just the pretext he was looking for to declare war on England. Everybody here prefers our uneasy peace to a renewal of open conflict.'

She listened to him in a state of profound agitation. As he spoke, she began to understand just how delicate their situation was and the nature of the responsibilities he had taken upon himself.

'It's one of those classic incidents in French Bay, with its human fauna from every nation,' he concluded.

Then he smiled. 'No treaty will ever sort things out as long as we have the kind of fogs we do, the kind of tides, the kind of holes and corners of rivers where people can lay up and hide . . . It's a land made for hit-and-run skirmishing, but, in spite of all that, I shall build you a kingdom here . . .'

'Is the expedition you are about to undertake a risky one?'

'It's only a question of helping the French, of making sure that the Indians of the area don't get involved in the conflicts, and, in short, of preventing Phipps from getting at the booty. He will be furious, but there is no question of our coming to blows.'

He clasped her in his arms.

'I would have liked to take you with me.'

'No, that's impossible; I can't leave Abigail alone. I've promised to help her at the time of her delivery and . . . I don't know why, but I am anxious for her. My presence is a comfort, so I must stay. Let us say no more about it,' she concluded bravely.

She went over and sat down in the chair and the kitten jumped up on her knees and curled into a ball. It seemed so friendly and pleased to be alive that it communicated some of its tranquillity to her.

But suddenly she felt heavy at heart again. He was going to leave her and she would have to struggle on alone. Against what menace?

Would the unknown ship be part of it, with her men who seemed to have been sent to dog their footsteps? Who had sent them? The Canadians? The English? It did not make sense. Their relations with their neighbours were much more straightforward. The English had other fish to fry and were not interested in bothering a man who was useful to them, with whom they had signed advantageous treaties.

Well, who was it then? Some personal enemy of Joffrey's? Some commercial rival trying to manoeuvre them out of their position? Had not someone already sold them out to Gold Beard? She felt strongly that she was the object of their attack, she was convinced that, had she not existed, Joffrey would have been left in peace.

She could not help telling him so.

'If I were not with you your situation would be much easier, I feel sure.'

'If you were not with me, I would not be a happy man.'

He took her two hands and kissed them.

CHAPTER 12

ANGÉLIQUE AND Abigail stood side by side in the tiny garden surrounded by tall clumps of flowers and grass. The garden, laid out around the Bernes' house and fenced in the New England manner, was one such as every settler's wife needed to help keep her family in good health in these areas where an apothecary might be found only at a considerable distance. Added to this there were a few vegetables – lettuces, leeks, radishes, carrots – herbs for seasoning, and masses of flowers for sheer pleasure.

With her foot Abigail pushed back a round velvety leaf that had strayed out of its bed.

'By the autumn there'll be pumpkins, which I shall keep for the winter. But I intend to pick a few when they are only as big as melons, to cook in hot ashes and eat like baked apples.'

'My mother loved gardens,' Angélique said suddenly. 'In the kitchen garden . . . I can just see her now, for ever toiling . . .'

Suddenly she could see her mother. Tall and aristocratic, a dim shape beneath her straw hat, with a basket on her arm and sometimes a bunch of flowers which she held clasped to her bosom like a child. It was a distant vision that had suddenly come into her mind for no apparent reason.

'Mother, protect me,' she thought.

It was the first time that such a plea for intercession had ever come from her heart.

She took Abigail's hand as she stood beside her and held it gently in her own; Abigail, tall, serene, brave . . . Perhaps she resembled the mother Angélique had forgotten?

That afternoon Berne had come to invite Monsieur and Madame Peyrac to do the Bernes the honour of sharing their evening meal.

This unexpected invitation seemed intended to prove that

72

the honourable and intractable Protestant and his co-religionists wished to make a new start after the heated exchanges
that had taken place on the occasion of Gold Beard's installation as Governor.[1] Being conscious of this desire for reconciliation, Count Peyrac had accepted the invitation and had
come with Angélique as dusk fell to the Bernes' house.

But the personalities of the antagonists were so strong and
their memories so charged with passion that the meeting had
not been free of emotional tension.

Leaving the two men alone, Abigail had taken Angélique
outside to show her the garden.

The friendship between the two women was stronger than
any quarrel. Instinctively they cut themselves off, refraining
from rigid judgements in order to protect the bond of mutual
affection between them.

Different as they were, they needed each other's affection. It
was a refuge, a certainty, a living thing that even absence could
not destroy, and that every tribulation suffered and strengthened rather than destroyed.

The fading silvery-grey brightness over the island-strewn
horizon seemed to be reflected in Abigail's fine-featured face,
heightening its beauty. The fatigue of her condition had not
impaired her features nor her lovely complexion. She still wore
the severe bonnet she had worn in La Rochelle, bequeathed to
her by her mother, who came from Angoulême where no one
troubled with lace and ribbons. This austere coif suited her
better than anything else.

'So you are happy, are you?' Angélique asked.

Abigail gave a start and, had it not been for the dark,
Angélique would have seen her blush. But she mastered her
emotion and Angélique sensed through the shadows that she
was smiling.

'How can I ever thank God enough? Every day I discover
new treasures in my husband's heart, the depth of his intelligence and his knowledge, his wisdom, the deep qualities of a
strong man, sometimes hard but full of sensitivity ... I think
that he really is ... a good man. But it is a dangerous virtue in
our age and he knows it.'

She added, musingly:

'I am learning to love a man. It is a strange adventure. A
man is something serious, something different, unknown, but so
very important. If they do not always understand us, do we

1. See *The Temptation of Angélique*.

73

women on our side make any attempt to understand them as the centuries have fashioned them, responsible for the world?'

'We are heirs to servitude, and they to domination,' Angélique replied. 'That is why the sparks sometimes fly. But it is also a fascinating adventure, trying to seek agreement through love.'

It was almost completely dark. Lights were beginning to shine from the houses in the fort, as white as opal against all that dark blue, and from the scattered islands pale, reddish-tinted stars of fires and lanterns shone out.

All of a sudden Angélique said:

'It's as if someone were watching us . . . Something moved in the bushes.'

They listened. Abigail put an arm round Angélique's shoulders and clasped her to her. Later she was to say that at that moment she had felt certain that some terrible danger hung over Angélique de Peyrac.

They both thought they heard a kind of deep, heart-rending sigh, but it might have been nothing but the wind in the pines on the cliff top.

'Let's go in,' said Abigail tugging at Angélique.

They turned towards the house and took a few steps towards it. But this time branches began to crackle and they heard an honest-to-goodness grunt.

'Oh!' Abigail exclaimed, turning round. 'That's what it is. It's the Mercelots' pig in our garden again. There's only a hedge on their side, and they don't bother to keep it in its sty, because it's less trouble to let it scavenge for food in the village streets and in other people's gardens.'

She strode towards the boundary dividing their property from the next.

The door to the house was open and a young woman holding a baby a few months old in her arms was silhouetted against the light. Abigail called to her.

'Bertille! Your pig has been trampling over my garden again!'

The woman crossed the threshold and walked listlessly towards them. Nevertheless she moved gracefully and seemed to be young and pretty. As she drew near Angélique realized it was Bertille Mercelot, the La Rochelle paper-merchant's daughter. The baby on her arm was dimpled and curly-headed. He sat very upright and looked as if he was examining everything with great seriousness.

'I have talked to my husband about it,' said Bertille plaintively, 'and he's finally agreed that we should build a fence and share the cost of the carpenter with you. But with all the trouble we've had over the past few days – those fights, those strangers, and the new Governor – he hasn't had time to attend to it.'

'I'll grant you that there were more urgent matters to see to than the building of fences,' Abigail agreed. 'But you should try to keep your pig in his sty. He has already caused us a lot of trouble.'

Angélique had managed to shoo the animal back on to its owner's land, where it galloped off. Bertille gave a sigh, bade them a brief, barely polite goodnight, then she went off too.

'So Bertille Mercelot is married, is she?' Angélique asked in astonishment. 'I didn't know. And there she is already with a child. We haven't been here a year yet, and nothing had been said about it then!'

'That's not her child,' Abigail explained. 'That is little Charles-Henri, you know, Jenny Manigault's baby, that was born just about the time we arrived. He'll soon be a year old, poor little thing. But of course, you probably don't know what happened to poor Jenny.'

'No, what did happen?'

'She was kidnapped by the Indians, towards the end of the autumn, barely two months after her confinement. A few of us were on our way to Camp Champlain in Gouldsboro, some on foot, some on horseback, when the redskins appeared hooting and yelling their war cries. Our men fought back, and the Indians were driven off but they took Jenny with them. She had lagged behind at the edge of the forest with her sister Sarah to pick berries. My husband, Gabriel, shot at one of the red devils. But another one hurled his hatchet at us and one of our men had his head split open. Sarah managed to get away and catch up with us. But we lost Jenny.'

Angélique was horrified.

'What kind of Indians were they? Iroquois? We might possibly . . .'

She could see herself rushing off to sue for the release of Jenny Manigault. But Abigail shook her head.

'No! For several days Monsieur d'Urville had the area combed, but they found no kind of lead. Monsieur de Saint-Castine helped us most obligingly, and decided in the end that it must have been a small tribe from the Upper Kennebec that had come down by canoe. As they are nomads, no one knows where to find them. They live somewhere up there more towards the English than the Canadian side.'

'What a terrible thing!' Angélique murmured. Suddenly the cool night air made her shudder.

'Monsieur Manigault nearly went out of his mind,' Abigail went on. 'He wanted to leave this place which he said was accursed and go off to Boston, but then the snow came and the storms, and he had to stay here for the winter. We were frightened that the baby would die without its mother's milk, but Madame Manigault is a very capable woman. She fed the baby with the milk from a few goats we have here and he survived. He is strong too, and we don't need to worry about him any more. His father was married again six months ago, to Bertille. She had always been crazy about him and did everything she could to get him.'

'Married again! . . . But . . . Jenny may not be dead!'

'That worried me too. But everyone said that it was unlikely she would have survived among those savages. So her father gave his blessing to the union. The poor young man was in despair and could hardly have gone on living alone with his orphan child, and Bertille would have forced him in the end to live in sin. It was all for the best, wasn't it? She's looking after the child . . .'

Angélique made an effort to be philosophical about this cruel accident and its outcome. She realized that for these Calvinists, with their own particular rules for living, in crossing over into the world of the redskins poor Jenny had passed decisively over into the Other World.

'Let's go inside!' said Abigail. 'I have made you sad . . . Here one mustn't think too much, one mustn't dwell on dangers, on bereavements or unavoidable mistakes, or one loses heart. We need all our strength to keep us moving forward, towards life, for the best . . .'

'Yes, you are right.'

CHAPTER 13

TWO LITTLE boys were playing backgammon on one corner of the table.

So absorbed were they that they sat hunched over the game with their straight hair, one golden, the other brown, falling down over their cheeks. An elderly Negro, his white hair looking like a cap of cotton waste, was following every detail of the game, also leaning forward with his chin on his dark hands.

A candle in a brass candlestick cast a gentle radiance over the scene, bringing a sparkle to the gold earrings that hung from the old Negro's ears, his jet-black nose and the dazzling whites of his eyes.

There was a stir as Angélique and Abigail entered the room. The two little boys jumped to their feet and flung themselves round Angélique's neck, while the old Negro hastened towards her with all kinds of good wishes. This was Siriki, the Manigaults' servant. The family had taken him in many years ago from among a group of slaves held in bond in La Rochelle at the time when Manigault listed trade in 'ebony' among his multifarious commercial activities.

Siriki proudly asked Angélique whether she recognized the blond child as Jeremy Manigault, whom he had brought up from the time he was a boy.

'Hasn't he grown, Madame? He's almost a man. And he's not yet eleven.'

Jeremy's cheeks were indeed plumper, his eyes bluer and his hair fairer than ever.

Laurier Berne, his opponent at backgammon that evening, looked puny beside him although he too had grown much stronger.

'Which of you two boys is winning?' Angélique asked.

'He is,' Jeremy replied, pointing indignantly at Laurier, 'he always wins.'

Abigail consoled Jeremy with a hug and a slice of cake.

'You can finish your game tomorrow,' she said. 'I'll put the board up on the shelf without disturbing the men.'

Jeremy, his mouth full, waved them all a general farewell then placed his hand in Siriki's.

The Bernes' house had been built halfway down the slope leading to the main square. It had very small windows so as to keep out the cold, and also because glass was scarce. Built in haste during the autumn, the Huguenots' houses were pretty cramped. The Bernes' consisted of two rooms, one for living and eating in, the other containing the parents' bed and a closet. There was a lean-to for storing logs and another for their ablutions. A loft beneath the roof reached by means of a trap-door and a short ladder completed the dwelling. Martial, the oldest son, had felt too cramped inside and had built himself a bark wigwam in the garden.

Laurier slept in the living-room while Sévérine occupied the loft.

Sévérine was there too. She had been burning citronella to keep away the mosquitoes. She was entering upon adolescence and was still skinny, with the same eager little face and wide mouth. But she had blossomed beside the patient Abigail.

Seated on either side of the table upon which reposed in state a long-necked black bottle of old rum, Joffrey de Peyrac and Gabriel Berne were engaged in animated conversation. Joffrey de Peyrac was recounting Honorine's exploits in Wapassou while Berne tried to outdo him by describing what she used to get up to in La Rochelle. They both agreed that she was a delightful child, and that you could not help loving her from the moment you first set eyes upon her.

'Even when she was a baby she was like that,' Berne said. 'I remember when I found her in the woods at the foot of the tree to which she had been tied . . .'

He broke off. His eyes met Angélique's which he saw filled with a sudden panic then went back to Joffrey de Peyrac, who was watching them both closely.

'That's an old story,' he said. 'It is part of the world we left behind us. I shall tell it to you one day, sir, if Dame Angélique allows me, or else she may tell it to you herself. Meanwhile let us drink to our health and that of our heirs present, absent or to come,' Berne concluded, lifting his glass.

Towards the beginning of the meal another tiny guest arrived unexpectedly. 'Oh, look what's just come in!'

'My kitten!' Angélique exclaimed.

It jumped up on her knees, placed its two front paws on the

edge of the table and introduced itself with a husky miaow, then demanded its share of the banquet.

'He's just like Honorine when she first came to our house,' said Séverine. 'You could see that she thought she was the most important person in the world . . .'

Angélique told them the story of the kitten.

'He's incredibly brave. I don't know how he manages, as tiny as he is, to find me wherever I am.'

They went on talking about cats while the subject of the conversation gorged himself on grilled fish. Although he was still sickly, now that he had found strength to clean himself, he turned out to be pure white with a cinnamon-coloured skull-cap and a few other odd patches. He was darker, almost black, round the eyes, with a patch of black on one ear, on a single paw, and at the base of his tail. His fur was long and thick. He had whiskers like pompoms and tufts of fur that sprang straight from his ears, giving him the appearance of a small lynx. He was a charmer and he knew it.

CHAPTER 14

ANGÉLIQUE FOUND the Duchess of Maudribourg reciting the rosary with all her flock, including Julienne, and her secretary Armand Daveau, kneeling stoutly in one corner.

It was very hot but no one seemed to be inconvenienced by the discomfort of kneeling on the beaten earth floor of the modest house where the benefactress had been accommodated. Angélique was later to discover that such pious sessions were of frequent recurrence in the circle of the King's Girls. The frail and lovely Duchess was the most earnest figure among them and kept her flock under firm control. Prayer seemed to be her favourite occupation, her eyes, upturned towards Heaven, shone with ecstatic joy and her complexion looked as if it was illuminated by some inner brightness.

Alone among the survivors from the wreck of the *Unicorn*, Job Simon, the tall captain with the port-wine stain on his temple, took no part in this pious exercise. He wore a melancholy expression as he sat on the sand outside the house, beside his carved unicorn – an alarming figure all hairy and flanked by his mythical beast – it was almost as if he was on guard over the assembled Vestals.

'Good news for you!' said Angélique as she went by. 'You will get your gold leaf. I asked Monsieur de Peyrac on your behalf.'

Suddenly met by the full volume of the intoned *Ave Maria*, Angélique was momentarily taken aback. But when Madame de Maudribourg caught sight of her, she immediately crossed herself, kissed the crucifix on her beads and put it into her pocket. Then she stood up and went to meet her visitor.

'I had been hoping to see you, dear friend. As you see, although it is very simple, we already feel at home. Some place where we could meet and pray together, that is what we most needed to recover our strength and face the future with courage.'

'That's splendid,' said Angélique, 'I am delighted to hear that you are in a fit state to cope with what I've come to tell you.'

'I am ready,' said the Duchess drawing herself up and looking fixedly at Angélique.

'There is going to be a reception on the beach today in honour of the Governor of Acadia, the Marquis of Ville d'Avray, who is our guest, and I have come to invite you and your girls to join us.'

Angélique had issued her invitation in a serious voice, but she smiled as she reached the end. The Duchess grasped her intention, grew pale, then a pink glow suffused her forehead.

'You are making fun of me, I do believe,' she murmured by way of excuse. 'I probably strike you as too devout, don't I? Forgive me if I shock you. But you see, prayer is something vitally necessary to me!'

'There's nothing wrong in that. It is for me to ask your forgiveness,' said Angélique, sorry now for having teased the Duchess. 'Prayer is a good thing.'

'And so is having fun, too,' the Duchess concluded gaily. 'A meal on the beach! What a lovely idea! We might almost be in Versailles, beside the "Grand Canal" ... The Marquis of Ville d'Avray, did you say? I think I know the name. Doesn't he have a hunting lodge somewhere between Versailles and Paris where the King likes to stay?'

'I don't know; you can ask him. My husband would also like

you to meet some of the prominent members of our colony.'

'Ville d'Avray! Do I gather he is the representative of New France and of the King in this area? And he has come to visit you?'

'We are old friends. This will be an opportunity for you to discuss your situation and how best to find a way out of it.'

Angélique was feeling her way. None of the King's Girls appeared to have spoken to their benefactress about the Governor's proposal of settling where they were. Would Madame de Maudribourg be agreeable to the idea of diverting her recruits from the sacred mission entrusted to them of going to Quebec to help populate New France?

For the time being she showed no concern about the matter. She gave her dark hair a quick brush, letting it hang loose over her shoulders, straightened the lace collar on the black velvet dress, then eagerly followed Angélique out.

According to the custom which had grown up of people gathering in front of the inn for meetings that were part discussion, part village fair, a number of trestle tables had been erected, and stood laden with a variety of refreshments: drinks, fruit, a number of fish and game dishes for everyone to help himself as he wished.

The older folk grouped themselves for preference round Joffrey de Peyrac, Count d'Urville and Colin Paturel, and around Manigault and Berne, while the English refugees, being new arrivals, stood timidly on one side but close to the Huguenots from La Rochelle, instinctively seeking those of their own religion in spite of the difference in nationality.

Facing them stood the sailors from the *Heart of Mary*, the most recent settlers, whom their French compatriots from La Rochelle had good reason to dislike, in a relatively quiet group under the implacable eye of Colin Paturel who, while welcoming this person or that in his capacity as Governor of Gouldsboro, never took his eyes off his erstwhile crew. His lieutenant, François de Barssempuy, helped him in his task.

A few redskins mingled with the officials, important Sagamore chiefs, but Angélique looked in vain for the tall scarlet figure of Piksarett. On the other hand, she did notice Jerome and Michael strutting about and poking fun at the olive-skinned Carib who belonged to the spice-seller. For the tropical islanders, from the world of bananas and cotton, seemed more outlandish to these folk brought up on bear grease and maize, than did a Frenchman from Paris or a Russian from the Siberian steppes.

As Angélique and the Duchess of Maudribourg drew near to the crowd, a heavily bedizened figure stepped forward and hastened towards them. With exaggerated gestures of greeting, sweeping the ground several times with the plumes of his hat, he bowed low before the Duchess. He was a short man, somewhat corpulent, but seemed very amiable and enthusiastic.

'At last,' he exclaimed, 'at last I set eyes on her whose matchless beauty is the talk of New France, even before she is known there. Permit me to present myself. I am the Marquis of Ville d'Avray, representing His Majesty the King of France in Acadia.'

Ambroisine de Maudribourg, somewhat surprised, responded with a slight nod. The Marquis went on volubly.

'So it was you who turned the head of that serious-minded d'Arreboust and brought damnation to that saint Loménie-Chambord. Did you know that they have blamed you for Pont-Briand's death?'

'Monsieur, you are in error,' the Duchess hastened to protest. 'I have not the good fortune of knowing these gentlemen, neither have I anyone's death on my conscience.'

'Then you lack good grace.'

'Not at all. You are making a mistake, I tell you. I am not . . .'

'Are you not the loveliest woman on earth?'

At this the Duchess burst out laughing.

'A thousand thanks, sir. But once again, I am not . . . the woman to whom you should be addressing your words. I am sure you mean them for the Countess of Peyrac, mistress of these lands, who might indeed be responsible, by reason of her charms, for the calamities you mention . . . Here she is . . .'

The Marquis turned towards Angélique whom Ambroisine was pointing out. He went pale, blushed, then stammered:

'Oh dear, what a mistake! Do please forgive me . . . I am terribly short-sighted . . .'

He began to fumble in the pockets of his waistcoat, which was embroidered with tiny pink and green flowers, very long as fashion dictated in Versailles, and flowing out beneath the tails of his coat.

'Where are my spectacles? You haven't seen my spectacles, have you, Alexander?'

He turned to a lad accompanying him, who for all his youth

looked as dour as the Marquis seemed jovial and exuberant.

'Spectacles!' the boy replied haughtily. 'What do you want spectacles for?'

'To see with, of course, great heavens! You know I'm almost blind without my glasses. I have just committed an unpardonable sin. Ah ladies, how I do apologize. But yes, indeed, dear Countess, you are blonde. That description seems more accurate. So you are the Lady of the Silver Lake, a tale that has gone the rounds of Quebec.'

He was beginning to recover from his embarrassment and to regain his fluency, while his ready smile and his gaze moved with evident pleasure from one lady to the other.

'What matter?' he decreed. 'The blonde is as good as the brunette. I would be wrong to be sorry for that. The more pretty women there are the happier one is! You know, life really is good!'

And he seized them both by the arm.

'You don't hold it against me?' he asked Angélique.

'Of course not,' she managed to get in as he turned immediately towards Ambroisine.

'And neither do you, I hope. That's the way I am. Frank, open, I say just what I think, and when someone fills me with admiration I am utterly incapable of controlling myself. You see, where beauty is concerned, every form of beauty, I have a passion for it, a real cult, and I just have to express it.'

'That's a fault that I imagine people are only too happy to forgive you.'

The Duchess of Maudribourg seemed to be brightening up. Her beautiful face which usually wore a sad expression was quite transformed, and she laughed indulgently.

'Count,' the Marquis called to Joffrey de Peyrac as the latter approached, 'you know, it's intolerable! You hoard up the most rare and wonderful things in your blessed Gouldsboro. Here you are with the two most beautiful women in the world.'

'Have you been introduced to the Duchess of Maudribourg?' Peyrac asked, making a gesture of the hand in her direction.

'We have just met.'

He kissed the tips of Ambroisine's fingers several times.

'Madame de Maudribourg has been our guest for some days now. Her ship went aground off the coast here.'

'A shipwreck! How dreadful! Are you telling me that this magnificent countryside and this lovely sea can be dangerous!'

'Now don't play the innocent,' said Peyrac with a laugh.

'You are one who should know after the exploit you have just accomplished, in passing through the Reversing Falls of the Saint John estuary with your three-master.'

'It was not I who did it, it was Alexander,' the Marquis replied with a swagger.

Joffrey de Peyrac introduced Colin Paturel, Governor of Gouldsboro, to the Duchess, and his lieutenant, Barssempuy, the captain of his fleet, Roland d'Urville, captain of his Spanish guards, Don Juan Alvarez, and the chief notables among the Huguenots from La Rochelle, then last of all Baron Saint-Castine whom Angélique discovered to be present, and his prospective father-in-law, Mateconando, Sagamore of the Souriquois of Penobscot, who appeared wearing the black Florentine beret presented to him by Verrazano on top of his long plaits.

The Duchess smiled amiably at them all.

'It seems as if these shores have more gentlemen of rank on them than the King's antechamber.'

'We are all gentlemen of adventure,' cried Lieutenant de Barssempuy. 'We carry aloft the banners of our fathers, while now in the King's antechamber only bourgeois or cowards remain.'

He was trying to create a good impression, for he was in love with Marie and feared the Duchess might frown on his candidature. Just to be on the safe side, he repeated his name which the Count had already called out and mentioned the titles of his peers in the region of Nantes from where he originated.

A certain controlled curiosity sparkled in Ambroisine's eyes which darted from face to face of those surrounding her. It was hard to know what she was thinking, but Angélique felt intuitively that she was enjoying herself in this unusual company.

Barssempuy tried to catch Marie's attention with a few signals, and found himself imitated, though with much less discretion, by Aristide Beaumarchand, who was trying to catch Julienne's eye.

But the King's Girls remained in a prim group under the aegis of their benefactress and of Petronella Dámourt, with the secretary Armand Daveau bringing up the rear.

Then the Marquis of Ville d'Avray discovered them.

'But here are yet more,' he exclaimed. 'Oh, what an admirable spot! Come, ladies, come and take some refreshment.'

He broke the circle and led them off towards the trestle tables. Angélique heard him saying to Ambroisine de Maudribourg:

'A shipwreck! But how appalling! Tell me all about it, poor child.'

She went over to Baron Saint-Castine who introduced her to his fiancée, Mathilde, the young Indian princess with whom he was in love. She was a lovely, delicately-built girl with heavy black plaits framing the golden oval of her face.

'Have you any news of our English mariner, Jack Merwin?' Angélique asked the Baron.

'Father de Vernon? He went off again. I imagine he must have been trying to link up with Father d'Orgeval on the Kennebec to report on his mission.'

'What is happening on the Indian war front?'

'Those on my lands are still quiet, but they are disturbed at the news that keeps reaching us, and I am finding it hard to contain them. The Abenakis to the west of the Kennebec are still harvesting scalps and prisoners. It is rumoured that they have put to sea with their fleets of war canoes to attack the islands in Casco Bay and track down the English in their furthermost lairs. If those islands go, New England will not easily recover from the blow.'

'And a good thing too!' shouted Ville d'Avray, who had overheard their conversation from where he stood nearby eating a crabmeat delicacy.

'It will be less of a good thing if that corsair Phipps captures the Administrator of New France,' rejoined Saint-Castine, 'and if, by way of reprisals all the English ships at present fighting in the Bay come and lay siege to my fort at Pentagouet.'

'Never fear, my good fellow, Monsieur de Peyrac will take care of the English,' the Governor of Acadia insisted with his mouth full. 'Have you tried this crab, Baron? It leaves the most delicate after-taste. Nutmeg, I wager. It is, isn't it?' he said, pointing a finger at Angélique, as if overcome by excitement at the discovery of a secret of the utmost importance.

She agreed that he had guessed right.

At the same moment two new arrivals drew the attention of the assembled company in two different directions. As half the heads were turning towards the edge of the woods from which a monk dressed in brown homespun had just emerged, carrying his Indian canoe on his head, the other half were looking towards the roadstead down which came sailing a heavy sloop weighing about thirty tons.

'There's Brother Mark, the Capuchin friar from Saint-Aubin on the Sainte-Croix,' Ville d'Avray cried, pointing to the friar, 'and here comes Grand Fontaine,' he ended, pointing towards the sea.

Grand Fontaine had been nicknamed Big-Woods on account of the magnificent oak forests that surrounded the property where he spent the greater part of his life. He was a giant of a man who was above all an inveterate hunter and fisherman and made a meagre living from the sale of a few furs.

He pushed his way unceremoniously through the crowd spilling out from the sloop; no sooner were his feet on *terra firma* than he recognized Peyrac and shouted from afar:

'The obstacle of the Saint John estuary falls was overcome by those pretty gentlemen from Quebec. But the silly bastards let themselves be taken from the rear by the English pursuing them. And now the English have blocked the mouth of the river. I can't get back to my place, so I've come to ask you to give me a hand.'

He came forward, followed by the motley crowd that had disembarked from the sloop. A handful of solidly-built Acadians, a group of women and children who were clearly either English or Dutch, some Malecite or Mic-Mac Indians, wearing their pointed embroidered hats, and standing out against them all, the tartan kilt of Cromley the Scot whom the Count had dispatched a short time previously with a warning message to all foreign settlements on French Bay.

'Yes,' repeated Big-Woods drawing closer, 'that flaming Governor brought off a feat we should all take our hats off to, but he's got us all in a right mess . . .'

'To whom are you referring, sir?' asked the Marquis of Ville d'Avray, drawing himself up to his full height.

'Oh, so you're here,' said Big-Woods, catching sight of him. 'You managed to get through ... from Jemseg? And you walked through the forest?'

'I always manage to get through where I choose to,' cried the Governor, his voice high-pitched with anger, 'and you will learn that I always manage to catch up with insolent people like you . . .'

Big-Woods was somewhat disconcerted; 'I did say that we should take our hats off to you for getting your ship past the estuary falls.'

He gave a sniff and drew his buffalo-calf sleeve across under his running nose.

'After all, we have been put in an awkward position because of you, up there, with all those Englishmen buzzing around like

86

a lot of wasps. You'd have done better to get away from the English by tacking back and forth across the bay rather than going up the river like that . . .'

'It was the only way of saving my precious cargo.'

'Yes, indeed,' said one of the new arrivals with a snigger. 'We thought as much. Precious it certainly is with all the furs you took in your raids on us.'

'There was no raid, as you call it, Monsieur Defour, at your place,' the Governor shouted, 'for the very good reason that when I reached your domains the four Defour gentlemen had gone to earth instead of behaving like loyal subjects of his Majesty and receiving his representative in an honourable manner. And as he fled one of them managed in addition to get the six soldiers from Fort Saint Mary to desert and offer their services to Monsieur de Peyrac.'[1]

'Well now, you should be pleased, since Monsieur de Peyrac is going to give you a hand. By bringing them here we merely did what you would have done anyway. And instead of thanking us . . .'

The two Defour brothers looked alike except that the younger one who had just come ashore was even taller and broader-shouldered than his older brother. Ville d'Avray glowered at them.

'Good! Well let's hope that soon we'll have the scoundrels together here so that I can clap them in chains and take them to Quebec under guard.'

The two brothers and Big-Woods burst into noisy, insolent laughter, loudly imitated by all their Mic-Macs, relatives or blood brothers.

Big-Woods drew an enormous peasant kerchief from his pocket and began to wipe his eyes from which ran tears of mirth.

'You are not on French territory here, Governor. Gouldsboro is a neutral kingdom, and we are neutral too.'

'A neutral kingdom!' the Governor repeated, his eyes popping from his head. 'What's this I hear? But this is rebellion! . . . Revolt against the Fleur de Lys! . . .'

Joffrey de Peyrac showed no interest in the quarrel. The rows between the Governor of Acadia and the people under his administration were notorious and were repeated on each of his annual visits.

Meanwhile the Count had been having a brief word with the

1. See *The Temptation of Angélique*.

Scots and a handful of refugees from the English and Dutch trading posts. It finally transpired that the foreign settlers in French Bay were more anxious about their Bostonian compatriot Phipps than the French, and that they had seized the opportunity of a visit to Gouldsboro while waiting for things to sort themselves out at the mouth of the Saint John River. An Acadian ship which was going by had been glad to take them on board.

'Have some refreshments,' said Peyrac after introducing them to the Reverend Patridge, to Miss Pidgeon and the Englishmen who had escaped from the Bay of Massachusetts.[2] 'In a few days' time you will be able to go home again. Old Chief Skoudoum has his redskins under control, and I shall go myself and pay him a visit to calm him down.'

'He has sent you this string of cowrie shells,' volunteered the monk in brown homespun. And he handed Peyrac a leather thong on which had been threaded a number of shells.

'Skoudoum sent for me specially from his village of Metoudic and then sent me on to you. These gentlemen from Quebec are asking him to bring out his warriors against the English. He has still not reached a decision and has sent you this.'

'Only a single strip!'

Peyrac stood thoughtful, turning the strip of shells over and over in his palm. It was a meagre offering, which might equally well mean: 'What shall I do? I am waiting', as 'This is a gesture of deference which I owe you before beginning my campaign, but I shall act as I wish.'

'What do you think, Father, you who have seen him?' Peyrac asked the friar, turning towards him.

'He will make no move before knowing your opinion. But he is nevertheless preparing a number of war cauldrons to please the French whose ships are threatened by the English.'

The monk spoke as if the matter were indifferent to him. He was young, with an energetic and attractive face, very sunburned, smooth-shaven, his auburn hair tousled by the wind, his habit tucked up high under a rope belt, with moccasins on his feet. There was something about him – although he had taken orders and was entitled to celebrate Mass – which led people to call him Brother Mark as if he were a novice or a lay brother.

'It suited you fine that Skoudoum sent you chasing off

2. See *The Temptation of Angélique*.

through the woods,' Ville d'Avray said to him somewhat tartly, 'you enjoy that better than saying paternosters, don't you? And you were able to go larking about in the rapids of the Saint John and the Sainte-Croix. How many times did you find yourself with your canoe on your head? How much foam did you drink among all the whirlpools and the rocks? These young people think of nothing but performing mad exploits against the waters,' he added, turning to Angélique. 'Look at this monk. He amazes even the Indians themselves by his boldness in sailing down dangerous watercourses. Do you think he gives any thought to the service of God for which he was sent here? Not on your life! And what about my Alexander? His parents entrusted him to me for me to make an accomplished gentleman of him and not some savage who dreams of nothing better than sailing up a river at the speed of ten galloping horses as he did last year up the Petitcodiac. This year he had to have the Saint John estuary . . .'

'So you admit that it was just to satisfy your young favourite that you've got us all in this mess . . .' Bertrand Defour began.

'But I never sent for Phipps,' Ville d'Avray shrieked back, beside himself.

'Nevertheless, the exploit remains,' Brother Mark said conciliatorily. 'Not only disadvantages have come of it. It was the memory of the way the French navigated up stream last year that so filled Skoudoum with admiration that he wondered whether he ought not to become their loyal ally.'

The Marquis's face lighted up and he gave one of those boyish smiles that took twenty years off him.

'Just as I said!' he exclaimed. 'It was not in vain that Alexander risked his life . . . and mine. You see, Count, without my Alexander we would all have been lost.'

'Careful now, we have not yet been saved,' Peyrac said with a laugh. 'And I don't want Skoudoum to become too attached to the French. Just at the moment I prefer his haughty ways. I'll have to do something to impress him too.'

He glanced around and then made his way towards a group of Englishmen sitting on the sand, quietly eating and drinking beer.

'Is Mr Kempton the pedlar among you?' he asked.

There he was, busy measuring up all the feet held out to him, and promising for the following day, or, at the latest, the following week, pairs of shoes as elegant as any in London and strong enough to stand the heaviest wear.

At Peyrac's request the little pedlar from Connecticut came forward, his neck swathed in yards of ribbon like a snake charmer.

'Mr Kempton,' said the Count, 'I need your bear.'

'My bear! What do you wish of him?' protested Elias Kempton suspiciously.

'I need his help, with a mission of the greatest importance. Such an intelligent bear owes it to himself to join the diplomatic service on behalf of England. I would like to take him with me to Metoudic to win over the chief of the Malecites, Skoudoum, who I hope will render me some important services, among others that of not siding with the French in this war.'

Elias Kempton shook his head.

'Impossible, Mr Willoughby must not be involved in such dangers. And in any case I cannot be parted from my bear.'

'But you can go with him.'

'Are there any European women there?' the pedlar asked suspiciously.

'Yes, indeed there are! And terribly deprived, too. They will welcome you with open arms.'

'That's different then,' Elias Kempton replied delightedly, his eyes twinkling.

'How incredibly lustful the English are!' Ville d'Avray remarked in disgust, nibbling away at a huckleberry tart, for he knew enough English to have followed the gist of the conversation.

'No, it's not what you think,' Angélique informed him with a laugh, 'that good gentleman is a pedlar from New England in search of customers. The bag he carries is bottomless; he always has something to sell, even lace cuffs and satin edgings. Naturally all the women are delighted to see him here.'

Kempton had made up his mind.

'Right. I shall inform Mr Willoughby and bring you his reply tomorrow,' he concluded, anxious to get back to his business. Then he went off calling: 'Fine shoes! Fine new shoes . . .'

'What an extraordinary man,' said the Duchess of Maudribourg, 'how lively and amusing everyone is here!' She looked at Angélique with all the enthusiasm of a young girl attending her first ball.

She seemed spellbound, forgetful of her responsibilities as benefactress. Some of the men among the new settlers who considered themselves 'bespoke' to the King's Girls took this opportunity to try their luck with the young ladies, enticing them over to the trestle tables where, under the pretext of offering them food and drink, they might manage a private word with the girl of their choice. Barssempuy was doing his charming best to overcome Marie's modesty, while the Quartermaster, Vanneau, had embarked on an account to Delphine Barbier du Rosoy of his campaigns in sundry parts of the world. Naturally Aristide Beaumarchand was putting himself out for Julienne who, from time to time, was unable to restrain a raucous laugh which she immediately stifled by putting one hand over her mouth, as she cast an anxious glance in the direction of the Duchess and Petronella Damourt. But even the fat duenna had relaxed her vigilance.

Angélique noticed that the Moorish girl, although most charming and pretty, seemed to have been overlooked. Colin Paturel's sailors, who were trying to behave respectably, did not want to pay court to a mulatto girl, lest it remind them of the West Indian girls met in their travels.

Angélique was thinking of going over to get the Gouldsboro girls to look after her, but at that very moment Yann le Couennec, who had noticed the girl standing alone, approached her.

'Do you speak French, Mademoiselle?'

'But of course!' the girl exclaimed. 'I was brought up in the Ursuline convent at Neuilly near Paris.'

'How delighted I am,' said the worthy young man. 'Would you care for some spruce beer, some white sumac lemonade or a little Spanish wine to gladden your heart?'

'Some Spanish wine, please,' the girl replied finding her smile again.

The Duchess, standing beside Angélique, had noticed what was going on.

'How kind of that young man to look after the child,' she commented with a sigh. 'My poor Mauresque! I did not want to bring her, but my friend the Marquise de Roquencourt was most insistent. I do not know whether she will find anyone to take her in Quebec. And I feel really sorry, for I have grown very fond of her. But I suppose she can always take the veil as a lay sister. She is very accomplished.'

Angélique wondered whether this might not be the time to speak to the Duchess about letting some of the King's Girls settle in Gouldsboro. But Joffrey de Peyrac came towards them.

'Didn't you tell me that Sagamore Piksarett turned up in Gouldsboro this morning?'

'Yes indeed. He came to claim my ransom, so he said, and wished to see you urgently. But I do not see him here.'

'What's all this about a ransom?' the Duchess asked, wide-eyed.

Angélique briefly explained that during a battle in New England she had been taken prisoner by the famous Piksarett. He had let her go free but in accordance with Indian laws of warfare, Monsieur de Peyrac owed him a ransom.

'How extraordinary it all seems,' said Madame de Maudribourg looking at her in astonishment. 'Why do you not get rid of these insolent Indians?'

'We must respect their customs . . .'

They called over the two braves, Jerome and Michael, who were eating venison near a fire. After wiping their hands on their moccasins and in their hair they presented themselves.

'Where is Piksarett?' Angélique asked them in the Abenaki tongue.

The two Patsuikett warriors looked at one another and seemed to hesitate.

'He's run away,' Jerome replied.

It seemed a strange word to use, especially about the intractable Piksarett. Peyrac got them to repeat it, then he asked Castine's advice. But there seemed to be no other way of translating the Abenakis' phrase. Piksarett had 'run away', why? In the face of what danger? Angélique and the Count looked at one another.

'I was going to ask him to accompany me on our expedition,' said Peyrac. 'Skoudoum cares a great deal about his alliances with the other Abenaki tribes and a visit from the Great Convert about whom he had spoken to me with interest, would certainly have delighted his heart. They would have discussed religion, smoked my best Virginia tobacco, and I would have had time to defuse the bomb.'

'Why don't you take Mateconando, my father-in-law-to-be?' the young Gascon baron proposed. 'He too is very eloquent on religious matters.'

'Peyrac my dear fellow,' cried Ville d'Avray, 'if you want to impress the Malacite chief you should take my Alexander with you. You heard what Brother Mark said just then. We must give this young hero his due after what he has done.'

'That doesn't stop it being a damn fool thing to do,' Big-Woods reiterated loudly.

'But think of the honour of such an exploit ... People as coarse as you simply cannot understand ...'

And they all began to argue furiously once more, Brother Mark even more heatedly than the others. People listened to him with a certain respect since it was claimed that not even the natives were as familiar as he was with all the falls in the network of streams, watercourses and rivers from Rivière du Loup on the Saint Lawrence down to the Kennebec along the Saint John, the Saint Croix and the Penobscot.

'They really do get worked up about this business, don't they?' Angélique remarked to Count d'Urville, who was standing beside her.

'If you knew the area, you would understand why,' replied the young Norman nobleman. 'There, one's whole life seems to be dominated by those constantly moving waters; the forest is alive with the sound of waterfalls ...'

Defour was saying: 'If only there weren't those tides of nearly eleven fathoms high ...'

'But *there are* tides eleven fathoms high,' Ville d'Avray replied, triumphantly, 'whereas in the Mediterranean the tides don't even reach one fathom.'

'Tides of eight fathoms are not unknown at the farthest tip of Brittany, but that doesn't make the Bretons behave like madmen.'

'No, they are worse ... But to return to our French Bay: what is the cause of such high tides?'

'Some folk from Saint-Malo explained it to me,' said one of the sailors from the *Heart of Mary* who happened to be a Breton. 'They've been coming over to fish here for as long as any one knows, their ancestors have been coming for centuries, long before Columbus. They know all the secrets of this coast-line.'

'And so?'

'They say that a sea-monster came and jammed himself in a crack on the seabed. And now every time he turns round the sea overflows.'

'Hold your tongue, you old humbug,' shouted Colin while a number of those present began to laugh. 'You cannot tell that kind of story nowadays.'

'And why not?' the sailor protested crossly. 'The men from

93

Saint-Malo even told me that occasionally around the five islands opposite Parsboro you can see the monster's eyes glistening under the water . . .'

'Oh, do hold your peace, old fellow,' Ville d'Avray urged him indulgently, 'if Monsieur Peyrac were to hear you, him a scientific man, he would make fun of you all right.'

'And why should that not be an explanation, even if it isn't a scientific one, as you call it?' said another Breton springing to the defence of his compatriot. 'After all not so long ago back at home in Brittany the land began to move over towards Pont-Brieuc. Merlin the magician had the people dig down into the earth and they discovered two gigantic dragons, one white and one red . . . It isn't natural for the sea to rise up the way it does suddenly and then go away again as if there was something pushing it from inside. There must be a reason for it.'

Ville d'Avray was forced to admit that the matter remained a mystery for him too. Then he looked up: 'Count, will you clear this one up for us?' he asked. 'I have a feeling that you may well be able to answer the question we've been discussing. What is it that causes the movement of tides particularly in our Bay, where we get these giant tides which in a few hours transform the landscape and make it almost unrecognizable? You come to a stretch of shore that runs along the edge of a forest and six hours later at the very same spot you find yourself standing at the foot of a cliff. It really is puzzling, isn't it?'

Joffrey de Peyrac gave the assembled company a friendly smile.

He was wearing the simple dark green velvet doublet which Angélique was fond of because he had been wearing it when she had found him again in La Rochelle. As she looked at him standing a few paces from her, the humanity in his eyes, whose burning intensity she had sometimes had to brave, but through which she also knew both passion and joy, she herself began to feel calmer. It seemed to her as if the touch of silver at her husband's temples had become a little more pronounced and she felt a tremor of tenderness in her heart.

'I would gladly answer your question,' said Peyrac, 'but I would be interested to see whether anyone here could do so instead of me. I shall offer a present to whoever manages to work out the truth by use of reason and on the basis of his observations. Come, gentlemen, you are all seafaring men, and you must certainly have picked up a great deal of information in the course of your travels. It will not take you long, I feel sure, to come close to the scientific and mathematical answer, of what it is that causes the movement of the tides.'

They all began to whisper among themselves, and to wrinkle their brows.

'I see Yann raising his eyes heavenwards,' said the Count. 'You're getting warm, my boy.'

'Should we be seeking the secret of the tides among the stars?' Yann asked.

'Yes, of course. Or rather, among the planets,' a voice affirmed. 'Since the tides are caused by the attraction of the moon.'

CHAPTER 15

IT WAS a woman's voice that spoke. All eyes converged on the point from which the voice had come.

The Duchess of Maudribourg, who was standing beside Angélique, courageously braved these stares, in which astonishment mingled with irony and disapproval.

She held her head high on her graceful neck and looked back with a slightly challenging smile.

A stupefied, almost scandalized silence reigned for an instant. They all awaited the verdict.

Peyrac took a few steps towards the Duchess.

'You have won, Madame,' he told her with a bow, 'and allow me to say that Gouldsboro is honoured to have within its walls, if I may so put it, a pupil of the great astronomer Gassendi, a Frenchman who was the first man in the world to measure the length of the terrestrial meridian in French Guyana.'

'The moon? What has the moon got to do with all this?' exclaimed the Governor of Acadia.

He looked like a clown gaping in astonishment. Then he added:

'To begin with, there are tides during the day as well as at night.'

'You astonish me, my dear fellow,' replied Peyrac. 'You should remember that as far as our world is concerned, which is after all a planet among other planets, the moon is always there, by night as well as by day, just as the sun is too.'

'And attraction, what does attraction mean?' asked Vanneau the quartermaster.

'Have you ever seen a magnet picking up needles?' asked Madame de Maudribourg. 'At certain times the moon does just that to us.'

Everyone grasped the simplicity of the image and there followed a further astonished silence.

Most of them were looking up at the sky. Then Ville d'Avray suddenly discovered the pale crescent of a moon in a pearly sky which was just beginning to turn golden with the approach of evening.

'Ah, so that's what you do to us, you wretch,' he cried. 'And now I would like to know why at certain hours, that minx up there decides to suck us up whereas at other times she leaves us in peace.'

Joffrey de Peyrac gestured in Ambroisine de Maudribourg's direction.

'The floor is yours, Madame.'

'You could explain it just as well, Count,' she replied with the merest trace of coquettishness. 'Is this an examination?'

He shook his head. His dark, attentive gaze lingered on Ambroisine de Maudribourg's face.

Angélique suddenly felt a pang of something inexplicable, an almost physical pain, as if her heart had suddenly shrunk within her, crushed in a brutal grip. It was a deep, insidious pain, a pain as of terror, and it took her several moments to analyse what it was that had caused it. It was that glance of Peyrac's. Then she understood. That was a look that *only she should have received*, she, Angélique, his beloved, his spouse.

The face of the young Duchess had acquired a kind of transparency like alabaster in the pearly light that hovered on the point of darkness, and her great, dark eyes sparkled with the clear light of intelligence. He was half smiling, but no one could have guessed the precise nature of his thoughts.

'An examination, oh no, Madame!' he protested. 'But I stand all too often on the rostrum. I'd like to be your pupil for a while.'

She burst out laughing almost like a girl, and made a movement of protest that swung her long black hair across her shoulders.

'What nonsense! I am certain that there is nothing I could teach *you*.'

'And I am quite sure you could.'

96

'But ... they are flirting! ...' Angélique told herself in horror. And it was indeed a kind of horror that nailed her to the ground as the words flew back and forth before her and she could hear, as in some distant nightmare, her husband's hoarse tones and the deep throaty laugh that accompanied Ambroisine's bewitching voice.

'Count, you are trying to trap me ... a scientist of your renown! Surely you are not suggesting that you really don't know why the high tide does not occur precisely when the moon is at its zenith but is always slightly out of phase ...'

'Unfortunately I don't, I have not yet been able to determine the mathematical cause of this phenomenon ...'

'You are making fun of me ...'

'No I'm not. Actually you have every right to make fun of me ... but it is only a trivial humiliation ... One can forgive one's ignorance when one has the good fortune to be taught by such a pretty lady ...'

'Wait a minute! Wait a minute!' Ville d'Avray called out. 'I want to understand this too! Let us begin at the beginning. How is it that the attraction of the moon, if we grant that there is such attraction, produces the tides? Now listen carefully, Alexander!'

'I know all that,' the young man replied sulkily.

Ambroisine spun round to face the lad with an expression that was both questioning and imperious. The boy had the wisdom to beat a hasty retreat.

'I mean that Father Maubeuge in Quebec told me about it, but I didn't pay much attention.'

'Father de Maubeuge?'

Ambroisine seemed to show considerable interest.

'He has been to China, hasn't he? And was one of the founders of the Peking observatory? I am greatly looking forward to meeting him!'

'Well, what about this moon?' Ville d'Avray asked impatiently. 'If the moon, as you say it does, exerts its influence more or less equally upon the whole globe, how is it that at certain places the tides are very slight while in others they are enormous?'

'A clever objection. This is indeed something that has been long discussed. Nowadays we have established that this difference is due to the viscosity of water which is not the same for all seas. The Mediterranean is an enclosed sea, which makes it very salty, and the moon's attraction is unable to produce a sufficient curve to counteract the viscosity of the surface, whereas on the other hand . . .'

'What do you mean by the viscosity of the surface?' someone asked.

'We mean the layer that constitutes the "skin" of the sea.'

'The skin of the sea!' Ville d'Avray exclaimed, almost laughing.

'Yes indeed, my dear.'

Angélique was getting a grip on herself again. Since the Marquis had begun to join in the conversation, which was no longer entirely between Count Peyrac and the Duchess, she had begun to feel better and the dizzy feeling that had swept over her so suddenly began to disperse.

She forced herself to listen and try to understand.

Ambroisine de Maudribourg's voice explained with great clarity that if you were to shoot a bullet obliquely at the surface of the sea it would ricochet off, thus proving that the sea set up a resistance to its penetration on account of its 'skin'. In an enclosed sea like the Mediterranean this skin seemed necessarily to contract and therefore to become very thick, thus resisting the attraction of the moon. On the other hand, the greater the surface area, the more the skin would stretch as it did here in French Bay or in the coastal inlet near the Mont Saint-Michel in Brittany, which are the end points of a vast ocean, and the more readily did the sea respond to the attractive force of the moon.

'Count Peyrac, does my explanation depart too far from the rigorous scientific truth?'

'No, it is quite correct and can be understood by all,' Peyrac agreed.

He nodded several times by way of approval. She looked at him ardently as if enraptured. Her lips were slightly apart, revealing the edge of her glistening, perfect teeth.

'All that seems logical enough,' the Governor agreed, 'but has anyone established when it is that gentle Phoebe exercises her influence over us otherwise than in our dreams?'

'The strongest influence occurs when the moon stands between the earth and the sun . . .'

The quartermaster broke in sharply:

'And why are there two tides?'

The Duchess explained in the strong well-modulated voice she adopted when talking about scientific matters, that at each of these the moon was not in the same position with regard to the sun. When it was in quadrature, that is to say at right angles to the sun, the two poles of attraction cancelled one another out resulting in a lesser pull whereby the sea rose less. This resulted in the neap-tide.

'It makes my head go round,' Ville d'Avray commented, sceptically.

He was watching Peyrac's reactions out of the corner of his eye, but the Count seemed in no way to be casting doubt on the assertions of this pretty woman. On the contrary, his chiselled features, deliberately impassive, revealed a certain satisfaction.

'And so Kepler's laws have been confirmed, have they?' he asked.

'Yes. As a matter of fact I have been in correspondence with him.'

The Count raised a quizzical eyebrow.

'With Kepler?' he asked, a shadow of incredulity in his voice.

'Why not?'

She stared boldly at him once again.

'Do you consider that a woman is unable to understand the laws he deduced from his observations of the phases of the planet Mars? Namely that planetary orbits are ellipses of which the sun forms one of the two foci, and that the area swept by the radius vector from the centre of the sun to the centre of the planet is proportional to the time taken to describe it, that is to say to cover the distance; and the laws stating that the square of the time taken for a planetary revolution is proportional to the cube of the major axis of the extension of the orbit.'

There was no doubt about it. Peyrac was profoundly moved by this exchange with the Duchess of Maudribourg, an exchange that remained a mystery to everyone else.

Angélique felt a sense of relief to hear the Marquis of Ville d'Avray, who never liked playing second string, again break the spell with a question.

'But let us get back to the moon! One further question, Duchess, for my guidance, concerning the tides. If I grant that a kind of swelling takes place on the surface of the earth which faces the moon at the moment of the pull, how is it that the same phenomenon takes place at the antipodes, on the other side of the globe?'

She gave him a smile of commiseration.

'But what is the earth, sir,' she asked gently, 'in the immensity of the planetary system which surrounds us? Nothing more than an infinitesimal dot. The influence of the moon, like that of the sun as well, of course, is not confined to a single point, namely the one where you happen to be. It literally encases us, passes completely through us, and it is indeed wonderful to reflect that this communion with visible and invisible systems surrounding us into infinity forces us to recognize the splendour of our Creator, God, our Father who is in Heaven,' she finished with fervour, raising her eyes towards the firmament.

A star appeared through the liquid gold of the evening light. And at that moment a flock of birds flew with a great beating of wings, over the silent gathering.

It was then that Angélique grew aware of something strange, something unusual that had occurred, something that no one save herself had realized. And even she had only noticed it fleetingly, as if it were taking place somewhere else and were no concern of hers. But the spectacle engraved itself in the depths of her eye in the most shattering way: *every man present was looking at Ambroisine de Maudribourg.*

The Duchess looked strikingly beautiful with her youthful white face ecstatic, as if lit by some sacred passion. Angélique would have been incapable of saying how many seconds went by, perhaps it was only a flash. And it could be that it never happened at all.

The benefactress turned towards Count Peyrac and asked in her distinguished society voice:

'Are you satisfied, Dominie? May I take off my academic gown?'

'Yes indeed, Madame. You have more than adequately answered these difficult questions, and we would all like to thank you very much.'

And still she looked him straight in the eye. Then she gave a little pouting smile.

'And what about my present?' she asked as if coming to some conclusion. 'Did you not say that you would offer a gift to whoever could explain how the tides worked and why they were so high in French Bay?'

'Yes I did, but . . .'

'But you had not reckoned with the possibility that it might be a woman who gave you your answer?' she said in a burst of laughter.

'Quite so,' he agreed with a smile, 'and although I had thought of giving these gentlemen a few twists of tobacco for their pipes . . .'

'You had thought of nothing for me . . . a woman.'

She was still laughing, but her laugh had grown gentler and softer, almost indulgent.

'No matter! I am not hard to please. I have lost everything in the shipwreck . . . the smallest object would delight me. But I do deserve my recompense . . . don't I?'

He glanced away as if fearing to look straight into those bold, candid eyes. He was just about to remove a ring from one of his fingers to offer it to the Duchess, but, on second thoughts, he delved into the leather alms-purse he wore on his belt and drew out a rough gold nugget the size of a walnut.

'What is that?' she exclaimed.

'One of the finest nuggets we have found in our mine at Wapassou.'

'What an extraordinary thing! I have never seen one before.'

She held out her hand.

He handed her the nugget with a smile and she lifted it up on the tips of her delicate fingers, allowing it to sparkle in the light of the setting sun.

Once again fear swept over Angélique, an anguish which could not be expressed in any cry, in any movement or any reaction on her part, before which prudence required her to remain motionless and impassive, for fear of seeing the precipice she had glimpsed open still larger and more terrifying beneath her feet.

CHAPTER 16

SUDDENLY THE silence was broken by shouts and scuffling, followed by bursts of laughter.

Cantor's wolverine came racing down the hill like a black cannon-ball, ploughed a furrow through the crowd, knocking over everyone who happened to be in his way, and came to a halt in front of Angélique, his superb bushy tail erect, his tiny rodent's face close to the ground as he turned upon her his great eyes that caught the red glow of the sky.

The Duchess of Maudribourg started back with a cry.

'Whatever is that monster?' she asked in terror. 'Angélique, I beg you, save me.'

'It's only a wolverine. He's not dangerous. He's tame.'

Angélique knelt down to pat the animal. She suddenly felt very glad to see the wolverine and sensed an easing of her anxiety.

'He's looking for Cantor. He's been quite distracted since Cantor left.'

'Your son would have done better to take him with him,' shouted Madame Manigault who had suddenly found herself sitting on her ample posterior, fortunately undamaged.

'But Cantor looked for him,' explained Martial Berne. 'We both searched for him when the time came to leave. But Wolverine had gone off into the forest to play with a bear, and Cantor had to set sail without him.'

'Ah, here is the bear,' said someone.

Elias Kempton joined the gathering, followed by his huge companion.

'I've brought you Mr Willoughby,' he declared solemnly to Count Peyrac. 'I've told him what you expect of him and he has no objection to accompanying you up French Bay, although he's very happy in Gouldsboro and is not that fond of sailing. But since it's a matter of prestige for England, he quite understands.'

'I would like to thank this loyal subject of the King of England,' said Peyrac, addressing a few words to the bear in English.

The bear had indeed prospered in Gouldsboro, where he was able to stuff himself with myrtle berries, hazel-nuts and honey. He looked twice as big as when he had first landed. He began to sniff around in all directions as if seeking a familiar face amidst those present, then rising up on his hind legs he made off towards Angélique growling and lurching as he went.

The Duchess gave another cry, stifled this time, and almost fainted. Those nearest the bear beat a hasty retreat. Almost in spite of themselves Joffrey de Peyrac and Colin Paturel began to make for the animal. But a few words in English from Angélique brought the bear down on all fours again, and she began to stroke him and talk to him.

'Beauty and the Beast,' said the Marquis of Ville d'Avray, delightedly. 'Really, what an extraordinary sight! . . .'

CHAPTER·17

'YES INDEED,' he commented again somewhat later, 'a most unusual spectacle! Your pale skin and graceful form beside that hairy monster! You're frightened of nothing. You are indeed as they say you are in Quebec . . . No, don't take that away, my good lady,' he said, holding back Madame Carrère, who was beginning to gather up the dishes from the tables, 'there's still some of that delicious crab left on that plate. Pass it over here! What was I saying? Yes, my dear Angélique, you are just like the pictures your devotees in Quebec paint of you. When I think that that serious-minded man d'Arreboust caused a scandal by coming to your defence on his return from the Kennebec country. I liked the way he spoke up courageously on your behalf, and it brought us closer together. He is quite obviously in love with you. And back in Montreal his wife is already deep in prayer for the salvation of his soul . . .'

Angélique was only listening to him with half an ear. People were beginning to drift away now. Sturdy young lads tackled the job of dismantling the trestle tables. The lilac-coloured dusk crept over the beach and the shouts of people who could no longer see one another rang out with perfect clarity, for the evening air was still, and the wind had fallen.

Angélique glanced around for her husband and could not see him.

'In Quebec, at the time of the great famine, when everyone thought you had all died in the depths of the forest, the Knight of Malta Loménie-Chambord asked for a novena to be said on your behalf. Some people thought this was excessive, but I went along. I have always enjoyed doing things for pretty women, even praying for them. It caused quite a riot. There are all kinds of interesting people in Quebec, you'll see. I adore the city. There is always something extraordinary going on. I was there already back in 1662, when a comet passed overhead, a sign of war, and burning canoes bearing all those who died martyrs to the Iroquois . . . You killed Pont-Briand, so they say.'

'Me? I've never killed anyone . . .'

103

'Well, he died because of you. He was a very good friend of mine, but overfond of the ladies. He thought he was irresistible. An easy prey for that clever Jesuit.'

'Who do you mean?' Angélique asked, her voice faltering as she spoke.

She had suddenly caught sight of Joffrey. He was standing at the inn door talking to the Duchess of Maudribourg, who was sitting on one of the wooden benches that surrounded the doorway.

'Sebastian d'Orgeval, of course,' Ville d'Avray replied. 'A splendid fellow! I'm very fond of him. At first we used to come to blows, but I'm not frightened of the Jesuits. They are people with a certain charm . . .'

Ambroisine de Maudribourg, her hands clasped round her knees, was sitting with her white face tilted up towards Count Peyrac. The Count's silhouette stood out sharply against the light, tall, supple, imposing against the fiery background of the bay. Every now and then people coming and going from the inn hid him from Angélique's view.

Ville d'Avray wiped his mouth with his little lace handkerchief and stretched himself contentedly.

'Isn't life good, Angélique? Isn't it just? . . . But you do not reply? It was something quite out of the ordinary to listen to that pretty Duchess instructing us all as she did, wasn't it? . . . Ah, I did well to leave Quebec for a while. After the winter, everyone gets very edgy up there. My servant-girl wanted to visit her family on Orleans Island. You know, the way all Canadians want to be on the move as soon as winter's over. Young Maudreuil seemed to have the fidgets too. He wanted to go off collecting furs up country like all hot-headed young men. And as for Alexander, he was itching to perform some nautical exploit.'

The beach had now grown dark. And yet no one had lighted lamps. It was so mild that people hesitated to part company and go home. They went on chatting idly in groups.

'Yes, life is good,' the Marquis of Ville d'Avray repeated, 'I like the atmosphere of French Bay. You feel those currents going by in the air? That is why everyone here lives on the edge of madness. Except your husband, who confines himself to creating mad projects in the sanest possible manner.'

'What mad projects?' asked Angélique, turning nervously towards him.

'Well, for example, the creation of this settlement. Catholics and Calvinists side by side . . . It simply won't work! When the children grow up, they will fall in love and want to marry . . . But their pastors or their priests will refuse to marry them, and their fathers will curse and their mothers weep . . .'

'Oh, do stop, you are making me depressed,' Angélique cried, unable to stand any more.

'But what is wrong? I had no wish to upset you. On the contrary, did I not tell you how much I like this place? What originality, what a variety of human types from the four corners of the world!'

Some birds flew overhead uttering piercing cries as they went.

'The summer is so short in these northern latitudes,' he said. 'One has to live feverishly, fix everything in a few months. But after that . . . you must come to Quebec, in the autumn . . . it's so beautiful. The ships have all gone, the Saint Lawrence hills are all pink, and the river is like a huge pale lake, standing at the foot of the Rock, slowly allowing the ice to cover it. You must come. You can spend the winter there. My house is at your disposal, yours and Monsieur de Peyrac's. It is one of the most comfortable in the city . . . You will like it there. No, no, it will be no trouble to me at all, I have a little place down in the lower town . . .'

'Excuse me,' Angélique called over her shoulder as she left him hurriedly.

She had just seen Ambroisine de Maudribourg's silhouette detach itself from the shadow of the inn and begin to walk up through the village. On an impulse she went to meet her. The Duchess was walking quickly, almost running.

They nearly bumped into one another and as she recognized Angélique in the dim light, Ambroisine suddenly looked frightened.

'What's wrong?' asked Angélique. 'You seem upset?'

'So do you.'

There was a silence. The Duchess's eyes looked like two dark holes in her marble face. She stared at Angélique with painful intensity.

'How lovely you are,' she murmured almost involuntarily.

'You were talking to my husband. What could he have said to upset you like this?'

'Oh, nothing, truly. We were just talking . . .' she hesitated for a moment then stammered: 'We . . . we were talking about mathematics . . .'

*　　　*　　　*

'So you went on with your conversation about mathematics with Madame de Maudribourg?' Angélique asked Peyrac. 'She certainly is learned.'

'Perhaps too learned for a pretty woman,' the Count replied off-handedly. 'No, actually, this evening we'd heard enough with that most impressive explanation of the tides. I confined myself to explaining to her that it might be possible for some of her protegées to settle here.'

'And what did she say to that?'

'She said she would think about it.'

CHAPTER 18

TWO DAYS passed bringing jobs to be done, problems to be solved, and shoals of visitors, who were more or less welcome, but who seemed to bear down on Gouldsboro as if it were the only place affording firm ground beneath their feet, and a guarantee of security during the tense period through which French Bay was passing.

Angélique had tried to understand what it was that had happened to her on the beach when she saw Joffrey looking at Ambroisine. But the incident was beginning to fade into the background. She could no longer explain the sensations she had felt. How could she believe in these while Joffrey was still there, sharing her nights with her? And it seemed to her that never had he shown so much passion. Everything was simple between them in the realm of love, and, if they each harboured some secret anxiety, this only intensified their feelings as they made love, discovering in one another the necessary strength.

'How happy I am!' he said to her softly. 'Your presence is everything to me.'

He no longer spoke of his departure, but she knew that at any moment he might be obliged to go. And this made all the more precious and intense the hours they were granted together. She blessed the night, the refuge of lovers. Night! That was when man's happiness or misery was decided.

The day after the lecture on the beach a small fishing smack from Saint-Malo put in for water, at the same time setting ashore a distinguished clerical gentleman, who hitched up his soutane with some show of irritation in order to avoid the pools of water along the beach.

'I say, if it isn't my Sulpician!' exclaimed Ville d'Avray on catching sight of the priest in the distance. 'So you've run out on the Jemseg lot, have you, my dear fellow? All those foul-mouthed Acadian squireens and that petty-minded little runt Carlon! You were quite right. Here at least it's amusing and the food's good . . . Is my ship still there and has no one tried to pillage it? Now don't tell me the English have got it!'

That was not what the Sulpician, Father Dagenet, had to tell him. The English were in fact still lying in wait, at the mouth of the river, for their prey to grow weary and try to bolt from the burrow. The Sulpician had become bored with it all and had set off first through the forest then by sea to join the Governor to whom he was attached as private chaplain.

'All the same it would have been better if you had stayed there and kept an eye on my baggage,' Ville d'Avray said reproachfully. 'But I can understand why you didn't. It's obviously so much nicer in Gouldsboro . . .'

Another arrival was Father Tournel, the chaplain from Port Royal. He had come across for news, on behalf of the chatelaine, who was worried at her husband's failure to return home. Hubert d'Arpentigny, the young Acadian landowner from Cape Sable, had also come over to accompany Madame de la Roche-Posay's messenger.

Peyrac said to him: 'Why don't you come with me when I set out to scare off the English from the Saint John estuary?'

'What would I gain by that?'

'The goodwill of Carlon, the Administrator, who's about to fall into their hands.'

Hubert d'Arpentigny consulted his steward, Pol Renart, and his Mic-Macs. Had he not indeed come over to Gouldsboro sensing that preparations for battle were in the air, and knowing that Gouldsboro was the one place from which it would be possible to conduct a sea campaign? War for what end? That was never easy to establish, but there was always the hope of capturing a few ships or sacking a fort or two, which would help the impecunious domains scattered along the coast of French Acadia to carry on for a little longer.

At such a time, when every hour was crowded with hectic activity, life had a feverish, tremulous intensity not unlike the bright, strong colouring of the landscape. The fine weather, unchanged for the past two days, had turned the sea a blue so intense that it was almost unbearable. It was also the season of willow-herb, the slender stems of which, mauve, rose-pink or red, sprang up from every crack in the ground. The tiniest sunny dell was gorgeous with episcopal purple, the smallest cranny in a cliff side was suddenly fringed with violet.

Their flowering marked the opulence of high summer. Yet the sea still continued extremely rough, ceaselessly throwing up plumes of snow-white spray along the shore, while the never-ending thunder of the waves against the craggy pink and blue cliffs boomed dully throughout the land making people feel keyed-up and avid to live as fully and passionately as they could.

Yes, there was war and love in the air, and also a haste to build, to bring to fruition things already established, to establish new couples, shelter them beneath a roof, surround them with gardens, to make new paths, new roads, to build a church where the new arrivals could bind their souls forever, and to build forts on the four points of the horizon to protect them forever from destruction.

The way in which, in the course of that summer, Puritans and Catholics, hunters and pirates, redskins and Acadians converged upon their settlement somehow defined their role, and it was clear that, regardless of the different opinions, sympathies or ambitions of its inhabitants, this independent port, rich and well protected, had already become established as precisely the kind of flourishing commercial centre that the whole of north-west America was crying out for.

Swept along by this current, Angélique put off till later the examination of her inner anxieties and worries. This was no time for emotional and spiritual niceties. An inner voice whispered to her that she must go on living 'as if nothing had happened'. And without either of them referring to these thoughts, she knew that Joffrey de Peyrac was doing the same.

But while appearing to be exclusively preoccupied with preparations for his expedition, was he nevertheless secretly thinking of those whom he had sworn to seek out and unmask, the mysterious prowlers of the Bay? He said nothing about it, and Angélique, following his example, did not broach the matter either, refusing even to think about it.

Could the demons be so easily deceived?

In the evenings people foregathered in the wharf-side inn with the visitors to Gouldsboro. In honour of the Governor and his Sulpician, the Duchess and her secretary, Monsieur de Randon and his blood-brother the great Mic-Mac Sagamore, Baron Saint-Castine and his father-in-law-to-be Chief Mateconando, Pastor Thomas Patridge and the various chaplains, a number of special dinners were held there.

During these meals the Duchess of Maudribourg, to Angélique's considerable relief, did not attempt to bring the conversation round to scientific matters again. Ville d'Avray, who was a great talker, kept the conversation going, and Peyrac, who suddenly appeared relaxed and full of gaiety in his old, somewhat caustic manner, full of unexpected flashes of wit, replied with much good humour. The ancient philosophers formed the subject of these exchanges, being neutral and relatively safe ground for guests of such diverse allegiances.

Even the Reverend Patridge, a man of considerable culture, deigned to smile. These Papists deserved to burn in hell but they were entertaining. It was astonishing to see, the shrewdness and subtlety with which the Indian chieftains joined in this kind of discussion. They ate with their fingers, belched, and wiped their hands in their hair or on their moccasins, but their philosophy was worthy of Socrates or Epicurus.

Alexander de Rosny, everlastingly and inexplicably sulking, was useful as a butt and a scapegoat. Ville d'Avray and Peyrac did their best to explain how it was that so handsome a young man came to be so grumpy by appealing to the transmigration of souls, reincarnation, possession by evil spirits, heredity, the influence of the planets, etc, etc. All this they suggested with no trace of ill will, but with considerable verve, and the young man listened to their propositions without the slightest change in his expression.

Such impassiveness finally induced a state of general hilarity, although Angélique noticed that the Duchess was not participating in it. Her smile lacked conviction and her great eyes seemed at times to wear a tragic expression. Of course her chief preoccupations were known to all. The dilemma had faced her the very day after she had so brilliantly expounded Galileo's and Newton's theories of the tides.

That morning, Madame Carrère had brought Angélique the Duchess's clothes which she had mended, except for her mantle which, so she said, required further attention.

'I have done what I could,' said Madame Carrère, 'but, you know, when things are torn to ribbons like that ... I've never seen the like.'

Angélique laid the pale yellow satin skirt, the blue bodice and the red modesty-vest over her arm and was on her way to the Duchess's house when she was intercepted by Aristide Beaumarchand, who seemed to have been waiting for her at a bend in the path.

It would have been an exaggeration to say that he no longer resembled the hideous pirate whose paunch she had slit open then sewed up again for him at Maquoit Point. But he was clean-shaven and wore his greasy hair tied back with something that resembled a leather thong, and his clothes were clean – although they hung loosely about his body, which had grown much thinner – and as he stood before her holding his hat in both hands across his stomach he looked almost respectable.

'I was waiting for you, Madame,' he said baring his scattered teeth in a broad smile.

'Oh yes,' Angélique replied, on her guard. 'I hope your intentions are honourable.'

Aristide pretended to be offended.

'But of course they are! Whatever do you mean? You know me, don't you?'

'Precisely!'

Aristide kept turning his hat round and round between his hands in embarrassment.

'Well, here goes!' he finally decided. 'Madame la Comtesse, I wish to marry.'

'To marry! You!' she exclaimed.

'And why shouldn't I marry like everyone else?' he asked, drawing himself up with all the dignity of a repented pirate.

'Is it Julienne you are in love with?' she asked.

It seemed somewhat inappropriate to use the word 'love' with reference to those two particular people, but after all, why not, as he himself had said? For it certainly was love they were talking about. One only had to see how Aristide Beaumarchand's leaden complexion grew almost pink while he modestly lowered his rheumy eyes.

'Yes, you guessed first go. She's the most remarkable one among them. And you see I'm not interested in just anyone, you have to have what it takes to get me interested, especially with young ladies. But she's really someone.'

'You're right. Julienne is a fine girl. Have you spoken about this to your captain, Monsieur Paturel?'

'Of course! I would never have taken the liberty of asking Julienne for her hand unless I had been sure I could offer her a secure future. I explained my intentions to Gold Beard. With my share of the booty that I've got buried somewhere, and the dowry you get here, I shall be able to buy a sloop which I shall use for coastal trading so that I can go from one outpost to another to sell my tafia.'

'Your *what*?'

'Just an idea of mine. I'm a great connoisseur of rum, you know! ... Oh, of course when I say tafia it can't be real tafia, real distillers' rum, because in any case there's no sugar cane around here. I mean a good "firewater", made with a base of the molasses left over from sugar refining. You see, it's for free. Actually, in the West Indies they will pay you to take the stuff away! Hyacinth will take care of that. So you see then I'll add water to it to make it ferment, give it a good bit of "sauce" to colour it up and give it a flavour; there's a whole choice of recipes, a bit of grated leather or burned oak, some resin, a bit of tar, and put it to mature in a barrel with a good piece of old meat inside and after that dole it out a pint at a time, jolly good rum and not too dear! People in the colonies here, especially the English, will like that, and I can barter some with the Indians. They don't worry too much about the quality as long as it's strong.

'I've talked to the Count about it. He understands me, because I know that that's his system too: you bring in goods that are cheap and make something from them which you can sell again for a lot of money. That's called industry, that is, only you have to know what you're doing and have some ideas . . .'

'And what does he say about it?'

'He didn't say no.'

Angélique was not totally convinced that Count Peyrac gave his unqualified approval to this scheme that involved brewing low-grade alcohol on his land and selling it as real rum to the settlers of French Bay, but Aristide Beaumarchand's genuine intention to lead a settled and industrious life certainly deserved to be encouraged.

'Well, I wish you luck, my friend. Don't you want to go back to the Islands any more?'

'No! I want to settle down. The Caribbean Islands are no place for a respectable married couple and especially not for a pretty girl like Julienne. Hyacinth would pinch her from me. But of course things are not all tied up yet until Old Poison has approved the scheme. That is why I wanted to ask you, Madame, to put our case to her.'

'Old Poison?' Angélique repeated uncomprehending.

'The benefactress! The old Duch! 'Cos she don't look like letting any of those King's Girls go. And she's got to be persuaded. And I'm not only asking on my own behalf. There's also Vanneau who's set his heart on Delphine and . . .'

'All right then. I shall ask Madame de Maudribourg if she has thought about the matter and I shall mention your name to her.'

'Thank you very much, Madame la Comtesse,' Aristide said humbly, 'as long as you have the matter in hand, I feel better about it. We know how it is with you, things get a move on, my oath they do!'

And he gave her a conspiratorial wink. Angélique was shocked by his lack of deference towards the Duchess of Maudribourg, but you had to take him as he was: a pretty low-grade pirate, a faithless creature who served neither God nor master and for whom the subtleties of tact would forever remain a closed book.

Marie told Angélique that Madame de Maudribourg was saying her prayers, but as soon as she heard Angélique's voice, the Duchess emerged from her retreat.

'I have brought you your clothes,' said Angélique, 'all except the mantle . . .'

Ambroisine stared at the yellow skirt and red bodice, gave a shudder and made as if to push them away from her.

'No, no, I can't! . . . I would like to keep wearing this black dress. Perhaps you would let me keep it, would you? I am wearing it as mourning for the ship and all the poor people who died such terrible deaths, and without benefit of confession, too! The memory of that terrible night still haunts me. Today is Marymass and we should already have reached Quebec. And there I would have been able to pray in the peace and quiet of a convent cell. I feel sure I shall find peace with the Ursulines. They are an order which I find meets my needs more than any other, for conversation within it most closely resembles what Our Lord had here on earth when he taught the souls of men. Why, oh why, instead of leading me to that peaceful haven has He cast me upon these wild and desolate shores?'

She seemed to be as bewildered as a child and her great eyes wandered with questioning and anguish in their expression, from Angélique's face to the startling blue of the horizon flecked with white which could be seen through the half-open door.

Such was her anxiety and her sense of discouragement that for a moment she communicated it to Angélique.

But Angélique had her haven, her port, in the man to whom she had linked her life. She was no longer in the position of asking herself whether she would be better here or there. And yet she could well understand the dismay of a young woman overburdened with responsibilities on finding that here she lacked people to whom she could turn for support and the religious atmosphere to which she was accustomed.

She put the clothes down on one of the seaweed-filled mattresses that had been laid out in straight rows along the walls for the King's Girls.

'Now don't think too much about all the things you are missing here,' she said. 'Soon you will be able to set off for Quebec and the Ursulines.'

'Oh! if only I could hear Mass.'

'You will be able to from tomorrow morning! The sea has just sent us a superabundance of clergy.'

'It is such a long time, already several weeks, since I was able to assist at the Holy Sacrifice. It always brings me comfort.'

'Did you not have a chaplain on board?' Angélique asked.

The Duchess's remark about the sailors who had died without benefit of confession reminded her that among the bodies washed up by the sea, none had been wearing a soutane or a religious habit. On reflection it did seem to her rather strange for a ship that had been chartered to carry out a religious mission on the orders of so pious a person as Madame de Maudribourg.

'Yes we did,' the latter replied in a toneless voice, 'we had a Father Quentin on board, a most devout soul, who wanted to devote his life to the salvation of the Redskins. But the poor man was drowned off Newfoundland. There was a thick fog and we almost struck a huge iceberg. All the crew were crying out "Mercy on us, we shall be killed!" I saw it with my own eyes, so close you could hear us scrape against it. The mist prevented our seeing the top of it . . .'

She looked as if she were about to faint, so Angélique drew up a stool, sat down, and motioned to the Duchess to do likewise.

'And what about Father Quentin?' she asked.

'That was the day he disappeared. No one knows what happened. I can still see that monstrous iceberg, still feel its deathly, ice-cold breath. I think it must have been haunted by demons . . .'

Angélique reflected that, however learned, pious and rich, the benefactress was really too impressionable a woman to undertake such a journey. Either her confessor had given her the wrong advice or had been mistaken in thinking that she was of the stamp of a Jeanne Mance or a Marguerite Bourgeoys, already famous throughout French Canada, who had lost count of the number of times they had crossed the Atlantic. Or possibly the Jesuit – for he must have been a Jesuit – had wanted to exploit to the full the mystical exaltation of this unfortunate young widow with too much money and make use of her in the service of the missions of New France for which their Order was responsible.

Angélique's heart filled with a kind of pity. Sitting there in her black dress with her hands crossed on her knees and her deep-set eyes looking into the far distance at some unspoken vision of desolation, with her fragile porcelain complexion and her thick black hair, the Duchess looked more strikingly like an orphan infanta than ever. But it was no easy matter to come to her assistance as she seemed to live in a world apart, which she herself had created.

'You must find me ridiculous,' she said, 'to be frightened of everything like a child . . . you who have lived through so many dangers and yet remain so serene and gay, so strong in spite of the fact that you have so often come close to death.'

'How do you know that?'

'I sense it . . . Of course I had heard you mentioned in Paris last winter before I set sail. People spoke of Monsieur de Peyrac as a gentleman of fortune whose ventures represented a threat to the settlements of New France. They told how in the autumn he had brought over a shipload of Huguenot settlers and a beautiful woman, but no one was sure whether you were his wife or not. And of course maybe you are not? Not that it worries me! . . . I shall never forget what I felt when I first saw you on the seashore, so beautiful and so reassuring among all those strange, fierce men's faces.'

Then she added dreamily:

'He is different too . . .'

'He?'

'Your husband, Count Peyrac.'

'Yes indeed, he is different,' Angélique replied with a smile. 'That is why I love him!'

She tried to find some way of getting Ambroisine back on the subject of the girls' marriages.

'But on the whole, Madame, in spite of the circumstances of your arrival, you have not found Gouldsboro too unpleasant a place?'

The Duchess gave a start and turned sharply towards Angélique, then asked her with an air of anxiety that made her voice tremble:

'Will you not call me Ambroisine?'

Angélique showed some surprise at her request.

'If you so desire. Do we know one another well enough for that?'

'People can feel close from the very first time they meet.'

The Duchess of Maudribourg was trembling and seemed to be extremely agitated. She looked away from Angélique and once more began to stare at the horizon through the open door as if there lay her only hope.

'Gouldsboro?' she murmured at last. 'No! I feel the presence of passions here that are strange to me, and since I have been here I have suffered from disturbing temptations of despair and doubt, and a fear of discovering that even before I had set foot here, my life had wandered on to a disastrous path.'

Her intuition might well have been right. Fresh from the atmosphere of the convent the young widow had maybe glimpsed that there was another life she might have known, a life of greater warmth and happiness ... Angélique shrank from exploring the matter any further. She found the Duchess of Maudribourg's personality very strange, although she could fully understand what troubled her, or even what had warped her and made her somewhat odd.

It was obviously not a good day to talk to her about practical matters such as the establishment of the King's Girls, but Angélique felt she had to get it over with as Colin's men were growing impatient, fearing they might lose their 'betrothed'.

'Have you considered the suggestions my husband made to you yesterday evening?' she asked.

This time it was with veritable panic that Ambroisine de Maudribourg looked at Angélique. Her face turned as pale as chalk.

'What do you mean?' she stammered.

Angélique was patient.

'He spoke to you, didn't he, of the plans some of your girls have made to settle here, where they could make good Catholic marriages with some of our men?'

'Oh, you mean that?' Ambroisine's voice was colourless. 'Forgive me. I feared . . . I thought you meant something else . . .'

She ran her hand over her forehead then laid it on her breast as if to control the beating of her heart. Then with fingers clasped she shut her eyes and spent a brief moment in prayer.

When she looked at Angélique once more, she had regained her composure. She spoke in a firm voice.

'One or two of my girls have told me of their feelings for the men who came to their rescue at the time of the shipwreck. But I ignored what they said. What a crazy idea! . . . To found a family in a colony of heretics? . . .'

'There are a large number of Catholics amongst us.'

The Duchess cut short the discussion with a sweep of her hand.

'Catholics who are willing to live side by side with notorious Huguenots and will even associate with them are, in my eyes, either pretty tepid Catholics or potential heretics. I cannot entrust the souls of my girls to such people.'

'But surely all countries, including France, now in this century present us with the same picture. Catholics and Protestants live side by side within the same frontiers and do in fact associate with one another in the interests of prosperity.'

'What a deplorable picture of shameful compromise. When I think of it, I seem to see Our Lord's wounds bleeding on the cross, which causes me great pain, for He died in order to preserve His Word and that it should not be changed! And now there is heresy on every side! . . . Does it really not distress you too?' she asked, looking at Angélique uncomprehendingly.

Angélique changed the subject.

'But didn't King Henry IV decide once and for all that French Protestants and Catholics were equal in the eyes of the nation? He ratified those decisions in the Edict of Nantes, and the Kingdom benefited from the fact.'

'Ah but, my dear,' said the Duchess with a smile, 'you have not heard the latest. It looks as if the King may revoke the Edict of Nantes.'

This news came as a great shock to Angélique.

'But that's impossible!' she cried. 'The King cannot revoke an agreement made in all solemnity by his grandfather before the whole French people and in the name of his successor!'

She could see disaster looming over the whole of France. If the Edict of Nantes were revoked, French Huguenots would lose all civic liberties. No longer would they be able to marry legally, their children would be treated as illegitimate and their signatures worthless. The only choice left to them would be to become converts or flee the Kingdom . . .

'No, that's impossible,' she repeated angrily, rising abruptly to her feet. 'That would mean handing over all man's striving for good to the despotism of kings . . .'

'You speak like an ancient tribune of the people,' Madame de Maudribourg remarked ironically.

'And you speak like a bigot of the Society of the Blessed Sacrament,' Angélique retaliated, heading for the door.

The Duchess was with her in a flash.

'Oh, please forgive me, my dear, dear lady,' she begged in a broken voice, 'I don't know what came over me to speak to you like that . . . to *you* who are charity personified. Please forgive me! You have so profoundly upset certain fixed ideas that helped me to live my life that at times . . . I find myself hating you! And envying you, too . . . You are so alive, so genuine. Oh, how I wish that you were wrong! . . . And yet I fear that you are right. Please forgive me . . . Here I find that I am weak and inconstant . . . And it makes me feel humiliated.'

Her hands clutched at Angélique's arm, trying to hold her back, while her eyes sought out Angélique's.

The deep gold of her eyes seemed to light up with unspeakable joy when Angélique's green glance, as dark as a tempestuous and violent sea in her anger, finally met hers.

'See how sorry I am,' she murmured. 'Forgive me . . . I am . . . a little like you, a woman accustomed to being listened to and obeyed. I know that aspect of my character leaves much to be desired: I am proud, but I would not have any shadow come between us, in spite of all our differences; for I know not how it has happened, but over these few days you have gained a hold over my heart which is not normally easy to win . . .'

It was as if in the depths of those lovely eyes a creature tormented with fear was calling out for help, a fleeting impression, but Angélique felt her irritation evaporate. She could not hold against Ambroisine de Maudribourg the fact that her view of life was based on a narrow religious ethic instilled into her since childhood – that everything that was not on the side of God and his Church was against God. And yet – or so she guessed – the Duchess's scientific knowledge, so rare in a woman of the time, disposed her to a broader view of life. The Duchess's hands slid down Angélique's arms, and warmly clasped her fingers.

'Let's make it up, and in future let us try to explain our different points of view without impatience. I think that we are both a trifle hasty like all French people.'

Her smile begged for things to be put right between them. At such moments she was so appealing that Angélique would have been ungracious to resist her.

'All right,' she said, agreeing to smile as well, 'I admit that we wandered on to dangerous ground with the Edict of Nantes, which after all scarcely concerns us any more, since you, like me, will spend the rest of your life in America.'

'Yes, that obliges us to consider other possible forms of existence, maybe to bend some of our ideas about life. I shall do my best!'

They both sat down again, and Madame de Maudribourg asked Angélique for details of the proposed marriages.

Angélique did her best to give a balanced account of the position of Gouldsboro and its dependencies in the delicate *pas de deux* which New France and New England were performing in this eastern region of the American continent.

As soon as there was talk of trade and business matters, the Duchess of Maudribourg grew attentive and stopped trying to behave according to elevated but unreliable mystical formulae. She was well informed about colonial trade, with France as well as with England. She understood what the figures signified, and was aware of what was necessary at the start of an enterprise for it to remain viable.

Like all French people interested in the colony she was keen to know about the fur trade. Angélique confirmed what she already seemed to know – that the redskins of the Pentagouet and Saint John rivers were those with whom most business was done. The former provided moose and bearskins, whereas the latter had more beaver and otter skins to offer. Canadian elk skins from the Saint John river had run that year to three thousand, while those from the Pentagouet river were double that number.

'That is why Baron Saint-Castine is so rich,' said the Duchess dreamily. 'In fact Gouldsboro could well become a free port . . .'

Angélique did not tell her that this was already the case. She must give the Duchess time to weigh her loyalty to the King of

France, which would automatically involve the salvation of her soul, and her financial interests. It appeared that she had always been capable of running this side of her life, but she did find herself in a dilemma.

'I realize from what you have told me and from what I have seen myself here that the future of America lies in the independence of those who wish to see her prosper and not in being subjected to distant obligations. My girls would certainly gain considerable material advantages by settling here. But wealth is not everything on earth . . .'

She gave a deep sigh.

'Oh, how I would have loved to discuss all this with someone from the Society of Jesus, and be advised by him. They are men for whom holy aims are the only ones that matter, but if these can be reconciled with comfortable material circumstances, they are only too pleased. A Jesuit might well see this as offering the possibility of counter-balancing the Huguenot and English influence in your territories. My girls are strong in their faith, which they would be able to communicate to their husbands thus maintaining the true religion in these parts. What do you think yourself?'

'That's one way of looking at it,' Angélique replied, repressing a smile. 'It's certainly better than seeking to root out heresy by violence alone.'

It occurred to her that the Jesuits themselves must sometimes have their work cut out with their apparently inoffensive and docile penitent, the Duchess of Maudribourg. She would know how to beat them at their own game when it came to specious reasoning, which no doubt explained her influence and reputation in theological circles. But the 'benefactress' in her nevertheless remained hesitant about the idea of diverting her girls from the mission to which she had pledged them.

'I promised Our Lady to help in the building of New France,' she said obstinately, 'and I fear lest in allowing myself to be won over by the advantages you have pointed out to me, I may fail to honour that sacred promise.'

'But nothing is stopping you going to Quebec with all the young women who do not wish to stay here. And the others, having found the happiness they came to seek in the New World, will serve as a token of alliance with our compatriots in the north. All we seek is friendly understanding . . .'

They went on talking together until darkness filled the house. Sandflies and mosquitoes began to buzz in the shadows and Ambroisine complained, as she accompanied Angélique to the door, of the torment these insects caused her as soon as dusk began to fall.

'I shall go and pick you a little lemon-balm from Abigail's garden,' Angélique said. 'If you burn the tiny leaves they give off a delicious perfume which has the property of driving away these evening pests of ours.'

Then the Duchess said, as if moved by some sudden impulse: 'Isn't your friend very near her time?'

'Yes, she is. I guess that within the week our colony will find itself with one more young member.'

The Duchess of Maudribourg was looking out across the island-studded bay which once again had been set on fire by the myriad lights from the setting sun. Their reflection brought a glow to her pale complexion and her eyes seemed to glisten with still greater intensity.

'I don't know why, but I have a foreboding that that young woman is going to die in childbirth,' she said in a flat voice.

'What *are* you saying?' Angélique cried. 'You must be mad!'

Then suddenly the Duchess's words gave shape and form to one of the vague apprehensions which had troubled her. Yes! She had not wanted to admit it, but she too feared for Abigail. She felt her heart miss a beat.

'I should not have told you that,' Ambroisine said in a voice full of fear, seeing Angélique as pale as death. 'Pay no attention to me! I say things without thinking. My companions in the convent called me a soothsayer and said I could foretell the future. You see, I was thinking of how difficult things might be for my girls in this land when they in their turn have to bring a child into the world, and I suddenly felt frightened.'

Angélique strove to calm herself.

'Have no fear on that score. Before then, Gouldsboro will have a better stocked pharmacopoeia and better doctors than Quebec. As for Abigail . . .'

Angélique drew herself up to her full height and seemed to grow taller through her will to face destiny. The sun shimmered on her pale golden hair.

'I am her friend, I shall be there. I shall assist her and this I promise you, *she will not die*!'

CHAPTER 19

THE ROADSTEADS were filling up with ships once more. But this was the third day and still Joffrey de Peyrac gave no signal for departure although everything seemed ready.

'What are you up to?' Ville d'Avray asked anxiously. 'Are you not going to begin your campaign?'

'There's plenty of time. Fear nothing for your friends. If they fall into the hands of the English . . .'

'I'm not worried about my friends,' cried the Marquis, straight to the point. 'It's my ship I'm worried about. Full of priceless objects, not to mention thousands of pounds' worth of furs.'

Count Peyrac gave a smile and looked up at the windy sky, which remained blue although traversed by a few large white clouds. But still he gave no signal for departure, nor did he offer any reason for delaying. But, in spite of all this, the atmosphere remained one of imminent departure and everyone bustled about their preparations.

Once again Elias Kempton the bear-trainer was wandering about the woods in search of Mr Willoughby who, forgetting the importance of his diplomatic role, appeared to have set off on some forest expedition with his friend the wolverine.

And now, in order to appease Monsieur de Ville d'Avray, who was growing alarmed, people began to talk of a first embarkation. The Indians would leave with Messieurs de Randon and d'Arpentigny. As if warned of their imminent departure by some secret current the entire population began to head for the port, and while those who were actually leaving had still not been informed of the fact they were plied with messages for 'the people at the upper end of French Bay'.

At this point a crowd of Huguenot children ran down to the beach, squeaking like a flock of sparrows.

'Dame Angélique, come quick!' came a shrill cry from young Laurier Berne. 'There's a *Jesuit just arrived*!'

Suddenly there was great excitement on all sides, even among the clergy present. Such was the influence of the Society of Jesus that religious of less renowned orders never felt at ease before one of its representatives. The Sulpician, the Recollects and the Capuchin gathered together to ask one another about the expected arrival.

'It must be Jack Merwin,' said Angélique, full of happiness, 'alias Father Maraicher de Vernon.'

It was indeed he. Setting off to meet him, guided by the children, Angélique descried the tall, dark silhouette of Jack Merwin the Jesuit at the top of the cliff, with the little Swedish boy beside him. A large group of the La Rochelle folk had gathered around him and, as she approached, she heard the sound of voices raised in anger. By chance at the very moment the Jesuit had left the forest with his tiny companion, the English from Camp Champlain, led by the Reverend Thomas Patridge, happened to be coming along the coastal path. Patridge had immediately recognized his most bitter enemy, twice hated, nay, thrice, as a Papist, as a Jesuit, and as the pilot of *White Bird* whose scathing insolence he had been forced to suffer for three days.[1] And after letting out a preliminary roar, he had immediately begun to abuse the Catholic priest, piling anathemas upon him in the best biblical tradition. Thus had he set the tone for the reception offered by the French Huguenots. The appearance of one of the hated Jesuits inflamed their deep-rooted fear and hatred.

She could hear Manigault questioning him angrily:

'What have you come here for? We are Huguenots from La Rochelle banished from our country by the King you serve and who serves you. We have not come all this way in order to have to go on dealing with people like you.'

Father de Vernon turned haughtily towards him.

'Are you the leader of this outpost?'

'It isn't an outpost. It's a French settlement, but a free one.'

'And which anyone can enter freely?' asked the Jesuit, fixing his piercing eyes on them.

'Provided he does not behave as an enemy, of course . . .' Berne replied after a moment's hesitation.

At this point Angélique arrived, somewhat out of breath. She had hurried, fearing lest there be some irreparable quarrel. The Huguenot children called out to her:

'Hurry up, Dame Angélique, hurry, the Jesuit is going to kill our fathers.'

1. See *The Temptation of Angélique*.

Father de Vernon's face grew slightly less sombre when he recognized her. At least that was the fleeting impression she got, if ever it were possible to say that one could read the expression of any feeling on that haughty countenance.

But when she held out her hand to him, he shook it unhesitatingly and affectionately.

She spoke spontaneously.

'Here you are at last! I was afraid you might not arrive until after my husband had gone. Is Piksarett with you?'

'No! Isn't he here? . . . He told me he was going to Gouldsboro to claim your ransom.'

'He did in fact come. But then he disappeared!'

'He's capricious,' said the priest, as one who knew the Indians well.

They were picking up the threads of their acquaintance at another level. Angélique began to realize that Jack Merwin's personality had remained stamped upon her, occupying a great deal of her thought and interest. Was he a friend? An enemy? Dangerous? Or capable of becoming an ally?

He was still wearing the same greenish-tinged soutane, a trifle too short, the soutane he had dug up from under a tree at the mouth of the Penobscot, but whose high black collar with its white facing and full cloak gave him the appearance of a Spanish prince which all Jesuits owe to the founder of their order, Saint Ignatius of Loyola. What made him seem different was the fact that he occasionally smiled and no longer chewed continuously on his quid of tobacco.

To sustain him on his walks he carried a long pilgrim's stick topped with a plain metal cross. This cross was a great cause of dismay to the Protestants, who feared to see it enter Gouldsboro. But they would have to come to terms with the Church that was beginning to rise on the other side of the harbour. So without undue protest they followed Angélique and the Jesuit down the main village street, while at the back Miss Pidgeon was trying in a whisper to hush the Reverend Patridge in his fury at this diabolical intrusion.

Halfway down the hill they caught sight of Count Peyrac coming up to meet them.

'Here comes my husband,' said Angélique, unable to hide the note of joy and pride in her voice.

CHAPTER 20

How SEDUCTIVE and youthful he was, the Master of Gouldsboro, with his bold, slightly uneven tread, and the elegant line of his vast cloak billowing behind him in the wind. From afar off she could see the dazzling whiteness of his smile. He raised his hands in welcome.

'Welcome to you, Father,' he called out affably as soon as he was within earshot.

'Well, I never!' Father de Vernon murmured.

For fate so willed it that Joffrey de Peyrac came towards him closely surrounded by all the clerical figures at that moment visiting Gouldsboro, each and every one of whom was anxious to be first to meet the awaited Jesuit, and had hastened after him.

Thus it was that the Master of Gouldsboro, reputed in Quebec to be a man without religion, presented him with an escort that would have done credit to a bishop. He did not fail to see the humour of the situation.

'Yes indeed,' he said as he cordially welcomed the new arrival, 'as you see, Father, you were the only one missing, for now we have a representative here of every order that is devoting itself with such courage to the spiritual welfare of New France.'

'So I see! So I see!' growled the seaman Jack Merwin running his most mercurial glance over the assembled habits and soutanes, a Sulpician, an Oratorian, a Recollect and a Capuchin; not one was missing. 'Yes indeed! It's almost a council! But how do you do it, Monsieur de Peyrac?' he exclaimed, deciding to treat the matter as a joke.

'How I do it? How I do what? Attract all the most saintly people in the country into my lair? . . . I'm sure I don't know. You must ask yourself, Father, what it was occasioned you to pay us a visit, and perhaps you will find your answer.'

Then in a more serious vein he added quietly, wishing to be heard by the Jesuit alone: 'Whatever your reasons, I am delighted, for I know that it is to you I owe the life of someone very dear to me, and I am happy to be able to thank you in person.'

Vernon gave a nod to show that he had understood what Peyrac meant.

'I wanted to make sure that Madame de Peyrac's journey had had a happy conclusion,' he remarked lightly. 'Having had the good fortune to act as her escort for some days, through considerable danger, I knew the unhappiness she felt at being separated from you, sir, and how impatient she was to join you again. It therefore gives me great satisfaction to see you both happily reunited in your domain.'

Angélique blessed the Jesuit's tact. What he had said was exactly right to sweep away the last traces of cloud between herself and Joffrey. She looked at him with affection as they made their way down towards the main square, the objects of veiled curiosity on the part of the inhabitants.

Colin Paturel introduced himself next, surrounded by his reformed pirates.

'My guess is you will have plenty of penitents this evening, Father, if you offer to hear confessions.'

Father de Vernon caught sight of the Governor of French Acadia.

'You are here, Monsieur de Ville d'Avray?'

'And why should I not be here like everyone else . . . and like yourself?' the Marquis retaliated.

Angélique left them for a moment and ran over to the house in which the King's Girls were lodged, where she found the Duchess of Maudribourg who, for once, was not at her prayers.

'Come quickly,' she urged her, 'this time I really have got your high-ranking priest to hear your confessions. An authentic Jesuit of noble birth. Father Louis-Paul Maraicher de Vernon.'

The Duchess was having her hair brushed for her by one of her followers. She seemed plunged in some melancholic reverie, but when she had grasped what Angélique was saying, she burst out laughing.

'You are adorable,' she cried, 'and so kind! You are always trying to give people things that will do them good. And yet I know you thought I was ridiculous with my demands.'

'Not at all! I know that life is hard for immigrants. Everyone needs help in finding màterial and moral comfort.'

'You are adorable,' the Duchess repeated tenderly. 'A real Jesuit! How wonderful!'

Ambroisine de Maudribourg stood up. From her carefully smoothed hair there exuded that special scent which had struck Angélique as she had nursed her on that first day, a perfume so bewitchingly delicate, and so much in keeping with the Duchess's personality that it seemed to ennoble her.

'But how . . . ?' Angélique began. But the end of her question eluded her, she knew not why.

The Duchess spontaneously grasped her arm and together they set off. On the way down a tiny shadow that seemed to stumble from stone to stone caught their attention.

'Oh! it's your kitten!' the Duchess exclaimed.

'But what is he doing here, the naughty little thing?' cried Angélique, discovering her protégé who was looking at her with his big eyes, his tiny tail pointing skywards. 'I always shut him in and lock the door; I don't know how he manages to get out. If he's not careful, something will happen to him,' she muttered to herself, picking him up in one hand. 'He is so minute, and yet I have never seen a living creature so full of life and ardour. Listen to the way he begins to purr when I hold him to me . . .'

CHAPTER 21

As soon as they arrived down at the harbour, Father de Vernon's eyes fell upon the fleet lying at anchor in the roadsteads.

'I know that you're a sailor!' Peyrac said to him. 'Let me give you something to drink, then we'll go and see the ships.'

Angélique and Ambroisine de Maudribourg joined them on the harbour breakwater where Count Peyrac gave his new guest a detailed account of the characteristics of each of his ships and longboats.

'How gay it is here!' said the Duchess in a whisper. 'There's always something going on! . . . That Jesuit really looks most distinguished. I don't know why it is but there is something about him that reminds me of your husband.'

'Yes, perhaps there is . . .'

Ambroisine's observation was right. Of more or less similar physical type, tall, well built, vigorous, the two men, the Jesuit and the adventurer, above all resembled one another through the inner strength one felt emanating from them. In addition they shared the ability to enjoy life in all its aspects, savouring, for instance, all the finer points of a handsome naval vessel.

Jack Merwin's dark eyes shone as he listened to Peyrac listing the different sections of his fleet which had been designed and executed for transport, fishing, coastal trade, or simply as fast ships, not in the sense that privateers and battleships were fast, but more in the nature of true destroyers.

'It is sometimes necessary to travel across the sea faster than anyone else, just as a well-rested and well-trained thoroughbred can overtake a team of six horses without difficulty. For this purpose I have this small, light sailing ship, that rides low on the water.'

'I see only eight crew and no kind of accommodation. And yet it isn't just a dinghy.'

'It's a sambur from Yemen on the Red Sea, made from Java timber that never rots. She's a fine windjammer that can do twelve knots on two sails in a good wind.'

'She's a very shallow-draught vessel.'

'And therefore capable of making her way up all the creeks around here.'

The *Gouldsboro* remained the pearl of this tiny independent fleet, already more powerful than in any other port of the region.

'I worked with Rieder of Boston in drawing up the plans,' Peyrac explained.

'He's from Rotterdam, isn't he?'

'Yes. We are pretty proud of the result, for we have managed to satisfy two conflicting demands on a pretty rugged coastline, namely that we should be armed like corsairs and at the same time able to carry on extensive trading activities.'

'And what about that caravel?' Ville d'Avray asked. 'She looks solid enough but hardly worthy of your up-to-date fleet. Just about acceptable for Christopher the Jew;[1] but what an admirable picture on the stern. What a beauty that Virgin is! You know, dear Angélique, she looks rather like you! . . . Don't you think so, Count? . . .'

There was a silence.

1. Christopher Columbus was occasionally known by this name.

If Angélique had had cause to congratulate herself on the Jesuit's tact, she could scarcely say the same for the Governor of Acadia. He really did have the art of saying things that were best left unsaid. Neither was it the first time that she had caught him at this little game.

'I'll get my own back on you for that,' she thought.

'That's my ship,' Colin Paturel broke in. 'The *Heart of Mary* . . .'

'Oh, really!' the Marquis replied in ecstatic tones, looking in all candour at the huge blond giant. 'Well, you must give my compliments to your painter, dear fellow! I'd like to have something like that painted on my ship. It's a masterpiece!'

'If your ship is not already in the hands of the English, or at the bottom of the Saint John river,' Angélique remarked to him in a murmur.

The open, happy face of the Marquis of Ville d'Avray suddenly crumpled in an expression of chagrin.

'Oh! it wasn't kind of you to remind me of that,' he said reproachfully. 'Here I was all happy, enjoying myself a little in this most interesting company, and now I'm tormented again. But what are you waiting for to go and drive the English off?' he asked, turning to Peyrac, trembling with rage and striking the breakwater with the end of his silver-topped cane. 'It's becoming intolerable! If this goes on, I shall complain of you in Quebec! Whatever are you waiting for?'

'Maybe I've been waiting for this!' the Count replied pointing to something on the horizon.

He took his field-glass from his belt and opened it up before lifting it to his eye.

'It's him all right!' he murmured.

At this very moment a ship began to come in, a small, squat yacht that rode well down in the water.

'It's the *Rochelais*!' exclaimed Angélique jumping for joy.

Ambroisine looked at her in astonishment.

Now it was the Marquis's turn to draw a small gold-banded field-glass from the pocket of his figured waistcoat. His sulky expression vanished.

'But who is this charming young man I can see at the prow?' he exclaimed with enthusiasm.

'That's the captain,' Peyrac replied, 'who also happens to be our son, Cantor.'

'How old is he?'

'Sixteen.'

'Is he as good a navigator as Alexander?'

'That remains to be seen.'

Angélique had not been expecting the *Rochelais* to return so soon. But she felt a sense of relief. The fact that her children were scattered like this – Honorine in Wapassou, Cantor at sea and Florimond deep in the forest-lands of the New World – caused her a deep unspoken anxiety. She would have liked to have gathered them all together once more under her wing, as all mothers do in times of danger. But at least Cantor was there.

As the tide was out, he could not sail right up to the breakwater; so he dropped anchor between the *Gouldsboro* and his father's chebec, lowered his longboat and all present walked down to the shore to meet him.

'What a handsome boy!' said the Duchess of Maudribourg to Angélique. 'You must be proud of him, Madame.'

'Yes, indeed,' the latter agreed.

She was pleased to see on his frank, round, still childish face, the valiant and slightly distant look of her Cantor, a young prince born to lead a different life from this, but who stepped ashore with the same courteous assurance he would have worn before the King. He greeted his father with a military nod of the head, full of respect, and kissed his mother's hand.

'Charming!' Ville d'Avray repeated.

'He's like an archangel,' said the Duchess of Maudribourg.

The Count introduced him to a few people who had come to Gouldsboro during the young man's absence.

These introductions were interrupted by the impetuous arrival of the wolverine who made his appearance in his customary manner like a cannonball through a game of skittles.

Cantor became a happy child again to welcome his favourite friend.

'He must have kept on watching for you at the edge of the forest, where he was playing about with the bear,' Angélique explained.

'And here's the bear,' someone said.

CHAPTER 22

JOFFREY DE PEYRAC made up his mind immediately.

'If the bear's here, we must get him on board at once; it's now or never. Mr Kempton, are you ready to sail this evening?'

'Yes sir! I had my luggage taken down to the port this morning as you told me to. And I've worn my feet to shreds running after this rascal who can't have been that far away and must've been laughing at me from behind a tree.'

Mr Willoughby came forward without hurrying, stopping from time to time to turn over a stone, or to rear up on his hind legs in order to sniff the air and look disdainfully about him.

'I'll teach you to play pranks on me, Mister,' the pedlar growled as he prepared a leash with which to catch the fickle beast. Meanwhile the atmosphere had suddenly changed and everyone was bustling about. It had been decided that as soon as the bear, a key member of the expedition, had been located again, the first contingent of the slower ships should set sail, among them the big sloop which had brought in the Acadians and their Indians, and which was to take them back again with arms and baggage in addition, plus the pedlar and his bear, Mateconando, his braves and his daughter, the two Patsuiketts, Monsieur d'Urville and his Indian father-in-law, Monsieur de Randon etc. .... This motley flotilla might well give the English pause. Peyrac and his faster ships would join them when they had already taken up their position to disembark somewhere in the region of the Saint John estuary.

Meanwhile the instigator of all this activity, the bear, Mr Willoughby, did not appear to have fully grasped the gravity of the occasion. With considerable agility and a totally British self-possession, he managed to elude all attempts on the part of his master to chain him and take him on board ship, a thing for which he had never had much liking. After a number of unsuccessful attempts, Elias Kempton began to lose patience.

'Now that's enough,' he shouted, suddenly turning his hat

round so that the buckle was at the back, an action which for him signified a raging temper; 'Willoughby, there's to be no more playing around with these good people any more! After all, you are only a bear!'

The bear's sole response was to lumber off through the group of Indians, then, finding himself suddenly face to face with Father Maraicher de Vernon, he reared up to his full height and brought his dangerous front paws with their long claws heavily down on his shoulders.

The Jesuit showed not the slightest reaction and stood his ground. He knew this unusual companion whom he had taken on board once before as a passenger from New York, and he greeted him courteously in English. Nevertheless, although the Jesuit was a tall man himself, when the bear stood on his hind legs like this he was still taller and his red jaws with their sharp teeth swayed back and forth just a few inches from the priest's face.

The laughter died away and Angélique moved anxiously towards them.

Stuffed full of fruit, fresh air, and freedom, the bear seemed to have reverted to the wild state. Then suddenly he got down and stood before the Jesuit swaying back and forth and growling.

'He wants to fight,' Kempton exclaimed. 'Did you ever see such a playful wag of a bear? He reckons that he hasn't had enough attention yet! What a play-actor! He wants to fight with you, Merwin.'

'No, don't!' Angélique called out nervously. 'Can't you see the animal is over-excited.'

But Father de Vernon examined his redoubtable interlocutor in a good-natured manner with a trace of a smile on his face. This was not the first time the bear had challenged him to a fight.

'Fight him, Merwin,' the pedlar insisted. 'Otherwise we'll never get round him. Go on, you could do that for him, couldn't you? After all he's done for you . . .'

One might well have asked what services Mr Willoughby had in fact rendered to the captain of the *White Bird*, but the little pedlar from Connecticut judged life according to his own particular reckoning, in the centre of which stood his friend and childhood companion, the bear.

Meanwhile the bear was showing signs of distress. He seemed disappointed. Was no one friends with him any more, and in particular the man who had always been, as he remembered it, a loyal and honest adversary?

'All right!' the Jesuit decided.

He took off his cloak, which he handed to the little Swedish boy, kicked off his moccasins, and hitched up his soutane under his belt, to expose his skinny, knotted calves. Then he took his guard before the bear.

The animal gave a grunt of satisfaction that sent a shudder of anxiety through the spectators.

'July is rutting season for bears,' somebody said. 'The Jesuit is crazy.'

'Never mind! The devil his master will sustain him,' the Reverend Patridge shouted with a burst of sardonic laughter.

The crowd had gathered round in a tight, compact circle. Even the Indians were quiet. The tall black pointed hats of the Mic-Macs oscillated back and forth, in a dense, attentive group.

Every eye was riveted on this unusual sight – a wild beast in all his primitive strength and a bare-handed man, standing ready to do battle. A single blow from those terrible claws could slit open a man's stomach or disfigure him for life. Mr Willoughby did not use his claws in his normal contests: Kempton had filed them down a bit for him. But today they looked particularly sharp, and he was growling as he swayed back and forth and his eye had a red glint in it.

Then suddenly he hurled himself at his opponent, who sidestepped this first attack and gave him a violent pummelling from one side. The bear seemed in no way perturbed and turned around. But already Vernon-Merwin had brought his knee up violently in the bear's stomach. Mr Willoughby received the blow as impassively as a tree trunk. But he did stop for a brief moment, and Merwin dashed round behind him and began to pummel him and heave himself against him in an attempt to make him lose his balance. The bear stood firm, then he in his turn tried to drive his opponent back by leaning against him. Had he succeeded and fallen on top of him he would have crushed him.

The man stood his ground, his feet set firmly in the sand. For a moment there they stood, back to back, struggling to see which one would first make the other lose his balance.

Elias Kempton was dancing up and down, jubilant, rubbing his hands together.

'Well done so far. Wonderful! They are extraordinary, those two!'

The bystanders were beginning to grow less anxious and to become involved in the contest.

'I bet the Jesuit wins!'

'No, that's impossible. The bear is too heavy!'

Suddenly Father de Vernon managed to slip sideways out of his uncomfortable position, and the sheer weight of the bear made him fall over backwards. He immediately retrieved himself by rolling to one side and found himself on all fours. He seemed nonplussed. The Jesuit stood waiting for him a few yards off. Mr Willoughby looked round angrily.

Then suddenly he hurled himself forward like a cannon-ball and tossed him almost into the air, rolling him over and over to a distance of several feet.

'The bear is cunning too,' one of the spectators remarked in a whisper.

Merwin lay half outstretched with his face in the sand, stunned by the blow.

'He's had it!'

'Are you beaten, Merwin?' asked Kempton.

Mr Willoughby seemed very pleased with himself. Swaying to and fro he approached the motionless body and sniffed at it. Merwin suddenly curled up and let fly with his two feet on the animal's nose, the bear recoiled, then literally ran away and stood at the opposite side of the ring, groaning with pain.

'You shouldn't have done that, Merwin,' Kempton reproached him. 'Bears have very sensitive noses.'

'Is this a fight or isn't it?' growled the Jesuit, panting as he got to his feet. 'He gives me no quarter either.'

'Careful!' someone shouted.

Again the bear made for Father de Vernon, who just managed to avoid the impact. There followed a series of cutting and thrusting in which the Jesuit's agility compensated, but with greater and greater difficulty, for the sheer brute force of his huge adversary.

First rearing up on his hind legs to dominate his enemy better, then going down on all fours again, to move more quickly, the bear showed almost human intelligence in his tactics. Meanwhile the valiance of the man, his boldness, his knowledge of the animal, his strength and suppleness, compelled the admiration of the spectators.

It was a good fight. But tension was mounting and there was a certain anxiety in the air.

'Give in, Merwin,' the pedlar advised him. 'Better for you to give in!'

He seemed not to hear. The evening light was beginning to flood everything with its saffron glow. Jack Merwin's face had an ivory transparency, and he looked as if he was smiling; his eyes with their mineral glint suddenly shone with a kind of gaiety that transformed him.

It was then that the bear took him between his paws. A cry went up from the spectators.

'Careful! He will suffocate him!'

The tall silhouette in its black soutane seemed to vanish between the huge paws.

Fortunately Mr Willoughby considered himself to have won and released his opponent, who slid to the ground and lay motionless. The bear began to look around proudly, waiting to receive his applause.

Then suddenly he staggered and he too collapsed, sending up a great cloud of dust.

The priest stood up and dusted himself down with a phlegmatic air.

'Shall we continue, Mr Willoughby?' he asked in English.

But the bear gave no sign of life. It was as if he were an enormous mossy rock, that happened to have lain there since all eternity. His eyes remained shut.

'I say, what's happening?' the little pedlar from Connecticut asked in astonishment as he approached the bear anxiously. 'Willoughby, my friend! There seems to be something wrong!'

The bear lay utterly inert. It was hard to believe that a few seconds earlier he had been parading about, grunting at the attentive admiration of the watching crowd.

Elias Kempton, thunderstruck, walked right round the animal, unable to believe his eyes.

Then he exploded in imprecations.

'You've killed him, you damned Papist,' he shrieked, tearing at his few remaining tufts of greying hair. 'My friend! My brother! You're a monster, a bloodthirsty brute, like all your damned popes.'

'That's a bit of an exaggeration, old fellow,' Merwin protested. 'You know perfectly well that any blow I could give him would have no more effect on him than an insect bite. All I did was to catch him by one paw and make him lose his balance.'

'All the same, he's dead!' Kempton wailed in despair. 'You're a brute, Jack Merwin. I should never have allowed him to fight you, you Jesuit! You've killed him, with your satanic spells!'

'Oh come on, that's enough nonsense!' the Jesuit replied impatiently. 'There can't be very much wrong with him — I just don't understand why he's not moving.'

'Because he's dead I tell you! My lady!' said the pedlar turning to Angélique. 'You're a healer, do something for this poor beast.'

Angélique could scarcely refuse the English pedlar's request, although she found it an embarrassing one. Never before had she had occasion to give first-aid to a bear of this size. Neither could she understand what could possibly have so suddenly laid Mr Willoughby low. She remembered the blow he had taken on the nose which had appeared to hurt him, and she knelt down in the sand beside the animal's head. Gently she felt his nose which seemed to be warm and soft. There was no trace of blood anywhere. She stroked him several times from his nose up to his forehead. Leaning over him she watched his closed eyelids through the tangled fur. One of them began to tremble, and opened just sufficiently to allow her to catch a glance that was so human and so sad that it took her breath away.

'What's the matter, Mr Willoughby?' she asked him gently. 'Do please tell me . . .'

The animal blinked, and she could have sworn that a tear trickled down his nose. Then he heaved a great sigh and closed his eyes again, as if refusing to have anything further to do with so galling a world.

Angélique stood up and walked over towards Kempton and Father de Vernon who were standing anxiously side by side.

'Listen,' she whispered to them in English, 'I may be wrong, but I think there's nothing wrong with him at all, except that he is extremely vexed. A fall like that, and defeat when he thought he was the victor . . .'

'Yes, of course,' Elias Kempton exclaimed, his face lighting up, 'I had quite forgotten: this happened once before! . . . We couldn't shift him for three days!'

'Three days! That's a fine thing for us!' Peyrac remarked in a burst of laughter.

'And you're laughing!' the pedlar said indignantly. 'But it

isn't funny at all. Your expedition up the Saint John river is up the spout! . . . It's your fault too, Merwin. You managed to make him look ridiculous several times, and above all you hurt his nose. I can understand his being vexed.'

Monsieur de Ville d'Avray, who knew no English, asked what was going on. When the situation was explained to him, he exploded.

'What! The fate of important officials from Quebec now hangs on the good graces of a bear! . . . This is intolerable! Monsieur de Peyrac, I order you to tell that bear to get up immediately or . . . I shall be the one who sulks!'

'Believe me, sir,' Peyrac replied imperturbably, 'things are not as simple as that.' He examined Mr Willoughby, who seemed to be sleeping for all eternity.

'Perhaps we could try to heal his wounded pride,' Angélique suggested. 'Supposing you were to pretend to be dead, Merwin?' she turned towards the Jesuit Father. 'He would then think that he had won and . . .'

'A good idea,' Elias Kempton agreed enthusiastically. 'He has a heart of gold, but he cannot abide being weaker than any man. As a matter of fact, it doesn't make sense. You ought to be dead, Merwin. So pretend you are . . .'

'All right!' the Jesuit agreed.

So he collapsed on the ground in front of the bear, and lay there motionless.

The pedlar urged his friend to open his eyes and examine the sad spectacle.

'Look what you've done, Mr Willoughby! You see, you are the strongest bear in all the world! You taught that arrogant man a lesson. It will be a long time before he's right again. That will teach him to fight the most wonderful, strongest bear in the world . . .'

'Mr Willoughby,' Angélique urged, stroking the bear, 'think of your victory! How will anyone know that you have won if you don't get up?'

At this point the kitten came and rubbed his grain of salt into the wound. He suddenly rushed in and before anyone could stop him, insolently biffed the bear several times on the tip of his nose. Angélique drove him away, but the tiny creature was fascinated by this furry mountain round which everyone was standing. Kempton continued his solemn entreaties.

'Just look at what you've done to that devil in the black robes. As a Papist, he only got what was coming to him but all the same you ought to remember that he did take you on board his ship.'

This barrage of persuasive words, coupled with the teasing of the kitten who was tickling him, finally succeeded in crumbling Mr Willoughby's mountain of wounded pride.

He opened first one eye, then both, then began to take some interest in Merwin's condition. He gave a sigh, then slowly he started to heave himself up on to his heavy feet.

He carefully approached the prone body, sniffed it, and turned it over. The spectators held their breath.

'Yes, you see you have won again, Willoughby!' Kempton told him insistently. 'Stand up, my friend! Let people applaud you. Go on, clap him, you silly lot,' he called to the crowd.

'Long live Mr Willoughby!' they cried.

As this delightful din fell on his ears, the bear began to look happier. He stood up on his hind legs and walked right round the circle receiving its applause and homage.

Meanwhile the little Negro boy, Timothy, quickly handed the pedlar his shoulder-bag, from which he drew a piece of honey cake, his customary treat for the bear when he won a fight. This he accepted, and while he was enjoying it his master slipped his chain round his neck. After which he drew out a huge linen handkerchief as big as a towel, with which he copiously mopped his brow.

'Safe!' he exclaimed. 'Well now, Monsieur de Peyrac, we shall meet again at Skoudoum's. You see, you can depend on my bear! You there, you red serpents, take my baggage and my bales of merchandise,' he said, turning to the Mic-Macs, who ran to obey him, delighted to be embarking in such entertaining company. 'Follow me, Mr Willoughby! Let us leave all these Papists to their stupid activities!'

Poor Mr Willoughby! Perhaps he was not completely taken in by the game, but his honour had been saved! He followed his master without protest.

When he had been heaved into the boat and this had been filled with Indians and Acadians and several others as well, and had been waved from the shore Father de Vernon was allowed to get up again.

He was covered in sand, scratches and bruises, and his soutane was torn.

Young Martial Berne appeared at that moment with a bucket of water, and the Jesuit spent some time plunging his face into it. Meanwhile the English, far from being indignant, were laughing heartily at what had just occurred.

'Things are certainly gay here,' Ambroisine de Maudribourg remarked, her eyes shining.

'Yes, we're a mighty long way from Quebec here,' the Marquis of Ville d'Avray added. 'Never in all my life have I seen a Jesuit play the fool like that! When I tell Monsignor Laval about this . . .'

'I would rather, sir, that you did not mention this . . . incident in Quebec,' the priest requested with great dignity.

'Oh! Should I forgo that pleasure?' the little Marquis asked with a laugh, looking at him with insolent jubilation. 'Such a very good story! All right! I won't say anything. But in future, you will have to grant me indulgences for my sins! . . . Tit for tat. Imagine for once having a Jesuit at my mercy!'

CHAPTER 23

SHE HAD heard her husband ask Cantor as he disembarked: 'Have you brought Clovis back with you?'

'No.'

'Why not?'

'He's vanished.'

She was in a hurry to join him again, far from this crowd that seemed to remain almost permanently on the shore of Gouldsboro.

At last he was there, and she shut the door of their room in the fort with a feeling of relief. Angélique blessed the calm night, heavy with stars, alive with the sound of the sea, which was to give them privacy for a few brief hours.

He came towards her laughing.

'You were so charming with that bear this afternoon, my love. There is no one else in the world like you! I was dying to take you in my arms.'

She noticed how gay he was. All the noise and uproar, the incessant comings and goings, the decisions to take and details to arrange, none of this seemed to make him weary.

'You are the only one, the only one in the whole world!'

She was struck by the extraordinary peace which suddenly descended upon her. 'He is the only one,' she thought as well, feeling the strength of his presence. 'Everything he touches. Everything is marked with his extraordinary stamp ... this man loves me ... I am his wife ...'

Only the sound of the kitten playing with the lead bullet which he had found again under some piece of furniture broke the silence. It was as if some will-o'-the-wisp, some tiny guardian spirit watched over their happiness.

'You are worried about something, aren't you?' Peyrac went on, 'I could see it when I came in.'

'I would like to spend the rest of my life like this,' Angélique replied, snuggling against his shoulder, 'and above all ... not have you go away ... Oh, how I wish you were not going away. I feel a terrible sense of anxiety ... *Don't go!*'

'But I must.'

'Why?'

'Because Monsieur de Ville d'Avray is *sulking*! ...' Joffrey replied, simulating horror.

'Oh, what does that matter! Let him sulk. For once he can leave us in peace instead of for ever making acid remarks. Have you noticed how he has grown as tight as a clam but that Alexander is talking now. I saw him in conversation with Cantor. The Marquis and his protégé must have agreed to sulk turn and turn about ...'

They laughed, but Angélique remained anxious.

'Were you waiting for Cantor before you decided to leave?'

'Partly ... yes.'

'Are you taking him with you?'

'No, I'm leaving you in his charge ... and in the charge of this little creature,' he added, motioning towards the kitten.

She went over and picked up the tiny light creature with the big eyes.

'And what dangers do you reckon these two will protect me from?'

Suddenly the thought of Colin crossed her mind. By leaving her alone in Gouldsboro, where Colin was henceforth Governor, was Joffrey de Peyrac trying out yet another wager?

Of course not. Suddenly it was as if each one of them, she, he, and Colin now occupied their right positions. Looking up at her husband's face, Angélique could see no trace of hidden thoughts. And she thought: what man has any part in my life other than he? This was such an unchangeable truth that she became aware that on his side too the frontier had been crossed, with its anxieties and its corrosive doubts.

And Colin, who was just and frank and straight, knew this too. If he remained in Gouldsboro, accepting a position that suited his gifts, this was because he had found his own personal niche, had reached a state of equilibrium. And his presence here, acting as it did as a buttress to Peyrac's, brought a warm sense of comfort to Angélique's heart. In a whisper she said:

'It's a good thing to have Colin here, isn't it?'

'Yes it is. If he were not fully in control here, I would not leave the place.'

These words filled Angélique's heart with a joy that was apparent on her face.

He looked at her and a ghost of a smile crossed his face.

'Our situation is still far too unstable,' he went on, 'too many enemies are trying to harm us. Now Paturel has an unerring shrewdness, an iron fist, and no one finds it easy to circumvent him. I've told him of everything that might harm us. He has a true feeling for what we represent here, what we can expect from these lands, from these men. He won't let anything slide, he won't let himself be caught . . . he has all these people in the palm of his hand. He really has a heaven-sent gift of power over men.'

'As you have too.'

'With me it's something different,' said Peyrac thoughtfully. 'I fascinate them, whereas he convinces them. I can distract them and attract them by keeping them amused, but I remain distant. Whereas he is close to them, he is of the same stamp. Yes, thanks be to God, Colin is here, and I can go about other matters.'

She guessed that he was not only thinking of the expedition to free the Quebec officials. His object in leaving Gouldsboro was above all to track down and drive out their mysterious enemies.

'What's happened to Clovis?'

'I had asked Cantor to bring him back from the mine between the Kennebec and the Penobscot where I'd left him. I wanted to question him about the misunderstanding we had at Houssnock when you set off for the English village thinking you were doing so on my orders. It was Cantor who brought you the message, but he told me he received it himself from

Maupertuis. The Canadians have taken him away, but Cantor thinks he remembers Maupertuis referring to Clovis as having passed on the order from me. So I'm sure that I can learn more from Clovis about the people who are plotting against us. And now Clovis seems to have vanished.'

'Do you think that that's their doing?'

'I feel sure it must be.'

'Who can "they" be?'

'Time will tell. And that time is close, for I intend to hound them down mercilessly. Their flag was spotted among some of the islands in the bay, so maybe they are connected with the company that sold the Gouldsboro lands to Colin.'

'And what about Father de Vernon? What could be his role in all this?'

'Your Jesuit, the sailor and fair-ground wrestler? ... It seems to me that you have snared him in your net, he is on our side.'

'What do you mean? He's like a piece of marble, a monument of coldness. If you knew how calmly he watched me drowning off Monhegan Point!'

'But he did dive in after you.'

'Yes, that's true.'

Angélique stroked the kitten dreamily.

'I must admit that I like him. I always did like priests,' she confessed with a laugh. 'I seem to find it easy to find common ground with them, without knowing precisely what it is.'

'You present them with a picture of womanhood they have never had before, for you are neither a sinner, nor are you pious. And this lulls their suspicions . . .'

'How did he know that Gold Beard had captured me? And who sent him to fetch me from the *Heart of Mary*?'

'You will have to hear his confession.'

'A Jesuit! I have undertaken many a thing deemed impossible – but confessing a Jesuit, never! But all the same, I'll try!'

CHAPTER 24

'GOODBYE,' SAID Madame de Maudribourg, clasping Angélique's hands, 'I shall never forget you!'

Her magnificent eyes scanned Angélique's face with desperate intensity, as if she had wanted to fix it for ever in her memory. She was pale and Angélique could feel that her hands were frozen.

'You despise me, don't you?' Ambroisine whispered. 'But I must obey the will of God. My heart is torn in leaving this place. Never has holy obedience seemed so cruel, but Father de Vernon was categorical. I *must* go to New France . . .'

'You've already explained that to me,' Angélique replied. 'Believe me, we too regret the decision you have taken to leave us. I can see a number of people in tears today.'

'But I *must* obey,' whispered Ambroisine.

'Well, then, obey you must. We are not the sort of people to exert pressure on an occasion like this, to try to keep with us anyone who does not wish to remain here.'

'How hard you are,' Ambroisine reproached her in a strangled voice.

'Well, what would you have of me?' Angélique protested, with mounting annoyance.

'Just that you shouldn't forget me,' replied Ambroisine who seemed on the point of collapse.

She buried her face in her hands, then turning from Angélique, slowly walked away. In the brightly-coloured clothes she had donned once again, she looked more than ever like a fragile bird.

Her brief stay in Gouldsboro had left her with some mysterious wound.

On the previous evening she had made her confession to Father de Vernon. Shortly afterwards Angélique had seen her return in a great state of agitation.

'He has strongly advised me not to leave my girls here,' she cried. 'He told me that I must leave this place where God and the King of France are not held in honour, and that my duty is to take my girls to New France, and that I have allowed myself to be led into temptation by your dangerous liberality. "Yes, I agree that it is a seductive atmosphere here," he told me, "but one where these young women would soon forget the paths of eternal salvation, and become solely preoccupied with material wealth . . ." '

'Wealth . . . in Gouldsboro! . . . A god-forsaken place where we live in constant danger of losing the few wretched possessions we have . . . He has no fear of exaggeration, that man Merwin. How I recognize him there!'

Angélique was deeply disappointed by the Jesuit's reaction. She had all too readily presumed that they had won his goodwill.

She was about to set off to find him to tell him what she thought, but Ambroisine warned her that the priest was camping that night in a neighbouring village to which the chieftain had invited him and that he had already set out.

'Monsieur de Peyrac's fleet impressed him. He said that all the private and military establishments of New France could not between them muster such a fleet either for trading or defence.'

'French colonial establishments are always poor, because they are neglected by France itself and by their own government. But that's no good reason to imitate them . . .'

Angélique had to tell her husband of Madame de Maudribourg's decision.

'Well then, she must go,' the Count replied with surprising sharpness. 'Only yesterday Father Tournel, the chaplain from Port-Royal, suggested that he might accompany the women across there, where Madame de la Roche-Posay would receive them on French territory.'

'Won't some of our men be bitterly disappointed? They had been talking about marrying.'

'Colin and I will explain things to them. Port-Royal isn't far, we shall tell them, and the experience of a few days' separation may well be a good thing before committing themselves for life, etc., etc . . .'

'And do you think they'll fall for that?'

'They'll have to,' he replied.

She had not altogether grasped the meaning of his reply.

It turned out that the prospective grooms of the King's Girls were present at the departure of their betrothed, without betraying any excessive anxiety or despair. But a strange silence reigned, an inexpressible unease. It was as if something quite different was happening from what they thought they were seeing.

Angélique became so acutely aware of this that she had to make an effort to remain calm.

The manifest distress of the benefactress did nothing to help. A kind of pity for this young, helpless woman vied within her against the irritation she felt over Ambroisine's excessive docility to the orders of the Jesuits. She was sorry that Father de Vernon was not present for her to tell him just what she thought.

Aristide Beaumarchand came out best in the whole affair, for he kept his Julienne. Apparently the benefactress had jumped at the opportunity to get rid of her black sheep. Angélique noticed that Julienne was absent, frightened lest the Duchess of Maudribourg, who was both fickle and authoritarian, might change her mind at the last moment.

Ambroisine had decided to leave Gouldsboro so quickly that many of the inhabitants had not had warning of it. Madame Carrère arrived at the last moment, protesting.

'No one ever tells me anything. People come and people go without a word. Madame la Duchesse, I do apologize, but I have not finished mending the holes in your cloak . . .'

'Never mind, you may keep it, my good woman,' Ambroisine de Maudribourg replied in a flat voice.

She looked about her as if seeking help.

'Monsieur de Ville d'Avray,' she cried suddenly, turning towards the French Governor, who was attending the departure with an air of genuine sorrow, 'why don't you accompany us? Your charming presence would be entertaining, and isn't Port-Royal under your jurisdiction?'

'An excellent idea,' the Marquis agreed with a youthful smile. 'I've a terrible longing to taste some of those Port-Royal cherries.

'But,' the Marquis's face wore a pained expression, 'I simply must wait for the cherry season. I really am sorry. Have patience, just a little turn round French Bay to taste Marceline's shell-fish *gratin* and then I shall join you, charming lady.'

This sudden reply involving cherries and sea-food was comical yet, strangely, it occurred to no one to laugh or even to smile. There was something unreal about the whole thing.

Angélique's feelings towards Ambroisine de Maudribourg

had fluctuated for a long time but now that she saw her about to depart, the sight of that face looking up at her stirred both pity and sympathy within her.

In this woman there was a kind of innocence, something broken, and Angélique was moved at the thought of a creature of such beauty, born with so many talents and destined for fame, yet weighed down with some inner infirmity which she could not define.

At times the sheer contrast between the mature personality of the Duchess and her unexpected childishness had considerably irritated Angélique. These contrasts were disconcerting to the observer, but were not devoid of charm for one who was happy to live under her spell. Her childish side became most apparent when the Duchess found herself before a male audience. Was it instinct or compensation? She was like an adolescent girl making her first attempt at seduction . . .

Angélique was not going to forget the fear she had felt the other day during that scientific discussion, when she had seen Ambroisine look at Joffrey de Peyrac with those magnificent eyes. But now she understood that, through fear, she had given an extreme interpretation to actions that were of no importance.

Joffrey de Peyrac seemed not in the slightest concerned at the Duchess's departure, even appearing impatient to see the shipwrecked benefactress set sail, while her whole attention was concentrated on Angélique.

'We could have become great friends,' she told her, 'you and I are very close in many ways, in spite of our differences.'

She was right. Although obdurate as a result of her pious upbringing which she seemed neither to wish nor to be able to overcome, she had the occasional flash of instinct in her judgements which were akin to Angélique's own intuitions.

One day she had said to her: 'You are threatened by some lurking danger.'

And now she seemed reluctant to leave her, and looked at her with despair.

Ambroisine accepted help from Armand Daveau and from Captain Job Simon to board the launch. The King's Girls had already been rowed across to the ship. This final trip would take the Duchess to the little thirty-tonner, of which Monsieur de Randon had accepted the command. After putting in at Port-Royal, the ship was to join Peyrac in the Saint John river.

Behind Job Simon came two ship's boys carrying a trestle on which lay the wooden unicorn. He had not quite finished re-gilding it and had made a childish scene when the word departure had been mentioned. 'You must come with me,' the Duchess had insisted, 'you are the only one left of the crew I took on . . .'

Ill-tempered, he was the last to embark after installing the glittering unicorn in the stern of the launch.

Seeing the creature rearing up, ungainly and powerful against the crimson evening sky, Angélique suddenly thought of the phrase used by Lopez, one of Colin's men: 'When you see the tall captain with the port-wine mark you will know that your enemies are not far off!' What could such words have possibly meant? In spite of the birthmark on his temple, these words could scarcely apply to poor Job Simon, the blundering pilot, accidentally shipwrecked in French Bay.

With one arm encircling the unicorn's neck he sailed gloomily away from Gouldsboro, raising his hand from time to time by way of leave-taking. The children responded by waving too, but there were no cheers.

Job Simon and his unicorn hid the other occupants of the launch from view. But there was one moment when the boat's position shifted and Angélique saw Ambroisine de Maudribourg looking in her direction. The fire that darted from those dark eyes caught hold of her in a commanding way that held a meaning she could not understand. 'We haven't seen the last of one another yet,' that devouring glance seemed to say.

Abigail was standing at Angélique's side at that moment. On impulse Angélique seized her friend's hand and was surprised to feel Abigail's fingers grip her own tightly as if the tranquil young woman had also sensed the strange atmosphere of the scene.

The red sun was beginning to descend rapidly through the bands of cloud that stretched across the horizon.

And when the gilded wooden unicorn was hoisted on board, it glistened in all its splendour, and the sun illuminated the single pink ivory horn rising from its head.

Soon after, the ship crossed the bar and was swallowed up in the evening dusk. Then the children came to life and began to leap about in the sand. Taking one another by the hand, they began to dance rounds and farandols to the accompaniment of happy cries.

Abigail and Angélique looked at one another. They did not exchange a single word, but they knew that they both experienced the same sense of relief.

The atmosphere on the beach had completely changed. Only a few of the men who had seen the women they loved go off, still remained care-worn and sad.

But on the whole it seemed clear that no one really missed the passengers from the *Unicorn*, that had gone aground a fortnight earlier near Gouldsboro. These departures meant less worry and less work for its inhabitants.

'Now it's our turn,' said Peyrac, throwing his cloak over his shoulder as the brisk evening wind began to tear at it.

'Are you off?' Ville d'Avray asked, excitedly.

'On the next tide.'

'At last! Angélique, my angel, life is wonderful. Your husband is a charming man. You absolutely *must* come to Quebec, both of you. Your presence there will be the delight of the next winter season ... Yes! yes, you must come, I absolutely insist.'

PART TWO

Gouldsboro
or
Duplicity

CHAPTER 25

'Oh, my love,' she said, 'I feel we've scarcely had time enough to love one another and to tell one another so, and now you're going away. It's horrible.'

Joffrey de Peyrac took her in his arms, and stroked her feverish brow. Suddenly there was a clap of thunder. Clouds had been gathering throughout the evening, forming a heavy grey mass. The muggy heat was giving way to sudden squalls of wind, and the wooden shutter banged against the wall.

'You can't leave during a storm like this, can you?' Angélique asked hopefully.

'A storm! It's only a squall. My darling, you're like a child this evening.'

'Yes, I am a child,' she replied obstinately, with her arms around his neck, 'a child who is lost without you.'

'But we must grow up, we must grow old, it's high time,' he said with a laugh as he covered her with kisses, 'and we must look the truth straight in the face: I shall be away for about six to ten days, and I am well armed. It's a mere excursion up French Bay . . .'

'That French Bay frightens me. People are forever talking about it and I imagine it like some dark hole, filled with the smoke of hell, peopled with dragons, monsters and idols . . .'

'There is something of that about it. But I know what the region of hell is like for I've stood on its threshold on several occasions. So take heart, my love, I assure you that they don't want me there yet.'

His jollity finally overcame her forebodings.

'I might even be back before Abigail's baby arrives,' he added. 'Don't forget to ask the old Indian woman from the village for help, she is famous for her potions to ease childbirth.'

She knew that he must go. Not only because of Phipps. There were also 'the others', those whom she herself had begun to call 'the demons'. She must not hinder what he had undertaken. She knew that, when he struck, it would be swift and hard, and that afterwards all would be well. But it was his absence she dreaded. She ran her hands over his shoulders, straightened his ribboned epaulette and his lace shirt-ruffle. These possessive actions made her feel better, confirmed that he belonged to her alone. He was wearing his magnificent English outfit of ivory satin slashed with crimson and embroidered with tiny pearls, and high soft red leather boots that reached to mid-thigh.

'I saw you wearing this once before,' she said as she examined the costume. 'Weren't you wearing it on the evening I returned to Gouldsboro?'

'Yes, that's right. I had to dress up bravely as if for battle. It's no easy role to play the deceived husband, or at least one who is regarded as such,' he replied, laughing at her impulsive reaction of protest.

Then drawing her to him, he clasped her in a great wave of passion, throwing his arms around her and holding her so tight against his chest that she could scarcely breathe.

'Look after yourself, my love!' he murmured, his lips against her hair.

She sensed that never had he been so anxious at having to leave her.

He drew back from her and looked lovingly at her while his finger gently traced the line of one eyebrow, then followed the oval of her face as if sensing its perfection.

Then he strode over towards the table and picked up his pistols, which he fastened in the holsters on his belt.

'We can't turn back now,' he said as if talking to himself. 'We must go ahead, must seek out and unmask the enemy . . . even if he turns out to be in league with the devil.'

He took her in his arms once more. His lips wore their habitual caustic smile, as if he were trying to belie the gravity of his words.

'We must have neither fear,' he said, 'nor doubt. You see . . . I was once afraid, afraid to lose you, and I doubted, and now I know that had it not been for your warning me, I should have fallen into the trap that had been laid for me . . . Lessons like that make one humble. And prudent. So remember, my love, *never to be afraid . . . of anything*, but to be vigilant . . . and the gates of Hell shall not prevail against us.'

CHAPTER 26

HE HAD gone.

And now already, after a wet and stormy day, it was evening again.

Their room in the fort seemed to have lost its warmth. Finding herself alone in it, Angélique had to fight down a feeling of icy apprehension, which was insidiously creeping over her.

She would gladly have chatted with Cantor, but the lad had gone off late in the afternoon with Martial Berne, and two or three other young men, on some secret mission of their own.

In the course of the day Angélique had visited Abigail.

'I've asked a great deal of you, haven't I?' Master Gabriel's wife had said to her. 'Had it not been for me, you would have gone off with Monsieur de Peyrac . . .'

'Had it not been for you, yes, indeed I should; but, my dear Abigail, you exist,' Angélique replied gaily, 'and so does the tiny precious new life that is soon to bring us all joy.'

'I can't help feeling a trifle anxious,' Abigail finally admitted in a voice suitable for the confession of some irreparable fault; 'I'm frightened of not being able to face the coming ordeal. Gabriel's first wife died in childbirth: I remember, I was there. It was terrible being so helpless! . . . And I feel that he too, as my time draws near, is haunted by that memory . . .'

'Now you're not to get agitated about things,' cried Angélique, pretending to be cross.

She sat down beside Abigail on the edge of the big rustic bed and told her about all the happy confinements she could think of.

'I can feel something like a large ball moving backwards and forwards across there,' said Abigail, placing one hand just below her ribs. 'Do you think it's the child's head? Does that mean that it will be a breech presentation?'

'Possibly. But there's nothing to worry about. Sometimes babies are born more easily in that position . . .'

She left Abigail reassured, but she herself had taken on all the anxieties she had sought to take from her friend.

She went to see Madame Carrère.

'You will give me a hand, Madame Carrère, won't you, with Abigail?'

The lawyer's wife wrinkled up her nose.

Her energy and drive, along with her eleven children whom she brought up under almost military discipline, were giving her an increasingly prominent position in Gouldsboro.

'Abigail is no longer young,' she said with some anxiety. 'Thirty-five is late for a first child. I wonder if the child is in a good position?'

'No it isn't, actually.'

'If it remains too long in the passage it will die.'

'No it won't die,' replied Angélique with quiet assurance. 'So I can count on you, can I?'

She also walked to the Indian encampment, where she found the old Indian woman who had been recommended to her, sitting at the back of her cabin smoking her pipe. They had agreed that she would receive a mug of alcohol, two loaves of wheat-flour and a scarlet blanket in return for her advice, and any remedies she might provide at the appropriate time. She was highly experienced and knew the secret of certain nostrums whose composition Angélique would have very much liked to know. They included a root extract capable of deadening pain without slowing down or stopping labour, and an ointment that made the final stage of labour quite painless.

As she walked back towards the village in the thin, driving rain, Angélique shuddered. Entirely surrounded by dark forests, Gouldsboro clung to the shore, a tiny speck between those two restlessly moving wastes – the forest and the ocean.

The absence of ships in the roadstead, the departure of most of the guests who had thronged their shores over the past few days – the Acadians, their redskins, the King's Girls and their benefactress, the bustling Marquis de Ville d'Avray and his retinue of clerics – along with the grey dusk wrapping itself about the thatched or clap-board roofs, seemed to emphasize the vulnerability of this handful of houses clustered together for survival, hoping against hope to triumph over the lordly elements that surrounded them.

And yet, that very sense of vulnerability suggested the opposite notion, that of the strength of the men huddled together beneath those wretched roofs, with the light from their hearths glowing through the windows as a symbol of their strength of will.

Gouldsboro was a place of truce. It offered a guarantee of rest to persecuted men of good will. Calling to mind the young Protestant Martial Berne, spontaneously handing a bowl of cold water to the exhausted Jesuit, Angélique asked herself whether after all some changes were not indeed taking place in this corner of the globe.

She walked as far as the Inn at the quayside, which, after the hustle and bustle of the past few days, seemed empty; Cantor was not there; so she drank a bowl of fish-soup then returned home.

She felt really anxious.

The kitten alone, like a bright little elf, whose delight at being alive nothing could destroy, brought a ray of light to her darkness. Occasionally it would sit down on its tail with full feline gravity, and putting its head on one side, look quizzically at her. Then it would begin to play again with renewed liveliness.

She had to admit that she was pleased to have it there. The coming night and the days to follow already seemed interminable. The sound of wind and rain always seemed to be magnified in this room, and mingled with the nearby breaking of waves, as the fort had been built on the end of a small promontory. Then suddenly towards ten o'clock, just when night had fallen, everything fell silent.

When Angélique went over to the window to fasten the shutter, everything had died down – the rain, the wind, and the noisy hammering of the great waves against the rocks. A thick fog was creeping over the countryside; she could see it coming in across the sea through the darkness like a tall white wall. It rolled over the beach where a few sailors' fires were still burning, and then it was all around the fort, billowing like thick smoke and smelling of sea and damp leaf-mould. Its chill breath filled the room.

Angélique plucked up courage and locked the shutter. Joffrey! Where was he now? Fog is never a friend to ships at sea.

She went about her few preparations for bed in thoughtful mood. She was not sleepy but felt in need of a rest. And yet she could not have gone to bed that night without carefully tidying the room, noting its every detail and the position of each item. This particular night she wanted to sort things out, to take stock, to make a fresh start. So she folded all the clothes, carefully laying them away in their chests; she made a list of all her phials, sachets, remedies and herbs, got rid of those that needed to be thrown out, and put on one side the things she wanted for Abigail's confinement. The wooden box with the illuminated pictures of Saints Cosmàs and Damian was roomy and practical, and she enjoyed putting everything away in it. Joffrey's thoughtfulness warmed her heart, even while her feelings of perplexity and mild anxiety seemed to grow stronger. Yet the expedition he was going on was no different from so many others which he had undertaken. What hitherto unknown danger could he possibly encounter after so long a life spent in parrying the blows of fate and the malice of men?

He would soon be back again, having brought peace to the area. Then they would both be able to return to Wapassou with a clear conscience, and, although the life they led there was even more exposed to danger than the life of the pioneers on the coast, she thought of it with a delightful feeling of going back home, to a place where she felt in complete security, with him. There they could live their real lives, in the unfolding of the constant stream of tasks and simple joys of their family life.

She felt no anxiety for Wapassou, from which their absence would in fact be quite a short one. Peyrac had left plans for enlarging the fort and its precinct which would keep the mercenaries fully occupied, felling trees or building. Nor were the miners to remain inactive: they were to extract silver and gold, and dig new galleries; all hands would be needed for tending crops, for hunting, fishing, and the maintenance of stores. Even the children would not be idle. Angélique could imagine Honorine picking berries and hazelnuts accompanied by her bearcub Lancelot.

As she was tidying the big leather bag from which she was rarely parted, she found the Wampum necklace Outakke, Chief of the Five Nations of the Iroquois, had sent her. She lingered over the symbolic mauve and white beads, in which she saw a pledge of their tranquillity at Wapassou. And in spite of the appalling difficulties of the previous winter, she looked back on it all nostalgically.

'That was happiness, in spite of everything,' she told herself. 'We are so well hidden out there, at the top of our sacred valley of the Silver Lake, that it seems as if even demons can't reach us there . . .'

The thought of demons once again disturbed her, for the merest trifle would cause her spirits to soar or plunge. Would he find 'them'? ... And what lay behind the tricks that were played on them?

Her thoughts returned to the dark, tumultuous sea. She found she could hardly breathe, then reproached herself for these baseless fears. Nevertheless before getting into bed she loaded one of her pistols and slipped it under her pillows.

The silence outside was so complete that she had a sense of being entirely alone in the isolated fort, devoid of any other human presence ... So strong was this feeling that she could not resist the temptation to open the door leading to the stairs. She could hear the sound of voices – some of the sentries drinking in the main hall with Colin's men and a few Indians. That made her feel better, and she decided to go to bed, although in spite of all her efforts she remained tense, as if waiting for something to happen.

Finally she fell into a troubled half-sleep in which she saw vague shapes moving through the nightmare fog of French Bay. Marceline-la-Belle and her twelve children amid shellfish flying in all directions, the marine monster buried deep in Parrsboro Bay turning over while the waters swelled like fermenting dough, and the Indian god Gloosecap rising up through it all like a giant, piercing the murky skies with its livid demon's face and transparent agate eyes.

She woke up and all the weird creatures that had peopled her sleep seemed to be standing around her still, filling the heavy darkness, watching her. Yet she could see nothing.

It was still the middle of the night. She could feel 'them' there. There was something strange about the silence. The dark seconds ticked by with stifling slowness.

Then at last she became aware of what it was that must have woken her, an almost imperceptible sound at her ear. The noise stopped, then began again. Was it the sound of wood? Or metal? But it was close, so close that all of a sudden she realized it must be an animal!

In panic, she was about to leap out of bed, then she remembered: an animal ... yes, of course, her cat! It must have somehow managed to clamber up beside her to sleep. But why was it making this strange noise? Was it ill? She listened, could hear it better now, and suddenly realized that it must be standing with its back arched, and its hair on end. Yes, of course ... In obedience to the hereditary reflexes of its kind when danger threatens, it was spitting and panting alternatively.

Then she understood.

Through the darkness the cat could see something that she could not, something that filled it with horror and fear.

A long shudder ran through her. For an instant that seemed interminable, she lay there paralysed, petrified.

What was there, there in the darkness? Something frightening, monstrous, invisible, but something the cat *could see*.

At last she managed to stretch out her hand, slip it beneath her pillow and grasp her gun. The touch of its polished wooden butt in her palm made her feel better.

She began to breathe more calmly, gaining control over her thoughts.

What she needed was light!

She stretched out her hand towards her bedside table and her fingers encountered the kitten's warm fur, which was indeed standing on end like a pin cushion. As she touched its coat the kitten let out a piercing miaow and leapt off the bed, to take refuge beneath some piece of furniture where it remained curled up in a terrified ball. Angélique felt around, seeking her tinder-box and candle. Meanwhile her heart continued to thump loudly, making her still more clumsy. There was someone there in her room, of that she felt sure, but *who*?

'Even if it's the Devil himself,' she said, her teeth chattering, 'never mind. I *must* see whoever it is!'

She could smell something! ... Something that came towards her and wrapped her round like a wave. There was some question she had to ask . . .

Her fingers struggled with the tinder-box. She must make haste before the wave overwhelmed her. At last she struck a spark. She did not manage to kindle the touchwood, but in the glow she had seen a *human being*!

At the far end of the room, in the corner to the left of the door, there stood a motionless, black silhouette, draped in long mourning veils.

But why this feeling of nausea? This unbearable scent. In this scent lay the whole explanation, the whole danger.

Angélique felt a sudden sweat of anguish break out from every pore in her body. When the tinder began to catch fire, she carefully placed it against the wick, waiting until the flame rose up high and clear, scattering the shadows and driving the darkness to the outer limits of the walls.

Then, taking hold of the candlestick, she examined the shadows. There was no doubt about it, there was someone standing there. A dark shape, like a ghost draped in black, someone who seemed to be wrapped about in a black cloak, whose deep hood entirely covered its bowed head, making it look like one of those statues of 'weeping' monks carved at the four corners of a King's sepulchre.

For an instant she tried to convince herself that it was an illusion, a phantasmagoric effect of a piece of furniture covered with some garment, that was playing tricks with her terrified mind. But at that very moment the shape moved and seemed to take a step forward.

Angélique's heart gave a lurch.

'Who's there?' she asked in a voice as firm as she could make it.

There was no reply.

Suddenly she found herself extremely angry, and putting the candlestick down on the table she felt about her with her feet for her embroidered leather mules and stood up, without taking her eyes off the silent shadow. Then, picking up the candle again, made her way towards the black ghost.

Once again the perfume that had sickened her reached her nostrils and suddenly recognizing it, such was her terror that she thought she would collapse in a faint.

Ambroisine!

At the same time her crazy panic left her, as she told herself:

'If it is *really* her, why am I afraid?'

The perfume brought once more to life the familiar presence of the woman who had been their guest for several days, a bright-plumed bird, with unexpected moments of melancholy, of incomparable charm and devotion, scientific bent and naïvety, of youthfulness and mature power, the benefactress with the mysterious personality.

Once beside her, Angélique sensed without a shadow of doubt that it was she, and when she laid her hand on the ghost's brow and threw back the black cloth hood, she was not surprised to discover the Duchess's gleaming eyes burning with a sombre fire in her chalk-white face.

'Ambroisine!' she exclaimed, recovering her poise with some difficulty. 'Ambroisine, what are you doing here?'

The Duchess's lips were trembling and she uttered not a sound. Then, as if drained of all strength, she fell to her knees and, clasping her arms round Angélique's waist, laid her head against her breast.

'I couldn't,' she cried at last in despair, 'I couldn't leave this place . . . leave you . . . As the coastline vanished in the distance I thought I should die of grief. It seemed to me that my last hope of achieving a serene and happy life had finally gone . . . I couldn't leave.'

She was shaken with convulsive sighs. Through her thin batiste shift Angélique could feel the Duchess's arms twining round her like a tropical creeper, supple but with an irresistible, burning grip. The weight of that head pressing against her sent an indefinable feeling of enjoyment and unease flowing through her.

She managed to set the candlestick down on a nearby table and taking hold of Ambroisine's hands that were digging into the small of her back, she succeeded in unclasping the clenched fingers and detaching herself.

At that moment the long-drawn-out call of the fog-horn, sounded on a conch-shell, rang out through the dense muffling swathes of fog. The prolonged mournful wailing sound made Angélique shudder, and for a moment more she wondered fleetingly whether the figure kneeling there before her in any way resembled the woman who had but a short time before embarked for Port Royal. Was it an apparition, a mirage, or a waking nightmare?

Ambroisine de Maudribourg's eyes as they looked up at her were extraordinarily beautiful. The light emanating from them seemed to strike to the very depths of her heart in a mute appeal.

The fog-horn sounded again, a warning of danger to mariners.

'But how did you manage to get through the fog?' said Angélique. 'Where are your girls? When did you come ashore?'

'My girls must be at Port Royal by now,' the Duchess explained. 'All of a sudden a fishing vessel passed us, heading for Gouldsboro, and I couldn't resist it. I asked the fishermen to take me on board. They put me ashore not far from here, and in spite of the mist I had no difficulty in finding my way. I made straight for the fort, where I knew you would be sleeping, and the sentries recognized me.'

'The sentries ought to have warned me . . .' Angélique broke in, somewhat annoyed.

'Never mind! I knew where your room was so I came up. Your door wasn't locked.'

Angélique remembered that the previous evening she had

gone out on to the landing to listen to the sounds about the fort by way of reassuring herself, and after that she had forgotten to bolt the door again. She owed this dreadful scare to her own negligence. She was bathed in perspiration and as weak as if she had been exposed to overpowering heat. Yet at the same time she felt cold and had difficulty in stopping her teeth chattering. This would be a lesson to her not to allow herself to give way to vague fears and impulses.

She would have liked to shake Ambroisine but she realized that the Duchess of Maudribourg was not herself. It was as if she had returned to Gouldsboro, walking to the fort through this mist, and right up to Angélique's room in a kind of trance, driven by some desperate and irrational force.

Her hands had grown cold and begun to tremble. She was still on her knees but seemed to be coming to herself and growing aware of her foolish behaviour.

'Forgive me,' she murmured. 'Oh, what have I done? . . . But you will not abandon me, will you? . . . Otherwise I am lost.'

She was rambling.

'Get up, and come and lie down,' said Angélique. 'You are at the end of your strength.'

She led the Duchess, who staggered as she walked, over to the bed.

As she helped her remove her black cloak, a kind of red flash seemed to envelop them both. The cloak was lined throughout with crimson satin that caught the light; lying across the bed it looked like a huge pool of blood, of a deep and sumptuous red.

She helped Ambroisine lie down between the sheets that were still warm from her own body.

'I'm cold,' the young woman moaned with closed eyes.

She was trembling convulsively.

'Where did that cloak come from?' Angélique asked herself.

Then once more, as she drew the covers up over Ambroisine, who lay rigid and almost unconscious, she began to wonder whether she was really there. The kitten leapt up on the bed, wide-eyed, then after a moment's hesitation, in a flash took refuge once again under a piece of furniture.

'What is he frightened of?'

Angélique shuddered and felt herself assailed by the same feeling of malaise that had attacked the Duchess. She lit a fire in the hearth then quickly made herself a cup of very strong

Turkish coffee over a small charcoal grill, which made her feel better and helped to clear her head.

'What a crazy thing to do! To have come back alone in this weather. These fine missionary folk haven't got their feet very firmly planted on the ground . . . America is too tough for these high-minded ladies . . .'

'Drink this,' said Angélique, lifting the limp head with one arm as she held the cup to Ambroisine's lips. 'It's coffee, the best remedy in the world. In a few moments you'll feel better. And now, tell me,' she went on, when she saw a trace of pink appear on the young woman's cheeks, 'did you come here all alone, or have you one of your followers with you? Your secretary, for instance, or Job Simon?'

'No! No one, I assure you! I took the decision all alone when I saw the Acadian vessel pass us saying they were heading for Gouldsboro. Gouldsboro! You! Your charming friend Abigail, all the delightful people here, days full of gaiety, the freedom here, the very air one breathes here . . . I don't know what came over me . . . I wanted to see you again, to convince myself of your existence . . .'

'And they let you go off like that?'

'They were all shouting. But my impulse was stronger than their reasons. They simply had to let me do what I wanted and continue on their way as I told them to do. I know how to make people obey me,' Ambroisine added, with a sudden flash of defiance in her great eyes.

'Yes, I know. But it was still a crazy thing to do.'

'Oh, don't scold me. I can no longer understand myself. Perhaps it's only now that I am doing what I need to do, and not bowing to perpetual constraints.'

As she spoke, her eyes began to glisten as if filling with tears. Her head leaned on Angélique's shoulder like an exhausted child.

'Try to be calm, and we shall talk about it tomorrow. Meanwhile you must get your strength back. It is the middle of the night and you must sleep.'

'Tomorrow I shall go back to the house where I used to stay. I enjoyed watching the sea from the doorstep. I shall be no trouble to you. I shall live there alone and pray. That is all I desire . . .'

'We shall see. Now go to sleep.'

She got into the bed on the other side, and was glad to have the chance of getting properly warm again.

She hesitated to blow out the light, and thought of lighting an oil-burning nightlight. But she could not face getting up again. Where was the kitten? Would he climb up beside her now, reassured? Before blowing out the candle she glanced at Ambroisine, who seemed to have fallen into a deep sleep. Her delicate features wore an expression of childlike calm.

Angélique shook her head. She was a poor soul.

She blew out the light, but not before carefully placing her tinderbox within reach. For a brief moment her mind wandered anxious and undecided, then sleep stole over her carrying with it into her dreams the light, pervasive perfume that hung over Ambroisine de Maudribourg's hair as she lay beside her.

She dreamed the horrible dream she had once dreamt before in which she was making love with some monster wearing a terrifying grin. She was overwhelmed by a feeling of oppression and struggled to escape the horrible embrace.

Once again she woke up, her heart thudding, and saw two eyes level with the ground, shining through the blackness. A nameless terror gripped her as she looked at them for what seemed like an eternity. At last she realized that they were the eyes of the kitten, crouching under a table on the opposite side of the room. He was not asleep, but continued his watch, strangely alert.

Slowly Angélique's heart grew calm again, and stopped beating crazy drum rhythms in her ears. She began to get her bearings again. It was still night, still silent, and no doubt outside, still that heavy relentless fog. Angélique thought about the little houses that made up Gouldsboro, trying to go through them one by one in her mind, each one isolated, wrapped around in these opaque veils, irrevocably buried . . .

After a while she stretched one hand out to the side.

The place was empty. This time Angélique said out loud:

'Am I mad or what?'

And she lighted the candle like someone about to settle her fate.

Ambroisine was there, kneeling a few steps from the bed, praying, hands joined, eyes turned fervently up to heaven.

'What *are* you doing?' Angélique cried, almost angry. 'This is no time for praying!'

'Yes, it is,' the Duchess replied, her voice deep and hoarse, as if terrified, 'I must pray. *The devil is abroad!*'

'That's enough nonsense! Come back to bed again.'

The more Angélique feared giving way to panic, the more

she raised her voice. She felt a cold shudder run down her spine. It was like the atmosphere that night when, as a child, she had slept at the Abbey of Nieul, and the young monk had turned back his sleeves to show her the marks of Satan. 'Look what the Evil One did to me, look!'

She gritted her teeth and clenched her fists to check the trembling fit that had seized her. Why was the kitten trembling under the table too, looking utterly terrified?

'Let me pray a little longer,' Ambroisine de Maudribourg begged her. 'It's nearly time for matins! The cock will crow and Satan will go away!'

'There's no cock here,' Angélique replied roughly, 'so if you wait for it to crow you'll fall dead with exhaustion.'

'Ah, did you hear it?' cried the young woman, an expression of relief coming over her distraught face.

Surprising as it might seem, Angélique did hear a cock crow in the courtyard of the fort, muffled by the fog. This sound so familiar to all country dawns calmed her nerves too.

'He's going,' Ambroisine murmured, 'Satan is going. He's frightened of the day, frightened of the light.'

'So there *are* cocks in Gouldsboro,' Angélique commented. 'I hadn't noticed. Please, Ambroisine, remember that we only have a few hours' more sleep before us, and come and lie down. I'm exhausted . . .'

The young woman obediently crept back to bed and slid between the covers.

'What torture!' she murmured, drawing the covers up around her and burying her pale face in the pillow almost voluptuously. 'How good it is beside you, Angélique! You are always serene, unattainable. You have a strength which I find more attractive than anything else. You never seem frightened of anything. Where do you draw your courage from? Is it inherited? Oh, why did I not inherit too? Why has the Devil dogged my footsteps ever since I was born?'

This time Angélique left the light on. She did not want to fall asleep again in spite of her tiredness. The plaintive voice beside her stirred her with a deep pity. A child was emerging from this broken personality, and it was a child begging for help.

Angélique stretched out her hand and caressed that heavy head of hair, gleaming with the tints of night and fire. Ambroisine's eyes softened and fastened themselves on her with a kind of childlike wonder.

'What a wonderful thing it is to look at you and listen to you!' whispered Ambroisine dreamily. 'You're so beautiful! But you have a sensitive heart too. You're able to love other people and to feel that you are loved. I never feel anything . . . except fear . . .'

She stretched out her hand and, timidly as if dazzled by a bright light, touched Angélique's hair, her cheek, her lip.

'You're so beautiful and yet . . .'

'Nonsense!' said Angélique who was anxious to discern behind these random words the chink in the armour which would open up to her the secret of this wonderful heart. 'You're beautiful too. And you know it! As far as not being loved is concerned, the devotion of the girls accompanying you, and of all the men as well, is a sufficient proof of the love that you inspire.'

Suddenly the question that she had wanted to ask several times recurred to her memory and she exclaimed: 'Ambroisine, that perfume in your hair! It's almost as if you had recently put some on. But didn't you tell me that you had lost the last bottle in the shipwreck?'

Ambroisine pulled a wry face and gave a faint smile. 'Well, you see this is a very good instance of your point that my followers are very attached to me. Seeing how fond I was of this perfume and fearing that I would run short of it in New France, my secretary, Armand Daveau, brought a spare bottle. Like the careful and painstaking fellow he is, he wrapped it up in water-proof canvas and sewed the packet into the tail of his frock-coat. When he heard me lamenting the loss of my toilet-case, he was able to provide me with this wonderful perfume.'

'What an example of the devotion that you can inspire even in a pen-pusher!'

Ambroisine also smiled, but her smile was a little forced and made two deep indentations appear on either side of her mouth.

'That clumsy bore!' she muttered.

Her gaze returned to Angélique and she said somewhat agitatedly: 'All the men like you, and that includes those worthiest of the name. Men like your husband for example . . . a man that every woman would want to be able to captivate, and all you have to do is to appear on the scene in order to fascinate him. He follows you about with his eyes, they soften when they look at you . . . And that other fellow, the great silent giant, what is there between him and you? And even that Jesuit with his magnificent manners. There too I felt that "aura" of intimacy, of complicity that you have the gift of creating between any man and yourself, even the simplest of men: that stupid soldier, that debauched pirate, and even that frightful Indian . . . he too loves you. He would kill anyone who touched a single hair on your head; I have sensed that. All you have to do is appear and immediately something changes; it's as if people felt happier. Even the bear adores you!' she exclaimed wringing her hands.

Angélique burst out laughing: 'What a diatribe! You're exaggerating, my dear woman!'

'No,' said Ambroisine, obstinately. 'You have the gift of love, perhaps you know how to accept love, to feel it. What a fortune I would give to have that gift! You're fortunate in your body,' she continued, 'that's the secret. You enjoy everything in your heart but also in your flesh – happiness and unhappiness, the sunshine, the birds that flit by, the colour of the sea . . . the love that people feel for you, and the love you give out.'

'What stops you doing the same?'

'What stops me?!' she shouted.

Her eyes wide with horror, the Duchess was contemplating deep within herself an unbearable vision. The bitter line of her mouth made her appear ugly and worn out, like an old woman.

'Forgive me!' she said, suddenly pushing away Angélique's arm placed affectionately about her shoulders. 'Leave me; I want to finish with life. I'll kill myself, that's all.'

'God forbid such a thing! You, so pious . . .'

'Pious! Yes indeed. I have to be something, since I am dead all over. I've found nothing else to help me to survive! Praying, being pious, busying myself about religious matters . . . You laugh at my devout practices, don't you? You cannot understand . . .'

Angélique continued to hold against her Ambroisine de Maudribourg's form which was trembling convulsively almost as if she was on the point of jumping out of bed and doing something desperate. In her delirium she seemed to be unaware that she was throwing herself about semi-naked. Her body had a strange youthful perfection – like the body of an untouched girl.

'I've been through many ups and downs, believe me,' said Angélique, 'and there's little of human suffering that is unknown to me.'

'No, no! You were strong ... whereas I ... You can't imagine what it is to be ...'

'What, Ambroisine?'

'A mere child of fifteen, delivered into the hands of a bawdy old man,' she cried, as if spitting out a poison which carried with it her very entrails.

She bent over, panting for breath.

'I shrieked,' she whispered, 'no one came to my assistance ... I struggled for a whole night ... In the end he got his servants to hold me down! ... And priests bless all that ...'

She threw herself back, pallid upon her pillow. The perspiration stood out in beads on her temples. A purple ring was visible on her closed eyelids. For a moment she looked as if she were dead.

Angélique wiped her face.

'You won't tell anybody will you?' stammered the Duchess in a scarcely audible voice. 'You won't tell anybody that I cried out ... I was very proud. A pure, spontaneous child, but proud ... In the convent I used to rule the roost over the other girls – the prettiest, the cleverest, the most popular. From my childhood up I had astonished theologians, mathematicians used to come to the convent simply to question me. I used to lord it over the nuns, the ignorant creatures ... And then the sudden humiliation ... To discover that all these wonderful qualities meant nothing, and that I was a mere prey that men and their laws were entitled to sell to the highest bidder with the blessing of a conniving clergy ... To a man rotten with vice who was fifty-five years older than me.'

She broke off, out of breath and on the point of vomiting. Angélique held her up and said nothing. What could she say? She remembered: for her too, married by proxy, everything might have been equally ignoble. But there had been Joffrey de Peyrac waiting for her in Toulouse and the extraordinary adventure of the passionate love born between the young virgin who had been sold and the great lord who had bought her.

At one time the Duke of Maudribourg had come to Toulouse to learn the secret of the transmutation of gold, and the Count had refused to admit him because of his reputation as a debauchee. That was the contemptible man to whom Ambroisine had been delivered up.

Dawn was coming. An uncertain half-light was replacing the night, dimming the halo of the candle. The kitten slipped out of its hiding-place and made for the door, mewing. Angélique got up to open the door for it.

She drew aside the wooden panel over the window-panes. The fog was still there, as white as snow. But a scent of wood-fire was creeping in. There were sounds of movement below in the guard-room. She wished that Piksarett would come back, all bedizened with red paint, to tell her 'You are my captive.' That was life, their life on American soil, far from the Old World. A sense of nausea continued to grip at her throat. She went back to Ambroisine, and made her drink a glass of cold water.

The Duchess appeared drained of strength, and kept her eyes closed. However she did say in a clearer voice: 'I haven't forgiven or accepted yet. It still burns me like a hot brand. That's why I'm all dead inside.'

'Calm down!' said Angélique, kindly caressing her moist forehead as if she were a child. 'You've talked, and that's a good thing. Now, try not to think about it any more. Here you are at peace, far from all obligations and from those who have witnessed your past. If you want to confide any more in me, I will gladly listen to you, later. But now sleep.'

She laid her hand on those bruised eyes, imposing on them a refreshing sense of peace.

'What a blessing to have met you!' sighed Ambroisine, who seemed almost immediately afterwards to sink into a deep sleep.

CHAPTER 27

SHE HAD to warn Colin Paturel of the Duchess's unexpected arrival. The Governor of Gouldsboro made no comment. He shook his head several times and merely invited the two ladies to dine with him that evening.

The absence of Joffrey de Peyrac, and of the Marquis d'Urville, of the Spanish guard, the Count's suite and even the Marquis de Ville d'Avray created a void. The silence prevailing in Gouldsboro, enveloped in its mists, was almost like that of winter, except for the stifling heat of the days, which at times seemed to arise from the unseen forest, bringing down strange tangy and animal-scented odours to the coast, so strong that they quite drowned the pungent smell of the seaweed and the tides.

Colin's men were working hard building their village and their church. But they were a silent lot. Barssempuy, his aristocratic, young, dare-devil's face darkened by sadness, directed them with a few laconic orders.

The Protestants were going about their daily lives, which had already assumed a routine course, and there was hardly a word exchanged between the two groups. What understanding there was existed at the higher level, since the La Rochelle worthies seemed to get on well with Colin.

Angélique found Manigault, Berne and Pastor Beaucaire in conference with him. She inquired about Abigail's state of health. Gabriel Berne appeared in high good humour.

'She's been feeling better this morning,' he said, 'in fact she's decided to do the washing. I think we've got a few days to go yet,' he added, pleased to think that the crucial moment was still some way off, a time he feared even more than Abigail herself.

Angélique paid a visit to her friend. Abigail was indeed looking better and was going gamely about her tasks, carrying baskets of washing to the river, where, in company with Sévérine, Laurier, Bertille and a few other neighbours, she set about rubbing in the soap and wielding the wooden beater vigorously.

'I didn't feel strong enough to undertake this work, and I feared that the house wouldn't be in order for my confinement. Thanks be to God, I feel well, and all these sheets and clothes will be hung out on the line by this evening. Tomorrow the sun will shine. I'll have time in the evening to fold everything up. Sévérine will help me to iron them, and there we are. I'll be able to rest with my mind in peace.'

Angélique promised to come and help her.

On returning to the fort, she found Ambroisine de Maudribourg already up and sitting by a tray of food that she had had brought to her. The Duchess was still hollow-eyed. She seemed to be under a sort of constraint and remained thus for several hours, looking fixedly before her. From time to time she picked up a scrap of bread and ate it mechanically, absorbed in her meditations. Angélique told her that she didn't want to isolate her in the outlying house where she had been lodged with the King's Girls. Angélique had reached an understanding with Aunt Anna, the learned old maid who taught the children during the winter. Aunt Anna owned a well-equipped room, next to her own modest accomodation, with a separate entrance, that was used as a classroom. It was not used as such during the summer and Madame de Maudribourg could occupy it at the present time.

'Aunt Anna is a very uninterfering sort of woman and very helpful. She won't bother you at all. But if you feel lonely, you will have someone to talk to. She is certainly much more able to discuss mathematics and theology with you than I am,' Angélique concluded with a laugh.

'Oh! You are an angel,' murmured Ambroisine, 'what can I do to show you my gratitude?'

'Just get better, that's all,' said Angélique lightly stroking the poor woman's forehead, 'don't think any more about hurtful things . . .'

But the Duchess de Maudribourg was in a state of shock. It would be several days before it would be possible to reason with her as with a person in full possession of her faculties.

Angélique left her after again repeating several times her advice that the Duchess should rest. She helped Abigail during part of the day, chatting gaily while carrying the basket-loads of washing from the river to the drying place. Abigail was planning holystoning her furniture after stocking her cupboards.

Angélique didn't dare say to her that this programme of work seemed to her a very heavy one for the coming week. She knew by experience that this burst of activity on Abigail's part was typical of a woman who was nearing her term and felt obliged to put everything in order so that she could devote her mind in peace to giving birth to a new life.

Towards the end of the day the mist dispersed and the sun came out.

'Look! My washing will be dry by tomorrow,' said Abigail. 'My arms are worn out. What a pity that Martial wasn't able to help us.'

'Where is he?'

'He's off patrolling the bay with your Cantor and some of the other young men. I gather that Monsieur de Peyrac has entrusted them with a mission.'

Her concern for Abigail and for Cantor too had to some

extent replaced Angélique's preoccupation with the Duchess de Maudribourg's problems.

'Why doesn't Cantor ever tell me anything, and why does he disappear just like that without giving me any explanation? I would very much like to have had him by me during this time. What mission has Joffrey entrusted to him? Is he supposed to be looking for the ship with the orange flag in the bay? I do wish he would come back soon . . .'

Fortunately, Ambroisine de Maudribourg seemed to be better. But she was still in a weak state and did not seem strong enough to attend the supper to which Colin had invited them. Angélique sent him an apologetic message. She herself would have preferred to stay at home that evening after the labours of the day and her disturbed night. She would have gone to bed early.

'What a feeling of peace one has here in this place full of your presence,' said Ambroisine gazing about her. 'I've spent my day in this room examining every detail of it and it has given me a strange sense of calm. I am feeling better. It seems as if wherever you live evil spells cease to act, as if there were some kind of truce with the evil that is abroad.'

Angélique was filling her earthenware stove with charcoal in order to make some Turkish coffee for herself and her guest.

She looked up at Ambroisine, intrigued, as she spoke.

'What do you mean by that?'

'Don't you feel some danger hanging over us all?' the Duchess asked, staring at her wide-eyed. 'It's hard to say, but it's almost as if some danger threatened *you* in particular . . .'

Angélique blew on the coals to revive them, before placing her Moroccan coffee-pot on the little stove. Now she understood what it was that had disturbed her about the Duchess of Maudribourg; something that did not square with her status as an aristocratic lady and a benefactress – certain gifts she had of divination, such as were found among gypsies, qualities akin to those of Angélique herself. For during the course of her adventurous life, people had often taxed her with being a witch or casting evil spells through her green eyes. These were natural aptitudes, which she never used for evil purposes, but which, she knew, brought her close to the phenomena of life, of children, of animals and of primitive peoples.

She said:

'You talk like Piksarett.'

'The tall Indian chieftain who came to claim you as his prisoner?'

'Yes ... he suddenly said to me: "Danger hovers over you ..." then he literally ran away.'

'You see?' said Ambroisine in alarm. 'I am right. And I also wonder whether that danger is an external one ... or lies within you ...'

'Within me?'

'Yes! Angélique, please don't misunderstand me but I have a certain amount of experience with human beings, and particularly women, for I have rubbed shoulders with many characters ... but yours is one of the most extraordinary I have ever encountered, and that's why I want to point out the dangers I can see in it, dangers that might well be your undoing. You think that everyone else is like you, that the straightforwardness of your feelings can be understood by everyone. It would be so easy to take advantage of you ... for, you know, basically you lack prudence.'

'Prudence,' Angélique repeated, after listening attentively to what she said.

'Yes ... or at least you seem blind to the dangers that might ensue from your conduct ... For instance, take this ... Piksarett. He entered this room, which is your room, as if he had a right to, as if he were master here, and leaned over this bed as if he were accustomed to watch you there, he even laid his filthy, smelly hand on my shoulder and laughed through all his red paint. I really did think it was the Devil. My girls and I shrieked as if we were possessed!'

'I did warn you that you had to get used to the savages' ways of behaving,' Angélique replied, finding it hard not to laugh.

'But you might have been in bed with your husband!' said the Duchess with an air of anxiety.

'In which case, if we had failed to take the precaution of bolting the door in the evening, since we are quite aware of what to expect from the people who live along these shores, well then, we would have had a good laugh with him. The redskins are modest people, even prudish, but they are not embarrassed by man's natural functions.'

'You are very indulgent towards them. Are you really fond of that man? That ... Piksarett? You know what they say about you in Quebec, that you sleep with savages.'

Angélique's reaction was sharp:

'In Quebec! I'm not surprised! They would like to see me

dead. They would say anything. They even call me a demon, because they have been turned into fanatics by a man who sees us as followers of the Devil, who have set foot on his territories in order to pervert them, namely Father d'Orgeval.'

'I have heard of him,' Ambroisine replied dreamily.

'We can do nothing against this detraction.'

'You might at least try not to give people cause for gossip. That is what I meant when I reproached you – only of course because of my affection for you – for not paying sufficient attention to the petty-mindedness of the world. Sleeping with savages, that's a terrible reputation for a white woman. How can your husband allow such a story to gain credit, by tolerating such familiarity with you? Surely he's not a complaisant husband, is he?'

'Far from it,' Angélique retorted, thinking of recent events.

'Well then, I can't understand why he . . .'

'No one asks you to understand everything about other people's lives,' Angélique broke in somewhat dryly, 'especially in a country where one has to learn to re-think many principles. Here you need tolerance.'

'Yes . . . but prudence too is a virtue.'

This time Angélique refrained from replying. Ambroisine was beginning to exasperate her, with her mixture of lady bountiful of the Blessed Sacrament, childishness, and deep psychological insight. Yes, Angélique was in fact hurt, and yet deep within her she could not deny that there was something in what the Duchess had said, putting into words, as she did, the danger that loomed from a world which would never be able to accept them as they were.

Piksarett . . . Outakke! . . . Could she ever explain what it was that bound her to these sons of the American forest-lands? To Piksarett she had given a cloak the colour of the dawn sky in which to wrap the bones of his ancestors and he, in exchange, had granted her the life of Outakke, the wounded Iroquois. And Outakke, the God of Clouds, had sent her a wampum necklace, to seal their alliance, and some beans and rice to save them from famine towards the end of the winter. These things were inaccessible to the old European cultures which had lost a certain sense of humanity and spirituality.

She put the coffee on one side to settle for a moment. Then instinctively she walked over to the window. The night looked as black as ink, too dark.

'Do you believe in Satan?' an inner voice inquired ... 'I don't know! But God, I do believe in God. Oh God, protect us!'

She made her way back towards Ambroisine who had crossed her hands over her knees and kept her eyes fixed on Angélique.

'I have hurt you! Please forgive me ... Perhaps I am too keen to know you so that I may help you. For you have done me so much good.'

'Oh don't worry about me,' Angélique replied lightly.

'But then who will worry about you?' Ambroisine exclaimed. 'Why did your husband not take you with him? ... If he loves you, he ought to have realized that you are in danger ...'

'He wanted to take me with him, but I could not leave Gouldsboro, for I must wait until Abigail has had her baby ...'

'Oh yes, you did tell me ... You certainly are very kind to everyone about you. She is a Huguenot, isn't she? She came to see me one day. I was most interested, for it was the first time I have ever spoken to a Protestant. She seemed charming.'

'Yes, she is charming,' Angélique replied with a smile. 'What did she want?'

'She wanted to know if I was going to allow my girls to marry the pirates who are around the place. I had the impression that she herself was not unduly concerned about the matter, but that she had been entrusted with some mission, by her husband or the leaders and pastors of their community. I think the Huguenots regard the place as theirs, and themselves as masters of a Protestant colony, and that they do not look very favourably on the installation of Catholic families here. But as I had already reached my decision, on Father de Vernon's advice, regarding my girls, I was able to reassure her.'

Angélique felt somewhat vexed on learning what Abigail had done.

'Why did Abigail not come straight to me and tell me of their concern about this matter?'

'That was what I asked her and she confessed that it was difficult for them to oppose your husband since he was the proprietor of the land, to whom, I gathered, they owed a great deal, as indeed they did to you, and that you seemed keen on the idea of colonization through marriage to satisfy the pirates and their chief Colin Paturel.'

'I am not particularly *keen* on the idea,' Angélique protested, her nerves once again all a-jangle, 'but in the state of disorder resulting from the fighting and the shipwrecks, it seemed to be a way of settling everything.'

'That was in fact what Abigail explained and I think that she would have been perfectly happy to accept this solution. But the men of her community seemed to think otherwise. They seem to be more or less hostile to their present governor. He is a Catholic, isn't he?'

Angélique made no reply. Ambroisine's words gave her still further cause for worry. Those Huguenots! Would one ever manage to conciliate them! They really were too intransigent.

She poured the coffee into two cups and placed them on the table, one in front of Ambroisine, the other for herself. She fetched a glass of cold water from a jug to go with the coffee and came back. The Duchess, who had been observing her anxious face, gave a sigh.

'Yes, I understand. What you are trying to do here is rather difficult. Reconciling the extremes! Is it a reasonable thing to attempt?'

'We are not attempting anything,' replied Angélique at the end of her patience. 'That is just how things happened! Chance. People asking for help, people without a stone on which to lay their heads. What else could we do but save their lives and make them welcome on some corner of the earth . . .'

She had just sat down opposite Ambroisine when someone knocked at the door.

It was Madame Carrère, once again carrying the Duchess's satin cloak over her arm.

'I saw you go by, Madame,' she said, addressing the Duchess. 'I said to myself: "Fancy now, she's come back!" And that was a piece of luck because I've finished the work at last so I can give it to you.'

'But that's marvellous!' Ambroisine exclaimed, examining the material; 'you can't see a stitch. You are wonderfully skilful, dear lady.'

'That's Turkish coffee you have there,' the good woman said, greedily sniffing the aroma that rose from the two china cups in their beaten copper holders.

'Yes, do you too like this nectar of the gods, Madame Carrère?'

'Do I! Yes indeed, I used to have it occasionally in a little oriental café in La Rochelle.'

'Well then, you have this cup that's ready here while the coffee is still hot, and I shall make another one for myself.'

Madame Carrère gladly sat down and drank the coffee to the last drop. Looking at the black muddy residue in the bottom of the cup she poured it into her saucer.

'There used to be a gipsy who told fortunes from the coffee grounds. I learnt a bit about how she did it. Would you like me to tell your fortunes?' she asked.

'Oh no, please not. All these things savouring of witchcraft are sins,' cried the Duchess, snatching the saucer from her.

Angélique motioned to Madame Carrère not to insist.

'All right then, I'll be off,' said the latter, getting up.

'Is it going to be fine tomorrow?' Angélique asked, thinking about Abigail's washing.

Madame Carrère went over to the window and sniffed the air.

'No,' she replied, 'the wind has veered again. It looks as if it's bringing us cloud, rain and even a storm from over there.'

Shortly afterwards they heard the rumble of distant thunder, and the sea grew dark, flecked with white.

'I shall see you back home before it begins to rain,' Angélique suggested. 'Put your coat on.'

She helped Ambroisine draw on the scarlet-lined black cloak in which she had returned the previous evening.

'Where did that cloak come from?' she asked. 'Did Armand Daveau have that too hidden in the folds of his coat?'

Ambroisine seemed to awaken from some dream.

'Oh, that's another of those incredible stories. Just imagine . . . it came from the captain of the ship.'

'What captain? What ship?'

'The sloop that brought me back to Gouldsboro yesterday evening. They told me they had recently ransacked a Spanish ship, and that they had a whole chest of women's clothing on board which they didn't know what to do with.'

'Did you not tell me that they were Acadians?'

'That was what they said they were. And why not? Haven't all French Acadians a weakness for pillage when they feel the need?'

As Angélique remained perplexed, the Duchess added:

'He begged me to accept his gift. I don't know what he wanted from me, he rather frightened me. But I was shivering, the fog had just come down and I was glad of the cloak.'

175

'What did this captain look like? Did he have a white face and cold eyes?'

'I don't know precisely . . . I didn't dare look at him. After my bit of daring I found myself all alone, without any luggage, amid those unknown sailors' – she gave a wan smile – 'you see just how far I was driven by my urgent desire to return to Gouldsboro to join you.'

'And what about the ship? Was it flying an orange flag at the bow?'

'Not that I remember. It was just a large boat, you know. But now that I think about it . . . just as I was climbing down into the sloop I mentioned, I noticed another ship passing us. And that one . . . did have an orange flag at the bow!'

CHAPTER 28

'DAME ANGÉLIQUE! Dame Angélique!'

Recognizing Séverine's voice, Angélique immediately understood.

She leapt out of bed, accompanied simultaneously by the wide-awake kitten.

The outside air seemed to be shaken with a confused noise: a storm!

Séverine stood on the threshold, her uppermost drugget skirt raised like a hood over her streaming hair.

'Dame Angélique, come quick! . . . It's Abigail . . .'

'I'm coming.'

She went back into her room to dress and pick up her bag which was all prepared.

'Come in for a moment. Dry yourself.'

The door slammed violently behind Séverine.

'It's the storm,' said Séverine. 'I thought I'd never manage to get here; there are great torrents of water streaming down the hill.'

'Why didn't they send Martial?'

'He's still not back yet, nor is Father. They came to fetch him yesterday evening to stand guard in the new fort beside the river, as a party of Iroquois had been sighted.'

'That's all we needed to happen!'

Joffrey was at sea. And Martial out bivouacking on the small islands with Cantor and the others. The storm might well hold them prisoner there for several days and meanwhile all the mothers would acquire a few more white hairs. And now to crown it all Iroquois had been sighted . . .

Abigail, whose first pains had just begun, was alone with little Laurier.

'Let us hurry . . . the rain seems to be easing off . . .'

The kitten, tail on end and head on one side, had been following this exchange with interest.

'Now be good,' Angélique told him as she closed the door. 'And please don't try to follow me, or you'll get drowned in the storm.'

There was only one sentry on duty at the fort, for the others had been co-opted to defend the settlement against the Iroquois.

Fortunately the rain was easing off.

'Go and waken Madame Carrère,' Angélique asked Séverine. 'And get one of her boys, if available, to run to the Indian village and bring back old Vatiré.'

She rushed off into the night towards Abigail's house.

A cold, wet wind was driving before it enormous, turgid clouds, black as soot across the grey texture of a moon-lit sky. From time to time they were traversed by streaks of lightning and the rumble of thunder mingled with the roar of the raging sea.

'Oh God,' she said, 'please God, take pity on Abigail.'

As she reached the hut, the sky was rent once more and the torrential rain began again.

She hurried inside.

'Here I am,' she called as soon as she had crossed the threshold, to reassure the poor lonely girl in the neighbouring room.

The fire in the hearth was out.

Little Laurier was sitting there on his bed in his nightgown, frightened and shivering.

'You go on up to Séverine's loft and get warm in her bed,' she told him. 'Have a good sleep, for tomorrow you'll be busy running round to all the houses telling them the good news.'

She went in to Abigail.

'Ah, there you are, there you are,' said the young woman in a shaky voice. 'What is to become of me? . . . Gabriel is not here!

And I'm already suffering so much that I don't feel that I can bear any more.'

'Come now, come, you mustn't get worked up so soon about things.'

She put down her bag and took Abigail's hand and the young woman clung to her.

As she felt a pain coming on again she grew tense.

'It's nothing,' Angélique assured her in her most persuasive tones. 'It's only a pain that comes and then goes away again. Keep your courage up for just a few seconds . . . there now, that's good. You see, it goes away again . . . Like the storm . . .'

Abigail gave a faint smile, then relaxed, and her whole expression grew calmer.

'I suffered less that time,' she said, 'probably because of your being here and your healing hand.'

'No, it's not that. It's above all because you are less frightened and tense. You see it's quite easy. All you have to do is not to be frightened.'

She wanted to move away to light the fire, for it was cold. But Abigail held on to her.

'No, please, don't leave me.'

She seemed as if she would lose her head again, so Angélique assured her that she would not leave her for a single moment.

'Is it really you, my brave Abigail, in this state?' she scolded her gently. 'I don't recognize you. You have to face harder things than this. What is this fear that has suddenly got the better of you?'

'I'm guilty,' said the poor young woman with a shudder, 'I have received too much . . . too many joys. I have been too happy in Gabriel's arms, and now the moment has come when I must pay for this pleasure. God will punish me . . .'

'No! No! My dear girl! God is not such a miserable wretch as that . . .'

Angélique's joke wrested Abigail from her anxiety, and although another contraction assailed her, she could not help laughing.

'Oh, Angélique, you are the only person who could think of a reply like that.'

'What reply? What did I say?' asked Angélique, who in her anxiety had hardly noticed her own words. 'Oh Abigail, you see how easy everything is now. You have just had a contraction and yet you are almost laughing . . .'

'It's true that I feel much better . . . but doesn't that mean that things are not going well and that labour is stopping?' she asked, once again full of anxiety.

'No, on the contrary, your contractions are longer and deeper because you're not resisting them. It is our fears that increase our difficulties. Why try to interpret the justice of our Creator? Tell me that, my dear friend. Trust the advice we were given in both the Old and the New Testaments, "Be fruitful and multiply . . . love one another." The conceiving of a new life is something sacred too as is the birth of a child. You have served God well in conceiving this child with joy. Now you must serve Him again by fulfilling with courage and joy what He asks of you today, namely to bring into the world a new being for His glorification . . .'

Abigail had been listening to her avidly. Already her eyes were aglow and her face transformed, having regained its habitual serenity.

'You are wonderful,' she whispered. 'You've told me exactly what I longed to hear. But don't leave me,' she added childishly, still clinging to Angélique's hand.

'I must light that fire . . .'

'Whatever is Madame Carrère doing?' she thought to herself. 'She's not the sort of woman to worry about poking her nose outside when it's raining. It isn't natural . . .'

Time seemed interminable. She dared not leave Abigail's bedside, for although she was now calm and full of courage, she was reaching a critical stage.

Finally Angélique heard with relief a sound at the door, but Séverine came in alone looking like someone just saved from drowning.

'Where's Madame Carrère?' Angélique asked.

'They can't get her to wake up.'

Séverine seemed completely at a loss.

'How do you mean, they can't get her to wake up?'

'She's asleep!' Séverine replied, flustered. 'We shook her, we tried everything. She's asleep, and snoring, there's nothing we can do.'

'And what about old Vatiré?'

'One of the boys has set off for the village.'

'What's going on?' Abigail asked, opening her eyes and growing agitated once again. 'Is there something wrong? Is my labour going on normally?'

'Yes, of course. Truly, my dear, I have never seen a confinement go so smoothly.'

'And yet the child is the wrong way up.'

'That will make things still easier if you are brave about it. When the time comes you must make a tremendous effort and not give up.'

She whispered to Sévérine:

'Run and fetch the nearest neighbour. Bertille . . .'

The unfortunate Sévérine disappeared into the darkness again, not even bothering to pull her skirt up over her head to protect herself from the deluge. She was very soon back again.

'Bertille doesn't want to come. She says she's frightened of the storm. And also that she's never seen a baby born before . . . and also that she can't leave Charles-Henri all alone. Her husband is on watch. I can help you, Dame Angélique.'

'Yes, of course you can. There's no time to lose now. Light a fire, and get some water on the boil. Then go and change your clothes, you poor child.'

'She's a good girl,' said Abigail softly.

Now she was astonishingly calm. Sévérine lit a fire, hooked a cauldron over it, and put on a dry dress before bringing Angélique a stool. Then she brought a second stool on which to place the instruments Angélique might need. Angélique gave her a small bag of simples with which to make an infusion.

'Let's hope that Vatiré gets here in time,' she thought.

She could see now that the baby was well down in the pelvis.

'I can feel a tremendous force inside me,' said Abigail, suddenly lifting herself up and propping herself on her elbows.

'It's coming. Take heart! Don't stop now . . .'

Then suddenly Angélique found herself holding a tiny reddish glistening bundle by the feet, and in sheer delight, holding it up like an offering.

'Oh, Abigail,' she said, 'oh my dearest, here's your baby! . . . Look! Look at it . . .'

The newborn baby's cry burst forth like a fanfare. Angélique had not even noticed in the emotion of the moment that tears were running down her cheeks.

'It's a girl,' said Abigail, with inexpressible joy.

'Isn't she beautiful,' Sévérine exclaimed, as she stood there very straight, arms outstretched, and fingers spread like one of the enraptured onlookers in a Christmas crib. Then she burst forth in a peal of wondrous laughter.

'What an idiot I look!' thought Angélique to herself. 'There they are, the two of them, completely natural and happy, and I am the one who's weeping . . .'

She swiftly cut the cord and wrapped the baby in a shawl.

'Hold her, will you,' she said to Sévérine. 'Hold her in your arms.'

'What a beautiful thing the birth of a child is,' said Sévérine in ecstasy. 'Why should people not want you to watch it?'

She sat down on a stool, clasping her precious bundle to her.

'What a pretty darling she is! She grew quiet as soon as I held her.'

The afterbirth followed without a hitch. The baby was tiny, and the mother had not even been torn.

The ease with which the birth had taken place had thrown them into utter confusion.

'I'm trembling all over,' said Abigail, 'I can't stop my teeth chattering.'

'That's nothing to worry about. I'll put some hot stones round your feet, and then you will feel better.'

She hastened over towards the fire.

'And now it's your turn to admire your daughter,' said Angélique when she saw her friend cosily tucked in, and propped up restfully on her pillows. She took the baby from Sévérine and laid her in Abigail's arms. 'She looks as sweet and lovely as her mother. What will you call her?'

'Elizabeth! In Hebrew it means House of Joy.'

'Can I come and see?' Laurier asked in his thin little voice from high up in his attic.

'Yes, come and help us get the cot ready.'

Rain was still pattering on the roof but in the tiny wooden house its noisy hammering did not reach the ears of those who danced their dazzled attention on the new arrival.

Master Berne came home to find the table laid with the best table-cloth, silver candlesticks and white candles made of beeswax, with the 'company' china set around a steaming soup tureen. The whole house was lit up and a fire burned merrily in the hearth.

'What's going on?' he asked as he laid his musket against the side of the door. 'Any one would think it was an epiphany meal!'

'Come and see, Father!' cried Laurier.

The poor man could not believe that everything had occurred without hindrance, and that the child was there and

Abigail hale and hearty. So great was his joy that he was unable to utter a word.

'And what about the Iroquois?' asked Abigail.

'Not a trace of Iroquois, nor indeed of any war-party, Abenaki or other. I'd like to know who sent us on that wild goose-chase on a hellish night like this!'

Some time later, Angélique left the happy family and set off back to the fort. Dawn was not far off, but the night was still black on account of the huge clouds piled up in the sky. And yet it had stopped raining. A surprising calm had followed the dreadful din of wind and thunder. Exhausted nature seemed to be panting for breath, and above the trickle of a thousand tiny streams, suddenly the sound of crickets could be heard like an orchestra celebrating the end of the storm.

Halfway back to the fort Angélique met a young lad soaked to the skin, carrying a lantern. It was Madame Carrère's eldest son.

'I've just come back from the Indian village,' he said.

'But you haven't got old Vatiré with you.'

'I couldn't have brought her to you even on my back. She must have bartered some spirits recently from the sailors because I found her dead drunk . . .'

CHAPTER 29

WHAT WOULD have happened if . . .

That was the thought Angélique could not get out of her mind . . . And her joy and relief at Abigail's easy confinement could not restore her calm. She would have liked to remember the past few hours only for their intense happiness, but a shadow lay over them.

What would have happened if Abigail's confinement had not proved to be an easy one? To start with, Master Berne's absence that evening had upset her. Her solitude had made Abigail lose her head, and Angélique had arrived just in time to save her from panic. Then Madame Carrère's indisposition, the absence of the old Indian medicine-woman, and the storm.

Master Berne had asked who could have played such a trick on them as to send them off on a wild goose chase after the Iroquois on such a night . . .

Angélique could not help feeling that there was some mysterious link between this and the false messages given to her and to Joffrey in an attempt to deceive them. Such breaches of faith, breaking as they did all the laws of the sea and of the New World, could only have originated from their enemies and could only have been premeditated. She must question Berne and try to find out who had reported the approach of an Iroquois war party, just when Abigail was about to give birth to her child . . .

And what about old Vatiré? That was plausible. The old Indian lady could have been tempted by alcohol, although generally speaking she was sober. She was no longer in the habit of going out to the ships and trading a few furs for a pint or two of brandy. Someone must have taken it to her! But why precisely, almost criminally, that very evening, that very night!

And then there was the storm, the storm on top of everything else.

'But *who* could turn on a storm just to harm us? . . . Oh, I am going out of my mind! It is ridiculous to read into these circumstances any evil design. Who would wish for Abigail's death? . . .'

She looked up at the sky all washed with pink as it emerged from the sombre tempestuous night. Grey tow-coloured clouds scudded over the horizon to make way for a pearly dawn. A bitter, cutting wind was all the reminder of the violence of the night.

Angélique found it impossible to sleep. She leaned against her window, watching for the full dawn, talking to herself and to the kitten, which sat listening to her, head on one side, as if sharing her anxiety.

As soon as she saw Gouldsboro begin to come alive, she could not resist going off to the wharfside inn, her little companion at her heels, springing over the rivulets of water that cascaded down the beach.

'What is all this about your being unable to waken your mother last night?' she asked one of Madame Carrère's daughters who was alone in the kitchen, hooking the saucepans up on the pot-hanger over the monumental fireplace.

'But it's the absolute truth. And she's still asleep,' the girl told Angélique with some anxiety. 'She doesn't seem to be sick, but it's not normal to sleep like that, especially through all the din we made around her last night.'

'You shook her? You shouted at her?'

'Yes, of course!'

'It *is* worrying. Even a very tired person wakes up when given a good shake. Something must have happened to her. Take me to her quickly!'

Madame Carrère was snoring noisily, lying on her back, the sheet pulled up under her chin, with her mouth half open. She looked as if she would sleep on peacefully till doomsday.

Yet her complexion looked normal and her heartbeat was firm.

Angélique gave her a good shake, and called her without producing anything more than a few groans. In sheer despair she prepared a very strong infusion to strengthen the heart, and although Madame Carrère's reflexes worked perfectly to make her swallow the drink they gave her, she still failed to wake up. After about an hour she seemed to be sleeping more lightly, so Angélique, after looking in on Abigail, returned to her bedside to watch over her. The poor woman only awakened towards one o'clock in the afternoon.

She seemed dazed and it took her some time to grasp why her family, all the neighbours, and Angélique were standing anxiously round her bed.

'It was that coffee of yours,' she said in some vexation to Angélique, 'I felt funny almost as soon as I had drunk it at your place. I remember feeling as if my legs wouldn't support me any more. I thought I'd never manage to get back to the inn, I was hardly able to undress. There was a taste of iron in my mouth.'

'My coffee? But I drank some myself,' Angélique protested. 'No,' she corrected, 'now I remember, I made myself some after giving you my cup, but I never drank it! But Madame de Maudribourg drank some and she . . .'

She broke off. Had anyone seen the Duchess of Maudribourg during the course of that day? Everyone shook their heads. Perhaps Aunt Anna asked her to stay for lunch and a chat . . .

Angélique ran off to the old lady's house. The kitten leapt along at her heels.

She found Aunt Anna on her threshold talking to a neighbour about the happy arrival of little Elizabeth.

'Have you seen Madame de Maudribourg?' she called to her, panting for breath.

Aunt Anna shook her head.

'No, I haven't heard a sound from there, I thought she must be away; maybe she went out before I woke up to hear the Jesuit say Mass.'

Angélique went round the house and banged on the door of the lean-to shed where a bed had been installed for the Duchess.

There was no reply, and the door was bolted on the inside.

'We must break down the door,' she said to the neighbour.

'But why?' he asked in astonishment.

'Knock again,' Aunt Anna suggested, 'she must be asleep.'

'Hi, my lady, wake up,' shouted the neighbour battering his hefty fist against the door.

'It's no use, I assure you, we shall have to break the lock.'

'Wait a moment, I think I can hear someone moving inside.'

They heard a slight sound, followed by hesitant footsteps approaching the door. After some fumbling, the bolts were slid back and Ambroisine appeared in the half-opened doorway in her nightdress, still half-asleep.

'What are you doing here?' she asked in some astonishment. 'I've only just woken up. What time is it?'

'Very late,' Angélique replied. 'Ambroisine, how do you feel?'

'Perfectly well ... thank you ... only my head feels heavy and I have a taste of iron in my mouth.'

Exactly what Madame Carrère had said!

There was no shadow of doubt; it *was* the coffee! It must have contained some drug which had made the two women who drank it fall fast asleep for many long hours.

In her memory she saw Madame Carrère coming in and saying to her: 'Oh, how good your coffee smells!' 'Have *my* cup,' had been her reply.

Had Madame Carrère not arrived at that moment, *she* would have drunk that coffee, and *she would have gone to sleep* just when Abigail needed her help. It would have been of no avail for people to shake her, to call her ... Abigail would have had to go through her ordeal alone, and with her guilt feelings and her tension, she would have given way to panic, surrounded by frightened and incompetent neighbours and the din of the storm. At the best the child would have died, and possibly the mother too!

So it was true, that someone had wanted Abigail dead! But why?

'What is the matter?' Ambroisine stammered, 'you seem unwell. Has something dreadful happened?'

'No, no, thank heavens. Go back to bed again, Ambroisine, you can hardly stand up.'

'I'm terribly hungry,' the Duchess wailed like a small child, putting one hand on her stomach.

'Aunt Anna, have you any broth to give her?'

'I've got some sorrel soup!'

'But what is wrong with you?' Ambroisine asked again. 'You are deathly pale ... Why have I woken up so late? Something dreadful has happened, hasn't it?'

'No, no, on the contrary! ... Something wonderful. Little Elizabeth has arrived ... Abigail's baby.'

She added with a kind of defiance: 'You see, she didn't die!'

'God be praised!'

Ambroisine de Maudribourg clasped her hands, bowed her head and fervently murmured an act of thanksgiving. Standing there in her delicate nightdress she suddenly looked like a kind of angel with a strange charm.

'But then why are you looking so upset?'

'It's nothing! Just the emotion and fatigue of the night. And you frightened me with that long sleep of yours ...'

'I must throw out that coffee,' she thought.

She turned round and saw the kitten standing behind her. His hair was on end, his back arched, and he was puffing and spitting, staring at no one knew what.

Angélique caught hold of him and lifted him up towards her face. She would have liked to have discovered his secret by exploring the depths of his wide-open agate-coloured eyes.

'What is it you can see?' she said to him in a whisper. 'Tell me. *Whom* can you see? ...'

CHAPTER 30

A PRIEST ... a Black Robe from whom to seek advice. That was the need Angélique felt as she went to look for Father Maraicher de Vernon. It seemed to her that a man endowed with a sacred character would be better able than she was to sort out what was happening to her. She felt inclined to tell him everything but was not sure whether she would do so. Yet the old reflex, born of a religious upbringing, mingled with prayers and processions, was impelling her towards him. He was 'the priest'. He had bought dearly – at the cost of his asceticism, his withdrawal from the world – the right of insight into the obscure mysteries that govern the actions of men.

Why had Father de Vernon set up the cross in this place, as if he reckoned upon staying a long time? Did he intend by this sign to take possession of it? There, stationed between Catholic Gouldsboro and Protestant Gouldsboro, was his tiny encampment, which also enjoyed an open view over Camp Champlain and the Indian village. The tall wooden cross rose up against a background of trees and sky. The clearing in which he had erected the cross, the cabin, the confessional and the altar, was fringed with willow herb and sprinkled with junipers and a few bitter-smelling plants.

On emerging from among the trees you immediately became aware of the thunder of the waves, and from time to time, white plumes of foam appeared over the rocky edge, like some huge inquisitive animal, peeping furtively into an unfamiliar world.

The little Swedish boy was sitting in front of the hut hollowing out a shepherd's pipe.

Then Angélique caught sight of Father de Vernon at the far end of a rocky promontory. His black soutane stood out against the horizon that had once again become brilliant blue flecked with white. He was standing with his bare feet firmly planted wide apart, heedless of the spray thrown up from time to time by the waves.

As Angélique approached him, she realized that he was

looking towards Gouldsboro with its roadstead, its beach, its port over to the left and its 'pale wooden houses'. He was tense with concentration, as if desperately trying to fathom the secret of the picture spread out before him along the curving shore.

He did not hear Angélique approach, and she felt suddenly convinced that he was conjuring up in his mind's eye the Quebec nun's vision and comparing it with what he saw.

When he turned towards her, she said to him with a slightly disillusioned smile:

'You're thinking that it was Gouldsboro that Sister Madeleine saw in her vision! . . .'

He stared at her, his gaze deliberately cold and vacant. She felt powerless to convey to him the truth about Gouldsboro, with its will to survive outside the realm of mystical conflict and to make its own contribution to the creation of happiness, prosperity, and love.

'But why Gouldsboro?' she sighed.

'And why not Gouldsboro?' he retorted sarcastically.

As she looked at his proud face, his haughty stance and his chill expression, she was assailed with doubt. Supposing he was the hidden enemy! Or rather, behind him, the fanatical figure of Father d'Orgeval! She could not forget that it had been Father de Vernon who had come to fetch her off Gold Beard's ship.[1] On whose orders was he acting?

But then she remembered Jack Merwin as he had been, chewing his quid of tobacco and manoeuvring his sail, and her apprehension fell away. This man who had saved her from drowning, who had borne her in his arms and given her hot broth to revive her, could not be her unmitigated enemy. She must find courage to face him and find out what his intentions were.

She looked up at him.

'Well, what do you feel about it?' she asked with bravado. 'Could the she-devil appear in Gouldsboro?'

'Yes, I think she could,' he replied looking her straight in the eyes.

Angélique felt herself grow pale under the sting of the answer.

'So you are our enemy then?'

'Who said I was?'

'You are under Father d'Orgeval's orders, aren't you? He has

1. See *The Temptation of Angélique.*

sworn to destroy us. So he has sent you to spy on us, to destroy us . . . I remember . . .'

She took a step back and cried out in a kind of despair:

'You stood watching me dying! Yes, when I was drowning off Monhegan Point, you watched me drowning . . . I saw it in your eyes when you refused to hold out a hand to help me . . . But it's one thing to decide, under orders, that someone should die and quite another to watch them struggling in the throes of death. That you could not do!'

As he listened, he watched her sharply but remained impassive. And when she fell silent, panting for breath, he asked her calmly:

'May I ask you, Madame, the object of your visit to my encampment today?'

'I'm frightened,' she said in a burst of frankness.

She had stretched out her two hands before her as she spoke, and was surprised when he – a Jesuit – grasped them and held them firmly for a moment between his own.

'I am glad that you have come to me in spite of the evil designs you attributed to me,' he said. 'I am at your disposal to help you find your courage once more.'

She no longer knew what to say. Merwin's action had been so unexpected . . . and such a comfort, too.

She looked anxiously at him trying to understand what it was that activated this inscrutable personality.

A wave broke over the end of the promontory and a great plume of snowy spray shot up beside them to an incredible height, and a wind-borne shower of sparkling salty droplets sprinkled them both. They moved a few steps apart, and now Angélique found herself hesitant to speak.

'I don't know what is going on here, but I have a feeling that someone is so bent on destroying us that I cannot bear it any more. Who could want to destroy us? Is it Father d'Orgeval, Merwin? If you know, I beg you to tell me. Was it he who told you that I was on board Gold Beard's ship? Was it on his orders that you came there to fetch me?'

He denied nothing, but neither did he admit anything. She felt that he knew more than she did about the mysteries that surrounded her, but that he had not made up his mind to tell her the result of his reflections. Was he on his guard against her? Was he working for their enemies?

'English Puritans, French heretics,' he said all of a sudden, 'a band of lawless pirates, gentlemen of fortune ready for any violent deed – there's the population of Gouldsboro for you. How could such a sink of iniquity manage to live peaceably and not attract suspicion from Canada?'

'That's a very summary judgement,' Angélique protested. 'You yourself have seen that our population consists almost entirely of industrious families with a patriarchal way of life, even the pirates have decided to turn over a new leaf. The atmosphere is one of considerable propriety. Of course we have some fun from time to time, but you yourself did not consider it beneath you to provide some of the entertainment. As for the English Puritans, you know very well that they are refugees from New England. Why should they be deprived of their right to live? Haven't enough people already died on the other side of the Bay ... Oh, Merwin,' she continued in distress, 'don't you remember the little English children on Long Island who sang us a ballad about their shells? And now they are dead ... rumour has it that the islands in Casco Bay have fallen into the hands of the Abenakis ...'

'Well now, that's where you are wrong,' he replied sharply. 'They are not dead. Those islands are still waiting for the Indian canoes to attack them, and those little English children for whom you are shedding tears are still, I warrant, looking for shells and singing. And all thanks to you, or through your fault, according to the way you look at it!'

'What do you mean?' she cried looking at him in amazement.

'I mean that the departure, or rather desertion of Piksarett upset all the Indians' plans. The Indian war died out like a fire without fuel. The tribes he had led from the north headed back towards Quebec with their hostages. Those that had moved down to the south to await his arrival saw that he was more concerned with following you, Madame, in your peregrinations, than with leading his troops into battle. So you see, there was no Indian war in our lands without the great warrior of Acadia.

'After a few skirmishes, the Indians gave up the pursuit. So there, are you satisfied with your handiwork! Yes, it seems you are ...'

He had seen her face brighten. For the news that the children of Long Island had been spared had given Angélique such a sense of relief and joy that she suddenly felt her face grow pink.

'So they're alive,' she said, with shining eyes. 'God be praised!'

The Jesuit stood stroking his chin as he looked at her, and a humorous glint appeared in his eyes.

'You must admit, Madame, that Father d'Orgeval has good reason to resent you. A campaign that falls flat on its face, his Great Convert, his favourite son, shamelessly shirking his duty as chieftain in a holy war, and all because he has met the Lady of the Silver Lake. That's the name by which you are known in Quebec, which is sharply divided about you. Your power over so awkward a customer as Piksarett obviously smacks of witch-craft to anyone who does not know you. And there had already been certain changes of opinion about you, that were difficult for my superior to stomach; for example when Monsieur de Loménie-Chambord, who is his best friend, became your most outspoken advocate. That really hurt. How can he fail to consider you a dangerous enemy, when Monsieur de Peyrac's settling on these shores already looks like undermining the basis of all our work in Acadia, and when your presence at his side seems to have deprived Father d'Orgeval as if by magic of his staunchest allies.'

'But all we wanted was a place in which we could survive. America is a huge country still scarcely populated. We wish no one any ill, so how are we bothering him?'

'You are setting an example that is at variance with what he would like to impose here. The people of Canada are very willing to convert this world to God, but they are happier on the loose roaming about bartering furs than cultivating fields in the shadow of a church. They are easily led into picking up the irreligious ways of those who may live months on end far from all the sacraments. So you see your example alone represents a temptation for them.

'They come to you because they find the best ironware here and also the possibility of doing some profitable trading with the enemy without getting their hands dirty. I have come across quite a number of these French renegades in the wig-wams round here. Man is by nature a sinner. He loves his own pleasure above all else. The English want to pray in their heretical fashion and are prepared to go to any lengths in order to win the right to do so, while the French want to roam about the woods and grow rich by trading furs . . .'

'And what about you, my Father, what is your special pleasure?'

Thus interrupted, the Jesuit paused for a moment, then replied, 'To gain new souls for the Church and to keep those she already possesses.'

Another wave broke. This time the white plumes that had spread out across the blue of the sky, as if in an outburst of magnificent anger, fell further off, but one of the breakers washed over the edge of the rocks, swiftly rushed towards them, and swirled round their feet right up to the ankles.

'We mustn't stay here,' said Father de Vernon, 'the tide is coming in, and the sea is treacherous as you and I have every reason to know.'

They walked for a moment in silence, side by side, following a path that led to the grassy esplanade. The willow-herb spread right down to where they stood, a frail, invasive, pink and mauve army.

Angélique felt his arm slipped under hers in an instinctive gesture of protection. This man certainly did not behave like an ordinary Jesuit.

But she was not expecting the deadly blow he was about to deal her. Suddenly he spoke:

'You will not survive! Your work is doomed to failure, for no matter how far one goes, a guilty life carries with it its own condemnation.'

'What are you talking about?'

'About you, Madame, you in particular, and your past crimes.'

Suddenly her blood boiled.

'You have gone too far, Merwin,' she cried, snatching away the arm he still held, while her eyes flashed with anger. 'What do you know of my past? I am no criminal.'

'Indeed? . . .' he said ironically. 'Is it virtuous women then, who are branded with the Fleur de Lys back in France? . . . Imperfect as justice is over there, I still do not think it has reached that degree of unpredictability . . .'

Angélique felt the blood drain from her cheeks.

With what docility and naïvety had she fallen into his trap! Apart from Count Peyrac, there were only two men in the whole world who knew that she had been branded with the Fleur de Lys – Berne, who had been present at the branding in the little courtroom at Marennes,[1] and this Jesuit, who had saved her from drowning at Monhegan. She remembered his bare hands on her flesh as he rubbed her down to revive her. It

1. See *Angélique in Revolt*.

was then that he must have seen the terrible brand of the Fleur de Lys on her bare back. She realized that some explanation was called for. Either she must tell him everything about herself or run the risk of his erroneous suppositions that would only make the lack of harmony between them and New France even more dangerous.

She began to recover her self-possession. If she was to tell him the truth, there was only one possible way for him to know everything there was to know about her without doubting her words.

'Father,' she said looking him square in the face, 'in spite of the small regard in which you must hold me – and I realize that you are aware of a secret which entitles you to such an opinion – do you think me capable of committing sacrilege? . . . I mean, to use the sacraments for purposes that are evil?'

'No,' he assured her spontaneously, 'I do not think you capable of that!'

'Well then . . . would you, Father . . . hear my confession?'

CHAPTER 31

THE SWEDISH boy had wandered away from the encampment, looking for hazelnuts in the undergrowth.

The confessional consisted of a piece of lattice-work fencing, with a seat on the confessor's side and bare earth on the other for the penitent's knees. The roof was rounded and the walls of elm-bark roughly assembled over a framework of supple poles but had neither doors nor curtains. Both confessor and penitent, while almost invisible one to another through the screen of reeds, could nevertheless, each from his own side, look out towards the sea if they so wished.

Angélique knelt down.

Father de Vernon took a white surplice from the stool, slipped it over his soutane and placed the embroidered stole round his neck.

Then he sat down and leaned forward.

'How long is it since your last confession?'

The question caught her unawares. It was lost in the mists of time. Then suddenly she saw again in her mind's eye the Abbey of Nieul, the high throne-like chair on which the Father Abbot had sat with his pale face framed in his white monk's hood, and the boundless affection in his dark eyes.

'Not for . . . four or five years, I think,' she replied.

The Jesuit started.

'And you make that admission without embarrassment . . . but, my child, have you forgotten all your duties towards God, the Church and yourself? . . . You have been living in a perpetual state of mortal sin, and you seem scarcely moved by the fact. And yet, were you to die tomorrow, you would be handed over to Hell and Satan for all eternity! . . .'

Angélique remained silent.

'Confess your sins now,' he said, 'so that at least you may be pardoned for this appalling negligence.'

'I want to make a general confession,' she said.

'Very well, I am listening.'

She could have chosen only to mention the sins she had committed since her last confession, but a general confession covered the whole of her life. He would know everything there was to know about her. But although in so doing she was possibly exposing herself to a representative of their worst enemies, she knew that in kneeling here as she was she had scored a point. For the seal of confession would bind him to absolute and complete secrecy.

It was an absolute rule. And never had there been a single example of a priest ever breaking it.

After reciting the Confiteor and affirming according to the established formula that she undertook to sin no more, Angélique began to wonder where she should begin.

Her life had not been simple. Circumstances had made her a rebel, not a criminal, and the reason why she had been branded with the Fleur de Lys was that that she had been mistaken for a Huguenot. This she explained to him.

'Why did you not exculpate yourself from this charge by refusing to allow yourself to be called a heretic, even if only to escape the terrible penalty they imposed on you?'

She had to explain to him how she had been in hiding, since the King's police had set a price on her head . . . There had also been her child, abandoned in the forest, tied to a tree . . . She had been leading a war: she was the rebel of Poitou.

He listened without apparent emotion and appeared unmoved by her admission that she herself had killed two men, brushing this information aside with a wave of his hand. But he lingered much longer over the question of her morality: her lust, her adultery, how she had deceived her husband over and over again . . .

'But I thought he was dead, Father!'

'And what about the virtue of purity? It would seem you care little for that, my child!'

She felt like shrugging her shoulders, like saying to him that it was of no importance. She was getting muddled! How far off it all was. Another life, another world!

What emerged from all this confused jumble was a sense of horror and powerlessness, and by contrast there arose within her an inexpressible feeling of relief at the thought that now she was free, loved, and protected on American soil.

'Don't you understand, Merwin, that at last we can live in happiness and freedom, free in our convictions and our preferences . . . Please, I beg you . . . Let us live!'

'My child, do not forget that you are here to confess your sins, not to look for excuses or gain support. All your life you have tried to ignore, out of weakness, thoughtlessness or discouragement, the Church's teachings telling you to be chaste and virtuous. Nevertheless I will give you absolution, for Jesus was indulgent to the adulterous woman, he was indulgent to the sinner who came to him out of love and anointed his feet with perfume . . . In this spirit, now recite your act of contrition.'

And he helped her to recite the words she had forgotten, then blessed her as he absolved her of her sins.

In spite of his culture, his austere and universal vision, his calloused hands and bare feet brought him close to her. His fight with the bear had won over the entire population of Gouldsboro, for the Huguenots had sensed his humanity. They felt that he too was a seafaring man, bound by the messages of the winds, the secrets of the swell and the storm, a man of the harbours and inlets of the American coastline. But what would be his final decision about them?

In spite of the great flood of hope and joy that had overwhelmed her after her confession – without knowing exactly why – Angélique wished to remain prudent.

There was a moment's silence.

Then he spoke again in deliberately non-committal tones.

'Please do not conclude that because I performed an elementary action of humanity on your behalf at Monhegan, that I should therefore be considered your ally. The distance between us still remains the same.'

'No, not quite the same,' Angélique replied with a sudden laugh. 'You have dragged me by my hair across the beach and I have been sick over your waistcoat. Whether we like it or not these things draw people together and create bonds, even between a penitent and her confessor . . .'

Her humour broke down the Jesuit's defences, and he suddenly began to laugh heartily.

'All right then,' he said, 'I grant you that even if in your independence, your . . . proclaimed neutrality, you are not explicitly on the side of New France's enemies, neither do you rank among her friends.

'You must admit that it is not easy to regard you as harmless,' Father de Vernon went on. 'Take for example your present Governor, Colin Paturel. He is a corsair who received his letters patent in Paris and acquired lands in the region by legitimate means, who at the same time undertook to serve the New France missions, and I find him here, an ally of yours, in other words on your side. How did you manage to get round him, so that even when deprived of his spoils, he grants you such obvious fidelity?'

'Perhaps Colin realized that people were trying to make use of him by sending him to conquer these lands, from those who had as much right to them as he had. Things turned out differently. He is a fair man and we were able to reach an understanding with him.'

'By what artifice?' the Jesuit repeated.

He was sniffing like a dog around these astonishing facts, around the mystery. Then in a moment of impulse he suddenly said:

'He is too much in love with you. And he puts that love before his duty. I don't like him.'

'Believe me, the feeling is mutual. He told me so. He thinks you are too violent for a priest. No doubt as a corsair he was not exactly pleased that you should come right on board his ship and make off with his hostage, the Countess de Peyrac, whom he had managed to capture . . . But he is a very devout man and he would not like to feel that you regard him as an enemy of God and of the Church.'

She gave a sigh and went on:

'So there you are! What would you advise me to do?'

'Go to Quebec,' replied Father de Vernon. 'They must get to

know you there. Your husband is considered a traitor, an enemy of France. Now he is a Gascon by birth, which is something he has in common with our Governor Frontenac. And you should go, especially, in order to allay their fears and doubts.'

'But you must be mad!' she exclaimed in horror. 'Quebec! You know very well I would be welcomed with a hail of stones. The King's Police might well arrest us and throw us in prison.'

'Go there with a show of strength. Your husband's fleet is already far more powerful than that of New France . . .'

'What strange advice coming from you,' she retorted, unable to suppress a smile. 'So you aren't our enemy after all, Merwin.'

He made no reply, but taking off his surplice, folded it carefully and laid it over his arm. She realized that he did not want to go any further.

'Do you intend to stay in Gouldsboro for some time?' she asked him.

'I do not know . . . Now off you go, my child. It's getting late. Some of the faithful may well be coming to say the rosary.'

Docilely she bowed her head to take her leave and began to walk off down the path. Then she changed her mind.

'Father,' she said turning round, 'you did not give me a penitence to perform.'

It was customary at the end of a confession for the priest to suggest a few prayers or some sacrifice or act of devotion to be performed by way of reparation for sins committed.

Father de Vernon hesitated for a moment then his brow puckered and his face assumed a commanding air.

'Well then, go to Quebec!' he reiterated. 'Yes, that is what I order you to do as a penitence. Accompany your husband there. Have the courage to face the city, with neither fear nor shame. After all, it could well be that something good for the land of America will come from all this!'

CHAPTER 32

IN SPITE of Father de Vernon's refusal to answer the question she had asked him, namely whether he was their enemy or not, Angélique felt hopeful.

He was less mystical than Father d'Orgeval, but also less vulnerable, therefore less susceptible to fanaticism. He feared nothing, neither the dialectics of the Protestants, nor the seduction of women, any more than the taverns of New York, the sea, pirates, wreckers, redskins and bears ... His report to his Superior would be that of a man who had reconnoitred the enemy at close quarters.

Would d'Orgeval allow himself to be persuaded?

She suddenly bumped into Cantor who was returning from the port with a band of friends, bearing nets over their shoulders with baskets full of fish, lobsters and shellfish.

The lad embraced his mother impetuously. He was as swarthy as a pirate and never had his emerald green limpid eyes shone with a greater innocence.

He offered no explanation for his absence and she did not want to ask him for one. After all he was the captain of a ship.

But his presence completed her happiness. How lovely everything was this evening! Danger and anxiety seemed to melt away.

She looked up at a flock of birds. The superb sweep and swirling density of these flights, which suddenly darkened the sky, never failed to compel her admiration. Birds meant Gouldsboro and its bay, its islands ... its hidden mystery, Gouldsboro where the visionary nun from Quebec had claimed that the mystical drama of the Demon who had appeared to her in a vision, would be played out.

'... My vision took place at the edge of the sea ... The bay was full of a multitude of islands that lay like sleeping monsters ... I could hear the sound of seagulls and cormorants ...

'Then all of a sudden a very beautiful woman rose out of the water and I knew that she was a demon ... her naked body was reflected in the waters . . . She was riding a unicorn . . .'

'Mere phantasy!

'Nothing is going to happen,' Angélique told herself. 'I shall make sure it doesn't!'

She turned round, and suddenly saw a woman standing looking at her a few paces off, with her dark hair writhing like serpents against the red glow of the setting sun.

'You forgot all about me,' said the voice of Ambroisine de Maudribourg. 'You were watching the birds . . . listening to the cry of the seagulls overhead. It was like celestial music in your ears . . . I saw you close your eyes and smile. How do you manage to love life so much? Those seagulls fill me with nothing but fear. I hear the cries of the dead or the damned, whereas for you they are an enchantment. You love them and you do not love me.'

'You are wrong, Ambroisine. I am very concerned for you.'

She went towards her.

'But every one who lives in Gouldsboro has a claim on my interest and my affection. Whenever you choose we can consider together which is the best decision to take, either that you should have your girls brought back here, or that you should join them at Port Royal . . .'

'But I don't want to go away,' cried Ambroisine wringing her hands . . . 'I want to stay here, on my own, with you . . .'

'But you know, you are their benefactress,' protested Angélique; 'those young women need you. Come now, Ambroisine, you are not a child . . .'

'Yes I am! I am a lost child!' the Duchess cried in despair.

She seemed in no state to listen to reason. Gone was the imperious woman, bold, sure of herself, who up to this point had led the life of a rich, noble and pious widow, given to good works and learned in scientific matters, a woman who never faltered and who had even achieved some measure of happiness and success – that woman seemed to have vanished. Something that had occurred over the past few days, on these shores had broken her.

Angélique laid her hand on Ambroisine's hair and stroked it as she would have done that of a child.

'It's all right,' she said reassuringly, 'have patience! Here you are safe and no one will hurt you. When you feel stronger again we can discuss matters. By the way, I am just off to see Abigail to take her a few gifts my husband and I have prepared for her.

199

Would you care to come with me? The sight of that lovely little baby should make you feel better . . .'

For Abigail there was a Bible covered in gold brocade trimmed with silver with two embossed metal plates depicting the Exodus from Egypt and Esther before Ahasuerus and a scarlet silk layette embroidered in gold with a matching pillow-case and insert for the top of a sheet. To this Angélique had added, for the whole family, a box of English sweets and two jars, one containing green ginger and the other orange flowers.

Cantor, Martial, and the other youths were there, bringing their noisy congratulations to mother and child.

Angélique feared that sooner or later the young woman would begin to tire of so many visits. Abigail herself was growing anxious; her milk was not coming in and she had a slight fever. Angélique promised to prepare her some herbal tea which she would bring the following morning. She gave instructions to Séverine and Aunt Anna to take it in turns to remain at her bedside, and also to Gabriel Berne, who was very attentive to his little family.

She went on to do a few other things accompanied by Ambroisine, but as soon as she was alone that evening her anxieties returned. She was annoyed with herself for not having spoken to Father de Vernon about the diabolical atmosphere that seemed to have come among them. Since he did not appear hostile, why not be more frank with him? But almost immediately her conscience brought her back to a sense of prudence. For a start, the hints, the facts that gave support to her anxiety were only tenuous. As soon as she attempted in her own mind to put them into a certain order, according to a certain logical sequence, she could not find a lead into them. An unknown ship manned by strangers who had appeared to have deliberately given them false information; a woman – two women – who had overslept, undoubtedly under the effect of some drug. But to talk about all this to a confessor who was himself mildly on the defensive with her, was no easy matter. She needed more reliable facts before she could even decide on the source of the danger.

Her mind went back to the matter of the drugged coffee, for without the slightest doubt the sleeping draught, which had put Madame de Maudribourg and Madame Carrère into so prolonged a state of torpor, could only have been placed in the coffee which the two of them, and they alone, had drunk.

Angélique carefully examined the remaining ground coffee,

which seemed completely normal and smelt delicious. If Joffrey had been there, he could have analysed it and found what substance had been added to it.

She thought of asking the opinion of the spice-seller. Perhaps he, with his delicate sense of smell would be able to recognize what was in this one. But she decided not to involve that pirate, who was not even a Gouldsboro man, in this business. In order to avoid any possible accident, even if only to the cat which kept sniffing at the coffee and might well get himself poisoned too, she decided somewhat regretfully to get rid of it.

She herself threw the contents of the tin into the sea then returned to her room, closely followed by the kitten that never left her heels.

How lucky for her that he was there! It was not much but his living presence calmed her anxiety. She lifted him up against her shoulder and stroked him as she stood looking out of the window at Gouldsboro in the night haunted by flashes of distant lightning.

CHAPTER 33

THE FOLLOWING day was particularly hot, for the wind had dropped, the sea was flat and listless, and both forest and earth exuded a white mist through which the sun seemed to shine as if through a layer of translucent porcelain.

Early in the morning, taking advantage of the fact that Ambroisine de Maudribourg was still asleep, Angélique walked up to the Bernes' house with the infusion she had promised. She gave a first cupful to her friend and left the jug on the edge of the hearth near the fire. Abigail was to have two or three cupfuls during the course of the day. But in any case, Angélique would come back that afternoon. Little Elizabeth was an adorable baby who already seemed to be smiling, or at least so Séverine was convinced.

Angélique returned to the Duchess, who was standing on her doorstep looking out at the sea.

'Would you like to come for a walk with me. I want to pick

up some amethysts and agates, to take back to Honorine, my little girl. Apparently there are some fine ones on the beaches ...'

In one hand she held a basket containing a bottle of lemonade and some maize scones.

They found a few stones and a large number of shells, and Angélique talked about Honorine, who would undoubtedly be delighted at all these finds. When they sat down a little later they both felt very thirsty, and Angélique put the bottle to cool in a rock-pool.

'I make this lemonade from the red sumac,' she explained. 'The white sumac is poisonous, it even kills the oaks and yews that grow around it; whereas the berries of the red sumac mixed with maple-sugar then fermented makes the most delicious drink.'

They waited until the bottle was well chilled before enjoying its contents. Ambroisine gave a sigh of childish satisfaction, then lay down on the sand and rested her head on Angélique's knees.

'And what if it were white sumac? ... perhaps we might die?'

'Of course not, don't worry.'

'Poison,' said the Duchess in a dreamy voice that seemed to come from a long way off, 'poison ... that's a word that has haunted me for years. To poison him ... yes, him, the monster ... I wish I had had the courage to do it. I could think of nothing else, my only consolation was to imagine him dying by my hand ... but I was frightened of Hell ... and then in the end he died ... of old age and debauchery ... and I am being punished for those wicked thoughts, by trailing my misery with me, by finding no rest anywhere, even in prayer ...'

'Why did you never remarry? It can't have been due to lack of offers.'

Ambroisine sat up with a jerk.

'Remarry! ... How could you ask such a thing? Oh, how cruel you are as a happy, serene woman! ... To find myself once again the prey of a man? No, I could never do that ... the mere thought of it makes me feel ill: the idea of allowing a man to touch me!'

She bowed her head and her hair rippled over her face, almost masking her delicate Tanagra figurine profile which the heat and her emotion had flushed red. The sun was beginning to turn her bare arms golden, and she ran a finger slowly down one of them in a melancholy caress.

'And yet I am beautiful ... am I not? Who would be able to cure me from so terrible an infirmity: the horror of love ...'

The worldly mask, so carefully erected for the purpose of her Court and scientific contacts, was crumbling. This sickness would be hard to cure. How could she be helped to restore confidence to this wounded femininity? She should have learned this from a priest, but Ambroisine, through long habit, would keep up the play-acting in front of a priest and not be sincere.

It seemed as if Angélique was the only person to whom she had revealed these deep wounds.

Angélique talked to her at length, in an attempt to bring back her zest for life and her confidence in it, and to remind her by various means of the mercy of God and of his love for all his creatures. Ambroisine remained silent and seemed indifferent to her arguments, but Angélique finally had the impression that she had brought her some little comfort.

'You are kind,' the Duchess murmured, putting her arms round Angélique in a spontaneous, child-like gesture, 'I have never met anyone so human as you.'

She closed her eyes and seemed to fall into a sudden restful, restorative sleep. Angélique left her to rest. The confidences she had received had saddened her. She gazed out towards the horizon, wishing she might see the sail of the ship bringing Joffrey back.

She was assailed by memories of those far-off days in Toulouse. She had been only seventeen, and at the age of thirty the great nobleman from Toulouse had seemed to her like an old man, and the wealth of experience that could be read in that sardonic, scarred face had been positively terrifying. He had already experienced all the passions, but where she was concerned, she whom he loved from the very outset with the truest affection, he had shown the greatest possible tenderness. She had been delivered up in all innocence to his every whim, but he had not let her down in love. How could she ever thank God enough for such a gift!

'What are you thinking about?' Ambroisine suddenly asked her in a voice that was all on edge, 'or rather *whom* are you thinking about? You are thinking about him, of course, about him . . . the man you love . . . You are happy, while I have nothing, nothing . . .'

In a frenzy she shook her head so that her hair flew in all directions, then suddenly growing calm again, she begged Angélique to forgive her irritability.

They returned to the village as the heat began to decrease. But still the wind had not risen and the air remained heavy, thick, and sticky against the skin.

Someone came to tell Angélique that Father de Vernon was asking for her, and was waiting somewhere near the fort. The Duchess of Maudribourg waved to him from a distance and made her way towards Aunt Anna's house.

The Jesuit father seemed surprised, almost annoyed.

'I thought Madame de Maudribourg had left Gouldsboro . . .' Angélique tried to explain.

'And what about the King's Girls, where are they?'

'In Port Royal.'

'And aren't they coming back too? I thought some of them were going to marry Gouldsboro men.'

'Did you not strongly advise against such marriages?' Angélique asked in astonishment.

'I?' he replied frowning in his most haughty manner. 'Why should I meddle in that sort of thing?'

'But I thought . . . Madame de Maudribourg told me . . . she must have misunderstood your views on the matter.'

'Yes, I suppose she must have!'

He gave Angélique a penetrating glance and seemed about to say something, but changed his mind.

'You wanted to see me about something?' Angélique asked.

He shook himself, as if regarding the thoughts that tormented him as inopportune.

'Yes . . . I wanted to take my leave of you, for I am leaving the region tomorrow at dawn.'

She was surprised to find how sorry she was. Fear, irrational fear reared its head in her breast.

'Are you going to join Father d'Orgeval?'

'Not for some weeks yet. But I must get a message to him sooner than that.'

'Are you going to plead on our behalf?'

He gave a mildly ironical smile, then he grew serious again, almost sombre.

'You must not count too much on my intervention,' he told her frankly. 'I hate these heretics under your protection.'

'But what about us, Merwin, you don't hate us, do you?'

She looked at him fervidly, urging him to indulgence.

'Me . . . you don't hate? . . .' her glance read.

He gave another smile but shook his head.

'You must realize that I cannot support those who themselves support the henchmen of Satan.'

'But you might suggest to Father d'Orgeval that he could spare us.'

She wished that he would weaken. So that she could retain at least the hope that she had touched that heart of stone. But he never faltered.

'Well then, at least when you see him, will you ask him something from me?' she went on. 'He can hardly refuse me that, even if I am his worst enemy.'

'What is it?'

'Ask him to let me into how he makes his green candles.'

Father de Vernon burst out laughing.

'You really are disarming,' he told her. 'All right! I shall put your request to him.'

And he held out his hand to her as if to seal an alliance. Here again he was not behaving like an ordinary Jesuit, but like a seafarer, a loyal companion who, unwilling to put into words what he feels, expresses his deep feelings in a gesture.

She too grasped that aristocratic hand with fervour, a hand made brown and calloused through the handling of sails. A thought crossed her mind: 'He must not go, for if he goes I shall never see him again . . .'

A flock of screeching birds threw a shadow over the beach and she suddenly felt as if something terrible was about to happen. Fate was on hand and about to strike. Fate. Suddenly it was there behind Jack Merwin, and the terror he saw in her eyes made him wheel round. Behind him, only a few paces away, the Reverend Thomas Patridge was standing motionless, weighty as a stone monument. His eyes alone moved, bloodshot, rolling and darting fire.

Father de Vernon pulled a wry face.

'Welcome to you, pastor,' he said in English.

The minister appeared not to hear him. His scarred face, a deep purplish red, betrayed a fury such as could no longer be expressed in words.

'You henchman of Satan,' he growled at last, as he approached the Jesuit. 'So at last you've got what you wanted, betraying the sacred laws of sanctuary, of honour and of hospitality.'

'What are you growling about there, you old idiot! Henchman of Satan yourself!'

'Hypocrite! Don't imagine that it will be as easy as all that to betray us into the hands of Quebec. I have fought against the redskins to defend my flock, and I shall fight you.'

His massive fist shot out and he struck Merwin full in the face.

'Die, Satan!' he shrieked.

The blood spurted forth, running from the priest's nose over his mouth. Then Patridge struck him again, this time in the stomach. He was about to strike him a third time when the Jesuit retaliated by jumping backwards and kicking his adversary on the chin so that his teeth crunched together.

'Death to you too, Satan!' he cried.

And the two men began to grapple with unbridled fury. In a flash a circle of spectators had formed about them, aghast, thunderstruck, unable to intervene. The quarrel had broken out so rapidly that Angélique scarcely realized what was happening. The deafening sound of the birds as they flew in a sudden whirl overhead, masking with their cries and the beating of their wings the sound of the blows and insults the two men were exchanging, helped to confuse the assembled spectators and give this deathly struggle the air of nightmare.

When the two men fell to the ground, locked in an infernal ferocious embrace, Angélique ran towards them, begging them to calm down and separate, and was almost knocked over herself by a sudden leap the pastor made in disengaging himself from some deadly hold. In so doing he drove his knee with all his strength into his opponent. The Jesuit took the blow in the region of his liver and gave a hoarse cry.

His arm, like a clamp, grasped the shoulders of the Englishman whose face was almost black with congestion, while he raised his other hand and brought it crashing down, edge side on, on to the base of his neck.

'Go and fetch Colin Paturel! He is the only one who can separate them! Quick! Quick! They'll kill one another!' Angélique shouted over the maniac screeching of the birds.

She rushed to meet Colin Paturel as he came striding over.

'Quick, Colin, please! They are fighting to the death! The pastor and the Jesuit!'

Colin rushed forward and pushed his way through the circle of onlookers; then suddenly there was total silence.

Further along the beach the noisy flock of seagulls and cormorants had come to rest on the rocks where they were now stalking up and down. Through the silence a slack wave broke with a silky whisper.

Horror-stricken, unable to utter a word, the men stood looking at the two crumpled bodies, lying like broken puppets on the sand.

'He broke his neck,' someone said.

'He burst his insides,' said another.

His eyes glazed and bulging, the pastor was dead. His enemy was still moving. Angélique fell to her knees beside Father de Vernon, and lifted his wax-like eyelids. His eyes were growing pale with a metallic, blind look about them.

'Father! Father!' she said. 'Can you see me? Can you hear me?'

He stared blindly at her then said in a faint voice:

'The letter ... for Orgeval ... it must not ...'

He gave a gasp, then for a few seconds a rattle came from his throat and he was dead.

In a broken, trembling voice, Angélique tried to explain to Colin what had happened.

'I simply don't understand ... Suddenly there was the pastor, beside himself with rage and he struck the priest ... Of course they have always been enemies ... when we were at sea off Casco Bay, they were always on the point of coming to blows ...'

Colin separated the two bodies and laid them out one beside the other, both big strong men in their black clerical clothes. He closed their eyes and asked for two kerchiefs. Two of the women untied their headscarves and Colin covered the two bruised faces with them.

'Who can say the prayers for the dead for this man?' he asked, pointing to the Reverend Patridge.

Pastor Beaucaire stepped forward, deathly pale, and recited the most important words from the Protestant burial ceremony to which the Protestants gave the response almost in a whisper.

'And what about for him?'

'I will,' stammered the young Capuchin Father, known as Brother Mark, who was still in Gouldsboro.

Being considerably agitated he got all in a muddle with his

Latin, his set prayers and his signs of the Cross. The great Jesuit Merwin would have given him a pitying smile.

'I want some men to serve as bearers!'

Four men stepped forward, but Colin was not satisfied.

'More than that, they're heavy!'

It took eight broad-shouldered men to carry them to their last resting place on the cliff top.

'You're to put them in the same grave,' said Colin.

That grave still stands there beneath the pines among the willow-herbs.

It is not known. It is not remembered. But if you were to brush aside the moss you would find that grey stone, half-broken, on which can still be made out, although much worn, the words the Governor of that distant time had engraved there:

> Here lie two men of God who
> Killed one another to the shout of:
> Death to Satan!
> May they rest in peace.[1]

CHAPTER 34

'WHERE'S THE little boy?' asked Angélique. 'Father de Vernon's young companion, Abbial Neals!'

She had run to the Jesuit's abandoned encampment, then, not finding the child there, had searched everywhere for him. Father de Vernon's baggage must be with him. Jack Merwin's last words haunted her: 'The letter for Father d'Orgeval . . . it must not . . .' That letter was of the greatest importance. Agitated as she was she felt quite sure that everything was explained in that letter. If only she could find it, she would know the identity of her enemies.

What exactly had he been trying to say: that the letter must

1. This fight between a Catholic priest and a Protestant minister is authentically recorded in American history, as is the inscription carved on their common grave.

208

not go to him, or on the contrary that it must not go astray . . .

She got Colin to organize a search for the boy. But when night fell they had to give up.

With the assistance of two English refugees from Camp Champlain they had more or less succeeded in piecing together the origin of the affair. Word had gone round among them that the Jesuit with the connivance of the local Papists, namely Madame de Peyrac and Colin Paturel, was going to take them as prisoners to Quebec. The native impulsiveness of the Puritan pastor had done the rest.

In the gathering darkness Gouldsboro, overwhelmed, lay silent. The cicadas and grasshoppers, masters of the field, sang their hearts out with an innocent exuberance that seemed to mock the sad inhabitants.

Finally Angélique went back to the fort; she dreaded the idea of being alone. When would Joffrey come back?

A minor anxiety added still further to her apprehensiveness. All day long she had not seen her kitten, nor did she find him in her room. Without his sprightly presence, the room seemed lugubrious and chill. The disappearance of the tiny creature struck Angélique as being just as final as that of Merwin, the Jesuit. And she found this absence added still further to her sense of bereavement.

She went downstairs again, determined to find him, but dared not ask the sentries if they had seen the creature. After all that had happened that day, her concern for a cat might have seemed trivial. And yet, for her, it had assumed overwhelming proportions. If she could not find him, if he was dead, she would regard it as a sign that ill-fortune had them all by the throat. She must find him. Just as she had searched earlier for the boy, so she went off now seeking the kitten through the village streets, quietly calling after him. 'Where are you, little one?' she called. 'Puss! Puss!' She searched in the shadow of hedges and leafy places. Then she went down towards the shore, and looked among the small boats that had been drawn up on the beach, among the fishermen's baskets, and over the rocks uncovered by the low tide.

The iridescent moon, enlarged by a misty golden halo, gave sufficient light to guide her steps.

In sheer despair she walked round the port a second time, searching the dark band of shadow at the foot of the wall. Then suddenly she stopped. Were those glow-worms? She glimpsed something shining there, right up against the palisade, in a patch of grass, something that looked like two golden eyes.

'Is that you, little one?' she whispered.

Nothing seemed to move, but she sensed a barely perceptible movement and her heart gave a leap of hope and joy. It was him, of that she felt certain. But why did he not move? . . . she went closer and bent down. This time there was no doubt about it. Two huge eyes stared back at her.

'It *is* you,' she said. 'But what's wrong? Don't you recognize me?'

She stretched forward one hand and as it brushed the kitten's body he gave a piercing cry and she quickly withdrew her hand.

'What's wrong? What's happened to you?' She rushed back to the guard-post.

'Give me a light, please!'

A man took down a lantern and offered to accompany her, but she refused.

She went back to the same spot praying heaven that the kitten would not have run away. Fortunately he was still there, curled up in the thicket, motionless, his head lowered as if in contrition. By the light of the lamp she could see that his little face was spotted with blood.

'What's wrong? What's happened to you? What have they done to you?'

She tried to take hold of him but every time she touched him he let out an agonizing miaow. She finally managed to wrap him in her shawl and hold him against her, where he lay trembling and mewing quietly with pain.

She took him back to her room. When she placed him on the table to examine him he gave one crazed leap off and tried to hide in a corner, according to the supreme instinct of animals who hide themselves to die. And yet he was unable to go very far, and once again curled up on the ground with his little head bowed, as if gathering up all his strength.

She knelt down beside him.

'It's me,' she told him gently, 'don't be frightened, I'll make you better.'

Doing her best not to touch him she tried to see where he was hurt. There was blood running from his nose. There were patches on his body where it looked as if the hair had been torn out and there were traces of blood there too. Had he had a fall? Had he been struck?

Very gently she lifted one of his tiny paws which he was

unable to tuck underneath him and which looked as if it bore traces of burns.

'Could he have stepped into a fire?'

A terrible suspicion was beginning to dawn within her, rising up within her like the surge of the sea, like a black wave ready to break.

'Someone has hit him! ... Someone has deliberately tormented him!'

Her heart almost stopped beating under the effect of the anguish and horror of it all.

'*Who could have done that, who?*'

And she looked around her in terror, searching for some presence in the shadows, trying to descry the face of the monster who wandered among them, invisible, sowing panic, despair and death.

CHAPTER 35

THEN, ALMOST furtively, she went out of the fort again. Clutching the little dying creature to her bosom, she set off towards the Bernes' house. She walked quickly through the darkness, frightened even of the moonlight that might reveal her presence. Fortunately the door stood open and the family were eating their evening meal by candlelight.

Angélique must have seemed upset for Gabriel Berne leapt to his feet and cried out, 'But child, what is wrong? Are you ill?'

' "They" tried to kill my cat,' Angélique replied in a voice that trembled in spite of herself. ' "They" have struck him and tormented him. He's going to die.'

'But who are "they"?'

'The demons ... who are trying to destroy us.'

They looked at her in horror.

'Angélique,' Abigail called, 'come and see me, will you?'

From her bed she could see what was going on in the next room.

'Angélique, come here,' she said gently but insistently, 'put the cat down on the bed. The children will look after him . . . and come and sit down here.'

She held out her hand, persuasive and friendly. Angélique put the kitten down, sat down herself beside the bed and collapsed exhausted against Abigail's shoulder.

'We shall not be able to survive,' she moaned. 'The forces of Evil will win. "They" will get the better of him in the end. He will never come back and I shall die if that happens . . .'

'Don't talk like that.'

Abigail clasped her to her heart. This evening it was her turn to bring comfort.

'Of course he'll come back,' she said reproachfully, almost in a whisper. 'You know perfectly well he will. He survives everything. You said so yourself one day. There isn't a battle from which he does not emerge victorious. In a few days' time, maybe even tomorrow, he will be back here, and then you will laugh at your fears.'

'But what have they done to my kitten?'

'An accident . . . a cart must have struck him, or an impatient sailor pushed him out of his way a bit too roughly . . .'

'He's just drunk a little water,' the children said.

That was a good sign.

'He will survive too,' Abigail assured her. 'Don't forget that cats have nine lives. And doesn't popular tradition have it that they are stronger than demons?'

In the face of such warm friendship Angélique began to feel better again.

'Please forgive me. I really am silly . . . it was the death of the Jesuit that upset me. I know he was a hard man but I was nevertheless very attached to him. And he would have become our ally . . .'

'Stay here with us for tonight,' said Master Berne. 'We should never have left you all alone after the terrible spectacle you witnessed this afternoon. Two men of God!' he muttered, shaking his head. 'Never have the heavens witnessed so desperate a fight . . . Please stay here, Madame, and sleep next to Abigail – I shall sleep in Martial's wig-wam.'

She tucked Laurier in, went up and kissed Sévérine in her loft, covered the fire in the hearth and threw a few leaves of lemon balm on to a little burner to keep away the mosquitoes and the sand-flies.

Then she drew the door half-to between the two rooms, retaining only one candle in Abigail's room, and attended to the baby.

This haven was full of tranquillity, human warmth and tenderness. The tight band round Angélique's heart began to grow less oppressive for here she was safe, among friends.

'While we're on the subject of Martial, do you happen to know what my Cantor is doing? They seem to be associated in some mysterious enterprise.'

'Young people love mystery and they love to feel important,' Abigail replied with a smile. 'Martial gave me to understand that Monsieur de Peyrac had entrusted them with some task to accomplish during his absence, something that involves their sailing among the islands. He did not tell me more than that, but I know that they are reporting to the Governor and taking orders from him each time they return to the fort.'

'Ah good!' Angélique replied and sighed. Better not to worry about Cantor.

Abigail's kindness, serenity, and affection were precious things. During her husband's absence she valued them even more. Far from separating them further and intensifying their educational and religious differences, America had brought them closer together. Lying back against her scarlet silk pillow, Abigail looked very beautiful, with her long golden tresses framing her delicate china-like face.

The baby was good and patient but was sucking vigorously at its fist.

'Have I fed her for long enough?' Abigail asked in some anxiety.

'Did you drink all that infusion I made for you?'

'Séverine forgot to give it to me,' the young mother admitted in some confusion.

'Although I left it where it was clearly visible. What a shame!'

She found the jug at the corner of the hearth where she had left it, but young Laurier had placed a basket of shell-fish in front of it on his return from his fishing expedition, which explained Séverine's forgetfulness.

'It's still warm. I'll give you a cupful,' said Angélique returning to her friend's bedside.

She began to pour out the liquid, but spilt a few drops of it on the scarlet pillow-case, which irritated her.

'Oh never mind. I'd rather make you a fresh lot. They are

very delicate leaves and I can see that the liquid has gone a nasty dark colour.'

She went over to the window and threw the contents of the jug outside, then held the shutter wide open and revelled in the scent of the night air. Lying as it did at the edge of the forest, the house was surrounded by delicate perfumes.

Angélique rinsed out the jug and while it was drying upside down on the wooden draining board, she prepared another infusion in a second container, which Abigail then obediently drank. Angélique took off the soiled red silk pillowcase and replaced it with some clean linen. She drew the baby's cot up beside the mother's bed, and then took another look at her poor little kitten, which was curled up in a corner, fighting with dumb tenacity against pain and death. She had done the best she could to dress his wounds with an ointment, and tried to get him to drink something, but he refused. And yet when she spoke to him he replied with a soft purring little note in his throat. Then she prepared herself for bed. She would leave the window wide open for it was hot. She blew out the candle, leaving nothing but a tiny oil-burning night-light in a coloured glass container in one corner of the room. She removed her bodice and her over-skirt and lay down beside Abigail.

From their bed they could look up at the misty blue night sky with its trembling stars. A light wind stirred the nearby branches and away in the distance they could hear the sealions calling to one another in the bay.

'Abigail,' Angélique said suddenly, 'you did not want the King's Girls to marry the men from Colin's crew, did you?'

Abigail gave a slight shudder.

'Well, I must admit that it would have created certain difficulties, but all things considered . . . it's nothing to do with me,' she replied hesitantly.

'But your husband, and Manigault and the others were against it, weren't they?'

'Yes, they were,' Abigail admitted frankly.

Angélique remained silent for a moment.

'Why did you go and talk to the Duchess of Maudribourg about it, rather than to me?'

Again the young woman shuddered.

'The Duchess wanted to know what I felt about it,' she stammered.

But Angélique had the impression that she had blushed in the darkness. Why did Abigail want to hide the fact that she had been sent by the Protestants to find out what the benefactress's intentions were? No doubt because she disapproved of the attitude of her co-religionists and her husband, and because she was friendly with Angélique, she tried to make light of the veiled opposition which the Huguenots would never cease to feel towards Joffrey de Peyrac.

A fleeting thought occurred to Angélique that perhaps it was among the Huguenots they should seek the ringleader of the plot that was trying to separate them, to demoralize them, and destroy the atmosphere in Gouldsboro. In their jealous eyes, the port was full of far too many undesirables whom Peyrac had admitted. She could quite well imagine one of them stirring up the irascible Patridge against the Jesuit whose presence among them was as intolerable as that of Satan himself.

But they possessed certain characteristics of unbending rectitude, of almost naïve, almost childlike honesty, which was very close to her own conception of life ... and she could not help liking them. Yes, liking them! So it was terribly hurtful to feel that they might possibly still be plotting against them. Suddenly life appeared hopeless, overwhelming ...

She felt Abigail lay her hand on hers.

'My friend,' the young mother murmured, 'don't be sad, everything will be all right. I am here and you are very dear to me. During the winter, how many a time did Gabriel and I talk about you, about Monsieur de Peyrac, about your sons and about Honorine, whom we so dearly love. How often we used to wake up during the night and listen to those terrifying snow-laden squalls blowing overhead, and we thought of you, so far away, lost in the depths of that wild forest, so much alone with your young children and a handful of friends ... It was then that we realized all that you meant to us ... Whenever my heart grew too heavy with anxiety, Gabriel would say to me: "Fear nothing, those people cannot perish! They have the mark of destiny on their brows, they will triumph over everything!" '

Angélique could have no doubts about the sincerity of so warm a friendship, and she put out of her mind all bitter thoughts, retaining nothing but the sweetness of the present hour and finding, in conversation with Abigail, all the comfort she so needed. She spoke of Joffrey, describing him as he had been before the Iroquois, and later at Fort Wapassou, helping each one to live his life.

'What a man! How could I fail to love him?'

Finally they fell asleep like two children.

Somewhere towards the middle of the night little Elizabeth began to cry. Angélique got up and handed her to her mother to feed. While the baby was being suckled, Angélique went over to see whether the kitten had not died. She could not find him. He had moved and she discovered him where he had clambered up into the armchair with its thick cushion. He had no doubt considered that someone as ill as himself had a right to something more comfortable than a wretched corner of a tiled floor.

He gulped down the milk she gave him.

'I think he'll recover,' she whispered happily to Abigail.

'Oh, I'm so glad! And I'm so pleased to see you smiling again.'

Before going back to bed Angélique held little Elizabeth in her arms for a while, rocking her back and forth as she walked round the room humming.

She stopped in front of the open window. The moon was lower in the sky but still flooded the landscape with its milky, unearthly light, and a great tranquillity emanated from this monochrome landscape, pearly grey on an ashen background.

Angélique looked down with a tender smile at the baby's tiny face as she slept in the crook of her arm. The innocence of that face was in harmony with the serenity of the night.

Then suddenly the peace was broken by a kind of lugubrious sob that ended in a terrible, prolonged shriek.

The shriek! It was like the one they had heard before!

And it came from close by.

Angélique leapt back from the window clasping the baby to her. An icy shudder ran through her body.

'What was that?' Abigail asked sitting up in bed. 'Who shrieked like that? I have never heard a cry like it before.'

'I have, once . . . perhaps it's a wild beast.'

'Close the window,' Abigail begged her.

Angélique handed her her daughter then went over to close the shutter, without daring to look out into the darkness. She placed the iron bar across the window.

All the old superstitions of their childhood, so common in the French provinces, flooded back into their memories: the werewolf, the cloven-hooved devil, the dragon, the chimera, and souls in torment.

Angélique decided that since America was a new land they should get rid of all these ancient fears.

On the other hand, there might well be more tangible dangers about them. But Angélique did not want to tell her friend about her certainty that there were unknown persons about who in some mysterious fashion were trying to harm them.

When they woke again the sun must have been already high in the sky, for it was very hot in the airless room.

Angélique thought she heard voices raised in argument, close by, on the other side of the shutter.

It was as if a crowd had gathered in Abigail's garden just outside the window.

She got up, still staggering and only half awake, and drawing the shutter, found herself face to face with a man in a cotton cap, another one wearing a fur hat and some women, among them young Bertille their neighbour.

'What are you all doing in Madame Berne's garden?' she asked.

CHAPTER 36

'YOU'VE KILLED my pig with your filthy concoction!' Bertille shouted bitterly. 'A pig that cost us a fortune. And because it was you, Madame de Peyrac, no one will say anything about it! We'll just have to accept our loss . . .'

'Don't be so aggressive, Bertille, and explain yourself.'

'You've killed my pig,' the young woman repeated.

They were all looking at something that seemed to be lying below the window. Leaning out, Angélique saw a pinkish mound on the ground: the Ramberts' roving pig, which did indeed seem to be well and truly dead.

'What happened to it?'

'You know, your pig used to gobble up anything it came across,' Hervé le Gall remarked to Bertille. 'It must have swallowed something sharp.'

'No, it didn't. Bertille replied obstinately bad-tempered, 'I know what I'm talking about. Yesterday evening I saw Madame de Peyrac throw something out of that window and here we find the pig dead at the very same spot.'

'It was some infusion,' said Angélique. 'It couldn't have drunk that.'

'It could have eaten the rubbish the stuff fell on.'

'It was just a perfectly harmless infusion, I tell you.'

'Then why did you throw it out?'

'Because it was no longer fresh, but it couldn't have harmed anyone in any possible way.'

'And why is your pig always in other people's gardens?' asked the neighbour in the cotton cap. 'Only yesterday it was rooting about in my corn.'

'Do you imagine we can keep it on a lead?' the man in the fur hat replied.

This was Bertille's husband, formerly married to poor Jenny Manigault. Angélique would not have recognized him, for he looked like a fur trapper, his face hardened and unshaven.

She asked them politely but firmly to go and fight it out somewhere else. Germain Rambert asked the other men to help him make a trestle on which to carry the animal who weighed at least two hundred pounds.

Around mid-morning, Bertille appeared again with little Charles-Henri on her arm. It was obvious that she had not come with much good grace, but had felt herself obliged to do so. Somewhat peevishly she asked Angélique whether she could give her an assurance that the infusion she had thrown out contained nothing poisonous. If this were the case, although the pig had died under suspicious circumstances, they might still try to salvage the two hams and smoke them, although it was too late to bleed the beast properly in order to make black-pudding and sausages.

At the mention of the word poison she at first shrugged her shoulders, then suddenly experienced a kind of shock; she had seen the terrible truth. She felt a cold sweat break out on her brow.

'Poison?'

'So it *was* poisoned!' cried Bertille in alarm, at the sight of her face. 'We shan't even be able to salvage a bit of bacon ... You'll have to pay us for this,' she cried, shaking the baby about in her anger.

'Don't be so excited,' said Angélique, 'and so full of recriminations, when it's all due to your own negligence. I assure you once again there was no poison in the liquid I threw out yesterday evening, but in any case I would advise you not to eat the flesh of an animal that has not been bled and that died from unknown causes. You should have fed it on your own garden produce and not on that of your neighbours.'

Bertille went off in a furious rage, shouting that she would complain to Monsieur de Peyrac when he returned. He at least would take a generous view of the matter, that she felt sure.

Angélique tried to dispel the terrible suspicion but could not do so. She tried to remember exactly what had happened on the previous day to the infusion which Bertille was blaming. She had prepared a quantity of it and had given a cupful to Abigail, who seemed to have been in no way upset by it. Then the jug had remained all day beside the fireplace as Sévérine had forgotten Angélique's instructions. When Angélique had gone to make good this neglect, she had clumsily spilt a few drops on the scarlet pillowcase. She had been exasperated and had then noticed the unpleasant colour the medicine had acquired during the day, and had consequently thrown it out of the window and washed out the jug and the bowl. These were made of Nevers porcelain, smooth, hardbaked, and shiny. Once they had been rinsed no trace would have remained of what they had held before. Angélique went outside and walked round the house to examine what was under the window. The place had been cleaned up, so, apart from footprints, there remained no sign of any foodstuff that might have led her to determine what had caused the animal's death.

'But why blame the infusion for killing the pig? It was Bertille who had suggested that. She always made a fuss about everything. Even if that drink had been affected by the heat or by lying around it could scarcely have done any harm. I have seen it used over and over again by nursing mothers . . .'

Once back inside the house she noticed the pillowcase she had removed from Abigail's pillow which she had thrown down in a ball in one corner.

On a sudden impulse she picked it up and spread it out. Where the liquid had splashed it, nasty white marks had appeared contrasting sharply with the brilliant scarlet of the silk. She felt herself grow pale. Such an effect could only come from some poisonous substance easing away the dye and even the material itself.

Angélique remained silent, holding the pillowcase open in front of her. That infusion she herself had prepared for Abigail, was she to think that some criminal hand had deliberately poured deadly poison into it? If so, had Laurier not put down his basket in front of the jug, thus hiding it from view, and had

Séverine not forgotten to give Abigail some of the contents during the afternoon, the young mother would have died a death as terrible as it was sudden. No, she must be going out of her mind! Who could wish for Abigail's death?

'Did you have many visitors yesterday?' she asked, turning towards Abigail who was staring at her but saying nothing.

'Oh yes, lots.'

'Who came? Tell me their names.'

'I can't remember everyone. There were times when I felt very tired and was dozing. But there was Monsieur Paturel and his lieutenant, Monsieur de Barssempuy. And also his quarter-master, Vanneau. He brought me a small object carved from meerschaum. Then the cabin-boy who was shipwrecked on the *Unicorn*. He wanted to give me something too, his carved wooden spoon. But I wouldn't take it, for it's all he has left, the poor lad. Oh, I was forgetting, Julienne came too, the King's Girl who married one of the pirates. She stayed quite a while. She wanted to help me in some way and offered to spin my distaff for me, which was a job I had had to leave undone. And she did it most diligently; she really is a very kind girl.'

'And who else?'

Angélique folded the pillowcase and wrapped it in a small piece of cloth before slipping it into her pocket.

'I can't remember. But I'll tell you if any name or face comes to mind. But why so many questions? And what did Bertille come and make all that fuss for? Is there something worrying you?'

'No. Bertille thinks that her pig died because he ate something nasty in your garden; she just loves to make a fuss.'

'But you know, she may be right. On the advice of the Etch-emin chief, Madame d'Urville's father, I planted some of those plants whose roots you eat, plants called potatoes. But they say that the fruit of the plant that looks like tiny tomatoes is poisonous. I warned the children to be careful of them and not to go picking them.'

'Oh, that must be it then,' said Angélique greatly relieved. But she still had to explain the marks on the pillowcase.

But she could not get out of her mind the picture suggested by her over-excited imagination: the picture of a criminal hand pouring a death-dealing potion into the medicine to be given to Abigail. Crazy and inexplicable as the idea might seem, the tension, the accidents and the bad luck of the past few days forced Angélique to regard it as a certainty. Therefore there

must be a madman at large among them, trying to spread disaster, attacking anyone according to his whim.

Angélique clasped her head in her hands. And what had happened to the Swedish boy and the letter?

She knelt down to look at the kitten, which sat motionless on
the cushion in the chair.

'You can tell me, *who* did you see?' she whispered to him.
'You, you know everything. Oh, if only you could speak!'

Had Joffrey been there, he would soon have been able to
determine what chemical or natural substance could have been
so virulent as to have bleached away the scarlet of the pillowcase, even to the extent of destroying the material in
patches.

It seemed to her that her husband had left Gouldsboro an
eternity ago. But when she counted up the days on her fingers,
they only came to five.

If all went well in the Saint John river with the English she
still could not expect him before a week was up.

So between now and then, what attitude should she adopt?
And who could advise her about those suspicious stains?

She suddenly remembered the spice-seller who had been a
member of the crew of the Corsair from Dunkerque, and who
had decided to remain in Gouldsboro with his Carib slave, after
the *Fearless* had sailed.

After instructing Séverine to keep an eye on every one who
came to visit her mother and her little sister, she went off to
question the spice-seller. But he had left Gouldsboro some two
or three days previously, no one knew whether by sea or
whether he had set off through the forest, for so many different
kinds of people disembarked here.

She would have liked to speak to Colin, but if her feminine
intuition made her certain of the danger hanging over their
heads, the actual evidence in her possession was thin and unreliable. Possibly for the first time in her life, she did not know
what she ought to do, even what she ought to think or decide.
At one moment she would be so convinced of the fearful and
pressing menace that it made her feel giddy, and then at
another her fears would dissolve and the situation would appear
perfectly harmless, and she would ask herself what, after all,
had happened that was so unusual.

Two men had had a fight and had died from the blows they
had dealt one another; a mischievous kitten had been given a
drubbing by a brutal sailor, while a greedy pig had been

poisoned by the fruit of the potato plant; an old Indian woman had got drunk on bartered alcohol ... These were the kind of incidents and accidents that made up their day-to-day lives.

The heavy heat which a capricious wind began to stir up towards evening finally set her every nerve on edge.

Angélique decided to walk over to Camp Champlain. It had suddenly occurred to her how deeply upset poor Miss Pidgeon must be after the sudden death of the Pastor, and she reproached herself for not having thought sooner about the poor English lady. There she found Miss Pidgeon, sitting alone on a tree trunk, her hands clasped around her knees.

She went up to her and sat down beside her, putting an arm round her shoulders and she said softly in English: 'My poor dear lady . . .'

Miss Pidgeon began to cry.

What dreams, what tenderness and devotion lay hidden behind that delicate faded face, the face of an elderly child of the American shores, who had grown up between the wild forest-lands and the sea, in the straitjacket of Puritan discipline. But every human being is entitled to his private dreams.

'Why did they get him worked up like that?' she finally managed to say. 'He was so sensitive! Almost anything upset him terribly . . .'

Angélique knew she was speaking of the Reverend Patridge, and indeed she was not altogether wrong. He was a sensitive man in his own way.

'He was so apprehensive for us, his flock, and for the way our souls would be affected by contact with the French. He was always exhorting us to pray. Why did they have to come and tell him that we were to be taken off to Quebec, escorted by the Jesuit, and forced to be baptized Catholics. It wasn't true, was it?'

'Of course it wasn't! Haven't I told you over and over again that here you are under the protection of Count Peyrac and are completely safe! Why ever did Patridge not trust me instead of losing his temper yet again?'

'That's true! But, you know, after all those blows on the head the redskins gave him, poor lad, he was so very sensitive . . .'

It was plain that it did the old maid good to talk about the irascible pastor with a degree of tenderness and familiarity she would never have allowed herself during his lifetime.

They talked for some time and Miss Pidgeon slowly drew

comfort from their conversation. Angélique, seeing that she was better, was thinking that she ought to set off home, when she heard the sound of a horse galloping towards them, and recognized Colin. After entering the camp he inquired after their whereabouts.

Still astride his horse he stopped before them and greeted them with a courteous nod, then turned to Angélique.

'It is getting late, Madame. It would be unwise of you to return to Gouldsboro without an escort. Indeed you should not have come here on your own, so I have come over to fetch you.'

Then, turning to Miss Pidgeon, he said in English:

'Tomorrow, Miss Pidgeon, I wonder if you would mind being present at the Council meeting, for I would like to ask you to give some English lessons to our young Huguenots every morning. They will be brought over in a light cart and for your services you will receive supplies, assistance and a salary.'

'So it really is true that we are not to be handed over to the Canadians?' exclaimed Miss Pidgeon, positively reassured.

'Of course you aren't. Wherever did you get that dreadful rumour from? I have just been telling your compatriots yet again that it is completely baseless. As soon as the troubles are over in the Bay of Massachusetts, you can return completely freely to New England. But meanwhile, think over my offer.'

CHAPTER 37

ANGÉLIQUE RETURNED to Gouldsboro riding pillion on Colin's horse.

She was obliged to hold on to his belt with both hands but told herself that she had no choice but to accept his help. If he had come there to fetch her back, boldly heedless of the delicate situation they were in after the recent drama that had almost destroyed the bond of love between Angélique and Count Peyrac, it was because he knew, he too, that the danger that hung over them was all too real and that it was his duty, come what may, to defend her.

'What a risky thing to do!' he growled at last. 'I can

understand why your husband sometimes loses patience with you. What an idea to set off alone along this dangerous road!'

At that moment they passed the new fort, which was now almost finished, and around which the sentries were beginning to light their fires.

'But what did I have to fear?' Angélique asked in surprise. 'It seems to me that the road between Gouldsboro and Camp Champlain is quite safe now. We no longer have any reason to fear a sudden attack by the Iroquois as we did last year.'

'It isn't only the Iroquois we have to fear.'

'So you're afraid too, are you Colin? What are you afraid of?'

He hesitated.

'How do I know? There's something evil about.'

'Don't be superstitious! Tell me what you mean . . . Tell me frankly.'

'I have nothing further to add to what I said to you on board my ship when the Jesuit came to fetch you away: "Take care, someone seeks to harm you." '

'And yet the Jesuit turned out to be friendly. He would have upheld our cause, of that I am sure. And now he is dead, God help us. And no one can find the boy either. Yes, you are right, there are evil things about.'

She gave him a jumbled account of everything that had frightened her: Madame Carrère's and Madame de Maudribourg's inexplicably long sleep at the time that Abigail had had her baby, a sleep that was certainly attributable to the coffee they had both drunk; the suspicious circumstances of the death of Bertille's pig . . .

'One can't link any of it together, and yet it seems as if someone is at the bottom of it all.'

They reached Gouldsboro and Angélique slipped down from the horse. Colin dismounted too and leading the horse by the bridle they walked together to the central square of the village.

'Speak out, Colin,' Angélique insisted, 'I have a feeling that something is on your mind that you don't want to say.'

'Only because it may have no connection at all with what is happening here. It was just an idea that occurred to me when they spoke about the shipwreck of the *Unicorn*, all those people who died of broken skulls. And Job Simon who kept on repeating: "The wreckers! they hit me!" Then I remembered that there was a man known in some of the ports as "the man with the lead cudgel"; sometimes he had a ship, sometimes he hadn't, but he's never been exactly poor. He had a whole gang of men similarly armed and when they were on the prowl in a town no one was easy, especially the other ships' crews. He hired out his services to raid an unattended ship or equally to press-gang young men into serving on board some ship, any kind of devilry where the sea was concerned, all along the coast. A queer cove ... He could have done something else, but he chose to do that ... I only came across him once in a bar in Honfleur.'

'What did he look like?' Angélique asked him, breathless.

'Difficult to describe. There was a devil inside him. He was a pale, cold man ...'

'That's him!' cried Angélique. 'Now I know it's him. He's the man who's prowling around our islands. I am sure that under the pretext of freeing the Quebec officials it's he that Joffrey has gone after and that is why I'm so frightened for him. The Englishman Phipps is less dangerous than these "invisible men". But why, if this is the man you are talking about, did he come to America? Why attack us? Why lure the *Unicorn* on to the rocks and massacre her crew?'

'Perhaps for the sake of Evil. When a demon has found a way of striking at people, he never tires of it.'

'But what possible connection could it have with what I was telling you earlier? Drugged coffee, and a poisoned pig ... You are in control of everything here, every ship or boat that puts in, and no stranger could wander around our houses without being noticed.

'And yet ... just imagine, Colin what a terrible thing it would have been to see Abigail die before my very eyes; I would have gone quite mad.'

'That's maybe what they're trying to do,' Colin replied.

Angélique looked closely at the rugged face of the man who had once been Gold Beard. He had always had an awareness of the hidden aims of his enemies. Ismail the King, the Cunning One, accused him of having second sight.

'If that's what they're after,' she replied, 'never fear. Whatever happens, I shall not go mad.'

Colin gave a deep sigh.

'How I would like to be able to protect you, the way I used to.'

'Don't worry,' she repeated. 'If "they" want to devour me, they will break their teeth, because I'm tough ...'

'You haven't changed,' he said.

'What matters is that I should be forewarned. It has done me good to talk to you, you see. After all, if "they" are strong, so are we.'

He bowed his head and took his leave of her. She knew that all that night he would be watching vigilantly over the settlement, going the rounds of the sentries, asking questions, checking the identity of sailors along the shore, and positioning his most trustworthy men at those points that needed special protection. She felt certain she would find one of them in the vicinity of the Bernes' house.

CHAPTER 38

AND YET when she took hold of the doorknob and began to open the door of her room, she knew instinctively that, just like the other night, there was someone waiting for her. On this occasion she did not have the courage to face the danger alone and called one of the men from the guard post below.

He went into the room before her, holding his lantern aloft.

There they found a frightened child clutching a bag to him. The light glinted on his blond hair. It was Abbial Neals, the orphan boy whom Father de Vernon had picked up on the quayside in New York.

She felt a surge of joy, of relief, and also, without quite knowing why, of apprehension.

As soon as the door was closed she spoke in English to the ship's boy from the *White Bird*. He did not reply, but merely passed her impulsively the bag he had been holding. It was a haversack made of untanned deerskin, and on opening it she saw that it contained all the dead Jesuit's possessions: a breviary, a stole, some box-wood rosary beads, a surplice and, in a quilted velvet pochette finely embroidered in silver and gold, the sacred objects needed for saying Mass.

With an impatient movement the child seized the breviary and handed it to her.

The book opened of its own accord round a folded piece of

parchment, which on opening it she saw to be an unfinished letter.

'My dear brother in Jesus Christ . . .' from the first words she realized what it was – the letter to Father d'Orgeval . . .

She was seized with fear. What terrible thing was she about to learn? . . . Had she a right to read this letter? . . To force, as it were, that secretive, close man to confess what he had sought to keep hidden from her in his lifetime!

Nevertheless, so urgent did it seem to her to understand the menacing situation that she began almost mechanically to unfold the letter and run her eyes over it.

She read:

'My dear brother in Jesus Christ, I am writing to you from Gouldsboro where I have come to complete the investigation you entrusted to me. And since, in line with the confidence you place in my judgement, you have assured me that my opinions will be received by you as the expression of the truth, with as much credence in my words as if you yourself had been able to judge matters on the spot, I shall speak out forthrightly, fearing neither to flatter you nor to displease you.

'A sacred objective, more important than our personal susceptibilities which as sinful men we are often inclined to experience, obliges us both to disregard our own feelings and desires and to seek nothing but the truth, in order to protect the numerous souls, at grave risk, that depend upon our ministry.

'And so I will begin by stating flatly from the outset that you were right, Father, and that the visions which God in his goodness was gracious enough to vouchsafe you, corroborating the vision of that most saintly nun in Quebec, have not deceived you. Yes, you were right: the Demon *is* in Gouldsboro . . .'

Angélique broke off, dumbfounded. She could scarcely believe her eyes. Was it Father de Vernon who was launching such an accusation? . . . The letters began to dance before her eyes.

'Yes, you were right: the Demon is in Gouldsboro, and I shudder as I write such words. However well prepared we may be to face satanic beings during the course of our religious life, it is nonetheless a terrible ordeal when this actually occurs. And it is with all the humility of a man who has at times felt himself weak indeed before so terrible an encounter that I am about to give you the details. Albertus Magnus[1] tells us that what makes the spirit of Lucifer so formidable is that it links the

1. *Treatise on White Magic.*

beauty of an angel to the seductiveness of the female character, before which any man of flesh feels himself particularly vulnerable, not only because of its bodily charms, but I think also because of the temptation to tenderness and self-surrender, which the unfading memory of our mothers and the happiness we received at their hands leaves in us. But fortified by your counsels and our training, I found it relatively easy to unmask the true nature of the woman whom I shall not hesitate henceforth to call the Demon, the very spirit of evil in a woman's body, of quick intelligence, lustful, criminal, sacrilegious, not even scrupling to employ her seductive powers on me and to use the sacrament of penance in order to circumvent me and make her my ally in her infamous projects...'

'Oh no, no!' exclaimed Angélique, almost out loud. 'No, Father, that isn't true. I didn't try to seduce you, it isn't true. Oh, Jack Merwin, how could this be? I thought you were my friend...'

Her heart was beating. A feeling of calamity swept over her until she felt giddy. She had to lay the letter down on the table in order to support herself and stop herself collapsing.

The fair-headed child was looking at her, his frightened expression no doubt reflecting the expression she herself wore; then he began to speak in a tremulous voice: 'Mistress, they are after me. For God's sake do help me!'

But she did not hear him.

Someone knocked at the door, then, receiving no reply, spoke:

'What's happening? What does the child want? Am I bothering you?'

It was Ambroisine's soft voice.

Angélique pulled herself together.

'It's nothing. Good evening, Ambroisine, what do you want?'

'Only to see you,' the Duchess exclaimed in tragic tones. 'I haven't even set eyes on you all day long and you seem surprised that when night falls I come to find out how you are.'

'How true, I have neglected you... please forgive me. I had a thousand things to see to.'

'You still seem anxious.'

'Yes I am. I have just experienced a terrible disappointment with regard to someone in whom I had placed my trust.'

Ambroisine laid her hand on Angélique's arm and said gravely:

'I think that you are finding Monsieur de Peyrac's absence unbearable. Something occurred to me: why don't you accompany me to Port Royal? With you I should find the courage to leave here again and take up my tasks, and to try to find the best solution for the girls in my care; to do this I have urgent need of your advice. The journey would enable you to join Monsieur de Peyrac two or three days earlier than if you wait for him in Gouldsboro.'

As Angélique hesitated in some surprise, she went on:

'Did you not know that he intended to put in at Port Royal before returning here?'

'No, I didn't.'

'At any rate he told me so,' Ambroisine assured her looking mildly vexed, 'that is . . .'

She looked like someone who has thought better of saying something, for her expression was embarrassed as if she had committed a blunder.

'He told the Governor too. I was present when he did so . . . Do come,' she urged. 'Let's leave tomorrow for Port Royal. It's better than waiting round impatiently here, and it will greatly help me to take heart again.'

'I shall think about it,' Angélique replied.

She was still feeling as if she had received a terrible shock. The discovery of the betrayal – yes, it was betrayal – of Father Maraicher de Vernon had left her in a state of terrified astonishment. Ambroisine was right. She needed to get moving, to do something, and above all to see Joffrey again as soon as possible.

She realized that she must read the letter through to the end, and was about to ask Ambroisine tactfully to leave her alone, but as she glanced down the table she realized that the letter she had placed on it had disappeared.

Her eyes travelled round the room. The child had gone too.

'Where's the boy?' she cried.

'He went off,' said Ambroisine. 'I saw him pick up his bag, put into it a piece of paper that was on the table and dart noiselessly over to the door. He's a strange boy, like a will-o'-the-wisp.'

'But we must catch him.'

She tried to rush over towards the door but Ambroisine held her back forcibly, clinging to her, her face suddenly pale with fear.

'Don't go, Angélique! I sense demons about the place! Perhaps they have invaded the mind of that child!'

'Oh rubbish!' cried Angélique. 'I must catch him.'

'Not tonight. When it's light again,' Ambroisine begged her. 'Angélique, please come with me to Port Royal. I can feel some evil spirit is abroad here. I mentioned it to Father de Vernon, and told him that Gouldsboro was a place that ought to be exorcized. And he didn't laugh either; I think he agreed with me.'

'People of his kind always try to make the facts fit in with their preconceived ideas,' Angélique said bitterly.

Suddenly she felt very weary.

'Angélique,' Ambroisine repeated, 'do come away with me, please. Don't you feel how brooding the atmosphere is here? It was partly for that reason I came back. I couldn't bear the idea of you alone here, possibly surrounded by people planning your downfall . . . I cannot do very much for you but at least I shall be by your side.

'It was also one of the reasons why I was in a hurry to get my girls away from the bad influence of this place. I cannot detect where the tension comes from . . . Perhaps from the English . . . They are evil people. They are heretics.'

'But we hardly see anything of them. They never leave Camp Champlain.'

'But could they not have been entrusted with a mission of destruction against you . . . And what about those pirates! . . . I can well understand that your Protestant friends don't feel easy with such a Governor. Why does your husband trust him? He even goes off and leaves him in sole charge of the outpost . . .'

She hesitated.

'I don't know whether it's of any importance, but I overheard a conversation between two of his men that aroused my suspicions. One of them said to the other: "Just a bit of patience, old feller. In a short while now everything here will be ours . . . Gold Beard gave us his word." Then they went on to say that when you've lost a battle you have to learn to be cunning, and that that had always been Gold Beard's strong point. And that he had accomplices in the Bay who would come to his assistance when the moment came.'

'Colin!' said Angélique with a shake of her head. 'No, that's impossible.'

'Are you sure of that man?' Ambroisine asked her sharply.

Yes, she was sure of him. And then suddenly she remembered. A man can change absolutely and completely, especially if he abandons himself to despair and resentment as Colin had admitted he had. Her heart gave way under this further weight of unbearable distress. If it was Colin, that explained everything! But no, that was impossible. Joffrey could never have been so utterly wrong about him. Unless of course he had done so out of calculation! What a calculation! She could not bear to think about it, or she would lose her head.

Whatever the situation, she must see Joffrey as soon as possible and tell him about these new dangers, these new suspicions, and try to sound him, to understand what he had in mind.

Now that Abigail had had her child she was free to leave. And if by going to Port Royal she could advance the longed-for reunion with her husband by a few days, she would be more than pleased.

'All right,' she said to Ambroisine, 'I shall accompany you. We'll set off tomorrow.'

PART THREE

Port Royal
or
Lust

CHAPTER 39

AT LAST they had got away.

With a small crew, the two women and their luggage, Adhemar still whining and fearful of the sea, but who found it nevertheless impossible henceforth to imagine living in America unless under the immediate protection of Madame de Peyrac, with Brother Mark, the Recollect monk, who had suddenly decided to be on his way again but who wanted to explore some of the rivers and rapids on the Acadian Peninsula, before returning to Saint Cross across the Chignecto Isthmus, with a handful of other folk who wanted a change of scene and a few visiting Indians, the *Rochelais* had left Gouldsboro, heading west towards the oldest French – possibly the oldest European – settlement in the whole of North America.

The terrible French Bay lived up to its reputation.

Short as the crossing was to Port Royal, a storm blew up that might well have sunk the little yacht twenty times over.

Getting through the narrows into Port Royal harbour took them two hours of fighting against line after line of gigantic waves with foaming crests. Every now and then through the mist and rain they caught sight of tall black cliffs topped with trees, on either side of the vessel and dangerously close.

Vanneau and the Acadian who was acting as pilot were lying across the tiller to hold it in the correct position. Twice Cantor, who was in command of the ship, fell and rolled against the rails because he had scorned lashing himself on to any fixed point.

Then when they reached the calmer waters of the harbour a fog fit to cut with a knife was awaiting them like some hostile sentry, barring their entry.

The ship nevertheless sailed on through it and travelled a few miles surrounded by the oppressive white fog, until the pilot suggested that they should drop anchor.

'We must be off the settlement, but it would be just as well to know where we're going before launching the boat. If we go any farther we might run into a ship lying at anchor outside the port. As soon as night falls, we may be able to make out the lights from the houses.'

This wait enabled the passengers and especially the two women, Angélique and the Duchess of Maudribourg, to rest and tidy their clothes and their luggage. Although they had been under shelter in the little cabin at the stern, they had been considerably shaken. The chest containing scalps that belonged to Saint-Castine had not been properly secured and had slipped and scraped Angélique's ankle. Shortly before his departure, Saint-Castine had returned to ask whether Monsieur de Peyrac had taken his chest with him to hand over to the Governor of Quebec.

'No, he didn't,' Angélique replied. 'He wasn't going to Quebec and it is very unlikely that we shall be going there.'

'Then would you take it with you to Port Royal? Monsieur de la Roche-Posay will have ways and means of seeing it reaches its proper destination. I must prove my good will to Monsieur de Frontenac and all the clique.'

This wooden chest, with its heavy bands of beaten copper, was extremely cumbersome. And in any case it did not seem a good idea to Angélique that she should be transporting this collection of English scalps across waters swarming with hundreds of ships from Boston and Virginia. But she could scarcely refuse to perform this service for Castine who at least was a reliable ally, for it was thanks to his intervention that the Abenaki massacres stirred up by the Jesuits had been brought to a halt on the west bank of the Kennebec.

And so she had taken the chest. Saint-Castine went on and on about his scalps until she could have screamed. The kind of thoughtlessness that characterized him, totally preoccupied as he was with his own concerns, his Indians, his scalps, his prospective father-in-law Chief Mateconando, and his fiancée Matilda, made Angélique feel that this was an incongruous detail idiotically introduced into the midst of her personal nightmare, still further adding to the chaos of her ideas and her reasoning.

What she wanted above all was to get away.

She left the kitten, now almost recovered, with the Berne children. Now that the tiny creature had managed to survive and that Abigail and her baby were well, there was nothing to keep her in Gouldsboro.

But when she had told Colin, he reacted to the announcement of her departure with unexpected violence, his face livid with contained anger.

'No, you are not to go! Madame de Maudribourg can perfectly well go on her own.'

This was a changed man she had before her! Gold Beard, the stranger! Remembering Ambroisine de Maudribourg's words, Angélique once again felt giddy with an anxiety that left her gasping for breath in an almost childish state of panic. But she had seen Joffrey lay his hand on Colin's shoulder as the two men's eyes had met. Such a look between two men spelt confidence, truth, rectitude. She had seen them through the window and *they had not known that they were being observed*. You cannot be mistaken about a look like that. Or else she, Angélique, was going mad! . . .

So deep was her perplexity that she took some time before replying to Colin, which she did more calmly than she might normally have done.

'But why do you object? Abigail's baby is born now. There's nothing to keep me here . . .'

Colin was containing himself with difficulty, although he made an effort, once over his first reaction, to speak with moderation.

'Monsieur de Peyrac will be put out not to find you here when he returns!' he said.

'But it's precisely in order to join him the sooner that I want to go to Port Royal since he intends to put in there on his way back from the Saint John river before returning to Gouldsboro.'

Suddenly the Governor seemed to grow calm, and a shrewd concentrated expression which she knew well replaced that of anger and anxiety, and his eyes narrowed.

'Who told you that? Who said Monsieur de Peyrac was putting in at Port Royal before returning to Gouldsboro?'

'But . . . didn't he say so himself before he left? He told you too.'

'I don't remember,' he muttered.

Deep within herself she was using all her strength to dam up the flood of suspicion ready to break over Colin. Why did he want to prevent her going? Was it because he regarded her as a hostage and did not want her to escape? Was his scant courtesy towards Madame de Maudribourg attributable to the fact that he realized that the intelligent and highly intuitive woman had seen through him?

She did not have sufficient facts and evidence to go on. She merely asked these questions while trying to calm her fear, and told herself that come what might she would leave Gouldsboro, since it was still possible to make good her escape.

The word 'escape' had come to her spontaneously. From now on, anything that seemed to present an obstacle to her setting off to meet Joffrey she would brush aside without a qualm.

Colin must have read the stubborn resolution in her eyes, for he said shortly:

'All right! I shall let you go, but on one condition ... that your son Cantor should accompany you ...'

Then it had been Cantor's turn to object violently to her decision when she told him of it.

'I'm not leaving Gouldsboro,' he declared. 'I have received no orders from my father to that effect. You can go to Port Royal with Madame de Maudribourg if you want to, but I'm not moving ...'

'You would be doing me a favour if you agreed. For various reasons Colin is reluctant to let me go unless you come with me ...'

Cantor shrugged his shoulders disrespectfully.

'You can let yourself be taken in if you want to,' he went on, increasingly inflexible, 'I know where my duty lies.'

'Well, where does your duty lie?' Angélique asked, beginning to feel herself losing patience. 'Explain what you mean instead of putting on these high and mighty airs!'

'Yes, explain yourself, child,' Ambroisine broke in, for she had been present during the conversation. 'Your mother and I trust your judgement. You should explain things to us and help us in our decisions ...'

But Cantor gave her a black, disdainful glare and with a lordly air stalked out of the room.

This renewed hostility on the part of Cantor, with whom her relationship had always been a difficult one, made Angélique feel thoroughly demoralized.

'Your son is anxious,' murmured Ambroisine. 'He's still only a child! Very much in love with you like all adolescents, the son of a beautiful mother, tremendously proud of his father. The other day, seeing him looking gloomy, I asked him why he did not seem to like Gouldsboro. He replied that he was not accustomed to enjoying the company of bandits. I thought it was just a quip, but I reckon it was something else ... Perhaps the Governor had threatened him! ... The lad doesn't know how to defend himself . . . He should trust you, Angélique; you ought to get him to talk . . .'

'It's not so easy to get Cantor to talk,' Angélique replied in some anxiety. 'And as for trusting me, I know he doesn't do that easily.'

She guessed only too well that Cantor's sensitive heart could not have failed to be wounded by the gossip that had gone around that summer concerning herself and Colin, and that this accounted for the lad's stiffness of manner.

Ambroisine observed her pensive face. Then she said in a tone of voice that was neither a statement nor a question:

'And you, you still trust that man, that Colin . . .'

'Possibly no,' Angélique replied, 'but I do trust my husband. He possesses such a profound knowledge of human beings, he could hardly have been wrong about that . . .'

She rejected the idea that Colin was a traitor, clinging to that glance she had seen pass between Colin and Joffrey, a look of understanding, and communication.

But now, finding herself off Port Royal, having finally managed to escape Gouldsboro and its oppressive atmosphere, all these things came back to her, and her ill-contained fears burst forth again, stifling her. All the distrust born of too many betrayals flooded back into her heart again. Was Joffrey there waiting for her behind that heavy curtain of mist, or was he going his own way far from her? And what about Colin? Had Colin flouted her? No, not Colin! She no longer knew . . .

In the end Cantor had come with her. When she was busily preparing for departure she saw him suddenly appear and begin arranging with Vanneau to get the *Rochelais* ready to take them over to Port Royal.

'So you're not abandoning me after all,' she said to him with a smile.

'I have received orders from the Governor!' he explained curtly.

What had Colin said to him to make him change his mind? Stifled fears still lurked within her. Colin! When she had told him of her fears that someone was on the prowl, out to poison, to kill, had he not shown very little reaction? Should he not have reinforced defences, tightened controls? And that story about the man with the lead cudgel, had that not been intended to put her off the track? Ambroisine had heard two of his men saying that he had accomplices in the Bay. But had she understood them properly? Colin! . . . When she had spoken of the ship with the orange pennant he had seemed to attach little importance to it. Did he know who "they" were ... His accomplices? Colin, their enemy! No! Betraying her? Suddenly she felt quite sure: no, it was impossible! She took a deep breath, feeling somewhat better on that score. But what of Cantor's hostility? Why should he behave like this? What was there about Cantor that she could never conciliate, never conquer?

Right now he was leaning over the rail not far from her, looking out likewise towards the invisible coastline. 'You handled the ship very well on this journey,' she said.

He shrugged as if unwilling to receive any compliments that might soften his critical attitude towards her.

'Cantor,' she asked point-blank, 'what did Colin say to you to make you change your mind about accompanying me?'

He turned his green eyes towards his mother and she admired his youthful beauty, through the iridescent mist that seemed to soften his features and hang like a halo round his vigorous young silhouette with its curly hair.

'He told me that I must go to keep an eye on you,' he said somewhat grudgingly.

'Can't I look after myself?' Angélique asked with a smile, placing her hand on the butt of the pistol she carried at her belt.

'You're a good shot, Mother, that I don't deny,' Cantor admitted without abandoning his haughty air, 'but there are other dangers of which you are unaware . . .'

'And what are they? Tell me .. I'm listening.'

'No,' Cantor replied shaking his thick hair; 'if I told you who it is I accuse, you would be angry and would merely think I was jealous and silly . . . so there's no point.'

He moved away as if to emphasize his detachment. What had he in mind? Who was it he dared not accuse before her? He always took such an extreme line ... She realized that there was something in him she would never overcome or conciliate ...

Once, in a moment of unbelievable delight, she had conceived a child, and now this child had grown to be a man and was like a stranger to her, appearing to remember only the pain she had caused him and none of the joys.

The mist lay moistly all about her filling her hair with rainbow-tinted pearls ... She felt cold and clasped her cloak tight about her. A shadowy form approached her and it was Ambroisine's turn to join her at the rail. She was wearing her black cloak with the scarlet lining. The red matched her lips which she had made up slightly, the black matched her eyes and her lily-white skin toned with the alabaster whiteness of the surrounding mist. She was very beautiful and seemed taller, less hesitant and strained than during the preceding days.

Port Royal, a Catholic settlement, provided with at least two chaplains, pious Oratorians, and crowded with visiting priests, where the atmosphere between the land-owning gentry and the industrious, intelligent peasant population was reputed to be patriarchal, would suit her better than Gouldsboro with its mixture of religions and variety of different backgrounds.

Angélique made an effort to smile at her.

'I warrant your girls will be delighted to see you again. They must have been very worried about you. Poor young things!'

The Duchess of Maudribourg made no reply but carefully scrutinized Angélique.

'You look like the Queen of the North,' she said all of a sudden, 'with that rainbow mist hanging about your hair. It's like a pale shimmering gold. Yes, Queen of the Snows. You would have been better suited in the role of Christina of Sweden than as a musketeer in petticoats.'

Vanneau and the Acadian pilot approached them. They too looked over in the presumed direction of Port Royal.

'The inhabitants must be anxious,' said the pilot. 'They must have heard the sound of our chain as we cast anchor. They don't know whether we might not be the English and most of them will be preparing to flee into the woods with their cooking-pots.'

'Unless they fire on us as soon as the fog has cleared,' said Cantor.

'It would surprise me if they had much by way of ammunition,' said the pilot, 'I hear that the Acadian Trading Company's vessel that brings in their supplies every summer was taken by pirates.'

As night began to fall, Angélique heard the pealing of a church bell and almost simultaneously a cold wind blew across the surface of the sea forming tiny choppy waves, half dispelling the fog, and a row of dim lights suddenly appeared along the shore. Then a further gust of wind, and the whole village of Port Royal sprang into view in the gathering dusk, its rows of wooden houses half-way up the slope with their tall steeply-pitched roofs, each one with a tall chimney rising out of the centre, from which a trail of smoke slowly rose up to mingle with the scudding clouds.

The French settlement was already about four hundred souls strong, so the general effect was imposing, and the houses stretched out along the shore as far as the broad meadows formed by the dried-up marshlands at the far end of the harbour, now covered with fruit trees and grazing sheep and cattle. The village was long enough to form two parishes, which enabled the inhabitants to process between the two churches on feast days. Apart from the lights of the houses there was little sign of activity at this evening hour.

Cantor had his father's flag hoisted, the oriflamme embossed with a silver coat-of-arms which was beginning to be known along the north American coast. They could only hope that those on shore could see the flag in spite of the gathering darkness and would be reassured. The longboat was launched and the passengers took their places in it.

As they drew near to the shore they began to make out a large assembly of people at the quayside, consisting chiefly of women and children. Their headdresses and white scarves fluttered in the shadows like a flock of seagulls.

'I can see Armand,' said Madame de Maudribourg. 'He's even fatter, poor man, the food in Port Royal must be too good.'

They fully expected a great welcome. The King's Girls were already waving their handkerchiefs, but some of the men, armed with muskets, called out to them:

'Are you English? Tell us who you are!'

They began to explain their presence when they were still at some distance and when the boat reached the shore everyone knew what was going on.

While Marie-la-Douce, Delphine, the Moorish girl, Henriette, Jeanne Michaud and the others, along with their inseparable Armand threw themselves at their benefactress's feet and round her neck, a distinguished-looking woman, still young, although her face was faded and lined, no doubt from excessive child-bearing, came forward to meet Angélique. By her dress, which was that of the prosperous middle class, sober but not lacking in elegance, and her hair which she wore in the French style, protected only by a small square of lace held in place by a pin decorated with a cameo, Angélique guessed that she must be Madame de la Roche-Posay.

'I am so pleased to meet you at last,' she said to Angélique with considerable friendliness. 'We have always had good relations with Gouldsboro. Do you bring me news of my husband?'

'I am afraid not, I myself have come here intending to ask you the same question.'

'They'll be back eventually,' Madame de la Roche-Posay sighed, philosophically. 'It always takes a lot of talk to sort out the affairs of the Bay.'

Madame de Maudribourg thanked the Chatelaine warmly for looking after her flock in her absence. Angélique noticed the same surprise in their hostess's eyes that they had all felt in Gouldsboro on discovering that the benefactress of the King's Girls was this pretty young woman.

Madame de la Roche-Posay accompanied them to the manor house, built partly of stone and partly of wood, on the site of Champlain's original house. This was where the proprietor lived with his family. In the main hall stood a row of children, nicely dressed and with neatly combed hair. They greeted the new arrivals, the girls with a curtsey, the boys with a faultless salute.

'But it's like being at court,' exclaimed Angélique, guessing that before her stood the numerous offspring of the Marquis de la Roche-Posay, well schooled by their governess, Mademoiselle Radégonde de Ferjeac.

The latter preened herself. She was the personification of everything that a governess of noble families ought to be, undoubtedly from a family that had itself been country gentry back in the time of Saint Louis but fallen on hard times. She was of indeterminate age, skinny, extremely plain, and strict.

'I must congratulate you on your pupils,' Angélique said to her, 'in these parts it really is miraculous to meet such well-brought-up French children.'

'I have no illusions about them, you know,' Mademoiselle Radégonde de Ferjeac sighed. 'As soon as the boys are grown up they'll be off to the woods and after the Indian women, and as for the girls, we shall have to send them off to a convent or to France in order to marry them off.'

'I don't want to go to a convent,' a sweet, bright-looking little girl of eight piped up, 'I want to go off to the woods too.'

'I was just the same when I was a child,' Angélique said with a smile: 'I think she'd get on very well with Honorine.'

'Who's Honorine?'

'My little girl.'

'How old is she?'

'Four.'

'Why didn't you bring her with you?'

'Because she is in Wapassou.'

She had to answer a great number of questions about Wapassou and Honorine.

Meanwhile the servants had entered and set out on the long wooden table a variety of dishes laden with food and pitchers containing refreshments. Two silver candle-sticks were lighted at each end of the table.

'These children have all too few opportunities to appear in polite society,' the governess said. 'As soon as I knew that someone had heard an anchor and chain from a ship in the port, I got the children dressed and set the kitchens to work.'

'And what if it had been the English?'

'We would have welcomed them with cannon fire,' said a lively small boy.

'But you know we've no ammunition left,' one of his older sisters told him reproachfully.

'Oooh! There's a French soldier,' they all shouted as they discovered Adhemar's presence. 'What luck! If the English arrive we shall have someone to defend us. Will you teach us to fire a cannon, Mister soldier?' asked the boys.

'How long will you be able to stay with us?' asked Mademoiselle Radégonde, turning towards Angélique and Ambroisine. 'In a couple of days' time we are giving a small party in honour of the anniversary of Champlain's landing at this spot. We are going to put on a play and hold a banquet . . .'

CHAPTER 40

HE WAS not there. She had always known that he would not be there! Joffrey! The quietness of Port Royal fell upon her shoulders like a leaden cloak. An idea crossed her mind, fleeting and terrifying: 'It's a trap! Another trap! . . . Colin was right not to want me to leave . . .'

Everything seemed suspicious. The calm of the evening, the

biblical serenity of the inhabitants, the children's laughter, the affability of Madame de la Roche-Posay. They were keeping something from her. It was unbearable.

During supper, Angélique listened carefully to the lady of the place who was saying that she feared that her husband failed to realize that this new French settlement would bring the English who would come and pillage them and ruin them with their reprisals, and that of course this would happen during the Marquis's absence, just when they were right out of ammunition with which to defend themselves.

'Did Monsieur de la Roche-Posay not give you any idea how long the French Bay expedition would last?' asked Angélique, searching desperately for some scraps of hope.

'No more than your husband did!' the Marquise lamented. 'As I said, those gentlemen have other things to think about than our anxiety.'

Angélique felt convinced that her words bore some hidden meaning or some warning which escaped her.

She noticed that Ambroisine de Maudribourg, during the meal, contrary to her normal custom, did not attempt to monopolize the conversation and to centre it round some scientific subject, which undoubtedly no one would have contested, but remained silent. She uttered not a single word, and scarcely touched her food, but wore an expression of distress on her pale face.

She insisted on accompanying Angélique to the door of the tiny house that had been allotted to her and where her trunk and her bag had been put.

Angélique felt how tense she was, possessed by some grave concern.

When the moment came for them to part, she took Angélique's two hands in hers, which were icy cold.

'Now the time has come,' she said in a voice she did her best to keep steady. 'I have been putting off this moment, through sheer cowardice. Angélique, you do not deserve to be deceived by anyone. That is why I must speak up, no matter how hard I find it . . . I have too much affection and respect for you . . .'

Angélique had grown accustomed to the oratorical style and the complicated preliminary remarks of the Duchess, but strangely enough on this occasion every word seemed to touch upon a tender spot of her anguish. What was she about to hear? Something that would destroy the very basis of her life and all her affections.

'I did not tell you everything when I asked you to accompany me here to Port Royal,' Ambroisine went on, 'for I was frightened . . . I knew he would come here . . . and I felt that I might not be strong enough to resist his charm . . . So I told myself if you were here too . . . things would be easier . . . But you must be warned . . . I cannot live a lie . . . I have already suffered enough from having to hide from you the fact that he has been making advances to me . . . It is not in my nature to dissimulate in this way . . . and yet I found I had to . . . for he expressly requested me to do so . . .'

'But *who* are you talking about?' Angélique managed to slip in.

'But . . . about *him*,' Ambroisine cried in despair, 'whoever do you imagine?'

She let go Angélique's hands and covered her own face.

'Joffrey de Peyrac,' she said in a muffled voice, 'your husband . . . Oh, how shameful I find such an admission . . . and yet I have done nothing, I swear it, nothing to provoke his passion . . . But the charm of such a man, how can one resist it? . . . When he told me what a rare pleasure it was for him to converse with me, when he begged me to wait for him at Port Royal, it seemed as if even the inflections of his voice gave promise of a paradise I had never before encountered . . . What a dilemma this encounter put me in! Not only did I fear the effect of so subtle a temptation on my soul and its salvation but felt horribly guilty towards you, Angélique, who had been so kind to me, in spite of the fact that he assured me that you were both, by tacit agreement, free to grant your love where you wished. That was one of the reasons why I returned so impulsively to Gouldsboro . . . to flee from him . . . and to find you again . . .'

She let fall her hands from her face and looked at Angélique with an air of perplexity and fright, seeking to fathom her thoughts.

But Angélique was in no state to utter a single word. Her suffering took a strange form, as if she could not make up her mind what she should accept or reject among the things she had just heard that pierced her heart to the core.

'Forgive my saying so,' Ambroisine went on softly, 'but you must agree that it is difficult not to be fascinated by such a man. I even had a fleeting sensation that with him I could be happy. You see, I am being frank. I don't want to pass myself off for better than I am . . . I have suffered too greatly at the hands of men. I think that something is broken inside me . . . Even with him . . . I couldn't . . . so why betray you so basely, you who are the loveliest of women? . . . I prefer to behave as a loyal friend . . .'

She made as if to take Angélique's hand but Angélique withdrew hers sharply.

'I have hurt you,' said Ambroisine. 'So you really care more for him than I thought? I had gathered that there was a certain coldness between you.'

'Whoever made you think that?'

'But . . . he did . . . when I told him that I did not think well of his advances, he, the husband of so lovely and seductive a woman, he told me that one wearies of beauty when it is not accompanied by a faithful heart, and that he had long since resigned himself to no longer having exclusive rights over your beauty.'

'But this is crazy,' cried Angélique, beside herself, 'he could not have said that . . . *that isn't him*! You're lying!'

Ambroisine looked at her horror-struck.

'Oh, what have I done?' she murmured. 'I have hurt you!'

'No, you haven't!' Angélique shouted back fiercely. 'I shall wait for some facts before I feel hurt . . .'

'What do you call facts?'

'That he should tell me so himself.'

'So you don't believe me?' the Duchess insisted. Then she added with a childish egoism: 'Oh, how you hurt me!'

'And you hurt me too!' Angélique cried out, unable to contain herself.

At last Ambroisine seemed to realize how deeply she had been hurt.

'What have I done? Oh, what have I done?' she repeated. 'I did not know you to be so much in love! Had I known I would not have said anything. But I thought I ought to warn you in good faith . . . so that you would have the chance to defend yourself . . . but I was wrong . . .'

'No,' Angélique replied with an effort, 'as you say, it's just as well to be warned . . . in time!'

CHAPTER 41

ANGÉLIQUE STILL felt stunned by these contradictory revelations. For quite a long time after retiring into the cottage she had been allocated, she remained seated on the trestle bed with its seaweed mattress without even thinking of lying down.

Stunned. She seemed to be floating under water, to be in a hypnotic trance. She tried to imagine Joffrey addressing Ambroisine in those seductive terms, with that warmth in his eyes, the tender caressing quality of his voice, enveloping the young woman in a charm that was difficult to flee from.

The idea seemed at one and the same time plausible and inconceivable ... Plausible! The ambiguous charm of this strange woman who had appeared out of the sea, the sparkle of her teeth when she gave that uncertain, timid, hesitant smile peculiar to her, the serious expression of those great dark eyes, a nocturnal giddiness that must have enslaved many a man, the fascination of a woman's mind with a thousand surprising facets: learning, wisdom, childishness, gaiety and despair, straightforwardness and cunning, and what more? ... Beauty, grace, everything necessary to hurl a man head-first into the open chasm that yawned at his feet.

It was plausible ... even for Joffrey de Peyrac ... and yet it was inconceivable, because he loved her, Angélique. Because they were bound together for all eternity and he could no more vanish from her life than the sun could vanish from the sky.

At times she felt as if she were suffering a kind of eclipse, as if her emotions had been anaesthetized, making it impossible for her to perceive her precise relationship with him and with other people.

She told herself that everything was spoiled, that everything tasted of ashes, and that no one would ever know how it had all happened.

But at one and the same time she remained firm in her resolution not to go into the matter deeply until she had seen Joffrey again.

She stretched out on her bed with infinite caution as if fearing lest she shatter like a delicate piece of glass the state of inner equilibrium she had managed to recreate within herself.

Then she slept. When she awoke it took her a long time to realize where she was. She remembered the name Port Royal but could not take in its meaning. As soon as her memory returned along with recollection of the disaster, she forbade herself to think about it.

Joffrey's arrival was the only thing that could resolve her dilemma and enable her to shake off the state of semi-lethargy in which she had taken refuge, and allow her to give way to the crazy despair she felt lying in wait at the back of her mind.

She must simply wait there like a person shipwrecked on an island, and refuse to give rein to her tormented imagination. But . . .

Never had a day dragged by so slowly . . . that day in Port Royal . . . it would remain forever in her memory like lead, like some vague nightmare.

When she came to think about it later, she had to admit that she would have been incapable of living through these two days of deadly uncertainty, without the single piece of evidence coming to hand that helped her to escape from the state she was in.

Thanks be to God, the incidents of the following night resolved this hidden crisis. Had this not been so . . . she humbly admitted that she had never been so close to losing her sanity, her faith, her joy in life, and to admitting herself vanquished.

During the morning she accompanied Madame de la Roche-Posay on a visit to a number of the families in the village, chiefly those that had lived there for several generations. Fine patriarchal families, originally from the Berry or the Creuse or the Limousin but now with a strong admixture of Indian blood.

In the majority of the Port Royal homes the daughter-in-law revealed beneath her white peasant coif the great black eyes of a little Mic-Mac girl whom the son of the family had brought home one day from his wanderings in the woods.

Pious, hard-working, and a good housekeeper, she gave birth to handsome children with black hair and eyes, and a very white skin, who grew up as good citizens dividing their time between working in the fields, going to Mass on Sundays, and eating hot-pots of bacon and cabbage. Many a Mic-Mac Redskin, covered in seal-oil or bear-grease, would come out of the woods and hang about Port Royal from morn till eve, claiming his right to sit at the fire-side as a relative come to visit his French relations and to admire his grandchildren.

This atmosphere derived from the antiquity of Port Royal, and also from its enclosed situation, being as it was an almost unsuspected haven, sheltered by the long promontory that closed off the basin on the shores of which it had been built. When the frenzy of French Bay put every ship in peril, the basin remained calm. And in winter snow fell there gently and silently and not lashed by the wind.

With the help of the Dutch, who had also at one time held Port Royal, the Acadian settlers had drained the marshlands and created broad acres of meadowland now used as grazing for cows and sheep, and planted magnificent orchards.

Madame de Maudribourg wanted to join the two ladies on their outing, but Angélique was in no mood to show her any amiability, although Ambroisine tried anxiously to catch her eye.

The group from the *Unicorn* had closed tightly around its benefactress. In spite of her occasionally naïve and sometimes thoughtless behaviour which Angélique was possibly alone in seeing, the Duchess really did exercise an extraordinary influence over those around her, a measure of authority from which no one escaped, neither the bespectacled secretary, nor old Petronella Damourt nor even the rugged Job Simon.

'The King's Girls are well-behaved, well-educated, nice girls,' Madame de la Roche-Posay remarked as the group went off again with Madame de Maudribourg. 'I would gladly keep them on here for our young men, but their patroness does not appear to be agreeable to this. And yet she showed no hesitation in sending them to me without the slightest explanation. I had to find clothes for them and feed them for several days at my own expense. She is a little strange, don't you find?'

That afternoon Angélique took the young Roche-Posay children up the steep hillside of the promontory at the foot of which lay the village.

From the top were visible on one side the green and storm-tossed waters of French Bay, while on the other side lay the basin stretched out, looking as dazzling as polished pewter, seen through the tree trunks.

There was not a sail in sight on the horizon, nothing but a few fishing vessels. They walked down again to the village. The Roche-Posay boys got on very well with Adhemar, and so as not to disappoint them, for he was affectionate with children, he agreed to go with them to have a look at the cannon that stood on one of the corner turrets and was supposed to defend the port. He had in fact learned quite a lot during the course of his years of enforced military service, and was able to explain to them how you handled the gun, how you cleaned it, loaded it and fired it. With a bit of searching around he discovered a few cannon-balls and piled them up in small pyramids beside the gun, which immediately began to look more reassuring. 'Just as well you came, Mister soldier!' said the children. 'Under pretext that we had no ammunition to drive away the enemy, we just let our defences go to pot . . .' Adhemar was extremely proud of his success.

And so the day wore on, slowly, gently, unbearable. As evening came, the sky grew stormy and charged with infernal tension, while serene faces masked incommunicable fears. And yet the evening meal taken in the hall of the manor house was an agreeable occasion. Madame de la Roche-Posay had invited, in addition to Angélique and the Duchess, some of the local notables, the two chaplains, and Armand Daveau the secretary.

Cantor was also present. It was he who unleashed the storm among the humans, while the storm that was still brewing in a sky full of great clouds heavy with rain had still not decided to burst, but made its presence felt only by the occasional low growl and silent, spasmodic flashes of fighting. A warm wind sent ripples over the cornfields and the clusters of pink, blue and white lupins that blossomed everywhere gave the entire village a permanent air of festivity.

The fare was delicious: crab seasoned with a pinch of ginger and a trace of liqueur, a haunch of roast venison cooked in pastry, a wide variety of salads and the famous Port Royal cherries, a brilliant coral pink, served in baskets. For dessert Madame de la Roche-Posay served a wine made from the wild vine, which was black as ink and very heady. Immediately the conversation grew animated. A skilful hostess, the chatelaine gave each of her guests an opportunity to shine. She had heard of Madame de Maudribourg's scientific reputation and asked her a few questions that were by no means unintelligent.

Ambroisine immediately launched upon some abstruse topic, which, however, she was so skilful in presenting that everyone present felt for a brief instant that they were particularly gifted in understanding mathematics. With the help of her personal charm she held everyone's attention. Angélique was vividly reminded of the scene that had taken place on the shore at Gouldsboro.

She could see Joffrey's attentive eyes fixed on Ambroisine. She found the image so unbearable that she preferred to put it out of her mind. It so happened that at that moment Cantor exploded. Ambroisine had been talking about her correspondence with the scientist Kepler. Cantor exclaimed:

'That rubbish again. But Kepler died ages ago, in 1630 . . .'

Ambroisine looked at him, astonished at the interruption. 'If I am not dead, nor is he neither,' she said with a trace of a smile. 'Just recently, shortly before I left Europe, I received a letter from him about the orbits of the planets.'

The lad gave a furious shrug of his shoulders.

'That's impossible. He was a scientist from the last century, I tell you.'

'Would you happen to be better informed about scientists than your father?'

'Why?'

'Because he himself told me that he had once entered into correspondence with Kepler.'

Cantor went puce in the face and was about to make a violent rejoinder when Angélique interrupted him firmly.

'That's enough, Cantor. There's no point in wrangling over the matter. After all, all German scientists' names sound alike and Madame de Maudribourg and you have probably made some mistake about it. Let us leave the matter there.'

Madame de la Roche-Posay changed the subject by suggesting a glass of Rosolio. It was the last of the barrel she had received from France the year before. If the Company's ship was late . . .

'The young men hereabouts are very hot-blooded,' she said when Cantor, after taking leave courteously, had left the room. 'The life they lead encourages them to fear no authority and even to despise it no matter where it comes from.'

The mosquitoes were beginning to buzz in the evening air that was still shot through with silent flashes of lightning. The guests took their leave and Angélique went off in search of Cantor, who was sleeping in a little lean-to up against a farm house.

'Whatever got into you this evening to be so rude to Madame de Maudribourg? Even if you do regard yourself as a pirate and a trapper you should not forget that you are a gentleman and that you were once one of the King's pages. You should show courtesy towards women.'

'I hate blue-stockings,' said Cantor with an air of superiority. 'I think it would be better not to teach women to read.'

'Ah, there you are, a true man!' Angélique exclaimed, ruffling his hair in a mixture of gaiety and irritation. 'How would you like to see me incapable of deciphering the merest scrawl?'

'It's not the same thing where you are concerned,' said Cantor with all the illogicality of an adoring son, 'but it's still true that a woman is incapable of loving learning for its own sake. She uses it, the way that woman does, to adorn herself like with a peacock's feathers, to seduce fools of men who let themselves be taken in.'

'Madame de Maudribourg certainly has a most unusual degree of intelligence,' said Angélique cautiously.

Cantor pursed his lips and looked away obstinately. Angélique sensed that he was dying to say something, but that he would not do so because 'naturally, she would not be able to understand him'. So she went off, reminding him that among the qualities expected of a young nobleman was also that of making oneself agreeable in company.

Night lay like a leaden weight on her shoulders. She felt the air to be thick, as if full of menace, and every house, closed up around the light of its hearth, seemed hostile, as if harbouring some hidden enemy who was following her every move.

She began to run. She felt an urgent need to take refuge in her cottage, even to barricade herself inside.

Before she reached her shanty she had to cross an open court-yard behind the main house, then, to get out again, go down a long vaulted passageway. As she proceeded down it she had the impression that someone was lying in wait for her, hidden in the deep shadows.

No sooner had her instinct registered the warning than two arms grasped her from behind, paralysing her movements. Their strength was irresistible. They felt like two burning serpents trying to wind themselves around her and suffocate her. It was completely dark beneath the porch and she could see nothing. Yet beneath the effect of her horrified surprise no single sound found its way from Angélique's throat. The arms clasped about her gave her an indescribable sensation, for *they were not the arms of a man.*

They were soft, warm and feminine, like the voice that whispered in her ear – she could not have said in what tongue – that gave her the same impression of fear and disgust. So intense and terrible was the sensation that she would have fainted from horror had not a sudden flash of lightning illuminated the porch enabling her to recognize in its light a face, close to hers and looking at her with astonishment, the face of Ambroisine de Maudribourg.

'Oh, it's you!' she managed to say. 'Why did you give me such a stupid fright?'

'Fright! What fright! My dear, I was waiting for you to take my leave of you, that's all, and you were walking so quickly, plunged in your own thoughts, that I had to stop you!'

'All right then! I am sorry,' said Angélique coldly, 'but it's very childish. In future please be more straightforward! You frightened me so much I'm still trembling.'

She had attempted to take a few steps but her legs felt like lead and would no longer support her and she had to lean against the mouth of the vaulted passageway. She took deep breaths in an attempt to calm the wild hammering of her heart, but the air that evening was dense, heavy, laden with scents exacerbated by the storm, and brought her no relief. She continued to feel on the point of collapse, filled with that sense of anguish that deprived her even of her reasoning faculties, and when once again she let her eyes fall on Ambroisine's face, her fear returned.

The dim light from the fire burning in the grate of the cottage where she was living, that reached them through the open door, casting intermittent rose-tinged glimmers, even the starlight among the clouds created a half-light around her and Ambroisine, which was rent from time to time by a dazzling, silent flash of lightning. Much later and afar off they heard the stifled rumbling of the thunder. And yet even when darkness returned once more, Angélique could see Ambroisine. It seemed to her that the whiteness of that face grew more and more intense until it too gave off an abnormal glow, and the dusky fire of those strange eyes with their golden glint grew brighter and charged with some evil power which left Angélique incapable of escaping their charm.

'You are angry with me,' said Ambroisine in an altered voice. 'You are estranged from me, I can feel it. Why? In what way have I hurt you, my wonderful one? How little I care for homage: it fails to move me, but a single smile from you is more precious than anything else in the world . . . my wonderful one! How I have waited for you! How much I have hoped for you . . . and now here you are before me, against me, so lovely . . . Do not judge me . . . I love you . . .'

She had wound her arms round Angélique's neck and was smiling. Her teeth glistened like pearls, sparkled like the stars.

Her words seemed to come from afar off as if borne on a dark, strange wind.

Angélique felt her flesh begin to creep.

It was as if she saw tongues of flame dancing round Ambroisine, gathering together and tracing against the phosphorescent background of the night those words that had haunted her ever since she had set foot in America, those words she had read, in the hand of the Jesuit, in his letter to Father d'Orgeval, those meaningless ritual words, unbelievable, ridiculous, and yet which, suddenly springing to her mind, drove themselves home with a terrifying relentlessness: the *Demon*! The *Succubus*!

'You are not listening to me,' Ambroisine suddenly said. 'You're just standing there staring at me as if you'd seen a ghost. What did I say that was so frightening? I said I loved you. You remind me of our mother Abbess . . . she was very beautiful and very cold but there was a terrible fire behind her impassive face.'

She laughed softly, slightly tipsy.

'I loved her to take me in her arms,' she murmured.

Her expression changed again and once again the kind of aura, which was possibly only visible to Angélique, seemed to emanate from her whole being, and especially from her face, her eyes and her smile, that glowed with a passionate exaltation.

'But you are even more beautiful,' she said tenderly.

Angélique told herself that she had never met anyone as beautiful. There was something supra-terrestrial about her. The beauty of the angels, she thought.

Her heart missed a beat but this time it was under the impact of an unknown sensation, that of detachment from the earth, as if she would communicate with some ethereal world invisible to humans. By some inner drive like the effort made by a drowning person to reach the surface of the sea, she managed to break away from this feeling of giddiness. Fear had given way before intense curiosity.

'What is the matter with you, Ambroisine? You are not your normal self this evening? You are like someone possessed.'

The young woman exploded in a strident laugh but then grew calmer.

'Possessed! That's a big word!' An indulgent smile was playing about her lips. 'How emotional you are, my friend! And how your heart is beating!' she said placing one hand on Angélique's breast.

Her voice rang with passionate affection.

'Possessed, no, but fascinated, perhaps? Yes indeed, fascinated by you! Yes, I am. Didn't you realize that right away? As soon as I saw you on the shore there over in Gouldsboro, I came under your spell and my life took on another meaning. I love your laughter, so gay, your love of life, the gentle way you handle other people ... but above all I feel overwhelmed by your beauty ...'

She laid her head on Angélique's shoulder.

'How often I have dreamt of doing that,' she murmured. 'When you spoke of Honorine, your daughter, I felt jealous. I would have liked to have been in her place, to have known the warmth of your body. I'm cold,' she said with a shudder. 'The world is full of terrors, you alone are a refuge and source of pleasure.'

'You must be mad,' said Angélique who was getting out of her depth. She had the impression she was living through a kind of dream. She could feel Ambroisine's nails lightly scratching at the material of her bodice, and the sound reached her ears as a terrifying rustling.

It cost her an immense effort to detach those clinging hands and force the woman back.

'You have had too much to drink tonight. That wine made from the wild vine was strong.'

'Oh, don't start playing the virtuous woman again! Yes I know it suits you wonderfully well! You are very good at playing the seductress, and all the men fall for it. They love virtue on condition that it is prepared to weaken before their passions. But between you and me there is no need for these tricks, is there? We are both beautiful and we love pleasure. Won't you grant me just a little friendship in spite of what I said to you yesterday evening ...'

She laughed in that low, soft laugh of hers that had something sensual, something spell-binding about it.

A flash of lightning that cast a crude and dazzling light into the dark corner in which their conversation was taking place gave Angélique a further sight of that face transformed by indescribable passion that endowed Ambroisine de Maudribourg with superhuman beauty.

'Why not? Are men all that important to you? Why do you seem disconcerted by my desire? You are no innocent, as far as I know. And you are sensual! You have lived at Court, you even organized the King's pleasure so I was told. Madame de Montespan told me many a spicy anecdote about you. Have you forgotten them, Madame? . . . Knowing what I know about you I find it hard to imagine that you would turn down any opportunity for pleasure when it occurred . . .'

Taking advantage of Angélique's astonishment on hearing references to Madame de Montespan and her earlier life in Court, the Duchess of Maudribourg had freed her wrists from Angélique's grip.

She stood there rubbing them gently as if Angélique had hurt her, while her burning eyes continued to observe Angélique in the shadows, which were rent from time to time by blinding flashes of lightning. Then suddenly an expression of bitterness twisted the corners of her mouth.

'Why are you so cold to me? If it were a man caressing you you would certainly react in quite another way, that I am sure. Have you never tasted the same kind of pleasure at a woman's hands? What a pity! It has its points.'

Then once again she gave that throaty laugh which was both irritating and appealing.

'Why should it be left to mere men to bring us delight? They have so little aptitude for it, the clumsy creatures!'

She gave another laugh, but this time it was a sudden burst of mirth, grating and metallic.

'Their skill is so short-lived, whereas mine . . .'

Once again she drew close to Angélique and her smooth arms, scented and warm, encircled her again.

'Mine is inexhaustible,' she whispered.

Her arms were smooth as velvet, but their very softness gave Angélique a sense of inexpressible horror.

She felt again that a supple serpent of immeasurable strength was entwining itself about her, coiling itself with egoistic sensuality around her body, overwhelming her with its sickly-sweet, avid caresses.

Whoever said that serpents were cold and slimy? This serpent, full of warmth and life, of overwhelming tenderness, of stealthy and insistent charm, with the dazzling light of its human eyes fixed on her, she knew that this was The Serpent, that had come straight from the enchanted mists of Eden . . .

So powerful was this impression that she would not have been surprised to have seen a forked tongue slither between Ambroisine's parted red lips. 'I shall tell you everything,' said the mouth close to hers. 'Do you refuse me the only pleasure I am capable of enjoying on earth?'

'Leave me,' said Angélique, 'you must be mad.'

The encircling arms relaxed their grip and the vision, both terrifying and heavenly, seemed to melt away and the darkness returned. The sounds and movements of the real world about her swam back into Angélique's ken: the strident note of the cicadas, and the rustle of waves along the shore.

She scarcely noticed the sound of retreating footsteps as the figure of a woman running melted away into the night like a white ghost.

CHAPTER 42

ANGÉLIQUE FOUND herself sitting on her seaweed mattress in the little clapboard house. She felt dazed, but at the same time the incident that had just occurred had had the effect of dispelling the oppressive tension that had haunted her all day long. She felt as if she had landed violently on her two feet again and experienced a certain feeling of relief. How often had she asked herself the agonizing question: who is mad? . . . Colin, Joffrey, me, the English, the Huguenots, Father de Vernon? . . . Now suddenly the answer was clear. It was *she* who was mad, the Duchess of Maudribourg.

Now in the light of this fact many things seemed to fall into place: Colin's words, and what the two pirates she claimed to have overheard had said, also the words she attributed to Joffrey, even what Abigail had said when she inquired on behalf of the Protestants whether the King's Girls were to remain in Gouldsboro, a mark of distrust that had hurt Angélique at the time. Suddenly she had a fleeting vision of the haughty face of the Jesuit puckering up his brows when

Angélique had said, 'You are opposed to the King's Girls remaining in Gouldsboro.'

To which he had replied: 'I? It doesn't concern me . . .'

And yet Ambroisine had undoubtedly told her: 'Father de Vernon is categorically opposed to the idea . . . he fears for the souls of my girls . . .'

All lies! . . . A travesty of the truth through the cunning of a deranged mind.

A certain logic emerged from these murky events. Ambroisine's transformation had been no transformation at all. That had been the way she originally was, while the person she had seemed to be to Angélique, a young woman dedicated to good works, pious, devoted, somewhat intoxicated by religion, then little by little revealing the hidden torments of her bruised soul, was nothing but a lie. The true Ambroisine was the woman who just then had uttered those astonishing words . . .

She remembered one of the things Ambroisine had said:

'We are both beautiful and we both love pleasure . . .'

This woman who had filled her with pity, what was she? Dangerous, amoral? Pitiable!

Who would talk openly about Ambroisine de Maudribourg? Her protégées adored her and obviously revered her.

Then she realized that she had never spoken to anyone about the Duchess of Maudribourg, never sought to find out what anyone thought of her, not even Abigail or Joffrey.

Joffrey had simply told her about the Duke of Maudribourg, her husband, which information corresponded with what Ambroisine had subsequently told her. The Count had also granted that she was very learned.

But what he thought about her, about the benefactress, that she did not know. She even had the impression he had wanted to hide something from her. Had she therefore been made a fool of?

She remembered the scene on the beach in Gouldsboro when she had noticed the fact that every man present, including Joffrey, had his eyes fixed on Ambroisine. Did they see her then as Angélique had seen her earlier on? Transfigured by some inner flame, some superhuman joy?

'Oh God, how lovely she is!' she told herself in horror.

What man could resist the attraction of this beauty if he once perceived it? Is that what happens to women when they really love someone and are filled with desire? . . . Is that what I look like when Joffrey takes me in his arms? . . . Yes, perhaps I do.

Yes, but after all, a woman making use of her charms, holding men's attention . . . that was not sufficient reason for Angélique to cry out: 'It is *she* who is mad! The lies, all the lies, come from HER . . .'

Then, thinking about the recent exchange that had taken place between herself and Ambroisine she realized that what had been so unusual about it was the indescribable terror she had experienced when Ambroisine had clasped her arms around her.

Now this mere action alone did not warrant such a terror, although its intention had been to surprise her, for until then never for a single moment had it ever occurred to her that the pious and ravishing widow sacrificed to the cult of Sappho.

That was certainly something to make her feel confused! . . . But not enough for her to have been petrified with terror as she had been.

During the course of her lifetime and especially during the time she lived at Court she had had to extricate herself from situations far more thorny than that of rebutting the amorous advances of another woman. At Court pleasure reigned supreme. It was the poison that intoxicated that avid crowd, for ever seeking madly to satisfy the senses constantly solicited by every kind of earthly pleasure.

In that part celestial, part infernal ballet that took place at Versailles, by dint of experience, and guided by her natural instincts, the innate respect she had for other people, which made her indulgent to human passions provided they contained no admixture of cruelty, Angélique had learned how to preserve her own liberty and her inner feelings without making enemies. Except for the King, of course! But that was another story.

So why this panic that had paralysed her so entirely at one moment as to deprive her of all reaction, like a stupid rabbit in front of a snake?

The snake! That image again!

'It must be because she is mad! True madness inspires fear . . . No, I have been frightened before in my life, and I have encountered madmen! But that was something else! It was like all the fears on earth come together . . . Evil! *Who is she?*'

A sudden inspiration brought her to her feet. There was someone in Port Royal who might be induced to unburden himself about the Duchess of Maudribourg, someone who detested her and made no secret of the fact. If only she knew the reasons for this antipathy it might help her to form a more accurate judgement about the strange creature.

She left the house. The distant storm was still rumbling on the edge of the dark horizon. But the village was wrapped in silence. She walked downhill until she reached the house that lay along the beach.

As she approached the hut where Cantor was sleeping she saw his lamp shining through the half-open sky-light and she stopped. Was he alone? Can one ever be sure with these young men! But casting a glance inside, she gave a smile. For he had fallen asleep with his hand still outstretched towards a huge basket of cherries which he had placed on a stool close to his bed. In spite of the powerful muscles of a handsome young man's body, over which he had carelessly thrown a blanket, to her eyes he still looked like the little plump-cheeked Cantor who used to fall asleep every evening looking just like an angel. With his halo of golden-blond curls, his sunburned face, his slightly pouting full mouth, his eyelids with their long silky lashes, he still retained all the innocence of childhood.

She crept into the hut and sat down beside his bed.

'Cantor!'

He gave a start and opened his eyes.

'Don't be frightened. I only came to ask your advice about something. What do you think about the Duchess of Maud-ribourg?'

She had caught him unawares so that he would not have time to be put on his guard and become distant with her as he customarily was.

He raised himself up on one elbow and looked suspiciously at her.

She picked up the basket of cherries and placed it between the two of them. The fruit was a delight to the eye and to the palate. The cherries were huge, brilliant, and a true dazzling red.

'Tell me what you think,' she urged him. 'I need to know what you know about her.'

He hesitated long enough to eat two cherries and spit out the pips.

'She's a whore,' he declared at last in solemn tones, 'the most appalling whore I've ever met in all my life.'

Angélique dared not remark that his life had only lasted

sixteen years and that as far as this rather specialized domain was concerned it was even shorter.

'What do you mean by that?' she asked in a neutral voice, taking a handful of cherries.

'I mean that she seduces all the men,' said Cantor, 'she even had a go at my father! . . . Even at me.'

'You must be crazy,' said Angélique with a start. 'Do you mean to say . . . do you mean that she made advances to you?'

'But of course!' Cantor affirmed, his voice a mixture of indignation and naïve satisfaction. 'And why not?'

'A boy of sixteen . . . a woman of her age . . . and . . . no, that's impossible, you must be crazy!'

Although she had been prepared since that evening to hear anything about her, the sudden shattering of the image she had formed of Ambroisine de Maudribourg, pious, prudish and even frigid, frightened of the love of men, somewhat childish, prim, engaged in good works, in other words Ambroisine, kneeling to recite the rosary for hours on end with her faithful troop of attendants, this was too much.

'But the King's Girls are so full of respect for her, revere her like a mother . . . if she were like that surely they would know it . . .'

'I don't know how she manages to get round them,' said Cantor, 'but what I do know is that she has set the whole of Gouldsboro topsy turvy . . . there isn't a man, I tell you, who has not been the target of her attacks, and who is to know which of them succumbed? I've got my own ideas about that and they don't improve my opinion of certain people . . .'

'But this is crazy!' Angélique repeated. 'If all this had been going on in Gouldsboro recently I would have noticed it . . .'

'Not necessarily!'

And he added with surprising wisdom:

'When everyone is lying, or is frightened, or feels ashamed, or says nothing for whatever reason, it is difficult to see things straight. You too, she managed to get round you in her own fashion. And yet she loathes you so much that I can't imagine how anyone could hate as much as she does . . . "Is it your mother who wants you to be a good boy?" she asked me when I repulsed her advances. "And you want to obey her like a good little boy, what a ninny you are! She can't keep you all for herself. She believes that everyone loves her and is only too happy to do what she wants, but it's easy enough to deceive her *y* playing on her pity . . ." '

'Did she say that? Angélique exclaimed almost choking. 'If she said that to you . . . to you . . . my son! Well . . . she really is *diabolical*!'

'Yes, she is!' Cantor replied.

He threw back his blanket and grabbed his jerkin.

'Come with me,' he said, 'I think that at this time of night I should be able to give you some interesting proof . . .'

They crossed part of the village, instinctively walking without making a sound as they had learned to do from their contact with the Indians.

Cantor seemed to be able to see in the dark like a cat, and guided his mother safely along until they reached a kind of small open square where the houses began to string out along the foot of the hill.

Cantor pointed out one of these, that appeared quite large and had a small wooden porch. The house was built at the edge of the slope that rose towards the line of trees and the summit of the promontory.

'That's where she's staying, the "benefactress",' whispered Cantor, 'and I wager that at this time of night she will not be alone.'

He pointed out a rock behind which Angélique would be able to hide without losing sight of the surroundings of the house.

'I shall go and knock at the door at the front of the house. If, as I imagine, there is a man inside who would prefer not to be recognized, he will make his escape through that window at the back. You can't fail to see who it is, for there's enough moonlight filtering through the clouds . . .'

So the lad went off and Angélique waited there, her eyes glued on the back of the house.

Several minutes went by, then she heard a scuffling noise and, as Cantor had predicted, someone clambered out through the skylight, leapt down to the ground and ran off as fast as his legs would carry him. At first she thought that the man making his escape had run off in his nightwear, until she realized that what she saw flapping in the wind as he ran was the homespun habit of Brother Mark, the Recollect, chaplain to Monsieur de St Aubin on the Saint Cross river. In his haste he had not even stopped to tie his girdle.

Angélique stood there aghast.

'Well?' asked Cantor when he had rejoined her a few moments later. He moved so swiftly and silently that she had not heard him approach.

'I'm speechless,' she admitted.

'Who was it?'

'I'll tell you later.'

'Do you believe me now?'

'Yes, indeed!'

'And what are you going to do?'

'Nothing . . . nothing for the time being. I shall have to think. But you were quite right. Thanks for your help. You're a good boy. I only wish I had asked for your advice sooner.'

Cantor did not like to leave her, for he felt that his mother was mortified and almost regretted the all too complete success of his ruse.

'Off you go,' she insisted, 'off you go back to bed, go back to sleep with your cherries.'

She was overcome with tenderness to see him going off, so young, so pure, still so straight. He had all the righteousness and beauty of an avenging archangel.

When he had vanished into the night she in her turn walked down towards the house, climbed the porch steps and banged on the door.

Ambroisine's voice replied from inside sounding somewhat irritated:

'Who is it, for goodness sake?'

'It's me, Angélique.'

'You!'

She heard Ambroisine get up and shortly afterwards the Duchess drew the bolt and opened the door a mere crack.

The first thing that Angélique noticed on entering the room was the monk's girdle lying on the ground beside the bed. Pointedly, she walked over and picked it up, then folded it, looking straight at Ambroisine.

'Why did you tell me all those stories?'

'What stories?'

A seal-oil night-light burned brightly on a stool, illuminating Ambroisine's pale face, her dilated pupils, her sumptuous hair tumbling over her shoulders, as black as the night itself.

'That you cared nothing for love, for men, and that you could not stand any single one of them touching you?'

Ambroisine looked at her in silence, while a glimmer of hope came into her face and a wheedling smile began to play about her lips . . .

'Jealous?'

Angélique gave a shrug.

'No, but I would like to understand. Why did you find it necessary to confide in me as you did? Telling me you were a victim, that the brutality of men had made you forever incapable of knowing pleasure, that they disgusted you, and that you were frigid and insensitive . . .'

'But I am!' cried Ambroisine in tragic tones. 'It was you who drove me to behave in this crazy way by rejecting my advances. So tonight I took the first man who sought my favours in order to get my own back on you, to try at least to forget the torment into which you had thrown me . . . and look what a terrible thing it was . . . a priest! I have committed sacrilege . . . seducing a man of God . . . but all the way from Gouldsboro he's been following me, pestering me, while I have tried in vain to remind him of his duty. You never understood why he wished to accompany you to Port Royal. Well, that was the real reason . . . and I don't know what is to become of me in the midst of so many torments, the concupiscence of men and your hardness towards me . . .'

She suddenly looked up.

'How did you know that I was not sleeping alone? Did you follow me? Did you want to know what I was doing? So you don't hate me after all? You are interested in what I do?'

So anguished and avid was the anxiety that lay behind those last questions, that for a fleeting moment Angélique felt her pity reawakened, and this must have shown on her face, for Ambroisine crossed the room and threw herself down at her feet, twining her arms about her once more, begging her to forgive her, not to reject her, and to love her. But this contact brought back all the sense of revulsion and fear she had felt earlier.

And now she realized the truth with terrifying clarity. The woman before her neither loved her nor even desired her as her lovely lying mouth had said she did. All she sought was *her undoing*! Driven by fierce hatred, implacable jealousy and who knows what delight in destruction, she wanted to see her fallen, dead, vanquished for ever. Angélique!

'That's enough,' she said pushing her away, 'that's enough, I've had enough of your raptures! Keep them for those who are taken in by you.'

Crouching at her feet with her head thrown back Ambroisine de Maudribourg looked at her for a moment in silence.

'I love you,' she whispered almost breathlessly.

'No you don't,' Angélique replied, 'you hate me and you would like to see me dead. I don't know why, but that's how it is.'

Ambroisine's look changed again and she began to examine Angélique with a cold, piercing attention that made her flesh creep.

'They told me you were not an easy opponent,' she murmured.

Angélique struggled to free herself from the clammy fear that was once more creeping over her. She moved towards the door.

'Don't go,' Ambroisine begged her, holding out her pearly arms, while her parted fingers looked like claws. 'I shall die if I cannot win you.'

Kneeling on the ground, half naked, against the splash of scarlet formed by her long satin cloak which the light made shimmer like pools of blood, she gave Angélique the impression that she was caught up in some nightmare from Dante's *Inferno*.

'I know why you despise me,' Ambroisine went on, 'you want to keep your passion for the man you love. But he does not love you. He is too fond of his freedom to tie himself to a single woman. How stupid of you to imagine that you hold sway over his mind and his heart! No one holds sway over him, nor is he tied to any one! He chose me when he wanted to . . .'

Angélique stood with her hand on the latch, her heart assailed with doubt and anguish. She became defenceless at the mere mention of his name and did not realize that Ambroisine had hit on the only way of keeping her there and making her suffer, and was revelling in the discovery.

'Do you remember that evening when he talked to me down on the beach. You were frightened . . . and how right you were to be frightened. You asked me: "What were you talking about with my husband?" and I replied: "About mathematics . . ." because I felt sorry for you. I was thinking about the passionate, exciting advances he had just been making to me, and saw you so anxious, so jealous . . . you poor thing! How foolish of you to be so desperately attached to him. You see, he deceived you quite unscrupulously . . . You didn't realize that he had arranged to meet me here in Port Royal! You didn't even know when he was expected back.'

'And he wasn't even here,' Angélique retorted, pulling herself together.

Had she forgotten her recent discovery that everything Ambroisine said was a tissue of lies? Once again she had fallen into the trap.

'But he'll come,' said the Duchess, quite unshaken, 'he'll come, you'll see . . . for *me*, and me alone.'

CHAPTER 43

THUS EVERYTHING seemed clear at present. Ambroisine de Maudribourg was mad or worse, wilfully perverse, destructive and a liar.

There was no longer any shadow of doubt about her hatred for Angélique, but what did this hatred spring from, and what did she hope to achieve by it? . . . Was it instinctive jealousy of any happiness, or an innate need to hurt, an urge to drag down, to pervert anything that seemed noble . . .

And why did this have to happen just when she and her husband found themselves grappling with dangers both definite and ill-defined that had recently been convulsing Gouldsboro? First the drama of Gold Beard and his pirates.[1] Then, just when they were in this generally precarious state in which their own weakness mysteriously threatened them in the depths of their being, what ill fortune had brought them from the depths of the sea this outsider, this woman born to sow discord, anxiety, doubt, the temptations of the flesh, remorse, secret shame, silence? . . . A shipwreck! The shipwreck of the vessel called the *Unicorn*, drawn on to the shoals of Gouldsboro by unseen wreckers. Its victims had turned out to be more dangerous than the devils that had struck them down. There had followed an infernal round of crime, lies, and attacks, all committed in a state of heedlessness that subsequently seemed inexplicable.

Throughout all this confusion, this horrible dream, this welter of uncomfortable sensations impossible to unravel, Angélique clung to the one thing she knew to be certain, at least for her, the love Joffrey had shown her that evening when he had sent for her and said: 'Let's have it out, my love!'

1. See *The Temptation of Angélique.*

It was he who had made the first move, as if he were anxious to dispel the clouds that lay between them, to build a barrage of love that would also serve as a defence against the new onslaught that was about to be launched upon them.

Ambroisine de Maudribourg had disembarked that very morning. Had Joffrey de Peyrac's intuition warned him about her? Angélique longed with all her heart to see him again, and called to him within herself, reassuring him about her trust and her love in this deceptive and disheartening world. It was a thin thread but a strong one that bound her to him and she emphatically repeated to herself that she would never allow the jealous woman in her to destroy that bond. No matter what happened, the memory of the words of love he had spoken to her that evening, the memory of the look in his eyes, both inscrutable and passionate – that memory would be her lifeline during the coming ordeal.

Angélique waited for dawn sitting on the hillside above the village. The thin mist was already beginning to disperse under the effect of the rising sun. Angélique was sitting not far from the spot where Lord Alexander the Scot had built his fort in 1625, and brought in settlers wearing tartans and tam-o'-shanters to live on the side of the French colony, the first Port Royal, sacked and burned ten years earlier by the Virginian corsair Argall on the orders of the New England Puritans. Lord Alexander's fort had itself been destroyed in turn, but the Scots remained, and there were little red-headed children among the black-haired Acadians.

All this past history of Port Royal meant little to Angélique that morning; for her it was a place without a name, or rather a ghostly backcloth whose apparent peace and friendliness sorted ill with the revelations the previous night had brought her.

Cantor was right. When some people are lying and others are scared, anything can be going on under your very eyes in your very own house, without your being able to tell where the trouble comes from. That was how things had been with Angélique while she was at Ambroisine's mercy ... and she knew she was not through with her yet although she had grasped one end of the thread, that she was not yet through with bitter discoveries ... horrible discoveries, perhaps ... Dawn was coming, with a sombre blue sky in the quarter where the storm had rumbled, gradually revealing the harbour with its pewter-like glints.

One of the Oratorians, Father Tournel, in his black soutane, crossed the main street followed by a lad who had got up early to serve Mass for him.

Angélique waited a little longer, then, when the sun peeped over the eastern crest of the wooded slopes she stood up.

She walked along the side of the hill to where, somewhat further on, there was a clearing through which ran a little stream that then tumbled on down to the village. Angélique saw the man she had come to seek, for she knew that he was camping here. Wrapped round in a cotton loin cloth, a man stood washing himself vigorously in the running stream. It was Brother Mark.

As soon as he caught sight of Angélique, he showed signs of embarrassment, snatched up his monk's habit which he had thrown over a bush, and pulled it on smartly, somewhat confused at having been caught unawares in so few clothes.

Angélique walked straight up to him, drew the monk's girdle from her pocket and handed it to him.

'You left this last night at Madame de Maudribourg's,' she said.

Brother Mark had a new cause for embarrassment. He looked at the girdle as if it had been a poisonous snake and his usually carefree, sunburnt woodman's face turned an even darker red.

He took the girdle, knotted it around his robe, then, still with eyes downcast, began to gather together the few objects that lay scattered in the grass around the fire over which he had cooked himself a bowl of sagamite. Then at last he resolved to look at Angélique.

'You are passing judgement on me, aren't you? For breaking my religious vows.'

Angélique gave a sad smile.

'It is not for me to sit in judgement on you, Brother, where that matter is concerned. You are a vigorous young man and it is your business how you reconcile nature and your vows. All I want to know is: why *that* woman?'

Brother Mark took a deep breath and seemed to be affected by some inner turmoil which prevented his finding suitable words.

'How can I explain it!' he exploded. 'She never left me alone. Ever since her arrival in Gouldsboro, she's been pursuing me. Never have I been assailed like that. She got a hold over me by wiles whose power I recognize without understanding where their deceptive charm lies.'

A profound state of melancholy replaced his earlier excitement. He nodded his head.

'You think that there is something in her that could single you out if you took the trouble to love her, to penetrate her mystery. But all you find is emptiness. Nothing but emptiness, all the more deadly because it is decked with all the graces, with so many seductive mirages ... and then deep down, like a serpent's fang, a terrifying will to destroy you, to drag you down as she sinks to perdition ... no doubt the only pleasure she is capable of knowing.'

He fell silent, his eyes on the ground.

'I have been to confession to Father Tournel,' he went on, 'and now I'm leaving. I think that all this has nevertheless taught me something that will be useful to me with those I am supposed to help ... As for the savages, what can I teach them? They know more than we do about things pertaining to the soul. Fortunately I still have the forest and the tumbling waters.'

As he was a very young man whose heart was for perhaps the first time bleeding to have to forgo once and for all something that really mattered, his eyes grew suddenly red as he looked up towards the thick foliage full of humming insects, but then he pulled himself together.

'The forest is kind,' he murmured. 'And nature is mysterious too, full of beauty and snares, I grant you, but not depraved; and animals too are courageous and simple in their innocence ... perhaps the reflection we receive from things, of God our Creator, is less dazzling than that we expect from human beings, but at least it is a faithful one.'

He did up his pack and threw it over his shoulder.

'I'm off,' he repeated, 'I am going back to the savages. The whites are too complicated for me.'

He took a few steps then turned round, hesitantly.

'Might I ask you to keep all this a secret, Madame?'

She bowed her head in agreement.

He went on:

'You, Madame, I don't know ... but maybe you are stronger than she is. But do take care ...'

He stepped towards her and whispered as if communicating some vital secret:

'Take care! She's a *Demon*.'

Then off he went, striding briskly. She envied him as he set off beneath the trees with their musky smell.

CHAPTER 44

BACK IN Gouldsboro Ambroisine had said to Angélique: 'Don't you feel as if you were threatened by some danger . . . there is a demon at large . . .'

The demon was herself. How clever of her to have diverted suspicion from herself by making the first move and being the first to accuse others . . .

By a series of delicate touches, by a phrase dropped here or there, she had done her very best to separate Angélique from all who could have protected her, enlightened her, or warned her: from Piksarett, from Abigail, Colin, Father de Vernon, her own son even, and most especially from Joffrey, her husband.

She had said about Piksarett: 'People say you sleep with the savages . . .'; about Abigail: 'The Protestants are opposed to Catholics being settled in Gouldsboro, but they don't want to talk to you about it because they know that you are attached to the idea . . .'; about Colin: 'Do you really trust that man? . . . He strikes me as dangerous . . .'; and about Cantor: 'Your son is restless . . .'; about Father de Vernon she had said: 'He does not consider Gouldsboro a sufficiently wholesome place for my girls'; and Joffrey: 'He shouldn't have abandoned you like this . . .'

When Angélique analysed all these ruses that had gradually bound her hand and foot, a cold shudder ran down her spine and her hair stood on end, while in the midst of her horror she felt a kind of admiration for such a considerable genius for evil.

And as for the way she had been outwitted herself, what skill Ambroisine had shown in her choice of words and in her hypocritical play-acting. By representing herself as a victim in need of help, she had won Angélique's attention. By telling her that she loved Gouldsboro, she had warmed her heart . . . She had revealed that she was from Poitou as Angélique was herself and had asked her whether she had gone out collecting mandrake roots on some moonless night.

'Oh, Cantor!' Angélique said to her son whom she went to see again in his hut after the departure of Brother Mark. 'She really is . . . a monster.'

Then suddenly she burst out laughing.

'To have been taken in like that! Never . . . never in all my life have I met anyone with such extraordinary insight into human weaknesses. She is fantastic!'

Cantor looked at her darkly as he went on emptying his basket of cherries. 'You are like my father,' he said, 'he is amused by Satan's antics and entertained by his Machiavellian ways as if they were some strange oddity of nature. But look out! We haven't heard the last of her yet . . . She's still here, just a stone's throw away, and she has us in her power.'

Angélique suddenly remembered Father de Vernon's letter, with those words he had written that had struck her to the heart, words in which she had read an accusation levelled at herself, those words the Jesuit had written to his superior.

What if his accusation had not been levelled at her . . . but at the other woman?

'The Demon is in Gouldsboro . . .'

This time the shudder that ran through her chilled her to the very heart, for Father de Vernon was dead, the letter had vanished, as had the boy in whose possession it had been . . . Her head was beginning to spin! In her attempts to unravel the tangled skein of evidence she was going to end up believing in visions. One thing alone now seemed urgent, she must get rid of this woman, render her incapable of doing harm, set a distance between them forever, but how?

Outside, Port Royal was awakening, stretching itself, coming to life. Soon people would come inquiring after the Countess of Peyrac. She would have to make her appearance and meet Ambroisine again in the full light of day; life must resume once more apparently where it had left off. She would sit at Madame de la Roche-Posay's table, and see the Duchess of Maudribourg opposite, with that face like an ill-used angel's, with those fine, intelligent eyes, and maybe she would smile at her with that disarming smile of hers, full of contrition. At the very thought she felt quite sick and she realized that her son, that shy, uncompromising young man, was the only person with whom she could share her secret, the only person to whom she could turn for help.

Apart from him, there was no one to assist her, and anything she might attempt to say about the Duchess of Maudribourg to those around her would be rated as calumny. Ambroisine was the very image of virtue. Angélique realized that she was dangerously isolated and, remembering Colin's insistence that Cantor should accompany her, she thought of him with gratitude.

Now that she in her turn had seen things as they were, she must get Ambroisine out of the lives of them all.

But it was not going to be as simple as all that. Where was a ship to take her away? The harbour was empty, apart from the *Rochelais* lying at anchor. There were a few large fishing vessels lying motionless at some distance in the heat haze that hid the opposite shore and the sunken meadows with their retaining banks along the mouth of a fine river.

The Acadians of Port Royal were poor people; their one and only ship of any size was at that moment part of the expedition up the Saint John river. They had long since given up any hope of competing with the New England or European flotillas, which during the summer months lingered in the waters of French Bay, but bought their supplies of cod for the winter months down in Boston.

That morning Angélique felt so oppressed by the atmosphere that she was surprised at the lightheartedness with which this small, remote community went about its business and its pleasures, which included, among other things, the joyous preparation for the following day's celebrations, while Angélique tortured her imagination to find a way of hastening the departure of Ambroisine de Maudribourg and her flock.

Should she be sent off on the *Rochelais*? And in what direction? Under whose command? She did not like the idea of involving Cantor any further in the affair.

So what then? They could hardly kill her or drown her, or lose her in the Indian forest! For a fleeting moment Angélique envied the easy conscience of the 'lace-bedecked assassins' she had known in the old days at Court who, so easily and without wasting scruples, paid some cut-throat from the Paris underworld to rid them of their undesirable acquaintances.

She had not reached that point yet.

There were times when, because the sun was dazzling and hot, and the flowers brilliant, because the people at the gates of their tiny gardens seemed simple and good, she found the memory of all the evil she had glimpsed while Port Royal slept, begin to fade; then the panel like that of a triptych, would open again, revealing its other side, and show Hell in opposition to Paradise, night in opposition to day, and she saw Ambroisine naked and white against the scarlet satin of her cloak, and heard the voice of the Recollect father whispering: 'Take care. She's a Demon!'

The Duchess tried several times to approach Angélique in order to speak to her, but the latter evaded all encounters. In spite of innocent appearances, the truth she had glimpsed during the night had been too stark. Her eyes had been opened and now she could see in everything and everyone about her nothing but debauchery, lust, ignominy, and hypocrisy, as she attempted to construct plans for Ambroisine's departure.

Mademoiselle Radégonde de Ferjeac, busily engaged in her preparations for the play she was to put on the following day, completed the picture. In her total indifference to the secret torments of human passions, she had everyone exhausted. Bustling here, calling for people there, giving orders somewhere else, she roped in all the little Mic-Mac children playing in the streets to join in the dances, she sent people off to pick flowers, supervised the carpenters who were building her a stage in the form of a raft – you could see better from the beach – cutting out costumes, ripping up lengths of material, plaiting garlands. She would allow no one to stand aside.

Job Simon was immediately assigned the part of the god Neptune, and Petronella Damourt, because of her plump cheeks, that of Aeolus, father of the winds. She handed them both their parts which she had written out during the winter evenings and urged them to study them until they were word-perfect. She ran from one end of the village to the other repeating: 'Let's hope there's no fog tomorrow!'

She wanted Angélique to play Venus and Ambroisine Phoebe the Sorceress.

Meanwhile Madame de la Roche-Posay, quite unruffled, or perhaps accustomed to this sort of thing, was busy making cakes, for tomorrow there was to be a banquet.

The following day, which was a holiday for everyone, gave no one time to worry about personal problems. And perhaps after all this was for the best! Still no sail had appeared on the horizon. Everyone had to attend High Mass in their finest regalia. The Indians had come down to the village in large numbers, through the forest in their bark canoes, and from the other side of the basin. They had brought furs with them but

Mademoiselle Radégonde de Ferjeac was inflexible. She put a stop to all bartering at the first hint of it, and sent all the chieftains and 'principal' Mic-Macs off to paint themselves from head to foot in honour of the feast, and to form a 'guard of honour' on the waters of the harbour by drawing up their canoes in a circle round the raft upon which the play was to be performed. They did as they were bade for Radégonde de Ferjeac had, over the years, become one of their familiar demons, whom they had learned it was pointless to resist.

After Mass, which finished very late, the sun was still shining so a large table was set up outside on which were served quails and partridges, 'most delectably gamey', as Governor Ville d'Avray would no doubt have put it, accompanied by the excellent bluish-mauve Port Royal cabbages, which had become famous throughout the Bay, and Acadian turnips, which were unique in the world. After that there came cheese and wine, followed by open fruit tarts.

This was only a snack to give the actors time to get ready. Some of the men carried the pews from the two churches down on to the beach, while the women and their older sons set up enormous cauldrons to cook the Redskins' sagamite of boiled maize and fish, to be eaten to their hearts' content after the party. At some of the other tables the chief sagamores would join the settlers, and be served with daintier food by an army of cooks dressed in white gowns and aprons, who were getting ready to come streaming out as if by some miracle from the manor-house kitchen.

Radégonde de Ferjeac was hurrying everyone on. With the assistance of Armand Daveau whom she had commandeered for the occasion as her personal secretary and who was following her about with a portable writing desk equipped with pens, ink and paper, hanging round his neck, she was busy putting the finishing touches to the preparations. The governess's chief concern was not that any of her actors, duly schooled by her, should forget their lines, but rather lest fog should come down for in summer it was liable to descend on them quite suddenly.

But fortunately the sky remained clear.

The raft was towed out some distance from the shore; the Indian canoes stationed themselves around it, while the actors got into a boat that was to row them out to the stage.

'Oh please don't make me do that,' begged Petronella

Damourt. 'Ever since we were shipwrecked, I've been terrified of the water.'

'What's all this weeping and wailing about?' Radégonde de Ferjeac rebuked her sternly. 'Come on now, get on board! You shouldn't have come to America if you're frightened of the sea and being shipwrecked.'

Neptune was magnificent, totally unrecognizable in a long blue-green robe, with his white beard and hoary head wearing a gold paper crown and brandishing a trident borrowed from a crab-fisher. Cantor was there too with his guitar, and Delphine du Rosoy was a nymph. There were angels, cherubs and demons, and by way of make-up Radégonde had borrowed some of the special paint the Indians used to paint their bodies blue, white, red and black, and had created some terrifying masks worthy of ancient Greek comedy.

The spectators took their places on the benches and, when these were full, sat on the ground. The raft was a good idea, for, since the beach was sloping, the spectators could both see and hear with ease.

Angélique kept an eye on what was going on and did her best, out of politeness to Madame de la Roche-Posay, not to appear preoccupied. The society in which she had been brought up had laid great stress on the virtue of self-control, a quality she found very useful. During her life Angélique had many times realized the importance of being able to hide her feelings, whether of fear, of anger or of impatience, beneath a natural smile, an exquisite urbanity that lulled the suspicions of her adversary no matter who he might be. But she did not lose sight of the fact that Ambroisine herself was of noble birth, and it almost became a battle between the two of them as to which one would appear most gay and apparently relaxed in order to convince the other how little she cared for the dreadful revelations of the preceding night.

From time to time Angélique caught sight of Cantor wrestling with his guitar and being ordered about by Radégonde de Ferjeac, in whom the poor boy had found more than his match. He had been forced to don a garland of roses and get up on the raft to accompany the actors.

'He's divine!' said Ambroisine de Maudribourg gushingly, turning towards Madame de la Roche-Posay and Angélique.

'He was once a page at Versailles,' Angélique replied, 'and has learned to deal with all kinds of situations, and to cope with all kinds of whims! That's a tough training, whatever people may think.'

Job Simon had obviously missed his vocation. He would have done better to be an actor than to navigate ships to the Antipodes. In his well-modulated stentorian voice he recited the verses of the worthy Lescarbot which had previously been heard on this very spot in the days of the first settlement. Spellbound, the audience became absorbed in the account of the mythological vicissitudes suffered by the heroes of the action and all eyes were fixed on the raft and the seascape that served as backcloth. Thus it was that no one saw it coming – Mademoiselle de Ferjeac's personal enemy, the fog.

For it crept up on them from behind. Spilling over from French Bay across the top of the promontory it rolled down towards the village like an avalanche. No sooner had they felt its cold breath than it was upon them. Within a few seconds, in all that vast crowd, each individual found himself as it were alone, scarce able to make out his neighbour. First the shore, then the raft, and then the Indian canoes vanished in turn, and the sounds of voices died away.

'It's the same every year,' wailed the unfortunate governess. 'These dreadful fogs always spoil our party.'

Invisible in the mist she called out to everyone to remain in their places. Perhaps the fog would clear! To fill the gap she announced that baskets of iced buns and fritters would be passed round.

The actors called through the mist for someone to fetch them off their raft, but they too received instructions to be patient. It looked as if this particularly dense fog, because it was carried on a swift-moving current of air, might rapidly clear.

Half an hour went by and the situation did indeed appear to be improving, when someone brought tidings that there was a ship in the harbour. The rattle of an anchor chain had been heard. While this report was still being discussed, the fog lifted to reveal the shape of a small three-master lying motionless off the coast. Immediately there was a great stir. The raft and its occupants were becoming visible again but the play could not be continued before the new arrival had been identified. It was still only a ghostly shape, a shadow of a ship which from time to time vanished completely in the mist.

But already Angélique knew that it was not the *Gouldsboro*, which was a much bigger ship, and Madame de la Roche-Posay did not recognize it as their hundred-tonner, in which her husband had set sail to help Joffrey de Peyrac in the Saint John river.

'Perhaps it's the Company's ship dispatched from Honfleur. It's late August, and high time for it to arrive.'

'But it's a very small ship for that.'

'Oh, they are a mean lot! We no longer expect much more from our partners over there: we know them!'

Everyone remained expectant; then, as if a curtain had suddenly been drawn aside, the last traces of mist vanished, revealing the full extent of the basin, and a number of longboats at a few cables' distance, full of armed men rowing as fast as they could towards the shore.

A single cry went up:

'The English!'

There was a general stampede. Clambering over the wooden pews, people scurried for their houses to pick up their most precious belongings and hide them from the enemy looters. In the absence of Monsieur de la Roche-Posay who had taken most of the menfolk off with him to fight, the settlement had no defence to offer. The Indians were so well aware of this that they chose to draw away from the beach in their canoes. They had not come to fight, and accustomed as they were to traffic with English ships in this region they preferred not to get mixed up in the white man's quarrels.

But some of the sagamores who had Acadian relatives offered their help and some of the peasants who were more hot-headed than the rest went to fetch down their muskets.

'Mister soldier,' cried the Roche-Posay children turning to Adhemar, 'let's man the cannon, quick. We're going to have a battle.'

Out in the longboats the English sailors were shouting at the top of their voices to urge one another on. The first of the boats came up with the raft on which the powerless actors, in their masks and fancy costumes, were milling about.

'But it's Phipps!' Angélique exclaimed, recognizing the Bostonian who had accompanied the English admiral when he put in to Gouldsboro some weeks earlier.

Then she suddenly wondered whether he had seen Joffrey, and whether he would be able to give her news of him.

The situation did not seem to her to be desperate in itself. Gouldsboro's relations with New England were too good to rule out the possibility, with the Countess of Peyrac herself present, of reaching some kind of understanding with the new arrivals.

She told Madame de la Roche-Posay, who was resigned to what was about to happen, having foreseen it all too clearly.

'Don't worry. I know the captain of that ship. We did him some small service, and he will surely not refuse to talk things over . . .'

So together they made for the shore to be the first to meet the assailants. But Angélique had not noticed the Roche-Posay children dragging Adhemar off towards the port.

She was just beginning to signal to Phipps and call to him in English when the situation was disastrously transformed by the activities of the Marquis de la Roche-Posay's belligerent offspring.

The English captain, who as a Puritan could be identified by his black clothes and tall hat, had just laid a grappling-iron on the raft in order to take it in tow and capture the weird-looking company in their masks and fancy clothes, when Adhemar, at the top of his tower, chose to light the wick. There was an explosion and, whether by chance or by skill, a cannon-ball whistled overhead and landed plumb between the raft and the longboat, which both began to rock, hurling everyone into the water.

'Victory!' shrieked the Acadians, showing greater satisfaction at seeing the English struggling in the water than anxiety about the fate of Neptune and his followers.

The English sloop had indeed been hit and was sinking.

Chaos ruled and Angélique was forced to give up any idea of making herself heard. By now they had a battle on their hands. It was brief but violent. Adhemar's lucky shot was the only one fired. More boats landed a little farther along the beach, and their contingents of heavily armed sailors rushed to the assault of the little fort and laid hands on Adhemar before he had time to renew his exploit. A few rounds of musket-fire put the seal on the capture of Port Royal that day by the English forces. Seeing that all was lost, some of the inhabitants, carrying their cooking-pots and leading their cows by the halter ran off to the woods, for one never knew to what lengths these New-England sailors might go once they had decided to sack a French settlement. The others, including Angélique, and, generally speaking, everyone who had been down on the beach when the ship arrived, making up that part of the audience that had been closest to the stage, and comprising the leading members of the community – Madame de la Roche-Posay, her children and household staff, the Duchess of Maudribourg and her protégées, the chaplains, the notables' families, and Angélique herself . . . were surrounded, ordered to keep quiet and roughly herded within the circle of their own church pews with muskets trained on them.

Meanwhile those who had fallen into the water from the longboat and from the raft were struggling to reach the shore. Phipps and Neptune were the first to emerge from the water, looking daggers at one another. The former had lost his puritan hat, the other his golden crown.

Phipps was foaming with rage. If his original intentions had been far from peaceable, they had now become frankly murderous. All he could speak of was 'nooses and gallows' and of razing the village down to the last shack of these damned 'Froggies'. He knew them too well to be willing to show them the slightest indulgence. This New England settler had been born in a small village in Maine, which meant that his childhood had been spent amid constant attacks from the Canadians and their redskin converts, and that a good many of his family's scalps hung as trophies in Abenaki wigwams or on the walls of French forts.

'I'll teach you to go in for heroics,' he shrieked when Adhemar was brought before him, bound hand and foot. 'Uproot that big cross over there on the beach and put up a gallows in its place for this rogue!'

Hearing these words, Adhemar, who had picked up a smattering of English during his voyage east of the Kennebec, realized that once again his last hour had come.

'Madame, save me!' he begged, looking to Angélique among the sea of heads.

The uproar was at its peak. To the wails of those who had been rescued from the raft, among them the unfortunate Petronella Damourt, who had once again narrowly escaped from drowning, were added the shouts of protest from the local inhabitants trying to stop the English sailors from battering down the doors of their houses with their axes.

Phipps gave orders for the looting to stop for the time being. Later they would see, and, if they had to burn the lot, they would do so! But before that he wanted to gain possession of the most important booty, in particular to confiscate the charter – commissions and royal patents – in the possession of the Marquis de la Roche-Posay, which proved that the King of

France was granting support to the settlers in the area.

He began to climb the slope towards the Manor House, and Angélique reckoned that the moment had come for her to act.

'I am going to try to make contact with him,' she confided in the Marquise de la Roche-Posay, 'it is essential to do so now before things take a turn for the worse. In any case he will be able to tell us what has been going on on the Saint John river. It looks as if he has just returned from there and, to judge by his ill-humour, events can hardly have turned in his favour. Perhaps we might also get news of our husbands . . .'

She remembered that when William Phipps had put in at Gouldsboro with the admiral who was Governor of Boston, a member of his crew had turned out to be a French Huguenot, a refugee from La Rochelle, who was distantly connected with the Manigaults. The latter had invited him to a meal during the few hours he spent in port.

Fortunately she recognized this man among their guests, and sidling over to where he stood reminded him of who she was and of his visit to Gouldsboro.

'I must speak to your captain,' she told him.

She had no difficulty in persuading him, for the man had seen that Monsieur and Madame de Peyrac had excellent relations with the Governor of Boston, so he allowed her to leave the other prisoners and accompanied her himself up to the house.

In the main hall Phipps and his men were frantically searching for the documents they wished to seize in order to prove their rights and expose the double-dealing of the French. They were hacking open sideboards and cupboards with their axes while others endeavoured to force the locks of chests in the hope of finding, in addition to the documents, jewels or valuable clothes which these depraved Catholics were said always to possess in great quantities.

When Angélique arrived, she found Phipps throwing the china off a dresser on to the floor.

'You must be crazy,' she said, addressing him in his own tongue, 'you are behaving like a vandal! Those things are precious. Take them if you must, but don't break them!'

The Englishman swung round, beside himself with anger.

'What are you doing here? Go back to the others.'

'Don't you recognize me? I am Madame de Peyrac, I entertained you some weeks ago and my husband helped you out of a tight spot during a storm.'

This did nothing to calm the irascible man.

'Your husband! Yes indeed! He's just played a fine trick on me up there.'

Angélique plied him with questions. So he had seen her husband, had he? . . . He had seen nothing at all. There had been a fog, worse luck, when he was keeping a close eye on those damn Quebec officials trapped in the river. The fog had hidden the manoeuvres of Peyrac's little fleet from him. However had they all managed to slip away under his very nose? Those damned French! Booty and a prize capture he had sworn to take back to Massachusetts by way of increasing his bargaining power with those pig-headed people up there in Quebec, in bloodthirsty Canada, and by way of vengeance too for the blood of massacred New Englanders . . . crying out for justice.

He spoke somewhat confusedly in the manner of taciturn people not used to voicing their thoughts or putting their feelings into words. This made his resentment even more violent, boiling within him without finding any outlet for his pent-up anger.

'They've ruined everything up there . . . those savages from the north with their damned Papist priests, settlements ruined, settlers massacred . . . it's hard to stop them.'

'I know. I was among them all just some weeks ago. At Brunswick Falls I only just managed to escape. Did you know that I managed to save some of your compatriots and bring them back to Gouldsboro in safety?'

'Then why does Count Peyrac stop me from fighting those wild animals, at least getting hold of their bloodthirsty leaders when the opportunity arises?'

'In order to stop the war! Don't you realize that he also was responsible for preventing Baron Saint-Castine from bringing in his Etchemins, as he had received strict orders from Quebec to do, and that, had my husband not done this, it would not have been merely the settlements lying east of the Kennebec that would have gone up in smoke but all those on the islands, the shores of Maine and Nova Scotia. The war was brought to a halt thanks to him and now the slightest spark could result in a catastrophe of far greater proportions over which his influence would be powerless . . .'

'But we must bring these damn Papists up with a jolt!' Phipps shouted in despair. 'If we don't deal them blow for blow, they will exterminate us in the end, no matter what our numbers are. A handful of fanatics up there among their snows and their forest-lands, and us down here, ten times more numerous but like a lot of bleating sheep ... But I'm not of that stamp. I was born in Maine. I'll teach them that these parts belong to me and I'll spend my life doing so if I have to! Come what may, I cannot return to Boston empty-handed. Port Royal will have to pay for Saint John ... I must have hostages and also this charter from the King of France ...'

His eyes searched the room for a likely hiding place.

'Ah, what about that chest over there?'

In one corner of the room where it had been placed upon her arrival, Angélique recognized Saint-Castine's chest full of scalps. Angélique moved swiftly between Phipps and the chest.

'No, not this chest, I beg you. Those are my personal things.'

She beat him to the chest and sat down firmly upon it.

'I would ask you not to open this, sir,' she said firmly. 'My husband and I are good friends with the English, since we hold the title to our lands from the Massachusetts General Court, but there are certain acts we could not tolerate without feeling obliged to lodge a complaint, regarding whoever perpetrated them as a godless pirate, and no longer the representative of his government. Now listen to me,' she said, seeing him somewhat taken aback, 'sit down and calm yourself.' She pointed to a stool in front of her. 'I have a proposal to make to you which, I think, should make everyone happy ...'

Phipps eyed her with some suspicion. Angélique trembled at the thought that she was sitting on three-hundred-and-fifty scalps taken from Englishmen by the Abenaki Indians. She had a horrible feeling that their rank smell was leaking through every cranny of the chest. But her authoritative manner triumphed over the hot-tempered English Puritan.

He seated himself and, as he was still drenched from his plunge into the sea, a pool of water began to spread over the floor around where he sat, which he eyed in some dismay.

'Now listen,' Angélique went on persuasively, 'what exactly do you want? Hostages, through whom to bring pressure to bear on Quebec in order to obtain proper respect for your treaties, or to exchange for prisoners who have been taken off into captivity up north by the Abenakis and the Canadians? But here, as you are doubtless aware, the people are Acadians, French, I grant you, but so totally abandoned by their government and the royal administration that they are obliged to trade with Boston and Salem in order not to perish ... I grant that you could take Madame de la Roche-Posay and her children as hostages, but who would care about them in Quebec?'

Phipps knew this; it had already occurred to him. He gave a deep, worried sigh, untied his white neckerchief and wrung it out with a melancholy air. Then he pulled off his sealskin boots one after the other and tipped the water out of them.

'Well then, what are your proposals?' he said with a sigh.

'I would suggest the following. A very rich and highly considered French noblewoman has recently arrived here in Port Royal, accompanied by a group of young women whom she was to accompany to Quebec to make wives for Canadian army officers and young noblemen. Their arrival in Canada is still awaited, for her ship was wrecked near Gouldsboro, and we don't know what to do with them. Might I suggest to you that you should take them all with you. This noblewoman is so well connected that her capture would cause concern even to the King of France himself and in any case she is so rich that, even though she has lost her ship, you would be able to obtain a considerable ransom for her. I even believe' – Angélique allowed herself to stretch the truth a little here – 'that among her companions is a young lady betrothed to a high-ranking personage in Quebec ...'

The Englishman's hard eyes narrowed with the effort of reflection. He wrinkled up his nose and gave a sniff.

'But if they were going to Quebec, however did their ship end up in these waters?' he asked, for as a seaman he regarded that aspect of the matter as somewhat suspicious.

'The French are no good at navigation,' Angélique replied off-handedly. And as William Phipps was of the same opinion, he let the matter drop.

When one of his men arrived carrying the Charter which had been found in the desk of the clerk of works, his mind was finally set at rest.

'Very well,' he said, 'I shall let things rest there. But I'm taking that soldier with me. That's only fair: he wounded two of my men ...'

The embarkation of the Duchess of Maudribourg, her secretary Armand Daveau, the duenna Petronella Damourt and the King's Girls, with Captain Job Simon and the surviving cabin boy carrying the gilded unicorn between them, to be carried off

283

to captivity in Boston by the English, passed off without incident in an atmosphere of semi-indifference.

The Port Royal Acadians were delighted to have got off so cheaply. As soon as they had realized that the situation was taking a turn for the better and that everything would be all right, they appeared laden with furs, cheese and supplies of vegetables and fruit, offering them to the sailors in the hope of obtaining some English ironmongery which was of excellent quality and greatly sought after. Bartering proceeded briskly along the beach: a big round cheese for a box of nails etc. etc.

No one paid much attention to the departure of the hostages whom the English, in a hurry to catch the tide, hustled somewhat roughly on board.

Angélique and Madame de la Roche-Posay, each happy in her own way at having come out of it all at such little cost, did make sure that the King's Girls were given baskets of food to help them endure the crossing.

Quartermaster Vanneau was there too, but Delphine Barbier du Rosoy did not look at him. With hanging heads and downcast eyes, as if resigned to their strange, chaotic destiny, the King's Girls followed their 'benefactress'.

The unfortunate Adhemar, loaded with chains, was the first to climb into the boat.

'Oh Madame, don't abandon me,' he cried, turning towards Angélique.

But she could do nothing for him. She did assure him, however, that Phipps had undertaken to spare his life, and gave him some hope that the English might send him back to France ...

When the time came for Ambroisine de Maudribourg to step into the boat she halted before Angélique, who saw this time that the unbelievable truth which she had glimpsed in a flash during that nightmare evening, was indeed the real truth.

Before her stood a woman who sought her destruction, her perdition ... even her death. As if throwing off her mask, knowing that the game was lost, the Duchess no longer tried to conceal her jealousy and detestation.

'Have we to thank you for this charming arrangement?' she hissed with an attempt at an insolent smile.

Angélique made no reply. The hatred flaring in Ambroisine's eyes wiped out every memory of what might, between the two of them, have been the beginning of some degree of understanding and friendship.

'You wanted to get rid of me,' the Duchess went on, 'but don't imagine that you have won as easily as that ... I shall continue to do my utmost to bring you down ... and the day will come when I shall make you weep tears of blood ...'

PART FOUR

The Upper Reaches of French Bay
or
The Aggressors

CHAPTER 45

THE FURTHER the boat penetrated into the upper waters of French Bay the starker everything seemed to become and the more strongly accentuated, as if calculated to astonish, to surprise, to startle; everything seemed to aspire to be gigantic, immoderate, imposing, impressive – the beauty of the landscape, the splendour of the trees, the height of the tides, the violence and savagery of the inhabitants, the denseness of the fogs, the flavour of the lobsters and shellfish, the depths of the fjords, the variety and number of waterfowl, nesting in the peat-beds of Trantamare, the intense colours of the minerals – the red of sandstone, the white of salt, the black of anthracite – the meandering courses of the innumerable rivers, the majesty of the waterfalls, the multitude of cascades, the fertility of the soil, the hosts of fur-bearing creatures and the superabundant stocks of fish in the sea.

And like the hiding-place chosen by some insane brigand to store his treasure-trove – perhaps the great god Gloosecap himself – the place offered an infinite variety of natural curiosities, the reversing falls at the mouth of the Saint John, the tidal bore of the Petitcodiac, the ice caves, the petrified trees . . .

Here the sea threw up on the shore lumps of coal, opals, amethysts, cornelian, copper . . .

That evening a stout twelve-ton cutter bobbed up and down on the waves as it hugged the northern shore of Chignecto Bay.

Angélique, who was sitting in the stern, watched with some apprehension as the tall red cliffs slid by, their summits hidden by a curtain of misty rain.

She had the feeling she was entering some forbidden land guarded by hostile gods.

The boat was rigged with a single square sail, but sometimes had to be rowed and did not make much way. Its crew consisted of a handful of Acadians and some Mic-Mac Indians, the latter there more as travelling companions than as sailors. The owner of the cutter was Hubert d'Arpentigny, the young nobleman from Cape Sable, and the pilot was his steward Pacôme Grenier.

Angélique bore the journey patiently, knowing that in a few days' time she would join Count Peyrac on the eastern seaboard on the other side of the isthmus. For now she was trying to outstrip him, which was perhaps foolhardiness on her part for which he would criticize her, since he had in fact more or less implicitly advised her, when he had left, to wait patiently for him in Gouldsboro.

But at that time no one had foreseen that within a few days – a fortnight at the outside – so many dramatic events would have occurred that made it urgent for her to join him. Angélique simply had to find him in order to bring him up to date on all she knew, guessed or felt, and to find out what he himself had discovered. While still in Port Royal she had learned that, without going back to Gouldsboro, he was sailing towards the Gulf of St Lawrence, which involved going right round the peninsula of Nova Scotia. She could not wait any longer. They must be together and united in order to fight, to summon up their forces, and tell one another what they knew for certain and what they feared.

Angélique could not manage to place all the Ambroisine de Maudribourg business in the context of their own struggle. It was like some diabolical intrusion, intervening just at the time when, surrounded as they were by these mysterious hostilities, they had both found it equally difficult to see from whence came the real dangers to them, who precisely was the enemy.

After talking to her son and learning from him how the Duchess had lied about certain matters in Gouldsboro, Angélique could no longer have any illusions about the evil intentions that had led the woman, after her shipwreck, to sow unhappiness and discord among those who had saved her life. A constant stream of memories, deeds, words, barely perceptible reactions came back to her, now taking on a new meaning. She remembered a comment of Adhemar's, the poor innocent, when one day she had said to him: 'Be careful not to waken Madame de Maudribourg,' and he had replied: 'Oh, creatures like that don't sleep; they only seem to.' A strange warning about Ambroisine's strange activities for, as Angélique now knew, Ambroisine was forever ferreting about in Gouldsboro, a warning which had gone right over her head, so easily had the Duchess succeeded in persuading her of her inactivity: 'I have been praying all day. I slept for a few hours . . .'

Then there had been the Indian Piksarett's reaction. She now thought she understood his sudden change of attitude when he said: 'Take care, danger threatens.' Ambroisine de Maudribourg had been standing a few paces from him. Had he, a redskin, so sensitive to the obscure meddlings of invisible spirits, sensed the demoniacal power that dwelt in this woman?

Angélique ran her hand over her brow.

'I'm losing my bearings . . . I must get back to more down-to-earth matters.' A jealous, twisted woman trying to destroy a happiness she found unbearable, that lies within the bounds of normality . . . What was less normal was the lengths to which this clever woman had been prepared to go to further her destructive schemes . . . Had she been standing under Abigail's window that night when Angélique had heard that inhuman cry? Was it she who had poured poison into Abigail's infusion? If it was, Angélique told herself, here was a woman who was capable of *anything*!

She did not dare delve any further into a matter which she was unable to support with proof. It seemed too crazy, too monstrous. When she had joined forces with Joffrey, she would show him the scarlet pillowcase; then she would dare to lay all the facts before him, and to try to understand why, why the Duchess of Maudribourg had been driven to behave as she had towards them. She herself was merely the victim of a shipwreck, the victim of dramatic and criminal actions. Did the wreckers in fact exist, who were said to have lured the *Unicorn* on to the rocks?

Angélique recalled all the traps that had been placed in their path since they had left Wapassou in the spring, more or less forgetting Ambroisine in order to go back to the very first indications they had had of foul play, which had been more obvious although also disguised and operating through deceit. But the time would come when the veil would be rent asunder and the mysterious occupants of the ship flying the orange standard would show their faces. They would become human beings who could be fought and overcome, and hanged outright for their foul deeds and their double dealing. But first they would talk, and through that it would be possible to trace the plot back to its source and find out from what quarter the blows came and who had paid for them to be struck. Now that Joffrey was on their heels, the end was not far off. She was quite confident about that.

She must put Ambroisine out of her head. Now she was far away and could no longer harm them. The English would not release their prey so easily as that. Ambroisine was just one of Satan's grinning faces, another of his jokes sent to confound human beings.

Angélique did not hide from herself the fact that this brief episode, in which she had felt the breath of ruthless hatred upon her, a will to destroy her such as she felt sure she had never before inspired, not even in Madame de Montespan – for Madame de Montespan wanted the King, whereas on this occasion the stakes provided no justification – this encounter in which she had come within an ace of defeat, had left its mark upon her. 'Oh well,' she told herself, 'that will teach you not to allow your judgement to be warped by your own weaknesses.'

Ambroisine had arrived at the very moment when she had been having doubts about herself, just when she had felt the foundations of her life to be threatened, when she found it difficult to escape from the whirlwind that had flung her personality to the four winds as if in despair, as if split in two: the successive shocks of her moment of aberration with Colin, her fear of a Joffrey she no longer knew, whom she must keep and win anew, her discovery of herself, and the fact that she had been forced to take a good look at herself, to question everything, to recognize herself and even to see herself in a new light, to accept herself as she was, to become aware of the necessity for alertness, and also of the wounds life had inflicted upon her, of the moral infirmities she still suffered from in spite of herself as a result, and which she must find courage to treat and to heal ... He would help her. She remembered the tenderness of his words that had reassured her, and called her back to him, and had been like balm to her crippled heart ...

But at a time like that the other woman, the jealous woman had found it only too easy to confuse and embroil her. Happily the danger was now past, and Angélique, as she watched the low clouds swirling around the tops of the reddish cliffs, gave a sigh of relief. She congratulated herself on having succeeded in getting rid of the dangerous creature in time. Phipps had been a heaven-sent blessing. Nothing would remain of this episode beyond the experience from which she would do well to learn a lasting lesson.

It was not the first time that she had noticed that when deceit and lies abound the only people to see through the enemy's game are simple, even naïve people like Adhemar, or, at the other extreme, those whose personal acquaintance with vice and dishonesty enables them to identify it more easily in others. Such had been Aristide and Julienne who had not hesitated to denounce the Duchess forthrightly. But who had listened to them? Mostly people whose credit was slender, often for good reasons, with the great of this world and 'respectable' people.

But at last all that was over.

In a few days' time Angélique would join her husband again; she would seek refuge against his heart, abandon herself to his strength. No longer would she be proud, for she had learned during this crisis how dependent she was upon him.

She had decided more or less at a moment's notice to make her way up French Bay. After the English had departed with their hostages, Angélique, still in Port Royal, had asked herself what she should do. Should she return to Gouldsboro? And supposing meanwhile her husband were to put in at Port Royal as Ambroisine had predicted? In the end she had sent the *Rochelais* back to Gouldsboro with Cantor to see whether there was news there. But no sooner had the little yacht crossed the harbour bar than another ship sailed in. This time it was Monsieur de la Roche-Posay returning to his domain.

He was accompanied by Hubert d'Arpentigny and his cutter full of Mic-Macs in their pointed hats. He had been taken by Phipps but released on account of his extraordinary appearance. The Puritan with the cropped hair could not make up his mind about the true identity of his prisoner who was said to be a French nobleman of ancient lineage. But the man wore his hair in black tresses bristling with feathers, a fringed leather jerkin; his skin was the colour of red clay and Phipps found his black eyes disconcerting; so he thought that for the time being he would prefer to release his catch.

The two men brought the news that after pacifying the approaches to the Saint John river, Joffrey de Peyrac on board the *Gouldsboro* was sailing for the Gulf of Saint Lawrence.

'The Gulf of Saint Lawrence!' cried Angélique horribly disappointed. 'But what business has he up there? And he is not even calling in here first . . .'

'He had no idea that you were here, Madame,' said the Marquis, 'and I understood that he did not intend even to put in at Gouldsboro. He seemed to be in a hurry to reach the southern shores of the Gulf of Saint Lawrence as soon as possible in order to meet old Nicolas Parys who owns those lands from Shediac to Canso Point and even Cape Breton Isle and the Isle of the Blessed Sacrament that lie opposite.'

Whatever Joffrey de Peyrac's objective was, he was moving still further away.

Angélique asked for maps; she could not bear the idea of waiting any longer. If the *Rochelais* had still been lying at anchor in the harbour, she would have immediately set off in pursuit of the *Gouldsboro*. And yet – what a nuisance – she had just sent it back with Cantor on board. She was almost in tears. Hubert d'Arpentigny was watching her and with that intuition commonly found in the very young who find it easier to understand the role of emotion in female motivation because they themselves are still governed by their feelings, he shared in her disappointment and impatience.

'And supposing you were to arrive there before him?' he suggested.

She looked at him without understanding what he meant, and he placed a finger on the map.

'If I take you up to the far end of the Bay, there, one of Marceline's sons or one of the Defour brothers will accompany you on foot across the few miles of land that separate the top of French Bay from the Gulf of Saint Lawrence. And there you are! You will come out somewhere between Shediac and Tatamagonge and Count Peyrac has only to suffer some small delay in sailing round the Peninsula[1] and you will reach Nicolas Parys's before him.'

So she had agreed. It would be a short journey; on the evening of the second day they should be off Penobsquid. Hubert d'Arpentigny said that they would put in at Carter's, an Englishman from Massachusetts who had had his ears cut off for making counterfeit money. He farmed a piece of land down one of the many red-sandstone fjords whose narrow mouths they would from time to time notice leading away down some labyrinthine river to the haunts of bear and moose.

'Don't miss the entrance,' Hubert d'Arpentigny impressed on his pilot. 'It should be easy, for Carter lights a fire every evening on a promontory and has two fishing families keep an eye on the spot. You can see the lights of their cabins slightly to the left of the fire.'

This advice was far from superfluous, for it was pitch dark.

1. The Acadian peninsula or Nova Scotia.

Angélique wrapped her sealskin coat about her for the damp, salt-steeped air was penetrating. She thought of Joffrey: every hour that passed brought her closer to him and she felt a desperate need to join him so that they could at last pool their defences. Their defences against whom?

She threw back her head and the low-hanging storm-clouds, swirling black and tormented like vapours from hell, seemed to reply to her question:

'From Satan!'

Fear, immediately suppressed, clutched at her throat, and she had the impression that the launch was bobbing up and down more violently on the swell.

'Ah, I can see lights over there,' she cried.

And the thought of those green dragon's eyes that guarded Chignecto Bay came back to her memory.

'That's Carter's hamlet!' Hubert d'Arpentigny exclaimed delightedly. 'Find the channel, Pacôme! In less than an hour, we'll be eating a flitch of good bacon and drying our boots.'

The swell began to shake them about by way of response. At first it was a series of crests and troughs that grew deeper each time as if under the effect of some irresistible impulsion from the depths of the sea. Soon the big boat seemed to be tossed about like a straw on the crests of waves that grew more and more gigantic.

'Find the channel, Pacôme,' Hubert d'Arpentigny cried out again as he clung to the side.

Then came the shock, as if a sharp piece of steel held in some gigantic hand had shot forward and buried itself deeply in the side of the boat; almost instantly Angélique found herself up to her waist in icy water.

'Every man for himself,' came the cry of voices. 'We have struck the rocks of Saragouche!'

In the darkness the heavy boat was now being buffeted from one rock to another, this deadly dance being accompanied by the screams of the shipwrecked sailors and sinister crunching sounds.

Acadians and Mic-Macs called out in their native tongue, while Hubert d'Arpentigny shouted in French for the benefit of his passenger.

'We are near the shore, Madame, try to . . .'

The rest was drowned by a further roar as the foaming sea boiled over them, covering them right over their heads, before hurling them down, streaming water, beside another reef.

Angélique knew that she must try to get away from the boat before it was smashed to pieces, otherwise she ran the risk of being too seriously hurt or stunned by a blow that would leave her unconscious at the mercy of the fury of the sea.

So terrible was her memory of the time she had nearly drowned off Monhegan, when she had been rescued by Father de Vernon – especially the sensation of being paralysed and dragged down to the bottom of the sea by the weight of her clothes – that she almost unconsciously found strength to untie her linen over-skirt and step out of it and to kick off her shoes. At that very moment a further shock of unbelievable violence scattered them all, and Angélique, clinging to a broken spar from the side of the boat found herself hurtling forwards. She knew the way the sea plunged in towards the beach, that it was essential to let go of her spar in time and grasp anything that came to hand before the retreating wave claimed her once again as its prey. She felt herself enveloped in shingle from the beach, struck a rock and clung to it.

In a moment she was dragging herself on her elbows and her knees across the sand, remembering what Jack Merwin had told her . . . 'Up to where the seaweed is dry . . . not before that . . . you mustn't stop . . . otherwise the sea will get you again.'

At last she felt the soft dry sand and collapsed on her back, panting for breath, scratched and torn all over but unaware of the pain in her body.

She was lying at the foot of a very tall cliff which, rising up before them, had accentuated the darkness in which they had been struggling. Now she was beginning to see more clearly and as she looked towards the Bay she could see the sea where the rocks among which they had gone down looked like blacker blotches ringed with white foam, for the stormy sky was dimly lighted by the moon which from time to time pierced the clouds and cast a brighter light before once again growing dim. But that was enough. Angélique could almost see the debris of the boat tossed hither and thither and even thought she saw men's heads among the eddies. Some way off, one or two of them were clambering ashore.

She wanted to call out but had not the strength to do so. And yet she began to feel more confidence. They would all be saved. Just another shipwreck! This coastline abounded in them, one simply had to get used to it! But what exactly had happened? Why had they seen those lights on the hillside if they had only reached the approaches to the rocks of Saragouche?

As this thought occurred to her, she half sat up and with particular concentration looked about her in an attempt to solve the mystery of this pallor stained with inky-black patches.

All her senses were on the alert. She thought she caught the sound of terrible cries mingled with the roar of the sea on the rocks, but it all seemed confused.

Why those lights up on the cliff? Like when the *Unicorn* had gone down!

Then suddenly a human form appeared a few paces from where she lay, stepping forward from the shadow of the cliff. It was someone come from the land. A man coming towards her, a black figure against the moonlit sky. He seemed to be scrutinizing the sea as it raged in the creek where Hubert d'Arpentigny's boat had been smashed.

For a moment he turned round, and Angélique had the impression that he was looking in her direction.

She was about to hail him but the sound died away in her throat, for, projected as he was like a figure in a shadow-play against the brilliance of the moonlight, she saw that in his hand he held a kind of short stick.

'The man with the lead cudgel!'

And everything Colin had told her about this criminal of the seashores flooded back into her memory. So it really was he! He was not a myth. The man Colin had spoken about, the murderer, the wrecker who lured ships on to the rocks and finished off the survivors with a lead-weighted cudgel.

And at the same instant she felt certain that these ghostly wreckers did exist and that they were going to kill her.

CHAPTER 46

SLOWLY HE began to walk towards her. He was taking his time. She was at his mercy. Cast up by the sea after an exhausting struggle, only half conscious, what victim could ever defend himself against blows dealt by these lurking murderers?

As she lay there powerless, Angélique realized that her half-naked body must form a white patch that made her clearly visible to her assassin. He came closer. Then for a moment, swallowed up by the shadow of the cliff, he disappeared from view. But she began to hear the sound of his boots crunching on the shingle. She felt around with her hand until she found a fairly large stone and threw it in the man's direction. The stone fell to the ground with a dull thud, having missed its mark. Again she threw another stone. She heard him give a mocking snigger. The man was enjoying her hopeless attempt to defend herself.

Then the snigger was suddenly cut short and the man gave a strange hiccough. Something fell to the ground not far from where she lay; the man had crumpled up.

For a moment nothing stirred and Angélique lay where she was, every nerve tense.

Then another silhouette stood out against the moonlight on the exact spot where the murderer with the lead cudgel had first appeared a few moments before. But this time it was a Redskin, for she could see his bow still flexed for the arrow that had just killed. Angélique's heart gave a bound of joy and relief.

'Piksarett!' she cried with all the strength of her lungs. 'Piksarett, I'm over here!'

For she had recognized unmistakably the feathered, gangling form of the chief of the Patsuiketts.

Taking new heart, she got up and went to meet him. After walking a few steps she stumbled over the prostrate body, and a feeling of revulsion and fear made her start back, and she almost fainted. She was shivering, soaked through, in her short petticoat and bodice that clung to her skin. During the shipwreck she had lost her sealskin coat and her fortunately minimal luggage, which contained no more than a change of clothes but had included her comb and tortoise-shell brush which she so loved. But there were other things to worry about before she wept their loss.

Piksarett was kneeling by the body. She could hardly make him out, but the musky smell of his body filled her with relief. It was indeed he.

He was busy removing the arrow which had struck his victim under the shoulder-blade. Then he turned the body over and in the darkness the dead man's face made a whitish patch with his open mouth a black shadow in its midst. She was unable to make out his features.

'And where were you off to again, captive?' came Piksarett's

297

voice. 'Do you imagine you can escape me? You see I got here in time.'

'You saved my life,' Angélique told him earnestly. 'That man was going to kill me.'

'I know. I've been on the lookout for them for several days. There are a lot of them, six or seven . . .'

'Who are they? French or English?'

'Demons,' Piksarett's voice replied.

This superstitious savage with his native simplicity had unashamedly put into his words what she already knew. Only 'they' were closer now. 'They' were revealing their identity instead of shrouding their actions in mystery; now their faces could be seen. It is true that such faces only reveal themselves at the moment of striking.

'You are cold,' Piksarett remarked, hearing her teeth chattering.

She trembled as she recognized his familiar voice.

'Dress yourself in this man's things.'

He unclasped the belt with a pistol attached and stripped the corpse of its jerkin, part leather, part wool. Angélique donned the garment and felt the better for it. She would dearly love to have seen the face of her invisible enemy, but Piksarett refused to drag him into the moonlight.

'Let us wait for dawn,' he suggested. 'I'm alone here and if "they" are still around, "they" might find us here. When day dawns "they" will go away.'

She would have liked to have asked him what he was doing there, why he was alone, he a Narrangansett wandering about in the land of Malecites, whether he knew the whereabouts of Michael and Jerome, and why he had run away from Gouldsboro. But the best way of ensuring that you get no reply from an Indian is to ask him questions, so she held her peace. She was dazed with fatigue and beginning to feel pain from the salt in her wounds. A little before dawn, Piksarett was intrigued by the light of a fire burning not far from them in the creek. He crawled towards it and returned to tell her that it had been lighted by a group of Mic-Macs in order to dry their clothes and grill some fish they had threaded on a stick.

'It must be the ones who were with us in the boat. Did you see any whites?'

No, he had not.

Angélique had been expecting to find that the dead man's face was that of the pale man who had accosted her one evening

298

in Gouldsboro, saying: 'Monsieur de Peyrac wants to see you on Old Ship Island.'[1] She was disappointed and also frightened to see that it was not he. So *he* was still alive, still more dangerous than the man who lay there. She could see that this man was only a thug, a brutish creature trained to strike without scruple or pity. She could see it in his low brow and his hard, scowling jaw. His hair was long and unkempt.

Before abandoning him to the crabs, Piksarett bent down and with a flick of his knife removed the unsavoury scalp and hung it at his belt.

'Our ancestors used to have to bring back the heads,' he explained to Angélique, who was startled at his action. 'Now the hair is enough evidence of our victories. Removing a scalp with a flint as we used to was a difficult operation. Fortunately white men have given us steel knives . . . come. Let us go to the Mic-Macs. They are not people like us, but they are after all Abenakis, Children of the Dawn.'

With the coming of day, the mist had begun to lift; it was not too thick and would clear with the heat of the day. As they approached the Mic-Macs, Angélique and Piksarett heard the sound of melancholy chanting, to which another group of voices gave the responses in a monotonous undertone.

'The death chant,' Piksarett whispered.

They found the great Mic-Mac sagamore Uniakke kneeling before the body of Hubert d'Arpentigny, whose skull had been fractured.

'They have killed my blood-brother,' he told Piksarett after the latter had gone through the customary approaches and given his name.

'They struck him down as he emerged from the sea. I saw them.'

Piksarett told them what he knew about the men who, taking advantage of the darkness and the difficult terrain, had lured the cutter on to the rocks.

'Take me to them, so that I may wreak vengeance for this crime. How I regret' – the Mic-Mac's square face, normally a brownish-yellow colour was so pale and ravaged with powerless grief that it seemed carved in ivory – 'how I regret not having been born an Iroquois or an Algonquin like those Hurons in the north, so that I could torture those wretches to death. But their scalps will hang in my wigwam or I shall never return to my own people.'

1. See *The Temptation of Angélique.*

'I have one already,' said Piksarett in triumph.

He proposed an alliance, which they sealed with a few rites, then offered to take them to a place where they could prepare a stewpot, after which they would hold council.

Angélique's teeth were still chattering, less on account of the cold than with horror. The nightmare continued, was growing more definite, taking shape. First it had been the victims of the *Unicorn* whose deaths had been blamed on the elements and bad luck, and now two Acadians and three natives had been murdered, and they were now certain that the deaths were intentional. The death of Hubert d'Arpentigny, the well-known nobleman, would undoubtedly cause a great stir in French Bay, even in Quebec, for in spite of the conflicts between the two regions, Acadia still remained in the eyes of the French Kingdom an integral part of New France, under the Government of Canada.

'Poor young Hubert d'Arpentigny, so full of life and passion! ... It's my fault,' she told herself, 'why did I stop him returning to his estate at Cape Sable ... It was my death they sought and he has been struck down ...'

An icy chill crept over her: 'Our name – my name above all – will once again be associated with disasters that have struck the French. First there was the vessel carrying the King's Girls, heading for Quebec, that foundered off Gouldsboro, and now this worthy young Frenchman has been murdered in my company ... How can I prove that it was a trap? No one will believe us ... they won't listen to the evidence of Mic-Macs ...'

More than ever now, with danger looming so close and growing more clear-cut, she felt she must join forces with her husband.

The group of surviving Indians divided in two. Six of them were to bury the dead until such time as they could take them back to their villages. They were to go to a nearby village of some kinsfolk in the hope of finding some canoes in which to travel across to the Peninsula bearing the sad news.

Uniakke and his lieutenant would go with Piksarett the Abenaki, who had undertaken to lead them on the path of vengeance. Angélique was pleased to hear Piksarett say that the first thing to do was to find the Man of Thunder, that was to say Joffrey, who was owner of the lands stretching from the mouth of French Bay to the source of the Kennebec.

'His enemies are now our enemies. He is pursuing them and

is at the moment off Shediac with Skoudoum and Mat-econando. He has ships, arms, cunning and knowledge. Let us ally ourselves with him and get his advice before setting off on our campaign against those who have killed your blood brother Uniakke; for, my brothers, we must be prudent. I do not know what kind of whites they are, these killers. They are neither English, nor French, nor pirates, nor men from St Malo ... They have a ship, possibly two.' Then he lowered his voice in conclusion:

'And also ... I think they are possessed by evil spirits.'

She noticed that Piksarett's prying eyes were for ever on the alert. He, the mystical savage, had an inborn awareness of these hidden threats, of these lurking perils that stole upon them in apparently harmless guise. She remembered his sudden change of mood when he had come to Gouldsboro in search of her ransom, the way he had begun to look around him as if sensing the approach of some noxious beast: 'Take care,' he had told her. 'Danger lurks about you!' Then he had run away! As Jerome and Michael had said ... On what track had he gone off then? It seemed as if she had led him to just the right place since he had appeared at the very moment when the trap which she, Angélique, had not discovered in time was about to ensnare her.

But now she felt reassured at finding herself in his company and under his protection, so she was in good heart when she followed him into the depths of the forest with the Mic-Macs. Piksarett the redskin already knew a great deal, and if he was unable to communicate it to her, because his information came from a special, indefinable sense, she could at least trust him. And in the situation in which she found herself she began to understand that it was precisely these powers she needed; for the anguish she had felt, especially since her visit to Port Royal, was less physical – although she now knew that her life was in danger – than moral, stemming from the knowledge that some-one was trying to hurt her and destroy something she possessed that was more precious than life itself.

Had her enemies been at Port Royal, as they had been in Gouldsboro, incredible as that might seem?

Before leaving the seashore, the Indians carefully searched the rocks again. There they found several objects that had be-longed to passengers aboard the boat, including Angélique's bag and her shoes. This discovery cheered her, for although her bag, apart from her tortoise-shell toilet-case, contained nothing of value, when one has been shipwrecked on a wild shore every-thing has its uses. She wrung out the water from everything she could. The rest could be dried out later. She had brought with her, with the intention of showing it to Joffrey when she met him, Abigail's scarlet pillowcase with its stains and holes. She was pleased not to have lost this important piece of evidence connected with a matter she had found very suspicious.

As soon as they left the shore, the land lay sweltering under the motionless, secret air. It was intensely hot and there was not a breath of air. It was already the end of the summer, preceding the glorious autumn. Everything was tinder-dry and the under-growth crackled beneath their feet. Soon would come the time of forest fires, mingling their purple and scarlet flames with the purple and scarlet of the trees.

But meanwhile the forest was still clothed in emerald green, with its cedars, its spruces and the sharpened perfume of resin and a myriad wild fruit-trees.

Piksarett led his companions off the beaten tracks leading to Indian villages. Not one of the three redskins seemed keen to encounter the natives of these parts, Malecites with green eyes, whose blood, mixed from time immemorial with that of Breton fishermen, indeed Vikings, the first to discover these lands, had made them talkative and mercenary, over-accustomed as they were to trading with ships and indulging in deadly drinking bouts. Towards noon they came out into a clearing that was so overgrown with tall grasses and bushes that they had to cut their way through it with their knives until they came upon three or four large wooden cooking-pots at the edge of the line of trees.

'I told you we should be able to have a feast,' said Piksarett, very pleased with himself.

'You who are a Patsuikett from the Merrimac River, you know this area better than we do, who live beside it,' the Mic-Macs admitted.

'Once the whole earth belonged to the Children of the Dawn,' Piksarett declared, having no scruples where exagger-ation was concerned. 'The memory lives in our blood, and it is this that guides us towards places where our ancestors used once to feast. Since the coming of the white man we have had iron cauldrons which we can take with us on our travels, but our lands have shrunk like a badly cured buckskin.'

In times gone by, the Indians used to make bowls in which to cook their sagamite by carving out pieces of tree trunk over a fire. Then they would fill them with water, and throw in hot stones to make the water boil. Then they added maize, fish or meat, fat, and berries from the woods. Nomadic tribes always knew where these wooden pots were situated throughout their lands. The people were more stable, for they were obliged to remain in the vicinity of their pots.

On the way the Indians had killed a caribou, and they boiled up its bones to obtain white fat to take with them on their journey. In a separate pot they cooked the stomach and its contents, which had a soft consistency and appeared greenish yellow. This dish tasted slightly bitter on account of the young willow leaves that the caribou eats during the summer.

Angélique could not bring herself to taste it. She was sitting down, resting her back against a tree trunk. She was utterly exhausted and in spite of their walk and the heat she still felt cold. The chill came from inside. After her narrow escape from drowning at Monhegan, Father de Vernon had made her eat a bowl of hot soup. And she had felt that never had she eaten anything so good. Now he too was dead. An idea born of this thought, like the cruel little serpents that tormented her ceaselessly, made her see his death in a new light.

'When they hear about it, they will say: "Do you know, at Gouldsboro they murdered a Jesuit, Father de Vernon . . . what a terrible thing! That Count Peyrac stops at nothing . . ." '

How could they ever reply to accusations like that, which seemed so credible?

She shuddered again. In her attempts to get warm she slipped her hands into the pockets of the jacket she was wearing, the jacket taken from one of the faceless strangers who had been pursuing them. At the bottom of one of the pockets she found a number of small objects: a tobacco-grater, some frippery for trading with the Indians, and, in another pocket, a folded scrap of paper which she took out and examined.

It was a sheet of fine parchment – she could have sworn it was slightly scented – with a few lines written on it. The writing alone filled Angélique with horror, for she could not tell whether it had been written by a man's hand or a woman's, by someone cultivated or uneducated, by a madman or someone sane, for it showed an admixture of virile strength and feminine affection, with great bursts of pride standing out like claws, and all the circumvolutions of guile, with heavy smudges of sensuality accompanied by the general elegance of the letters, indicating that the writer was accustomed to handling a pen.

She read:

'Sow calamities along her path that she may be accused of them.' And a bit lower down was added:

'I'll be waiting for you tonight if you're good . . .'

There was something unhealthy and frightening about these words.

The signature was illegible, its individual letters indecipherably entwined, forming a shape that looked like some hideous beast. Angélique had the feeling that she had seen this signature before somewhere, but where?

She held the parchment with the tips of her fingers, resisting her impulse to cast it into the fire to purify herself from its contact.

CHAPTER 47

THEY WALKED for another whole day along little-trodden paths, used only by wild animals and hunters.

Between the trunks of oaks and silver firs they glimpsed the dazzling surface of numerous beaver lakes. The Indians walked so fast that Angélique had some difficulty in keeping up with them, and had it not been for her they would have gone even faster. They might even have run, for they were capable of running for hours on end without a break, often at a speed which a white man regarded as the fastest possible. Judging by what they said to one another Angélique knew that they considered themselves to be closely pursued by danger, but could scarcely leave her behind since she too was in peril and must be delivered safe and sound to the Man of Thunder, her husband. Then, and only then could they regard themselves as having escaped the evil spirits. When they had to ford rivers Piksarett carried Angélique on his back. The friendship and solidarity she was shown by these savages, their intuitive understanding of the situation – which even for her still remained confused – were invaluable to Angélique during those difficult days. White men with their more sober and materialistic minds, by laughing at her vague doubts and fears, would not have inspired her with the same confidence, nor offered her the same comfort.

As they were eating that evening after the day's march, the boom of a cannon being fired quite close to where they were set the echoes flying.

'There's a ship over there calling for trade,' said Uniakke.

Intrigued, they carefully made their way to the edge of the cliff that bounded a broad, calm river. These deep clefts, breaking the coastline as they did at frequent intervals, enabled ships to penetrate a considerable distance inland up the estuaries.

A small yacht lay at anchor, its scarlet flag reflected in the emerald green waters of the river.

'It's the *Rochelais*!' Angélique cried, scarcely believing her own eyes.

Already she could make out Cantor's fair hair on the deck of the ship, along with the familiar shapes of Gouldsboro people, Vanneau and Colin's lieutenant Barssempuy.

They slithered down the steep bank.

'Ah, I knew I'd find you,' said Cantor catching sight of his mother.

Shortly afterwards he joined her on the tiny beach at the water's edge.

'However did you guess that I was in these parts?'

'Sniffed you out,' Cantor replied laying a finger on his nose.

'Well you certainly are a son of these parts,' Angélique exclaimed, embracing him in great delight. 'You're as good as the Indians!'

What a nice boy Cantor was with all the insolent confidence of youth, full of vigour and passion!

'I went back to Port Royal to bring you news of my father which they had received in Gouldsboro, but you were no longer there. They told me, though, that you had set off towards the east, so I followed in your tracks as far as Carter's, who said he had not seen you, that your boat had been wrecked, but that you were safe, and that you had set off into the interior with the redskins. After that it was easy to work out where you would be likely to be each day and find a point where I could probably reach you. So I had the cannon fired somewhat at random in these coves, and you heard it.'

Angélique had taken in only one word:

'So you've news of your father?'

'Yes, he sent a letter to Colin to tell him that he was making all speed to the Gulf of Saint Lawrence, sailing round the Peninsula, and that he could not hope to be back within three weeks at the earliest. He sent him some instructions concerning Gouldsboro.'

'And was there nothing for me?'

'Yes, there was a note for you.'

'Well, give it to me,' said Angélique, holding out her hand impatiently.

Cantor seemed taken aback, then replied in some confusion:

'Oh Mother, forgive me, I forgot to bring it . . .'

Angélique would gladly have wrung his neck.

'But it was a very short note,' Cantor went on greatly dismayed to see how upset she seemed, 'there can't have been anything very important in it!'

What more was there to say!

'I brought you some things,' Cantor went on timidly, aware that he had gravely sinned against that incomprehensible code that orders the lives of those people still difficult for an adolescent to establish contact with, namely adults. 'It was Abigail who got your things ready. She even included some warm winter clothes, saying that possibly you might have to go to Quebec . . .'

'Did your father mention me in his letter to Colin?'

'No, but Colin decided that I should pick you up at Port Royal and take you in the *Rochelais* to the Gulf of Saint Lawrence thinking that you ought, come what may, to join my father.'

So Colin would have approved her decision to set off to the Chignecto Isthmus.

While they were talking, Malecite Indians had been coming out of the forest carrying skins of beaver, otter, mink and silver fox. In order not to offend them, Barssempuy agreed to some trading being done. Ironmongery from Gouldsboro was of excellent quality and the natives were pleased, in spite of the fact that they did not obtain as much alcohol as they would have liked.

When they had gone, Angélique and her three redskins went on board the *Rochelais*, and they weighed anchor as darkness fell. They had agreed not to attempt to circumnavigate the Peninsula, which would have caused them to back-track and delayed them by several days. They were already too far to the east, so they would follow Angélique's original idea and anchor the *Rochelais* in the upper reaches of Chignecto Bay then cross the isthmus on foot, which would take them three or four days at the outside. Angélique was already dreaming of the moment when they would come out on the shores of that vast bay, facing in the direction of Europe, the summer haven of cod-fishers, who were then to be found all along the beaches, fishing, cutting up and salting cod. At this time of the year the stench of cod was so powerful that it could be smelt several miles inland.

Would she also catch sight of the *Gouldsboro* lying off shore? What was Joffrey doing up there? How she wished she had that message from him which Cantor had thought un-necessary to bring her! Every word of his to her at that moment would have been sheer delight. She would have kissed the words he had written. For they spelt certainty, and the warmth of his presence, for which she felt a burning need. Less on account of fear of the dangers that hung over her – she had survived many another peril alone – than because of her need to feel sure that in a vile, false world, all too easily subject to the lowest instincts, he at least was there, and he was a man who loved her, a man who was straight in all his dealings.

Furthermore she was not well.

The *Rochelais* had arrived just in time to save her from having to give up. Without counting the numerous bruises she had suffered as a result of the shipwreck, the cut on her foot had turned septic. The damage had occurred on the first trip of the *Rochelais* to Port Royal, during the storm, when she had been struck on the leg by Saint-Castine's chest full of scalps.

And then the very first thing she caught sight of as she en-tered the cabin in the stern of the ship that evening was that famous chest with its three hundred and fifty English scalps.

'Am I dreaming?' she exclaimed. 'I thought I'd left that in Port Royal!'

'Monsieur de la Roche-Posay gave it to me,' Cantor ex-plained. 'He thought it was an excellent opportunity to get it some of the way towards Quebec, but I also think that he was not too keen for it to remain in his house.'

So one way or another they all hoped that this evidence of Baron Saint-Castine's zeal in the King of France's cause would finally reach its destination.

So Angélique resigned herself to its presence. In the other trunks that Abigail had prepared she found what she needed to treat her wound, to dress herself properly and begin to look human again. She was not at all sorry to be rid of the wrecker's dreadful jacket, but took care to remove from it and carefully put away the mysterious note in that disturbing handwriting that read:

'Sow calamities along her path that she may be accused of them . . .'

CHAPTER 48

THE FOLLOWING morning, leaving Shepody Bay into which the Petitcodiac flows on their left, the *Rochelais* began to make its way up one of the most remote reaches of French Bay, where they knew they would find among the blue herons, the peregrine falcons, the black ducks and the white eiders, some of those specimens of humanity of whom Angélique had heard tell – people who belonged neither to God, nor to the Devil, who lived for themselves alone, deep in their retreat, watching out for their enemies from the heights of red and black cliffs – and anyone was an enemy who entered the meandering tree-lined fjords – namely Marceline-la-Belle, the Defour brothers, a hermit and a handful of other people . . .

The woman with her eleven or twelve children owned a modest country house with a saw-mill and a flour-mill, and a storage depot for goods to be bartered with the Indians.

Renting out the hunting and fishing rights she had inherited from her late husband, she held the lands in fief and offered her protection to a number of Frenchmen, coastal fishermen or small farmers who had settled there with their wives, their Indian concubines and swarms of young half-breed children. There were altogether some ten houses and sixty to seventy people.

The *Rochelais* cast anchor below this wildly beautiful domain.

A path, lined with lupins, led up to the stoutly built stone and wood house. The profusion of these flowers with their gigantic stems, sky-blue, pink and white, made the surrounding land look like a royal park.

On reaching the house they found it empty and the whole place deserted, although the embers were still hot in the grate and there were hens cackling in the yard.

'They must have taken flight with their cooking pots when they saw our sails,' said one of the crew who knew the area. 'It's the usual practice around here, especially in these isolated French hamlets that have no means of defending themselves. When English marauders are around it's better to camp out in the woods for a few days than to be taken off prisoner to Boston. The French can't stand the idea of having to eat that Puritan barley-gruel!'

The party from the *Rochelais* decided to try their luck with the Defour brothers, who lived about half a league away, and were lucky enough to find the third brother, Amadeus, at home. He at once offered them the most generous hospitality. The older brothers had not yet returned from their expedition up the Saint John river. Meanwhile he and the youngest of the four, with a cat for company – for they had a cat who was just like them, big, fat and taciturn – had stayed behind to look after the house and to hunt and fish. They had to make ready for winter, to accumulate and exchange furs brought to them by the Indians, to harvest their few cereals and potatoes, to fatten their pig and put their game to smoke. There they lived the life of rustic noblemen, saving against that distant day when they might return rich to the Kingdom of France, or possibly without the intention of returning but merely in order to have a sense of ease and prosperity till the end of their days. One could readily understand that people like them did not want to be disturbed by governors, by Jesuits, or by tax-collectors.

On the other hand, where their friends were concerned, their generosity was boundless. The oldest brother had already proved this by his raid on Fort-Marie to obtain reinforcements for Count Peyrac. They liked to show their generosity at the expense of the King of France. Amadeus immediately agreed to take Angélique over to the other side of the isthmus to the Gulf of Saint Lawrence. He would take some of his men with him to carry the baggage. It would be a matter of two days' walk, possibly less, since the marshes and peat-bogs were almost entirely dried out at this time of the year, which made them easy to cross.

But in spite of her impatience, Angélique was unable to set off the following day, for her foot was hurting her and her leg was swollen. The wound she had received, which she had neglected at Port Royal, had grown worse on contact with the sea water. It was beginning to look like an ulcer, resistant to all treatment. So Angélique decided that she must rest her leg for at least another day and try a different kind of herbal poultice, which she hoped would be more effective than the one she had used hitherto.

In order to be able to set out as soon as possible, she did her utmost to rest completely. So isolated was this spot at the end of the earth, at the top of French Bay, its furthest inlet, where the waters rise twelve metres every twenty-four hours, that she felt completely protected from mankind and that no one would possibly come to look for her here.

What an illusion! For during the afternoon, as Angélique was crossing the main living-room, she found standing there, apparently expecting her, none other than the Marquis de Ville d'Avray, in his flowing frock-coat, his flowery waistcoat and high heels, resting one hand on his silver-topped cane, while in the other he held that of a small plump child of about four, with golden curls emerging from beneath his red woollen cap and who resembled him strangely.

'Angélique!' the Marquis exclaimed. 'How delighted I am to see you again!'

He added in offended tones:

'I learned that you were staying here! We can't have this! You never told me you were coming and you might have gone off again without coming to see me ...'

'But I didn't know you were in these parts.'

Angélique's eyes moved hesitantly from the Governor to the little boy.

'Yes,' said the Marquis proudly, 'this is my youngest! Isn't he delightful?'

And he added in order to clarify the situation:

'He's also Marceline-la-Belle's youngest. You don't know her, do you? What a pity! You should see her opening shell-fish! ... Say how-do-you-do, Cherubino! He's called Cherubino ... Isn't it just the perfect name for him? Why ever have you come to stay with these miserable people the Defour brothers, instead of staying with Marceline?'

'We did call there, but she was not in!'

'Oh yes, that's true! We all took refuge in the forest with our cooking-pots. It's an old custom among French Acadians. As soon as they catch sight of an unknown ship, they pick up their cooking-pots and go off and live with the redskins for a few days ... It's most amusing! But it so happened that I was almost certain I recognized one of Monsieur de Peyrac's ships, so I insisted that everyone should return to the house that evening.'

He looked around him in some irritation.

'However do you manage to get on with these insolent brutes? Not only do they deride me and refuse to pay their letters patent and dividend but – do you know the story? – they have corrupted Alexander ... yes corrupted him. They have engaged him to sail their merchant craft up the Petitcodiac bore. So you see Alexander is lost to us. He will become a brutish creature like them, and eat with his fingers, and sleep with the native women ... It's most tiresome! But I have written to Quebec to complain about them ... I shall read you the letter before I send it off. How long will you be staying with us?'

'I should have liked to leave tomorrow,' Angélique replied, 'but I have hurt my leg and the wound is a long time healing. I fear that I should not be able to walk far without trouble.'

The Governor immediately showed great concern:

'And here I am keeping you standing up! My poor child! Here, please sit down. Show me this wound of yours; I have some knowledge of pharmacy.'

He was in fact extremely competent and they agreed that the ulcer should be treated with pimpinella or Aaron's rod.

'I'll find some before the day is out. I know everyone round here. I am even on excellent terms with the witch-doctor in the next village. But you must be reasonable, my child. You will not be able to undertake any long walks for several days and you know it.'

'Yes, I do!' Angélique sighed, bowing her head.

She secretly decided that she would ask Piksarett and the Mic-Macs to set off as scouts along the coast and take a message to her husband.

The Marquis seemed delighted.

'So we shall have you with us for some time!' he said joyfully. 'You'll see how pleasant it is here. I come here every year. Marceline keeps a few of my clothes and looks after them so I have no need of luggage. It makes a pleasant rest in the midst of this exhausting tour of inspection. My duties as Governor are so exhausting, especially when complicated by ill-will here and there. You saw the trouble we had on the Saint John river!'

'Yes, speaking of the Saint John river, how did it all turn out?' Angélique asked, longing to hear him speak of her husband.

Monsieur de Ville d'Avray gave her some details:

'Monsieur de Peyrac performed some admirable manoeuvres and Skoudoum came to his assistance. The English were completely outwitted, particularly as there was a fog you could have cut with a knife. I retrieved my ship the *Asmodeus* without loss nor bloodshed ... I would have liked to have thanked him for his help but he more or less vanished from sight; he seemed to be in a hurry to get the job done ...'

The Marquis gave her a knowing wink.

'No doubt so that he could get back to you as soon as possible, dear lady!'

'I haven't seen him since,' Angélique replied. 'But as I learned that he had sailed for the Gulf of Saint Lawrence I thought I would try to join him there.'

'You will join him there, have no fear, little lady! Meanwhile you will be here for the feast of Saint Stephen. It's wonderful! Each year I hold a party on my ship on that day. It's my feast day, yes, as I am called Stephen. You will come, won't you! Smile, Angélique, life is wonderful!'

'Not as wonderful as all that!' came the voice of Amadeus Defour as he entered the house. 'And especially not for those who run into you. Governor, what are you doing in my house?'

'I have come to greet personal friends of mine whom you have so outrageously commandeered,' Ville d'Avray replied, drawing himself up to his full height. 'Furthermore you forget I have the right of inspection in all territories dependent on my jurisdiction, your house included. It is my duty to take stock of how much you are stealing from the State and from me.'

'And to see how much you can steal from the worthy folk who, as you say, come under your jurisdiction?'

'Worthy folk! ... ha ha ha! Are you referring to yourselves when you talk about "worthy folk"? You are a lot of dissolute unbelievers, who never attend Mass. Father Jeanrousse said you were a lot of pagans.'

'We have no chaplain and Father Jeanrousse said himself that he is not here for the benefit of the whites but only to convert the redskins.'

'And what about the hermit up on the mountain side? You could confess to him . . .'

'Granted we don't go to confession, but we still are honest folk.'

'Honest! My poor friends. Do you really think you can deceive me and that I don't understand what is going on up the Petitcodiac. You get your furs and your timber over to the Gulf of Saint Lawrence in record time, and sell it to ships that put in at Pointe-du-Chêne or Saint Anne before they head off back to Europe. More goods leaving Canada without paying any taxes. You are nothing but a lot of rogues! Do you know what will happen when I tell them that in Quebec?'

Amadeus made no reply but went and poured himself a glass of spirits from a bottle beside the fireplace.

'You pay me ten per cent of your profits,' said Ville d'Avray following his movements with an eagle eye – and there was no longer a trace of either naïvety or joviality in his blue eyes – 'and I shall keep my mouth shut.'

'That's not fair! It's always us who have to pay,' Amadeus protested. 'You don't ask as much as that from Marceline, yet God knows how much she makes on the side with her underhand deals.'

'Marceline is a woman who is overrun with children and she hasn't much in the way of means,' the Governor declared solemnly, 'in spite of its demands the law knows how to show indulgence towards widows and orphans.'

'Yes indeed. In the way of means and indulgence, Marceline has managed to fix you up all right, whereas we folk don't possess the same means, far from it!'

'I'll give you a good beating, you peasant,' cried Ville d'Avray brandishing his cane.

'Let's see you try,' the colossus replied taking guard with his fists up.

The Marquis curbed his ill-temper.

'Not in front of the child. He is so very sensitive, you will upset him. Control yourself, Amadeus!'

They agreed on a truce, although Cherubino with his red cap did not seem in the least upset by this exchange of pleasantries.

The Marquis took hold of his hand again and signalled to Angélique.

'Let's go outside,' he murmured.

Standing on the threshold, he turned back to face the room.

'All right then, I'll agree to five per cent, but only on condition that you show me a little deference. I am not demanding. You and your brothers come to Mass on Saint Stephen's day and share my birthday cake with me on board the *Asmodeus*. People must be able to say that the Governor of Acadia is shown some consideration in his own province. Whatever would they think otherwise?'

Once outside in the shelter of a huge bank of lupins he explained to Angélique:

'You know, the trouble with all these people here is that they are jealous! You see, each of the four brothers is the father of at least one of Marceline's children . . . and very handsome children they are too, that I grant you, but even so mine is the best looking of all,' he concluded casting a satisfied glance at the chubby little lad with the blue eyes. 'After all, it's only to be expected; I am the Governor! But let us forget this incident. I shall have you sent the necessary medicine, and as soon as you are better, please come over and see us. Marceline wants to meet you, and you will see that she is an extraordinary woman.'

CHAPTER 49

AS OFTEN happens when one has heard a great deal about someone, possibly too much, Angélique did not feel over-anxious to make the acquaintance of the famous Marceline. That female prodigy whose volubility and fecundity, boldness of spirit and skill at opening shell-fish seemed to have won the admiration of every male in French Bay made Angélique feel a trifle irritated with her in advance.

But Ville d'Avray had kept his word. He had sent her plants and ointments whose efficacity she immediately noticed. Within two days she was feeling considerably better and decided she must pay the Governor a neighbourly visit. So she set off along the path that led from one domain to the other, Piksarett, the chief of the Patsuiketts, accompanying her. He had refused to go ahead as a scout as she had asked him.

'You are in danger,' he had declared. 'I don't want to lose you before obtaining your ransom. Uniakke and his brother can go on to the coast and look for the Man of Thunder. Give them a message for him, and if they find him perhaps he could come to meet you.

But when she came to write the message, she did not know what to say: should she warn him? Should she say 'I am at Trantamare . . . I am waiting for you . . . I love you . . .'

Suddenly the bond that linked her to him seemed not to have been broken, but to have become lost as if engulfed in darkness. What had happened?

She crumpled up the note and threw it away.

'Let the Mic-Macs tell him what has happened: that I have been shipwrecked, that Hubert d'Arpentigny has been killed, that they tried to kill me, and that I am here . . .'

So the two redskins set off. She decided it was better for her to remain with the Gouldsboro people and Cantor.

CHAPTER 50

MARCELINE'S HOUSE was vast, comfortable and extremely well appointed. Angélique found Monsieur de Ville d'Avray relaxing in a huge cotton hammock suspended from two beams, while his young son played on the floor beside him with some pieces of wood.

'This is an authentic Caribbean hammock,' the Governor explained. 'Extremely comfortable! You have to know how to lie in it – diagonally from corner to corner – and then it's marvellously restful. I bought it for a few twists of tobacco from a Caribbean slave who was passing through with his master, deserter from some pirate ship.'

'The spice-seller!' Angélique exclaimed. 'When was it that you saw them?'

Less than a week ago the two men had been making their way towards the coast, there to pick up a ship to return to the islands. They seemed destitute, and Ville d'Avray had had no difficulty in acquiring the native's hammock, 'for next to nothing', and his 'caracoli', a talisman carved in some mysterious metal which he wore round his neck set into a disc of hard wood. The Marquis showed her the amulet.

'It's a very rare thing to come by. The Caribbeans won't part with them, for they are about the only things they have to hand down to their heirs. Monsieur de Peyrac will tell you that this yellow metal which looks like gold and, like gold, will not tarnish, is not in fact gold nor even a gilded silver alloy. They obtain it from the Arouags of Guyana, their sworn enemies, when they go to visit them bearing gifts before entering into combat with them ... I'm delighted with my acquisition, it's a valuable addition to my collection of American curios ... I believe that you have some Iroquois beads, a most beautiful wampum necklace, given you personally by the chief of the Five Nations.'

'Outakke ... yes, he did ... but I shall never sell it ... nor indeed give it to you "for nothing" as you seem to be hoping ...'

'Does it mean so much to you? You seem very attached to it ... It has happy memories for you, has it?' the Marquis asked her somewhat briskly.

'Yes, indeed ...'

Angélique remembered the moment when she had held that wampum necklace in her hands, while the fort filled with the smell of haricot-bean soup brought by the Iroquois to save them from starvation. Never would she forget that moment. 'These beads are for you, Kawa! The White Woman who saved the life of our chief Outakke ...'[1]

The Marquis glanced out into the courtyard where Piksarett, surrounded by a group of children, was telling tales of his numerous exploits as Great Warrior of Acadia.

'People say in Quebec that you sleep with the savages,' he said with a smile. 'But that is just gossip,' he added firmly, noting Angélique's reaction, 'and I never believed it ...'

'Then why do you repeat it to me?' Angélique asked, angered. 'What need have I to know all the unpleasant things that are said about me in your scandalmongering little town? They've never even set eyes on me!'

'But you know the facts are astonishing, my dear! Outakke, as unending an enemy of the French as he is of every member of the white race! And to you, a woman! Such an honour ...'

'I saved his life. So he saved ours. After that what was so strange about our exchanging gifts?'

'And what about him?'

1. See *The Countess Angélique*.

Ville d'Avray gestured with his chin towards Piksarett.

'What about him? . . . Piksarett, the Abenaki. He's the opposite of Outakke: the deadly enemy of the Iroquois, equally untamable in his own way, mad keen to fight for his God and for his friends. And yet he abandoned his war campaign no sooner than it had started in order to tag along after you like a lap-dog! The Jesuits must have loved that!'

He grinned broadly.

'You must admit it's enough to make people talk! . . . Whatever is it that makes these red serpents so attached to you?'

'I don't know, but it's not what you suggest. In any case you know as well as I do that no redskin, no matter who he is, would even entertain the idea of entering into an amorous relationship with a white woman. They are repelled by white skin.'

'There have been some cases, though,' Ville d'Avray replied pompously. 'I admit that they are rare, but they have always involved women with interesting personalities. Even among the English. There have been women who left everything in order to go off into the forest with some handsome smelly Indian. Women are primitive creatures beneath the skin . . .'

'At the moment it is he who is following me,' said Angélique, beginning to lose her temper. 'And for goodness sake don't make any such allusions in front of him, or your scalp will find itself hanging at his belt a minute later and you might think you would have done better to remain at Court rather than causing mischief among us here in the wilds of America with your tittle-tattle. Furthermore I don't know to what extent you are aware that what you are suggesting is an insult to both me and my husband . . . And it would be better for your own safety if he doesn't get to hear about it . . .'

'But I was only joking, come, come!'

'Your jokes are in rather poor taste!'

'How touchy you are,' the Marquis complained, 'but come, Angélique, what did I say? There is nothing to make such a fuss about! Why do you take everything so seriously? . . . Life is wonderful, my child! Smile!'

'That is just typical of you! First you make me furious and then you indulge in the pleasure of consoling me and encouraging me to look on the bright side of life . . .'

'That's the way he is and there's not much we can do about it. We just have to put up with him,' said Marceline as she entered the room. 'He's exactly like his son: lying, delicate; he

317

needs someone to take care of him, the poor little thing! He's only a child! What do you expect! Mischievous, sly and thoughtless like all children. Mischievous but amusing. And we forgive him because he's not a coward although he's spoilt. And not basically nasty. He only lies about small things, not about the big ones . . .'

She went on in this vein for a while without it being clear whether she was speaking of the father or the son . . .

She was tall and strongly built but less masculine than Angélique had imagined her. Also more distinguished. Her thick, auburn hair was beginning to turn silver at the temples, which contrasted with her tanned face, a trifle ruddy, that radiated youth and wholesome healthiness. She could well understand why it was that homesick adventurers liked to lay their heads on that capacious bosom, finding that their zest for life was renewed through contact with her boundless energy, even though left as poor as Job . . .

Marceline, orphaned, penniless, persecuted, several times married, widowed, a mother and abandoned, had created her own happiness from the merest trifles. Her 'misfortunes' would have been enough to explain her putting a noose round her neck. But she looked on her life as consisting of a mixture of good luck and happy coincidences. She could have sold joy as she sold shell-fish and coal.

'My other children are well behaved but a bit simple,' she explained to Angélique. 'Of course they are! All their fathers couldn't be governors . . . but this little one makes us keep the old brains up to scratch! It's a good thing too . . . If you never have to use your head you become stupid! And when his father arrives, there's all hell let loose. By the end of summer you can be sure that everyone here is at daggers drawn! He can turn a whole town topsy turvy, my goodness me! I can't help admiring him! I don't know how he manages to find so many different ways of vexing, hurting and annoying people . . . it's an art, I'm telling you . . . I couldn't do it. I'm no good at being nasty to people, that's been my undoing.'

As she spoke she was busy scrutinizing Angélique carefully. Finally she said:

'Well, you'll pass! I'm pleased: you're as good as he is. I mean. You're just the wife he needs! Who am I talking about? About Count Peyrac of course! It worried me. People talked about you. They said you were very beautiful. Too beautiful even. That frightened me. Very beautiful women, and from the nobility too, they're often bitches! You see he came here when he was first exploring the region, before we heard he'd brought you back from Europe. He's a man ... how can I put it? He's different ... quite different from the usual run. He's head and shoulders above all the others, even him,' she declared, referring to Ville d'Avray as if he was not there. 'There's something about him that makes every woman, no matter who she is, want him to show some interest in her, even if only by looking at her – as he knows how to look; it's a strange sensation, you feel he sees you, that you are something, someone – or even just by smiling, or saying a phrase like ... "How welcoming your house is, Marceline. You've given it a soul ..." You feel all the bigger for it ... you say to yourself: "Did I really do that, did I give a soul to my house? And are people aware of it? ..."

'So I said to myself, a man like that could never find a woman who was up to him. For him a woman could only be a distraction, a passing whim, and he's no man to marry a nobody so that she can serve him and he can show her off in drawing-rooms ... and I said to myself he's not going to find that rare bird he needs on the high seas or in these wild parts ...

'And then blow me if I don't hear that there is a Countess de Peyrac in Gouldsboro. I was so curious that I almost took to my boat to go and have a look at you. And now here you are, and I'm very pleased; there really are some nice things that happen in this world.'

From the moment she began to speak Angélique had realized she was talking about Joffrey, and the open enthusiasm with which Marceline expressed herself brought such joy to her heart that it almost made her weep. She could see him here, when he had first arrived, still solitary, banished from France, rejected by his own kind for the sin of intelligence and big-heartedness, and her heart felt as if it would burst with love and nostalgia. She herself, so far away, over there in France, hounded like an animal. While he was here, having lost all hope of ever finding her again. Both of them made wretched with pain which they thought would never find consolation on this earth. Then the miracle that had reunited them suddenly began to seem other-worldly. Noticing the sudden tears that rose into Angélique's eyes, Marceline broke off, anxiously.

'Please forgive me,' said Angélique, wiping her eyes, 'what you are telling me touches me to the heart! You have moved me more than I can ever say. And just at the moment I am terribly anxious about him.'

'Everything will sort itself out,' said Marceline kindly. 'The Governor has told me about it. You are trying to join him on the coast but are unable to continue your journey because you have hurt your foot. Have patience! We may possibly hear news of him quite soon. My son Lactance has been over in Tormentine these past few days, taking some goods over there. I'm expecting him back tomorrow or the day after and if he has seen Monsieur de Peyrac he will tell us so.'

This possibility made Angélique feel more calm.

Marceline's presence really did have a tonic effect on everyone, leaving them with the impression that, as she had said, 'everything would sort itself out'.

Together they ate a light meal with much merriment: some cider and a game pie.

Then Ville d'Avray read Angélique the letter he was sending to Quebec to denounce the appalling behaviour of the Defour brothers. It began as follows:

Your Excellency,
    I find I have no more grounds than before for satisfaction with the behaviour of the Defour brothers. The one who has just returned from France is no more appealing to me than the others. Their characters have been utterly spoilt by the FREEDOM they have enjoyed and the habit of being masters of their own behaviour, a deplorable custom among those who inhabit the maritime provinces of Acadia, a habit they have learned from the Indians. It is therefore vital for us to keep an eye on these dangerous men whom I already brought to your notice last year . . . etc, etc . . .

Some of Marceline's children came in to be introduced. The oldest was a girl called Yolande, as tall as her mother but lacking her natural femininity.

'She's a real tartar,' Marceline said proudly, 'she can knock a man down with one blow of her fist.'

Angélique asked the Marquis privately which of the children had been fathered by the Defour brothers.

'I am not at all sure,' he replied. 'All I do know is that there are some among them. I can feel it.'

Suddenly everyone's attention was drawn to a tiny dot on the horizon: it was a ship, and they all went outside to look.

Yolande asked whether they should get down the cooking-pots and take refuge in the woods.

'No,' said the Marquis, 'I can see now who it is. It's the Flemish argosy of those bloodthirsty drunks, the Defour brothers. Good, they'll all be here for Saint Stephen's Day. Perhaps Alexander too!'

He rubbed his hands together.

'Ha ha! I'm going to make them sing the Mass.'

Angélique said nothing but stared at him.

'What is wrong?' the Marquis asked. 'You look thoughtful.'

'Something struck me but I cannot think what it is,' she replied, 'it concerns you, and it's very important, but I can't quite get straight what it is. Ah, yes, I have it! ... Of course ...'

The scene she had been trying to remember flooded back into her memory.

'The first time I met you on the beach at Gouldsboro you told me you could see nothing, even close to, without your glasses. And here you are, with no glasses on, not only seeing that distant boat but managing to identify it.'

The Marquis looked abashed and began to blush like a child caught out in some piece of wickedness, but soon managed to pull himself together.

'That's right! I remember ... As a matter of fact my sight is excellent and I have never needed glasses in my life ... but on that occasion I was obliged to put on that little act ...'

He glanced around, then drew Angélique away into one corner in order to have a private word with her.

CHAPTER 51

'... IT WAS all because of that woman who was with you.'

'The Duchess of Maudribourg?'

'Yes ... When I caught sight of her my blood froze in my veins ... My only fear was lest she recognize me or realized that I had recognized her. So to avoid that I made up the first story that came into my head, which seems to have had the desired effect, since even you were taken in ... I have some talent as an actor ... Monsieur Molière used to say to me ...'

'Why were you frightened that she might know that you had recognized her?'

'Because she's a formidable woman, my dear! You mention the name of the Duchess of Maudribourg in certain private circles in Paris or in Versailles, and you will see the faces grow pale. I myself had met her once or twice, at Court of course, but especially at those Black Magic gatherings which one more or less has to attend if one is to get anywhere. It's very much the fashion now. Everyone attends them in the hope of meeting the Devil. I myself haven't much time for that kind of thing. As I told you I'm a simple, good-natured man. I like to live in peace amongst my friends, my books, beautiful objects and in a beautiful country. Quebec suits me . . .'

'Why didn't you tell us what kind of a person this woman was after chance had brought her to our settlement?'

'Do you imagine I wanted her to slip me a poisoned draught? She's a poisoner, my dear, one of the most skilful . . . and, you know, the situation really was rather delightful . . . flirting with that devil with the angel's eyes. When I think that she had the insolence to say to me . . . "You are in error, Monsieur . . . I have nobody's death on my conscience . . ." she who sent at least a dozen individuals to join the majority, not to mention her aged husband, some servant-girls she did not care for, and a confessor of hers who refused to give her absolution . . .'

He burst out laughing behind his hand.

'She's of illegitimate birth, the daughter of a lecherous lady of noble birth, who was something of a witch and had her by her chaplain or her valet or her brother, or some clod-hopper or other . . . no one knows. People put the odds on the chaplain, because he was an excellent mathematician, which would explain her undeniable scientific ability, although there was a time when theologians thought that she held these gifts from the Devil . . .'

He went on with some concern:

'I never did manage to find out who was her mother . . . Madame de Roquencourt knew her, but I never managed to worm the truth out of her . . . all I know is that it was one of the great names of the Dauphiné.'

'I thought Madame de Maudribourg came from Poitou . . .'

'She'll say absolutely anything on that score. It all depends on whom she has set out to seduce . . . Madame de Roquencourt took an interest in the child, heaven knows why . . . Perhaps she had some special reason to be friendly with her mother . . . or perhaps she too fancied the chaplain . . . he was by no means an uninteresting man, that chaplain. A kind of spontaneous scientific genius. It was only by taking orders that he managed to educate himself. His daughter inherited his gifts, and the satanism too! Have you heard mention the trouble they had at the Convent of Norel?'

'No.'

'It all happened about twenty years ago when she was there. She must have been about fifteen. But it was by no means the only convent in which the Devil had a good frolic. There was Loudun, Louviers, Avignon, Rouen, it was all the fashion at the time . . . At Norel the satanic activity was led by a certain Yves Jobert, who was spiritual director to the convent and who got the nuns to dance about naked and make love to one another even in the church and in the garden. He taught that sin must die through sin and that in order to imitate the innocence of our forefathers people should go about naked like them and follow the dictates of their senses rather than control them. It's a theory that is not without its attractions, but the Inquisition did not see things in that light. They made Yves Jobert suffer the torture of the boot before burning him alive along with some of the nuns.[1] She, Ambroisine, got off scot free because she's cunning. The Duke of Maudribourg married her. So at last she was able to put a coat of arms on her bastards' banner – gules a lion sable. He thought he was on to a good thing because he was in the habit of treating himself to young virgins and getting rid of them later when he began to get bored with them. But he met his match in her. Where vice and poisoning were concerned he had nothing to teach her. Naturally none of this is known officially, or hardly . . . The names involved are too important. But I know everything that goes on, it's hard to hoodwink me . . . so you can understand why I was upset at meeting this greedy Messalina in America. But I think I managed to extricate myself quite well from that awkward situation . . . Angélique, you seem cross, why?'

'Because you didn't warn me. Having that woman in our midst put us in mortal danger.'

1. The authors would like to remind their readers that the facts described here by Ville d'Avray are authentic. During the Age of Louis XIV witchcraft played a prominent part. Both the Court and convents witnessed the most outrageous behaviour. Thousands of newborn infants were slain during Black Masses. The 'Poisons Affair' in France and the Salem witchcraft trials in America took place a few years later.

'Oh nonsense! She hasn't killed anyone here that I know of.'

'No, but she might have!'

Angélique was trembling inwardly. Now she felt sure that Ambroisine had tried to poison Abigail.

'Angélique, you've changed completely,' cried the Marquis in despair. 'You're behaving as if you really were angry with me!'

'I could gladly kill you,' Angélique replied looking at him coldly.

Her glance can scarcely have been reassuring for the Governor recoiled.

'Not in front of the child!' he said hastily. 'Please, Angélique, be reasonable. It's as if you are really reproaching me for something serious.'

'Indeed I am! You knew the most terrible things about that Duchess and yet you said nothing to us about them. That's where you are to blame!'

'But no, on the contrary, I believe I showed skill and calm. Had I denounced her I might possibly have brought out the worst in her. Who knows? Did she not come to America in order to make amends? Conversions are very popular among our beautiful criminals. When they've had enough of the pleasures of Venus, they turn religious and get a lot of attention that way, believe me! Mademoiselle de La Vallière wears a nun's habit now, and Madame de Noyon who poisoned all her newborn children and two of her lovers – I am the only one to know that – has been at Fontevrault for some years now and they're talking about making her Abbess...'

'Oh, do stop talking about this shameless world!' cried Angélique hastening towards the door.

The Marquis of Ville d'Avray hurried after her in some agitation.

'Angélique! How easily you are upset! Come now! Let us not quarrel over trifles, come! Do at least grant that I tried to do everything for the best...'

She gave him a black look ... she did not believe in his protestations of innocence. If he had said nothing it was no doubt partly out of fear of Ambroisine but also because he adored getting other people's affairs in a tangle from which he derived a sense of importance.

'You judge me too harshly,' he said, truly saddened. 'But never mind! One day you will get to know me better and will regret your harshness. But meanwhile let us not spoil our excellent relations on account of someone who matters so little. She's far away now and can harm no one . . . Come, Angélique, smile, life is wonderful! You will come to my birthday party, won't you?'

'No, I'm not coming.'

CHAPTER 52

HE MADE such efforts the following day, coming to call on her at the Defour brothers' house and overwhelming her with protestations of friendship and the honourableness of his intentions with proofs to back him up as far as the Ambroisine affair was concerned, that in the end she gave way. All right then, she would come to his birthday party! All right, she did forgive him! Yes, she agreed that it was thanks to him that her foot was almost better now! That it would be ungracious of her to sulk, and to miss the fantastic party they were going to hold on the *Asmodeus* and also to miss the extraordinary spectacle of watching Marceline opening shell-fish . . .

Furthermore, his heart was heavy on Alexander's account. He had come back with the two elder Defour brothers, saying that he wanted to go on navigating the rivers instead of returning to Quebec with his patron . . . The interview had been stormy.

'How ungrateful the young are,' the Marquis said with a sigh. 'Angélique, don't you add to my sorrows!'

All right then, she would come over that evening and decided that she must do something about her appearance for the occasion.

She had been unable to sleep that night and her face looked drawn and sickly. She reproached herself for having reacted so violently to the revelations of that scandalmonger Ville d'Avray. Angélique herself had lived at Court and these things were nothing new to her.

Had she forgotten the Black Masses glimpsed through those secret nights at Versailles, when the dwarf Barcarole had been her guide and protector against the criminal plots of the

Marquise de Montespan? 'I was less vulnerable then, less easily upset by human turpitude . . .'

Here in these virgin lands, in the intoxication of her authentic, dazzling love, she had begun to forget. Her life had taken on another meaning, more complete, more wholesome, more creative, more in harmony with her inner nature. Would 'they' pursue her all the way here in order to make her pay for the times she had erred? It all seemed like a nightmare! Where could she find innocence if it was not at the ends of the earth? Through the window that stood open to the night she could see Piksarett the Indian watching over her. Another world, another people. Cantor, her son, was sleeping nearby. She thought about Honorine . . . about Séverine . . . about Laurier and about little Elizabeth in her rustic cot, and Abigail . . . and she got up in a state of agitation to go and look at the stars, and to seek in the limpid night sky she knew not what necessary strength.

'No, "they" will not prevail against us . . .'

She was still thinking of Joffrey de Peyrac, seeing him as the only one among so many human beings whom she had met whose background she shared, with whom she had been able to sign the spiritual pact of friendship and of love. This heightened their solitude amongst men, but also made it impossible for them to stray along other paths than those marked out by their destiny.

'How could I ever have lived so long without you? You alone know me and recognize me . . . you who know how much we are alike, although I am a woman and you a man. Was there any time in my life when you did not exist? No, for it was my vision of you that preserved me, in spite of my weakness as a woman, and prevented my joining the common herd, where I would have been swallowed up and lost . . .'

Towards late afternoon she set off, accompanied by Cantor and Piksarett, to Marceline Raymondeau's house. The Defour brothers were already there, having got out their best cloth suits and buckled shoes from a chest, clothes they scarcely wore from one year's end to another. They entered more or less cheerfully and seemed more or less at ease, but on this occasion they were obliged to please the Governor.

That morning had found them at the chapel of the hermit, a hoary Recollect in grey homespun, to attend the religious service. They sang the hymns with ill grace but in stentorian voices.

'Dreadful,' said Ville d'Avray as they came out. 'They nearly deafened me. Ah my dear, you will hear the singing in Quebec! The Cathedral choir and the Jesuits' choir . . .'

'You seem very sure you are going to see us in Quebec. As far as I am concerned, the project does not seem at all likely to come off. We are now in September, I don't know where my husband is . . . and in any case I cannot spend the winter so far from my little girl whom I have left in an isolated fort on the frontiers of Maine . . .'

'Bring her with you!' said Ville d'Avray as if it were the simplest of things to arrange. 'The Ursulines will teach her the alphabet and she can skate on the Saint Lawrence . . .'

In spite of the attractions of the festivities that were being prepared and that had brought Acadians from far and wide, including a few English and Scots settlers, as well as the chiefs of neighbouring tribes, Angélique felt that she could not join in with a light heart.

She was far from being in the same state of mind as at Monhegan two months back. What a memory! There she had leapt over the midsummer fire to exorcize the evil spirits and had danced wildly with the Basque captain Hernani D'Astiguarra,[1] under the disapproving eye of Jack Merwin, the Jesuit, and of Thomas Patridge, the Pastor, and now both were dead . . . What a lot of trials and tribulations they had seen! When would this accursed summer come to an end? . . .

Coloured lanterns had been hung along the ship's rigging and were reflected in the calm waters of the fjord where the *Asmodeus* lay at anchor.

Cantor tuned his guitar, now recovered from the shake-up it had been through in Port Royal.

They were to be taken out to the ship by boat there to partake of a banquet, after which there would be singing and dancing.

But Angélique was doomed that evening not to be able to fall in with the wishes of the unfortunate Governor of Acadia, for during the final burst of preparations, as darkness began to fall, a young redskin came up to her and told her in excellent French that the hermit on the mountainside had asked her to go to his chapel where there was a man who wished to speak to Madame de Peyrac and her son Cantor. Angélique's reaction was violent:

1. See *The Temptation of Angélique*.

'I don't care for messages like that; a man ... that's too vague! Let him say who he is and I will go.'

'He said the message was from Clovis.'

CHAPTER 53

CLOVIS! IT really was he.

When Angélique and Cantor entered the hermit's cave they had no difficulty in recognizing, by the light of a smoke cresset, the short, stocky Auvergnat with his coal-black eyebrows and his small piercing, hostile eyes. He nevertheless got up when they arrived and stood before them, cap in hand, in a relatively deferential attitude. His shirt was stiff with grease, and he was ill-shaven and hairy, a real man of the woods!

'Clovis! You here?' said Angélique. 'We thought we would never see you again! Why did you desert?'

He sniffed several times, putting on the obstinate look he always wore when she remonstrated with him.

'Didn't want to,' he replied, 'but they promised me a Caracas emerald, and at first sight what they asked me to do didn't seem all that dreadful. Then after I got involved, I realized that whichever way I turned, my life was a goner. So I did a bunk . . .'

'Who are "they"?' asked Angélique who had immediately grasped that Clovis was referring to their mysterious enemies.

'How do I know? ... People who are out to do you no good! But why? And for whom? ... That I don't know.'

'What did they ask you to do for them against us?'

Again Clovis sniffed. The difficult moment had come.

'It was at Houssnock,' he explained. 'A joker turned up and gave me a few trifles and promised that if the job was a success I'd get an emerald. He told me there was the ship of some pirate in the bay that they were in cahoots with that had ransacked all the treasures of Spaniards in Caracas, and that they would get an emerald for me from him. And what they wanted me to do didn't seem all that bad.'

'What did they ask?'

'Not much,' said Clovis shaking his head.

'But what?'

'He wanted me to get you, Madame la Comtesse, to go off to the English settlement without Monsieur le Comte getting wind of it. There had been talk of someone accompanying the young prisoner across the Kennebec, and it all seemed simple to me: I told Maupertuis and his son that Monsieur le Comte had asked them to accompany you and your son to the English village, and that he would wait for you at the mouth of the river. They didn't say a word. Canadians always jump at the opportunity of dashing off into the woods without asking questions. They told the young gentleman here' – Clovis motioned towards Cantor with his chin – 'and he saw nothing funny about it. Young people too like to get away without worrying too much about it . . .'

'Thanks a lot,' said Cantor, realizing that they had traded on his adolescent impulsiveness in order to trick his father and lead his mother into a trap.

At Houssnock, Angélique, seeing him arrive with a message from his father to say she should set off alone for Newehewanik, had done as she was told without herself investigating the sources of the order.

This plan had been drawn up in so Machiavellian a fashion and with such an intimate knowledge of the personalities concerned that Angélique felt some doubt as to whether Clovis could possibly have thought it up himself.

'What was the man like who came to you in Houssnock?'

As she asked the question she was already sure what the reply would be. So she gave the answer herself, as Clovis went on standing there dumb.

'A pale man, wasn't he, with chilling eyes?'

'The first one was like that,' Clovis replied. 'But I met others. There are a lot of them. They're sailors. I think they've got two ships. They follow the orders of some chief one never sees, someone who gives them orders but who isn't with them. They only meet from time to time. They call him Belialith. That's all I know.'

He began to bend down as if to pick up the bag – scarce filled – that composed his baggage, as if he had finished what he had to tell them.

'I suppose you know, Clovis, that at the English village we were ambushed and were within an ace of losing our liberty, if not our lives . . .'

'Yes, I heard that,' he replied, 'and that's why I ran away. What's more, they'd deceived me. No emerald for me. The pirate who had them had joined Monsieur le Comte. I ought to have guessed that if Monsieur le Comte was in that region, he'd pull the chestnuts out of the fire. It was by no means the worst thing I did, entering his service, and I should have stuck there.'

'Yes, you should,' said Angélique severely, 'but you've always been a difficult man, Clovis, and rather than remain faithful to one master whose kindness you well knew as indeed you did his power, you preferred to give way to jealousy and bitterness, especially towards me. You were delighted to see me get into difficulties, weren't you? Well, I hope you're satisfied: I did, and they haven't finished yet. But I am not so sure that you have been the winner either, in this nasty business.'

Clovis bowed his head and for once seemed to accept the rebuke.

In spite of the way he had behaved, she felt some pity for his hounded solitude. He was a narrow man, although not lacking in intelligence, and quite good at his job as a blacksmith, but too primitive to be able to stand alone in a world that was crafty and cruel to the simple-minded. She knew his secret, the passion of a man who had spent his life staring into a dancing flame, seeing treasures reflected in it; it was his love for gems and precious stones with which he one day hoped to create an exquisite shrine for the famous sanctuary of the little Saint-Foy-de-Conques, in his native Auvergne.

She went on:

'When you realized you had done wrong, why did you not go straight to Monsieur le Comte and tell him?'

He gave her a furious, indignant look:

'What the . . .! Do you take me for a bloody fool? Wasn't what I'done bad enough already? More or less sent you to your death, you! Madame la Comtesse. And can you imagine me explaining that to him, to his face . . . Do you imagine he can show pity, him, towards someone who had tried to harm you? I can see you're a woman, you go around imagining that men are all honey and sugar inside, like you women . . . I know him, I do, I know him better than you! He would have killed me . . . or worse! He would have looked at me with such a look in his eye that I would just have ceased to be a living person . . . I couldn't face that. I preferred to go away . . . You see, you . . . for him . . . you are his treasure . . . and when someone possesses a treasure, it's something that burns you there,' he said, laying one hand on his breast. 'No one has the right to touch it, nor to try to take it away ... I know what I'm talking about, I do ... I too have a treasure. And it's because I don't want to lose it that I'm not going to hang around here any more ... Because "they" are on my tracks. "They" are dangerous,' he continued, lowering his voice, 'the sort of folk that chill you to the bone. There's the Brute, old One-Eye, Saddy, the Invisible Man – he's the one they send ahead because no one ever notices him, he's so like someone everyone has seen before. A crew like that are the limbs of Satan on earth. Maybe they'll want to know where I've buried my treasure, but, nothing doing, they won't catch me.'

He slung his bag over his shoulder and set off towards the mouth of the cave. But Cantor leapt up and blocked his way out.

'Not so fast, Clovis! You haven't told us everything.'

'What do you mean I haven't told you everything?' the man asked, bridling.

'No you haven't! You're still hiding something, I feel sure!'

'You're just like your father,' Clovis growled, his eyes flashing hatred. 'Come on now, me lad, let me pass. I told you I don't want to get myself done in for this. Enough to have done my best to save your lives ...'

'What do you mean?' Cantor insisted. 'What danger have you tried to save us from?'

'Yes, tell us,' Angélique insisted, seeing from the man's expression that Cantor had guessed right. 'Clovis, we have always been good friends and you have lived with us in Wapassou. Show your loyalty and help us as far as you possibly can.'

'No! No!' Clovis replied resolutely, looking about him with the air of a hunted beast. 'I can't. If I mess things up for them, they'll kill me.'

'Mess up what?' cried Cantor. 'Clovis! You can't allow them to get the better of us. You're one of us ...'

'I tell you they'll do me in,' Clovis repeated in despair. 'They will kill me. They stop at nothing. They're demons ... they're always following me, I've always felt them on my tracks ...'

'Clovis, you are one of *us*,' Cantor repeated, staring straight at him with his green eyes, like a serpent trying to hypnotize its prey. 'Speak ... or else ... you may escape them, but you will never escape divine justice, nor your little Saint from the Auvergne.'

The miner leaned back against the wall, looking like a cornered wild animal. He murmured:

'You told me once, Madame, that I needed to do penance. How did you know?'

'By your eyes, Clovis, for you are a man who has not yet made up his mind whether he is on the side of good or evil. And now the moment has come to choose.'

He hung his head, then said:

'They're going to blow up the ship!'

'Which ship?'

'The Governor's ship that's lying at anchor not far from here.'

'The *Asmodeus*?'

'Perhaps!'

'When?'

'How do I know? Now, in an hour's time, possibly two, but certainly tonight while the festivities are going on on board.'

Then, seeing the expression of horror that came over Angélique's and Cantor's faces, he went on:

'That's why I fetched you both here, the two of you . . . when I learned, being in these parts, that you were attending the festivities. I didn't want to see you blown up with the others . . . There, I've told you everything . . . now let me go . . .'

He pushed roughly past them and ran out of the chapel. They heard him slithering down the side of the ravine like a wild boar crushing down the brushwood.

Blessed be the Creator who made red Indians as swift on their feet as a running stag. Piksarett, as he set off on the path leading to Marceline-la-Belle's domain, bounding over obstacles, scarce touching the ground, literally flying at times, streaking through the night like lightning, like the wind, might have given the gods a high idea of human kind.

Warned by Angélique of the danger hanging over the Governor's guests on board the *Asmodeus* he had dashed off, soon overtaking Cantor who had already set off at a run. Cantor had stamina, but Piksarett had wings.

Angélique followed as fast as she was able with her bad foot. Her anxiety was such that she was breathless when she reached the Defour brothers' concession. And still there was a half league to go.

She came to a halt. Further back along the path she had cried out to Cantor to hold back, but in vain. The brave lad had rushed on to the assistance of his fellow men, risking his own life in order to warn them in time, as the noble redskin was doing too.

And what if the vessel blew up while they were both on board, before they had succeeded in persuading the carousing guests to abandon ship?

Angélique was so petrified that she was incapable of any thought beyond this, even of uttering a prayer.

'It's impossible,' she repeated to herself, 'it would be too horrible. It shall not be.'

With every second that passed, destiny was settling the fate of a number of human lives, perhaps even her son's. Deep in the bowels of the *Asmodeus* there was a deadly something nibbling away at time, advancing inexorably towards disaster. At what moment in time would the inevitable progress of this deadly device and Piksarett's and Cantor's mad dash intersect? Before they arrived? While they were on board? Or after it had been possible to save everyone?

She went on more slowly, and as she was about halfway to her destination, a blinding flash seemed to come from the heart of the dark forest and a deafening boom made the cliffs echo.

How she managed to reach Marceline's domain, she would never know!

She saw the ship, a mass of flames, slipping down into the dark waters. Then her eyes ran back to the shore where, by the light of the blaze, she could see a large crowd gathered on the beach, with the Marquis de Ville d'Avray shouting as he paced agitatedly up and down.

Piksarett and Cantor had arrived in time.

Piksarett had suddenly burst in upon the revellers on the poop-deck.

'Get off this ship,' he had cried, 'this ship has death in its entrails.'

The Marquis de Ville d'Avray was the only person present to take him seriously, all the others being more or less drunk and hearing nothing. But the little Governor was very capable of rising to certain situations. With his son tucked under his arm, by main force and determination, assisted by Piksarett and Cantor, he had succeeded in herding everybody on to the deck and in getting them down into the various boats waiting to row them back to land.

Back on the beach people began to look at one another uncomprehendingly.

'What's going on? Where's my glass?'

Ville d'Avray dusted his cuffs and looked up at the tall Piksarett.

'And now explain yourself, Sagamore!' he said solemnly. 'What does all this mean?'

His reply came in the form of a thunder-clap that shook the bay. Flames shot up all round the ship and in a few seconds it was ablaze, had begun to list, then to sink, carrying with it to the bottom of the sea the entire cargo of furs and precious goods belonging to His Excellency the Governor of Acadia.

CHAPTER 54

COULD A beginning ever be made in counting up the treasures he had lost? Apart from the furs, there were thousands of pounds' worth of bartered goods – English of course – and jewels and Spanish *doubloons* – acquired by the Governor in exchange for his patronage or his influence on behalf of the tiny isolated settlements in the Bay, which had often acted as receivers of these pillaged goods. And there were arms, ammunition – to sell to whom? In exchange for what? The Marquis de Ville d'Avray's affairs bore witness to the boundless interest he took in everything under the sun and to his keen sense of market, aesthetic and luxury values. There had been wines, liqueurs and rum from the islands. The gifts he had received from Peyrac in Gouldsboro were among those whose loss he most bitterly mourned. The only items saved were the parts of the Dutch porcelain stove, for the Marquis had brought them ashore shortly before in order to show them to Marceline and to wrap and pack them more thoroughly before setting off on the return journey to Quebec along the coast of Nova Scotia, which was often very stormy.

During that night and the whole of the following day the shores around the point where the *Asmodeus* had gone down looked like an ants' nest turned upside down. How could such a dastardly crime have been committed? It might have been put down to negligence, to a fire caused by sailors who had got drunk and knocked over their lanterns or gone stumbling about the holds without remembering how explosive the atmosphere was, as sometimes happened during the dry heat of late summer. Some of the goods piled up in the holds fermented, a barrel of 'tafia', made too strong and badly sealed, began to distil alcohol, which impregnated the overheated air . . . It only needed a single spark . . .

But they knew that the blow had been a calculated one – with criminal intent.

Someone brought Ville d'Avray a small piece of a rather odd-looking cable, discovered by a redskin in the sand of a neighbouring creek.

The Governor examined it, shook his head and said bitterly:

'Brilliant! Really brilliant!'

It was the remains, either forgotten or abandoned as unimportant, of a most effective portable sabotage device. He explained that when the pirates in the South Seas wanted to exact vengeance for unfair competition, or chastise those who failed to pay up or forgot their promises, they had displayed considerable ingenuity in fabricating time-fuses, which produced neither smell nor smoke and could be placed close to the powder-magazine by an accomplice who had all the time in the world to make good his escape. This fuse was of particularly brilliant design consisting of a narrow fish-gut tube, packed like a miniature sausage-string with tiny lumps of tinder stuck together by some black substance which Ville d l'Avray hesitated to identify, but which Angélique recognized as Chile saltpetre, for it was the substance Count Peyrac made most frequent use of in his work. The whole thing was impregnated with a kind of Indian resin.

'That makes it possible for the contents of the casing to burn slowly without making any smell or smoke,' the Governor explained. 'Someone managed to place one end of this fuse near our powder magazine and must have lighted it yesterday or the day before. Nothing would have put it out, nor revealed its presence before it reached its objective . . .'

'But surely the ship was guarded, wasn't it?'

'Yes, but by whom?' bellowed Ville d'Avray. 'By a pack of lazy good-for-nothings who get drunk, exploit me, and spend their time running after the Indian women ... And with all the comings-and-goings and preparations for the party, anyone could have come on board with that fuse coiled up under his hat ...'

He looked suspiciously in the direction of the Defour brothers.

'Hey, lay off!' said the oldest brother. 'Are you accusing us? That's coming it a bit thick, Governor! You're forgetting that we were on board with you tonight and that, had it not been for the Narranganset, we would all have been blown to smithereens together ...'

'That's true! Where is the Narranganset? ... How did he come to hear about this! He'll jolly well tell me even if I have to have him tortured for it ...'

Angélique intervened to spare Piksarett and told them that it was she who had been warned just in time about the explosion that was about to take place, and that, had it not been for the miraculous fleetness of foot of the Indian, they would not have been saved. But she refused to tell them Clovis's name or to describe him, although the Marquis, all a-quiver and in a terrible state of agitation, plied her with questions. The representative of the Governor of New France in Acadia was prepared to launch every savage in the area in pursuit of this man and roast the soles of his feet in order to force out of him any possible information about the real instigators of the disaster. Angélique admitted that for some months there had been a gang of malefactors prowling in the area who, it seemed, had been out to harm Count Peyrac and his friends in particular. But she gave her pledge that the man who had risked his life to warn her of the danger was not one of their accomplices.

'But I still would like to get my hands on him,' cried Ville d'Avray. 'He would tell me everything, everything! ... We must as soon as possible put these bandits where they can do no more harm.'

And with that sentiment, the entire population, including the Defour brothers, entirely agreed. There was growing indignation among the settlers in the area and also among the Indians, who had been told that the English had sunk a ship bearing gifts to them from the King of France. They were coming out of the forests ready to go to war with whatever enemy the Governor might specify.

Angélique's obstinacy in refusing to give Ville d'Avray any details about how she had come by the information, put him into a rage. The loss of his riches, and especially all the objects he had so lovingly collected, certainly meant more to him than the saving of his life. In his misery he began to ramble wildly.

'And how am I to know that it wasn't *you*, Madame, who stirred up this plot against me? How do I know it wasn't your work, or that of your people? I am sufficiently well aware that Monsieur de Peyrac would stop at nothing to ensure his supremacy over these French territories. He has proved his cunning on more than one occasion. And we know how devoted you are to him. "Let's get rid of the Governor of Acadia and all who remain loyal to him" ... What a wonderful idea! Then he would be master of everything ... Ah, now I see it all.'

'Are you speaking about my husband and me!' Angélique cried, beside herself with anger.

'Yes I am,' he said stamping his foot, puce in the face. 'And this is the proof!'

He waved the piece of fuse with its composition tinder.

'An item as out-of-the-way as this could only have come from his diabolical workshops! ... His workmen and his miners are more skilled and more industrious than any others on this earth. That is already well known throughout America. Would you deny it?'

In a flash Angélique realized that Clovis might have had a hand in the fabrication of this slow-burning fuse. To even the least well-informed, any such complicated contrivance, requiring a knowledge of science, bore the hallmark of Gouldsboro and Wapassou. The help Clovis had given to their enemies could not have consisted solely in sending her off on a wild-goose chase to the English village!

Horror-struck, she examined the tell-tale piece of fuse. She herself might well have lost her life in the explosion, but as neither she nor Cantor had been actually present at the time, her position became suspect. Suddenly the phrase she had read on the piece of paper found in the wrecker's pocket took on a a terrible meaning: 'Sow calamities along her path that she may be accused of them! ...'

Seeing that she found nothing to say, Ville d'Avray was triumphant.

'Ah, you seem abashed! So there is truth in what I say. How was it that you alone, Madame, with your son, were the only ones absent during the festivities?'

'I have already explained that to you,' Angélique said with a sigh. 'We were sent for . . . and if you think a moment, Marquis, had I wanted to kill you all I would scarcely have bothered to send Piksarett and my very own son to you so that they ran the risk of being blown up with you.'

'That was just play-acting . . . or remorse. Women are subject to that kind of vacillation.'

'I've heard enough of this! You are talking nonsense. It's partly your fault too that all this happened.'

'Whatever do you mean? That's the limit,' he cried, his voice a high falsetto. 'I am ruined, and in despair, I nearly lost my life, and yet you accuse me!'

'Yes, for you should have warned us back in Gouldsboro, you should have told us about the dangers resulting from the Duchess of Maudribourg's arrival.'

'But where's the connection? How could anything I might have known about the Duchess of Maudribourg have any possible connection with the band of criminals you tell me about and the loss of my ship?'

Angélique ran her hand distractedly over her brow.

'That's true! You are right! And yet I feel there is some link between her and all the disasters that keep on striking us . . . Because all this is the work of the Devil and she is possessed by the Devil.'

The Governor glanced around him in fear.

'You speak about her as if she were going to return,' he wailed, 'that would be the last straw!'

He sat down on a stool and wiped his eyes with his lace handkerchief.

'Forgive me, Angélique. I admit that I was talking wildly. My impulsive nature often gets me into trouble, but my instinct is sound. Forgive me. I *know* that you took no part in this; on the contrary, you saved our lives. But you must admit that my friendship for you and your husband has cost me dear. You might at least help me to find that man.'

'That I cannot do, and in any case he will be miles away by now.'

It was the first time that it had ever occurred to her that there could be any link between Ambroisine and the unknown persons who sought their downfall. It seemed crazy and illogical, but an indefinable something in the sequence of events had no doubt bit by bit put the idea into her mind, and now under the stress of emotion, her subconscious thoughts had come to the surface.

338

Everything was fluid and uncertain, the objectives aimed at defied logic, but on all sides there were the marks of a kind of relentless will to destroy by any means, however roundabout, attacking with equal force both body and soul.

The net was being carefully drawn around her, so that if she escaped death itself, it was only to feel the agonizing approach of spiritual tribulations. Was she as well armed against this assault as against attacks on her life?

The blows struck were becoming more violent, more cruel, more accurate. And the blow she received the very day following the disastrous night in which the *Asmodeus* was sunk made her spirit reel.

CHAPTER 55

ANGÉLIQUE HAD remained at Marceline Raymondeau's to help her to calm the Marquis de Ville d'Avray and cheer him up. The receding tide had uncovered the wreck, and some of the company had gone on board in an attempt to save anything that could be salvaged. The Indians were preparing their war cauldrons, when simultaneously a caravan from the east coast approached from across the marshes, bringing merchandise and news.

Marceline called Angélique, took her into the house then to her own room 'so that they could have a chat in peace and quiet without being disturbed by all this hullabaloo.'

Big Marceline stood courageously in front of Angélique and looked her straight in the face.

'We women must stick together,' she said, 'and often the best thing to do is to speak out. I've bad news for you, Madame.'

Angélique stared anxiously at her but said nothing.

'My oldest boy has just come from Tormentine,' said Marceline.

'He didn't see my husband?'

'Yes he did, *he saw him*, but . . .'

Marceline drew a deep breath before going on:

'He was there . . . but he was there with that woman, you know, that woman the Governor was talking about . . . the

Duchess of ... I don't know what ... you *know* ... Maudribourg.'

'He can't be!' Angélique cried in great agitation.

And yet her own cry of fear and despair never reached her ears.

The revelation struck her like a whiplash, and a nameless dread ran through her body as if her blood was draining away.

It seemed to her now that she had always been sure that this horrible moment would come! But still she could not focus her mind on it. No, she could not ... She repeated in a toneless voice that seemed not even to cross her lips:

'That's impossible! I saw that woman set off for New England with my own eyes ... a prisoner of the English who took her away as a hostage.'

'You saw her leave ... but you did not see her arrive there.'

'What does that matter? She's gone, I tell you ... gone! Gone! ...'

She repeated the words as if in an attempt to suppress, to wipe out Ambroisine's existence ... to perform the miracle of her never having existed.

Then she tried to calm herself.

'I am a child,' she thought to herself, 'a child who does not want to suffer, to mature ... Something broke inside me the day they took Joffrey away, and ever since then my greatest fear is to have to live through that a second time ... to be betrayed a second time ... What used he to say? That one must not be frightened of anything ... of anything. Look the problem straight in the face and it will bring its reward ... Have the courage to retrace your steps and the monsters will vanish ... I cannot live my life apart from him without dying ... I cannot ... so what shall I do? ... I must keep on ... I must know the truth ...'

Marceline had been watching her. Angélique knew that in her eyes there was no doubt about her misfortune. The Acadian woman had deliberately used the common expression: 'He is "with" that woman.'

But to Angélique it meant nothing. Merely that Ambroisine *was there* on the eastern seaboard, whereas she should have been in Salem or in Boston in New England.

'I'm surprised at him,' Marceline went on, shaking her head. 'He's not the sort to let himself be hoodwinked by a trollop. But

with men you never know! We women have our hearts here,'
she said placing one hand on her ample bosom, 'but with men
. . . it's lower down . . .'

Angélique suddenly thought she was going to be sick.

She could imagine Ambroisine, with all her mysterious sensuality . . . the seductive powers of an infernal angel, combined
with intelligence and knowledge, and at the least Peyrac's ever-
active curiosity of mind . . .

'No, it's impossible . . . impossible.' She did not consider him
fallible . . .

'Men, there's so many things about them you just can't pin
down,' Marceline went on. 'We women are not cunning enough
to understand what makes them tick. We're just not important
enough in their lives! Much less important than adventure,
conquest and ambition!'

She was right . . . and yet she was also wrong.

For he was different.

Suddenly Angélique blessed her dear love for being so
different from 'the others', so difficult to fathom, to understand,
a closed book even to her, capable of unbelievable harshness,
and of unimaginable tenderness and goodness, and capable also
of admitting that she alone, Angélique, had triumphed over his
deep distrust of sentiment, that she had forced the gates of his
heart, almost in spite of himself, that she alone had managed
truly to conquer him, and enslaved him without his fearing or
scorning himself.

She blessed the anger that had swept over him when he
had thought her unfaithful, so unusual a manifestation of his
nature that it had revealed to him the full force of his love for
her.

'Before, in spite of the love I felt towards you, I could
manage to live without you . . . but now I could no longer do so
. . .'

In spite of these words which she ran over in her mind as if
they were a life raft, the thought of Ambroisine's presence over
there filled her heart with so burning a fear that she could
hardly breathe. How had that dangerous siren managed to
escape from Phipps?

'Are you quite sure it's her?' she asked.

'Not a shadow of a doubt. She's there with a whole band of
King's Girls. They say it was Monsieur de Peyrac himself who
took them there and that he may escort them all the way to
Quebec.'

Once again Angélique felt the ground give way beneath her feet.

Had Joffrey de Peyrac learned of Ambroisine's capture by the English? When he had sailed past Port Royal and Goulds-boro without putting in, was he trying to catch up with her and free her?

Angélique did not wish to reveal her doubts to Marceline, not even to make protestations of confidence in her husband. Their relationship was too personal, too delicate for words to explain it, and even her distress or her unwavering confidence in him concerned no one else.

'Right,' she said at last, 'we shall see.'

'Do you still intend to go?'

'But of course! I absolutely must see him, and it's all the more important after what has just taken place here. But may I ask you, Marceline, not to tell Monsieur de Ville d'Avray about the Duchess of Maudribourg's presence on the eastern sea-board. I want to ask him to accompany me there because I need him as a witness, and if he knows that she is there he may refuse to come with me.'

'All right then,' Marceline agreed, and her handsome brown eyes glowed with admiration as she looked at Angélique:

'You are a great lady!' she said softly.

They went out on to the open ground in front of the house.

Down in the bay human cries mingling with those of the cormorants and seagulls seemed to have taken on a new ring. The entire population was converging upon one point of the beach, while people shouted to one another, pointing out some-thing in the direction of the rocks.

'It looks as if a drowned man's been washed up in the bay,' said Marceline, shielding her eyes with her hand.

A few moments later a lifeless body was drawn up on the shore.

'Perhaps it was someone left on board whose disappearance wasn't noticed,' suggested Angélique.

'Who knows? ... There are so many people hanging around in these parts at this time of the year ...'

Cantor broke away from the groups gathered around the body and came striding up towards the two women along the lupin-lined path. When he reached them, all out of breath, Angélique could see from his face what he was about to say:

' "They" got him,' said the lad. 'It's Clovis!'

CHAPTER 56

ANGÉLIQUE HAD no need to persuade Ville d'Avray to accompany her. It was he who took the initiative, declaring in
tones that brooked no reply:

'I'm taking you away from here. We cannot sit around here
waiting for God knows what to happen. I must get back to
Quebec as soon as possible to report to Monsieur de Frontenac
what is going on in Acadia. Old Nicolas Parys, the king of the
eastern seaboard, has certain obligations towards me. He will
surely manage to find me a ship and something with which to
fill it: furs, salt and coal. I don't wish to return empty-handed
to Quebec, people simply wouldn't understand it. And that old
rogue of a wrecker must have quite a bit of booty stowed away
somewhere. He'll jolly well have to scrape the bottom of the
barrel for me, or I'll have his rights over Canso and Royal Isle
withdrawn . . .'

There remained the difficulty of how they were to transport
overland – and it was frequently marshy land – his fairly heavy
baggage – for in the end the Governor had managed to salvage
quite a lot. There was also the Dutch porcelain stove and Saint-
Castine's coffer.

Alexander came to their rescue by suggesting that he might
load it all on to 'his' vessel, the Flemish argosy belonging to the
Defour brothers, and take them, at the speed of a galloping
horse, up the Petitcodiac into its uppermost navigable reaches,
from which point on there was a well-organized porterage
system. Within four days the consignment would be on the
beach at Shediac and all they would have to do was to send a
boat from Tormentine to collect it.

The Governor's face lit up.

'Brilliant!' he cried. 'I always said this lad was brilliant!
Come and embrace me, Alexander. I see that I have not
laboured in vain to train your intelligence. All right, so you are
a trifle frivolous, a trifle flighty, but if you can use your passion
for navigating ships over waterfalls and bores to help those who

343

love you, I can forgive you a great deal ... There, my friend, there, my blessing upon you ...'

He settled a few further details. He would have preferred Alexander to escort his baggage all the way to Tormentine, for he was frightened it might be stolen on the shore at Shediac. 'With all these foreign cod-fishers that descend on our coasts during the summer ...'

He gave Alexander a considerable sum of money with instructions to find reliable guards for the goods or to charter a boat himself to carry them, then took the money back on the grounds that young people were too crazy nowadays to have money in their pockets, and finally handed it back to him with all kinds of advice which the boy listened to with his customary bored expression. He was only waiting for the final words before leaping aboard his ship and setting sail.

'How is one ever to understand these children,' Ville d'Avray said with a sigh. 'The summer drives them all mad. He'll be back when winter comes, warming his feet at my porcelain stove and eating my toffee-apples ... one of my servant's specialities ... you'll see! But we're not there yet. At the moment I must find a ship and salvage whatever can be saved ... Oh, this land of Acadia! A thorn in my flesh! A real witch's cauldron! ... I'll never come back here again ... and yet I'm very fond of Marceline and my little Cherubino!'

Angélique for her part dispatched the *Rochelais* with Vanneau the quartermaster and a small crew to sail round Nova Scotia and meet up with them in Tormentine or Shediac, after putting into Gouldsboro to inform Colin Paturel of their whereabouts. She kept Lieutenant de Barssempuy and a few of the men as an escort.

She would have preferred to see Cantor remain in charge of the *Rochelais*, but the lad refused to leave her side. 'In a couple of days' time I shall be with your father,' she told him, 'and a few days later you will join us there ... you have nothing to fear where I am concerned ...'

But he remained obdurate without giving any precise reasons. She had to make an effort to hide her own anxiety from him and not to tell him what she had learned concerning the Duchess of Maudribourg. But perhaps he knew it intuitively or had overheard some gossip.

So she did not insist. All things considered, she found his presence a pleasure and a comfort.

Naturally Piksarett was one of the party, still proud of his exploit. He seemed in good humour, although Angélique, who had begun to know him well, sensed that he remained on the alert as if advancing into enemy territory.

'These Malecites are a pack of stinking animals,' he told her. 'Their sole allies and friends on earth are alcohol and goods from ships. Beyond that, they can scarcely tell an Iroquois from one of their brother Abenakis . . .'

The local natives remained in a state of agitation and effervescence, talking of war, of vengeance, and of gifts they had been promised but had not received. A large band of them followed the travellers without anyone being able to find out why. Ville d'Avray was convinced that it was in honour of him, the Governor of Acadia. But Piksarett considered that nothing good would come of this rowdy escort. The Indians of the region had already got together a large quantity of alcohol on board the seasonal fishing-vessels, and the time was approaching when, after pooling within each tribe their provisions of fire-water, they would embark upon one of those mad autumn drinking bouts that always ended in a number of deaths and terrible crimes, and that had already assumed the traditional form of a magic ceremonial.

Fascinated by the approach of the trance-like state induced by the white man's poison, 'the King of France's milk' as they called it, and knowing also what it would cost them to be involved in the subsequent orgy, but without having the strength to resist it, they were growing more and more nervy and suspicious, discontented with themselves and with everyone else, and were losing their customary good humour.

Fortunately the presence of two of the Defour brothers along with several of Marceline's sons, who were all local people and had relatives or blood-brothers among the Indians, ensured the safety of the travellers.

And in any case they would soon be on the other side of the Chignecto Isthmus. On reaching the Gulf of Saint Lawrence they would have left that closed world, imprisoned by its tides, its storms and its fog, the inward-looking world of French Bay, and would emerge into a wider landscape. From the eastern seaboard the view was outwards, towards Europe, not away from it, as here.

Angélique's impatience not only to clarify her own situation but to get away from these wild lands, forsaken by God and by men, was such that she hurried the party along the Chignecto trails at a speed which only the Red Indians managed to equal without difficulty, and that had the Marquis complaining constantly that he could not keep up.

But Angélique was as indifferent to his complaints as she was to the landscape through which they were passing.

She must arrive as soon as possible. She strode on, plunged in her own thoughts, that jolted about in her head without her always daring to follow them through to their conclusion or to face boldly up to them.

She trembled at the thought that Ambroisine might make an attempt on Joffrey's life. Ville d'Avray had told her that she was a poisoner!

She had killed several times.

But Joffrey was not a man to let himself be killed as easily as that, still less to allow himself to be taken advantage of by anyone, even a seductive woman, who might have homicidal designs upon him . . . She knew him. She thought of his unusual lucidity of mind, the distance he always kept between himself and others, his mind full of shrewdness and mastery, in which there was a certain element of contempt and distrust for human nature.

These features, which had sometimes distressed her, because she felt that she would never fully be able to get through to him, she was now delighted to know he possessed, for they were a guarantee that he would not allow himself to be outwitted by any Ambroisine.

He was too experienced . . . she told herself – especially where women were concerned. He had always known what he was doing . . . 'even with me . . . although he sometimes failed to recognize the depth of my feeling for him . . . but then I'm not easy either . . . and perhaps I myself, in my wariness of life and men, failed also to recognize the strength of my love for him . . . Oh, if the slightest harm should come to him, I would die! . . .'

There were moments when, like a person condemned to death, she relived scraps and fragments of her life . . . their lives apart, yet shared, for they had remained united through their memories, their nostalgia, all the different faces he had assumed for her, the love she had borne him in her youth, as Comte de Toulouse, and later her wild, hidden passion which as Dame Angélique of La Rochelle she did not want to avow, for this pirate, the Rescator, who had bought her.

Yes! She too, in her mature years, had fallen in love with the man he had become, and that without even recognizing him!

The Rescator who, in her eyes, would forever remain somewhat inscrutable, but who was awaiting her out there on the eastern seaboard, and who suddenly, when he smiled or took off his mask, would become the warm-hearted companion of Wapassou once more, her friend in their moments of pain or joy, a man whose delicacy and understanding were almost feminine. When would she be able to reach him at last, when could she be assured of his reality, of his life among the living – how quickly a dead man vanishes from the land of the living! ... When would she feel his presence and recognize him in all his gestures, his expressions, the sound of his voice, each thing particular to him, revealing him by his attentive love, and those things to which it seemed to her she had not paid sufficient attention, even his sudden withdrawals, his anger or his irony, or the coldness which had so frightened her because her still childlike being saw in it a threat to herself rather than a manifestation of his superior yet very human personality, while he sought to reach harmony with the world, to dominate it, not allow himself to be crushed by it or to be dragged down into its all too easy moral decay.

In this universe which he challenged, she had bit by bit become – like a star drawn into the orbit of a galaxy, slowly pulled closer and closer to the central planet – his chief preoccupation. He had admitted as much to her: 'I have fallen in love with you, with the woman you have become ... and because I do not yet know whether I have triumphed over your heart, today, for the first time in my life, I have known the pain of love ... I, Comte de Toulouse, I have to admit it: were I to lose you I should be destroyed ...'

Even if he were exaggerating somewhat, hearing such words from his mouth was almost too much for her fearful heart.

Did it not all mean that it was too good, too extraordinary a love to be lived, and that it was all about to end, that she would arrive too late ...

So she strode on, swift as the wind, borne on by her urgent need to reach him, to clasp him at last in her arms, alive, alive ... anything that might happen after that, whatever she might learn thereafter would no longer have any importance ...

PART FIVE

The Gulf of Saint Lawrence
or
The Crimes

CHAPTER 57

THE BRETON fisherman from Quimper, who, weary of fishing all day long alone in his little boat, had 'gone up river', in other words gone off to catch forty winks in a remote creek, frequented only by seagulls and petrels, could scarcely believe his eyes when he saw emerge from the woods a blonde woman as elegant as a queen, accompanied by a nobleman wearing an embroidered, although dusty, frockcoat, an officer, a handsome fair-headed boy looking like a page and a band of befeathered Indians. It was as if the entire court of Versailles was making a tour that year in these remote regions of North America, and delighting in disporting themselves along those noisome, mist-shrouded shores, with their infernal exhalations, thick with mosquitoes during the oppressive heat of the day, while the damp, icy nights gave notice that their teeth would soon be chattering in the polar gales of winter.

They already had that Duchess in Tidmagouche, and now here came this other fine lady stepping out of the wild forest as if she had been for a stroll in a park, and bearing straight down on him.

Soon the new arrivals assembled in a group around the man where he still lay, bewildered, on the sand.

'Where are you from, my friend?' asked Ville d'Avray.

'From Quimper, m'lord.'

'A seasonal worker. Does your captain pay his dues?'

'To old Parys, yes.'

'And to the Governor of the Region?'

'Oh, he can go and take a running jump in the lake . . .' the man replied with a noisy yawn, as he lay still stretched out on the sand. After all, he was at home here, on these shores where his grandfather, his great grandfather and all his ancestors for centuries back had come to catch and salt cod every season.

'Just look at the insolence of these boors,' cried Ville d'Avray, striking the sand in fury with his cane. 'Cod is one of the riches of Acadia. They call it green gold. But all these Basques, Portuguese, Normans and Bretons regard it as perfectly reasonable that they should grow fat here at the expense of the State and without paying a penny for the privilege.'

'Grow fat, that's easily said,' the man protested, deigning to sit up. He tugged up his breeches to reveal his skinny calves, abraded by the salt.

'We toil and moil for four months at a stretch and don't go home much richer for it. Hardly enough for a few binges before setting sail again.'

'He speaks French pretty well for a Breton from Quimper,' Ville d'Avray remarked, quickly recovering his calm again. 'Where is your captain from?'

'From Faouet.'

'A Cornouailles man too, but from the north. They speak the same Gaelic dialect as the people from Cornwall in England. What is your captain's name?'

'If you went and asked him he would tell you.'

'Very well, that is what we intend to do. For we have no boat and you are going to take us to him in yours.'

'All these people?' said the man in some dismay.

Angélique interrupted.

'Just a moment, Marquis. We must find out where this man's ship is anchored, and if it is in the region we are making for, Tidmagouche near Tormentine.'

It transpired that this was in fact where these Cornouailles Bretons had set up their cod-drying platforms for the summer season. They had been in contract for 'centuries' with old Parys who lived at Tidmagouche during the summer and ran its trading post.

'The gravel beaches are excellent and the bay is huge. There's plenty going on to keep us entertained without impeding the work. Pirate vessels sometimes moor there before going off again and we have a good booze-up together.'

'Isn't there a French noblewoman there, the Duchess of Maudribourg?' Angélique asked in a voice which she hoped sounded off-hand.

'Yes indeed, and a good-looking piece too! But she's not for us. She's for the pirates and for the old man. Actually, I know nothing about it. Maybe she's for no one. We fishermen have nothing to do with people like that. We might make up to some of the girls accompanying her, but they're pretty well guarded and in any case during the season we're working so hard that we are not exactly on form and our captain keeps a close rein on us.'

Angélique feared the man might link Joffrey's name with Ambroisine's, but he said not a word, and she was too faint-hearted to choose to ask him any questions.

The Marquis de Ville d'Avray's eyes nearly started out of his head.

'What's this I hear? What did you say? That the Duchess is there and you knew it! And you didn't tell me!'

'I thought it unnecessary.'

'Unnecessary! It's a most serious matter, on the contrary. Had I known that the hussy was there, I would never have come. I would have gone to Shediac with Alexander.'

'Exactly! I wanted you to come with me, for I need you as a witness.'

'Charming! And who told you she was over here on the Gulf of Saint Lawrence?'

'Marceline!'

'And *she* didn't tell me either! That's women all over,' exclaimed Ville d'Avray bitterly, beside himself with indignation, 'they cajole you, are all over you, so that you think they love you ... then at the first opportunity they gang up against you and send or drag you off to your death without the least scruple.'

He set off resolutely towards the edge of the woods again.

'I'm going back.'

'No,' Angélique begged him, seizing him by his coat-tails. 'You can't abandon me like this.'

'Do you want her to murder me?'

'No, I want you to help me.'

'She will unmask me ...'

'No she won't, you will be able to lull her suspicions, you have a flair for acting, you told me so yourself! So please use it! ...'

'But she is more than a match for all the actors in the world.'

'Never mind! I need your help,' Angélique begged him urgently. 'It's now that *everything* is at stake ... *there*, on these shores. And it's going to be horrible, horrible ... I know it ... you cannot abandon me ...'

Her voice was trembling in spite of herself and she thought she was about to burst into trears.

'My husband will surely be there ... you must talk to him, tell him what you know about her, convince him ... if need be ...'

The Marquis looked up, saw the pathetic look in Angélique's eyes and realized what was tormenting her.

'All right!' he said at last. 'Never let it be said that I would leave a pretty woman in difficulties without doing my best to help her.'

He threw out his chest, leaning on his silver-topped cane, and drew himself up to his full height.

'All right,' he repeated, 'let us go and tackle the Demon!'

CHAPTER 58

IT WAS a world stinking of fish the whole summer long, that, from Cape Gaspé in the north, where the Gulf of Saint Lawrence joins the river of the same name, along a string of beaches and bays crowded with boats, with ships at anchor, with 'platforms' – kind of wooden tables standing on piles, for 'dressing' the cod – a vast fringe of bits of fish thrown away and a parallel fringe of clamorous sea birds, as far as Canso in the south, consisted of nothing but mile upon mile of fish drying on hurdles. The kingdom of the cod, known as Bay Verte! Mist often hung translucent and yellow like a sulphur-laden vapour over it all. Then the capes and promontories would vanish from sight, isolating each man in his wretched domain, between the sea with its metallic sheen and the forest lands along the cliff tops. There was nothing beyond, not in front, not behind. The spruce trees, a kind of Canadian fir, standing erect like tall, black distaffs, seemed to form an impenetrable barrier between the sea and the land beyond, gathering together, imprisoning beneath their guard a handful of houses, a few hamlets, a wooden fort with its enclosure and a few bark huts in its shadow, inhabited by Malechite Indians stupefied with alcohol.

Beyond the mists lay the Gulf. For having his feast day fall on the day the Frenchman Jacques Cartier set up the Cross at Gaspé, Saint Lawrence had been amply rewarded.

A river several thousand miles long, a bay as large as France itself, encircled by huge islands: Anticosti in the north,

Newfoundland to the east, and in the south Saint John Island.[1] and, next to it, treeless, its red cliffs looking like a ruby set in the sea, Royal Island,[2] a ring of anthracite round a vast lake. In the centre lay the archipelago of the Magdalen Islands: Demon Isle, Bird Island, Wolf Point, Havre-Aux-Maisons, and La Grosse ...

The prisoners of the 'strand' knew nothing of life in the Bay and took no part in it.

Every June the people on these flotillas from the European seaboards flocked to these shores like an irresistible migration of nesting birds, each one settling in his own corner from which he never moved.

The first one to arrive was called 'master of the strand'. He would set himself up with his crew and live there for months on end as if in his own private bounds.

This was how the shores of Tormentine-Tidmagouche appeared to Angélique when she reached them towards noon.

Cape Tormentine which gave its name to the area was much farther to the north and could not be seen from where they were. In fact this particular shore had no name, it was just a place for catching fish, engaging in criminal activities, or selling one's soul to the Devil ...

There the final scene was to be acted out, as she had told Ville d'Avray. She watched the shore slowly approaching to the leisurely stroke of the Breton fisherman's oars. The sun was still high in the sky, a whitish dazzling patch behind the mist. The sea was wrinkled with tiny sparkling waves. The dinghy which Angélique had boarded with the Indian Piksarett was making little way, for its single sail would have been of no avail in the slack wind.

Piksarett, tall and gangling, draped in his black bearskin and clutching his spear, his bow and his arrows, had insisted on accompanying Angélique in the boat, that was too small to accommodate more than two people in addition to the fisherman and his tackle.

The others had to walk, which would take them several hours, for the paths followed a roundabout course in order to skirt the bogs and marshes lying behind the settlement.

Angélique jumped out of the boat on to the sand regardless of the fact that she wet her legs up to the knees.

1. Translator's note: Saint John Island is now known as Prince Edward Island.
2. Translator's note: now called Cape Breton Island.

The Breton fisherman pointed out the houses standing in rows to the west of the beach, at the foot of the cliffs and part of the way up them. They seemed to grow untidily out of the landscape like wild plants, some large, some small, some with shingle roofs, some with straw, some even roofed with a kind of mossy growth. The wooden fort dominated them all, looking like a chunky black animal all hunched up upon itself, while further along on the edge of the promontory invaded by the army of firs, close to the silhouette of a cross, stood a tiny chapel with a narrow white-painted belfry.

Angélique hastened along the shore, oblivious of the activity along the beach where the fishermen were working. They themselves paid no heed to her and did not seem to see her.

Then, quite suddenly, she found herself surrounded by the King's Girls. Their faces appeared as in a nightmare: Delphine, Marie-la-Douce, Jeanne Michaud and her child, Henriette, Antoinette and even Petronella Damourt, their faces looking chalky and wan against the pallor of the sky.

And indeed they were as pale as death as they recognized her, suddenly standing before their eyes.

'Where is your benefactress?' asked Angélique.

One of the girls motioned in the direction of the nearest house, and Angélique rushed to it, and was inside in a flash.

There she saw Ambroisine de Maudribourg . . .

CHAPTER 59

THE DEMON was sitting by the window, her hands clasped on her knees in the attitude of meditation and prayer she so often adopted.

She looked round and her eyes met Angélique's. A smile flickered over her lips and she said simply:

'You! . . .'

She did not seem surprised. Her lips curved in the merest trace of a smile, and in that smile could be seen all the evil that lay hidden behind her gracious appearance.

'I didn't think we'd meet again . . .'

'Why?' Angélique retorted. 'Because you instructed your accomplices to have me killed?'

The Duchess's thin eyebrows shot up in astonishment.

'My accomplices?'

Angélique's eyes scanned every corner of the room.

'Where is he?' was her keenest thought. But beneath Ambroisine's ironical glance she held back the words that burned her lips.

'You see?' said the Duchess, shaking her head. 'I am not to be outmanoeuvred as easily as all that. You thought you were getting rid of me for good by handing me over to that Englishman . . . Well, here I am, a free woman and a long way from New England.'

'How did you fix things with Phipps?'

'You'd like to know, wouldn't you?'

She gave her throaty, bubbling laugh.

'A clever woman can always get round any man well endowed by nature . . .'

She scrutinized Angélique with mocking curiosity.

'But why have you come here? To look for *him*? . . . You're certainly not afraid of getting hurt, are you?'

At that moment Angélique's eyes lighted on a garment hanging on the wall in one corner of the room. It was Joffrey's doublet, the dark green velvet one with the silver embroidery, that he usually wore.

Ambroisine followed Angélique's glance and her smile grew more pronounced.

'Yes indeed!' she said off-handedly. 'Yes indeed, my dear, *that's the way it is*!'

Without thinking, Angélique rushed across the room. At the sight of that garment, her whole being had been shaken. She laid her hands on it: she would have liked to have buried her face in it. She ran her fingers back and forth over the cloth, trying to call to mind his familiar, adored presence.

'Did you understand what I said?' Ambroisine reiterated, her voice metallic. 'He's living here with me: he is my *lover*!'

Angélique spun round and once again her eyes took in the room.

'As you say! . . . But where is he then! Let him tell me so himself! . . Where is he?'

The Duchess's face betrayed a momentary hesitation.

'At the moment he's away,' she agreed. 'He sailed a couple of days ago, I'm not quite sure in what direction, Newfoundland, I think, but he'll be back . . .'

Angélique realized that she was not lying and did not know at that very moment whether she felt bitterly disappointed or a certain sense of relief at having to put off the moment when she would face him in front of Ambroisine.

'He asked me to wait for him here,' the Duchess went on in honeyed tones, 'he assured me he would be back in a week at the latest, and begged me not to leave . . . He's crazy about me . . .'

Angélique was looking right through her as if she had been transparent and as if the words were not reaching her ears.

'Do you hear me?' the Duchess repeated in a voice that betrayed impatience and irritation. 'Do you understand me? . . . I'm his mistress, I tell you.'

'I don't believe it!'

'But why not? Are you the only woman in the world whom anyone can love? We are lovers, I assure you.'

'No! You're lying.'

'How can you be so positive?'

'I know him too well. His instinct is sound and he has wide experience – of women too. He isn't a man to let himself be got round by a creature as vile as you.'

The Duchess gave a mocking cry and feigned ironical surprise:

'But what have we here! Anyone would think you loved him! How crazy you are! *Love does not exist* . . . It is nothing but an illusion, a legend that men have invented for their amusement on earth . . . the flesh is the only thing that counts and the consuming passions it inspires . . . As I said about Phipps, there's no man a clever woman can't get round when she knows how to set about it!'

Angélique burst out laughing. She had just had a vision of poor Phipps grappling with this lewd woman . . . Had the unfortunate man succumbed to such an assault? No doubt! For Puritans are ill-prepared for this kind of temptation, the fear of sin, in their souls, being equalled only by the fascination the power of Evil has for them.

Her sudden mirth disconcerted Ambroisine who looked at her uncomprehendingly, stupefied.

'You're laughing! Are you crazy? . . . Can't you understand that he too is fallible. All men are, I tell you! You only have to find their weak point.'

'He hasn't got a weak point.'

'It appears that he has ... since ... what I told him convinced him all too easily of how wrong he would be to disdain the pleasures I was offering him for a woman such as you ...'

Angélique stopped laughing.

'What did you tell him?'

Ambroisine ran her tongue greedily over her lips. A glint of triumph came into her deep golden eyes as she noted the anxiety Angélique had betrayed.

'Oh, it was all too easy ... When he joined me at La Hève where I had asked Phipps to put me ashore ... I told him that the first thing you had done after he had left Gouldsboro was to seek out Colin Paturel and to give yourself to him ...'

'You said *that*!'

'How pale you are all of a sudden ...' murmured Ambroisine, examining her with cruel attention ... 'so you see I wasn't too far out in my conjectures concerning you nor about that handsome, silent Norman. You fancy him ... and he's in love with you ... and so are others ... all the men love you and desire you.'

Her expression suddenly changed and she said through clenched teeth:

'Dead! I'd like to see you dead!'

Then with a terrible cry, she went on:

'No! No! Not dead! ... If you died, the light would go out of my life! Great Heavens! How can I at one and the same time want to see you dead and feel such despair at the mere thought that you might vanish from this world ... Oh, I came too late! If only you had loved me, we would have merged into one. I would have lost myself in you. I would have been your slave and you would have been mine.

'But you have grown attached to men, those unspeakably foul creatures! ... Men have enslaved you!'

She began to say the most disconcertingly obscene things that Angélique gazed at her wide-eyed as if she were actually seeing serpents emerging from between those lovely lips.

Paradoxically it was this hysterical outburst on the Duchess's part which saved Angélique from a similar attack.

When Ambroisine had told her of what she had accused Angélique to her husband, Angélique had seen in a flash just what damage such an accusation could have done to Joffrey de Peyrac. Their relationship since their reconciliation was still delicate, for it was only a short time before that she had seen

Joffrey's face transformed by terrible anger at the thought that she could have given herself to Gold Beard.

Slowly, gently, with infinite caution, gathering up their courage, pocketing their pride, delving into the depths of their love for strength to face such an ordeal, they had succeeded in healing the deep wounds they had inflicted on one another at that dramatic moment.

But with that wound still fresh in Peyrac's heart, how corrosive must Ambroisine's words have been!

She felt herself grow faint as if before some catastrophe which she had tried in vain to ward off, to prevent.

All was lost. Stunned as she was, she had but one idea: to flee blindly before her.

It was at that moment that Ambroisine, breaking into demented abuse, had to a certain extent brought her to herself again . . .

Her reaction changed direction and her anger with Ambroisine seared her like a red-hot iron.

'That's enough!' she cried, stamping her foot on the ground and shouting louder than the Duchess herself. 'You are odious, you are disgusting! Of course men are not saints, but it is women like you who degrade them and make them stupid. Be quiet! I order you to be quiet! Men are entitled to respect!'

They both fell silent at the same moment, and stood facing one another, panting for breath.

'You really are extraordinary,' Ambroisine said, looking at her as if she suddenly had some monster standing before her. 'What! I've just dealt you a mortal blow . . . and you needn't deny it. I saw it . . . I have just proved to you that your love, your idol, your god is fallible after all . . . and yet you still manage to lecture me . . . to stand up for men, for all men . . . Upon my word, what kind of a person are you then?'

'That doesn't matter . . . I loathe injustice and there are certain truths which I shall not allow you – learned, intelligent and influential as you are – to bury in your mire. A man is someone serious and very important, and just because their minds are sometimes a closed book to us women, that is no reason for us to take revenge for our inability to follow them, by dragging them down and reducing them to slavery. Abigail was saying something on the same lines to me the other evening . . .'

'Abigail!'

Once again the Duchess shrieked in hatred.

'Oh, don't mention that name to me . . . How I hate her!

359

That hypocritical heretic. I loathe her ... You looked at her
with such affection. You were always talking to her ... I saw
you through the window. You laid your head on her shoulder.
You slept at her side ... you held her child in your arms and
covered it with kisses ...'

'So that cry we heard in the night was *you*! ...'

'How could I look at such a scene without dying in agony ...
there you were, happy to be with her ... alive and happy ...
and yet she should have been dead a hundred times over ...'

Angélique took a step towards her. She felt as if her heart
was about to stop beating.

'You tried to poison her, didn't you?'

She spoke in an undertone, through clenched teeth.

'And you even arranged things so that she might have died in
childbirth ... When you guessed that her time was near, and
that no doubt it would be that very night, you came and put
some drug in my coffee ... But it was Madame Carrère who
drank it ... it so happened ... otherwise I would have slept all
through that night, and you knew that Abigail might die if she
were deprived of my help ... And you had someone take alcohol to the old Indian woman so that she was incapable of
helping ... then later you put poison in the infusion I had
prepared for Abigail ... You had heard me tell her she must
drink some several times during the day ... You went back
there during the afternoon and mingled with the visitors in
order to commit your dastardly crime ... Fortunately Laurier
put his basket down in front of the jug, and Séverine forgot
about it. Then that evening I threw the mixture out of the
window ... and Bertille's pig died ...'

She spoke as if in a dream, horrified.

'You wanted me to murder Abigail by my own hands!'

'You loved her,' Ambroisine repeated, 'and you didn't love
me ... You were always taken up with all kinds of things other
than me: with her, with the children, with your kitten ...'

'My kitten ... so it was you ... *you* who struck him, tormented him ... Now I understand ... It was you he could
see through the darkness when his fur stood on end with
fright ...'

Angélique was standing close to Ambroisine, bending over
her, her eyes flashing.

'You sought his death too ... but he managed to escape you
in time ... escape from your clutches ...'

'It's all your fault ...'

An expression like that of a cunning little girl came into the Duchess's face.

'You always did your utmost to make these things happen . . . If only you had loved me . . .'

'But how on earth do you expect anyone to love you in any kind of way?' Angélique cried, seizing her by the hair and shaking her mercilessly. '*You are a monster!*'

So beside herself with rage was she that she could, or so it seemed to her, have shaken the woman's head off. But she stopped when she saw from the expression on Ambroisine's upturned face that the latter was enjoying her violence.

She released her hold suddenly and the Duchess more or less collapsed on the beaten earth floor. As had happened that other night at Port Royal when she had knelt naked on her scarlet cloak, a kind of ecstatic glow spread over her face with its half-closed eyes.

'Yes,' she murmured, 'kill me . . . kill me, my beloved.'

Angélique, quite beside herself, began to pace round and round the room.

'Some holy water! Fetch me some holy water!' she cried. 'Please, some holy water! With such creatures I can understand the necessity for the sprinkling on of holy water and ceremonies of exorcism!'

Ambroisine burst into strident laughter; she laughed so much that tears came into her eyes.

'Oh, you are the funniest woman I have ever met,' she managed to whisper at last. 'The most delectable . . . the most unexpected . . . Holy water! . . . You should have heard how you said that! . . . You are irresistible . . . really! Oh, Angélique, my love!'

She got to her feet as if exhausted, examined herself in the little looking-glass that stood on the table, licked the tip of her fore-finger and smoothed her delicate eyebrows.

'Yes, you know, I have laughed more with you than I have ever laughed with anyone else . . . You know how to make me gay . . . Oh, those days in Gouldsboro . . . with your presence, your sudden changes of humour full of fantasy . . . My love, we were made for one another . . . if only you would . . .'

'That's enough!' Angélique shouted again and rushed out of the house.

She was running like one demented, twisting her ankles on the stony ground.

'Madame, what is the matter?'

The King's Girls came towards her, white-faced after hearing the shouts and screams that had come from the house in which the two women faced one another.

'Where is Piksarett?' Angélique asked them, still panting.

'Your redskin?'

'Yes, where is he? Piksarett! Piksarett!'

'Here I am, captive mine!' said Piksarett's voice as he appeared before her. 'What do you want of me?'

She stared at him, distraught, unable to remember why she had called for him. He was so tall that he towered over her, and in his face, the colour of baked clay, his keen, black eyes sparkled like jet.

'Come with me into the forest,' he said, using the Abenaki tongue, 'come and walk along the forest paths ... It is the sanctuary of the Great Spirit ... pain is deadened there ...'

She followed him as he strode swiftly away from the village towards the edge of the forest. Then he disappeared among the close-growing trunks of firs and pines sprinkled with grey dust from the drought. But the bushes in the undergrowth were beginning to glow red and at times they crossed great open spaces covered with purple bushes of myrtles and huckleberries that spread out like a sumptuous carpet all along the coastline.

Then they found themselves in the black shadows of the trees. Piksarett strode swiftly on, and Angélique followed him without difficulty, borne on by the blind necessity not to stop, for had she halted, the burning flood she felt beating at the gates of her heart – whose terrible pounding made it impossible for her to breathe properly – would have overwhelmed and crushed her.

When they reached a clearing from which they could see the sea through the reddish trunks of the fir trees, Piksarett came to a halt. He sat down on a tree trunk then, looking up at Angélique, he considered her with eyes full of mockery.

Then the burning flood swept over her.

As if she had been struck a blow she fell to her knees beside the Red Indian and, burying her face in the black bearskin, she burst into heartrending sobs.

CHAPTER 60

'WOMEN ARE entitled to weep,' said Piksarett with astonishing kindness, 'weep, my captive! The poisons in your heart will be washed away.'

He laid one hand on her hair and waited. She cried as if her whole being had crumbled, without even being able to see at the bottom of this chaotic chasm what precisely had caused her pain. It was a total surrender, the dykes had finally burst and courage had capitulated to human weakness, a physical need that saved her from madness, and as happens on those rare occasions when one accepts oneself as one is, inwardly reconciling what one knows about oneself with what one does not know, in the end she found that letting herself go like this brought balm to her heart. The pain that had been rending her grew less, and in its place she began to feel a sweet, calming something that lulled her distress.

The echo of the disaster died away within her, slowly giving place to a deathly silence but one in which soon there began to rise up again a creature bruised, crushed, and weakened ... This creature in her own image looked into the depths of her soul and said to her: 'And now, Angélique, what are we going to do?'

She dried her eyes. Alone she could not have borne this shock, but Piksarett was there. Throughout those terrible moments Angélique had never ceased to be aware of a human presence watching over her. All was not lost. Piksarett had kept faith with her.

'He's not there!' she said at last in a broken voice. 'He's not there! He's gone off somewhere else, I don't know where. What is to become of us?'

'We must wait for him,' Piksarett replied, staring at the white horizon through the trees. 'He is on the trail of the enemy, but he will come back.'

'Wait for him,' Angélique repeated, 'here? Near to that woman. To have to meet her every day, to see her mocking me, triumphant. I can't do it ...'

'Well, what do you want to do then,' the Abenaki exclaimed ... 'concede her the victory?'

He leaned down towards her, pointing an imperative finger towards the village.

'Observe your enemy, never give her a moment's peace, watch her every word in order to expose her lies, set the trap that will be her undoing; how can you expect to do all this if you refuse to live in the same place? That woman is full of demons, I know it, but you are not yet vanquished as far as I know.'

Angélique covered her face with her hands and in spite of herself she was shaken by a sob. How could she explain to Piksarett what had hurt her worse than all else?

'One summer I went to the Valley of the Five Nations,' Piksarett told her, 'alone ... Each night I entered one of the villages, and went into one of those long houses in which more than ten families sleep, and took the scalp of a sleeping brave ... By day they were on my tracks ... every instant I had to foil their ruses ... I no longer recognized my own breathing, nor even the sensation of my own life, so careful had I to be to render myself invisible and prepare my exploit of the following night. They knew that it was I, Piksarett, the chief of the Narranganset, but they never caught me, not even caught sight of me. When I had twenty Iroquois scalps hanging on my belt, I left that land. Now in the Valley of the Five Nations it is said that I am capable of transforming myself into a spirit at will.

'And thus will you remain here among your enemies, stronger and more skilful than all of them, preparing their defeat and your triumph.'

'I'm frightened,' Angélique murmured.

'I can understand that. It is easier to fight men than demons.'

'Was that the danger you saw hovering over me when you came to Gouldsboro to seek my ransom?' she asked.

'Yes. Suddenly there was a shadow there, and I could hear the rustling of evil spirits. It came from among the people gathered in that room. It had already closed around you ... I had to go away in order to escape that deadly influence and recover my lucidity of mind.'

'But why did you not warn me?'

'Women are not easy to convince, and you even less than other women.'

'But I would have listened to you, Sagamore. You know that. I trust your intuition ...'

'What could I have said? Could I have pointed out that woman who was your companion, your guest, your friend, and say: "She is full of demons. Take care: she seeks your death. Worse, she seeks to destroy your soul . . ."? You white people make fun of us when we speak like that . . . you treat us as if we were small children or senile old men whose minds are befogged. You will not admit that invisible things can sometimes be quite clear to our eyes . . .'

'You ought to have warned me,' she repeated, 'now it's too late, for all is lost.'

'I did warn you. I said: "Danger hovers over you. Pray!" Did you do so?'

'Yes . . . I think so.'

'Then why are you in despair? God harkens to the just man when he calls to Him from the depths of his distress. Who says it's too late or that all is lost?'

She did not dare explain to this noble Indian – who like his fellows was so utterly a master of his senses by tradition and temperament – the nature of the doubt that tormented her concerning the man she loved.

'Listen! She says that my husband has fallen in love with her and has repudiated me in his heart!'

'She's lying!' Piksarett affirmed categorically. 'How could that be possible? He is the Man of Thunder. His powers are countless! And you, you are Kawa, the fixed star. What would he be doing with a woman like that?'

He spoke in accordance with his own logic, which for him was irrefutable. The depraved concupiscence of white men was beyond his primitive understanding.

'I must admit,' he agreed, 'that white men are somewhat perplexing. The habit of pressing a trigger to defend their lives has made them forget how to save themselves by building up the resistance of their souls and their bodies. The slightest effort exhausts them, a brief period of hunger depresses them, they cannot do without women, even the night before a battle, and never think that they might risk facing the enemy in a state of weakness and distraction . . .'

'But the Man of Thunder is not of that kind.'

'You speak about him as if you had met him,' she said.

She listened as he spoke, looking up at him with eyes bright with hope. That wrinkled clay face, covered with tattoo marks, between those two plaits of hair threaded with the feet of a red fox, that stood out from beneath his topknot stuck with feathers, and festooned with rosary beads and medallions, seemed to her at that moment to be the kindest face in the world.

'I sense him through you,' Piksarett replied. 'The man you love could never be vile, nor base, nor treacherous, or you could never love and serve him. Now, you do love him. Therefore he is neither base nor vile nor treacherous. Never have doubts about a man when he in the warpath, O Woman! ... You weaken him at a distance and make him a prey to danger.'

'You are right.'

She wanted to believe him, although she still felt numb in that terrible spot where Ambroisine had struck her. That mention of Colin's name had been at one and the same time like a forgotten nightmare and like a weapon which still possessed a redoubtable power. Joffrey might still be feeling the effects of it whereas she herself found that it no longer meant anything at all. She wondered with a kind of astonishment how she could ever have been sensually tempted, even for a single moment, by any other man than this. What kind of a woman was she then, those few weeks ago? ... It all seemed like years ago, and she did not recognize herself. At what moment had she ceased to be that uncertain child, dependent on her past and her inadequacies, in order to become the woman she was today, having found her guiding star, her self-assurance ... but too late, perhaps ...

Was it when she had leapt over the fire among the Basques at Monhegan?

Hernani d'Astiguarra had shouted:

'The person who jumps the midsummer fire the Devil cannot harm for the rest of the year!'

That was a memory that comforted her. Piksarett was right. Fate was offering her a reprieve. She should use these days before Joffrey's return to unmask Ambroisine.

She had once been perfectly capable of fighting Madame de Montespan[1] on equal terms. Today the stake was no longer the King, and her opponent was even more formidable. But she had acquired other arms too. The success of her life and the benevolence of fate towards her had fortified her soul. To him who has never won, defeat is indeed bitter. But she, who had been vouchsafed these wonderful rediscoveries in this world, could scarcely jib now at having to pay the price for them, perhaps for not having sufficiently appreciated their miraculous value at the time!

1. See *Angélique and the King*.

The final act was approaching which would seal the pre-
destination of their love.

Was she going to retreat now?

Piksarett saw her eyes flash and her nostrils begin to
quiver.

'Good!' he said. 'What would I do with a captive who was a
coward? I would be ashamed of asking for her ransom, so little
would she be worth ... You know, it is not easy for me to be
here either. I am all alone here as I was when I walked the
Sacred Valley of the Iroquois. Uniakke is hiding somewhere in
the forest with his father. I have promised them that I will
hand over the men who killed their blood brother, but they are
unable to be of much use to me as they are strangers here and
fear evil spirits. I am all alone and I feel more uneasy than
when I wandered alone in the Sacred Valley of the Iroquois,
my enemies. But never mind! Cunning is our ally. Don't
forget that, and no matter what happens, conserve your
strength.'

They began to walk back slowly. From afar off, the site of
the village was revealed by the cry of seagulls, the nauseous
smells, and then, as they rounded the bend, they saw the hidden
shore with its scattered houses. Sailors worked busily all along
the strand around their platforms that reached down to the
edge of the water to receive the evening's catch, some working
as cutters, others as salters, yet others extracting the oil, and
some way off in the roadstead they could see the Breton ship
bobbing up and down at anchor with its sails furled.

There, as Piksarett had told her, she would remain watchful
and strong in the midst of her enemies.

And for a start she would go and take Joffrey's doublet away
from Ambroisine.

CHAPTER 61

THAT DOUBLET was the only trace she had been able to find of
Joffrey de Peyrac's visit to Tidmagouche.

If it was true, as Ambroisine had stated, that he had sailed
two days earlier after spending more than a week in the port,

his stay, with all the havoc usually created by a ship's crew on shore leave, had left remarkably few traces. It was almost as if he had never been there. She must question the local people: the fishermen, the few farmers she had glimpsed, and also Nicolas Parys, the proprietor of the land along the coast, who had invited them to dine with him that evening in his fortified dwelling up on the cliff.

The rest of the party had arrived towards the end of the afternoon. They were all exhausted and devoured by mosquitoes and leeches from the marshes.

The Marquis de Ville d'Avray came towards supper time and scratched at the door of the hut where she had installed herself with her son and her luggage.

'Are you ready, my dear?'

Angélique admired the way he had succeeded in cutting a dash in a plum-coloured silk frock-coat that revealed a waistcoat embroidered with tiny roses, and a pair of buckled shoes on his feet.

'I always carry a change of clothes with me,' he explained.

He looked better for having framed his face, swollen with mosquito bites, with a powdered wig.

'I know what the old man's like. He expects a certain amount of protocol. But that apart, I warn you here and now that we shall find ourselves among the most colourful gathering of bandits you are likely to meet for a hundred leagues in any direction. Nicolas Parys has the gift of surrounding himself with the scum of the earth. He seems to attract them, unless it is that people are debauched by contact with him.'

He looked about him in some apprehension.

'The absence of the Count puts us in an even more difficult situation. What bad luck! What did he want to go off to Plaisance for! But they say he should be back in under a fortnight! In any case we must stick together,' he whispered. 'I have asked to be housed somewhere near you. And watch your food, too. Eat only food taken from the same dishes as the other guests and wait until they have begun to eat before putting anything in your mouth yourself. I shall do likewise, and I have told your son Cantor to do the same.'

'If all the other guests have the same idea as us and we all sit there waiting together,' said Angélique with a nervous laugh, 'it will be very funny!'

'It's not a joking matter!'

Ville d'Avray was sombre.

'I am very worried. Here we are in the cave of Messalina and King Pluto.'

'Have you seen her?' Angélique asked.

'Who do you mean?'

'The Duchess!'

'No, not yet,' the Marquis replied in a voice that proved that he was in no hurry to do so. 'What about you?'

'Yes, I have.'

The Marquis's eyes brightened.

'Well?'

'We exchanged a few words, fairly cutting ones, I admit, but as you see, we are still both alive.'

The Marquis of Ville d'Avray looked closely at Angélique.

'Your eyes are red,' he said, 'but you do not seem downcast. That's good! Have courage. I have a feeling it's going to be a close-run thing.'

For once the Marquis of Ville d'Avray's acid tongue seemed to have done less than justice to the truth, for his description of Nicolas Parys and his guests had in fact erred on the side of charity.

In characterizing them as a gang of bandits, he had not succeeded in adequately conveying the sense of disquiet one felt in the company of Nicolas Parys, his guests and his neighbours. Their characters seemed to be the result of a number of factors – a harsh life, unbridled debauchery, and rapacious greed to hoard up anything that came into their hands and to make money in the neighbourhood of this eagle's eyrie. A kind of hereditary nobility gave these exiles in the land of America a taste for ostentation, which was somewhat coarse and degenerate but quite impressive.

There were no women present that evening, apart from Ambroisine and Angélique, and a few Indian concubines wandering around the houses, insolent or dazed with alcohol.

Nicolas Parys had had a daughter by an Indian woman he had married. He had had her brought up by the Ursulines in Quebec and had married her off to the son of some squireen in the neighbourhood, giving them as fief the Canso Peninsula and Royal Isle.

In the smoky light of the great resin torches held in iron rings on the walls and in candlesticks, the table seemed to fill the room as for a banquet, heavily laden with victuals of all kinds among which stood, in a straggling row, wooden bowls for the guests, with a few non-matching spoons and knives lying beside them.

It was obvious that most of the diners would have to make do with their fingers instead of forks.

On the other hand, the wine was served in huge gold or enamel goblets, which Ville d'Avray immediately eyed greedily as he did also the small cut crystal glasses in which the spirits were to be served.

Here drink was king, as was obvious from the ceremony with which it was surrounded and from the red noses of the participants. There were barrels in the corners, casks standing on end, jugs full of wine and long-necked black flasks full of rum.

The general effect, seen through the smoky half-light, reminded Angélique of the atmosphere she had once before encountered during her Mediterranean travels, in a small chateau in Sardinia owned by a nobleman who was half-wrecker, half-pirate and had the same wolfish look and the same dangerous arrogance as her present hosts.

There were five or six of them – possibly more, it was not easy to see – round the table, and when the ladies entered, their rubicund faces lighted up with welcoming smiles, while, at a signal from Mr Nicolas Parys, they bowed after the French manner. This gallant gesture was, however, interrupted no sooner than begun by the eruption of two monsters that had been lying before the hearth, and that leapt up with fearsome growls and bore down upon the new arrivals.

Old Parys took down a whip from the wall and struck out blindly at the animals. He finally succeeded in calming the two monsters, which turned out to be huge dogs of an unknown breed. They were found, it appeared, on the island of Newfoundland, where they were said to be a cross between bears and mastiffs abandoned on the island by some colonial expedition, and they did indeed recall both these types of animals by their great size and their thick fur-like hair. Their master said that they could swim like porpoises and that they caught fish.

The reason for their sudden anger was the appearance of Cantor's wolverine, which had boldly entered the room at Cantor's heels with the other guests.

The animal was now standing rigidly at the door, his thick tail fluffed out, baring his evil-looking jaw with its pointed teeth, ready to take on the giants in single combat.

'What the deuce is that?' cried one of the men.

'It's a wolverine,' said Nicolas Parys, 'the most ferocious beast in the forest. It must have come out of the woods by mistake but it's strange that it doesn't seem frightened.'

Cantor interrupted:

'He's tame. I brought him up.'

Angélique noticed that Ambroisine was trembling from head to foot.

'Your son's brought that horrible creature with him again! It's intolerable,' she said in a voice which she found it hard to keep from rising to a screech. 'Look at it! It's dangerous! It ought to be killed!'

Such was the detestation in her eyes as she looked at Cantor that it was almost as if she was speaking of him, and Angélique trembled for her son.

'Why kill him? Leave the animal alone, I like him,' said old Parys, then turning towards Cantor:

'Good for you, my boy! It's no common thing to tame a wolverine. You're a real backwoodsman you are! And as handsome as a god with it! I say, Governor, here's a lad to your liking, isn't he? Eat up now, set to, my boy! Ladies, help yourselves!'

The owner of the coasts of the Gulf of Saint Lawrence had a slight hump and was half-blind, but his overbearing personality which, through a mixture of graft, boldness and contriving had made him king of the east coast, could be felt in every move he made. In his presence people instinctively accepted his domination.

One of Marceline's sons or one of the Defour brothers seemed not to have taken enough trouble over his dress, and Parys requested him to go away and put on his 'court clothes' as he called them. The man protested, saying that he had just come up from the marshes . . .

'All right, you'll do then!' conceded his host. 'But go to my room and get a wig to stick on that brutish head of yours, and we'll call it a day, this time.'

He had placed the two women at opposite ends of the long table, while he himself sat in the middle, and his rheumy eye went from one to the other with evident satisfaction while his mouth spread in a toothless grin. But his lack of teeth did nothing to hinder him doing full justice to the feast, which consisted largely of game accompanied by highly-seasoned sauces, and of three or four sucking pigs roasted in their crackling over hot coals. For a brief space the only sound in the room

371

was the sound of cracking bones, chewing jaws and the lapping tongues. Two great cobs of brown bread with almost black crusts were provided so that those keen on sauces were able to fill their wooden bowls to the brim, and everyone did so.

Through the smoky haze Angélique could see Ambroisine's pale, charming face at the other end of the table, blurred by the steam from the food, mingling with the smoke from the tobacco smoked by some of the Indians. She looked like an apparition glimpsed through the incense of some evil sacrifice, and in the pearly whiteness of her face her dark eyes seemed immense. Angélique felt these eyes fixed upon her, while her half-opened lips smiled, revealing the flash of her childish teeth.

There was a feeling of tension in the room.

'You can't see a thing here,' whispered Barssempuy, leaning towards his neighbour, the Marquis.

'It's always like that here,' Ville d'Avray replied, likewise in a whisper. 'I don't know whether he imagines the lighting is excellent, or whether he does it on purpose, but it doesn't worry him. He can see in the dark like a cat, and he is watchful as a cat too.'

It was indeed a fact that old Parys's eyes never stopped examining his surroundings over the bones that were piling up in front of him, while all the others coped as best they could with what they had on their plates.

Nicolas Parys's eyes lingered on Angélique and on Piksarett, who, without a by-your-leave or a may-I, had seated himself on his 'captive's' right, and on Cantor who was sitting on her left.

Then, when the wines had been poured into the golden goblets, tongues were loosened and people began to swap stories.

At first, misled by the semi-darkness, Angélique had imagined that all the men present were strangers to her, but then she recognized one of them as the captain of the *Unicorn*, Job Simon, the man with the port-wine stain. His bushy beard and bristling hair had grown even greater, and his stoop seemed even more pronounced than before while his protruding eyes beneath his beetling brows stared fixedly before him.

The secretary Armand Daveau was also there, and she wondered that she had not recognized him immediately, and how she could have confused him with this 'band of malefactors', as he had always seemed to her to be a man of distinguished, even if somewhat obsequious, manners. But now – either through a trick of the light or of her anxious imagination – Monsieur Armand's slight paunchiness struck her as unhealthy obesity, while his somewhat full chin and thick lips, open in a smile that sought to be forever amiable, betrayed a distasteful sensuality. Behind his spectacle lenses, his eyes stared out fixed and bright, while the frames of his glasses suddenly seemed enormous, making him look like some cruel, slightly crazy owl.

Also present was Nicolas Parys's chaplain, a perspiring, congested Recollect, his face inflamed with alcohol.

Not far from her sat the captain of the cod-fishing vessel that lay at anchor in the Bay, the man from Faouet. He was of a different type, somewhat spare in build, a man hewn out of granite. She noticed that he was drinking like a fish but without losing control. The only visible sign of his potations was the progressive redness of the ridge of his thin nose. Apart from that he remained bolt upright on his bench, scarcely ever laughing and eating heartily.

Ville d'Avray lightened the atmosphere by recounting with much wit a number of broad jokes which all present could understand and which put them in good humour.

'Let me tell you what happened to me one day,' he began in his soft voice.

He had the gift of keeping his audience on tenterhooks until one of his listeners would growl:

'Governor, you're having us on.'

'Well, yes, I am,' he would agree, 'it was only a joke.'

'You never know with him whether he's lying or telling the truth,' said somebody.

'Do you know what happened to me on my last birthday?'

'No.'

'Well, I'll tell you; as is my custom every year, I had gathered all my friends together on board the *Asmodeus*, that delightful ship, a small, floating Versailles . . . you all know it . . . and the party was at its height when suddenly . . .'

'What happened?'

'The ship blew up.'

'Ha! ha! ha!' the guests laughed in noisy mirth.

'Well may you laugh,' said Ville d'Avray in pained tones, 'and yet it's the truth. Isn't that right, my dear Angélique? And you, Defour, isn't that what happened? The boat blew up, caught fire, and sank . . .'

'Well I'm hanged!' said Nicolas Parys, startled in spite of everything. 'How did you manage to escape?'

'By divine intervention,' Ville d'Avray replied piously, turning his eyes heavenwards.

Angélique admired Ville d'Avray's ability to appear so much at his ease; he was eating heartily and seemed to be paying no more attention to the advice he had given Angélique concerning poison. It was only fair to say that in so dark a room there was nothing one could do but address a prayer to heaven with every mouthful and then think about something else. In spite of herself, Angélique hesitated when the Breton captain passed her a jug full of some unidentifiable liquid.

'You must taste this sauce, Madame, every part of a fresh cod can be eaten ... the head, the tongue, the liver. You mix them into an oil-and-vinegar sauce with a spot of red pepper ... Do taste it.'

She thanked him and engaged him in conversation so that he should not notice that she was not doing justice to the dish in question. She asked him whether he was pleased with the season's fishing, and how many years he had been coming across to this particular place.

'I was more or less born here. I used to come over with my father as a ship's boy. But you mustn't let America get too much of a hold on you. If I'd listened to old Parys, I'd be a human wreck by now. Four months in every year is plenty! During the last few weeks we are half round the bend. It's the drought, and working like slaves ... I've still got piles and piles of cod to salt and holds to fill, I can't see the end of it ... My son is sick, he always gets like this towards the end of the season, when the dust falls from the trees ... He can't breathe. I have to leave him on board the ship in the roadstead, where there's more air ...'

In spite of the Marquis's gift of the gab, Angélique found that whenever her eyes met Ambroisine's, she could not help going tense inside. Quite unconsciously, she would turn from time to time towards the door. Was Joffrey suddenly going to put in an appearance? If he could have appeared there on the threshold, with his tall condottière's silhouette dominating the assembled company, and his eagle eye scanning that motley collection of faces in the semi-darkness, what a relief it would have been! Perhaps a caustic smile would have played over his lips on seeing them all, and herself among them. He knew who was who, but feared no one. Even these men would certainly assume a changed manner and a different tone when they spoke

to him, of that she felt sure. Oh, why was he not here? . . .
Where was he?

A terrible fear swept over her. Supposing they had killed
him? Supposing that, here, on this lost strand, in this foul den
at the ends of the earth, driven on by the Demon, they had
killed him!

Under Nicolas Parys's gaze which she became aware constantly came back to her, she forced herself to eat some food,
fearing lest he consider her a coward. Fortunately Piksarett sat
beside her, cheerfully tearing his meat with his weasel's teeth,
while Cantor was busy eating with the clear conscience of a
young man who has covered many a mile in the day.

The old man wiped his greasy lips on a corner of his wig.

'Well, here you are, Madame de Peyrac,' he said all of a
sudden, as if in response to some unspoken thought of his. 'I'm
glad you've come to visit me. It has confirmed me in my wish to
see you reign over this part of the world.'

'What do you mean, Monsieur?'

'I'm fed up with this rotten place. I want to go back to
the Kingdom of France and have a little fun. I would like to
sell my lands to your husband . . . But for what, that's the
question . . . I asked him to tell me the secret of making gold
in exchange. He's quite willing, but it seems complicated
to me . . .'

'No it isn't, on the contrary, it's very simple,' Ambroisine's
bewitching voice broke in. 'You have such a sharp mind, dear
Nicolas, I am astonished that you should allow yourself to be
put off so easily. Monsieur de Peyrac has explained it all to me;
there is nothing magical about it, it's just a question of chemis-
try, not of alchemy.'

She began to describe one of the processes for making gold
which Joffrey de Peyrac had evolved especially for the mines in
this region. Angélique recognized as she spoke the familiar
terms Joffrey de Peyrac used when explaining his work to
her.

'How learned you are, my dear little lady,' exclaimed Ville
d'Avray delightedly, looking at Ambroisine, 'it's a pleasure to
listen to you, and indeed, how easy it all sounds. It seems to me
that I would do better to make my gold in the manner you
describe rather than by such old-fashioned methods as making
people cough up their taxes, or collecting buttons from the
coats and uniforms of men shipwrecked along our coasts . . .'

Nicolas Parys sniffed and wrinkled up his nose several times, staring fixedly at the Marquis, who was smiling innocently.

Angélique took advantage of the somewhat heavy silence that reigned for a moment in order to ask a question.

'So you've seen my husband recently, have you?' she asked, trying to make her voice sound firm and natural. 'Has he been here?'

Parys turned towards her, looking disconcerted and somewhat surly, and observed her in silence.

'Yes,' he replied at last. 'Yes, I've seen him . . .' and he added in a rather odd voice, '*here* . . .'

CHAPTER 62

'DIDN'T YOU notice the buttons on his jacket, then?' Ville d'Avray asked her as he escorted her back to her house. 'Solid gold, stamped with a coat of arms. The worthy officer who decked his uniform with those has a long time since been meat for crabs. Perhaps not in this area, but there's no shortage of coasts where shipwrecked people can be stripped of their possessions. It's an industry that pays, provided you know how to set about it. It's said that he has a chest containing more than a thousand buttons, all solid gold stamped with coats of arms from all over the world. It was only a rumour, but now I am sure it's true. Did you see how he winced when I referred to certain ways of acquiring gold?'

'Were you wise? You shouldn't provoke him like that, he may be dangerous.'

'No, it's all right! He and I always exchange a few digs like that. All things considered we are good friends . . .'

He seemed pleased and relaxed.

'In fact it all went off very well! We managed to get away from that gathering still in good health! . . . That's something positive. I'm delighted with my evening . . . Sleep well, Angélique my dear. Everything will be all right! . . . Have confidence . . .'

But he did not add his habitual: 'Life is wonderful, so smile!'

'I'm right next door,' he whispered to her. 'If you need anything at all, just call me . . .'

As he raised her hand to kiss the tips of her fingers, she held him back in a sudden convulsive movement.

She could no longer contain herself, she must confide in someone.

'Do you think he really came here?' she asked, her voice uneven and shaking. 'It's like a nightmare . . . where is he? It's terrible to be chasing after him like this. It's as if he was avoiding me, as if he was fleeing before me . . . Where is he? Maybe they've killed him? Perhaps he'll never come back? You know everything that goes on, and I'm sure that you have already found out what's happening. You must tell me the whole truth; I would rather that than live in uncertainty.'

'He was here, that is correct,' the Marquis replied in measured tones, 'he was still here a couple of days ago.'

'With her?'

'What do you mean, my child?' Ville d'Avray asked gently, clasping both her hands in his as if to sustain her.

'What are people saying about him . . . and about the Duchess of Maudribourg?'

'About him? . . . Well, people know him, they either fear him or respect him. He is Monsieur de Peyrac, Master of Gouldsboro, and rumour has it that Nicolas Parys wants to sell him his lands on the Gulf of Saint Lawrence, which is why they met here last week.'

'And what about her?'

'How much do you know?' the little Marquis asked her.

Angélique capitulated.

'She told me that he was her lover,' she confessed in a voice choking with emotion.

Then she poured out, pell-mell, all that had occurred between herself and Ambroisine.

Ville d'Avray said nothing, but listened gravely to Angélique, who felt that she had a sincere friend in him, someone of greater worth than he at first appeared.

When she had finished, he shook his head doubtfully. He seemed neither disturbed nor upset.

'Opinions vary here about our dear Duchess,' he said. 'Some praise her to the skies as if she were a saint of irreproachable virtue, like the Breton captain who bids fair to becoming converted in order to please her. Others, less gullible, have a fair idea of what she's really like, but it looks as if she's managed to preserve her reputation. If some of the lustful males around her are made welcome in her bed, it's a well-kept secret.'

'Just like at Gouldsboro and Port Royal,' Angélique replied wearily. 'Some lie, others keep quiet out of shame or fear, while others are deluded and worship her.'

She hesitated for a moment, then, deciding to keep back nothing of her humiliation, went on:

'There was a coat of Joffrey's hanging on the wall in her room.'

'Play-acting!' was Ville d'Avray's spontaneous reaction. 'That was a trick to undermine your morale. She knew you would come and it's you she's trying to hurt . . . She stole that coat . . .'

'Are you sure?' implored Angélique.

'Almost certain of it! It's just like her. It's a typical feminine trick, that one. You shouldn't fall for it. But what is far more worrying is that she has prepared the minds of those who might have been won over by your charm when they met you. Some here regard you as a dangerous intriguer, while others see you as a depraved creature who sleeps with redskins, or as an incarnation of the Devil in the service of heretics, bent on driving the good French Catholics from the lands that God has given them. In so far as Monsieur de Peyrac is liked, you become a Messalina who makes him wear the horns, and in so far as he is feared, you are a willing tool in his hands.'

'And yet I thought that Nicolas Parys spoke to me if not exactly amiably, at least without any open hostility.'

'The old man's another matter. He believes only in himself, and not even an Ambroisine will prevent him thinking what he wants. But he's got into his head the idea of marrying her, and is courting her assiduously, and heaven knows just how far he can be bamboozled by that siren with the forked tongue.'

Angélique paid relatively little attention to the lies Ambroisine had been spreading about her. She was far more keen to take hope again in matters concerning her husband.

'So do you think she is lying yet again about Joffrey?'

'It looks like that to me . . . You tell me that she rages against men, that she wants to kill Abigail, that she grinds her teeth at the thought of *you* receiving love and homage . . . in other words, not *her* . . . I see nothing in all that that points to a triumphant mistress, sure of the love of a man she has taken from her rival . . . and I would even wager that, if she attempted to catch our recalcitrant Count, my Lord de Peyrac, in her snares, she may well have suffered a crushing humiliation. Her bitter protestations seem to prove that.'

'So you don't believe he really is her lover?'

'On present information, no,' he affirmed energetically.

'What a nice man you are!' she said, giving him a hug.

Fortified by this new hope she felt she would manage to get some sleep.

Cantor was lodged in the next hut, and she could hear him turning over in bed and occasionally snoring lightly on the other side of the wall.

This gave her a sense of security as did the presence of Sagamore Piksarett who was sitting in front of the house, wrapped in a bartered blanket, beside a little fire which he fed with twiglets.

The night was cold and wet. The smell of salt and of cod seemed to penetrate everywhere and stick to one's skin. A thick fog hung over the hamlet. Angélique had given up trying to light a fire in the hearth and had wrapped herself straight away in the blankets she found lying on the hurdle that served as a bed. These rooms, which were empty for certain periods according to the comings and goings of the fishermen, were all alike, containing as they did the same roughly-made furniture: beds, tables, stools, a box containing logs, and a few saucepans, pitchers, and water-bottles.

The room she occupied was fairly large and contained also two benches with arm-rests made of billets with the bark stripped off that stood on either side of the chimney-piece, and a worm-eaten chest in one corner. There were cobs of maize and animal skins hanging from the beams.

Angélique shivered. Her mind remained on the alert, and she would occasionally come to with a sensation of having had a horrible nightmare. Nicolas Parys's huge Newfoundland dogs were wandering about the village, for they were unleashed at night, and on several occasions they began to growl as they approached Piksarett, sniffing and snuffling around the cracks in the walls of her hut. It reminded her of the fear of wolves, long since, in the country districts of France.

In fact the Duchess had not denied anything when Angélique had accused her of trying to poison Abigail, and of trying to kill her kitten. When Angélique thought about this, about the tiny innocent creature in the hands of that cruel woman, the horror she felt for Ambroisine made her feel quite ill. Cruelty to animals or to small children is always particularly horrific, for

379

the supreme dastardliness of an attack on creatures who cannot defend themselves, deprived as they are, not only of physical strength, but of the means of communication offered by the power of speech, remains among men the mark of Satan himself. Man is appalled to recognize in such acts the worst in himself, the bottomless pit of his own depravity, his fall from grace, his possible madness and possible eternal damnation . . .

The reflection of Satan in the heart of man, Satan seeking his own reflection, his own grimacing face, in a mirror made in God's image!

'When I was a little girl,' thought Angélique, 'I used to feel sorry for the Devil, who was always portrayed on the doors of our churches as being so very ugly . . .'

Her mind wandered for an instant back to those churches in Poitou, and the swollen faces of those stone carvings, that delicate tracery, those bunches of grapes and pine cones, and the interiors of the churches, as dark as caves . . . the bread blessed on Sundays, the incense . . . the perfume of exorcized generations . . . Over there, in the Old World, through good years and bad, for century after century, Satan had made alliance with men and had assumed his bestially hideous guise.

But here, in these virgin lands, he was taking over the mastery, and, awesomely resuming his true aspect, that of an angel . . . Ambroisine!

'I'm raving,' Angélique told herself, coming back to reality again, as if she had missed a step on the stairs. Her heart was pounding within her. She closed her eyes, determined to sleep, but her mind would not stop going round and round these confused thoughts.

'Why did she tell me that she was from Poitou since it isn't true . . . Just to ensnare me, to lull my suspicions . . . Not a single word that did not reach its object, that did not weave the spell that was to blind me, and hide from me everything she wished me not to know.'

She avoided thinking of Joffrey . . . she must wait for him, that was all. Ville d'Avray confirmed that he had set sail for Newfoundland. Newfoundland? That great island to the east, that was the end of the world . . . Would he ever come back? Would he come back in time?

It seemed to Angélique that she was reliving outside time the long wait she had had to endure throughout her life, and that what was about to happen was like a symbol of the battle she had had to wage against the forces of despair, in order to deserve, yes deserve, the miracle of having found him once more on this earth.

Had they really appreciated this overwhelming happiness at the time?

When, aboard the *Gouldsboro*, the Rescator had removed his mask,[1] and revealed the features of Count Peyrac to the woman who had once been his wife, they had clashed, too battered by life to recognize one another in the serenity of their first love.

Now it seemed to her that the whole drama was being played out once more, but in its pure state, and with unbelievable violence, that in these few days she was to lose him and to find him again. And all her anguish would be re-kindled, re-born. And the joys as well, perhaps, later.

She awakened feeling calmer and more sure of herself. This was the first day.

Before getting up she continued her review of all the facts, in a state of half-sleep, as one might work out in advance every detail of a battle. And, first and foremost, she was aware of this intuition that never ceased to torment her, the idea that some link existed between Ambroisine de Maudribourg and the wreckers who were pursuing them in order to destroy them.

'They've got a leader,' Clovis had said, 'someone from whom they take their orders, someone on land called Belialith.'

Belialith! That was a satanic kind of name, with over-tones of a kind of ambiguous femininity.

She struck a light and put it to the wick of the seal-oil night-light she had placed on a stool, then felt for the envelope she had slipped under her pillow, and took from it the piece of paper she had found in the wrecker's pocket.

Once again she read those words, then raising the paper to her nose and shutting her eyes, tried to catch the scent given off by the paper.

'I'll come tonight if you are good . . .'

Ambroisine!

She had a vision of the wrecker with the bear's head and the blood-stained cudgel. Ambroisine . . . Ambroisine enslaving that coarse brute with her depraved caresses . . . anything was possible. And if that was true, then all of a sudden the words spoken by Lopez, Colin's sailor on board the *Heart of Mary*, made sense: 'When you see the tall captain with the port-wine stain, you will know that your enemies are not far off.'

1. See *Angélique in Love*.

Job Simon, the captain of the *Unicorn*, the vessel chartered by the Duchess of Maudribourg to bring the King's Girls to Quebec ... But he seemed a good man and had been the first to denounce the attack of which he had been a victim.

Where was the bridge linking these three unknowns: the ship with the orange pennon and its crew of bandits, the *Unicorn* carrying Job Simon and the Duchess, and the *Heart of Mary* belonging to the corsair Gold Beard, now Colin Paturel; for he too, albeit indirectly and unwittingly, seemed to have been part of the plot to destroy Peyrac and ruin Gouldsboro.

Angélique was trembling with excitement, for she felt she was about to reach some important conclusion.

Then suddenly she felt discouraged again. No, it didn't make sense! There was one detail, and by no means a negligible one, that would always demolish her theories: and that was that those very wreckers, whom she was accusing of being accomplices of the Duchess of Maudribourg, had decoyed the *Unicorn* on to the rocks and slaughtered her crew. They could hardly have received such an order from Ambroisine herself since her own ship was involved and she herself was on board and had been saved from drowning only by some miracle.

By some miracle! ... unless ... unless the time had come for the fulfilling of the vision of the nun in Quebec.

The Demon riding on a unicorn ... stepping out of the waters on the seashore at Gouldsboro ...

A woman with a child in her arms had stepped out on the sand, her little feet shod in precious leather ... her ankles decked in scarlet silk stockings, as she stepped forth elegantly ...

Her clothes were torn and dirty ...

Madame Carrère, who had cleaned and mended them, had said:

'There's something I don't understand about those clothes ... something funny ... it's as if ...'

Had she meant that they had been torn and soiled on purpose?

Now Angélique reproached herself for not having questioned Madame Carrère more closely, for not having forced her to reveal all that was in her mind.

CHAPTER 63

ANGÉLIQUE DETERMINED to remove Joffrey's doublet from Ambroisine's possession, and waited for her enemy to leave her room to attend Mass.

She saw a great band of people, with the 'benefactress' at their head, setting off towards the promontory where the bell on the tiny chapel was calling the faithful to prayer.

Here in Tidmagouche, the Duchess seemed to be holding court after the manner of a queen. As the first to arrive, she had firmly taken root. It would be a difficult matter for Angélique to dethrone her. She seemed to need not only her girls, her secretary and Job Simon to escort her, but all her admirers and suitors to a man. Nicolas Parys was there too, with some of his guests of the previous night, including the captain of the cod-fishing vessel, quite a number of Breton fishermen, and of course Ville d'Avray, very relaxed, bowing this way and that, as he walked along the sandy track, with as much grace and affectation as if he had been walking down one of the avenues at Versailles.

As soon as the procession disappeared from sight round the edge of the woods, Angélique made her way swiftly to Ambroisine's room. There she seized Joffrey's doublet and clasped it to her heart. Then she began to look about her.

The idea occurred to her to make the most of this opportunity to try to find out more about her enemy. So she began to open her trunks, her bags and the drawers in the various pieces of furniture.

She turned over clothes and underwear, all of which gave off that heady perfume that had struck Angélique from the very moment the Duchess had set foot on the beach.

What a strange moment that had been, timeless and immeasurable. She shuddered as she thought about it. What was its hidden meaning?

Where did this shipwrecked woman get all these dresses from? Her trunks were full of them. Presents from her admirers? From Joffrey? A sudden anguish seized her, but she forbade herself to think any more along those lines.

She continued her investigations, but found nothing that could throw any further light on the situation. Then suddenly a piece of paper fell from the pocket of one of the dresses. It was a letter that ran to a number of pages. Angélique picked it up and immediately recognized it as Father de Vernon's letter.

CHAPTER 64

How HAD the letter got into the hands of the Duchess of Maudribourg? Had she had the Swedish boy, the bearer of the Jesuit's message from beyond the grave, followed and killed? Why had she wanted to get hold of that letter at all costs? And why was she keeping possession of it? What vitally important secret was contained in those lines that Angélique had not succeeded in reading to the end?

After the first words, she had been so upset that she had found herself unable to go on, and had put the letter down on the table; it had been at that moment that *Ambroisine had entered the room and the boy had run off*. Many a time since she had blamed herself for her impulsiveness and sensitivity, which had prevented her from finding out the full content of that letter, upon which the fate of all of them might hang.

One of the things that had impelled her to try to join Peyrac as soon as possible instead of waiting patiently for him in Gouldsboro had been precisely her obsession with that vanished letter, which seemed to accuse her in such dangerous and damaging terms, and which might well reach its destination, and fall into the hands of the ruthless Father d'Orgeval, before she and her husband had time to work out a plan of defence against such dreadful charges.

But now that she had found the letter again here, in the Demon's lair, she realized that a slow process had been going on within her, guiding her towards an understanding of the meaning behind the Jesuit's words, which at first sight had rent her heart, coming as the revelation of betrayal by a trusted . . . a dear friend . . .

Clasping her precious booty to her, the green velvet doublet and Father de Vernon's letter, Angélique slipped furtively back to her own room, barricaded herself in, then, laying Joffrey's doublet on the table beside her, unfolded the sheets of the bulky letter, which, grown crisp from dryness, crackled in the silence of the hut. Her eyes immediately lighted upon the words she had already read.

'Yes, Father, you were right ... the Demon is in Gouldsboro ... creating an atmosphere of licentiousness, lechery and crime ...'

But now as she read, the Jesuit's long, elegant handwriting did not seem hostile or accusing. Her friend stood there before her. From those lines emerged the truth about him as a person, distant, cold, yet warm-hearted. Through this letter which she held once again in her hands, she realized that he was going to speak to her in an undertone, to tell her in confidence his terrible secret. Since his letter, bearing his last message, had failed to reach the man to whom it was addressed, Father de Vernon was delivering it to her, Angélique, the Countess of Peyrac, as he had tried to do as he lay dying. 'The letter ... for Father d'Orgeval ... it must not ...'

Now she understood the meaning of those last words. Gathering together the last of his strength, he had begged her not to let the letter fall into _her_ hands. 'The Demon ... see to it, Madame. I alone know the truth, and if she gets hold of it, she will suppress it ... Then evil and lies will continue to lead men's minds astray, and to plunge them in misery and in sin ... During these few days I have spent in Gouldsboro, horrified by the intuition that assailed me, I have put all my mystical resources and my will for good to work to discover the truth ... and having discovered it, unmasked it, denounced it in this letter, now I am about to die without having brought it to the light of day ... Do your best, Madame, to get in before those Demons ... This letter ... for Father d'Orgeval ... it must not ...'

It was as if he had explained all this to her, in a low voice, as she sat beside him. Then, summoning up all her strength, and almost piously, Angélique began the remaining part of the letter, which she had not had time to read before.

'Yes, Father, you were right ... the Demon is in Gouldsboro ...

'A terrible woman indeed ... who hides her instincts for, and her knowledge of, every vice beneath an appearance of charm, intelligence, and even pity; a woman who does her utmost to

385

destroy those who come near her, just as the carnivorous flower of the American forestlands decks itself in bright hues and exudes sweet scents the better to attract the insects and the birds it wishes to devour. She does not hesitate to commit sacrilege. She approaches the sacraments in a state of mortal sin, tells lies in Confession, and even goes so far as to lead into temptation the ministers of God in their priestly robes. I have been unable to determine whether she is a victim of what is known in theology as "obsession", in other words, whether she is besieged by demons exterior to her own soul and person, that cause her to act almost unconsciously – a state of mind akin to and easily confused with madness – or whether we are faced with one of those relatively common cases of "possession", where the demons enter the body and mind of a human being and take over his or her personality, or whether finally – a rarer and more alarming case – we are faced with the incarnation of some evil spirit, some demoniacal emanation from the Sephirothic Tree, kin to one of the seven black principles of Gouliphah, a succubus in this case, which has received the power of incarnation in order to be able to spend some time among human beings to sow destruction and sin among them.[1]

'Although you know, as I do, that this is a rare occurrence, it should not be ruled out as a possibility in the present case, for it bears out most precisely, Father, your own opinion on this subject, which has been your principal concern for the past two years, and fits in equally well with the revelations of the visionary nun in Quebec whose ideas so impressed you at the time.

'Threatened by the forthcoming appearance of a demon succubus in the Lands of Acadia, your watchfulness for this country which is dear to your heart made it impossible for you to neglect such a warning, and forced you to study the interpretation of this vision and to look for premonitory signs, in short, to track down this phenomenon, its occurrence and possible consequences, just as we are forced to do in the forest.

'That track led you to Gouldsboro, a new settlement on the shores of Pentagouet, established abruptly and almost in spite of us by a gentleman-of-adventure owing allegiance to no particular flag and more or less an ally of the English. Inquiries instituted by you revealed that he was of French origin and of high birth, but banished from the Kingdom for long-past

1. Some of the terms in the Jesuit's letter have been taken from a seventeenth-century letter about a case of demonology.

386

crimes of witchcraft. Everything tallied with what we knew. Then a woman joined him, handsome and seductive. There was no further shadow of doubt . . .

'My mission to New England took me away for some months, during which I lost track of the affair, and it was no doubt precisely because of my ignorance of the affair, I might almost say my indifference to it – which left me freer in my judgement, without preconceived ideas or strong feelings in the matter – that you commissioned me, immediately I reached Acadian waters in my sailing ship, to check your conclusions with my own eyes and to send you a complete report on the matter, concerning not only the precise political implications of what is going on in Gouldsboro, but also the true mystical identity of the antagonists. You advised me to go to Gouldsboro and establish personal relations with these people, to observe them and sound them out, and then, once I had formed an opinion, to communicate it to you candidly and in detail.

'And so here I am once again this evening, in Gouldsboro where I have just spent a number of days, and after several weeks of investigations and careful observation, praying the Holy Spirit to guide me in all lucidity and justice, here I am drawing up my report to you, and affirming – alas! – yes, Father, that those heaven-sent warnings and your own apprehensions have not deceived you. The Demon is in Gouldsboro. I have seen her here. I have spoken with her. I have trembled to meet her eyes that quiver with fleeting flashes of hatred when they meet mine. You know the subtle divinatory instinct of such creatures with regard to us, the soldiers of Christ, whose mission it is to unmask them and who possess the necessary weapons so to do.

'Having said all this, I must now, dear Father, report to you a situation for which I feel you to be unprepared, and which causes me to fear lest, receiving my testimony in all its abruptness, you tend to dismiss it as the result of some passing aberration . . .'

'Oh, these Jesuits with their round-about ways of putting things,' exclaimed Angélique impatiently.

She forced herself not to skip lines or turn pages without reading them thoroughly, in order to reach the conclusion more quickly. Her heart was beating fit to burst.

He really was laying it on thick, this Merwin, with his rhetorical ways of wrapping things up! She did not seem to realize that Ambroisine would soon be returning from Mass with all her troop, that she would notice that someone had been rummaging through her things, and that the letter she had kept had vanished.

Angélique got the better of her impatience. She must read the whole thing without skipping a single word, for it was all extremely important; nothing must remain imprecise, and, in spite of everything, she did understand the Jesuit's beating about the bush, since it had devolved upon him to pronounce judgement on a diabolical mystery, on a situation that was the precise opposite of what it incontrovertibly appeared, and he was aware that even a man of unusual ability would be hard to persuade that he had been the dupe of his own passions, when he had thought them justified by the claims of the Good. This was, she realized, precisely what Father de Vernon was trying to do in writing to that most remarkable and redoubtable Father d'Orgeval, their indomitable enemy – hers especially – and that she must not forget that he too was present in this dialogue, since it was he that Merwin had been constantly addressing while his pen ran on, honestly yet prudently, across the paper. He must surely be conscious of certain aspects of his superior's character, since he expressed the fear that the latter, on receipt of his testimony in all its abruptness 'might dismiss it as the product of some passing aberration due to human weakness, to which we are all liable to fall victim one day.'

'And so I would ask you, my dear Father,' he went on, 'to be good enough to remember the impartiality which I have always attempted to show in the various missions with which you have entrusted me over the past few years, whether dealing with the Iroquois or New England, whether with the Government of Quebec, or with Versailles or London.

'Disapproving as I do of all excess, all enthusiasm, all premonitions, I have always sought to present the facts in their true contexts, basing my conclusions only on my own personal observations and aided, I repeat, by the Holy Spirit to whom I never fail to pray daily to open my eyes to the truth and the truth alone.

'And so today I shall name the woman whom I regard as the instrument of Satan amongst us, in full awareness that my only duty towards you is to hand over this naked, clear truth, as you asked me to express it and as it has become evident to me, and in spite of the fact that I cannot fail to see the confusion that my revelations will entail. And now, to broach this matter of your doubts in my regard, I am well aware that you expect a certain name to come from my pen. But that is not the name I am about to give you.

'When you sent me instructions regarding this new mission, you asked me to try to find Madame de Peyrac, who had escaped you in Newehevanik, but whom you believed to be travelling somewhere in the region of Casco. I well knew that you had made up your mind about the spouse of the man who is now Master of Gouldsboro and of the greater part of the Lands of Acadia from the Upper Kennebec to beyond Mount Desert.

'Everything about Madame de Peyrac – her reputation for beauty, charm, wit, seductiveness – conspired to pinpoint her as the woman whose damaging influence on your work you feared. I myself inclined to this opinion, and I must admit that I was curious to come with her in order to be able to observe her at leisure and at close quarters. With the help of good luck and some complicity I managed to find her fairly quickly. I took her on board my ship, and during the subsequent journey, that lasted several days, it was an easy enough matter for me to form a judgement of her. A boat, alone on the sea, is a closed world, and it is not easy for those aboard to pretend to be other than they are and to avoid showing their characters in their true light. Sooner or later comes the flash that reveals the depths of the soul.

'Madame de Peyrac struck me as a feminine personality, unusual indeed, but lively, healthy, courageous, independent-minded without being self-important, intelligent without ostentation. Her actions and her attitudes have a freshness about them that is very attractive. And yet one can find in the intentions behind them nothing more than the expression of a natural wish to live according to her tastes and personal temperament, which is sociable and inclined to cheerfulness and action.

'Thus I came better to understand how it is that she retains the devotion of the savages, including that wild creature, the Iroquois Outakke, who is no easy character to manage, and most particularly, the Narranganset Piksarett, whose unpredictability did so much to damage your military campaign. I see no evidence of either evil spells or depraved intentions in these most unusual attachments. Madame de Peyrac amuses and interests the Indians by her liveliness, her skill with arms, her knowledge of plants, her specious reasonings, which in no way fall short, in imagination and shrewdness, of those of our redskin friends, with which we are only too familiar.

'The fact that she already speaks a number of Indian dialects as well as English and Arabic does not seem to me to be a sign of diabolical powers as some might consider, but merely an indication that she possesses gifts in this direction and is keen to communicate with her fellow men, that she cares about learning and is willing to make the necessary effort to acquire it. This I say because it must be admitted that few women are so inclined, either because of a laziness of mind inherent in their sex, or because of the practical nature of too many of the tasks assigned to them.

'In short, the fact that she does not fit into the common mould does not seem to me to brand her as an enemy of goodness and virtue.

'When we reached Pentagouet I did not see fit to detain her any more and I let her go back to Gouldsboro. The following week I went there myself, and it was then that I met the Demon . . .'

Angélique broke off, her heart beating fit to burst, and turned over the last page of the long letter. She was so absorbed and so much on tenterhooks that she scarcely took in the fact that it was to her that Father de Vernon had been referring in the lines she had just read, lines that revealed something akin to love for her.

There was something uncertain, unformulated, something deep and tender that took on the value of a declaration, spoken as it was by this voice from beyond the grave. Shattered, she experienced a sensation of heart-rending sweetness.

'Oh, Jack Merwin! Oh, my poor friend!' she murmured.

She should never have doubted him. It was an unworthy thing to have done, and she was cruelly punished for it by the remorse that overwhelmed her. On that earlier occasion when she had read the first lines of this letter she had been frightened of discovering in it a truth that was too cruel. She had given way to emotion and fear. Her hesitation, her momentary lapse had constituted that iota, that tiny margin of time which had decided the life or death of an innocent child, the poor little messenger from the dead priest, and had given victory to that evil spirit over the judge upon her trail, who was denouncing her in this very letter which she, Angélique, had feared to read any further, seeking to run away from it in case she should read her own condemnation in it.

Joffrey used often to say to her: 'You must never be frightened . . . of anything.'

And now the drama was unfolding, opening out beneath her eyes.

'And who is she, you may well ask me, if not Madame de Peyrac?

'Well, here is the answer. Recently a shipwreck on these shores cast up a noble lady benefactress on her way to Canada with a number of young women and girls who were to be married there. It is she whom I would point out to you as that redoubtable creature, raised up out of the depths of hell, to seek our unhappiness and our perdition.

'Her name? It is known to you.

'It is the Duchess of Maudribourg.

'I am not unaware of the fact that she has been your penitent for many a long year, and is even related to you, and I have heard that you encouraged her to come to New France, to place her vast fortune at the disposal of our work of conversion and expansion in the interests of the most Holy Catholic Faith.

'But my surprise lay in finding her here and in rapidly unmasking her fearsome perversity. Now she tells me that she has been commissioned by you to destroy the pride and insolence of your enemies personified, Count and Countess Peyrac, and that she was in this region under your orders, performing a holy mission in which I was to support her . . .'

'What? What's this? This is something new!' cried Angélique, stupefied. Then, simultaneously realizing that someone had been banging on her door for some time, she folded up the letter and slipped it into her bodice. In a kind of trance she went over and opened the door, and stood abstractedly looking at the Marquis de Ville d'Avray as he gesticulated before her like some delirious puppet.

'Have you passed on or are you trying to make me die of fright?' he ranted. 'I was about to break the door down . . .'

'I was resting,' she said.

She hesitated to tell him immediately about her rediscovery of the letter; the revelation she had just received of possible collusion between Father d'Orgeval, who was bent on getting rid of them, and the corrupt great lady, just arrived from Europe under the cloak of benefactress, cast a totally new light on the role of the latter and the astonishing coincidence of her arrival in the region of Gouldsboro!

Ville d'Avray came in followed by two of his men bearing his Caribbean hammock which he got them to sling from the beams.

'I've been put in a regular hovel,' he explained. 'I can't bear to go back there, even less to hang my hammock there. So I am coming to take a rest in your room. In any case, it would be better for us not to be too far apart.'

Angélique left him to settle in and went off in search of Cantor. Here, just as in Port Royal, life seemed to be going on in the most natural manner possible. It was just a French coastal settlement in the last days of summer. There were seasonal fishermen, Indians bringing in furs, a few farmhouses, with forestlands lying behind, people coming and going, some passing through bringing in news then setting off again, others camping out while awaiting the arrival of a ship and the possibility of setting off to Europe or Quebec. People were trading, gossiping, making plans and projects; the middle of the day sent everyone off to sleep, whereas the evening livened them up in a slightly artificial way, their reaction being to forget that they were far from their own folk in a savage continent. Fires were lighted along the beach, and pipes filled, Nicolas Parys held open house, while the wail of Breton bagpipes could be heard somewhere through the darkness. Late into the night there would be the sounds of sailors returning drunk from the Indian village.

It seemed like a gathering of worthy folk, brought together in the great shake-up of exile.

As in Port Royal, Angélique had the feeling of being isolated from her own people, of being alone to bear the burden of an incommunicable secret. There were times when she might have thought it all a dream, had it not been for the Jesuit Father's letter, which she carried hidden in her bodice and whose contact reminded her of those strange and categorical statements: 'a succubus intent on evil . . . her name is known to you . . . it is the Duchess of Maudribourg . . . she says she has been commissioned by you . . .'

Ambroisine commissioned by Father d'Orgeval to subjugate 'from inside those dangerous conquerors of the shores of Acadia, installed at Gouldsboro . . .' and yet it could not have been Ambroisine who misdirected her at Houssnock, nor sent her to meet Gold Beard on Old Ship Island. So what then? She must have accomplices! And feverishly Angélique assembled in her mind various scraps of evidence in support of the theory that Ambroisine was not acting alone, that she was only the guiding spirit, the instigator of this plot to bring them down and destroy them without pity. If that was so, it followed that everything, or almost everything that had happened during the course of this accursed summer had been planned with this aim in mind, even that the *Unicorn* had been deliberately wrecked on the shore of Gouldsboro. But that was madness! Ambroisine herself had been on board, and she would never have run such a risk, crazy as she might be ... The King's Girls would never have allowed themselves to be sacrificed in such a way ... It had to be borne in mind that the poor creatures had only just been rescued, and that part of the crew had been massacred and the rest drowned ...

Who were the survivors from the crew? The ship's boy and the captain, Job Simon, who had been the first to denounce this criminal outrage, who had cried out that the wreckers had lured them on to the rocks and finished them off with blows from their cudgels ... His despair at the loss of his ship was not feigned. But there was one thing about him that remained unexplained. And that was that, as captain of that vessel, he did not seem aware of the error he had made by ending up in French Bay when he should have been heading for Quebec. Was he not perhaps mad as well? As she looked at him wandering about in the distance, swinging his long arms, ungainly and stooping, his great, shaggy head straining forward as if searching in vain for something, and nodding from time to time, Angélique did begin to wonder. All these unfortunate people seemed to have been overwhelmed by their misfortunes. And it was wrong to say, as she had had the impression earlier on, that everyone appeared serene and normal. It was as if her eyes had been opened and she noticed the haggard, suspicious or frightened expression on certain faces, their pallor, their drawn faces, those bitter lines that had suddenly appeared at the corners of their mouths, their determination to keep silent, their hunted looks, or the repressed hostility which expressed itself in backs turned towards her as she passed, or alternatively, glances that followed her all too persistently.

She walked through the settlement from one end to the other, conscious of the prevailing atmosphere, but also indifferent to it, for her mind was taken up by a much more pressing problem – she could not find Cantor. After walking the length of the beach she climbed up towards the hamlet. The houses were built around a kind of small square from which one could look out over the horizon. She raised her hand to shade her eyes, in the fearful hope of catching sight on the gold-flecked sea – honey-coloured as if already touched by the melancholy of autumn — of a sail that would grow larger as it made its way towards the entrance to the bay. But the horizon was bare.

As she turned round, she saw that Ambroisine was standing behind her.

The Duchess's eyes were flashing.

'You have taken the liberty of searching through my things,' said the Duchess, her voice harsh and quivering. 'Bravo! You aren't exactly troubled by an excess of scruples, are you?'

Angélique gave a shrug.

'Scruples? With you? . . . You must be joking.'

She realized as she saw Ambroisine's delicate nose tremble and grow pinched in her anger, that the Duchess had miscalculated what Angélique was capable of doing. Choosing her victims most frequently as she did among people of good class, of lofty mind, who were inclined to see the best in their neighbour, she traded on their native delicacy and the reactions instilled by their upbringings to fool them with impunity, relying on their inability to use in their own defence the dastardly means she herself used in attack: lies, calumny, indiscretion . . .

Now she was beginning to realize that in Angélique she had encountered an ermine without fear of being splashed with mud.

'You took that letter, didn't you?'

'What letter?'

'The letter from the Jesuit, Father de Vernon.'

Angélique considered her in silence as if seeking time for reflection.

'Do you mean to tell me that you had that letter in your possession? How could you have? . . . So you will stop at nothing. You had the boy who brought it to me killed, didn't you? You had him killed by your accomplices . . . Now I remember, he was trying to tell me something; he was saying: "They" are after me, "they" want to kill me, for heaven's sake help me . . . And I wasn't listening to him! Poor child! I shall never forgive myself! . . . You had him murdered!'

'But you're crazy!' cried Ambroisine, her voice rising sharply. 'What ever are you talking about with all this story of accomplices? . . . That's the second time . . . I haven't any accomplices . . .'

'Then how did that letter get into your hands?'

'The letter was lying on the table between us, I took it, that's all.'

'Then why did the boy run away,' Angélique thought, 'when *she* came in . . . ? He was frightened of her! Just like the kitten . . . He knew she was possessed by evil; but where is he now?'

She thought of little Abbial, the Swedish boy who had come to ask her help after the disappearance of his benefactor. It was unforgivable!

'You've got that letter, that I know,' Ambroisine went on; 'well, so much the worse for you. Don't imagine you will ever be able to make use of it in any way against me. The Jesuit is dead. The words of a dead man are always subject to caution. I'll say that you cast a spell on him, that you made him write that letter in order to ruin me because I was about to denounce the dreadful things going on in Gouldsboro; I shall say that you debauched him, that he was your lover . . . and it's true that he loved you! That was obvious. I shall say that once you had that trumped-up letter in your possession, and were certain that its evidence would incriminate you, you had him murdered in Gouldsboro, in your den of bandits and heretics, for who would ever know how he died there? And what witness called to give evidence would people believe – except me, who was present at the time, and who can tell in Quebec how I saw a horrible Englishman hurl himself at the unfortunate priest and murder him while the crowd, with you in the forefront, roared encouragement and laughed at the crime . . . I shall tell them how distressed I was to witness such a spectacle and how difficult I found it to get away from that dreadful place, over which you hold sway, without risking my own life . . .'

She gave a gracious sweep of her hand that seemed to invite Angélique to gather around her all the inhabitants of Tidma-gouche.

'Go on then . . . point me out to them! . . . Call out to them: "Here is the Demon! It's the Duchess of Maudribourg . . . I am making an explicit charge against her." . . . Who will believe you? Who will support you? . . . Your name is already a legend among the French in Canada and elsewhere, and I have taken care since I have been here to add a few spicy details . . . They regard you as impious, dangerous, evil, and so far your conduct has in no way belied what I have said . . . You came out of the woods accompanied by your savages, you have attached yourself to that man Ville d'Avray, who is hated here and regarded as the greatest robber they have ever known as Governor in these parts, and . . . did anyone see you at Mass this morning? . . . I was there . . .'

She shook her head with a tinkling laugh.

'No, Madame de Peyrac ... this time your beauty will not save you. My position is too strong ... Even were you to go brandishing your letter in Quebec or elsewhere ... If it's a choice between you and me, Sebastian d'Orgeval will believe me.'

'So you do know Father d'Orgeval, do you?' Angélique asked.

Ambroisine stamped her foot in rage.

'You know perfectly well that I do since you have read the letter! Don't try to put one over me, you can't win.'

She held out her hand:

'Give me back that letter.'

Her eyes flashed, darting flames. Angélique reflected that such was the force of her spitefulness that simple, emotional people must easily be overruled and frightened by her when she spoke to them like this and forced to obey her as if in a dream.

She refused to let herself be discountenanced and replied quietly:

'Calm yourself! People are looking at us over there and your reputation as a virtuous, mild woman might be undermined by these little fits of temper.'

She walked past Ambroisine and returned to her room.

That night, after barricading herself in, she finished reading the Jesuit's letter by candlelight.

In the last lines of his missive Father de Vernon showed signs of being somewhat in a hurry.

'I have a number of interesting things I'd like to tell you about the settlement of Gouldsboro, but space and time prevent my doing so here. I shall give this letter to Saint-Castine's messenger. I am leaving, for I no longer feel safe here, and yet I do not want to go too far from the area as I feel that my presence might in some measure impede to some extent the evil deeds being hatched here. The best thing would be for you to try to join me in the village of X where I am meeting Father Damian Jeanrousse. There we can discuss matters together and I shall convey to you by word of mouth the nature of the observations upon which I have based my judgements.'

There followed various polite expressions which, in spite of their somewhat formal language, revealed the affection and respect which the two priests felt for one another.

Angélique had given up the idea of mentioning the letter to

her son or the Governor, for she could not disguise from herself the fact that Ambroisine was right. When she had asked who would believe her, who indeed would? Such a letter could, by a few clever insinuations, be turned against her, Angélique. She could find in it no evidence to support her theory that Ambroisine had accomplices, that she was not acting alone, that she was only the guiding spirit of a vast plot, conceived against all reasons to destroy them. Outside a certain context the Jesuit's statement would appear wild, unacceptable, the result of hypnosis. And he was no longer there to reveal and to prove the facts and the deductions that had led him to his conclusions. The accusations he levelled against Ambroisine seemed to be as baseless from the theological point of view as they were from the political. They constituted an attack against a person belonging to the upper ranks of the nobility, widely known, who had no mean a reputation in the higher spheres of theological learning, and it looked as if she had separated her fields of action pretty skilfully, retaining an irreproachable reputation among those whose support and approval she sought, and letting herself go whenever she was sure that any exposure of her activities could be turned to her own advantage.

So Angélique, in spite of the weapon she held in her hands in the form of this evidence, still found herself in a delicate position. But she preferred not to dwell on the fact that evening, and to cling to the comfort she experienced at having once more found in Father de Vernon's letter a friend who, beyond the bounds of death, would still watch over and defend her.

CHAPTER 65

ON THE second day after their arrival in Tidmagouche, Lieutenant Barssempuy asked to see her. He had a request to make of her.

In spite of the fact that he had done her a bad turn at Maquoît Point, when, as Gold Beard's lieutenant, he had taken her prisoner, she got on fairly well with this young gentleman-of-fortune, who was capable, like all his kind, of both the best and of the worst, but was not without basic good qualities. He was courageous, gentlemanly, enterprising, had received a good education in some chateau where he had grown up, no doubt the fifth or sixth child in a large family of some ruined nobleman. Now that everything had been settled with the pirates from the *Heart of Mary* and Gold Beard had become Governor of Gouldsboro, Barssempuy his lieutenant professed total devotion to the Count and Countess of Peyrac.

It was he who, at the time of the wreck of the *Unicorn*, had found Marie-la-Douce lying wounded among the rocks. He had carried her back in his arms and had fallen very much in love with her. Unfortunately the departure of Madame de Maudribourg with her protegées when they set off for Port Royal had broken off this romance.

Angélique noticed that his face looked drawn and no longer like that of a fearless pirate, glad to be alive and to find himself still on this earth every evening. He asked if he might speak to her, but as Ville d'Avray, who was relaxing in his hammock, did not seem to be inclined to leave them, he assured her that he would be quite happy to say what he had to say in the presence of the Governor. It concerned something that Angélique and the Marquis de Ville d'Avray had said in his presence on the previous day when their party had reached the coast and Madame de Maudribourg's name had been mentioned.

'Monsieur le Marquis himself seemed alarmed at the idea of meeting her again. It was then that I understood that my personal feelings about that dangerous, perverse woman, were not mistaken; and now, more than ever, I tremble for my sweetheart. You may remember, Madame, how much I fell in love with that delightful girl. I felt like this from the very first moment when I discovered her covered with blood. And yet I am a tough man, and I must confess that until now I always laughed at the thought that I might ever give way to so violent a passion. And yet that is how it is! And at first I thought that my feelings were reciprocated. We confided in one another to some extent. She comes from an excellent family, but is poor and has no dowry, so she was put into a convent to take the veil as a lay sister. It was in that convent about two years ago that Madame de Maudribourg suggested she might become her lady companion. I had the impression in Gouldsboro that she was by no means indifferent to me. So when I saw how devoted she was to her protectress, I went to see the Duchess to tell her of my wish to marry Marie and to give her an account of myself. Madame de Maudribourg assured me she would mention the matter to Marie, and shortly afterwards brought me a negative reply, asking me not to pursue the matter, and telling me that Marie was an impressionable girl who was too upright and honest to have the slightest inclination for a pirate, who clearly must have blood on his hands, and that the very idea horrified her, etc. etc. . . . This was a terrible blow to me, and it so upset and distressed me that I don't know how it happened, nor how she set about it, but the Duchess so managed to console me . . . that I ended up spending the night with her . . . the Duchess . . .'

Such was the look of astonishment on his face as he confessed what had happened that Ville d'Avray began to chortle with laughter over in his corner.

'Now I realize that I was just one of her innumerable victims, and that Marie is no doubt another, and I want to do my utmost to get her out of her clutches. Chance had it that in escorting you here I have found the girl I love again, when I thought she must be sailing under different skies and that I should never see her again . . .

'It seems an ideal opportunity to save her . . . but she is avoiding me. Perhaps you might be able to speak to her and persuade her how much I love her and want to help her.'

'I'll try.'

Since she had discovered Ambroisine de Maudribourg's true nature, Angélique had begun to wonder, with some anxiety, about the relationships existing between the 'benefactress' and the young women around her. They were a group of well-behaved pious girls, recruited from orphanages and the foundlings' hospital to be married off in New France: girls like Marie-la-Douce, the sensible Henriette, the charming, timid Moorish girl, Antoinette, and some others, all quiet, docile, sweet girls, a discreet young widow like Jeanne Michaud and her little boy Pierre, young ladies from the lower ranks of the nobility, poor but chosen for their good breeding, their open natures and cultivated minds, and even including some personalities by no means colourless and lacking in character like Delphine Barbier du Rosoy or Marguerite de Bourmont, not to mention the old duenna Petronella Damourt, a kindly, good-natured soul, though a trifle simple.

Now, some of these women had known the Duchess for a long time. Petronella seemed almost to have brought her up. Others had known her for only a few months, since she had selected them for the expedition to New France. All these girls without exception adored her. Julienne was the only one among them — and she was a girl from the streets, of quite different type from the others, who must have slipped in among the rest to avoid being shipped off to the Islands — who detested her and had made no bones about saying so.

But the devotion of the others towards the Duchess seemed to be boundless.

Was there not even something excessive, something abnormal in these manifestations of loyalty? She remembered the wild outburst of emotion when it had been announced that their 'benefactress' had been rescued from the waters, how they had thrown themselves at her feet, embraced her, clasped her around the knees, weeping tears of joy. And on another occasion, that first evening, when they feared the Duchess might die, how disproportionate their panic had seemed, as they begged Angélique to remain at the sick woman's bedside, all those crazy girls clinging to her dress, that strange insistence . . . What did they know about the Duchess?

Were they themselves dupes, oblivious of everything, spellbound, terrorized? . . . Lieutenant Barssempuy's request presented her with an opportunity of finding out more about the matter.

She approached Marie-la-Douce behind one of the houses of the hamlet. The young woman had gone out to pick flowers on the clifftop and was returning down a path that led behind this empty hut. In this place Angélique hoped that the Duchess would be unable to see her speaking to one of her protegées.

Marie started back when she saw her, but Angélique stopped her, saying:

'Don't run away, Marie, I must speak to you without witnesses and we haven't much time.'

With her bunch of flowers in her hands, the young woman stared at her, unable to conceal her fright. She was quite pretty and her expression was both timid and intriguingly spontaneous. Her greatest assets were her lovely neck and sky-blue eyes, her delicate blonde hair and her frail, simple, flower-like grace. But she had grown very thin recently, for she was probably exhausted and not fully recovered from her injuries after so much travelling and so many changes.

She was pale and her skin and lips seemed to be chapped from the dry air and the salt. But above all she had a hunted look apparent in her dilated, slightly-staring pupils, and her mouth half-open as if she had difficulty in breathing. Angélique also felt as if some cable within her was stretched to breaking-point.

This was no time for beating about the bush.

'Marie,' she began, 'have you seen "them"? You said when they brought you to me: "I can see the demons, they hit me in the darkness . . ." You saw the men who came out of the darkness with their cudgels to finish off the shipwrecked people . . . Now tell me, tell me everything you think you know or you suspect . . . We must put an end to these crimes . . . It's she, isn't it, it's *she* who gives them their orders?'

The young woman listened to her with a panic-stricken air. All she could do was to shake her head in terrified denial.

'You have been living with her, close to her, for the past two years,' Angélique went on, feeling that her minutes were numbered, 'you must know what kind of a person she is. And now you must speak up in order to help me, before we are all killed, destroyed . . . tell me.'

Marie-la-Douce gave a start as if she had been burned.

'No, never,' she replied fiercely.

Angélique suddenly grasped her by one thin wrist.

'But why not?'

'I shall never forget all she has done for me. I was alone in the world, without any other future than the walls of that convent. She took an interest in me, enabled me to live again, to blossom, to be happy in fact . . .'

She lowered her eyelids.

'It's so good to be loved,' she murmured.

To what extent Ambroisine's clever amorality had taken advantage of the naïvety of the young orphan girl, who had remained in a state of childishness as a consequence of her dreamy nature, her solitude and her ignorance of life, it was hard to tell.

'If that was all it was,' said Angélique, weighing her words, 'I would not judge you harshly. But she is worse than that, as you know. She is capable of anything. The very abyss of perdition, Evil in its pure state. Loved, did you say? Barssempuy loved you. He wanted to marry you. Did she even tell you about his approaches to her? No, I can see that she didn't from your expression of astonishment. She may even have said unpleasant things about him in front of you, while telling him that you wanted none of him . . . and while she seduced him herself. And that is the diabolical woman, the terrifying woman who stole your beloved from you, whom you seek to defend and protect from due punishment! . . . Tell me what you can, I beg you. Tell me everything!'

'No! I know nothing,' cried the young woman, struggling to free herself, 'I tell you, I know nothing . . .'

'Yes you do. You suspect things, you guess things, you live too close to her not to have noticed certain things . . . She has accomplices, hasn't she, those wreckers who tried to kill you all on the beach? You see, she sacrificed you, to be killed like the others . . .'

'No, not me . . .'

'What do you mean by that? Why not you?'

But Marie-la-Douce, wresting her wrist from Angélique's grasp, ran off as if the Devil himself was at her heels . . .

She must try again, Angélique told herself.

Now she felt sure that the Duchess's entourage could give her valuable information. But it would be no easy matter. She had come to realize that these defenceless or artless girls were kept silent by fear, shame, docility, or the ingrained habits of the lower orders of society that prevent their judging the affairs of the great by ordinary everyday standards. A mixture of stupidity, ignorance, naïvety and innocence. How cleverly Ambroisine had played on it all in order to achieve her ends!

'You seem sad,' Ville d'Avray said to her, swinging back and forth in his hammock and nibbling at some popcorn Cantor had cooked for him over the fire. 'Come now, my dear Angélique, you should not let yourself become downcast, nor take human baseness too much to heart. Encountering it and putting up with it is part of our earthly obligations. But there are compensations. You will see, when we are in Quebec and enjoying a little glass of rossoli, by the fireside, as we listen to your charming boy playing his guitar, you will forget all this . . . and we shall all laugh about it together.'

But in spite of his encouragement, Angélique did not feel inclined to laugh at anything. She kept on looking out of the door or through the window, not knowing just what she was looking for. Perhaps the silhouette of a sailing ship growing larger on the horizon and entering the roadstead?

Towards the end of the afternoon she suddenly rushed outside, thinking she saw a tiny dot in the dazzling metallic glow of light towards the east. With her hand over her eyes, she stood watching.

She heard Delphine du Rosoy not far from her call to Marie-la-Douce and say:

'Madame de Maudribourg has gone to pick huckleberries with Petronella and the Moorish girl. They are waiting for you at the Breton cross to help carry the baskets...'

The young woman set off along the path trodden by the worshippers that morning on their way to Mass. For a split second Angélique hesitated, wondering whether this was not a suitable occasion to make another attempt to persuade Marie to talk. She must have thought things over, and even from this distance Angélique could see that the poor girl had red eyes and a swollen face. But if she tried to follow her and speak to her on the cliff-side path she ran the risk of meeting the Duchess of Maudribourg on her way towards them. So she went back to her room.

From his hammock the Marquis could see all the comings and goings through the door as well as through the window.

'The catch will be poor today,' he said, 'the cod will be badly salted and there'll be a lot of cut fingers among the "choppers"...'

'Why do you say that?'

'Because Madame de Maudribourg is paying those gentlemen a visit. I can see her over there mingling with the fishermen like a queen among her vassals, escorted by our Breton captain, who is dancing attendance on her. He claims he's as hard as steel, but she has soon softened him up...'

Angélique followed the direction of his gaze and there indeed, at the water's edge, beside the platforms where the Bretons were busy at work, she could see the figure of Ambroisine holding the attention of all present.

She was indeed holding court down there, for a ship about to sail for Europe had put in to take on fresh water and was lying at anchor in the roadstead. Some of the passengers had come ashore to stretch their legs.

'If that ship is bound for France it might be a good opportunity for me to send a message to a very dear friend of mine in Paris. I'll go and see.'

He got down from his hammock.

'But why did Ambroisine have Marie-la-Douce sent off to meet her in the opposite direction from where she was?' Angélique wondered.

She went out on to the doorstep and looked towards the promontory. Barssempuy was standing a few paces from the house, in despondent and idle mood, whittling a piece of wood.

The sight of the young man who was in love with Marie-la-Douce, suddenly, through some association of ideas, triggered off a reflex reaction in her and she ran towards him.

'Come quickly,' she said to him with lowered voice, 'come with me, quickly. Monsieur de Barssempuy, Marie-la-Douce is in danger!'

Without asking questions he followed her and together they set off up the path leading to the Breton cross.

'What is the matter, what do you fear?' he asked at last, when they were out of sight of the village.

'They're going to kill her,' she replied, her voice coming in jerks, 'maybe I'm mad, but I feel sure they will. They're going to kill her. Someone saw me talking to her this morning, they must have questioned her and forced her to reveal what we were talking about.'

Now they were running, and they arrived panting at the promontory where the chapel stood with its wooden cross.

'She's not here,' said Angélique. 'Is this the right place? She was told to go to the Breton cross . . .'

'That's further on,' said Barssempuy. 'It's a stone cross that was erected two hundred years ago by the Breton fishermen. Right on that headland over there!'

'The highest cliff!' exclaimed Angélique in despair. 'Come on quickly, she mustn't be allowed to reach it. We haven't time to get round the cove, let's go down on to the beach and call her from there . . .'

Not without difficulty they slithered down the slope to the beach which was all stones and pebbles at this point, and they found the going hard. The cliff seemed to get further and further away.

'Ah! I can see Marie,' cried Barssempuy.

A frail female figure had just appeared against the whitish sky. It was moving along the promontory towards the Breton cross that stood like a Celtic menhir at its very utmost extremity.

'Marie,' cried Angélique with all her strength. 'Marie, stop! Get away from there!'

It was too far. Her voice could not carry that distance.

'Marie! Marie!' cried Barssempuy in his turn. 'Ahh . . .'

The same wild shriek came from them both at once. Then they both fell silent, their heartbeats suspended in horror as they watched the young woman spinning as she fell.

'Someone pushed her,' Barssempuy panted, his face haggard,

'I saw it . . . someone . . . came up . . . behind her . . .'

They began to run again, stumbling over the stones, the rocks, and the piles of seaweed, stumbling, as in a nightmare.

They discovered Marie-la-Douce in the hollow of a rock, just as on the day when Barssempuy had found her after the wreck of the *Unicorn*. The young man was unconsciously making distressed gurgling noises as if struck a mortal blow in his entrails.

'Do something, Madame, do something, I beg you!'

'There's nothing I can do,' said Angélique, kneeling beside the twisted body. And she too unconsciously groaned, so heart-breaking was the sight of this slim, shy creature so cruelly done to death.

Marie-la-Douce opened her eyes. Angélique was aware of the still lucid mind awake behind those blue eyes that seemed to reflect the sky.

'Marie,' she said, holding back her tears, 'Marie for the love of God who is going to take you to Him, say something . . . Did you see your murderer? Who was it? . . . Say something, I beg you, to help me.'

The bloodless lips moved. Angélique bent over her to catch the scarcely audible words which came from them in an exhausted breath, her last: 'At the time of the shipwreck . . . she was not wearing . . . her red stockings . . .'

CHAPTER 66

'EXPLAIN IT all to me,' begged Barssempuy. 'How did you know that someone was going to make an attempt on her life? Tell me who these criminals are. I'll hunt them down until I find them. I'll exterminate them.'

'I'll tell you everything if you calm down.'

Assisted by Ville d'Avray, by Cantor and the two other men from the *Rochelais* who had come with them, it cost her an immense effort to calm the young man's despair, and to per-suade him not to do anything extreme, by crying murder among a lot of people who were already over-excited, whereas only patience, tenacity and coolheadedness could enable them to face up to such a cunning enemy, and to unmask him whoever he might be. If he knew that he was accused, or suspected, he would in future be on his guard, and it would become more difficult and more dangerous to gather clues and to find a trail, the moment not yet having come to accuse the Duchess. All the men present were under her spell. Barssempuy would be regarded as out of his mind, and there would certainly be someone prepared to cook his goose under one pretext or another. He finally allowed himself to be persuaded and remained sitting by the fireplace, downcast and dejected.

The following day they bore Marie-la-Douce to her last resting place. The King's Girls wept. They spoke of Marie-la-Douce as their sister and companion. They said that she was a foolhardy girl, and that she would always go gathering flowers in dangerous places, believing them to be the prettiest ones . . . She had fallen . . .

At the last blessing in the little cemetery with its simple crosses leaning this way and that, Angélique found herself standing next to Delphine Barbier du Rosoy, a girl of noble family, whom she liked. She had shown a great deal of courage and presence of mind at the wreck of the *Unicorn*, and she stood out clearly from the other girls in upbringing, judgement, and education. They naturally turned to her, and Angélique noticed that Ambroisine spoke to her with a respect that she did not show to the others, as if she wanted to give her special treatment, in order to win her good graces or to prevent Delphine from seeing through her, because of the girl's particular sharpness of mind.

Now, seeing her tearful and sobbing wretchedly like a child, which was not in keeping with her moderate, well-disciplined nature, Angélique was moved to pity for her:

'Can I help you, Delphine?' she asked in a whisper.

The girl looked at her in surprise, then wiped her eyes, blew her nose and shook her head.

'No, Madame, alas! You cannot help me.'

'Well, you help me, then,' said Angélique suddenly making up her mind. 'Help me to bring to book the Demon who is dogging our steps and bringing misfortune to all of us.'

Delphine gave her a furtive glance then remained silent, with bowed head. But on the way back to the settlement, she murmured as she passed closely by Angélique: 'I'll come to your place with a few of the girls shortly before the midday meal.

We'll say that Cantor suggested we should sing some songs
. . .'

'To sing songs?' spluttered Cantor. 'Those girls have got no
sense at all! We've buried one of their number today and they
want to sing songs! It doesn't strike me as a very clever sort of
excuse . . .'

'You're right, but no doubt that was all poor Delphine could
think of on the spur of the moment. There are times when ideas
just fail you.'

'All right, I'll sing them some hymns,' said Cantor. 'That
will strike an appropriately serious note!'

When the girls turned up, Angélique noticed that it was at
the time when Nicolas Parys regularly came to pay court to the
Duchess. She drew Delphine aside while Cantor was engaging
the attention of the group.

'Delphine,' said Angélique, 'you know the source of the evil,
don't you? That woman! . . .'

'Yes,' said the girl sadly. 'I was taken in by her for a long
time myself, but in the end I had to face the facts. In France no
one was able to see the situation in its true light, but here there's
something . . . wild, primitive in the air that makes people
reveal themselves as they really are. Little by little at Gouldsboro, and at Port Royal, I came to see the truth and I realized
what sort of a person *she* was.

'Indeed, even earlier on, I didn't approve of her constantly
compelling us to lie in order to cover up the attacks she suffered
. . . Out of modesty, she used to say, so that it would not be
known that she was visited by the spirit of God. I ought to have
understood earlier that such attacks were a symptom of
madness or possession, and not of mystical ecstasy as she
wanted us to believe. How naïve we were! Julienne was the
only one to see the truth straight away, and we detested and
despised her, the poor girl! And now what's going to happen?
We're helpless, in her power, at the ends of the world. Yesterday, when I saw that ship in the roadstead setting sail for
Europe, I would have given anything to be able to go on board,
to run away, it doesn't matter where. May God have pity on
us!'

'Delphine, do you think that the Duchess is in touch with
another ship, with accomplices to whom she could give orders
to help her in carrying out her criminal designs?'

Delphine looked at her in astonishment: 'No, I don't think so,' she stammered.

'Then, why are you convinced in your heart of hearts that Marie was murdered? . . . By whom? Even if it was done on the orders of your benefactress, she wasn't able to push her over the cliff herself. She was down here, with the cod-fishermen, I saw her.'

'I . . . I don't know . . . It's difficult, impossible to find out everything about her, at times it's almost as if she had the gift of being everywhere at once . . . And she also lies so much and her lies have such a ring of truth about them that one gets quite lost and one can't say exactly whether she was in such and such a place or not . . .'

'And . . . Marie's last words . . . can you explain them to me? . . . She murmured: "At the time of the shipwreck, she was not wearing her red stockings." '

Delphine stared at her.

'Yes, that's right,' she said as if in answer to a question she had never dared to ask herself; 'those red stockings! . . . The ones she wore when she disembarked in Gouldsboro, I had never seen her wearing those before . . . and I think I can truly say that she didn't have them in her luggage on the *Unicorn*, for I often tidied her things . . . and if Marie-la-Douce said that . . . She knew better than anyone else since she got into the boat with her . . .'

'What do you mean?'

'I never felt quite sure about what I saw. It was so dark and after all it didn't mean anything! After the shipwreck, everything got in a muddle in my head. I couldn't manage to place events in their right order. First we heard that our benefactress had been drowned, then that she had been rescued, and that she had saved the life of Jeanne Michaud's child. There seemed to be something that didn't fit. But now I am sure: it was *before* the *Unicorn* struck the rocks that I saw the Duchess with Marie, the baby and her secretary getting into a rowing boat. Then almost immediately afterwards we heard those terrible crunching sounds and people began to shout: "Every man for himself, we're going down." '

'That would explain everything. She left the ship *before it sank*. During those two days when we thought she was drowned she must have joined her accomplices on board their ship, probably that sailing vessel we glimpsed lurking among the islands, and there she found clothes to change into, for example those red stockings which she thoughtlessly put on before coming ashore in the guise of a wretched shipwrecked woman.

'But what about Marie? She was among those who were nearly drowned . . . Do we have to suppose that they pushed her overboard from the rowing-boat . . . No, that would be too horrible . . . But why not? Everything is horrible in this business; everything is possible . . . everything! . . . In any case we shall never know that, for Marie's dead.

'No! No!' Delphine repeated in anguish. 'No, it isn't possible. *I* must be mistaken . . . we had already struck the rocks when I saw that scene . . . I am no longer sure of anything. It was dark. Oh, I'm going mad . . .'

There was a noise at the door.

'Is it her?' murmured Delphine, growing pale with fright.

Fortunately it was only Petronella Damourt who had come to call her flock back to a sense of propriety and discipline.

'You ought to be doing your mending and telling your beads. You took advantage of the fact that I was having a little snooze to go off and enjoy yourselves. Madame will be very displeased!'

'Don't be hard on the young folk, Petronella my dear,' Ville d'Avray said, putting on his most gallant and charming manner to calm the duenna. 'Life is so dull on this coast, waiting about for who knows what. How could they fail to respond to the gracefulness of a good-looking young man with a guitar?'

'It just won't do!'

'Come now! You're pretending to be stricter than you really are. You deserve to have a little fun too. Come and sit with us for a while. Do you like popcorn? Sprinkled with a little soft brown sugar, it makes a delicious sweet . . .'

Delphine whispered in Angélique's ear:

'Petronella is the one you ought to question. Try to get her to talk. She's a little simple-minded, but she's been in Madame de Maudribourg's service for a number of years and is very proud of the fact that the Duchess tells her everything; she sometimes says she knows things that would frighten a lot of people, but that it's not possible to live close to such a saintly person who has ecstasies and visions without sharing some terrible secrets with her.'

CHAPTER 67

FOR SOME time Cantor had stopped playing his guitar. He was listening attentively.

'What's that . . . that noise?'

From the direction of the fort came the sound of frantic, distant barking. The lad went out on to the doorstep, moved by a sudden presentiment.

'The Newfoundland dogs! What are they after? . . .'

The sound of furious barking grew louder, the frenzied baying being reminiscent of a hunting pack in full cry.

'Someone's let the dogs off the chain.'

Two hounds appeared, racing down the hill, hot on the track of a sort of dark-coloured ball that was fleeing before them.

'Wolverine!'

Dropping his guitar, Cantor rushed to the rescue of his pet. Wolverine was galloping for refuge in the house, where he knew his master would be, but he ran like a fat weasel and was being overtaken by his ferocious pursuers, which were covering the ground in a series of enormous bounds.

The three animals arrived almost simultaneously in a cloud of dust in the little public square of the hamlet. Seeing himself overtaken, Wolverine turned and bared his fierce fangs, ready to challenge his assailant and spring at this throat. A full-grown glutton can easily kill a moose, a lynx, or a mountain lion, but Wolverine had two opponents to cope with. While the first cautiously held back, contenting itself with barking noisily at a distance, the second sprang at full tilt on to Wolverine's back and sank its fangs into his spine. Wolverine turned and clawed its belly open. Then the other dog sprang. But Cantor was coming. With raised knife he stepped between the animal and his wounded glutton, and the hound fell back with its throat cut.

All this took place in a matter of seconds in the midst of a flurry of dust, a welter of blood and an infernal racket of barks, growls, and death rattles, over which could be heard the high-pitched shrieks of the King's Girls and their duenna.

As if by magic, a circle formed. The entire population of Tidmagouche came rushing as if summoned by enchantment towards the scene of the drama – the Breton fishermen and their captain, the Indians who happened to be hanging about the place, the few permanent Acadian residents, Nicolas Parys, his suite of concubines, servants, woodsmen and the yeomen who were his drinking companions. They all gazed at the dogs which had just expired in a pool of blood, and at the glutton, which was also bleeding and kept on darting its blazing eyes around and threatening anyone who came near it with its sharp teeth. Cantor stood at its side, his knife in his hand and his eyes as bright as the animal's.

There was a hesitant silence, then the owner of the place, old Parys, advanced towards Cantor.

'You've killed my animals, young man,' he said angrily.

'They were attacking mine,' retorted Cantor boldly. 'You yourself said that they were dangerous and that they had to be kept on the chain. Who let them go? You? Or her? ...' he added, pointing his blood-stained knife in Ambroisine's direction.

The Duchess was standing in the front row, putting on precisely the startled expression to be expected of a well-bred lady faced with such a repugnant spectacle. In spite of her self-control, Cantor's attack caught her off balance, and she threw him a look of bitter dislike, but she quickly recovered her self-possession, and put on once more her gentle, serene expression that had something childlike about it and made people feel protective towards her.

'What on earth has got into him!' she exclaimed in frightened tones. 'The boy is out of his mind.'

'Stop treating me like a child,' rejoined Cantor glaring at her with detestation. 'There's no such thing as children for you – only males to satisfy your pleasures! ... You think you're clever, but I will tell the world what an unprincipled wretch you are ...'

Angélique came and stood beside her son and quickly laid her hand on his arm.

'Calm yourself, I beg you, this is not the right moment.'

She had the alarming impression that none of those present, at least among the men, was ready to listen to such accusations against the Duchess de Maudribourg. They were still at the stage of boundless fascination with her and were blind or bewitched. And indeed Cantor's words roused a storm of angry protests.

'Yes . . . the young fellow is out of his mind!'

'I'll make you swallow your own words, you whippersnapper,' growled the captain of the *Faouet*, stepping forward.

'Come on then, I'm ready for you,' retorted Cantor, brandishing his long woodsman's knife; 'you'll make one more vicious animal whose throat I cut, whippersnapper or no whippersnapper.'

The Breton fishermen were outraged by this reply to their captain and began to growl and step between the two men.

'Don't go near him, captain. He's dangerous, that lad . . . And be careful . . . he's too good-looking to be human . . . he may be . . .'

'He's an archangel,' said Ambroisine in her soft voice.

Then, in the breathless silence, she went on:

'But an archangel defending the Devil. Look! . . .'

And she pointed to Cantor's feet where the wolverine still crouched at the ready, baring his white teeth in a cruel snarl. His black fur stood on end, his tail erect like a brush, quivering in the air, while his wide eyes stared about him with a fixed and terrible expression that did not fail to frighten the spectators.

'Isn't that the very face of Satan himself?' Ambroisine repeated, feigning a shudder.

The effect of such words on superstitious minds, when spoken by a feminine persuasive voice about an oddly-made, unfamiliar animal that looked the very incarnation of those grinning stone monsters, those gargoyles on cathedrals that spout out rain-water, and also looking remarkably like the hairy representation of the Evil One which European men had been accustomed to contemplate since their earliest childhood on the façades of their churches and in the illuminations in their missals – the effect of such words was to give concrete shape to the mystic fear they felt at the sight of Cantor's fine looks as he stood there in youthful anger among the blood-stained animals, and likewise at Angélique's beauty as she stood at his side, with the plumed and tattooed Indian behind her, his spear in hand ready to defend her, the inscrutable guardian of these two people with the same unusual green eyes. What they all were capable of taking in, in spite of themselves, in the dark recesses of their minds and with the primitive intuition of peasants and fisherfolk, of the invisible drama that was being played out between the antagonistic forces in this scene before them, triggered off within them a sense of fear which could only find outlet in some act of overt violence.

'We must kill that animal . . .'

'Look at it.'

'It's a demon.'

'Even the Indians call it accursed.'

'It will bring us bad luck.'

'Kill it!'

'Strike it down!'

For one moment Angélique had the feeling that this crowd of over-excited men armed with knives, sticks and stones was about to sweep herself and her son irresistibly aside in order to seize the unfortunate wolverine and hack him to pieces.

But the resolute stance of Cantor, herself, as she laid her hand on her pistol, and that of the men who had accompanied her from French Bay and now stood ranged behind her, the Defour brothers armed with their muskets, Barssempuy with his cutlass, Marceline's oldest son grasping his Indian tomahawk and club, and the two men from the *Rochelais* who had armed themselves with hefty cudgels, not to mention Piksarett with his spear, all conspired to check the hysterical fury that threatened to burst out.

Then Ville d'Avray intervened.

'Let us not lose our tempers,' he said advancing with measured tread to the centre of the circle around Angélique and her supporters. 'My friends, it is the end of summer and you're all a bit on edge; but that's no reason to start killing one another over two dogs and a weasel.

'Moreover, you're forgetting that I am the Governor of Acadia and that I do not tolerate bloodshed or brawling in the territories under my jurisdiction. A thousand pounds' fine, prison, even the gallows – those are the penalties which will be incurred, according to the law, by those responsible for causing disorders, if I report the matter to Quebec.'

'You'd still have to be in a position to send in that report, Governor,' interrupted a powerfully-built, youngish Acadian, who turned out to be Nicolas Parys's son-in-law. 'You've already lost your ship and a large part of the fruits of your plundering; you're not going to risk your life for a weasel, as you call it. Gluttons are the worst pests in the forests; they rob all the traps. Even the Indians say they're possessed by demons.'

'There's no call for you to interfere just because it belongs to this good-looking young man and you want to do him a favour . . .' chimed in the captain of the cod-fisher sarcastically.

He broke off under the chilly gaze of the Marquis, whose light blue eye passed from one to the other and was as hard as stone.

'Be careful both of you! I can be nasty when I want to!'

'That's right, he can,' confirmed one of the Defour brothers, stepping forward. 'I can promise you that. In any case, you Bretons,' he went on, thrusting out a threatening finger in the direction of the captain and crew of the cod-fisher, 'you're strangers here. *Our* difficulties with the Governor or with the animals of *our* forests are a matter for us Acadians, and are no concern of yours. Clear out of here and let us settle our affairs among ourselves; otherwise we'll drive you away from our shores in the future, and then bang goes your cod-fishing!

'As for you Acadians from the East Coast, if you want things to get hot, you'll get heat all right and a lot more than we ever get out of the rubbishy coal full of sulphur that you have the cheek to sell ten times dearer than ours at Trantamare.'

'What are you insinuating with your talk about sulphur?' demanded Nicolas Parys's son-in-law coming forward with clenched fists.

'Stop!' rapped out the Marquis de Ville d'Avray placing himself authoritatively in his plum-coloured frockcoat and flowered waistcoat between the two giants. 'I said that I wasn't going to have any brawling, and I mean to be obeyed! Everyone is to go back to his work. The incident is closed. As for you Gontran,' he said to Nicolas Parys's son-in-law, who had insulted him, 'you can expect to have to turn the pockets of your coat inside out when the next collection of unpaid taxes is carried out. My God! I won't forget you . . . nor you either, Amadeus,' he said giving Defour a friendly slap on the arm. 'You were magnificent. I can see that year in and year out we have learnt to appreciate one another. It's a pleasant surprise, but there's nothing like adversity to show what a man is really like.'

Smiling with satisfaction, he watched the crowd disperse. Cantor bent over his wounded glutton, and servants came forward in silence to pick up the carcasses of the dogs.

The Marquis de Ville d'Avray's eyes were moist: 'What Amadeus did greatly touched me,' he told Angélique. 'You saw the spirit and the skill the numb-skulled brute displayed in my defence, didn't you? Ah! Acadia! I adore it! No doubt about it, life is wonderful!'

CHAPTER 68

'POOR WOLVERINE, they've hurt you,' said Cantor dressing his pet's wounds. 'They say you're a demon; but you're only an innocent animal. They're the demons, the human beings.'

He went on philosophizing, kneeling beside his glutton which he had laid before the fire to attend to him. Wolverine had lost a lot of blood, but his wounds were only superficial and he would soon recover. He listened to Cantor talking to him, watching him attentively, and his eyes, when he did not need to defend himself and to face an enemy that he had to terrify, had deep golden lights in them, and the soulful, anxious expression of the dumb creature that cannot express itself, but that understands.

'Yes, you understand,' said Cantor stroking him, 'you know where evil and madness lie. It would have been better if I had left you in the forest rather than bring you among the savage beasts called human beings.'

'In the forest he would have perished,' pointed out Angélique, depressed by the bitterness in her son's words. 'Remember that when you found him, he was too young to survive alone . . . All you could do was to bring him up. It's one point in favour of human beings that they are able to modify the relentless laws of nature.'

'The laws of nature are straightforward and simple,' retorted Cantor pedantically.

'But just as cruel in their demands. Your glutton knows it, and he prefers to be with you among human beings rather than to have perished miserably in the forest without his mother. You can see that in his eyes.'

Cantor gazed thoughtfully at the big hairy animal, which in spite of its apparent weight, could be so quick and agile.

'So it was your fate to come among us and share our lives, then?' he said questioningly looking Wolverine in the eyes. 'But for what purpose? What will your role be among us? For a

415

glutton is not just any sort of animal, and it's true that he is possessed by a particular kind of spirit, and that's why the Indians fear and hate him so. The woodsmen say that he is the animal closest in intelligence to human beings. It's as if he can judge them according to their moral value and instinctively recognizes their true nature. A glutton can identify a bad man and constantly keep on pestering him. Perrot told me about one particularly unsavoury specimen who had taken refuge in the forest. A glutton from the neighbourhood, whose female he had killed, took a set on him. He even went so far as to make holes in his buckets and wreck his cooking pots. What can a man do without a bucket or a crock to his name, in winter time in the forest when he can't even melt a bit of snow over the fire? The fellow had to clear out and make his way back to civilization as best he could. The glutton didn't give him a moment's peace. The man was half out of his mind and said that he'd been persecuted by an invisible demon.'

'How interesting!' said Ville d'Avray. 'I should take one of these animals back to Quebec, we'd have great fun.'

'The fact remains that Piksarett has left us,' said Angélique. 'He claimed he had to join Uniakke, but I felt that he was put out by the row over Wolverine. Do you think he'll come back?'

'He'll come back if he's got any sense. What lies between the Indians and the glutton is a kind of rivalry between forest creatures fighting for their lives. The wolverine demolishes their traps without being caught because it knows that the trap is set to capture and kill animals. It's a lethal device that must be destroyed, and the glutton also renders any prey caught in a trap unusable in order to punish men and discourage them from laying further traps on its territory. Naturally this puts the Indians in a rage, since often the wolverine proves the stronger and, where he is king, those areas have to be abandoned. The Indians say that they are accursed and that a demon defends them . . .'

Conversing in this manner, they kept their minds off more tragic anxieties. Night brought them some respite. By barricading themselves into their shanties, and organizing a watch shared between Ville d'Avray's and Angélique's men, it was possible to have a reasonably quiet night. But the recent tragedy of Marie-la-Douce and the incident concerning Cantor and his wolverine that had nearly got out of hand, had upset them all and made it hard for them to sleep. So they threw an armful of broom on the fire and sat talking until late into the night before breaking up to snatch a brief, troubled sleep.

Angélique had taken this opportunity to show the Marquis a handkerchief embroidered with a gryphon which she had found among the Duchess's possessions, and he confirmed that it was indeed the emblem of the Maudribourgs. From his fob pocket he drew a small magnifying glass with which to examine the embroidery.

'This must have been done by a Flemish seamstress. She has the same seal embroidered on the lining of the cloak she wears, near the neck-line, the embroidery of her coat-of-arms all being done in gold and silver; the most extraordinarily delicate piece of work.'

'That cloak!' exclaimed Angélique. 'Yes, that was where I noticed that lion rampant ... but that means ... that she came back to Gouldsboro with a cloak bearing the Maudribourg arms! ... She can hardly claim that it was given to her by an unknown ship's captain! ... Now everything is clear. They must be her accomplices she goes to see among the islands, to whom she gives her orders.'

She was feverishly excited by her discovery. She had tugged one thread and now the whole skein was following after: the roving ship with its orange flag, beginning to lay a false trail, then Ambroisine, arriving from Europe on the *Unicorn*, leaving the ship before it was wrecked, and reappearing in Gouldsboro as an unfortunate victim of the wreck, stripped of all her possessions the better to mislead people, to lull suspicions that might otherwise have been aroused.

Angélique also felt certain that there was some connection between the seal of the lion rampant and the signature on the note she had found in the dead wrecker's coat.

She saw links everywhere, striking coincidences, all kinds of evidence, but then there were moments when what she wished to establish escaped her, slipped from her comprehension like a drop of mercury that people wear themselves out in their fruit-less attempts to catch. Nothing really fitted. They were only tiny details, light as straw, that the wind bore away.

Barssempuy and Cantor were for setting fire to the whole place and killing all these bandits and their dangerous female. Angélique and the Governor of Acadia advocated a more patient attitude, one of indifference that would lull their enemies into a false sense of security. For every day gained brought Count Peyrac's return nearer.

'But why isn't he here already?' Cantor repeated. 'Why has he abandoned us like this?'

'He doesn't even know that we are here,' Angélique pointed out. 'It's my fault as well. I never seem to manage to remain where he thinks I am. And I can quite understand his occasional exasperation. I shall never do it again . . .'

What she was experiencing, living in close proximity to this woman who claimed to have seduced Joffrey, discovering with every hour that passed some still more disturbing and dangerous aspect of her power and cunning, seemed to Angélique to be the most tremendous ordeal she had ever had to face.

She felt the strain in her very body, and while her mind stood firm, repelling all doubt and seeking to remain under proper control, an unbearable anguish would occasionally take hold of her, and she had the impression that her whole inner being was melting, was dissolving, and that she was about to faint in a spasm of fear, a kind of panic that shrieked wildly at her: 'All is lost . . . all! all! . . . You will not triumph this time . . . *She* is too strong for you . . .'

With an effort she pulled herself together and grew calmer. But such was her distress that she remained icy cold, covered in perspiration. Several times during the night she had to get up to go to the water-closet.

It was a somewhat primitive, uncomfortable spot, at some distance from her room. Angélique would have preferred to have to cross the Atlantic or miles of desert alone. The night, murky with mist and a hidden moon, seemed heavy with evil spells, pitfalls, and nameless horrors. The dank smell of brine and fish wafted up from the beach like the stench of an open, putrid pit around her. She feared lest she stumble into it and be engulfed there. Where was Love in all this nightmare? Where was security of joy, and the happiness of being alive? The teeming monsters of hell had clambered out of their chasms and were crawling up the sands towards her . . . The Demon would kill Cantor . . . Joffrey would never come back again . . . Honorine would be left an orphan . . . There would be no one to look after her. She would be of less account on this earth than a lost kitten . . . and what about Florimond? . . . How could she ever have allowed him to go off into the depths of those unexplored forest-lands, into such danger, without realizing that he would never escape them and that she would never see him again . . .

The hooting of an owl sounded both mocking and sinister to her ears.

Everything was lost, everything . . . and now came death and defeat . . .

CHAPTER 69

AND NOW it was the third day of this period of waiting. It was Sunday, an opportunity to show they had not given up and to avoid letting themselves be put in an untenable position. Angélique and her friends – few as they were, in face of the general hostility, of the mob's suspicions and dangerous fear, that Ambroisine was so skilled in fostering with her poisonous charm – must now allow themselves to become isolated, must keep going for as long as possible.

Under the aegis of Ville d'Avray, whose social sense in such a situation was invaluable and had full scope to operate, they all attended Mass together – including the two men from the *Rochelais* who were Huguenots but knew when to bow to circumstance. They had known far worse in La Rochelle. And if they had, once again, to hoodwink these damned papists, they would be as sharp as the situation demanded!

Cantor was the only one to object to the idea. He feared, he said, that if he left his wounded wolverine behind, someone might well finish him off in their absence. Angélique made him promise not to make a fuss.

Mass lasted two hours. The entire white and Indian population of the settlement attended piously and no one seemed to mind the sermon preached by the officiating Recollect, who went on and on about the necessity to call on the intercession of the Virgin Mary and all the saints of the Breton calendar when assailed by demons, in particular those of the air that entice men to leave their work and their worldly obligations for a carefree life of vagabondage, and all the pitfalls inherent in such negligence, etc. . . .

'The sermon was a bit on the long side,' said Ville d'Avray as the crowd began to disperse after the final genuflexion. 'It always astonishes me to see these ships' crews so devoutly swallowing their chaplains' interminable sermons. But where sailors are concerned, provided a preacher talks a lot about angels, saints and the devil, whether he makes a fricassee of them or a salad, he has always done his duty. All sailors, especially the Bretons, are only too ready to fall to their knees. But you see, I think it has calmed them down . . . The fact is they're worried. There's an ill wind this year on the "strand". Some of them are beginning to desert, a young lad vanished a couple of days back. The captain has been ranting and raving about it, and he asked the chaplain to call them to order. But then why has this very man let himself be caught in the snares of our dear Duchess? She has upset his judgement and discipline has suffered. So much the worse for him and all those who let themselves get into her clutches. And now even that old reprobate Parys is talking about marrying her . . .'

'You're a knowledgeable man,' Angélique said to him, 'do you know how to tell character from handwriting? I've been meaning for a long time to show you a document that intrigues me.'

Ville d'Avray confessed that he did have some knowledge of graphology, in fact that he had quite a reputation for his skill in the matter.

On their return home, after the Marquis had installed himself in his hammock, Angelique handed him the paper she had found in the wrecker's pocket.

He had livened up considerably, and it was with some eagerness that he seized the small piece of paper which Angélique passed him.

But no sooner had his eyes fallen upon it than he changed colour.

'Where did you get this scrawl?' he asked, gazing piercingly at Angélique.

'I found it in the pocket of a jacket,' she replied.

'Yes, but surely there's more to it than that.'

'What is so extraordinary about this cryptogram?'

'But . . . this is extraordinarily like Satan's writing.'

'But has anyone ever seen his writing?'

'Yes indeed they have! We have a few specimens of it. The most remarkable one, from the most authentic source, dating from the last century, from the time of Doctor Faustus's trial, was written out under Satan's dictation. All the experts agree that it contains the characteristics of the Spirit of Evil. Usually Satan uses the signature of one of the seven principal demons. And so in the Faustian document, he signed the name Asmodeus. What about this one? . . .'

He examined the contorted signature, which to Angélique had looked like some mythical animal.

'Belial!' he murmured.

'Who is Belial?'

'One of the seven black principles in question. He is a demon who appears as someone very beautiful and is Lucifer's most active agent. His character is ferocious and treacherous, but his beautiful, young and charming appearance almost makes one doubt the fact. He stimulates the genetic, erotic instinct, but also the instinct of destruction and is reputed to be the most perverted of all the demons of hell. And also one of the strongest since he commands eighty legions of demons, in other words over half a million evil spirits.'

Ville d'Avray shook his head thoughtfully.

'Eighty legions! We're in a nice mess!'

'Do you think as I do that that writing could be *hers*?'

'This writing looks like a woman's . . .'

'Belialith!' Angélique murmured.

They remained silent for a considerable time.

He stretched out again in his hammock and yawned.

'Why did you call your ship *Asmodeus*?' asked Angélique.

'Just an idea that came into my head. Asmodeus was the superintendent of Hell's gaming-houses, it was he who tempted Eve in the earthly paradise, he is the Serpent! I liked him. I rather like playing games with demons. After all they are only poor devils. And no one ever feels sorry for them . . . theologians are wrong to accuse them of all wickedness. It's the spirit of evil *plus* man that is horrible.'

Angélique looked at him without being able to conceal her astonishment.

'You say some very profound things.'

He reddened slightly.

'I have studied some theology, even some demonology. I had an uncle who was a bishop and who wanted to leave me his living. For a while I studied theology and all that to please him. But you know, I didn't want to stick in the same place all my life and so I gave up all idea of inheriting my dear uncle's substantial revenue from his abbacy. And yet I rather enjoy discussing these matters with a few chosen friends. In Quebec I shall introduce you to Brother Luke who plays tarot better than anyone I know, and to Madame de Castel-Morgeat who is more learned than any abbess, and also to little Madame d'Arreboust if she will deign to leave her Montreal retreat. She is a most interesting woman whom I love like a sister. She only comes to Quebec for my sake. Not even for her own husband, although he deserves better than that. He's an excellent friend of mine. But of course, come to think of it, you know him. He even came to pay you a visit this winter in your fort at Wapassou . . .

'Another one you made fall head over heels in love with you . . . Just like Loménie-Chambord. And you lose heart over eighty legions of evil spirits and a single demon incarnate? I must admit that the demon has turned out rather well, but come, come now, Angélique, this is a mere nothing for you! . . . But why are you looking at me in that strange way, dear lady?'

'Do you think that we are perhaps both going mad?' murmured Angélique.

CHAPTER 70

'WHAT I don't understand,' said Angélique looking closely at Petronella Damourt's round face, that seemed to have grown puffy and pallid, as she sat before her by the fire, 'what I don't understand, is why Madame de Maudribourg took Marie-la-Douce with her in the boat rather than you. Of course she did not know that the *Unicorn* was about to be wrecked, but if she had taken you with her you would never have had to go through that terrible ordeal.'

'Yes, that's what I keep telling myself,' the governess exclaimed with such force that she almost split the cup of infusion she was holding.

Angélique had succeeded in persuading her to come into her room. Sitting on the bench facing her, the good stout lady had allowed herself to be prevailed on to drink some medicine that Angélique recommended for her stomach pains. She drank it noisily. She too had changed. As a result of too many exhausting plunges in the water, and too much excitement and fatigue for an old woman like herself, who was of a wheezy, stay-at-home nature, some signs of senility were beginning to appear in her behaviour. Her hands and her lips trembled slightly, and her big pale eyes had a fixed expression. There was a constant hint of a vague smile in them. She seemed to be always relishing in a conceited sort of way the satisfaction of sharing an important secret. Seeing her so vague, Angélique realized that she would gain nothing by asking her precise questions. Chancing her hand, she began to talk as if she knew all about the governess's inner preoccupations, and it seemed to her that her remarks were finding a response in the poor woman's confused brain.

'You're quite right, Madame,' agreed Petronella nodding her crumpled, somewhat crooked bonnet, 'it's no proper thing for a body to experience in her life, this business of being drowned, or very near. The water was so cold, and it got in your eyes, your ears, your mouth, and I just don't know when it's all ever going to end. We'll never be done with these beaches, and these boats. My heart won't stand it, I'm sure.'

She was becoming agitated, and Angélique took the cup from her hands.

'You ought to have got into the boat with her,' she said in a reassuring voice, 'it would have saved you from a cruel ordeal. I'm surprised she didn't ask you to accompany her since she's so fond of you and can't do without . . .'

Angélique was feeling her way slowly and cautiously, going back to a scene which she felt sure had greatly distressed the governess.

'The fact is she knows I don't care for her brother,' said Petronella.

Her brother? . . . Angélique's heart gave a sudden warning bound, but she refrained from asking a question . . . Without saying anything, she handed her another bowl of infusion, and Petronella sipped at it absent-mindedly.

'But I did hope that we'd be shot of that fellow in America. And just think, he was waiting for her here. It was he sent the boat to fetch her. But I told her, and so did Monsieur Simon the captain, that it wasn't wise. It was dark, and the sea was far from smooth, "and there may well be some nasty reefs hereabouts, and I don't know these parts," the captain told her, "and since we can see the coast and the lights, wait till we're at anchor." But what was the use? No point trying to make her listen to reason when her brother was calling her.'

She took another greedy gulp.

'Ah, that's a bit of all right!' she sighed.

Angélique was holding her breath, fearing to distract her by a single word from the thread of her vague thoughts.

'It's not that she obeys him,' the stout lady resumed, 'she doesn't obey anyone, but she needs to see him; it's as if he was the only person in the world with whom she had an understanding, her Zalil. I've never understood. He really is a fright that man, with his long gloomy face, his cold fishy eyes, and not what you'd call easy to get on with either. I don't know what she sees in him. And anyway you can see for yourself, straight away he brought us bad luck being in these parts. We were shipwrecked and a lot of very nice people were killed.'

'Why was her brother waiting for her in French Bay?'

Her questioning tone seemed to raise Petronella from her unconscious monologue, and Angélique realized that she had blundered. The old lady eyed her suspiciously.

'What's all this I've been telling you? You're making me talk nonsense!'

She attempted to get up, but hardly succeeded in stirring. Sudden terror appeared to nail her to her seat.

'She forbade me to talk to you,' she stammered. 'What have I done? What am I doing?'

'She'll kill you? . . .'

'No, not me,' said old Petronella in a sudden burst of pride and fervour. Her reaction was identical with Marie-la-Douce's.

'So we know she is capable of killing,' said Angélique quietly.

Petronella Damourt began to tremble. Angélique urged her to speak, trying to awaken her conscience, to make her understand that she would make up for her half-complicity with her mistress's criminal activities, of which she must have been aware over recent years when she had served her devotedly, by helping Angélique and her friends. It was no use. She couldn't get another word out of her, not even any confirmation that the boat that they had sighted several times belonged to Ambroisine's brother, the pale man.

She knew nothing, so she said. Nothing! Nothing! And she affirmed it with chattering teeth. The only thing she knew was that if she took a step outside this house, 'they' would kill her . . . and she seemed resolved to stay put till the end of time.

'Well she's a big barrel to have tied to our coat tails,' said Cantor when Angélique had informed him and Ville d'Avray of the situation. 'But we can't chuck her out, she's frightened of being murdered.'

'Perhaps she's not far wrong,' said Ville d'Avray.

During the evening the Duchess de Maudribourg sent for her

companion. Angélique informed her that the old lady was indisposed and that she was keeping her with her for the night so as to be able to look after her. She was frightened that Ambroisine might show up, but she did not appear.

It was a disturbed night. Petronella did not emerge from her prostration except to groan and weep. Moreover, she was suffering from stomach pains, brought on again by her terror. Angélique had to accompany her outside several times, for she would not have allowed her to go a single step alone. Everywhere she saw monsters and hidden murderers. Finally Petronella remembered that she had some medicine in her reticule which she had found a great comfort in her disturbances. Angélique administered it to her and at last they were able to get some rest.

In the morning she seemed better. They had a serious talk around the table on which Ville d'Avray's cook and his assistant served up the first meal of the day. They tried to persuade the poor governess that she should keep up an appearance of naturalness, and that she should go back to the King's Girls. It was the best way not to arouse suspicion. Monsieur de Peyrac would soon be there and everything would be all right.

She seemed to pluck up courage. Ville d'Avray put her completely right by telling her that he had guessed as soon as he had set eyes on her that she was from the Dauphiné and they talked about her native province.

In order not to be dependent on Nicolas Parys's hospitality, Angélique had arranged to take her meals in her own lodgings with Ville d'Avray, Cantor, Barssempuy, Defour and Marceline's son.

In spite of everything, they were cheerful moments, made pleasant by Ville d'Avray's lively manner. It was a way of drawing close together and not feeling themselves too isolated in this sinister atmosphere.

Suddenly the Duchess de Maudribourg appeared on the doorstep. She was accompanied by her usual devoted male attendants, old Parys and the captain of the *Faouet*, who owned a concession a few leagues away and who was only too glad to come so far each day in order to meet the beautiful Duchess. All this fine company appeared to be on their way home from Mass. The Duchess was wearing a dress of flame-coloured shot silk, which gave her dark hair a reddish tinge, so that when she stood against the light she seemed to have a sort of halo. She came in saying:

'I've just looked in to find out how you were getting on, Damourt. What's been wrong with you, my dear?'

The fat governess went pale and began to tremble all over. The expression of fear which came over her bloated features so transformed her that she looked like a hideous caricature with her eyes starting out of her head, with her trembling cheeks and her thick hanging lip from which crumbs of cake fell. It was such a distressing sight that even the urbane Marquis couldn't find a word to say or any bright remark to make to break the frozen silence.

'What on earth's the matter with you, Petronella?' asked Ambroisine with a hint of surprise in her angelic voice. 'Anybody would think you were scared of me.'

'Didn't I always look after you proper, Madame?' quavered the old lady, while her deformed lip was twisted into a kind of pitiful smile. 'You was like my own child, wasn't you? . . .'

Ambroisine cast an astonished glance around the assembled company.

'What on earth is up with her? She doesn't seem to be in her right mind! . . .'

'I spoilt you proper, didn't I?' went on the unfortunate creature. 'I let you enjoy yourself any way you liked, and I even helped you . . .'

'She seems to be going out of her mind,' whispered Ambroisine looking at Angélique. 'I noticed that she's been a bit odd recently. Pull yourself together, my dear Petronella,' she went on more loudly, drawing close to the old lady who looked like a large fat toad fascinated by a snake, 'you're a little tired, aren't you? But it's nothing . . . all you need's a bit of looking after. Have you got the medicine that usually does you good? Ah yes, here it is . . .'

With a great show of concern she took from the governess's embroidered reticule the flask containing the tablets that Angélique had given her the previous night, dropped two of them into the bowl beside Petronella, poured in a little water with her white hand and lifted the bowl to the patient's lips.

'Drink up, my poor friend, drink up, it will do you good. I'm very sorry to see you in such a state. Come on, drink up . . .'

'Yes, Madame,' the woman stammered, 'you're very kind . . . Yes, yes indeed, you've always been kind to me . . .'

Her hands which were endeavouring to hold the receptacle trembled so violently that the liquid was spilt on her blouse.

Ambroisine went on helping her. The poor woman drank clumsily and noisily like a big scared doll.

'What a disaster!' commented the Duchess in an undertone, addressing the assembled company. 'The stresses we've been constantly exposed to have deranged her mind. She was too old to run such risks. I did try to persuade her not to follow me to America. But she was unwilling to leave me . . .'

Suddenly Angélique caught Cantor's expression as he stood with his wolverine at the fireside. The lad's eyes and the dog's were fixed on Ambroisine and were shining with the same frightened hateful glare.

'Oh! I feel awful!' groaned Petronella Damourt, putting her two hands on her stomach. 'Oh! I'm going to die!'

Tears started from her eyes and bathed her wax-coloured face.

Angélique stood up, resolving to shake off the strange apathy which was nailing her to her stool.

'Come, Petronella!' she said authoritatively. 'Come my poor dear. I'll help you to the toilet.'

She went up to the old lady and bent over her to help her up.

The Duchess muttered in an undertone: 'Doesn't the old woman disgust you? You really are . . . very kind. *I* couldn't. What a dreadful thing it is when people go into their dotage! . . .'

'She's going to kill me,' groaned Petronella Damourt, while Angélique was steering her not without considerable difficulty along a rough path that they had taken several times since the day before, 'she's going to kill me, like she killed the Duke, and the Abbot, and Clara, and Theresa, and the Abbess, and the young man who saw her through the window, and the valet, who was a good fellow, and I didn't want it . . . Wasn't right what she did. I told her. But she laughed . . . she always laughed when she saw people dying . . . And now she's going to kill me . . . You said it, Madame, I'm going to die, and she'll laugh; I'm going to die, I feel it. May God forgive me my sins . . .'

'Stay there,' said Angélique whose flesh was creeping from this nightmare monologue, and who felt almost as sick as the unfortunate creature, 'don't you move from this place until you've recovered.'

She propped her up in the toilet.

'Don't come back until you feel calm again. I'm going to try to persuade the Duchess to leave you with us. I'll tell her that you have an illness that may be infectious . . . Keep up your courage and don't show any fear before her . . .'

Ambroisine was still in the room, very seductive, a queen among her subjects. Ville d'Avray was saying to her: 'The Dauphiné is a beautiful region, we were just talking about it. Do you know, Duchess? . . .'

He had recovered his ease of manner, perhaps was even over-doing it. The Dauphiné was not exactly a highly appropriate subject, since Ambroisine had disguised the fact that that was the region from which she had come, having persuaded Angélique that she was from the Poitou in order to get on friendlier terms with her.

'It is an unruly, independent-minded region,' the Marquis explained. 'It's because of those remote upland regions where the people live isolated in their valleys for at least ten winter months. The bears, the wolves . . .'

Thus they talked in desultory fashion, and Angélique had the impression that because of Ambroisine's presence, her radiant beauty and the disguised feelings of all present, that they were plunged in a sinister and unreal atmosphere. The persisting smell of the tide and putrefaction on the beaches where the cod were drying, where the heaped-up livers were melting in the sun over the gratings, and exuding their valuable but mal-odorous oil, heightened the pervading sense of nausea. Time no longer seemed to have any dimension.

'Old Petronella hasn't come back yet,' Cantor suddenly interjected, having remained silent up to that point.

'Quite right! We've been chatting for more than an hour,' observed Ville d'Avray consulting his gold-chased watch, 'and she's still not back.'

'I'll go and see what's become of her,' said Angélique quickly, getting in before Ambroisine.

But they followed her, moved by a presentiment, which grew stronger as they descried before them the first nucleus of a crowd of people.

Collapsed and half-wedged in the narrow space among the traces of her vomit, the old lady was dead. Her skin was grey and appeared to be speckled with black.

'How dreadful!' murmured the Marquis de Ville d'Avray raising his lace handkerchief to his nose. Angélique was frozen with horror and reluctant to understand, to believe in such a crime.

'Can she have poisoned her just now before our very eyes!

428

... At our table! When she was so kindly preparing her medicine. She must have slipped some poison into the drink! She made her drink her own death under our very eyes!'

She looked at Ambroisine in wild surmise and saw the trace of a fleeting smile on the Duchess's lips, which was meant for her and expressed delight in her triumph and a kind of satanic defiance.

CHAPTER 71

'FATHER *must* come now,' said Cantor in a plaintive, almost childish voice, 'otherwise we're all done for. What is this nightmare? Am I dreaming? ...'

His sharp, authoritative young manner was crumbling at this glimpse of the abyss.

'Come, Cantor,' said Angélique holding out her arms to him.

He sat down beside her, laying his forehead on her shoulder.

'You must get away from here by boat,' she said, 'you must go and look for your father wherever he may be, and you must tell him to hurry.'

'Leave by boat?' he commented despondently. 'That's not so simple. Ships come only rarely to the Bay. The *Rochelais* can't get here for two weeks yet. I'd be quite capable of reaching Newfoundland or exploring the whole Gulf in any old tub, but we haven't even got that.'

They were sitting together around the fire, the little band of faithful folk who had rallied round Angélique, her son and the Marquis de Ville d'Avray. It was the evening of the day that had seen the body of the old lady who had died that same morning laid to rest.

Her burial could not be delayed. It seemed that her flabby, faded flesh, already bloated while she was still alive, was visibly decomposing. A grave had been hastily dug, the last blessing mumbled, the protective earth thrown over her and a cross set up at her head. A wind of panic was blowing over the King's Girls, who were pale and silent, over the superstitious Bretons, who were muttering that a jinx was on the place, and over the permanent inhabitants, Acadians and Indians, who feared an outbreak of plague or smallpox . . .

The atmosphere of hostility and suspicion towards the new-comers, particularly since the scene with the wolverine, was growing even more marked.

'You must get out of here,' replied Angélique, feeling that Cantor was more at risk than anybody else at the present time. 'If you can't do so by sea, you must head overland, as you did when we were at Macquoit Point, and try to reach some point of the coast, some port, Shediac for example, where you might find a boat of some kind.'

'Can I still do it?' wondered Cantor. 'If Ambroisine's cronies are lurking in the forest, I shan't be able to get through.'

He was referring to what Piksarett had reported on his return from the forest, namely that he had noticed two sailing ships moored broadside on in a neighbouring cove and, among the crews, some of the faces of the wreckers he had glimpsed in French Bay. Might it not be that these miscreants, who were beginning to go on the prowl in the surrounding woods, bartering alcohol with the native women, were the advance guard of reinforcements summoned by the diabolical Duchess.

They turned to Piksarett, who was sitting at the fireside smoking his pipe.

'Can Cantor set out through the woods without danger?'

He shook his head.

'So we're encircled, then?' said Cantor.

Angélique went on questioning Piksarett.

'Do you really believe that those prowling sailors are in league with the woman full of demons? . . .'

'The spirit tells me so,' answered Piksarett slowly, 'but inner certainties are not enough, especially where white people are concerned. I told Uniakke: "Be patient, you can't go lifting white men's scalps on the coasts unless you want your actions to be interpreted as a sign of madness and provocation to war . . ." They must reveal themselves and show themselves in their true light so that their wickedness is known. For the moment all they do is trade a little alcohol in order to corrupt the women. They melt pitch on the beach and caulk their ships like all the sailors who come here in the summertime. It's not enough to wipe them out. We must wait. Perhaps one day one of them will come and join the woman. Perhaps she will try to meet up with them. We'll know about it; the woods have eyes.'

'Wait!' exclaimed Cantor. 'We'll all be dead tomorrow.'

He started to his feet.

'I'll kill her!' he said wildly. 'It's a sin to let creatures like that live. They should be killed before they kill you. I'm going to kill her!'

'Let's go,' said Barssempuy, rising to his feet. 'I'm with you, my lad.'

Angélique intervened.

'Be quiet both of you. Today if she were to die without apparent reason in the eyes of the people here, we'd die too. We must hold on until the truth becomes obvious. Then punishment will follow.'

'Your mother's right, my lad,' agreed Ville d'Avray. 'If we rush things, your father, the Comte de Peyrac, may well find a pile of corpses here. Drunken Indians in the forests, the ne'er-do-wells ripe for anything at the orders of a possessed lunatic woman, the woman scared, the men at the end of their tether, all these things put together ... Bloodstained beaches at the end of the summer on these accursed coasts is a mere commonplace. And how it could ever be sorted out, the devil only knows.'

'But I can't leave you; she'll kill you, Mother.'

'No, not me,' retorted Angélique.

Then, remembering Marie-la-Douce's and Petronella's words, she corrected herself: 'Not me, not yet. She'll only kill me when she feels that she's finished, annihilated, doomed ... We still have a few days before us.'

'Yes, you set out, my lad,' insisted Ville d'Avray. 'You are now more in danger than anybody else because you're vulnerable. Ah! youth! What unutterable grace! What a moving sight it is to see a young man rising up in anger against the baseness of the world! ... We must try to find a ship! ...'

Angélique had in mind to approach the Breton fishermen to see whether they couldn't provide a small boat for Cantor to get away in. She tackled Captain Marieun Aldoch in the hope of winning him round, and suggested she might go and nurse his sick son, whom he kept on board his vessel anchored in the roadstead. But the man proved hostile and suspicious, and she couldn't get anything out of him.

When Angélique passed by with Piksarett at her heels, mutterings and even sniggers followed her. Some of the men spat on the ground, others made the sign of the cross.

But towards evening on the sixth day, Providence came to the rescue in the form of a large boat, with a square sail, which entered the roadstead and ran right up to the shore before casting anchor, the occupants obviously intending to land and fill their casks with fresh water. The people of Tidmagouche shouted to them to keep off, that they didn't want any strangers here and that they would fire on them. But the skipper of the sloop was having none of that, and Angélique recognized his grating voice even from a distance.

'A fine thing it would be if there was any coast in the world in which a Brother of the coast could not put ashore! . . . Avast there, you lubbers, or I'll riddle your addled pates for you. I've got just the medicine for you right here!'

Aristide Beaumarchand, with a pistol in each hand, came up the beach followed by Julienne and the Negrillo Timothy, both laden with empty casks and demijohns.

Angélique rushed down to meet them. They didn't appear particularly surprised.

'Pleased to see you again, Madame. Hasn't the *Fearless* arrived yet?'

'The *Fearless*? . . .'

'They're a rough-looking lot you've got here,' went on Aristide, 'and I've seen some ripe specimens in my time.'

'Did you just happen to put in here?'

'Yes and no. We knew that Monsieur de Peyrac had arranged to meet the *Fearless* here at the beginning of the autumn, and Hyacinth is supposed to be bringing me a supply of tafia.'

'Is he expected here soon?' she asked, appalled at the thought that Hyacinth Boulanger might come and add one more specimen to this collection of bandits.

'Hard to say. It all depends on the wind from the Caribbean. But since they're not at the rendezvous, I'm off. The locals don't look as if they appreciate visitors.'

'They're out-and-out bandits; be careful not to leave your boat unattended,' advised Angélique glancing anxiously in the direction of the shore where more and more people were congregating.

'No danger of that,' sniggered Aristide, 'the old gig is well defended.'

Mr Willoughby was installed in the front of the boat, growling threateningly at anyone who ventured too close.

'We teamed up with the heretic from Connecticut,' explained the former pirate while they were filling their casks at the spring that gushed from the cliffside and ran away into the sand. 'We do a bit of coastal trading. He sells his stuff and I sell mine. We've done some good business all the way round Nova Scotia, but in these parts there's nothing doing. That's Canada for you. The people don't want anything to do with rum; they prefer their rotgut grain alcohol. We'll just have to manage as best we can until Hyacinth turns up at the rendezvous. I was thinking of staying on here for a bit, but the place stinks, and I'm not talking about their damned cod either . . . better not to hang about.'

'What about Monsieur de Peyrac?' asked Julienne.

'I'll hang on for him hereabouts. He can't be long now.'

'Can't be much fun for you here on your own,' said Julienne, sensing that there was something unusual going on, although it was not her way to be lightly surprised by anything.

'It's dreadful. Really, you two are a heaven-sent blessing,' said Angélique.

'Think so?'

Aristide gave Angélique an old-fashioned look. It was the first time that anyone had ever said anything of the sort to him and Julienne.

'Yes. We've got ourselves caught in a trap and we can't even get out to go and fetch help. You must take Cantor off with you.'

She quickly put them in the picture. How, since the beginning of the summer certain malicious people, perhaps in the pay of governments that wanted to discourage the Peyracs from settling in this part of America, had been trying to damage them in every possible way, and were finally plotting against their very lives. It appeared that the Duchess de Maudribourg was more or less their secret leader.

Julienne went pale on hearing that the benefactress was in the offing.

'Are we never to be shot of that bitch?' she groaned. 'Crook, daughter of a whore, murderess . . . she's everything! Doesn't seem as if the Lord looks after his own properly! . . .'

'So that's the way of it,' said Aristide, 'the girls on the *Unicorn* were really meant for us? . . . Didn't I tell you! We didn't take anything from anybody . . . And are you going to be left like that, Madame? I've got obligations to you. You sewed up my paunch for me, didn't you?'

'Save Cantor, so that he can send my husband to the rescue. You will have more than repaid your debts and made up for the bad turns you did me in the past.'

It was all managed very neatly. So that no one could attempt to interfere at the time of his departure, Cantor, who had been forewarned by his mother, suddenly dashed down the slope, with his glutton at his heels, at the very moment when the boat was beginning to pull away from the shore. Aristide was holding in the sail, and pouring out a flood of colourful abuse upon the dumbfounded spectators. Cantor pushed his way through the crowd, entered the water, threw Wolverine into the boat, and hoisted himself up into it in his turn with the assistance of Julienne and Elias Kempton.

'Be seeing you,' shouted the pirate in his rough voice, while the sloop and its motley cargo slipped away into the rising mists of evening.

Who would think of pursuing them? . . .

CHAPTER 72

SEVEN DAYS. Marie-la-Douce was dead, Petronella also. Cantor was in danger and had fled with his wolverine. The days dragged on, at once dreary and agitated. The crisis came with all the suddenness of a thunderclap, and it was as if they had been in a dream.

Ambroisine crossed the threshold and made straight for Ville d'Avray's hammock. He was away; this was the time of day when he went to the port to have a chat with Nicolas Parys. He had already formed habits to which he was strongly attached . . . The Duchess lay down in the comfortable hammock with evident pleasure, and, with her arms crossed behind her head, she gave Angélique a quizzical look.

'You've been in a great hurry these recent days, it would seem,' she said in her fluting voice. 'I admit that you were too quick for me. The handsome archangel has flown. Pooh! He was only small fry. I have other means of striking at you.'

Angélique had just sat down at the table on which she had placed her looking-glass. It was a relief to know that Cantor was out of danger. He would find his father, as he had done before, although a mere child at the time. Consequently, Ambroisine's intrusion did not particularly disturb her. She undid her hair and began to brush it slowly.

'What are you hoping for?' went on Ambroisine in her smooth way, with a note of ironical pity in her voice. 'To win your Count de Peyrac back? My poor thing, you don't know him properly at all; look at the things you failed to notice when we were still at Gouldsboro. I almost felt sorry for you. I didn't like to see you being taken in to that extent, for after all we both come from the aristocracy of Poitou, and that creates a bond between us . . .'

'Oh don't bother,' broke in Angélique coldly. 'I know perfectly well that you're not from Poitou. And as far as being an aristocrat is concerned, I know that your quarterings are few and far between and the bar sinister very much in evidence.'

Her feminine intuition had enabled her to sense the only chinks in Ambroisine's armour, and she had not been mistaken.

The Duchess reacted violently.

'What are you insinuating?' she cried half sitting up. 'My quarterings are every bit as good as yours!'

Then, suddenly changing expression as she often did:

'How do you know that? Who told you? . . . Ah! I think I can guess. It was that little rat Ville d'Avray. I just knew he'd recognized me. His play-acting didn't take me in.'

'What's Ville d'Avray got to do with it?' rejoined Angélique, who trembled for the poor Marquis and regretted having provoked Ambroisine and set her sharp mind in action.

'I'll tell you the whole truth. One day when you were delirious you gave yourself away by referring to your father the priest. Being begotten by a clergyman is never a certificate of legitimacy for us Catholics. As to finding out that you were born in the Dauphiné, it was Petronella Damourt who told me.'

She did not feel guilty for having told this white lie. The poor governess had no more to lose now.

'The old louse,' hissed Ambroisine. 'I was quite right to . . .'

'. . . kill her,' said Angélique, finishing the sentence for her, and going on calmly brushing her hair. 'No doubt in view of what she was on the point of telling me about you, you acted wisely.'

Ambroisine remained silent for a considerable time. She was breathing with difficulty and her nostrils were pinched. Between her half-closed eyelids she examined Angélique shrewdly.

'I realized it straight away,' she said at last, 'as soon as I saw you on that beach, beside him; I knew that you would not be an easy opponent. Afterwards, I felt easier in my mind. You seemed to be so kind and loving. Kind and loving people are quite defenceless. But I soon changed my mind again. You're tough, and unpredictable . . . What's the best way to outwit you and charm you? . . . That's what I still keep asking myself. What does the secret of your charm and your seductiveness consist in? . . . You really are, I think, a human being without artifice. Eve must have been like you.'

'So I have been told before; that's an old one!'

The Duchess's little teeth sparkled like a she-wolf's, ready to bite.

'But the fact is that the demon got the better of her,' she hissed. And then after a pause: 'What is there between the Comte de Peyrac and you? Tell me.'

Angélique turned and looked at her.

'What there is between him and me can't be understood by creatures of your type.'

'Really! And what is my type then?'

'The Devil's!'

Ambroisine began to laugh, a mocking laugh but with a ring of pride in it.

'It's quite true. I just don't understand,' she replied, 'I admit it. And yet I'm very learned in all sorts of sciences. But straight away you were a mystery to me . . . there on the beach . . . and then, when I woke up, ill from that terrible sleep . . . I had seen monsters lurking in wait for me . . . a demon with eyes on his behind, and another one with a goose's beak . . . I knew their names . . . They terrified me . . . And when I woke up both of you were at my bedside . . . I sensed that he was burning to take you away to love you, and that you were impatient to follow him, that nothing really existed for you except the moments that were to follow for you, you alone, for your two beings, for your two bodies, and that by some unknown grace you were going to be as happy as if you were in paradise. For me the coming night would be terrifying and bitter, while for you it would be divine . . . What cruelty there was in your haste to leave me. I was only flotsam tossed up by the sea.

'When you went away, I suffered dreadfully. I felt as if my soul was torn from my body. I cried out like a damned soul sinking into hell.'

'I remember that cry! But I went back and asked Delphine

and Marie-la-Douce, who were at the window and who didn't appear to know where it was coming from . . .'

Ambroisine smiled her hateful, beautiful smile.

'What do you imagine? That they don't know how to put on an act? . . . I've trained my faithful girls properly! They would lie to the King himself to please me. And at the time they were frightened that they had done something to displease me. Hadn't I ordered them to keep you all night at my bedside, at all costs? I *did not want* him to take you away! But they had failed . . .'

She gritted her teeth.

'Oh, you were always foiling my plans. Sometimes you frightened me, you seemed to be on the point of seeing through me. I had immense difficulty in distracting your attention. Even luck seemed to be on your side. For example when Madame Carrère came in and drank your coffee, it was almost as if you had summoned her . . . Ah! Gouldsboro . . .' she murmured with a shake of her head, 'I don't know what it is about that place . . . I didn't feel easy there. Everything I tried seemed not to go as it usually did . . . why? why?'

Angélique had stopped moving in order to concentrate on what she was saying.

'Perhaps it's America,' she said, 'perhaps it's the New World which has saved us from his evil spells. Here one is obliged to live openly. There is no painting nature over. And then again, people are trained by necessity to be on their guard against everything: the Indians, the sea, the veering winds, and pirates who may suddenly appear from nowhere. That makes them more attentive, less easy to ensnare in this poisoned honey.'

Ambroisine was going on dreamily, lying with her arms crossed behind her head.

'I remember . . . in the beginning . . .'

Angélique had to admit to herself that in this slightly veiled voice that sometimes faltered and hesitated, there was a charm that was difficult to resist, that one could not help listening to in fascination.

'In the beginning . . . I saw you enthusiastic about so many things . . . it was a matter for both wonder and fear. I didn't know how to capture your attention. You were passionately absorbed in this love . . . it was your pole-star . . . you were absorbed in your friends . . . Abigail . . . and even in this country . . . Yes, you loved this country . . . and me you did not see. I learned to hate the sea . . . and the passing birds . . .'

She paused and seemed to reflect.

'He! . . . I was sure that I would get him away from you one day . . . I didn't want to know what there was between you . . . but Abigail, what agony! . . .'

She resumed with clenched teeth and implacable intensity which made her wide eyes suddenly blaze.

'I learned to hate the sea because you loved it, and to hate the birds because you found them beautiful . . . How strange their flight was when they passed by in their thousands, in clouds that darkened the sky . . . When your face was raised towards them, I wanted to distract you from the love you felt for them . . .'

She sat up again.

'But today you see them no longer,' she said in unspeakably exultant tones, 'you don't even know that the wild geese of autumn are covering the sky at this moment . . . At least I've achieved that – you no longer see the birds.'

She fell back as if exhausted.

'Oh, why did you love so many things, so many people and not me? . . . not me alone?'

She seemed to spit out these last words in a convulsion of rage in which all her overwrought self-absorption found expression.

'It was then that I swore to destroy you, *him, both of you,* by treachery, debasement, death at last, and the damnation of your souls! . . .'

The passion which rang in this dreadful statement struck Angélique like a blow, and for a long time the spasm which seized her seemed to be descending into her in deeper and deeper circumvolutions until it reached a zone of naked, abject fear which remained the only sensation she was capable of feeling at that moment.

'If she talks like this,' she said to herself like a child with terror, 'she must be sure of her victory. What are her powers? From whom does she hold them?'

She had already once before heard such hatred in a woman's voice, Madame de Montespan's . . . But this was even worse! 'The damnation of your soul.' Who could utter such a threat without being penetrated to the very marrow by an unrelenting hatred?

What was the good of struggling? She would never escape from such a will of destruction directed against her! . . .

She feared that her fingers on the handle of the brush and

comb would begin to tremble. Above all she feared that in a reflex of self-defence and horror she would rush upon the criminal woman and render her incapable of doing further harm by killing her, as she would have done to a wild beast that was attacking her. 'But be careful,' an inner voice warned her, 'such acts, however justified they may be, will cost you dear, and him even more so, and your children. What does one do when faced with a wild beast when one is unarmed? One keeps cool. Remember! That's your only chance . . . if there is one at all.'

Slowly she began to run her brush through her hair again. Then she shook her hair out over her shoulders.

Ambroisine was watching her without speaking. Night was coming.

Angélique rose and fetched a pewter candlestick from the chimney-piece, placed it beside the mirror on the table and lit the candle. The mirror showed her her reflection, a pale face half submerged in darkness as if under the surface of water. But she was surprised to find in her drawn features an unexpected, youthful expression. It had always been that way: anxiety and distress lent her features a youthful expression.

Ambroisine resumed:

'Abigail and her children, your favourites, those stinking Indians that you made laugh, the wounded men who waited for you as if you were their mother, and your kitten, and the bear . . . I was jealous of the bear and I was even jealous of old Miss Pidgeon when you went to console her after the death of that fat fool Patridge.'

'Did you kill him too?'

'I? What *are* you saying?'

The Duchess opened wide, innocent eyes.

'Don't you remember that he fought in single combat with Louis-Paul de Vernon?' said Angélique. 'The Jesuit had seen through you and he had to die. But how were you going to do it without attracting suspicion? A Jesuit doesn't let himself be killed as easily as that. Then, you yourself or one of your confederates spread a rumour among the English that they were to be taken off as prisoners to Canada. You knew that that was all that would be required to make the Pastor as dangerous as a wild boar.'

Ambroisine appeared to be delighted.

'Clever, wasn't it?'

Angélique's longing to strangle Ambroisine, or at least to

439

strike her, made her feel quite sick, but she betrayed no emotion, guessing that if she let herself go, she was in danger of going beyond the bounds of prudence.

Ambroisine appeared to be weary of failing to make her lose her temper. She got up from the hammock and went over to Angélique, who was watching her every movement. The young woman now had the same effect upon her as a venomous creature, and the mere smell of her scent made her feel ill; Ambroisine seemed amused to see her grow pale.

To give herself a countenance, she opened her handbag and began to put away her toilet accessories. Ambroisine mechanically glanced inside the bag and uttered an exclamation:

'What's that?'

She had glimpsed the lead bludgeon that Angélique had taken from the hands of the man Piksarett had killed on the beach at Saragouche.

'How did you come to possess such an object?' asked the Duchess gazing cruelly at Angélique, her eyes starting out of her head.

'One of the rogues in the Paris underworld gave it to me a long time ago.'

'That's not true!'

'And why not?'

Angélique's eyes were blazing:

'What concern is this wrecker's weapon to you, Madame de Maudribourg? Of what interest is it to you? How is it that you know that I could only have got this weapon from one of the bandits who finish off people wrecked on the shores of French Bay this season? You're the one who orders these crimes, aren't you? You're their mysterious leader? ... Belialith! ...'

She seized Ambroisine by the wrists.

'I'll unmask you,' she said with clenched teeth. 'I'll have you arrested and imprisoned ... You will be dragged to the Place de Grève! ... I'll denounce you to the Inquisitioner and have you burned as a witch! ...'

Angélique's rages had always disconcerted her opponents. They flared up at the very moment when those concerned were misled by her distinguished great lady's manners into thinking that she could never give way to vulgar outbursts of the type associated with the common people, and achieved their effect largely through the revelation they brought of the vulnerability of her heart.

'But you're frightening,' moaned Ambroisine. 'How can *you*

440

be so vindictive? . . . Oh! let me go, you're hurting me.'

Angélique released her so suddenly that she staggered backwards and half-collapsed on the hammock, where she sat rubbing her bruised wrists.

'You drove my bracelet into my flesh,' she complained in a tearful voice.

'I'd like to drive a knife into your heart,' retorted Angélique angrily, 'but that will come one day! You won't lose anything by waiting.'

Ambroisine again gazed at her in astonishment. Then throwing herself back in the hammock she began to toss and turn this way and that, twisting her arms and giving little inarticulate cries – babbling incoherent words that gradually became intelligible.

'Oh! Satan, my master,' she moaned, 'why did you compel me to attack her? She is unbelievably cruel . . . I can do no more. Why *her*? Why did he force me to attack *her*? Why did he come pestering me with his blue eyes as piercing as sapphires? . . . Why do you allow such beings to exist on the earth, you who are so easily moved by the baseness of others . . . deceived even by the perfection of beauty of a type often associated with foolishness, and unconsciously lulled into a sense of false security by an apparent offhandedness that they take for an admission of defeat, by verbal passages of arms in sophisticated style, whose latent hazards they do not discern . . . the most cunning enemies, the cruellest . . . could believe themselves masters of the situation and of the emotions of a woman upon whom they had made every possible onslaught . . .'

Angélique's anger was like a storm that blows up in a few seconds out of a cloudless sky – and before there is time to take in sail the treacherous unforeseen wave overturns the boat. The intensity of the feelings she was expressing had been such that it seemed that destiny was speaking through her. At the moment when, bending over the Duchess, she pronounced those terrible words, the flame of the Inquisition's fire seemed to blaze up between them, soaring aloft, crackling, roaring and consuming in cruel convulsions the fleshy body of the Demon, and Ambroisine herself had not remained unaffected by the force of the vision thus conjured up.

'Who is the master of the Universe . . .? "He" is stronger than you! . . . When will you finally bring him down? He has already escaped you once . . . oh my lovely childhood! He and his blue eye and his hands covered with blood! . . . He and Zalil streaming with human blood. We were all in Satan's hands! But he escaped you ... And now "He" is terrorizing me ... He has delivered me up to this dreadful creature ... to her, Angélique! She's called Angélique! Have pity! Have pity!'

She gave one more desperate groan, then relaxed and remained motionless, rigid as if in a state of semi-catalepsy. Angélique witnessed this delirium in a mixture of fear and depression. This woman was wicked, demoniacal, and above all, a raving lunatic. What possible way was there out of the situation?

When silence fell again, she remained, drained of strength, standing beside the table, listening to the flurries of wind around the hovel. From time to time the sound of men's voices could be heard, as they straggled up to the hamlet from the beach, and the call of a conch-shell, very far off, reminiscent in its nostalgic tones of the distant barking of sea lions.

A sinister limbo-region for beings who had lost God's favour, a purgatory where abandoned souls were destined to be the prey of the spirits of evil, and of torment so as to appreciate more fully the value of the Gods, on the day when it was vouchsafed to them to see the light once more ...

Ville d'Avray scratching at the door and coming in, with his amiable smile, his red heels, his flowered waistcoat and his plum-coloured frock-coat, struck Angélique as the most incongruous sight that could have been seen in this accursed place. But even the Marquis's smile was wiped from his face as if by magic when he caught sight of Ambroisine lying on his hammock.

'She's taken my hammock!'

He looked as put out as a spoilt child on finding that somebody else had been playing with his favourite toy. Severely annoyed, he went and sat on one of the log benches near the fireplace.

Angélique reported to him, in an undertone, her recent conversation with the Duchess and the threats which had been levelled at her.

Immediately his temper flared up.

'This time she's gone too far! Very well then! I will use my authority as Governor to have her arrested and put under surveillance.'

Then, realizing how unrealistic that plan was, he shook his head.

'There's nothing to be done, alas! We're caught. She's got in before us and now she's beginning to go on the rampage, while we stand helplessly by, a little group of undesirables who are increasingly at her mercy.'

He lowered his voice still more:

'The place is full of suspicious characters. I made the point to Nicolas Parys, the Bretons would be better occupied getting on with their cod-fishing than idling about the place armed to the teeth. I asked him what it all added up to. He said that they were not men from Marieun Aldouch's boat. "Well, who the dickens are those uncouth fellows who come lighting fires on your territory without asking permission?" I asked him. He seemed rather embarrassed. "I think," he said, "they come from two ships anchored to the south, on the other side of the Cape." I cottoned on. Our Duchess is bringing her accomplices in.'

He gave a wink.

'The eighty legions,' he whispered. Then recovering his gravity: 'Well, we'll fight on, that's all. From now on our safety depends on our cool-headedness, our vigilance and a rapid intervention on the part of Monsieur de Peyrac. We must hang out until then. Nevertheless, once we're out of this hornet's nest, I'll complain to Quebec, I'll take the matter even higher, I'll write to Paris. The people over there *will* persist in regarding the colonies as a dumping ground, and packing off their undesirables there, mad men and mad women too important to lock 'em up in the lunatic asylum at Bicêtre, like any ordinary Tom, Dick and Harry. You think, my dear, that it's just bad luck that you go off to the end of the world and there run into a Duchess possessed by the Devil playing fast and loose in complete liberty, but you're wrong! It's a result of the policies deliberately pursued by our royal officials. At the ends of the world, that's where you meet these mad women that the convents won't put up with any longer, nor the Court, nor the exorcisers, nor anyone in a decent position. It's just too bad for the people in the Antipodes who get landed with them. "They ought to have stayed at home", that's their view. When I think of all the bother I've had with this Messalina – my *Asmodeus* at the bottom of the sea, my birthday celebrations interrupted when they were just getting going properly . . . and you didn't even see Marceline opening her clams. It's heartbreaking! A whole season written off in fact. And who's to blame? Government officials blinder than moles, over in Paris, with their goose-quills stuck behind their ears, laying down the law on emigration policy to the colonies. But things are not going to go

on that way! I'm going to write to Monsieur Colbert himself –
I know him personally and so do you, I think. He's a hard-
working, able man, but he's too busy ... and what can you
expect from all these middle-class people that the King
favours, they don't grasp the finer points. They toil away like
beavers imagining that the world can be made to go round with
a blueprint on paper and that all you have to do to keep human
beings on the straight and narrow is to add up columns of
figures in a ledger. Oh well, nothing much you can do about it,
the world is changing!'

'Don't talk so loudly, she'll hear us.'

'No! she's in a state of catalepsy, and is completely unconscious. It's a cowardly way of running away from the strain of
living and from facing up to the consequences of one's
actions.'

He took his snuff box out of a pocket in the skirts of his coat
and took a pinch. His loud sneezes did not raise Ambroisine
from her leaden slumbers.

'Madness, possession, diabolical incarnation? ...' He did
not feel able to give a final verdict.

'It looks as if this evening she's been playing on admissions,
defeat, and the fear you aroused in her in order to move you to
pity; but don't let yourself be taken in. With creatures like her
it never means anything.'

Then, raising his voice and striking a different tone: 'Don't
stay standing there like a candle, Angélique,' he said. 'It's fresh
this evening. Come and sit by the fire and tell me all about your
past dealings with Monsieur Colbert. After all, we are on the
same side, aren't we?'

On emerging from the kind of lethargy that had overcome
her, the Duchess de Maudribourg found them talking quietly
by the hearthside about cocoa prices on the world market.

'Would you like me to see you home, dear lady?' offered the
Marquis gallantly, seeing her get up.

But Ambroisine merely threw him a baleful glance, made
straight for the door and went out.

CHAPTER 73

DEMONOLOGY, POSSESSION, madness!

Haunted by these words, Angélique awakened from her feverish sleep and for a few moments, everything seemed calm.

It was night on the Gulf of Saint Lawrence, with men asleep and snoring, an Indian crouching beside the embers, gnawing with his little, weasely teeth at a lump of elk fat, while the moon floated through the translucent mist . . .

Her fears and suspicions, everything seemed insane. She found it hard to remember that over the past few days two women had died, and that hidden threats hung over them, born of the homicidal fantasies of a crazed woman.

From the depths of the night came a harsh, rhythmic, hypnotic sound — the drums and shrill flutes of the redskins. 'They're beginning to drink themselves into a stupor,' Ville d'Avray had said. In the forests all about them whole peoples were about to break out in frenzy, to steep themselves in the magic of alcohol, of fire-water, the limpid, burning, corrosive source of dreams that linked them to their invisible gods.

Behind them lay those dangerous woods: in front lay the salt sea with its fog-bound horizon, whence it seemed that no help could ever come.

The fact remained that the sea had brought them Aristide with his boat, as welcome as any Noah's Ark. It was almost as if the Demon had been hoodwinked and had let these grotesque specimens of mankind slip by, mistaking for her own these drifters, who wandered wherever the crest of the wave swept them, peddling hardware and adulterated rum — the negrito, the bear, the whore, the hawker, the n'er-do-well . . . Wearing the masks of ancient farce, they had blundered into this well-regulated tragedy, without it being possible for anyone to say from what wings they had emerged, and it was perhaps a sign that the Demon was beginning to weaken before the blab and swagger of human beings and their incredibly untidy way of living, that he had suddenly and unscrupulously mixed up the playing cards which had been dealt out in such a calculating manner. Cantor had got away, Cantor would find his father, as he had found him in days gone by . . .

Ambroisine's cries, during that attack, whether feigned or real, had betrayed a certain degree of anxiety, a certain bewilderment. Certain images lost their impact, were deflated like a gold-beater's skin at the pin-prick of a simple, earthly reality. Angélique, tossing in her half-sleep saw a sapphire-coloured eye appear on Ambroisine's forehead, as she rode that mythical animal, the cruel, white unicorn that lives in the depths of the forest.

CHAPTER 74

THE UNICORN with its twisted horn was trying to enter the house, and as it battered the door frame the sun's rays glittered on its back of pure gold.

At last it succeeded in forcing its way into Angélique's room and behind it reared the hideously ugly tousled head of Captain Job Simon.

He stretched his long, gangling body to its full height, and his tousled grey hair almost touched the ceiling beams.

'I'm entrusting her to you, Madame,' he said in his thick voice. 'I'm going, but I can't take her with me.'

'But I don't want that creature here with me,' cried Angélique.

'Why not? She's not vicious.'

He laid one hand upon the neck of the gilded wooden unicorn.

'And she's lovely,' he murmured with love in his voice.

Angélique noticed that he had his sailor's bag slung over one shoulder.

'Are you leaving us?'

'Yes, I'm off.'

His face looked haggard, patchy with grey whiskers. He looked away.

'The other day it was the lass. Then the day before yesterday, Petronella . . . she was a good woman. We got on well together. I can't stay and watch this sort of thing any more, I'm going. I've had enough! I'm leaving with the ship's boy, he's all I've got . . .'

'You'll never get through,' said Angélique in a half-whisper. ' "They" are in the woods, "they" are even here now . . .'

Job Simon did not ask to whom she was referring.

'Yes I shall. I'll get by . . . only her . . . my unicorn . . . I'm leaving her for you to care for, Madame. I'll come back and fetch her whenever I can . . .'

'You'll never come back,' Angélique repeated. 'She'll never let you escape, she'll send her men after you, you know, those men who sank your ship and killed your crew.'

Old Simon looked at her with a frightened air but said nothing.

Then he made his way heavily over towards the door where the ship's boy with the wooden spoon stood waiting for him.

'Just one word, captain . . . before you take your secret to the grave,' Angélique asked, calling him back. 'You always knew you were nowhere near Quebec, didn't you, you a professional navigator? You knew you were meant to go to Gouldsboro in French Bay. How could you ever have allowed your reputation as a navigator to suffer so? And to have kept silent after what happened?'

'She paid me to do it,' he replied.

'How did she pay you?'

Once again he stared at Angélique with fear in his eyes. His lips began to tremble and she thought he was about to speak. But then he changed his mind and lowering his head went off followed by the ship's boy.

Soon after, Angélique, sitting wearily, alone with the unicorn, saw the Marquis de Ville d'Avray come in. In a state of great excitement he closed the door, locked it, then went over to check that the window was tightly closed and that no one could hear what he was about to reveal to her.

'I know *everything*,' he declared delightedly, 'and when I say everything, I *mean everything*.'

In his jubilation it did not occur to him to sit down and he went on talking as he paced up and down the room.

'Old Job Simon came to confess to me. He told me he would have gladly told you everything, but that he felt too ashamed, what with you being a lady, and all that. "Just because one has behaved like a so-and-so that isn't sufficient reason to go on doing so to the bitter end." Those were his very words, I'm just passing them on to you. In short he told me *everything* that he himself knew, and if you link it all with what Monsieur Paturel told us and the suspicions we have had about the Duchess of Maudribourg's association with those wreckers' ships, everything fits together and is perfectly clear! As I suspected, the whole thing seems to have started in one of those stinking holes in Paris where the royal officials push their pens. Job Simon in search of a lading, anxious to charter his ship, and looking for a sleeping partner, found himself enrolled in the plot which was already being hatched over there last year, whose objective was to cause the failure of any independent colonization schemes of Monsieur de Peyrac, your husband, on these shores which we consider – with justification, I might add in passing, dear Angélique, and without any trace of acrimony – as belonging by right to France ... It was therefore a question of discouraging an intruder from settling in French Bay, and they – here again we ought to determine who: let us call them the powers-that-be, decided to mount a joint action in order to rout out from the lands around Gouldsboro these troublesome people who were proving to be somewhat too enterprising, somewhat too sure of themselves, somewhat too rich, somewhat too unusual, somewhat too ... everything, goodness knows. Dangerous, in fact: in other words your husband and his followers.

'Then letters patent were given to the navigator Gold Beard, likewise in search of lands to populate, and it was left up to him to conquer the area shown to him, indeed sold to him, and to drive out the heretics who had settled there without authorization. That I imagine must have been how one of Colin's men, accompanying him to Paris, the man called Lopez whom you mentioned to me, came, while waiting around at Versailles, to exchange a few words with Job Simon, who had also been summoned there. Job Simon vaguely remembers him. They both found out that they were involved in the same business, namely to dislodge a certain Peyrac from the coast of Maine. And this would explain the words used by Lopez: "When you see the tall captain with the port-wine stain, you will know that your enemies are not far off."

'So much for the action that I might call exterior, or martial. Gold Beard could either have conquered the lands of Gouldsboro or have failed to do so ... which was in fact what happened, since the handful of wretched heretics he had been told about turned out to be your tough nuts of Huguenots from La Rochelle.

'They also feared that, even if Gouldsboro should fall to him, this might not be sufficient to destroy a man who already possessed numerous outposts and mines, and exercised great influence in the land. And this was precisely where a subtle machination came into play, that makes me vaguely suspect the source of the most virulent antipathy to Count Peyrac. Yes, on my oath,' Ville d'Avray went on meditatively, 'it was such a skilful plan that it makes me tremble with fear and admiration – I adore intellectual combinations, the skill of a brain capable of controlling human beings like so many pawns on a chess board, moving them from a distance by sheer insight into their innermost selves. So they decided – now listen closely – not only to try to crush Count Peyrac's growing material strength but also to destroy his *moral strength*. A disheartened man, who has lost his driving power, is no longer attached to a mere piece of land that holds bitter memories for him. At the worst he will leave the place, at the best commit suicide, or let himself die, and in any case one is rid of him! And it would seem that our diabolical Duchess was put in charge of this psychological side of things. Oh! what skill! It's staggering. Obviously it wasn't Job Simon who explained these subtleties to me. I'm piecing together the picture from what he told me and from what he thought he had understood, the poor man! He was just an unsophisticated fool to be used to provide an innocent-seeming cover for the arrival of the seductress upon the scene of action. A "benefactress" who was rich, pious, with her head in the clouds, accompanying a group of young women to be married in Quebec, being shipwrecked on the coast of Maine, and ensnaring the lord and master of the region in her coils ... that was a scheme worthy of her greedy, cunning imagination ... The only difficulty lay in persuading Job Simon to humour her every whim and to keep his mouth shut ... A Breton is no easy man to persuade, but our Duchess has her methods, and we know what they are. So much for the *Unicorn*! ... at least for its role in this plot ...'

'Sit down, will you, you're making my head go round,' Angélique interrupted, 'and please would you open the door again. It's stifling in here.'

Ville d'Avray opened the door.

'It's fascinating, isn't it?' he murmured. 'Have you anything to drink?'

Angélique pointed to a jug of water standing on the table. He quenched his thirst then delicately dabbed his lips. He was thinking hard.

'I presume,' he went on, 'that the Duchess of Maudribourg was entrusted with this delicate mission because it offered an opportunity of sending her a long way away, but also because she possesses a considerable fortune, enough to pay handsomely for assistance required, which is an important factor.'

Angélique decided to mention Father de Vernon's letter, which revealed some kind of collusion between Father d'Orgeval and Madame de Maudribourg.

'So everything is explained, everything falls into place. If she is his penitent, he must have sent her here to do penance. Was he really aware of her virulence and all the damage she could cause? Or will he admit that his predictions fell short of reality? Handling demons, like handling dangerous snakes, is not the easiest of skills to acquire.

'But what I find above all outrageous is that all these gentlemen in their cassocks should have started meddling in the affairs of Acadia without even informing me. They share out the cake in advance, they install themselves, they rule the roost, they send us black or white demons, and where do I come in? It's fantastic cheek! ... Not to mention the highway robbers with a price on their heads who are sent to plague our coasts. All kinds of people are mixed up in this affair – honest folk, pirates, somewhat dubious, but men of considerable stature like Gold Beard, downright criminals, and as we know, messengers from Hell.

'Let us recapitulate: Gold Beard is first to set out. After wintering in the Caribbean where he did various deals with the Spaniards, he sets sail, come the first days of spring, for Gouldsboro, attacks it and fails, and withdraws. But he is quite determined to get the better of Count Peyrac. So he captures the leader of his mercenaries, Kurt Ritz. And after that it was your turn, since chance had brought you to Casco Bay.[1] For meanwhile you have come into the picture. At first there was only Peyrac, a gentleman of fortune, lording it at his will over land and sea. Then suddenly there was a woman beside him, a woman who, like him, won men's hearts, fascinated them, added the strength of her presence to his own which had already shown how out-of-the-common it was. This was too much! Remember now: they had to break his moral strength. He was to be attacked at this vulnerable point. The ship or ships bearing Ambroisine's accomplices reached the mouth of French Bay. At Houssnock they tried to make you fall into the

1. See *The Temptation of Angélique*.

hands of the Canadians. Were you to die or be taken captive to Quebec, in what a weak position Monsieur de Peyrac would be when the French laid down conditions for his surrender. But you escaped them. Chance brought you to Gold Beard's ship. Father de Vernon came to take you off it again. On his return from New York, he had been sent a message instructing him to get hold of you. But by whom? Was this a step decided on by Ambroisine's accomplices or by the man I guess pulls all the strings in this affair? Gold Beard bowed to the Jesuit. From then on you were in the hands of those who wanted to force Monsieur de Peyrac to give up. But here again things did not turn out "as usual", as our charming Duchess was later to complain. Father de Vernon, who knew that you were an important pawn in the game that was being played, but who saw no urgent reason either to kill you or to hold you in captivity, allowed you to return safe and sound to Gouldsboro.

'From that moment on, I must admit that I am a trifle muddled. It seems that some men from an unknown ship tried to use Gold Beard to cause trouble between you and your husband in order to provoke a general massacre among all your people ... What exactly happened, my dear Angélique? ... Tell me about it.'

'No,' Angélique replied, 'those are personal problems, and in any case I am terribly tired.'

'That's mean of you,' complained Ville d'Avray, disappointed, 'I go to unbelievable lengths to unravel all this tangled skein instead of you and you refuse to confide in me ...'

'I promise I'll tell you all the details one day ...'

'When we're in Quebec?' exclaimed Ville d'Avray joyously.

'Yes, that's it, when we're in Quebec,' Angélique agreed. 'But for the moment suffice it to say that you have guessed rightly. They'd calculated everything so that we'd kill one another. Do you think that Ambroisine was in the offing at that time?'

'No, but her accomplice, the bandit in charge of the two ships, was. He may well have been responsible for that Machiavellian plan. He is as diabolical a male as she is a female, I'll tell you about him in a moment.'

'I've seen him. He's the pale man, isn't he? I only saw him once, when he came and told me: "Monsieur de Peyrac wants to see you on Old Ship Island." It's strange, I was very tired after that long day of battle which I'd spent assisting the wounded. All I thought was: how pale he is, like a dead man.

But he did not frighten me, and I followed him without misgivings.'

'That is one of the characteristics of infernal spirits that take on human form. If they were to frighten people, no one would fall into their snares. And they usually appear when one's intuition is weary and one's vigilance relaxed.'

Angélique could still see that scene. She had followed the man across the Bay uncovered by the receding tide. And there on the island was Colin waiting for her ... while Joffrey de Peyrac had been told in an anonymous note that she was on the island *with her lover*. So he had gone there, and had seen her on the island with Colin ... a whole night long. The two of them ... and him, watching ...

The Marquis paused, waiting for her to tell him her secret, then seeing that she said nothing, went on:

'Very well!' he said with a sigh. 'I won't insist. You can tell me all about it in Quebec when we are sitting comfortably by my Dutch stove. Meanwhile, I'll merely recall that your enemy Gold Beard suddenly found himself Governor of Gouldsboro, while Monsieur de Peyrac remained proprietor of the territory. A fine turn of events, which cannot exactly have pleased our Machiavellian plotters. It must have been at that stage that the *Unicorn* appeared on the scene. Whether Ambroisine always intended right from the start to sacrifice the ship, her crew and even the girls in her charge, in order to make her allegedly unexpected arrival appear more convincing, or whether she reached this decision when she realized that, after all the efforts that had been made, neither Monsieur de Peyrac's armed strength nor his morale seemed to have been in the slightest impaired ... My guess is that she had always planned to commit these crimes, being obliged to eliminate certain persons who it had not been possible to take into her confidence or who knew too much. And then there always comes a moment, with certain people, when the lust to kill becomes a mania and gets out of hand. Only terrible catastrophes and a vast number of victims can give them a sense of power or even satisfy their erotic feelings. With those accomplices waiting for her on the beach, armed with lanterns, Job Simon, who had never been in the area before, thought he had reached his destination. They sent out a dinghy to pick her up before the ship struck and sank ...'

'Why did she try to save Jeanne Michaud's child?'

'Just another piece of play-acting! A device to reinforce the impression that she was a woman of moral grandeur, virtue, dedication and selflessness. She must have been composing in her own mind her future "Life of Saint Ambroisine" in the style of the reading-matter in which she had steeped herself in the convents. The scene of her arrival as victim of a shipwreck was most moving, wasn't it?'

'Yes, indeed it was!'

'But skilful, cunning and perverse as she is, had she not on occasion sacrificed prudence to her femininity?' thought Angélique. She had gone off to join her accomplices and there put on her red stockings, although she knew that they might cause surprise, even doubts and suspicions, even in a simple girl like Marie-la-Douce, who, as her chamber-maid, knew exactly what her mistress had brought with her on board the *Unicorn* from France. Then on another occasion it was that scarlet-lined cloak that she brought back from a trip at sea, and Angélique had wondered at it, and at her perfume . . . yes, her perfume! Had anyone ever been rescued from a shipwreck with shining, perfumed hair? . . .

'And I, a woman, I let myself be taken in by that!' Angélique told herself.

But of course her hair should have been soaking wet and sticky with sea water. Whereas what had first struck Angélique had been the scent and the beauty of that dark hair, like a silken mantle spread over her shoulders. She cared for her hair with a kind of idolatry. Never could she have steeled herself to neglect that hair, nor to go without her perfume even for a few days. And it had been a case of feminine aberration when she had said to Angélique:

'My perfume . . . do you like it? I'll give you some.'

And Angélique had replied: 'But I thought you had lost the bottle in the shipwreck.'

And the reason why Madame Carrère had been worried by the Duchess's clothes, repeating on several occasions: 'Those stains, those tears, there's something funny about them', was it not because, as a careful and experienced housewife, it had seemed to her that the damage *had been done on purpose*. Doctoring clothes of fine quality so that they resemble garments damaged by salt water, rocks, sand and seaweed, is not an easy skill to acquire, nor a gift given to everyone, and furthermore, Ambroisine, who seemed to be particularly attached to these brightly-coloured things, had found it impossible deliberately to spoil them really effectively. These were tiny details, the slightest slips in a plan prepared by a master hand, but which in an obscure way had awakened the suspicions of the victims and enabled them bit by bit to discover the trick and to analyse how it had been done.

'And what about the leader of the gang with the leaden cudgels, the pale man, who is he? Petronella told me that he was Ambroisine's brother.'

'Job Simon said he was her lover, her acknowledged lover. All right then, let us say her brother and her lover. Incest isn't the sort of thing to put her off.'

'Yes, I can see that; the son of some abandoned priest or of that high-ranking witch who begot him with Satan one witches' sabbath night. Do you know, they say that the seed of Satan is icy cold. How disagreeable that must be! What do you think? . . . But why are you laughing, Angélique my dear?'

'You do ask such funny questions,' she replied, exploding with mirth.

Dusk had fallen, a deep pulpy orange colour, the stink of cod became still more oppressive while their anxiety and suspense grew to more dramatic proportions. But a crack was becoming apparent in the façade of Ambroisine's behaviour.

As she had passed by Angélique's room she had heard her laugh and the kind of detachment and calm displayed by Angélique and the Marquis de Ville d'Avray stirred up her doubts and fears. She was unable to understand the reason for her feelings and it was as if the suspicion she might be dealing with a hitherto unknown species of creature, stronger than herself, occasionally dismayed her. The spirit may be willing but the flesh is weak, and the body of the Demon was also beginning to flag beneath the tension of those interminable hours. The mask, so carefully preserved, was beginning to crack, revealing the marks of age on her lovely face, as if under the accumulation of wickedness, lies and crimes, a ripe abscess was beginning to burst and to exude, drop by drop, into the light of day, an expression of the most terrifying dementia.

By now Angélique was beginning to cough and she felt herself burning with fever, while dark rings surrounded her enlarged eyes.

Another night to get through.

'You are not well,' Ville d'Avray told her as he was about to leave. 'Allow me to help you undo your dress and put you to bed.'

Angélique refused his help, thanking him and saying that it was nothing, just a bit of a cough that had come upon her. She would go to sleep and tomorrow would feel better again.

'But you are wrong not to accept my help,' said Ville d'Avray, mildly put out. 'To my sick friends I'm a veritable sister of mercy. You're too independent, Angélique, too sure of yourself, for a woman . . . Well, at least prepare a warm stone for your feet.'

When he left her that evening she had to admit to herself that he was right. She was aching all over and had the greatest difficulty in preparing herself for the night. She could not even summon up enough strength to warm a stone in the hearth, as he had advised her to do. So with icy cold feet and a burning face she tried to get to sleep. Her bed felt hard, her covers weighed down upon her. She was stifling. Awakening from a restless sleep which she found it impossible to estimate as having been long or short, she got up to unbar the window. Piksarett was keeping watch outside while the Governor's men along with Barssempuy and Defour likewise took turns at keeping watch. She had nothing to fear, although it seemed to her that no guard, no walls could protect her adequately from the threats that hung over her . . .

She wanted to leave the candle burning, but the wind blew it out. She found it impossible to sleep again and now she felt cold.

Through the open window the night was beginning to grow grey, although still opaque and scarcely contrasting with the dusky black foliage of a tree against the roof, but sufficiently grey for her to have glimpsed a human shape flitting by, blocking for a brief moment the rectangle of the window. Immediately she realized that someone had entered her room and was standing against the wall on the right.

With one hand on her pistol butt she lay there on the alert, trying to catch the sound of breathing. Nothing. Nothing but the tiny tinkling of shells followed by a familiar smell. Piksarett! The redskin! . . .

Then she gave up any idea of striking a light. If he had decided to watch over her in her room, he must have his own reasons! And surprisingly enough, she fell asleep almost immediately, relaxed at last.

She awoke to the sound of a struggle.

It sounded like an animal leaping heavily on to the floor. Dawn was still far off.

This time Angélique did strike a light and saw Piksarett overpowering someone on the ground.

'He entered your house.'

'Who is it?'

The candlelight revealed the gaunt, terrified face of a young sailor, probably a Breton from one of the cod-fishing vessels.

'What are you doing in my room?'

The boy's lips trembled and he was unable to utter a single sound. The thought crossed her mind that perhaps he did not know any other tongue than his Celtic dialect.

'What did you want of me?'

Finally he managed to speak.

'To ask for your help . . . Madame.'

'But why?'

' "They" are after me,' said the young man, whom Piksarett was holding on his knees before Angélique. 'For four days now I've been trying to escape from them in the forest, I can't shake them off my trail. It's the Pale One who's the worst, the cleverest. I don't know who "they" are but I know they want to kill me.'

'But why should they want to kill you?'

'Because I saw who pushed the girl over the cliff the other day. But he saw me too . . . and ever since then I've been on the run from them . . .'

She remembered the Breton captain complaining that his men were beginning to desert and that one of his lads had vanished . . .

'You're one of the cod-fishers, aren't you?'

'Yes . . . I do the drying, up and down the "strand" all day long. I'm less under surveillance than the others. It was hot and I wanted to go and pick some raspberries. I know a good place for them near the Breton cross. There was a ship just put in for water, and work was slack, so I made the most of it, and went up there. And . . . I saw him . . .'

'Who was it?'

The wretched boy glanced fearfully about him and whispered:

'The man with the glasses, the pen-pusher who works for the Duchess.'

'Armand Daveau?'

He nodded.

He told them how he had seen the young woman arrive and the secretary say something to her, and point to two baskets standing beside the cross. She had set off to collect them when the secretary, following swiftly behind her on tip-toe, and choosing the moment when she was only a short distance from the edge of the cliff, had given her a violent push.

'It never occurred to me to hide, and when he turned round, he saw me ... so I ran off into the woods ... I wanted to get back to the beach and tell my captain, then I thought that that would be useless. He's mad about that Duchess, quite lost his head over her has Marieun Aldouch. And yet he's a tough nut too. But she ... I thought I'd try to make for another beach up north, and get away with some fishermen from Saint Malo when they sail for home at the end of the season. I know the area and knew how to get there. I've been here every year ever since I was old enough to be a ship's boy. But I soon realized that there were men out after me. So I went to earth, and hid as best I could, but get away from them, impossible! Then it occurred to me to come to you for help, to you, Madame, because I knew that you have nothing to do with this gang of thugs. One night when I was up a tree and they didn't know, I heard them talking round a fire, talking about the Duchess who is their leader, whom they call Belialith, and they talked about you too, and Monsieur de Peyrac your husband. They said that she would have to make up her mind to kill you before he came back, because although she's a formidable woman, you might prove more than a match for her. That was what gave me the idea of trying to get back to the village under cover of night and come back to you for help and assistance.'

He clasped his hands together and held them out to her, trembling.

'If you really are more than a match for her, noble lady, come to my help!'

Piksarett, in spite of the Breton's rough accent, seemed to have followed the gist of his story.

'What can we do?' asked Angélique, turning to him.

'I shall take him to Uniakke,' the redskin replied, 'he's in a strong position, and now we are here in force. His relatives the Mic-Macs have come up from the big village of Truro, and I'd like to see the Malecites try objecting to that. And in any case they are drunk and no longer know what they're saying, nor what they want; one day they listen to the men in the two ships, lying at anchor behind the Cape, who bring them fire-water, then the next they listen to Uniakke, who is a great chief and who tells them that the wild geese desert the ponds of tribes who go mad in the autumn at the very moment they are preparing to visit them.

'They too will join us when the day of vengeance comes, and the day is nigh when the Children of Dawn will come out of the woods to take the scalps of your enemies and of those who killed our brothers.'

CHAPTER 75

IN ORDER to make their getaway and reach the refuge of the woods, they had to make the most of the remaining darkness. Piksarett had his bow and arrows, and under his protection, the young man would be able to reach the Mic-Mac encampment safe and sound. The two figures slipped outside and were immediately swallowed up by the darkness.

Angélique was shivering, racked with fever. She was coughing and felt tempted to curl up once more under her uncomfortable blankets but told herself that she must make good use of the fact that she was up and about to attend to herself a little – make herself a drink, put a dressing on her foot, which was once again showing signs of turning septic – otherwise she would find herself devoid of strength, and any one could come and strangle her in her bed like the bewitched queens of yore, without her even being capable of pressing the trigger of her pistol.

She threw a handful of gorse on to the still glowing ashes and hobbled across the room to fetch some water from the bucket and fill a small pot which she hung over the fire. Then she tore up a piece of lint, prepared some balm, selected some herbs to make an infusion and sat down on the hearthstone while she waited for the water to come to the boil.

Her efforts had exhausted her and she was bathed in perspiration, so she wrapped a blanket round herself, fixing it firmly round her shoulders in Indian fashion. She rested her forehead against the stone hearth and watched the flames dancing, letting herself drift into a state of half-sleep in which her thoughts, lucid and bright, kept floating – painlessly, she might have said – through her head but had no power over her actions.

As for the woman who entered the room, taking advantage of the half-open door which Angélique had not thought to lock, not even to close after Piksarett's departure, she became aware of her less as a human presence than as a spirit that glided towards her, a ghost which might equally well have entered through the walls, and had lost its power to frighten because it was no longer a thing of flesh and blood.

It occurred to her incidentally that Piksarett was no longer there to defend her, that she might well have to call for help, to arm herself. But her instinct told her that the danger did not threaten – not yet – her life. So she made no move. The spirit was paying her a visit. It was all a game, blows would be exchanged, a little blood spilled, a scratch inflicted. It was nothing! The other woman would retire, licking her wounds. She must hold out. Tomorrow, or the day after, Joffrey would be here . . .

'I saw a light in your window . . .' said Ambroisine. 'Weren't you asleep? . . . Don't you ever sleep?'

She wanted to take her revenge. She leaned on the cowl above the rustic fireplace and the glow from the flames, lighting her features from below, threw them into relief as is frequently done in pictures of Mephisto, at the time when he rose up before Faust's eyes from the flames of Hell; outlined in black, her long eyes looked like liquid gold, the curve of her eyebrows seemed enormous, the bony structure, thus thrown into relief, stripped her face of its habitual grace and transformed it into a mask made up of shadows and planes of alabaster whiteness.

She looked neither beautiful nor ugly. Merely strange. Like a statue with hollow eye-sockets through which a pair of human eyes looked out.

It occurred to Angélique that, seated as she was on the hearthstone, she was lighted in a different manner, which gave her the advantage. But this relative satisfaction was fleeting, for she was seized with a fit of coughing and had to go in search of her handkerchief.

'You are ill,' said Ambroisine with intense jubilation. 'You see what power I have over you. In just a few days you have lost your exuberant good health.'

'Anyone can catch a cold,' Angélique replied, 'these are things that constantly happen to people without any necessity to summon up all the minions of Hell to help.'

'And you're still joking,' said Ambroisine, grinding her teeth, 'you are incorrigible! Don't you realize that you are going to die . . . You should already have died a hundred times . . . The reason why you are not dead already, is that I didn't *really* want you to die . . . but the day I sign the decree . . .'

'No, that's not the reason. It's because I have *baraka*.'

'*Baraka?*'

'It's a charm. The Arabs said I had *baraka*. *Mektoub*: "thus it is". It means that I cannot die by the contrivance of my enemies.'

'What nonsense!'

But Angélique's explanation had given the Duchess cause for anxiety. She began to pace up and down, draped in her great black cloak. Now she looked beautiful again with her hair spread out over her shoulders, her perfect face, bold and full of life, and her red lips revealing the glint of the edge of her teeth.

'Tell me,' Angélique asked her suddenly, taking advantage of the momentary dismay she sensed, 'what is Father d'Orgeval to you?'

'I've known him all my life,' Ambroisine replied. 'The three of us grew up as children together in the country, in the Dauphiné. There never were three children as strong as we were. We were full of fire, inhabited by a thousand lively spirits. Our chateaux were close to one another – dismal, haunted places, and those who lived in them were stranger and more unpredictable than the ghosts. There was his father, a fierce, terrifying man, who used to take him with him to massacre Protestants, then there was my mother, the magician, who knew the art of poisons, and my father the priest, who used to call up the Devil, and my nurse, Zalil's mother, who was a witch and taught him to nail bats on to fences round the fields and to put dead toads on people's doorsteps. But he was the strongest of all of us with his magical blue eye. Why did he betray us? Why did he join that army of black men with their crosses on their hearts? He wanted to range himself on the side of Good. He is mad. But one can never wipe out what has been. He knows me, he knows what can be got from me, and sometimes I enjoy serving him as I did in the old days. On the very edge of Hell we become accomplices again . . . Do you understand? For example, the day you are vanquished . . . then I shall have come back to him again . . . And perhaps he will think of me. His scorn, his abstractedness, his superiority, all these are like a red-hot iron to me. One day I shall ask Zalil to kill him.'

'Who is Zalil?'

Ambroisine made no reply. She gave two or three convulsive shudders and closed her eyes as if reliving the days that were gone.

Things were falling into place. Zalil must be the Pale Man, the brother whom Petronella Damourt had mentioned. 'There was my nurse, Zalil's mother! . . .' An infernal alliance, but one which had grown less daunting as it took on earthly shape: a noble lady, using her fortune to make conquests and do good works, in the name of God and the King; her lover, a pirate, who helped her in this work. A terrestrial plot. Of these three children 'shot through' by fire, each one had gone his own way. One had become a Jesuit, another the noble Duchess of Maudribourg with her dazzling intellect, while the third had become the man with the lead cudgel. The fanatical passions that lived on with them continued to be the common factor linking their different fates.

'So you see,' said Ambroisine, opening her eyes again with a smile, 'I'm telling you everything and now you are beginning to know it all. And that is why you will have to die now. I have hesitated for a long time! I left it to fate to decide. I was fascinated to see how you managed constantly to triumph over danger. The *baraka*? . . . No, I don't think so. It was my indecision that protected you. But now my mission has lasted too long, and I must make an end of it. You will die tomorrow.'

She spoke in a monotonous, affected voice. This lack of harmony between her sophisticated tones and the content of her words betrayed a certain disorder in her thoughts. Angélique replied in the same tone.

'Thank you for warning me. I shall endeavour to make the necessary arrangements, in accordance with your plans.'

Ambroisine cast her a furious glance.

'Do you always joke about everything?'

'Oh no, not always, not by any means . . .'

'You really do look dreadful,' the Duchess of Maudribourg went on, apparently reassured by Angélique's obvious malaise. 'You are not as strong as you make yourself out to be, but I like to see you putting up a good fight. You have the vitality of a seagull. Do you know who once made that compliment about you to me? A man called Desgrez. A very curious man, too curious . . . In other words a policeman. I must admit that one of my chief reasons for leaving France was so as not to have to run into him too often. He was somewhat too interested in my friend Madame de Brinvilliers, your neighbour in Paris; but perhaps you don't remember her . . . But she remembers you, and the parties you used to give in your house at Beautreillis.[1] What a monster that François Desgrez is! I told Marguerite that she ought to follow my example and get out . . . it will cost her dear if she doesn't . . . But so much the worse for her. But it was he who, one day when we were talking about Madame du Plessis-Bellière, the King's mistress who disappeared so mysteriously, said that you had the vitality of a seagull . . . He seemed to know you well . . . strange, isn't it? I was already attracted to you through your legend . . . and here I find you with the man I have been commissioned to destroy in America . . . The world is dominated by a handful of people . . . All the others have just walk-on parts, they're mere dust . . . What a pleasure to have to face you and triumph over you. My pleasure was already increased tenfold . . . To know you well enough to make you stumble, you who had held your own against the King, to have you at my mercy. Every human being possesses a chink in their armour, some crack through which fear will come welling up, and through which their strength will seep away. I was determined to find that crack. What an exciting mystery your personality was! It was not an easy matter. Your perspicacity, that instinct of yours which I felt to be ever wakeful. How frightened I was that day when you said to me: "It was not mere chance that brought you here . . ." I don't remember now how I managed to distract you from that idea!

'But now here at last you have been defeated, you are lost . . . and that is why I have decided that you are to die.'

'No, that is not the reason. The truth is that you want to get rid of me before he gets here. Someone you are frightened to confront, my husband, Count Peyrac. Tomorrow he may be here, and then all your lies will be made manifest, and the entire structure you have created to deceive those about you will crumble. Then you will find yourself alone, with no one to succour you, and will have to face the punishment that awaits you.'

Ambroisine showed no shock at her words, merely surprise.

1. See *Angélique: The Road to Versailles*.

'You do surprise me,' she murmured disdainfully, 'are you still not convinced that your Count Peyrac no longer belongs to you? . . . What do I have to show you by way of proof in order to convince you that he is my lover? How naïve you are! As soon as he set eyes on me in Gouldsboro, he was fascinated by me, he told me so . . .'

As soon as Ambroisine mentioned Joffrey, Angélique felt as if her blood withdrew from her veins. She had the impression that her heart grew smaller, stopped beating. That was it, in her case, the crack Ambroisine had mentioned earlier with such knowing and diabolical intuition . . . that crack which all human beings have within them, through which 'fear wells up and one's strength seeps away'.

She said nothing, gathering all her willpower together so that nothing should be apparent.

'What a sensation!' the Duchess murmured. 'From the very first moment to arouse the admiration and desire of such a man! I had heard said of him that although he was a man of free morals, he was not an easy man to seduce. That one woman only seemed ever to have captivated his heart, if he had a heart. The woman who lived with him at the moment and who claimed to be his wife. It was going to be a difficult road . . . yes, indeed . . . but all the more exciting for that. *You! He!* And from the very first moment, from that very first look, such a victory . . .'

'You're getting a bit muddled, I think,' Angélique remarked coldly. 'Didn't you tell me just recently how you had suffered when you woke up and saw the two of us at your bedside, and realized that we loved one another . . .'

'Ah yes, but how silly I was to worry about that . . . The very next day he sent me a love-letter! And now you're busy consoling yourself with the thought of the loving words he spoke to you that night . . . But he had already set eyes on me, and wanted to lull your suspicions, so that he should be free to pay his court to me . . .'

Joffrey! Joffrey! Standing there at Ambroisine's bedside, his enigmatic glance fixed on that divine figure, which, acting the part of a sick woman raving in delirium, she had revealed shamelessly to him. And Adhémar, the tragic fool, busy commenting on the scene:

'That's what you'd call a handsome woman, you really can say that's a fine figure of a woman, can't you, Monsieur le Comte?'

How vile! How unbearable! Angélique felt a wave of hysterical laughter begin to sweep over her at the mere thought of Adhemar. She must control herself and not let herself go. There in spite of everything was Adhemar's face superimposed on her vision of that unbearable scene. It was irresistible! Oh, how it hurt!

Not to know what Joffrey was thinking at that moment! How painful it was to her that he should still be so little known. Would she always be alone on earth?

'How difficult you are to hurt,' whispered Ambroisine as she observed her with cruel attention . . . 'You are so beautiful and so moving . . . that I would almost like to . . . cede you victory . . . but that's impossible! . . . I want you to know everything . . . Yes, the day after that he sent me a note, practically a letter, in which he told me in unforgettable terms what an impression I had made on him, that he also knew my Sorbonne degrees, that he was delighted to have me in his domains, and rejoiced at the prospect of being able at last to discourse with a truly learned mind, for he was cruelly deprived of such pleasures in America, and that in addition to this satisfaction, it was a still greater pleasure to him to meet so pretty a woman, and so on with so many delightful compliments that I had to re-read the letter several times in order to take it all in . . .'

Angélique's arm had risen almost mechanically towards Ambroisine.

'What do you want?' asked the latter, breaking off and looking uncomprehendingly at the open hand.

'Show me that letter.'

A glint shot through her enemy's wild eyes.

'You really are extraordinary! Aren't you frightened of suffering?'

'I have known worse,' Angélique replied with an air of detachment, thinking within herself that this was untrue and that never had she known anything worse than what she was experiencing at this moment, this crushing agony that forced her to doubt him, to be on the point of receiving the tangible proof of his betrayal and of losing him forever.

'And supposing I were to tell you that I didn't keep the note.'

'Then I would tell you that you have lied to me and that I don't believe a single word of all you have just told me.'

'In that case so much the worse for you.'

Ambroisine raised her hand to the pearl-studded alms-purse she always wore at her belt.

'I did keep it. I like re-reading what he wrote to me in those first days of our acquaintance . . . I know how to savour what comes from him. Men enjoy flattery. Perhaps you were not sufficiently appreciative of the way he treated you, since he has grown weary of you.'

The whole of Angélique's life hung on those female fingers, as they searched among the various objects in the purse.

'If she can't find it, she's lying,' she told herself again.

'Ah, here it is,' said Ambroisine.

Angélique recognized the vellum Count Peyrac used in Gouldsboro and when Ambroisine had opened the letter as she turned it towards her, she also recognized from afar his rapid scholarly handwriting.

'Give it me!' she repeated.

As she sat there huddled up on the hearthstone, clutching her blanket about her, holding out one hand, she realized that she must look like a beggar.

But she was too weak to stand up and face Ambroisine on equal terms.

'You are so pale,' Ambroisine remarked with a spiteful smile, 'you are on the point of collapse . . . It's curious but you are really the only person who has ever inspired me with something like pity.'

Then, appearing to make up her mind, she went on:

'No, I don't want you to read the words of love he sent to me . . . they would finish you off . . . I want to spare you.'

And she leaned forward to catch a flame to the letter she held in her hand.

But Angélique was too quick for her, and shot out her own hand, grasping Ambroisine's and tearing the letter from it.

'Tigress!' cried Ambroisine.

She looked down in dismay at her wrist, which was oozing a few drops of blood. Angélique's nails had dug into her flesh.

'By burning that letter she wanted to leave me in doubt,' Angélique thought, 'so that I should never know what he *really* wrote to her.'

She was trembling so violently that she had to wait a moment before she could decipher the words that danced up and down before her eyes. She already knew, because of what Ambroisine had done, that all she would find would be harmless words.

And indeed all it consisted of was a series of mathematical formulae and some figures.

But so terrible had been the experience she had been through that she did not even feel any relief upon the discovery of Ambroisine's lie.

'So once more,' she said, looking at Ambroisine, 'once again you have tried to deceive me . . . you never received any love-letters from him . . . Just another of your vile games. You managed to get him to write you this on some pretext or other, or else you stole it from him in Gouldsboro, just as you stole his doublet. You were forever ferreting about everywhere, preparing your schemes. But your tricks are pretty crude . . .'

A cock crowed outside. Dawn was breaking.

Ambroisine carefully dabbed at her delicate skin where it had been broken.

'You really are unbelievably nasty and brutal,' she said.

She backed towards the door with that shifty, childish look she wore every time things didn't go the way she wanted them to . . .

'Don't look at me like that. Your eyes haunt me. When you are dead, I shall stab them through and through.'

CHAPTER 76

UTTERLY EXHAUSTED, Angélique barricaded her door and fell on to her bed. Oh! These appearances that Ambroisine put in! On every occasion she poured out a corrosive fluid that sapped all resistance. 'The next time . . . I shall be unable . . . unable . . . to bear her any longer . . .'

All Ville d'Avray's verve and his very French courage, in the style of the little lace-bedecked Marquis, would no longer be capable of safeguarding her from the demoniacal hold Ambroisine was gaining over her.

A demon succubus, with a ravishingly lovely face, sweeping back and forth on a whirling gust of wind. A nightmare! A symbol! The eternal enemy hovering at her bedside, trying to force her door, the door to the fortress of her heart, where she kept her love . . . Once already the accursed legions had despoiled it all.

She was shaking with fever. Her mind was wandering. She

had told Colin to have no fear, for she would never become mad!

And now the Demon had led her to the very gates of peril. Then she had a burst of renewed energy: 'No, I will not give you *that*, you vile creature, you demon spirit! Impure spirit!' Holding the crumpled piece of paper with its cabalistic signs clasped tight between her fingers brought her no relief. Her fear had been too profound, was too closely linked with the fear that had haunted her for many a long year, a fear stirred up by the strange evocation of old names, so totally unexpected in this place, that she thought she must have dreamt that she had heard them come from Ambroisine's lips: Desgrez the policeman, the house at Beautreillis, the Marquise du Plessis-Bellière . . . the lovely Marquise who had so mysteriously vanished. It was she, who had landed up today in a hovel in America, once again playing out her destiny, as if life would never finish sharpening its pen to write up before her, in constantly more demanding terms, its eternal challenge.

Everything was converging at a single point. It was like one of those balls of prickly debris carried on to a beach by a storm; gradually it grew bigger and bigger and rolled towards her to crush her. She saw an avalanche of faces tumbling about her: the Pale One, Old One-Eye, Saddy, the Invincible Man, all eighty-four legions! . . .

CHAPTER 77

'MADAME DE PEYRAC! Madame de Peyrac!'

Someone was drumming on her door and she heard women's voices calling her. With an effort she shook off her painful torpor and staggered over to remove the bar she had placed across the door after Ambroisine's departure.

The sun was already high in the sky and it was very hot. At first it seemed to her dazed eyes that someone had placed two tall tree trunks on her threshold, encompassing a tiny poppy, then her troubled vision grew clearer and she realized bit by bit that it was tall Marceline with her daughter Yolande who stood there holding by the hand between them Cherubino with his red cap.

'It's us, come to see you,' said Marceline cheerfully. 'We were worried about you. So Yolande and I said to one another, let's go and make a trip to the East Coast.'

She came in, and after closing the door, said:

'To tell the truth, I had a message from your friend in Gouldsboro, Madame Berne. She asked me to keep an eye on you, saying that she was very worried about you, that she felt sure that you were in danger . . . And if your looks are anything to go by, Madame la Comtesse, she mayn't have been that far wrong.'

'I'm not well,' Angélique murmured.

'That I can see, poor thing. But never fear. Now I'm here and you will be able to stay in bed and I shall look after you properly!'

Dear Abigail. Angélique felt her affection through Marceline's presence as she began to peel vegetables to make stock.

'You've caught a chill. It's always like that on the coast. It's a rotten place! During the day you're burning hot and at night the icy fog goes right through you. Everyone's coughing and spitting . . .'

The Marquis, attracted by the general commotion, joined them and upon catching sight of Yolande and Cherubino, threw up his hands in dismay:

'Great heavens, woman,' he cried, turning to Marceline, 'how could you possibly bring that sensitive child and that pure young girl to an infernal place like this? I hardly dare to say so, but we are literally under attack from demons.'

'There are no demons that can't be got the better of,' Marceline retorted, settling her Cherubino on her knees, 'I couldn't have left him behind, he would have got up to too much mischief. And talking of demons, you can count this little lad among them. As for Yolande, she's capable of knocking Satan himself out with a single blow. Aren't you, Yolande? Don't worry about us, Governor! It's you who shouldn't have left Madame de Peyrac here, all helpless, sick as she is; that wasn't right of you, I declare . . .'

'But I did offer to look after her, but she wouldn't have it . . .' Ville d'Avray lamented. 'Great ladies lack the necessary simplicity.'

The wind was changing. By her mere presence, the tall, straight-speaking Marceline, who would not readily allow Ambroisine to distil her poison, was driving back the circle of darkness.

This became still more evident when that evening a strange ship sailed into port, and they saw the Basque harpooning captain, Hernani d'Astiguarra, walking up the slope followed by some of his crew. A young whale had got caught up in forty fathoms of net and the Bretons had been busy trying to disentangle it ever since the previous day. The men were extremely worked up about this set-back, and they at once set on the Basques who had come to recover their prize, insulting them, swinging blows at them, and even pelting them with stones. The reaction to this attack was prompt, for Hernani was not a man to be lightly taken advantage of.

'Avast, you Breton lubbers,' he cried, brandishing his terrible harpoon, 'or your stinking strand will be covered in blood. My oath, your brine has gone to your heads!'

'They're quite crazy,' he told Angélique a little later when they had renewed acquaintance, and she had invited him to take a little refreshment with her. She no longer had the little barrel of armagnac which he had given her, but they talked about it, and about Monhegan and midsummer night.

Well looked after by Marceline, she was already beginning to feel better, and the arrival of the tall Basque captain who had shown her such friendliness seemed a good omen.

He examined her carefully with his glowing eyes, no doubt noting the signs of tension that still remained on her pale face.

'Yes, the autumn wind is devilish along these shores,' he agreed. 'You mustn't let it make you ill, Madame. Remember that you jumped over the midsummer fire, and I'd thrown a pinch of wormwood into it, to drive away the evil spirits. Whoever jumps over that fire is proof against the Devil for that year.'

Then she told him briefly about her difficult situation. He understood completely, for he was an intuitive man, and anything to do with devils is of deep concern to the Basques, going back a very long way in the traditions of this people of unknown origin.

'Don't worry,' he said, 'I shan't abandon you. I have far too pleasant memories of you. I shall help you jump that fire again if I have to. I intend to remain in the area until Monsieur de Peyrac de Morens d'Irristru comes back. It will give me the opportunity to greet a brother from my own illustrious land and to come to his assistance if need be.'

Marceline with her bold jollity, Hernani and his men, who

kept the Bretons guessing, while they kept one eye on Ambroisine's accomplices – who, armed with muskets, had infiltrated the place in ever-increasing numbers – had brought not only moral but material assistance. They were like a token that Joffrey was near, about to arrive. Cantor must have found him and told him to make haste.

And now it was the tenth day.

Angélique was hastening along the path up to the Breton cross, in order to hold back Piksarett who had been reported as advancing with an Indian band to scalp everyone in Tidmagouche.

This was no moment to unleash slaughter.

That morning a man had arrived at the outpost shouting that the Indians were on their way, that they had already wounded one of his companions with an arrow, and that they were led by the great Narranganset. Angélique was summoned, fortunately being, thanks to Marceline's nursing, up and about after a peaceful night.

Groups were forming and people were arming themselves. The women and a handful of children present were advised to go to the centre of the hamlet. Nicolas Parys had his culverines aimed.

'It's years now since the natives hereabouts have shown any hostility towards us,' he explained to Angélique, who had just arrived, 'they're an indolent lot and not at all in a hurry to go to war. But, if excited with fire-water, they could follow some great chief, like the sagamore who accompanied you, Madame. What has he told them? That's his business. But we're in a fix. I gather that there are a lot of them, quite determined to have all the white scalps from Tidmagouche. We're going to have to fire on them and it'll be a nasty business. We must try to calm them down and you must persuade the Patsuikett chief to call it off. Just because he is the greatest warrior of Acadia, he thinks he can do anything.'

'Which way are they coming?'

'From the direction of the Breton cross promontory. They've been seen deploying their forces along the edge of the woods, and no doubt they'll try to half encircle the settlement before charging in on us.'

'I'll go and meet them,' she said.

Ville d'Avray wanted to accompany her, but she refused his help, as she did that of Hernani and Barssempuy, who both suggested going with her. The sight of an armed man, no matter who he was, might upset the Redskin. He would not want to give in to the Governor, nor to a Basque, nor to any pirate lieutenant, in fact not to anyone who had no connection with the Children of Dawn. Whereas Angélique, his captive, might find it easier to produce arguments that would convince him.

'It's nothing,' she assured them. 'Everything will be settled very soon.'

Just as she was about to leave and set off, Ambroisine gave a cry and rushed towards her.

'Don't go,' she cried, 'they will kill you. You mustn't go . . . I don't want you to . . . I don't want you to be killed!'

She clasped Angélique to her with such desperate force that Angélique nearly suffocated beneath her clutches. Ambroisine had dressed that day in the clothes she had been wearing the day she arrived in Gouldsboro; the scarlet bodice, the yellow skirt, the duck-blue mantle, and it was just like a renewed nightmare to be clasped in her arms again, as if this demented convulsion was the conclusion of the drama, the duel to the death, that had set them face to face.

'Not you!' she cried. 'Not you! I don't want them to kill you! Oh, please, please, don't go off to your death! . . .'

'Let me go,' Angélique murmured through clenched teeth, resisting her urge to push Ambroisine away violently, by grasping hold of her hair. And in any case she would have been unable to do so, for at that moment Ambroisine's strength was superhuman; it was like the strength of an octopus, or a serpent winding itself round its prey in order to smother it.

It took the concerted efforts of Ville d'Avray, Barssempuy and Defour to pull Ambroisine away, and she fell to her knees in a crumpled heap, half-fainting, shrieking stridently, writhing under the effect of some violent attack.

'Hysterical and mad,' Angélique told herself as she hastened up the path. 'God deliver us from her before we all become like her. And now it's Piksarett who's lost his head!'

All this must be brought to a rapid halt, for it was becoming increasingly difficult to prevent jangled nerves from exploding into violence . . . Then she stopped for a moment, as she caught sight of the Breton cross. Just one more bend in the path and she would come out on to the open space beside it. But something held her back as she was about to set out again. She did not know exactly what it was, but it was something that *should not have been*! . . .

She thought about the Breton cross. It was there that Marie-la-Douce's assassin had appeared ... from there also that the suspicious men from the ships came. Rooted to the spot, she stood waiting. Waiting to know what was preventing her from going on and forbidding her from taking a further step.

Something that should not have been!

Then through the rustic calm of this path winding along with the cliff on one side of it, the thick woods on the other, it all became clear and obvious ...

The birds were singing ...

And she remembered certain tales the woodsmen used to tell about their experiences with the redskins: 'A whole throng of them can advance without a single twig snapping or a rustle of leaves betraying their presence. The only indication you have of their approach is that the birds stop singing. A sudden silence in the forest is always a warning that the redskins are close ...'

Yet, the birds were singing.

Therefore there were no redskins. There was no band of Indians hiding in the nearby leaves.

There was no Piksarett.

Piksarett! The Indians! Just a pretext to get her to leave the settlement alone.

A trap! And a trap into which she was about to run head-long.

She dashed for cover in among the trees, and once there, she began to think.

'No Piksarett, no redskins. Just another story. But no doubt in their place there were murderers waiting there beside the Breton cross to kill her. Had not Ambroisine told her that other night: 'You are going to die!'

Taking care to keep hidden she crept from trunk to trunk, and moved forward.

Then she saw 'them' at the edge of the wood.

There were five of them.

Five bandits armed with pistols and cutlasses, each man having also in his hand, as a mark of recognition, that deadly weapon, a short black stick. Among them she recognized the Pale One, the man of whom Colin had spoken, the man with the lead cudgel, the White Devil, the accursed brother of the Demon.

Thus, had she gone on up the path, she would have found herself face to face with them. She might not even have noticed them until a little later, after she had moved on into a completely exposed position.

And that would have been the end of her.

What if the birds hadn't been singing!

Of course, she did have her gun, but would she have been able to load it in time?

Now she must act with the greatest possible caution, and try to retreat towards the hamlet without attracting their attention, as the undergrowth was rather scant, and in any case, she must be armed.

She drew her pistol in order to load it, but her fingers searched in vain around her belt for the bag of bullets and small box of primer which she had checked over that very morning.

Then she realized with horror, that Ambroisine, in clinging to her with protestations of despair, had removed them from her belt . . .

'She's done for me!' thought Angélique fearfully. 'She's done for me, well and truly done for me!'

This homely phrase seemed hardly adequate to express her astonishment.

Although she had been warned, although she had been on her guard, although she knew full well that they were living in proximity to one of the most dangerous creatures the human race had ever seen, and were in mortal danger at every second, she had once again allowed herself to be completely taken in.

Oh! Ambroisine! Ambroisine the Accursed, playing on human impulsiveness to make people impale themselves on the snares she had prepared for them.

If the birds had not stopped her by their singing she would have found herself face to face with these bandits, utterly defenceless.

But demons do not ever reckon with birds.

She could see the men beginning to show signs of restlessness and to consult one another, no doubt surprised that she had not appeared. One of them advanced cautiously in the direction of the path while another entered the woods to her left.

She took cover behind a bush, having no other resource for the moment but to remain motionless.

At that critical moment there was the sound of a cannon being fired in the distance, followed by several other reports from the south. It was probably some ships calling the natives to come and bargain with them, as so often happened.

But the cannonade continued, and the men lying in wait for her seemed to grow anxious. They drew together again, and she could see them from a distance, arguing violently. Then, reaching a decision, they moved off and swiftly disappeared in the direction from which these muffled explosions had come.

She had the impression that her immediate danger was past, but prudently remained motionless for some time.

She felt that by now she could try to return to Tidmagouche, but the distant uproar, that seemed like the sound of a battle, intrigued her.

So she decided to emerge from hiding and risk a few steps, when she suddenly thought she saw, coming from the south, the silhouette of a redskin walking swiftly, darting in and out among the trees, and shortly afterwards Piksarett emerged a few steps from her. He caught sight of her:

'What are you doing here?' he exclaimed angrily. 'It was reckless of you to leave the shelter of the houses! I warned you that the woods were infested by your enemies. Do you want to lose your life!'

She had no time to explain the trap into which she had fallen.

'Piksarett, what's going on over there?'

A smile lit up the redskin's face, as he pointed in the direction from which the cannon and musket-fire was coming.

'He's on his way!'

'Who?'

'Your husband! The Man of Thunder. Do you not recognize his voice?'

Angélique began to rush madly forward. But Piksarett leapt after her in order to precede her and show her the way.

They ran thus for a few minutes while the sound of battle drew nearer.

Then suddenly they found themselves on the edge of the cliff above the Cape where the two bandit ships were sheltering. The smoke and the smell of gunpowder rose among the trees and along the inlet, but the uproar seemed to be less, although there were still a few isolated bursts of fire and the sound of voices giving orders, while others cried for mercy. The brigands were surrendering . . .

Angélique saw the *Gouldsboro* lying hard up against one of the ships – the ship with the orange pennon – which it had grappled. On the deck the crew were having their wrists bound. Four or five other sailing vessels of different sizes filled the Bay, blocking every way out, preventing any possible escape.

Angélique looked eagerly for Count Peyrac but could not see him.

Then at last she caught sight of him, running up the beach, his pistols in his hands, followed by a few of his men, bent on capturing a group of bandits who had taken shelter behind an upturned boat.

It was *he*! . . . No, it was not he . . . his tall silhouette moved so swiftly, too swiftly, through the vapours and layers of stagnant smoke. It was like in a dream . . . a vision . . . him . . . disappearing . . . reappearing again . . . him, all her life! Her whole life had been like this. With him passing back and forth through the mists of memory . . . in her dreams . . . the picture of love . . . of paradise . . . her . . . she could see him, recognize him . . . it was he. He put his pistols back into his belt, while Count d'Urville made fast the prisoners. Then he turned towards Angélique . . . it was he!

She began to shout, calling to him with all her strength, without even knowing whether she was uttering his name . . . paralysed by the paroxysm of her joy, she found herself unable to move, then, regaining her power of motion, she began to fly towards him without any sensation of touching the ground, and scrambled down the slope that led to him, still calling out in the terrible fear that he might once again vanish from sight, vanish once more, leaving her alone on earth . . .

Hearing her shout, he ran forward with open arms. They met and threw themselves upon one another's hearts.

And there everything faded away – her doubts, her fears, the threats, the power of evil!

The strength of his arms, that rampart, his chest like a shield to defend her, and his warmth to protect her from the icy chill of loneliness, and – felt in his wild, passionate embrace – the sensation of his love for her, immeasurable, boundless, that seemed to run right through her, enveloping her, flooding her with inexpressible happiness.

'Oh, you're alive . . . you're alive!' he repeated in a broken voice. 'What a miracle! I have suffered a thousand deaths! My crazy darling! What traps you managed to fall into again! There, there! It's all over . . . Don't cry . . .'

'But I'm not crying,' Angélique replied without realizing that her face was covered in tears. 'Oh, how long it's all been,' she said between two sobs, 'all this time . . . all this time without you . . . all this time far from you . . .'

'Yes, terribly long!'

He rocked her as he held her against him, while she gave way to all the tears she had forbidden herself to shed during the past few days in order to preserve her strength.

No longer to have any doubts! To know that he was there! Alive! And that he still loved her! . . . What boundless bliss. He held her away from him a little so that he could see her better.

An opal-coloured sky above them, and their happiness in which they were alone.

'See what your eyes are telling me!' he murmured. And he fervently kissed her eyelids.

'They still have their old power to move me, but they are all ringed with black. What has happened to you, my treasure? What have they done to you, my love?'

'Oh, it's nothing! Now you are here! . . . I'm happy.'

They hugged one another again. It was as if Joffrey could not convince himself of the miracle that he held Angélique safe and sound in his arms, after the terrible fear that had gripped him when he had learned from Cantor that she was at Tidmagouche, face to face with the hatred and demoniacal lusts of that crazy, perverted creature who went by the name of Ambroisine de Maudribourg.

A formidable name.

An indescribable ordeal! But one which seemed, for the two of them at that wonderful moment, to take on its full significance.

With his lips against her hair, he prolonged his kiss.

'Time has ceased to exist,' he said in his deep voice. 'You see, my dear heart . . . the hours which we must live . . . are always granted to us . . . God willing. The impulse we never experienced before when we found one another after fifteen years' absence, that impulse to come together we have just experienced today. How much I feel now that you are mine at last!'

CHAPTER 78

ANGÉLIQUE STAYED behind the house, beside the open window. Joffrey de Peyrac had told her to wait there.

He himself circled the house, reached the door and went in.

Angélique knew that he had appeared in the doorway and that Ambroisine de Maudribourg was looking at him.

And without witnessing anything of the scene, she could guess the expression on those seraphic features, the flashing of those magnificent black eyes with their golden lights.

At the same time, Peyrac's men, who had approached overland, were surrounding the settlement and had seized the fort, while the ships of his fleet, towing their two prizes of war, were entering the harbour.

The heat was intense; a kind of torpor, a spell of terror, hung over Tidmagouche.

The beach and the hamlet were taken almost noiselessly, without a single shot being fired. Men who had been taking their orders from Ambroisine found themselves with their wrists bound without realizing what was happening to them. *She*, the Demon, still did not know.

She was looking at Peyrac as he stood before her.

Angélique heard that soft voice, slightly veiled and fragile, say:

'Here you are!'

She gave a shudder. How badly Ambroisine had managed to hurt her, so that the very sound of that voice filled her with horror and fear.

'It was high time that he arrived,' she told herself, 'otherwise she would have destroyed me . . . Oh Joffrey, my love!'

Then she heard his calm, confident footsteps crossing the room.

She knew that his eyes remained on the ravishing face of the Demon, but that nothing could be seen of what was going on in his mind.

'You have been a long time,' said Ambroisine de Maudribourg.

Then there was a silence, and Angélique thought she was going to faint. Every second that passed was charged with unbearable tension in which the outcome, victory or defeat, of some combat of giants was being decided. Two forces involved, both equally powerful, equally well armed, equally sure of themselves and of their strength.

It was Ambroisine who spoke first, and her voice betrayed her nervousness beneath the inscrutable eyes that observed her.

'Yes, you are too late, Monsieur de Peyrac.'

Then, in a tone of inexpressible triumph, that trembled with satanic joy:

'You are too late! *She is dead.*'

She must have smiled as she spoke this, with her eyes flashing.

'Has the hunter brought you her heart?' Peyrac asked.

This ironical allusion to the story of Snow White in which the wicked designs of the queen are thwarted, made Ambroisine furious with rage.

'No . . . but he is going to bring me her eyes. I have insisted on that.'

Then, in her madness, her thoughts ran on wildly:

'They are two emeralds. I shall have them set in gold and shall wear them over my heart.'

Now Angélique understood. Joffrey de Peyrac had always suspected Ambroisine de Maudribourg of being a perverted creature whose mind was already distraught or possessed. As he stood looking at her now, he must be wearing the same expression as when he had stood at her bedside listening thoughtfully in her delirium. His wide experience and also a particular sense some men have about this kind of woman, must have warned him about the kind of person she was.

'I see that you don't believe me,' Ambroisine went on in that abrupt and slightly strident voice she adopted with anyone who appeared not to be taking much notice of her words, 'you are just like her! She never would believe me, she just laughed . . . yes, she laughed! Now that laugh is dead! She will never laugh any more! . . . Never! It's your fault. You are like her, you want to make people believe that love exists, that *your love* cannot be destroyed by anyone. Senseless people that you are! There is no love . . . And so much the worse for you for having tried to prove that there was ... I have destroyed your love ... she is dead, do you hear me! Dead! Dead! Go and look and you will find her shattered body at the bottom of the cliff, and two black holes where her eyes were ... Now at last she will never look at me again ... as she alone knew how to look at another human creature. No one has ever looked at me like that ... When she looked at me she saw me "before", she saw me in my human guise. "After" she saw my spirit, but she never turned away from me and she never fled from me. That was what was intolerable. She always looked at me straight in the face, and she always spoke straight to me, to me alone. She knew to *whom* she was speaking and yet she was not afraid. But now no one will ever look at me like that, no one will see me as I am ... Oh, what agony!'

The crisis was approaching. Her rapid fire of words was interspersed with moans.

Angélique, her nerves stretched about to breaking point, felt like blocking her ears.

'She is dead, I tell you! She is dead! What will become of me now! And it's all your fault, your fault, you miserable man! ... Why did you repulse me! ... Why did you treat me with disdain and mockery! ... How could you dare to! ... And yet you are *nothing* ... Where do you find your strength? ... Had I been able to force you into subjection like the others, I would not have killed her ... I would rather have seen her suffer, die of grief, and that would have delighted my heart ...

'My mission would have been accomplished. Whereas now! ... She is dead and you are triumphant! ... What will become of me! How can I ever remain on this unspeakable earth! Kill me! Make an end of me! Kill me! But why don't you kill me! ... Don't you care about the fact that she is dead? ... You're not even weeping! Whereas I; I feel like weeping ... At such a disaster ... And I cannot. I *cannot*!'

A hoarse moan burst forth from the Demon's throat, almost identical with that inhuman cry which had already rung out through the night on two separate occasions, in which powerless rage mingled with implacable hatred, the echo of some fathomless despair.

'Kill me! ...'

Peyrac's voice then was heard, level and as if indifferent, and it immediately had the effect of relieving the unbearable tension.

'Why are you in such a hurry to die, Madame? ... And at my

hand? Would you have yet another misdeed attributed to me? ... The ultimate trap? ... No, I shall not grant you that ... Your death will come in its due time. Now the time has come for the revelation of your crimes, so please will you accompany me so that people may see you with your accomplices.'

'My accomplices?'

Suddenly the Duchess of Maudribourg seemed to have found her balance again.

'I have no accomplices! What *is* all this?'

'Would you please come with me,' the Count repeated. 'I intend to confront you with them.'

Angélique heard the Duchess get up, and she and the Count left the house together.

The Duchess did not at first notice Angélique. She was looking towards the roadstead, now filled with sails and ships, then towards the beach that was black with people. From a distance it was hard to distinguish the different crews, the Bretons and the Basques, Peyrac's men and his prisoners.

'Kindly come down to the beach,' the Count invited her. He was laying on the courtesy.

She turned towards him and it was then that she saw Angélique standing a few paces from her.

Not a tremor crossed her features, but she rapidly looked away again as if seeking to wipe out this vision, to obliterate the fact.

She ran her hands over her bare forearms with a shudder.

'Would you give me my coat, Delphine?' she said out loud in a perfectly natural voice. 'It's very cold.'

The sun was burning hot, but this request did not seem a strange one, for so painful was the occasion that Angélique herself felt chilled to the heart.

The Duchess draped herself in her great black satin cape with its scarlet lining, embroidered with the black rampant lion of the Maudribourgs, and began to walk down towards the shore.

There she stopped, and examined the crowd turned towards her. Mingling with the anonymous faces of ships' crews and armed men, with the fishermen and the prisoners, certain faces stood out. They were all there: Job Simon and his ship's boy, Cantor, Aristide and Julienne, Yannle Couennec, Jacques Vignot, Hernani d'Astiguarra, Count d'Urville, Barssempuy, the Marquis de Ville d'Avray, Enrico Enzi, and Peyrac's four Spanish guards ...

Angélique immediately recognized Brother Mark among them. He was standing with a group of Frenchmen, among whom could be seen a man dressed carefully although without ostentation, a man with an authoritative and crafty air, who was watching the scene with mingled interest and scepticism. He greeted Ville d'Avray and exchanged a few words with him. She later found out that this was the Administrator, Carlon, the important Canadian official whom Peyrac had managed to extricate from a tricky situation up the Saint John river. The other man was Monsieur de Vauvenart and she could also see Big Woods and a cartographer from Quebec whom Angélique had met in Katarunk.

Ambroisine's eyes had come to rest on certain people, known and unknown, but she did not flinch. She had merely glanced at those who headed the prisoners, among them the man with the pale, marble-like face. Finally she turned towards Peyrac, whom henceforth she pretended to be the only person she could see, and said in a quiet voice intended for his ears alone:

'You are very strong, Monsieur de Peyrac. I am beginning to understand why you have so many enemies, and why they so passionately seek your destruction.'

Then, in a louder voice, her cajoling siren's voice:

'What do you want of me, dear Count, and what is the object of this gathering? I am at your disposal, but I would like to know . . .'

Peyrac took a few steps forward.

'Madame, here is Monsieur Carlon, the Administrator of New France. You know Monsieur de Ville d'Avray, the Governor of Acadia. In the presence of these two important officials I wish to accuse you, Madame, of numerous crimes and malpractices which you have committed in this region of French Bay, crimes committed by you yourself and by these men here present, under your orders, crimes whose violence and horror cry out for condemnation and reparation before the tribunal of men, if not before that of God. I accuse you of causing, among other things, the loss of the vessel *Unicorn*, chartered largely at the expense of the French Crown, and of ordering the cold-blooded massacre of her crew and of the young women intended to populate Canada who were on board that ship, likewise of causing the death of a young Canadian nobleman, Hubert d'Arpentigny, in the shipwreck of his vessel in which my wife was travelling, of sinking by means of a mine the vessel *Asmodeus*, a disaster from which Monsieur de Ville d'Avray and a large number of people only escaped by a miracle, and of having in this very place, had a young woman done to death, and of having by your own hand poisoned an old woman . . .

'Not to mention the numerous attempted murders at different places, and acts of piracy along our coasts, etc. . . . The list is a long one . . . And I shall confine myself to these few precise accusations.'

Carlon the Administrator had been listening carefully, his eyes going from Peryac to the Duchess of Maudribourg.

It was the first time he had seen her and, although fore-warned, since he had been told what was going on by Peyrac, it was obvious that he found it hard to associate so many terrible and sordid crimes with this ravishingly beautiful young woman who stood there before them all, alone, frail, with her long black hair flying in the wind, looking like a frightened child. She gazed wide-eyed at Peyrac as if he had suddenly gone mad, and she shook her head gently and murmured:

'But what are you talking about? . . . I don't understand.'

And Angélique, who was looking at Carlon, saw that he was being taken in by her frail, waif-like manner.

He stepped forward and gave a little cough.

'Are you quite sure of what you are saying, Count?' he asked abruptly. 'It seems a bit steep to me! . . . How could such a young woman all alone do all that? . . . Where are these ac-complices of hers to whom you allude?'

'Here they are,' said Peyrac, pointing to the group of pris-oners at the head of which stood the Pale One, their captain. Among them also figured the man with the pearls, Saddy, the Invisible Man, the one they used to send out as a scout to mingle with village people and ships' crews because he looked like any other sailor and people were always under the im-pression that they had seen him before or knew him a little. 'All of them hand-picked,' Clovis had said, for they had all been chosen by Ambroisine and her brother with that unfailing in-stinct for the criminal propensities that would make them skilful allies, each man secretly attached to her through the gift she had given them, at least on one occasion, of her magnificent body.

They would never be made to betray her. They never even blinked when Carlon, pointing to Ambroisine, called out to them:

'Do you know this woman?'

The Pale Man let his stony glance fall on her, then slowly shook his head and growled:

'Never seen her.'

He expressed himself in such a way that some of those present were under the impression that they were victims of some terrible error.

Carlon frowned and stared sternly at Peyrac.

'I must have some admissions,' he said, 'or else some witnesses.'

'I have a witness,' the Count replied without any sign of emotion, 'and of some standing too! And I had quite a job to find him. I had to go all the way to Newfoundland. But here he is.'

CHAPTER 79

HE MOTIONED with his hand and a man of about fifty stepped out from a group behind him and stood before Carlon. He was wearing heavy wooden clogs and coarse woollen clothes, his dress contrasting sharply with his distinguished face that wore an expression of gentle benevolence.

'Allow me to introduce Monsieur Quentin, an Oratorian. He set sail with the *Unicorn* as its chaplain. He was not long in discovering the true character of this expedition and of the "benefactress" that led it. She thought that he would be an easy prey to her advances, but he repulsed them and, as he knew too much about her, it was decided that he should be got rid of. So he was thrown overboard off Newfoundland. Fortunately a fishing vessel picked him up in time. The King's Girls here present and the captain of the *Unicorn*, Job Simon, can scarcely deny that they recognize him as the chaplain who accompanied them on part of the voyage and who they were told had been accidentally drowned.'

'No doubt I was wrong in being so naïve,' the Oratorian declared, addressing Carlon. 'When I realized from the outset that the state of morals on board the *Unicorn* was so deplorable, because of this woman, I thought it would suffice for me to remonstrate with her in order to put matters right. But I found myself pitted against a very powerful adversary. I myself

483

became the butt of her assaults, and every day saw an incessant battle in which I tried to maintain my religious vows and to help the innocent souls who had fallen into her power. Believe me, sir, that when such things happen on board a ship that is only a few fathoms long, and from which one cannot escape, it is very ... embarrassing.'

'Do you mean that Madame de Maudribourg suggested you should become ... her lover?' Carlon asked in doubtful tones. Apparently he found the suggestion funny and did not believe it.

Ambroisine cried out in tones of despair:

'Monsieur Carlon, I don't know whether this man was thrown overboard or whether he threw himself overboard, but I did notice that from the earliest days it was he who was mad, and it was I who found it exceedingly difficult to escape his lubricious advances ...'

'Lies!' cried a voice.

And Brother Mark hastened to join the circle.

'Monsieur Quentin is not the only priest Madame de Maudribourg has tried to lead into temptation. I can bear witness to this, because I also have been one of her victims.'

'It's more understandable, where you're concerned,' the Administrator murmured, looking at the handsome face of the young Recollect.

He was beginning to feel out of his depth.

'If I understand rightly, the crew of the *Unicorn* threw Monsieur Quentin overboard? ... So Captain Job Simon is an accomplice too.'

Old Simon gave a savage roar.

'It wasn't my men who did it,' he shrieked, rushing forward, 'it was the three thugs she forced me to take on board with us in Le Havre. Yes, I'm a bloody fool ... she'd got me. I knew we weren't going to Quebec, but to Gouldsboro instead, I knew that I must say nothing about it, I knew that she was a whore and a trollop, and I knew they had murdered the chaplain, but what I didn't know ...'

Bristling and gigantic, he stood out, a tragic figure, against the white sky.

'... what I didn't know was that there we would find a group of bandits under orders from her to sink my ship and massacre my men ...'

He was threshing about in all directions, tugging at his beard, tearing his hair, throwing his arms heavenwards, and seemed himself to be so completely crazed, that clearly Carlon was beginning to ask himself whether he had not entered a mad-house.

'But you are out of your mind, captain! If Madame de Maudribourg was herself on board, she could hardly have sought to have the ship wrecked on the rocks. She would have been risking her own life.'

'She left the ship ... just before ... I didn't ask myself why, but afterwards, I understood ... Bit by bit, in Gouldsboro. I went on pretending not to have understood because I knew that if she realized I was no idiot, she would kill me ... like the others ... Killing presents no problems for her ... When I think of it! My *Unicorn*! My lovely ship! And all my men, my brothers, massacred ...'

He shook his fist at Ambroisine and it was he who spelled out the terrible accusation:

'Demon! Demon! ...'

CHAPTER 80

SUDDENLY SOMEONE shouted:

'Look out! He's breaking away!'

Taking advantage of the fact that all eyes were turned towards Job Simon so that no one was looking at the captives, the Pale One had made a getaway. He was running towards the sea and had begun to leap over the rocks uncovered by the low tide. His flight was quite pointless, for even were he to reach the sea and plunge into it and swim for hours, what would have been his chances of escape or survival?

But so diabolical a creature was he that everyone had the impression as they saw the silhouette of the White Devil grow smaller in the trembling haze of mist and heat, that he was about to vanish from sight, swallowed up by the horizon, as he had appeared one evening over the dazzling plain of uncovered seaweed, and that nothing could stop him from reappearing one day to pursue his evil purposes on earth.

'Catch him,' they shouted. 'Catch him.'

Now he looked like a hobgoblin leaping about at the far end

of the rocks. He reached the sea, the sea which had always been the accomplice of the murderer with the lead cudgel; he was going to join the sea again and it would hide him from the eyes of men. It was then that Hernani d'Astiguarra leapt forward from the right. His long legs carried him from rock to rock, leaping like a dancer. Then he came to a halt and stood still, a black silhouette against the yellow sky, while his arm carrying the harpoon drew back then was released with all the strength of a spring.

The arrow whistled away, carrying the line behind it, that unrolled, leaping and twitching like a mad serpent that has been cut in two.

A terrible cry rang out across the Bay.

Hernani the Basque walked back up the beach, the rope wound round his shoulder, hauling his prey up behind him.

When he reached Count Peyrac and Angélique, he grasped the harpoon at one end and threw down before them, as he would a shark, the man's impaled body. Then he grasped it by the hair and lifted it up so that all might see and recognize the hideous face with its staring glassy eyes, its wide open mouth, a face scarcely more livid in death than in life.

The Beast was dead . . .

CHAPTER 81

AND THROUGH the horrified silence there came a cry that was so inhuman that no one knew whence it had come.

Still less could they believe that it came from the gracious woman standing there in her dark cloak, a frail victim with the face of an archangel.

They only realized this when she rushed forward, still shrieking, and threw herself like one demented on the lifeless body.

'Zalil!' she cried. 'My brother! My brother! No, not you . . . Stay with me! You are my strength! . . . Don't leave me on this unspeakable earth! They will get the better of me! Zalil! . . . If you leave me, I can't remain here . . . Remember our pact! Your blood carries mine away with it . . . You will tear me from my body . . . I don't want to, I don't want to . . . Don't do that, you wretch! . . . Come back! Come back! . . .'

Petrified with stupor the witnesses of this hysterical scene of despair suddenly became convulsed, as if panic had seized them and was about to make them disperse and flee. But instead of this, the movement of panic drew them into a compact group, filled with horror, outrage and lust for vengeance, and with one accord they turned on the stricken woman.

Torn from the corpse which she had been clutching, punched and kicked, her hair torn out in handfuls, her clothes torn to ribbons, she was soon no more than a disfigured and blood-stained body whose very screams died away, so great was her suffering . . .

Moved by an impulse, Angélique rushed forward into the throng to try to stop the crazed attackers and tear their prey from them.

'Stop! I beg you,' she beseeched them, 'do not disgrace yourselves . . . Barssempuy, get back. Brother Mark, not you, you are a man of God . . . Job Simon, you are too strong to take advantage of your strength . . . Don't be a coward! . . . She's a woman! And you, captain, why are you striking her?'

Beside themselves with rage, the men went on shouting, crying out their despair, their secret, irreparable tragedy.

'She led me into temptation!'

'She sunk my ship!'

'She killed my brothers!'

'She murdered my betrothed!'

'My ship! . . . My brothers! . . . My beloved, dead! Through her fault! Her! The Demon! . . . She's a serpent! She must be crushed. She's a monster! A monster!'

'Marceline, Yolande, help me!' cried Angélique.

The two solidly-built women came to her assistance and between the three of them they managed to drag the Duchess's broken body from the crowd, while Peyrac, by his authority, calmed the wildest of the attackers, and the Spanish soldiers crossed their pikes to hold back those who were on the point of joining the hunt. All this took only a few seconds, yet such was their devastating, cruel rage that everyone stood panting for breath as if exhausted.

The men let them pass. They were women. It was their right to save the life of this other woman delivered up to the violence of men.

But Angélique refused to sit in judgement on the frenzy

shown by these unfortunate men, nor did she pride herself on her own act which had been more a reflex reaction against this bestial violence than any desire to succour her enemy. Would she have been capable of doing such a thing had she had this horrible creature to thank for Abigail's death, or Cantor's, or Joffrey's? . . . And if, after an exhausting battle, in which she had probed the depths of all her own weaknesses, she had not been victorious?

Yes, she was the victor.

Ambroisine the Demon was nothing more than a blind, disfigured wreck, denounced to the whole world by herself, whom nothing now could save from the justice of men if she managed to survive and escape that of God.

The proof of her crimes was now too convincing, the witnesses were all too many.

It was the end of her reign and her power on earth. Her accursed brother, the White Demon, had dragged her down with him to defeat and death.

She opened her eyes and said in a whisper:

'Don't hand me over to the Inquisition!'

She lay where they had thrown her down on a bed of seaweed in Angélique's hut, all bruised and bloodstained, with the tatters of her yellow, blue and red satin clothes exposing to sight her flesh that was one open wound; she might have inspired pity in them, had not the look of those eyes as they shone through her swollen eyelids still given the three women the sensation of being watched by a creature bent on their destruction.

'Why did you save her life?' asked Marceline in a whisper.

'Yes, why did you?' the Marquis de Ville d'Avray repeated, standing behind her as he entered the room, accompanied by Count Peyrac and Carlon the Administrator.

And yet in spite of themselves they all shuddered at the deplorable state of this unfortunate woman, only a short while ago so full of triumphant life and beauty.

'Her final snare,' whispered Ville d'Avray, 'the ultimate snare of Satan: pity. The human form given up to blind fury is a pitiable object. We are all too fond of the image of our own flesh and weep over its misfortunes. Yet we should beware, my friends. For as long as there is breath in her body, we are in danger. And even were she dead, things would not be much better. For she would become still one more evil spirit wandering around Demon Isle, drawing ships on to the rocks.'

He shook his head.

'Ah! The immortal soul! What a filthy invention! Now we're in a nice mess! Have you any solution to propose, sir, you who claim to have an answer to all problems?'

Carlon shook his head. Events had clearly passed beyond the customary concerns of his sedate, methodical mind. His eyes travelled from the battered body which no one seemed to be bothering to tend, to the faces of everyone else present. The significance of their expressions escaped him, for he had not yet understood what the vision of this wounded woman as she lay there represented to each one of them. He was as pale as death and it was obvious that he kept on asking himself whether it was not all a dream.

Big Marceline dealt him the final blow by suddenly raising her head as if at some sudden alert, and saying:

'Redskins!'

'Redskins! What do you mean?' Carlon moaned.

'They're coming!'

Count Peyrac dashed over to the door and they all followed him.

From the neighbouring forests that surrounded the settle-ment, came a low roar, as the war drums rang out and the advancing braves shouted in chorus.

Piksarett!

They had almost forgotten about Piksarett and his brothers! Piksarett and his people! Piksarett who had said: 'Have patience! Uniakke and his people and all the tribes of the Children of Dawn are gathering in the forest. They await the hour when I shall signal them to seek vengeance from those who killed our blood brothers, our allies, and who sought to humiliate you and cause your death, oh my captive! . . .'

Earlier that day the palefaces had tried to settle their conflicts according to their own laws, but now the hour of the redskin had come. The long, patient watch of the great Abenaki at Angélique's side, the share he had borne in his own heart of all the anxieties and dangers she had run, of which he had never failed to see the gravity and cunning, all the irritation he had built up against those palefaces, strangers and evil men, come to disturb the peace of his friends, and of the woman who had given him a cloak the colour of dawn in which to lay the bones of his ancestors, people who maliciously perverted the native populations of the coast, all this was to be duly accounted for by merciless slaughter.

'This is it! ...' Marceline murmured. 'They've begun to charge!'

The rhythmical roar had changed pace. Now it was like the rumble of a storm, of a tidal wave, like the sea spilling over its banks and advancing towards the human beings.

Almost immediately the edge of the woods became festooned with a tawny fringe that seemed to swell visibly as they watched.

Of course Angélique, Count Peyrac and their faithful followers had nothing to fear, since it was on their account that Piksarett and the Souriquois and Malecite tribes were advancing on Tidmagouche, but there was no guarantee that the inhabitants of the hamlet or the fishermen from the Breton cod-fishing vessel would be spared.

The men on the beach had already heard the sound which big Marceline's experienced ears had picked up, and Nicolas Parys went by, urging his own people on.

'Quick, run and take shelter in the fort!'

'Stay here, Monsieur Carlon,' the Count called to the Administrator. 'The Indians don't know you, and your life might well be in danger. Don't leave Monsieur de Ville d'Avray and my wife. You have nothing to fear as long as you stay with them. But don't leave this house.'

He hastened down to the sea.

'Where are the King's Girls?' asked Angélique.

She saw them higher up the slope, near the fort where Nicolas Parys was busy pushing everyone he could inside the shelter of the pallisade. Two of Peyrac's Spanish soldiers manned the tower, for their presence, which Piksarett would recognize, would act as a safeguard to those beneath their protection.

Already Cantor and Count d'Urville could be seen running down the beach shouting to the Breton fishermen:

'Be careful! The Indians are coming! They want to scalp all strangers! Get into your canoes, come and take shelter in the fort! ... Hurry up!'

'All the Basques may shelter under my banner!' called Peyrac. 'But above all, don't shoot!'

The red tide broke over the village, men swarming from all sides, with that spreading, irresistible movement that had already struck Angélique at the storming of Brunswick-Falls, a tide that submerged everything in a few moments.

One might well have feared that beneath that blind flood of

men innocent people might have lost their lives, including some of Peyrac's men or some of the sailors from the Basque ship who had helped catch the bandits.

But Piksarett, that swift, avenging archangel, seemed to fly from one end of his army to the other, pointing out the guilty, whom his practised eye had learned to recognize with infallible accuracy, during his long, patient wait.

Not a man escaped. Uniakke and his Mic-Macs, who had come from Truro, used their own avenging hands to scalp Zalil's helpmates, the band of wreckers responsible for the loss of the *Unicorn* and of Hubert d'Arpentigny's boat, as they were for the blowing up of the *Asmodeus*.

Angélique, Marceline and Yolande, along with the Governor and the Administrator, remained standing at the door of the hut.

'And what if they try to seize the Duchess?' said the Marquis. 'It won't take them long to find out where she is hidden, a woman full of demons . . .'

'They'll not come in here,' said Angélique. 'I shall speak to Piksarett.'

They stood there tense, listening to the cries that rose up all around them, cries of victory mingling with cries of terror, pain and agony, while the odd shot rang out in desperate defence.

Strangely enough, the area in front of them remained empty, as if the Indian forces had deliberately avoided crossing the centre of the deserted village.

Then suddenly a lone man dressed in black wandered out on to the little square. He stood there a few paces from them, strange and apparently vacant, bizarre, staring blindly about him as the sun, at its zenith in the blazing sky, was reflected from the lenses of his heavy spectacles. They recognized him as the Duchess's secretary, Armand Daveau, the pen-pusher with the heavy, sensual chin, the man with the endlessly benevolent smile, the man who had murdered Marie-la-Douce.

He went on smiling in a distracted way. Then seeing them standing at the door of the house, he took a few hesitant steps towards them, while they instinctively recoiled from him.

'Don't stay here,' Marceline cried, driving him away with a sweep of her hand. 'Run to the fort if you want to stay alive. The Indians are after you . . .'

He laughed smugly.

'People have cried wolf before, and they were wrong!'

'But now it's true! Listen! Can't you hear! If the Indians catch you you're as good as dead.'

'Why would they want to kill me?'

'Because you are a criminal,' Angélique shouted at him, 'you killed Marie-la-Douce by pushing her over the cliff, and it's not the first time you have dealt such a blow in the service of your diabolical mistress . . .'

He drew himself up to his full height, pink with ecstatic vanity.

'I have always striven to do right, for the greater glory of God.'

The folly of trying to absolve himself of the most odious of crimes, and his self-complacency, had something repulsive about them. With death and punishment hard on his heels he refused to seek flight, for it would have constituted an admission of guilt. His monstrous vanity paralysed him, denying the reality of all warnings of danger as he had his whole life long, had denied the warnings of his conscience, while bit by bit he had allowed himself to become enslaved by his passion for a perverted, demoniacal woman.

When the Indians burst into the square he took refuge behind Angélique, throwing himself at her feet, clinging to her and begging her to save his life.

'Leave him to us!' said Piksarett fiercely.

Two Indians seized the man by the wrists and dragged him some distance away on his knees. Piksarrett's hand, armed with a knife, rose up against the sky, as he clamped his victim's neck with one knee and grasped the murderer by his scant hair with the other hand.

They heard a terrible shriek.

Thus it was that few of the Demon's accomplices escaped the Indian knives. Every member of the two crews in her pay died.

Five of the Bretons from the cod-fishing ship were also victims of the massacre which in Tidmagouche earned the name of the 'bloody strand'.

Count Peyrac, by his personal intervention, at the very last minute saved the lives of the captain of the *Faouet* and Gontran-le-Jeune, who had neither of them had time to take refuge in the fort with Gontran's father.

Piksarett and his redskins did not pursue those who had

managed to escape in their dinghies to the ships lying at anchor, or who had hidden among the rocks.

Rallying his forces, the great warrior of Acadia went back through the hamlet to take leave of Angélique, who was still standing at the door of her house, surrounded by Marceline, Yolande, the Marquis de Ville d'Avray and Carlon the Administrator, more or less stupefied with fear.

'I have to accompany Uniakke and his brothers to Truro,' the Abenaki declared, addressing his captive, 'but I shall see you again in Quebec. You will need my help again there.'

Then, turning to Peyrac who had accompanied him:

'I have watched over her through innumerable dangers, let me tell you, Ticonderoga,[1] but I do not regret the trouble it has caused me, since the demons have not prevailed against her. That is a prayer to God said during Mass, "that devils should not prevail", and God has hearkened to us since his enemies have now been destroyed.'

He stood in all his proud majesty, bedizened with warpaint, and the blood ran in streaks down his legs from the scalps hanging from his belt. Beside him Angélique appeared frail, a white woman come from other parts, from a foreign world, but it was she whom the Iroquois called Kawa, and Piksarett was well pleased to share the privilege of defending her with his distant, inveterate enemies. He lowered his malicious, triumphant gaze upon her.

'Do you remember, my captive, when you stood before a door at Katarunk. I knew that Outtake the Iroquois, my enemy, was on the other side of that door, but I consented to grant you his life. Do you remember?'

She nodded.

'Well then,' the savage went on, 'today too I know who is on the other side of that door,' and he pointed to the doorway of the house in which the wounded Demon was lying, 'but as of yore, I grant you her life, for it is your right to decide upon it.'

He made as if to take a solemn farewell, but then, turning back one last time before going away, he declared: 'She was your enemy! Her scalp belongs to you!'

Ambroisine's scalp! She thought of that splendid head of hair with its enchanting perfume! ... A feminine, living sweet thing, an expression of earthly beauty, created for the zest of living, for pleasure and love, and, like every human thing, created for happiness, joy and tenderness, like Angélique's own

1. Nickname given to Count Peyrac by the Indians.

hair, over which she felt Joffrey's hand brushing in a possessive and passionate caress.

'Her scalp! . . . What use would I have for it? . . .'

Twilight was falling on the blood-stained shore above which a dark cloud of birds was rapidly gathering. Together with the savages, the smell of murder and harsh vengeance was departing. They must make haste to sort out and bury the bodies which gave an impression of a kind of innocence in the blind abandonment of death.

Confused by a sudden lassitude, Angélique imagined Ambroisine's dark hair touched with fiery lights hanging from her belt. Perhaps that was what becoming mature, growing up, achieving wisdom and serenity meant – to be left, after so much wickedness, fear, hatred, burning indignation and desire for death, with only a feeling of pity for a woman's hair, grieving that the demons should have had power to use human beauty in order to drag it down and to consign it through evil to horror and repulsion.

They had passed beyond the sphere of commonplace, everyday notions. That was evident from the words, and the particular way those who had been deeply involved in the recent tragic events had of talking simply about subjects which, in any other circumstances, would have called for fear and condemnation – an attitude which somewhat shocked the 'outsiders', those who had only been involved in the affair for the last few hours.

'That Piksarett is marvellous,' commented Ville d'Avray delightedly. 'Now we have nothing to worry about! The cleaning up operation has been carried out very efficiently. Everything's in order. No trial, no religious or lay court! We won't have to bother about producing endless evidence, which might very well have resulted in our ending up in the dock ourselves, and – who knows? – being burnt at the stake by the Inquisition. Perfect, perfect! Those Indians are very useful at times, I must admit, in spite of their dreadful habit of covering themselves with smelly grease.'

'You appal me!' exclaimed Carlon in high dudgeon. 'I'd hardly know you. You, such a fastidious man too! Your cynical way of talking about this incomprehensible, inhuman slaughter leaves me gasping! . . .'

'Believe me, it was the best solution. Everybody knows where legal proceedings can lead when poisoning and magic are involved . . .'

'But I was involved in this skirmish,' exclaimed the intendant in dismay. 'I'll have to put in a report on it to the Quebec Grand Council.'

'Don't you do any such thing! It's too complicated! Let's just wipe it out, wipe it out! Just as the wind and birds will wipe out all traces of this day from the beach. Just because a few skulls have been peeled, there's no reason for us to deliberately jump into a cesspool reeking of sulphur. Just keep your mouth shut! And in return I'll tell you the whole story. I know every detail. That will fill in the winter evenings for us.'

'But . . . there's still this Duchess de Maudribourg.'

'You're right. Dead or alive we've still got her on our backs.'

Ambroisine de Maudribourg was still alive, although she appeared to be on the point of expiring. Marceline, in her devoted stout-hearted way, was the only one with the moral strength to attend to her at all. Meanwhile, old Nicolas Parys called the company together in the main room of his fort.

'Now look,' he said to Peyrac, 'I've got a proposal to make to you about getting rid of that woman. You know that I want to go away and leave my lands to you. We have still to agree on the price, but I won't be greedy. What I want is to marry that Duchess de Maudribourg. I like that kind of she-devil and I'll soon get through her money; then, when there's no more left, she'll give me the secret of making gold; she knows it.'

'But, you're out of your mind!' exclaimed Ville d'Avray. 'The witch will cook your goose, she'll poison you the way she did her late husband the Duke, and any number of her other lovers.'

'That's my affair,' growled the old King of the East Coast. 'Well, is it a deal? . . .'

And as night was falling, he had his smoky torches lighted in order to draft a bill of sale and a valuation of his property to be assigned to his successor, Count Peyrac.

CHAPTER 82

BUT TOWARDS the evening of that day, in the gathering darkness, a cry went up.

'She's escaped! . . .'

A wind of panic began to blow, and Angélique came close to sharing the superstitious terror felt by some of the people. Living or dead, the shadow of Ambroisine continued to hover over the place. They had had too much to suffer from her maliciousness and cunning to have really believed that they would so soon be safe from her evil spells. And now they discovered big Marceline half-stunned, leaning against the hearthside, the bed on which the Demon had been laid, empty, and the window facing the woods ajar.

'I was poking the fire,' Marceline related, 'and my back was turned. How was I ever to imagine that she'd get up, half-dead as she was, and never stirring her little finger for all these hours! . . . She crept up behind me and gave me such a push as you'd never believe. I think she wanted to make me fall into the flames. I struggled. As I turned I caught a glimpse of her face. Horrible! Her hair was like a mass of wriggling snakes. And in the middle of her wounds and bruise-marks her eyes were glittering like the Devil's, and her teeth . . . her teeth, take my word for it, two were longer and more pointed than the others—real vampires teeth! . . . My heart very near gave out. I think I fainted right out, and bashed my head against the fireplace as I fell. When I came to, I saw that she had jumped out the window. Look and see if she didn't bite me with her fangs . . . No, I tell you, I'm ripe and ready for Hell! . . .'

Resolutely, she exposed her strong, white neck for examination. She was prepared for anything, but Ville d'Avray assured her in a very learned, theological way, that she bore no trace of bites and had nothing to fear from this supreme attack by Satan's minion.

Nevertheless, excitement was running high. Joffrey de Peyrac succeeded in establishing calm by pointing out that it was quite possible that a person like the Duchess de

Maudribourg, endowed with psychic powers beyond the ordinary run should suddenly recover superhuman force, in spite of the seriousness of her injuries, and thus be able to get up, run and flee blindly in a last burst of frantic vitality, but, in any case she wouldn't get far in the forest.

A few men were sent out to look for her, but they came back without having found any sign of her. The fact was that it was completely dark, the forest was hostile, and there was a heavy brooding atmosphere over the shore, where the task of burying the dead was being completed, and no one had any heart to rest that night.

A vision haunted Angélique and she felt a shudder run down her spine. She saw . . . yes, she saw . . . It seemed as if, before finally breaking and setting her free, the bond that had bound her through the violence of a treacherous, bitter struggle to her most formidable enemy, who had been sent to destroy her, still bound her to the woman she had learnt to know in order to defend herself against her, and *she saw her* . . .

She saw that demented woman, fleeing in her tattered satin robes, fleeing wildly through the untamed American forest . . . And in hot pursuit came a dark shiny ball tumbling down the ravines after her, slipping under the brushwood, drawing closer ever closer to the fugitive, springing upon her shoulders, bearing her down and rending her with its claws, while the fiery eyes and demoniacal snarl of lips drawn back over sharp canine teeth stood revealed. The monster! . . . The monster referred to in the prophecy . . . 'And I saw emerging from the brushwood a kind of hairy monster which threw itself upon the Demon and rent her to shreds while a young archangel with glittering sword rose up into the clouds . . .'

'Where's Cantor?' exclaimed Angélique.

She began to look for him everywhere, going from one group to another, trying to pick out his proud figure, his fair hair. If she had found him, she would have called to him, 'Cantor! Where is your glutton? Where is Wolverine?' But she saw neither Cantor nor the glutton. Marceline, surprised at her agitation, having already recovered from her shock herself, said to her: 'What are you anxious about? What do you expect to happen to your Cantor! It's long since that he stopped being a baby, that lad! But I know how it is, we mothers are all the same! . . .'

Worn out, Angélique went and sat on a bench outside her house. She drew her coat closely about her. It was the final anxiety, the last period of waiting, the last time that she would withdraw within herself in the isolation of this tragedy, felt by her alone, and that she was about to leave as one leaves the country to which one has paid a passing visit, and to which one will never return, but from which one carries away some prized treasures.

The moon rose behind the cliffs. Fires were still burning everywhere on the beach. The ships' lights danced in countless numbers on the harbour waters. From the vessels to the shore there was ceaseless toing-and-froing. The surviving Bretons, crestfallen and in poor shape, were making ready to depart, and hoisting the last casks of salted cod on board their vessels.

Count Peyrac came out of the shadows and sat down at Angélique's side. He put his arm round her shoulders and drew her against him. She wanted to talk to him about Cantor and the vision that was besetting her, but she kept silent. She must savour these moments, find a way out of the nightmare, cure herself from the cruel confrontation.

It seemed to her as if she were a different person, or rather as if she had acquired something that had been out of her reach up to that time and that made her different. This still ill-defined something added to her personality and strengthened it. But she did not know very clearly what the future had in store for her, and that was the reason why she felt it necessary to hold her peace. Later she would discover that she had become more forgiving, more indulgent to human weakness, but also more remote, less directly concerned with those about her, freer in heart and mind, better disposed towards herself, more capable of enjoying the savour of life, more closely linked to the invisible, to what is never spoken, and governs deep down the acts of human beings. This was a wealth beyond price, a treasure beyond estimation that the wave of evil was leaving deposited on her soul as it withdrew.

Little by little this period of waiting was changing its meaning, was finding an outlet in the direction of confidence, happiness, and the joy of things of which we have certitude.

From time to time, Joffrey kissed her on the forehead, and stroked her hair. They spoke very little during that night, which still stood between the unknown following day and the burden of a tragic day, full of blood and anathemas, a night of waiting. The Count merely explained why he had sailed in the direction of the Gulf of Saint Lawrence the previous month without even stopping at Gouldsboro. While still in the Saint

John river settling the business of Phipps and the Quebec officials, he had received a message from the East Coast to the effect that information of the utmost importance could be supplied to him concerning the *Unicorn*, the Duchess de Maudribourg, and a plot against him.

That was why he had hastened to the Gulf. This message bore out his own intuition that the Duchess de Maudribourg and the ship with the orange banner which was spying on them and plotting against them were in some way connected. The suspicion had occurred to him the day that the Duchess disembarked so splendidly at Gouldsboro. He too had sensed, but more clearly than Angélique, that there was something that did not ring true in the benefactress's stage-craft. Moreover, having examined the hulk of the *Unicorn*, and the bodies of the victims of the shipwreck, he had already formed the impression that there was something fishy about the affair, and Simon's reticence about his error of navigation intrigued him . . .

After the Duchess's spectacular arrival, so miraculously – and elegantly – saved from the waters, fainting at their feet, getting all the attention and sympathy, his anxiety had increased. What was the meaning of this motley collection of people and ships all converging upon Gouldsboro? His instinct refused to see in it merely the hand of chance.

And so, during that very day when Angélique was watching at the Duchess's bedside, he had had a further conversation with Colin Paturel, and had questioned him closely. He wanted to find out everything about the circumstances in which Colin Gold Beard had come by his letters patent for an expedition to North America, and in what precise terms the position to be taken, Gouldsboro, had been represented. 'A pirate and a few of his hangers-on to dislodge . . .' he had been told, and Colin now remembered that in order to encourage him in the venture, he had been told on several occasions 'that he would not be alone there', and that he would be assisted when the need arose, that there was an important name behind all this, one of the largest fortunes in the kingdom, and that, in a nutshell, means would be found of repaying him for the service rendered by cleaning up the place and establishing a genuinely French colony there. In the still somewhat vague light of this report, Peyrac had been able to form a clearer idea of the coalition against him, which had doubtless been hatched in Paris at someone's definite instigation in Canada, and he had sensed that the vague threats and the concealed but undoubted will to destroy him mercilessly, himself and his family, were taking on a more definite shape . . .

'All of a sudden, I don't know why, it struck me that the most urgent thing to be done, was to be reconciled with you, my dear . . . So I sent Enrico to fetch you . . .'

There had been the appearances and the facts, and then, on the other side, the schemes hatched to take advantage of good will and good nature. That evening in Gouldsboro the Demon had been already installed. But love had outstripped her, and that was why, having a presentiment of her defeat, she had uttered that cry from the other world which had chilled them with terror.

'When I think of her,' said Angélique, 'I begin to understand the Church's fear and distrust of women . . . Was she ever a woman? . . .'

The day was dawning with unusual brilliance, and in the first rays of the sparkling sun, she saw Cantor coming along the path which followed the contour of the slope above the village. He was walking with an easy relaxed stride and looking out towards the sea over which the sun was spreading a sheet of gold. Against this profusion of glory, his youthful good looks were further heightened, with his blond hair haloed by the light, his clear bright eyes, the freshness of his complexion made more pronounced as if by a touch of sparkling dew, the proud self-assured grace of his walk, and something pure and incorruptible that shone forth from his entire person . . .

'The avenging archangel!' Wasn't that how Ambroisine herself had described him?

'Where have you been?' asked his father when he halted before them.

'Where did you sleep?' asked Angélique.

'Sleep? . . .' answered Cantor with a touch of haughtiness. 'And who slept down here on the coast last night?'

'What about Wolverine, your glutton? Where is he?'

'He's running loose in the woods. After all, you mustn't forget that he's a wild animal.'

He came forward to greet his father and kiss his mother's hand. Then, as if an idea had suddenly struck him, becoming a child again, he said excitedly: 'What's all this talk about going to Quebec and spending the winter there? I'd love that. After Harvard and theology, and Wapassou and famine, I could just do with a bit of society life. My guitar is going rusty from having no chance of strumming out tunes for pretty girls. What do you say, Father? . . .'

Ambroisine de Maudribourg's body was found, dreadfully mutilated, at the edge of a marsh. It was thought that she had been attacked by a wolf or a wild cat. Only some tatters of her gaudily coloured clothes – yellow, red and blue – made it possible to identify her. The Tidmagouche chaplain, who had been kept busy burying all these people, and had been almost put out of mind of his customary potations, came to see Peyrac.

'Should I give her the last blessing?' he asked anxiously. 'I'm told that the woman was possessed of the Devil.'

'Give her the blessing!' replied Peyrac. 'In any event, she's now only a lifeless body, which is entitled to human respect.'

CHAPTER 83

As THE chaplain was going out, Ville d'Avray came in and broke up the painful atmosphere by declaring right off the cuff: 'No doubt about it, I've examined them both, and it's the smaller one I like.'

'The smaller one?' asked Peyrac with a trace of a smile.

'The smaller of your two ships, taken as prizes . . . for I have no doubt, my dear friend, that you are going to make me a present of one of them. My friendship for you and Madame de Peyrac has cost me dearly enough! The loss of my *Asmodeus*, apart from anything else. You know I'd spent a fortune on fitting her out as splendidly as possible. Not to mention the endless risks I had to run on account of that Demon, just because I happened to be in your part of the country, and was more or less obliged by circumstances to take sides with you. No, I consider that it is only fair that I should become owner of one of those pirate ships by way of compensation for my losses. Don't you think so?'

'I entirely agree,' said Peyrac, 'and I may add that I'll pay for the repair of the poop-castle and for the redecoration of the after-quarter. I'm prepared to bring one of the very best painters from Holland to decorate it in accordance with your wishes.

And this will still be but a poor return for the invaluable services you have rendered, Marquis.'

The Governor of Acadia reddened with gratification, and his plump face lit up with a childlike smile.

'So you don't think I'm being too greedy? How delightful of you, my dear Count! I expected no less of you. But there's no need to go bothering the Dutch. I have an excellent artist, Brother Luc, on hand in Quebec. We'll make an absolute gem of it . . .'

Little by little life was resuming its normal course. Having shown valour and the better side of himself in his combat with the Demon, Ville d'Avray was again becoming the fussy self-important man, taken up with his own interests and pleasures. But Angélique would never forget what a stout heart was hidden beneath the embroidered waistcoats and the lace frills of the little Marquis.

'He was wonderful!' she told Joffrey. 'If you only knew. During those last days at Tidmagouche it was so awful. Ambroisine was tormenting me in dozens of different ways. She had a way of suddenly popping up and each time she brought with her danger, doubt, and despair, which finally wore down all resistance. If it hadn't been for Ville d'Avray, I don't know how I'd have been able to hold out, to stand up to so much clever spitefulness. He made the painful tension fade away and made even the most dramatic situations seem uncomplicated by the outrageous things he said. He helped me to preserve my certainty that you would come back and that all would work out well in the end. Was it to fetch the key-witness, Monsieur Quentin, the chaplain, that you went to Nova Scotia?'

'Yes! The message that reached me on the Saint John mentioned important information. Here I have learnt the history of the *Unicorn*'s chaplain, who was picked up on the coasts of Nova Scotia, and who seemed to know a great deal about the ship and its owner.'

'But who sent you that message on the Saint John river?'

'Nicolas Parys!'

Angélique's eyes widened.

'Nicolas Parys? I thought he was dangerous! . . .'

'So he is, and cunning and unscrupulous, and vicious and debauched, but we're not enemies. That story about the chaplain thrown overboard that was brought to him from Nova Scotia, in which Gouldsboro was brought in, struck him as suspicious, and he had me informed so that I could come myself to clear up the whole affair. In any case, he detests any sort of intrusion of newcomers into the affairs of Acadia, of a good part of which he regards himself as king, and as he hoped to make a deal with me for his lands, he preferred to play fair and warn me that there were people on the prowl who were trying to do me down. But that didn't stop him falling for the poisonous charm of the beautiful Duchess once he got to know her.'

'But how did she get here?'

'On the *Gouldsboro*. I found her at La Heve, where Phipps, scared out of his wits, had dumped her, preferring to deprive himself of his hostages rather than to continue to grapple with such a temptress. I could hardly leave women in such an abandoned place, and I was obliged to bring them here where they had more chance of finding a ship for Quebec.'

'And then it was your turn to grapple with the temptress?'

Peyrac smiled without answering, and Angélique went on: 'No doubt it was on that trip that she purloined your doublet. She must have guessed in her diabolical way that one day she would be able to play on it in order to drive me to despair; but how did she know that I would come face to face with her again at Tidmagouche? ... She foresaw everything ... Before leaving Gouldsboro, had she arranged to meet you at Port Royal ...'

'Arranged to meet me? ... Why on earth should I have gone making arrangements to meet that witch?'

'She tried to persuade me that you had.'

'And you believed her? ...'

'Yes ... at times.'

'And that frightened you in your turn?'

He smiled as he looked her in the eyes.

'You? The seductress who had never seen her wiles fail to take effect even on the heart of the greatest monarchs and the fiercest tyrants?'

'Wasn't she a rival to be reckoned with? Terribly clever and well equipped ... Better equipped than myself in many ways that might have pleased you – knowledge, for example, and ...'

'It was a very artificial sort of knowledge and with a touch of madness about it that was more likely to put me off than attract me. How could you ever doubt my love? How could you ever have any fears as far as I was concerned? Aren't you aware of your matchless charm and your magical power over me? How could you ever have a rival in my heart? What folly! Don't you know that a genuine woman's personality, mysterious and artless at the same time, which is a very rare gift, arouses a man's passion much more strongly than unprincipled women imagine.

'Of course the attraction of the flesh for men cannot be ignored, and men who are by no means fools can be captivated by the glamour of a beautiful figure, but, as far as I'm concerned, already being under the spell of your bewitching charm and beauty, what could I have expected to get from that woman in spite of her undeniable advantages? In any case, she sensed my suspiciousness from the very beginning, and not being able to exploit those advantages as far as I was concerned, she pretended to leave Gouldsboro guessing that it was my mistrust of her that was keeping me there; and then, as soon as my back was turned, and I'd sailed for the Saint John, being easier in my mind because of her departure, she came back to ensnare you in her net, my love, my most precious treasure. You can see that, distrustful as I was, even I did not succeed in foiling all her schemes!'

'She was terrifying!' murmured Angélique with a shudder.

It would have taken a considerable time to list all the traps that Ambroisine had laid for them, both those into which they had fallen, and those that by some miracle and by an unseen protection they had succeeded in avoiding ... How, driven by jealousy and devilish hatred, she had wanted to kill Abigail, because Angélique loved her, either by depriving her of possible assistance during her delivery, when she had had alcohol taken to the old Indian woman, had spread the news that a band of Iroquois were approaching in order to get Master Berne out of the way, and had poured a drug into Angélique's coffee – but Madame Carrère had drunk it ... And Ambroisine had pretended to have been drugged too in order to avert suspicion. And later on, coming back to visit Abigail again, she had poured poison into the infusion that Angélique had prepared for her ...

The spice-seller and his Carib slave emerged from the forest at Tidmagouche at this juncture, and cleared up the mystery of the scarlet pillowcase. It was he who had sold the Duchess de Maudribourg the violent poison she had poured into the infusion. The fellow had a bit of practically everything in his stock! Joffrey de Peyrac established that it was not a vegetable preparation but iron arsenate. He had also given technical advice on the manufacture of the explosive fuse that had blown up the *Asmodeus*. On learning this, Ville d'Avray wanted to have the pirate arrested, but it became apparent that this Antipodean vagrant had also been to some extent a victim of the Demon and her satanic confederates. Hunted by them because he knew too much and realizing that, like Clovis, his life was in peril, he had wandered wretchedly about the forest in order to get away from them. He was utterly exhausted.

'All right then!' agreed the Governor of Acadia. 'I got his Carib's hammock and his greenstone. I'll leave him his life.'

The poor wretch lay down on the beach with his arms behind his head, his olive-skinned slave squatting at his side, and waited for the *Fearless* that was to pick him up there towards autumn and take him back to the Islands.

Phipps was the first to arrive, running the risk of entering French waters in order to try to join up with the Count de Peyrac. He had heard that the latter would be going to Quebec to negotiate on the situation of Maine and he brought various proposals from the Government of Massachusetts in that connection. He had also been commissioned to investigate the death of the English pastor who had been killed by a Jesuit at Gouldsboro. And, finally, he was bringing back the French soldier Adhemar, as the Puritans had declared themselves incompetent to pass judgement on the fate of such a personage. It was just as difficult to try him as to hang him, and they decided that the easiest way out was to let him quietly go back to the French.

Adhemar came ashore like a conquering hero, but Phipps had lost a lot of his swagger. He gazed apprehensively around and although assured that he was in neutral territory here and had nothing to fear from the Canadians, this was not enough to restore his confidence. He only regained his calm on learning in passing of the Duchess's fate and that he no longer ran any risk of finding himself face to face once again with such a disturbing woman.

The tragic outcome had also profoundly affected Nicolas Parys. The old bandit had taken very badly this blow to his designs on the Duchess de Maudribourg's fortune, and perhaps also to the senile passion she had aroused in him. His hair went white in two days, his stoop became more pronounced, and he sold off his lands to the Count de Peyrac by a number of hastily prepared contracts, and in spite of Ville d'Avray's protests, who pointed out that the Quebec Government ought to be informed of these dealings, and in spite of his son-in-law's outcry, who kept talking about inheritance and rights of succession. 'Canso is enough for you, you fat pig,' was all that Parys had to say to him. He went down to the shore of his American kingdom for the last time one windy morning, which was already a foretaste of the end of the season, to embark on the Breton cod-fishing vessel.

The breeze was sharp that morning, and those waiting by the landing-stage were impatient with the Governor-Marquis de Ville d'Avray and old Nicolas Parys for spending so long endlessly whispering with their heads together as if they were at confession. At last they finished their conversation, which must have been very important to judge by the expressions on their faces.

Muffled in his long overcoat and clutching his money-box tightly under his arm, the old Lord of the East Coast got into the waiting boat. Shortly afterwards the Breton fishing-vessel hoisted sail and drew away from the shore. It would never again return to Tidmagouche.

Ville d'Avray walked back up the beach rubbing his hands.

'A good bargain! When I was saying goodbye to the old miscreant, I said to him: "I'll let you off the money that you owe me for last year, provided that you give me the recipe for the sucking pig that we ate in your ill-lit hovel the first night of our arrival." Do you remember, Angélique? No? . . . Of course we were all a bit preoccupied that night, but the sucking pig was absolutely delicious, and I know that the old coot is a gourmet and sometimes takes a hand in the cooking himself. He was in fact a cook before he turned wrecker and landowner. Well, the fact is, that I'd got him just where I wanted him, and he had to tell me the whole secret – he had no alternative. I know his secret right down to the last grain of pepper . . . It's a Caribbean recipe that a buccaneer pal of his taught him, and no doubt it comes originally from China. You make a big hole in the ground, fill it with hot embers . . . you also need a special concoction to baste it with, but we've got first-class resins here. I'll send some of these barbarians out to collect a supply in the forest . . . Marceline, Yolande, Adhemar, come on all of you . . . to work . . .'

He took off his hat, his frock-coat, and rolled back his lace cuffs.

'Now that we've got the quality here, we'll prepare a regal banquet ... And you too, Englishman, take off your sugarloaf hat and come and lend me a hand with the roasting ... We'll give you a real entertainment in the French style. It'll make a change from your New England barley broth!'

So at last there was going to be a chance of admiring big Marceline at work opening her shellfish with lightning speed, while trestle tables erected on the beach, as evening was closing in, were set out with delicious-smelling dishes. Everyone had wanted to do his bit, and even the Administrator, Carlon, had joined in the preparation of a sauce.

When night fell, torches and fires were lighted all round.

'Come on, you Basques! Let's dance!' exclaimed Hernani d'Astiguarra. 'One last farandole before we go back to Europe!'

In spite of the endeavours of the demons to grieve human beings of good will, the summer season was drawing to a beauteous close. On the following day the Basques set sail for Europe, then Phipps for New England.

What were they waiting for under this opal sky? There was no sign of rain as yet. Dust was falling from the trees, from the pines, and black spruces, which stood bristling like giant distaffs along the cliffs. The smell of fires was borne on the breeze from inland.

His period of captivity among the Puritans seemed to have had a stimulating effect upon Adhemar. He had been promoted chief cook to the entire noble company, and had made himself a white cap which went wonderfully well with his crumpled uniform. When dinner time came, he announced proudly: 'Yolande and I have cooked you a marvellous lobster! Just come and try it.'

'He's pretty good, that boy,' was Ville d'Avray's verdict, 'I'm almost tempted to take him on myself, and you, Angélique, ought really to engage that little Yolande as your chambermaid. She's a charming young creature once you get over her rough manner. I'm very fond of her, and I'd like to give her an opportunity of getting out of this uncivilized hole, especially as she seems to be getting on very well with this fellow Adhemar ...'

Angélique looked at 'little' Yolande carrying in baskets of dripping shellfish with about as much grace as a Turkish docker. She found it hard to imagine her as a lady's maid.

'Well then, she can be your bodyguard,' suggested Ville

d'Avray. 'You might find that useful in Quebec . . .'

'But, do tell me,' broke in Carlon, who happened to be there with some of the members of his suite, 'tell me, Count,' and he turned to Joffrey de Peyrac who was also present, 'tell me whether it's just a joke or seriously intended. I keep on hearing the Marquis talking to Madame de Peyrac as if there was no doubt about it, that you and your wife are thinking of going to New France and even to the capital to spend the winter there.'

'But of course they're going there,' stated Ville d'Avray, with a toss of the head. 'I've invited them to stay with me, and I won't have anybody behaving uncivilly to my guests . . .'

'But you really are going too far this time,' spluttered the Administrator of New France. 'You talk as if it was merely a matter of attending some midnight feast in the Marais district in Paris! When you get an idea into your head, you won't look the facts in the face. You're not in the middle of Paris here, but thousands of leagues away, responsible for immense deserted and dangerous territories. Monsieur de Peyrac's position is that of an intruder whom it is more or less our duty to dislodge from his position, and if he were to take it into his head to go to Quebec we should have to consider him as an enemy entering our territorial waters. Furthermore, you are not unaware that the town is very much divided on the subject of the Countess, his wife. For more or less rational reasons, people have become very worked up about her, all sorts of obscure powers are attributed to her, absolutely dreadful stories have been told about her. If she's so imprudent as to go to Quebec, she'll get stones thrown at her!'

'I have cannon-balls to reply to stones,' retorted Peyrac.

'Wonderful! I'll make a record of your statement!' exulted Carlon, sarcastically. 'Did you hear that, Marquis? . . . there's a fine beginning for you!'

'That will do!' said Ville d'Avray imperiously. 'We have just eaten an excellent lobster together, which is a proof that everything can be settled. I'll talk your language, Mister Administrator. Politically speaking, Monsieur de Peyrac's visit is a necessity. As we are so far away from the sun, in other words the whimsies of Versailles and its Parisian officials, let us take advantage of the fact to act like reasonable people, in other words people who have the sense to sit down round a table and to talk to one another before coming to blows. And that's why, and not simply for frivolous reasons, as you're insinuating, that

I'm insisting so strongly on this visit taking place. And it is indispensable that Madame de Peyrac should accompany her husband, precisely because by doing so, she will give people a chance to get to know her better, and so put an end to the anxiety and hostility aroused by all this tittle-tattle, which is quite baseless but has been put about systematically for the very purpose of stirring up opinion against any solution of our conflict with the Count by other than violent means.'

'Put about by whom?' questioned Carlon aggressively.

Ville d'Avray let the matter drop. He knew that Carlon, as an inveterate Gallician, was devoted heart and soul to the Jesuits. This was not the moment to stir up the fire smouldering beneath the surface ashes.

'You must admit that I'm right,' he went on persuasively. 'You had an opportunity both here and on the Saint John river of seeing for yourself that Monsieur de Peyrac, who founded the Port of Gouldsboro, and has established himself along the Kennebec, is no playboy, not the sort of man who would let himself be easily dispossessed, and that the wise course, I repeat, is compromise if we want to preserve the peace of New France in general, and Acadia in particular.

'I see how it is! I see how it is!' commented Carlon bitterly. 'I bet you already arranged with him to get your share of the dividends.'

'What's to stop you doing likewise?' retorted Ville d'Avray.

While listening to this heated and trenchant exchange, Angélique had vainly attempted to open her mouth. She considered that, after all, she had a right to her say. But she saw Joffrey signalling to her not to interfere. Later, taking her aside, he told her that for some time past he had shared Ville d'Avray's opinion about the necessity of going in person to discuss things with the Quebec Government. In spite of the boldness of such a dangerous step for himself, not only considered as an ally of the English, but as a person formerly convicted by the Inquisition, as well as for her, as a person banished by the King of France, and in spite of the risk of falling into a trap, and finding himself ensnared in the midst of French Quebec, their position in North America was now such that he could reasonably talk on an equal footing with the representatives of royal authority in these distant colonies. This very fact of remoteness changed the whole basis of the meeting, and the isolation in which the Canadians lived, these Frenchmen of the New World, far from their homeland, not to mention the way in which they were neglected, made them more independent, more capable of settling questions of direct concern to themselves, according to the needs of the present situation and without bothering too much about the past.

Peyrac was already assured of the sympathy of the Governor, a Gascon like himself, Monsieur de Frontenac, which was an important card up his sleeve. Another person, at the centre of these strong feelings, who had as yet not taken sides either for or against them, was the Bishop, Monsignor Laval, a strong personality, whose support or abstention could settle a great many things.

Finally there were the Jesuits, openly hostile and above all the most influential of them, that Father d'Orgeval, who seemed to be the instigator of the devilish plot of which they had almost been the victims. Up to that point, he had avoided a face-to-face confrontation. The presence of his opponents in Quebec would compel him to show himself and face them openly or, if he still avoided them, to find his position inevitably weakened, for he must be well aware that in such political encounters, the absent are always wrong.

Everything, therefore, militated to encourage Count Peyrac to undertake the expedition, and even before leaving Gouldsboro for the Saint John river, he had secretly made up his mind, with the reservation that he would give up the idea again if unforeseen events made it impossible to put it into effect before the autumn. Meantime, with a view to this visit to the small, lively capital of New France, he had arranged to meet up with the *Fearless* in the Gulf of Saint Lawrence early in October, after commissioning Vanereick to proceed to the rich Spanish towns on the Caribbean to purchase presents for the leading people in Quebec.

Being well aware that the principal objection Angélique would make to this proposed journey was not the fear of facing Quebec, but the distasteful prospect of being separated for a whole winter from her daughter, and without much chance of having frequent news of the child, he had sent a message to the Italian Porgani, who was in charge of his outpost at Wapassou, instructing him to escort little Honorine to Gouldsboro, where, in accordance with further instructions he had given Colin, a ship would pick her up and bring her to the Gulf of Saint Lawrence, where her parents would be waiting for her. She ought already to be on the way, sailing round the peninsula of

Nova Scotia, on the *Rochelais*. There would only be a few more days to wait.

These obstacles overcome, Angélique gave herself up to joyful anticipation of seeing her little girl, who seemed never to have been so dear to her, and also to the excitement she felt at the prospect of this trip to Quebec. She listened more attentively to Ville d'Avray's lyrical descriptions as he worked out in great detail, almost hour by hour, a programme of festivities and entertainments for her winter in Quebec, which made the best that Versailles had to offer pale in comparison.

'Versailles! Don't talk to me about it! It's too complicated an arrangement to be handled properly. It's vastly overrated. You need a small social group in order to have real fun.'

Of the two expected ships, the *Fearless* was the first to arrive. The captain had had the good idea of mooring in the reddish waters of the creeks on Royal Isle, and Vanereick, accompanied only by his first mate, came to visit the Count de Peyrac at Tidmagouche, and bring the goods that he had been commissioned to purchase.

So they were spared the sight of the hangdog faces of the crew and if Aristide Beaumarchand met up with his 'brother of the coast' of lamentable memory, Hyacinth Boulanger, in order to purchase treacle scourings for the concoction of his hooch, that didn't put anybody out.

Vanereick's choice of presents for the ladies and influential people in Quebec was excellent. The convents would be delighted to receive religious paintings of first-class quality. There were church ornaments and altar vessels of gold and pewter, and in the lay sphere, trinkets, jewels, a little gold and enamel angel by a well-known Italian artist of the fifteenth century, a goblet of solid gold, also of Italian origin, in the form of a seashell, its base made up by a chased-gold tortoise, encrusted in tortoiseshell, and bearing on its back a green jade lizard. Joffrey de Peyrac set this little marvel aside 'for Madame de Castel-Morgeat'.

The most precious item consisted of two 'Agnus Deis', a kind of little gold reliquary, containing a wax pellet. The fact that these pellets were produced during the Pope's Easter Mass at Rome made them very sought after amulets because of their rarity and because they were supposed to carry the very special protection of the Saint and the Virgin Mary. Vanereick had got them from a Spanish Bishop, no one knew whether in return for a service rendered or by means of threats, but they were absolutely genuine and there was no question of forgery.

Peyrac set one aside for Monsignor Laval and the other – which gave rise to some surprise – for the woman who ran an establishment in the slum district of the town, and who had a certain amount of unofficial influence on the male population of the city – Janine Gonfarel.

There was also a profusion of material of all sorts – velvets and silks, dresses and falderals which Angélique sorted out and put away with the assistance of the King's Girls.

They were of course going on the trip, and it was hoped that following their intended destiny, namely of marrying some good Canadian bachelor or other, they would forget the terrible adventure in which they had been involved. Delphine had taken charge of them with authority and competence. She often talked over matters with Angélique. The events in which she had been involved had a profound effect upon her, and she asked Angélique if she would take her as a lady companion when she was at Quebec. Angélique had already accepted Yolande as chambermaid, and she thought that these plans were premature, and that Delphine would recover and would be pleased to be presented to young officers at Quebec, according to the terms under which she had been originally taken on. She told her to go on looking after her companions until they arrived in the capital of New France.

'In any event, we don't know what sort of reception we'll get there. You may be obliged to dissociate yourself from us.'

It was also necessary to settle the fate of poor Job Simon, the ex-captain of the wrecked *Unicorn*, who was wandering about like a lost soul accompanied by the cabin boy, who had also survived. Count Peyrac suggested putting him in command of a cod-fishing vessel belonging to the Gouldsboro fleet, which would henceforth cruise in Tidmagouche waters, and support the colonization of the place based on trade in dried fish, and the provision of reception and supply facilities of fresh water and food for ships arriving from Europe, which would make it their first port of call after crossing the Atlantic. Porterage over the Chignecto Isthmus would assure communication with French Bay and Gouldsboro.

Angélique had been intrigued to see the old captain with the port-wine stain pop up again safe and sound. In the hornets' nest in which they had all found themselves at the time he had decided to run away with his cabin boy, she had not for a moment imagined that the poor man would ever be able to escape the murderers lurking in the woods. He told her what his scheme had been.

'I didn't set out through the forest. I knew that "they" would very soon catch up with me. I went and hid in a hole in the rock, a sort of cave that I had found. We stayed there, me and the boy, for the few days still to run before Monsieur de Peyrac arrived.'

'But what did you live on?'

'One of the Bretons, a lad that I'd made contact with – he comes from the Isle of Sein like me – brought us food each day. We were damned well off . . .'

He too would soon get over his fantastic adventure, the poor captain, and the sight of the *Unicorn* regilded, with its ivory bowsprit, thrusting through the foam would console him little by little.

Before returning to her concession of French Bay, big Marceline came to see Angélique.

'Monsieur de Ville d'Avray wants me to let him take Cherubino with him so that he can have him educated in Quebec,' she explained. 'Up till now I've refused. He's still very little, just a child, and he's no plaything to be shown off in drawing-rooms. But now that you're going too, and Yolande, it's different. If the lad's with his sister and under your protection, I'll be easier in my mind, and for this year at least I can do Monsieur the Governor this favour, but on condition that you have the final say in everything that concerns the boy . . .'

Then the sail of the *Rochelais* appeared over the horizon, and there was a moment of great rejoicing. Everybody was down on the beach when the longboat brought in the passengers, among whom could be seen Elvire Malaprade's white coif and the small form of Honorine all wrapped up in her cape.

Angélique waded out into the water to be the first to grab her and press her to her heart. She did not weary of kissing her and gazing at her, finding that she had changed and grown and was more beautiful than ever.

Life was resuming its peaceful, familiar proportions, rainbow-tinted with happiness.

Octave Malaprade and his wife, the nice Protestant woman Elvire from La Rochelle, had insisted on accompanying Honorine themselves to the end of her journey. They brought all sorts of detailed news about life at Wapassou, and would be going back to spend the winter at Gouldsboro where they had left their two boys, Thomas and Bartholomew. October was coming on, and it was getting dangerous to make the return journey to the Upper Kennebec unnecessarily.

There had been so much talk at Tidmagouche about Honorine de Peyrac that even those who didn't know her, in particular the King's Girls, were delighted at her arrival. She was passed from arm to arm and her healthy looks and copper-coloured hair falling on her shoulders were much admired. Cantor came at the run, with Wolverine at his heels.

'Ah, here's the little redhead!' he exclaimed. 'How do you do, Mademoiselle? . . .'

He took her by the two hands and began to dance a jig with her, beating out the words: 'We're going to Quebec! We're going to Quebec! . . .'

When the hubbub of the arrival had died down a little and Honorine had got her breath back, she went and stood directly in front of Angélique and announced solemnly, 'The kitten's here too. I've brought him for you. He wanted to see you again.'

Thus everything was working out well. The kitten was there, the little ship's cat, pitiful and bold, which had popped up before Angélique that evening which now seemed so far off, when she was watching for the first time at the Duchess de Maudribourg's bedside. The little innocent, playful creature had come into the lives of the human beings to play some ill-defined role as a warning and as a protection.

There he was now on the table, in the state-room in the poop-castle on the *Gouldsboro*, and Honorine and Cherubino sitting on either side of the table were watching him giving himself a thorough wash. He had grown too, he had a fine thick tail, a long neck and a delicate head. He had kept his grace and his exclusive feelings for Angélique. The swell rocked the *Gouldsboro*, as the splendid ship headed under full sail to the north through the islands in the Gulf of Saint Lawrence.

On the way they had put in at Shediac where Ville d'Avray wanted to pick up his luggage, and in particular his Dutch stove. Packing-cases and bales were waiting for them intact and spared as by some miracle, but naturally Alexander had not been there for some good time.

'Don't cry,' said big Defour to the Governor as he took his

leave of them, 'we'll send you your fair-haired boy back one of these days ... when he's tired of shooting the rapids. What do you expect? Boys will be boys! ...'

The fleet accompanying the Count de Peyrac to Quebec was made up of five vessels: the *Gouldsboro*, the two ships seized from Ambroisine's pirates, commanded by Count d'Urville and Barssempuy, then two little Dutch yachts, of one of which, the *Rochelais*, Cantor had assumed command, while Vanneau was in charge of the other.

On board the *Gouldsboro* as guests, were Carlon, his geographer, and Ville d'Avray.

'As guests or ... hostages?' asked the Administrator Carlon at times, quizzically.

The Marquis shrugged his shoulders and enjoyed life. Everything would work out all right in the end! He kept glancing proudly at 'his' ship, and thinking up decorations that he might have done to it and about the name he would give it.

'What's become of your chaplain?' Angélique asked him one day. 'He did join up with us at Gouldsboro, but since then it seems as if he'd vanished into the wilds.'

'That's about the size of it ... He didn't want to accompany me to Trantamare. He doesn't like Marceline. He wanted to go back to Quebec. I told him: "What does it matter? Walk to Quebec then." Well! that's just what he did do. He set out ... on foot. There's something in the air in Acadia that makes even the staidest Oratorians unreasonable. But don't worry. He'll be the first one we see when we reach the dockside, I'll wager you ...'

They passed a flotilla of Indians from the north, stunted, little yellow men. People said that they were cannibals and called them Eskimos, the meaning of which is 'raw-meat-eaters'. A little brandy was bartered with them for a magnificent white bearskin, which Count Peyrac had made into a coat for Angélique, and there was enough over to make one for Honorine as well. She looked charming in it. A real little snow-princess with red hair on this sumptuous white background.

'Your daughter is exquisite, Count,' said Ville d'Avray, 'she bears herself like a queen and she has such an interesting face. But tell me where does she get that head of Venetian auburn hair from? ...'

He looked fondly at Cherubino.

'I'll have a little blue velvet suit made for him ... Ah, family

515

life! It really is delightful, after all ... Supposing I were to marry Marceline, what do you think?'

There was a storm of protest. Marceline at Quebec! Out of the question! French Bay would lose one of its proudest ornaments.

Another child joined in Honorine's and Cherubino's games with the cat, young Abbial, the Swedish orphan-boy, who had been picked up on the docks of New York by Father de Vernon. They had caught sight of him getting out of the longboat on the day that Honorine arrived, and it was a great relief for all to learn that the little stranger had not also been a victim of Ambroisine's criminal associates.

At Gouldsboro he had emerged from the forest shortly after the departure of Ambroisine and Angélique for Port Royal. He was brought before Colin Paturel and had explained that he had run away for fear of that demon woman against whom Father de Vernon had warned him, instructing him to take his luggage and the letter it contained to Madame de Peyrac and to her alone if any disaster occurred. It was apparent that the Jesuit had had a presentiment of his forthcoming death. After the disappearance of his patron, the boy had tried to come back into Gouldsboro to join Angélique. But a man had come towards him and moved by an obscure instinct he had guessed that the man wished him ill and had run away. For several days he had sensed that menacing strangers were on his tracks. Finally, one evening he had succeeded in creeping into the fort to wait for Angélique there. But when he was delivering the letter to her, Ambroisine had suddenly appeared once again before him. Terrified, he had run away once more, taking refuge in the forest where he lived like a wild beast, prowling round the outskirts of the settlement until he realized one day that the wicked woman had gone away and he had dared to reappear and put in an appearance before Colin Paturel.

He would be taken to Quebec because he was baptized and Father de Vernon had so wished it, moreover his slight testimony supporting the fact that the letter had been written by the distinguished Jesuit would perhaps not be without its use. The pawns were taking their places on the chess board after the game had been played out during the summer. Cantor recalled that when his father had commissioned him to explore the islands in the Bay of Mount-Desert, off Gouldsboro, he had found on one islet recently left by a crew that had refitted there, a standard with the arms of a lion rampant. That was where the ship with the orange flag must have put in. It was there that the Demon had come to join her brother in order to fetch her scarlet-lined cloak and her red stockings.

'Why didn't you tell me that?' Angélique asked her son. 'I had enough bother trying to establish that Ambroisine had accomplices ... That would have helped me. We would have gained some time.'

'It would perhaps have made you dubious about me. You didn't suspect her at the time and my position was an awkward one.'

Certain things were becoming clear, but others still remained in the shadows, and it would take time to disentangle the skein woven by Ambroisine's deceitful mind, to work out what had on particular occasions been her precise intentions. One thing seemed certain, the plot against Gouldsboro and against the moral force of those who had created it had been contrived long since, doubtless even before Angélique arrived there. Her arrival and that of the Protestants had only increased the urgency of destroying a settlement which was claiming to be an independent state and an ally of the English. Already in Paris, these same lands had been sold to a corsair, Gold Beard, on condition that he established himself there, and the Duchess de Maudribourg had been asked to take a levy of King's Girls there in order to gain remission of her sins. Furthermore, she must have been given carte blanche in order to establish herself at Gouldsboro.

There was no doubt, the choice was a good one. What was poor Pont-Briand, who had been sent to undermine Angélique's fidelity, compared with that masterpiece of seductiveness, Ambroisine-the-Demon? 'A temptress in every shape and form,' said Ville d'Avray ironically.

Had Father d'Orgeval foreseen the possible criminal extremes to which his 'penitent' would go, or had she exceeded her instructions when she found herself up against opponents of unexpected strength? That was a matter to be cleared up in Quebec, between men of good sense and good will.

Angélique sometimes thought of the town which they had to conquer, a town on a red rock, waiting for them on the shores of the great river, while they sailed over the turbid waters of the sea which was already showing the signs of winter, amid the purple of sunsets and the mother-of-pearl sheen of the polar dawns. Off the big island of Anticosti, inhabited by huge white bears and screeching birds, Joffrey de Peyrac mustered his fleet. While the scattered ships were coming up and manoeuvring into the lee of the island, at a short distance from one another, Count Peyrac led Angélique into the luxuriously-appointed room in the poop-castle which was the retreat of the two of them on board the ship. That state-room on the *Gouldsboro* was already full of memories for them. It was there that Angélique had come to implore the Rescator to save her Protestant friends, and it was there, a second time on her knees before him, she had begged pardon for them, there that for the first time he had removed his mask showing her – oh joy too violent to be borne! – his face restored to life, there that for the first time after fifteen years' absence, he had taken her in his arms again and loved her, and the room with its precious objects, its oriental comfort, palely lighted by the great window of gilded and panelled wood, would always tell of the heart-rending and wonderful stages in the renewal of their love.

'I've a present for you,' said Joffrey de Peyrac pointing to a jewel case on the table. 'Do you remember what we were saying to one another the other day? That we would never part again?'

'Perhaps it was presumptuous!' agreed Angélique. 'But I felt at that moment as if, even if in reality life did compel us to part again momentarily, the bonds uniting us could never again be broken.'

'Yes that's exactly the way I felt. And the moment seems to me to have come to . . .'

He broke off and taking Angélique's two hands he held them for a moment in his own, as if he was gathering his thoughts together.

'The moment seems to me to have come to reaffirm in the face of the world the sacred ties which have bound us for so long and whose symbol was so cruelly snatched from us in the past.'

He opened the jewel box and she saw, lying on a black velvet pad, two gold rings. He put one of them on the ring finger of his left hand, as he had done once before when receiving the nuptial blessing of the Bishop of Toulouse, and then placed the other on Angélique's finger. Then he once more kissed the two hands he was holding, murmuring fervently: 'For life, for death, and for eternity, is not that so, my dear child, my love, my beloved wife? . . .'

The ships were now mustered under the lee of the island. On a given signal they moved off on their course to the north-west.

The following day, which was the second of the month of November, under a clear, cold, cloudless, winter sky, they passed Cape Gaspé and entered the mouth of the Saint Lawrence.

The Ferdinand and Isabella Trilogy
Jean Plaidy

Castile for Isabella 40p

With fifteenth-century Spain rent with intrigue and threatened by civil war, Isabella became the pawn of her ambitious, half-crazed mother and a virtual prisoner at the licentious court of her half-brother, Henry IV.

Numbed with grief and fear, Isabella yet remained steadfast in her determination to marry Ferdinand, the handsome young Prince of Aragon, her only true betrothed . . .

Spain for the Sovereigns 45p

With the might of Portugal humbled, the Court of the Sovereigns saw the rise of Torquemada, the establishment of the dreaded Inquisition, and the coming of Columbus who left the woman he loved to make a dream reality.

Daughters of Spain 45p

During the last years of Isabella's reign it seemed there was a curse on the Royal House which struck at the children of the Sovereigns.

Tragedy followed tragedy – the Infanta Isabella, a broken-hearted widow; Juana, driven to madness by her husband's philandering; and the sorrow of parting with young Catalina, destined to become Katharine of Aragon, wife to Henry VIII and Queen of England. . . .

These and other PAN Books are obtainable from all booksellers and newsagents. If you have any difficulty please send purchase price plus 7p postage to PO Box 11, Falmouth, Cornwall. While every effort is made to keep prices low, it is sometimes necessary to increase prices at short notice. PAN Books reserve the right to show new retail prices on covers which may differ from those advertised in the text or elsewhere.